# THE SOLDIER'S LEGACY

Book Six of The Dark Angel series

COURTNEY LILLARD

ISBN: 979-8-9914485-1-2

Cover Design by Etheric Tales & Edits | MC Damon

# ACKNOWLEDGEMENTS

This book is dedicated to everyone who contributed some fraction of their time to help shape the person I am today, including my parents, siblings, friends, teachers, and colleagues from across the country. I also must thank my husband, Darren, who not only gave me the push I needed to begin writing seriously and reads the drafts but who also listens to my ideas with honest, eager ears.

# A NOTE FROM THE AUTHOR

The Dark Angel series has gone through several editions. This final version combines what used to be the first two books, The Shadow's Grasp and The Guardian's Deception, into Part One and Part Two of the former. The Demon's Curse also used to be the first book in The Yeluthian Duology, a sequel story meant to be two books. This book has been altered to continue The Dark Angel series as its fourth book. This decision was not made lightly considering the amount of effort it takes to rebrand a series, as well as my readers who were familiar with the original book order, but each part of the story has been kept the same. Chapter titles have also been added, and the rest of the series will follow a new order, so to speak.

This note serves as a notice for those of you who may see The Guardian's Deception, whether online or a physical copy. That book will now be considered the second half of The Shadow's Grasp, and the rest of the series will be numbered appropriately. The Yeluthian Duology is no longer its own entity since The Demon's Curse is now Book Four.

# Contents

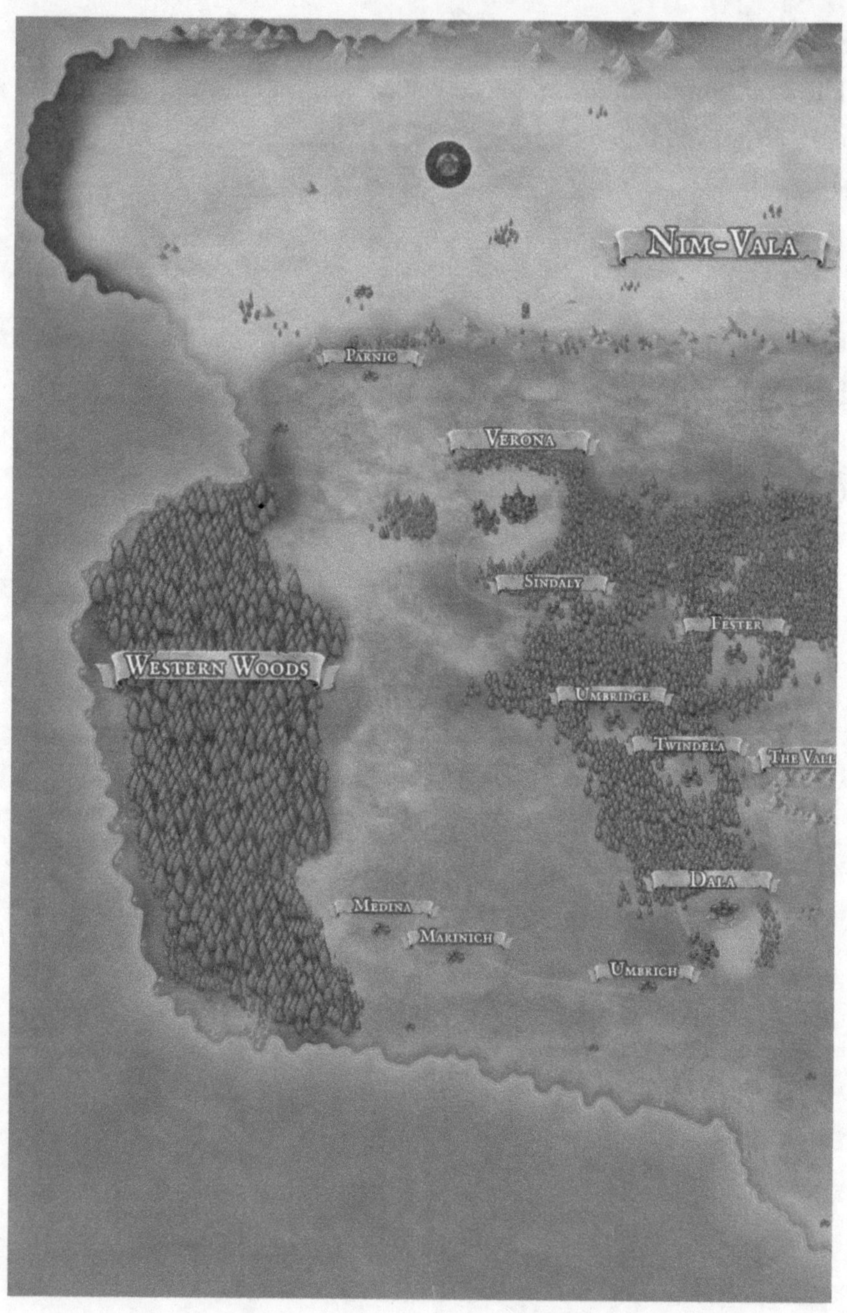

Nim-Vala
Parnic
Verona
Sindaly
Fester
Western Woods
Umbridge
Twindela
The Vall
Dala
Medina
Marinich
Umbrich

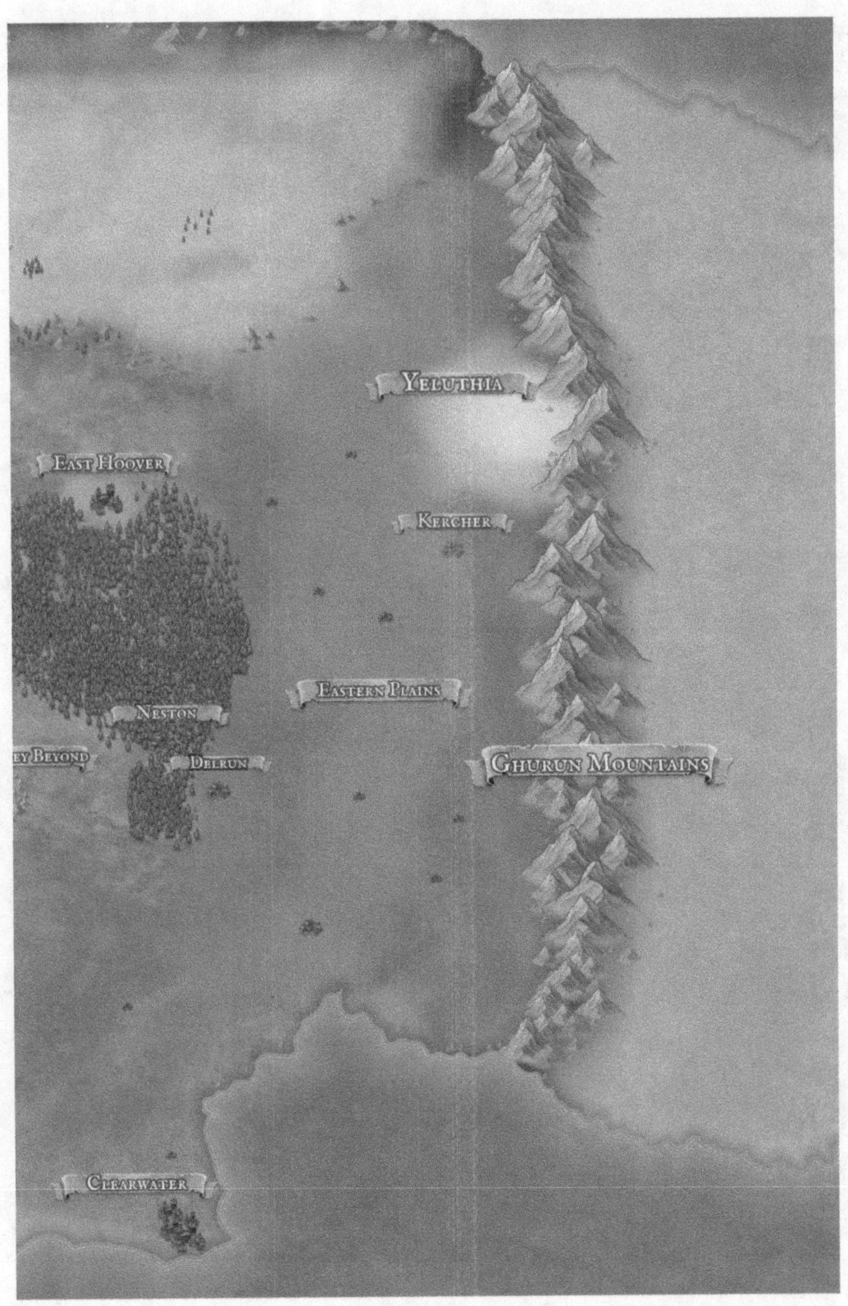

Yeluthia
East Hoover
Kercher
Neston
Eastern Plains
Ghurun Mountains
ey Beyond
Delrun
Clearwater

# Part One

# Return to Form

s he wandered through General Casner's camp along the northern border of Asteom, Will reconsidered his expectations of the near future and found himself a bit disheartened.

*I shouldn't be disappointed there's been no action, but I figured Finn would return and the Nim-Valans would turn up*, he reflected before spotting his friend Clara talking with a familiar group consisting of Bryn, Mary-Ann, and Lissa. *Perhaps I'm just impatient, though I haven't decided what I'll do once this mess with Lupin is taken care of.*

Instead of letting the thought weigh him down, he waved to the others he grew familiar with in the town of Muld as he approached.

"Where have you been?" Bryn chided and narrowed her eyes. "We agreed to help you forage in the woods before it got dark, but it looks like our time is limited."

He adjusted his glasses in a nervous manner while chuckling weakly. "Sorry about that. The medical station attendant caught me watching her tend to a soldier's ankle and asked for my input."

Before he could explain how the woman had been wrapping the area incorrectly, thus resulting in her hesitation under his curious gaze, Mary-Ann interjected with an unexpected comment.

"Careful, Will. You're going to make Clara jealous."

The mumble prompted giggles from everyone except the aforementioned light mage and Will, who stared at them without fully comprehending the jab.

"Weren't we just complaining about how late it is?" Clara added after despite her flushed cheeks. "If we don't leave now, we'll never find the items in time."

"It's not urgent," he attempted to reassure his friend.

However, the others turned to march away without her, leaving him baffled by their behavior.

"Did I say something wrong?"

The soft, blue eyes lingered on him before Clara took his elbow to lead him forward.

"Don't mind them," she grumbled while doing so. "I assume the soldier needed special attention?"

At her prompting, Will shared the brief encounter and how he took on the persona of an instructor walking the woman through each step. They eventually caught up with the rest of their group and searched for the various medicinal plants while he rambled about his tendency to intervene at the medical station. By the time they finished, night fell upon the land to drive them back to camp.

"I'll return these to the healer on duty," he shared before thanking each girl for her contribution. To his surprise, Clara remained when the others began departing.

"Would you like some company?" she asked in an innocent manner and with a smile that stirred a warmth in his chest.

Together, they delivered their prizes to the grateful, older woman. Then, they decided a stroll around the perimeter would help tire them further.

Will truly came to enjoy Clara presence ever since they established temporary lives in Nim-Vala, spurring a sense of unease he attributed to his lack of understanding her impression of him. Nobody ever saw him beyond his intellectual status and hobbies, especially since he rarely made time to do much else; however, he felt himself grow as an individual.

*I not only learned how to defend myself, but also how to protect others with a weapon and my instincts. I trust people like Clara and Finn, people who have my best interests at heart.*

Although the notion built his confidence, he couldn't refrain from comparing his current position within the camp to his previous life in Verona. The friends he met and built relationships with over the years thought he died during the ambush nearly two years ago. How he would be able to face them now was anyone's guess.

*I know Marcus, Grace, and Aaron will be just as relieved as Coura was, and I want to give them that peace of mind. Still, I don't plan on leaving the border until matters are settled. I'm not sure what I'll do or where I'll go then.*

"Is something bothering you?" Clara asked as he dove deeper into his neglected sense of direction.

He glanced at her without hiding his alarm. "Me?"

She frowned and nodded slowly to mock his obliviousness.

"It's nothing."

"Are you sure? You look upset."

Will rubbed the back of his neck before braving a response. "What do you plan on doing once this is all over?"

"I don't know," she mumbled halfheartedly while raising her eyes to consider the question. "If the general invites the light mages to stay on the border, I might remain here. That is, after I return to the capital to let my family know I'm alive. It just depends on the situation and how many others volunteer."

"I see."

Clara returned her gaze to him. "What about you?"

"It's like you said," he replied with a shrug. "Depending on what happens to Asteom's ties with Nim-Vala, I could stay or go back to Verona. I'm not a soldier or a healer, so I hardly serve a necessary role here."

Admitting that surprisingly didn't bother him as much as it had in the past, though he attributed the muted feeling to his successful adventures alongside his friends.

Evidently, Clara didn't feel the same. She halted, spun to face him, and place both hands on her hips. "You're wrong about that. You just explained how you helped a healer wrap an injured ankle because the light mage never learned. It's not just at the camp or in Nim-Vala either. I remember you bragging about potions the palace's medical station stocked up on because of their usefulness, and Lady Emilea always urged her students to utilize what we can without using magic. Your insight is exactly what Asteom needs."

By the end of her explanation, Will felt himself blushing and ducked his head to hide his cheeks as best he could. He cleared his throat after mustering the courage to elaborate on his comment.

"Thank you for that. In a way, not being needed has been the toughest part."

This time, his friend fixed him with a bemused expression. "What do you mean?"

"I don't have an assignment like a soldier or mage. The freedom to choose my next course is both a blessing and a curse when my heart is pulled in two directions."

"You want to return to the capital, don't you?"

He shook his head, crossed his arms, and averted his eyes. "Yes, and no. I would like to see my friends in the palace again, especially since they don't know we survived the Nim-Valans' ambush, but you, the other light mages, and Finn are my friends too."

A pause stretched between them for a minute until Clara rubbed her hands together and spoke softly.

"It may be selfish, but I want you to stay."

His eyes lifted and found hers. "Really?"

"Of course. We can return to Verona when this is over."

"And then?"

Her eyelids lowered while a slight smile graced her lips. "Who knows."

Will's heart thundered in his chest at the open-ended invitation to remain together even after the conflict ended.

As if to remind him of the situation, a shout off to his right drew their attention, abruptly concluding the moment. Many others joined the first before men and women began hurrying around the area.

Clara moved before he could decide what to do next, so he followed her back to the medical station where a handful of soldiers were being admitted. Blood caked their limbs and heads, though all appeared in decent conditions.

"What's going on?" his friend asked her superior, the older woman they gifted the foraged items to earlier.

A stern glance from the healer let them know they would need to wait for answers. In the meantime, both Clara and Will assisted where they could to tend to the troops. From what he could tell, none had been seriously wounded, though the gashes bled enough to concern everybody. Only when the injured lied on their established blankets did the pair hear about what took place from an acquaintance.

"The Nim-Valans ambushed the place where the demon's body was being guarded," he told them quietly so as not to disturb the atmosphere. "These five arrived and went straight here while their healthiest comrade stayed to explain the results of the combat to General Casner. That's all I know."

Will thanked the man for the information before turning to address Clara; however, she began walking toward the tent's flap and exited as he scrambled behind.

"Are you going to see the general?" he asked once he caught up and recognized the direction she was heading in.

She nodded and held her chin higher.

Instead of commenting on the purpose of that discussion given their positions in the camp, he let her lead them onward until a crowd at the center of the site forced them to halt. They could barely make out their leader's voice, yet they couldn't mistake the news: The advisor's body had been retrieved by northern troops who crossed the border.

*Would they remove the ancestral weapon without understanding the situation?* Will wondered against a sense of dread clouding his mind. *If they do, we'd be dealing with a repeat of events similar to what happened in the Valley Beyond and with Coura.*

The thought spurred him to take a step into the mob. Clara called his name yet he continued shoving his way past the bodies of his allies until he reached the front. There, he found General Casner speaking with two healers while a third supported the aforementioned soldier. Scarlet stained the man's peppered hair, and his eyes drooped to reflect his exhaustion. A minute later, the light mages dragged their newest patient away, then the general addressed the crowd.

"The assistant general and I are going to put together a team to replace the troops posted at that location. I'm sure you all understand the danger this attack poses, so be on your guard!"

"Yes, sir!" a majority of the onlookers replied.

With that, their leader disappeared inside the tent, leaving the soldiers and mages to disperse.

Will planned to confront their superior with his concern until Clara seized his elbow.

"Where do you think you're going?" she practically snapped. "The general is already figuring out the assignments. You'll get in his way if you interrupt."

Her words seemed to rouse him from his stupor. "If the Nim-Valans remove the sword Finn used to seal the demon, everyone will be in danger."

"You told me about that after you and Master Byron returned, remember? I'm sure he informed General Casner too."

When Will didn't attempt to continue striding toward the centermost tent, Clara released his arm.

"I intend to volunteer if they don't put me with that group," she went on in a calmer manner. "I'm sure it wouldn't be a problem if you do too."

He considered the idea before another came to mind. *What about Finn? Should I remain here until he returns? Would he bring a better update from Nim-Vala? He might set off to find Lupin's whereabouts-*

"What are you thinking now?" Clara inquired, interrupting his thought.

After pausing to wrap his head around the idea of tracking down the northerners in order to ensure the ancestral weapon's position, he addressed her. "I think finding and trailing the Nim-Valans might be worthwhile. Finn hasn't come back yet, so he won't hear about our dilemma until then."

"You want to meet up with him?"

Will nodded and waited for a lecture on the danger he would be putting himself in. To his surprise, his friend crossed her arms and stared at the ground, as if mulling over the plan.

"We should be able to reach Muld in less than a week," she muttered. "The people there would help us, I'm sure of that. If he hasn't been in that area lately, he probably went to the inner circle."

"I'll visit Muld first, just to be safe," he said pointedly, drawing her attention. "If he isn't there, I'll head to the capital."

"I'm going too."

"No, Clara. You're needed here. Besides, I'm more inconspicuous since I pretended I lost my hearing."

The light mage opened and closed her mouth twice before fixing him with a displeased expression.

"It's not that I don't trust you. Believe me, I would rather have you along."

"I know, but I don't like where that leaves me."

Will couldn't come up with any other words to reassure her, so he remained silent and waited for her to give in to his reasoning. After a sigh, she stepped forward, wrapped her arms around his waist, and spoke into his ear.

"Be careful. I'll tell General Casner what you're up to and be at the border with the new group if you need anything."

His arms raised to return the embrace while he promised not to get in trouble.

***

Byron set aside the letter in his hands for the second time that afternoon with a pleased smile. Few people ever wrote to him during time in Verona, though he never had someone anticipating his return in East Hoover.

*Cintra sure knows how to put me in a better mood*, he reflected and rose from his desk. *Of course, Symon's antics and problems are often more amusing than distressing.*

Business with the Magical Arts Academy and the surrounding areas sounded normal, which proved to be a relief given the sense of frustration and impatience looming throughout the palace. His partner ended her message by reminding him of her blessing, allowing him to stay in the capital city until the issues resolved.

*Unfortunately, the timeframe continues extending.*

The king's council met every other morning to discuss their current situation with the demons, ancestral weapons, and Nim-Vala. It seemed as though a new tidbit of information came up during each discussion, prompting the need for such frequent gatherings, and Grace lent them her goddess gift whenever they summoned her to ask. With her ability, they could keep in contact with King Arval and those in Yeluthia, Assistant General Calin in Dala, and General Casner on the northern border. The strain of using magic over such a distance left the Yeluthian ambassador and Master Jenna, who contributed her light energy, drained for a day or two.

*Their tenacity makes me feel useless*, he grumbled in his mind. Still, his steps didn't show his despondence as he crossed the third floor toward his former student's room.

It became a habit for him to visit Coura at least once a day over the past week, whether in her quarters or outside between training sessions, and share what arose from the council's meetings. The two even touched on dark magic, though away from prying eyes, reminding him of their original time in the palace when the demon's power remained secret. He found he enjoyed picking her brain and hearing what insight she offered on the subject of the demons, Nim-Vala, and even the Yeluthians' potential decisions. They would talk until he ran out of items to discuss or they had someplace to be.

The hint of a smile crept up on him when he recalled his desire to leave Verona for the lesser activity in East Hoover, and he attributed his pestering to that mentality since he wouldn't be able to communicate with those in the capital after their current business concluded.

*Hopefully that will be sooner rather than later*, the concerned part of his mind echoed.

Before he could return his thoughts to the present, a familiar voice called his name. His eyes caught Lydia standing in the middle of the hallway farther down. The woman's inky hair had been tied into a braid, which trailed over one shoulder, and her prominent chin stuck up a bit.

"Good morning," he began before remembering the time. "Or should I say, good afternoon."

Her lips curved into a pleased smile; however, he sensed something off about her behavior and realized she did not act as casually as she normally did around him.

"Good afternoon, Master Byron. I would like a word with you if you're available."

"Of course."

He prepared for a brief discussion in that moment until she cleared her throat and motioned to the busying corridor. It was then he understood she meant for them to talk in private.

"Why don't we head to the queen's garden?" she suggested as he opened his mouth to propose the same.

In another few minutes, the pair found a secluded section in the outdoor area where they wouldn't be bothered.

"Now then, we should be alone here," he concluded and dropped to sit on the only bench overlooking a patch of colorful flowers.

Instead of joining him, Lydia stepped in front of him, placed both hands on her hips, and leaned forward to put her face on the same level. Her lips dipped into a slight frown, which startled Byron enough to raise an eyebrow.

"Can you inform me of the situation taking place on the northern border?"

The question caught him off guard. "Have you not heard?"

"Not a word," she admitted while shaking her head. "The conflict in Dala is another subject I'm in the dark about as well."

For a moment, Byron stared at her in mild disbelief. *She stopped attending the council sessions ever since my return, so I figured she planned to stay out of the issues until they're resolved.*

*Perhaps I've been ignorant, especially since I never bothered to approach her about it.*

A wave of guilt washed over him then, and he cleared his throat to cover the feeling. "Before I explain, why don't you attend the sessions with the king's council? If you're curious, you should be present for our discussions."

She shifted in place to emphasize the awkwardness of her following response. "I haven't received an invite with information about when it takes place for weeks now."

"You mean…"

"Perhaps they assume I don't need to be there because you provide insight and input on behalf of the dark mages. I understand their point, so I tried not to become involved."

Byron studied the woman for a few seconds, shook his head, and released a sigh. *I've been ignoring Lydia and letting the council believe I'm resuming my responsibilities until I decide to return to East Hoover. Meanwhile, she's been shut out when she should be up to date and filling that position.*

Although part of him accused the council of not following through with the transition, Bryon put most of the blame on his shoulders. Mainly, he internally scolded himself for talking with Coura and Clearshot about the situation instead.

*Clearshot is a friend who's in a similar position between the conflict, but I shouldn't be going to him first. He's been through enough and holds no power in the palace. Meanwhile, Coura was directly involved and might not want to be as informed. Besides, she never approaches me about the subject. I need to remember Lydia is my replacement, not her.*

"I'm sorry," he apologized and met the matching set of emerald eyes. "My mind has been occupied with problems I left to avoid. Now that I'm choosing to be here and face them again, I stopped considering the next steps."

Lydia visibly relaxed and even shot him a hesitant smile. "I appreciate that and understand how preoccupied you and the council have been."

"That's no excuse for outright dismissing you. They trust my judgement and must not have thought anything different when I resumed my role; however, it is no longer mine to hold."

"Master Byron…"

He rose to place his hands on her shoulders. "You are the palace's dark master mage, Lydia. I rushed the process and need to accept the consequences. From this moment forward, I will make sure you're invited to attend the meetings as well in order for them to view you as such and ask for your input. I'll be there as a witness, share my input, and accept assignments, but you will be in charge."

"Yes, sir!"

With the weight off his shoulders, he returned to his seat and motioned for her to join him. "Let's begin by catching you up on matters along the northern border and in Dala."

***

The odd peacefulness spreading throughout the southern base put Marcus on edge instead of reassuring him the people moved past the demon and its creatures. He hated the thought of relaxing when the potential for danger remained; however, he kept such pessimism to himself since he couldn't imagine bringing down everybody's spirits.

Although a majority of the beasts had been killed during the weeks following their final ambush, those that escaped still lingered at night, prompting the soldiers to resume their patrols and the citizens to continue lighting lamps and torches at every hour.

That afternoon's announcement would update the routine.

"Are you sure you're not prematurely advising them to dismiss precautions?" he asked his fellow assistant general that afternoon as the two sat in the meeting chamber to go over the changes.

As expected, Calin shot him an annoyed glare in response. "If you keep questioning this decision, which we *both* agreed to, I'll demote you."

"You don't have the authority," Marcus grumbled and scratched his beard.

The Dalan soldier crossed his arms. "I don't care. Why are you on the fence again? You said you believe it's important for us to move on from the attacks."

"I know, but the demon bothers me."

"It's body is under constant surveillance, it hasn't moved a muscle since it dropped to the ground, and its creatures aren't interested in retrieving it. What's the problem?"

He pressed his lips together against the pit in his stomach, then he sighed in resignation. "I suppose I can never trust the current state of our situation whenever demons and their magic are involved."

Instead of a jab, which Marcus fully expected, Calin offered a sympathetic glance. "I don't either, but our resources and troops will recover sooner with the additional attention. Strategically, it makes sense to move on. Not all at once, but each step at an appropriate time."

"You're right."

"Come on," his comrade chided with a grin. "Let yourself unwind for the time being. This is the best shape we've been in for months!"

He grunted in confirmation and rose from his seat while shoving the doubts aside. Then, he returned the gesture when another subject came to mind. "Will you unwind too, or do you plan on being high-strung until the king's council announces your promotion?"

The question earned Marcus a groan from the older soldier, who pressed both hands on the table to lean forward, drop his head, and sulk. He placed a reassuring hand on Calin's back with a chuckle.

"You would think they'd get a spare minute to send us a letter," the man whined a bit dramatically. "I already sympathize with the Yeluthian ambassador, so I wouldn't ask her to spend more time using that ability of hers."

"I'm sure if it really mattered Aaron would inform us of a status change."

Calin turned to stare at him for a moment with an unreadable gaze. "Or General Tont?"

Marcus repressed another groan, though one possessing frustration instead of weariness. "I wouldn't hold your breath on that."

When his fellow assistant general didn't press the point, he figured they were finished with the discussion. They departed and moved toward the mess hall for dinner; however, Calin led him out through the southern exit, into the city, and to the tavern they frequented over the months since his reassignment. That usually meant the Dalan soldier intended for their conversation to be private.

"Let's get back on track," the man began once the pair received their bowls of stew and mugs of ale. "You already realized I'm hoping for a promotion after General Tio's death, may his soul rest in peace."

"Believe me, it wasn't that difficult," Marcus muttered before sipping at his drink.

"It makes sense since the base needs a permanent leader," Calin continued without acknowledging the comment. "I've already got a few individuals lined up to be my assistants, so I don't need you to stick around anymore."

"How unfortunate."

"I'm sure the palace will welcome you back."

"I meant unfortunate for your potential assistants."

Calin rolled his eyes before fixing him with an attentive stare. "Enough jokes. I'm ready for that next chapter of my life and to build my own reputation in Dala instead of being seen as General Tio's underling. I want to hear about your plans. At the moment, we're still equals."

In order to give himself time to consider the question, Marcus shoveled a spoonful of stew into his mouth and took his time chewing the meat and vegetables. *I honestly haven't considered changing my position or location because of the amount of business we've been dealing with. Besides, if Father intended to promote me, he would have done so as soon as the council heard about the* fight *here. If immobilizing a demon isn't enough to improve my reputation, I doubt much else would suffice.*

"I wouldn't mind sticking around until the creature has been dealt with permanently," he replied when he could speak. "Even if I become a general too, it's beneficial to keep multiple leaders, just in case."

Calin leaned back in his chair with a thoughtful expression. "True. I imagine you would help with training your replacement while supervising the base and continuing recovery efforts in the city."

Marcus nodded. He prepared to mention the potential length of time that effort would require until a loud thud sounded from the entrance as a trio of soldiers burst into the tavern. He and Calin were instantly on their feet, and his heart sank when he recognized them as guards from the field between the city and base. As soon as the men spotted the assistant generals, they darted across the room and saluted briefly.

"There's trouble," their leader began in a grumble, though the concern on his face betrayed the severity of the issue.

Calin pointed toward the door. "Explain on the way."

Marcus dug into his pocket, retrieved whatever coins he could find during those precious seconds, and tossed them on the table before following behind. From that spot, he listened to the guard while ignoring the discomfort of his tensing muscles.

"Something attacked those of us on duty as soon as the sun set," the soldier began and pointed to the leather bracer he wore on his right arm. The piece bore a single gash along his forearm, which dripped blood.

"Another one of the beasts?" Calin asked with more curiosity than concern or anger. When the man shook his head, the assistant general raised an eyebrow.

"No, sir. It was…something else."

"What are you hinting at?"

"Gage caught grass to the south move and yelled, but half of us dropped to the ground before he finished the message. Then, our lights went out one by one. I noticed a shadow approaching, raised my weapon, and the creature struck my arm. Before I realized it, my legs had been swept from under me."

Silence lingered between their group as they neared the edge of the city. Finally, Marcus decided to continue the questioning when Calin didn't go on.

"What about you two?" he addressed the remaining guards. "Did you see this shadow?"

They glanced at each other and hesitantly nodded.

"It's like he said," the first answered at a lower volume. "The figure didn't look like what we faced, but it moved just as swiftly, if not more precise."

"Let's check on the rest of the squad and figure out our next steps," Calin said after. This time, his voice reflected the same confusion Marcus experienced.

The five reached the clearing where various individuals, both their troops and random citizens, began gathering and observing a pair of flames at the demon's location. Waves, relieved sighs, and mumbled greetings met their group as the rest of the guards filed around them.

"Any sever injuries or casualties?" the Dalan assistant general practically demanded.

"Most of us got minor wounds we started tending to, but we have a young man who fell unconscious."

"Was he hurt?"

"Not that we can tell."

Calin glanced around the area. "What else happened?"

Marcus caught the troops hang their heads or look at a comrade uncomfortably, like a child about to be lectured for misbehaving. He held his breath until the soldier who spoke revealed the reason for such tension.

"It's the demon, sir. The body vanished."

"What!" Marcus and Calin exclaimed at once.

"The magical dagger is gone too."

"Did you search the area?" Marcus practically demanded.

"All but two of our lamps went out when we fell, but we started after we could move. Nothing seems out of the ordinary. We should be able to do more when the sun rises."

Calin growled a curse, and one sat on Marcus' tongue.

"It could be lurking around the field or head toward the city," the former muttered. "Keep scouting this area for clues. I'm ordering a full lockdown until morning at the soonest. Assistant General Marcus and I will warn the city and base to raise defenses, and the outer squad should be joining you shortly."

While the soldiers replied with another salute or grunts in confirmation, Marcus addressed the guard who shared the insight. "Before we split up, you mentioned you dropped to the ground."

"I'm not sure how, but I suddenly couldn't move my body," came the unusual response. "I lost my balance when my legs stopped working."

"Would you compare the sensation to being bound with rope?"

The man's eyes widened to show his alarm. "Exactly like that, though I've never been tied up."

This time, Marcus released the curse waiting on his lips, silencing the guard.

"What is it?" Calin interjected.

He met his comrade's stare. "We're dealing with a dark mage, somebody powerful enough to use a binding spell."

"Binding spell?"

"I can explain later, but it's just as it sounds. I've been trapped in one before, and it brought me face first into the dirt."

A pause stretched between the two until the soldiers shuffled in place, as if questioning whether or not they should continue with the plan. Calin looked them all over before repeating his order.

"Scout the area, search for clues, and wait for further instructions." He immediately stepped closer to Marcus for a private discussion, prompting the others to walk away. "Tell me what this means?"

Marcus shook his head in a helpless manner. "I have no idea. My first thought is that a follower of sorts came to rescue the demon since its body is gone and none of our troops were targeted. Additionally, whatever attacked them fled or is hiding nearby."

"Are you talking about a crazed worshiper or something?"

"Like I said, I don't know what to think. That's my best guess though."

Before Calin could reply, voices from some of the guards sounded in a panicked manner.

The assistant generals rushed over in response and found a young man, presumably the person who fell unconscious during the incident, sitting in the grass with a bewildered expression while his companions shook his shoulders.

"What's going on?" Marcus pressed when nobody elaborated.

"Damian just woke up," one of the guards shared, confirming his assumption.

Calin stepped forward to kneel with the others and address their potentially injured companion. "Are you hurt?"

For a moment, the soldier's dull eyes lingered on the assistant general before they went wide. His hand snapped to his chest while tightening into a fist. "S-Sir! I-I c-can explain…"

"Easy now. You fell unconscious during the attack."

A tense pause stretched between them until the young man dropped his head. After a few seconds, Marcus noticed his shoulder shaking.

"S-Sir, I didn't mean to," came the quiet, choked response.

"Mean what?" Calin pressed in a gentler manner.

"I… The demon, it…"

A jumble of incoherent words followed until the assistant general shook the soldier's shoulders with a bit more force.

"Out with it, Damian," his comrade growled, reflecting the group's impatience.

The comment had the young man glancing up again to reveal tears streaking down his cheeks; however, he spoke free of his emotions. "I don't know what happened. One second I was looking around the field when we heard footsteps. Then, my body moved on its own."

"What?" somebody exclaimed only to be shushed by multiple people, including Marcus.

"A shadow approached in a rush, like a gust of wind, and I felt a touch on my shoulder," the soldier continued, though in a wavering voice. "When it disappeared a second later, my legs went toward the demon's body. I tried fighting it, but I wasn't strong enough. My hand reached for the dagger and then…"

"Did you remove the ancestral weapon?" Calin asked in disbelief.

"I'm sorry, sir."

"What happened next?" Marcus demanded after. "We need to know the entire story."

The horrified gaze transferred to him. "My arm burned, as if it caught on fire, so I threw the dagger away. That's the last thing I remember."

Calin and the rest of the group shared their remaining questions or pushed for details while Marcus fell silent. A chill swept through his body when he recalled a similar experience.

*In the palace when I went after Hendal and the first demon, we stopped on the lowest level to search for the ancestral weapon. Coura described a similar sensation when she held the golden sword. This soldier couldn't have been completely possessed, but did someone with dark magic use him to remove the dagger? Is that why he felt pain when he touched the weapon? Was the attacker's only goal to retrieve the body then?*

Many more questions swirled around his head. Meanwhile, the rest of the group finished their interrogation and Calin continued issuing orders. The young man would be brought to the medical station in the base, the search would commence as planned, and he would return to the city to share the news. When they broke apart after, Marcus went to his comrade's side.

"We have a serious problem," he prefaced only to be rewarded with a deep frown.

# Trouble Brewing

The king's council meeting that morning went about as expected, except Lydia had been present to observe and share her input. Byron made sure to provide opportunities for her to speak on behalf of the dark mages and found himself pleased with her insight, which nearly matched what he would have said. He told her as much after.

"You flatter me," she joked as they strolled through the halls after remaining together for lunch. "Honestly, I don't mind speaking in front of others like that. I just need to understand the circumstances and where I should be, if that makes sense."

"We all view the world differently though," he added while hoping she would take the compliment to heart. "You will get more chances to grow in this position, so maintaining an objective perspective is critical. At least, that's how I've always done it."

"And I see no reason to doubt you."

He laughed when she shot him a playful wink before the two went in separate directions.

*I suppose I merely feared the unknown, which I often plan accordingly for. In this case, I'm glad she's confident as well as capable. Her outgoing personality reassures me she can handle the role. I'll need to officially confirm and announce her promotion soon then.*

Once he made a few mental notes, he dismissed the topic as he reached his destination and knocked on the wooden door. The faint call for him to enter from the other side had him turning the knob and stepping into Coura's room. As usual, she lied on her bed staring up at the ceiling without paying him much attention.

"Did you eat lunch yet?" he asked by way of greeting.

"I'm not hungry."

"Lydia and I just left the mess hall, and it appeared to be filling fast," he shared before recounting the day in reverse. First, he bragged about the woman's ability to keep up with the pace of the meeting given the specific subjects the generals rose, such as potentially reissuing the assignments around Verona in order to send support to the border and continue their search for the Nim-Valans who invaded Asteom. Her presence at the meeting also encouraged Jenna to speak up when they discussed the entirety of the mages.

"Nothing new to report aside from that," he concluded after a few minutes.

Coura remained silent throughout his update and after.

"How are you doing?"

"As well as I can," came her indifferent reply. "Has Grace been all right?"

Byron nodded despite his former student's eyes remaining elsewhere. "She has the day off, but we'll utilize her ability tomorrow for an update from General Casner. I'm curious how they're fairing given how we left the situation there, though the troops seem to be reorganized."

His former student hummed in response but didn't press the subject. The space fell silent after, which allowed him to reflect on her reserved behavior.

*She mentioned her throat's been bothering her, so perhaps that's why she doesn't speak. I suppose I talk enough for the both of us anyway.* That thought spurred an uncomfortable realization, one he hadn't considered until that moment. *Is she even interested in what's going on? These day-to-day updates allow me to view the entire picture in steps, whereas she becomes invested in the results. Before I went to Lydia, I hurried here to share the details. I assumed she would want to hear them as well.*

Upon further consideration, his gut told him he was moving in the right direction, especially given his replacement's progress. He said Coura's name to draw her eyes before releasing a sigh and scratching his neck.

"What is it?" she asked after clearing her throat.

"I believe I owe you an apology."

That had her sitting up. "For what?"

At her prompting, Byron explained his habit of visiting in order to confer with her after each council meeting and how he didn't consider her feelings on the matter. She studied him while he spoke then remained quiet when he finished.

"You probably think I'm being too sensitive," he added with a shrug, as if expecting her typical retort. "If you'd like me to quit updating you, just say so."

Instead of a jab at his expense, Coura stared at her hands and wore an unreadable expression.

Byron tilted his head. "What's wrong?"

"Nothing."

"I didn't mean to hurt your feelings."

"It's not that," she began while continuing to avert her eyes.

"Then what is it? You're starting to worry me."

Although he again attempted to make light of their odd conversation, he grew tense when she opened and closed her mouth twice without answering. He understood she hesitated because of indecisiveness, so he figured keeping his comments to himself would provide an opportunity for her to reach a resolution on her own.

That course of action led her to rise, approach her wardrobe, and throw the doors open. She wordlessly shoved the hanging pieces of clothing aside, piquing Byron's interest, before removing a long bundle of fabric. After turning without closing the wardrobe, Coura set the wrapped item into his hands and dropped onto the bed again.

"What is this?" he found himself asking. Whatever was underneath felt harder than he anticipated.

"Just open it," she grumbled while pulling her feet onto the bed to sit cross-legged.

Byron obeyed, though slowly at first. He had no idea what his former student hinted at; however, the last thing he expected to see was a glint of gold. Once he did, his entire body froze.

*Is this… An ancestral weapon?*

Indeed, the unmarred sword resting on his lap had no doubt been crafted by the experts among the Yeluthians. His energy reacted in the same manner as it did when he first encountered one years ago, leading him to marvel at its still-sharp blade and polished surface. A sense of ease relaxed his entire body while his mind raced at the same time with eager ideas.

*I can't believe it's in our possession! The council will rest easy knowing we have a means of attempting to end the demons we ensnared. Where on earth did Coura happen to stumble upon this?*

He prepared to ask and even cast her a look to reflect his optimistic mindset until he read the mixture of shame and timidness written across her face. It was then he recalled how only two of the golden swords existed: one resided with the Nim-Valan advisor while the other had been what they discovered in the palace's basement.

"You didn't," he began in a mumble when he understood how she obtained the item.

Coura responded by averting her eyes.

Byron's hands gripped the ancestral weapon tighter to reflect his rising temper. "Did you return to where you trapped the original demon we dealt with?"

Again, she chose not to answer. That tipped his disbelief into anger, leading him to scowl and raise his voice a bit with the intent to force her to listen.

"No wonder you've been coughing and complaining about your throat. Do you remember the shape you were in after you went there the first time? What if something attacked you? Did anybody know you left? How could you even consider acting so recklessly?"

While he lectured Coura on the severity of her decision, she pinched the bridge of her nose yet waited to reply until he ran out of breath. Even then, he still fumed.

"I'm sorry, but we needed that sword and a way to test whether or not its power is capable of defeating a demon for good."

"I hope it was worth the risk," Byron grumbled. His instinct to remind her of the dangers associated with impatience remained, but he kept it contained. "What did you do?"

"I planned to behead Soirée and find out what would happen to her energy."

"And?"

"She was… Soirée wasn't there."

A stunned silence filled the space.

"What?" he managed to whisper against a wave of dread. Suddenly, her reserved mannerisms made sense. "Coura, tell me what happened."

At his prodding, his former student shared how she returned far beneath the surface, discovered the remains of the boulder she initially pinned the demon to, and departed with the golden blade when her body protested the environment.

"I couldn't stay long, but I saw no clues," she concluded and paused to clear her throat. Already her voice started fading. "Still, I would imagine she'll return to the surface."

"Then what?"

"I don't know."

"What do you think the creature will do?"

"I don't know," she snapped, revealing a mixture of frustration and fear she bottled a second later.

At that, Byron suppressed his own emotions in order to put himself in her position. *Coura's been bonded to that being for most of her life, so it will likely come after her again. If it doesn't plan on using her, it might just aim to exact its revenge. We're vulnerable at the moment and dealing with Nim-Vala. It might be better to utilize the ancestral weapon while keeping her inside the palace for her own safety.*

Part of him knew she would argue against the restriction, yet he couldn't think of a better option. That was also why her next comment didn't startle him as much as he expected it to.

"I intend to search for her before she starts causing trouble again."

Byron studied the young woman in front of him for a minute. Coura didn't let her determined expression falter during that time, so he shoved his doubts aside.

"What you choose to do now is your decision," he began and crossed his arms to project his displeasure. "I wouldn't recommend going alone. Not only would you be facing a demon by yourself, but the Nim-Valans who crossed the border might get in your way."

"Don't we want to find them?" she countered.

"Yes, but that's a separate problem. If they aren't causing trouble, they should be arrested, which you have the authority to do as a soldier. It would detract from your business, and more than two or three at once would be taxing to transfer."

"Fine, I get it," she admitted and rubbed her eyes. "I'll ask my father or Commander Detrix when I see them. I'm sure they'll have some recommendations."

"A wise course."

Coura appeared to be contemplating the situation, so Byron figured he could leave her to do so at her own pace. As soon as he got to his feet, he rewrapped the ancestral weapon before deciding to deliver the item to the council the following morning. His former student stopped him when he approached the door after he shared this.

"What is it?" he asked with his hand on the knob.

The hardened expression she wore melted into a more vulnerable gaze as she extended a hand toward him. "I'll bring the sword to Aaron this evening. We're meeting after dinner."

Byron raised an eyebrow. Despite his desire to pry into that relationship, he forced himself to remain out of their business. "I'm sure I'll hear about it during the next council meeting, but let me know if you learn anything else going forward."

After she promised to do so, she bid him farewell for the evening.

***

Not even the pleasant atmosphere of the queen's garden could ease Coura's tense muscles and twisted insides as she

24

traversed the brick paths. She hadn't spoken to her friend after her return from the border, and that had been a brief update alongside Byron and Evern. Part of her knew he would only summon her if it related to business with the demons, Nim-Valans, or Hendal, yet the other side hoped he merely wished to reconnect after the months apart.

*Should I let myself be that naïve?* she wondered as she nodded to the guards on duty and entered the private section. *I can't say which reason I'm more worried to approach with him.*

The king of Asteom sat on a bench farther from the opening and twirled a leaf between his hands in a carefree manner until she appeared. Then, the rich, sky-blue eyes shifted to her, stopping her in her tracks. They stared at each other for a moment before Aaron addressed her.

"You look better than when we last met," he started with a hint of humor.

Coura's lips curved into a slight smile in response. "I'm hearing that a lot lately."

"I can understand why. You've been all over the country, risking life and limb to assist in our efforts to achieve a peaceful resolution. Just thinking about it makes me tired."

While she chuckled at the final comment, he patted the space beside him as an invite for her to join him. The offer relieved whatever uncomfortable sensation plagued Coura since she figured it would be a casual visit. Unfortunately, he dove into a serious topic as soon as she dropped onto the cool stone.

"I hate to do this now, but we need to talk about your future in Verona."

Coura frowned despite her best effort to appear unbothered. "What do you mean?"

"General Terrell visited me this afternoon to apologize for your disobedience and discuss a suitable punishment for freeing the former high priest."

"I suppose I should have seen this coming," she muttered before releasing a sigh. "What did you two settle on?"

When Aaron didn't reply, her heart sank. *Did he mention why I freed Hendal and where we went? The potential for danger should lessen the issue given Lupin's involvement in the palace.*

Her friend averted his eyes and continued before she could ask. "The general blames himself for not paying enough attention to you and your situation, though the council assumed your involvement wouldn't be necessary."

"Nobody expected the demons to return," Coura added and placed a hand on the hilt of the golden blade buckled to her side.

"Nonetheless, you played a part in breaking a criminal out of prison. The blame falls squarely on your shoulders, and General Terrell's reputation is tainted since he couldn't control a soldier under his authority. Before you argue, that's the truth. I can't make exceptions; not even for those I'm close to."

"I understand."

"As for your punishment, he requested to have you removed from his company."

"What does that mean?" she pressed without masking her shock. "Am I being reassigned?"

"Not exactly. When a soldier is dismissed from their position, they're either picked up by another general or no longer part of the army."

Coura could only stare at her friend in disbelief. *I'm no longer... What am I going to do?*

Only then did Aaron turn and meet her gaze. "We reached an agreement since you're unique. You technically belonged to his troops and Commander Detrix's company, which means you'll still remain a Yeluthian soldier unless the commander changes his mind. I plan on mentioning this to him tomorrow. What happens after falls under his jurisdiction."

"I guess it could be worse," she said after a minute of silence stretched between them. "I didn't know what to expect, but I'd wager an ordinary citizen would be arrested."

"You're right. Your loyalty to the kingdom saved you from such a fate."

A gentle breeze drifted by, carrying the chill of the fall season on the horizon. Coura allowed herself to relax while she accepted the change, just as Sage Vidar taught her to do with her magic.

"Thank you for sticking up for me," she finally responded and attempted a smile. "I'm embarrassed, yet I don't regret my actions. If I did, I'd have to admit the results weren't worth it."

He returned the gesture. "I figured you would feel that way. You shouldn't be ashamed of what transpired. Nobody will know or acknowledge why you supported the former high priest."

"At least I won't be tied down anymore." The comment had been thoughtlessly spoken until she remembered Soirée and the potential danger Asteom again faced. She prepared to unsheathe the golden blade and hand it over to initiate that conversation, but Aaron placed his hand on top of hers, distracting her from the topic.

"What about my proposal? Would that tie you down?"

The jarring change of subject startled Coura and spurred a blush. "I didn't mean it like that!"

He laughed at her reaction, and she joined him a second later. Once they quieted, he leaned closer until she accepted his offer for a kiss that lasted long enough to restore her faith in their relationship. Any doubts subsided as she recalled wanting nothing more than to ensure they could remain together. When he broke away, she leaned her head against his shoulder and let the renewed vow push her forward.

"Back then, I wasn't certain what it meant to marry you. I got scared I wouldn't be able to live up to your expectations, as well as the kingdom's. Now I know I can protect others and live my own life."

Aaron didn't reply, allowing her to go on.

"I believe I found my place in the world fighting for Asteom and with Yeluthia, but I could never forgive myself if I let the past keep me from moving forward." At that, she straightened, slowly unsheathed the ancestral weapon, and hurried to explain Soirée's lingering involvement before he could interrupt.

Her friend's face reflected his mixture of alarm, excitement, and concern, yet he kept whatever he planned to say behind his lips until she finished. He then paused to marvel at the weapon before addressing her again.

"Although this is a useful tool in our current dilemma, we're backtracking because of the first demon's escape. I suppose we need to just be thankful for our blessings and expect trouble at every corner."

"Aaron, I need to find her and make sure she doesn't hinder the progress we made," Coura began. Her resolve strengthened when he nodded in response to her statement. "I promise we'll discuss my position in Verona, marriage, and whatever you want when I put an end to these demons. I'll have no reason to be afraid of anything by that point."

He raised an eyebrow before attempting to pass the golden sword back. "I can accept your decision."

The warmth the ancestral weapon radiated continued soothing her Yeluthian power even as she rejected his offering. "Use this to get rid of the other two. I don't believe Soirée will try killing me just yet, so I'll return once the southern base and border are secure again."

"Are you sure?"

Coura knew he disliked leaving her without a means to defend herself against a demon; however, she already struggled with that choice during the days following her return from the creatures' realm. *I'll be searching for Soirée anyway, and I have no idea how long that will take. Besides, I meant what I said. She might be angry with me for trapping her below the surface, but we still share a bond. If I'm useful to her, she wouldn't toss me aside so easily.*

"I'll be fine," she reassured her friend and rose to stand. "Just try to fix at least one problem before I get back."

"I'll do my best," came his amused response before they parted ways.

***

The atmosphere of the council's meeting chamber felt oddly lighthearted when Grace entered that morning with Dianne accompanying her. She arrived every other day in order to continue communicating with the locations guarding the demons' bodies, which allowed her to strengthen her goddess gift's reach as well as contribute to the kingdoms' cause. That sensation, along with the increased morality around the palace, aided her confidence.

"Welcome Ambassador Zelnar," King Arval greeted her with a smile. "We have an update before you begin. This will need to be shared with General Casner as well."

"Yes, Your Highness."

Upon hearing her polite response, her uncle glanced at Aaron, who also appeared in a better mood than normal. Their behavior piqued her interest, yet she struggled to compose herself when her friend revealed the third ancestral weapon in their possession. Unfortunately, her elation was short lived.

"If you remember, this sword is one of two with the second being used to seal the being acting as a Nim-Valan advisor," Aaron continued and let his smile fade. "It seems the first demon we faced previously is free."

*I recall hearing about Coura and how she used her goddess gift to trap that creature in a place far below the planet's surface,* Grace thought as she nodded to acknowledge his words. *Although I am curious why she returned there, we are facing a new issue we would otherwise be uninformed about. It seems the council is aware of this and reached the same conclusion.*

"Asteom has the support of our people, unlike the years before your arrival," King Arval mentioned, as if reassuring her of their current path. "At the moment, we have an opportunity to destroy our enemies to the north and south, allowing King Aaron and his people to rebuild and fortify those areas."

"I understand. Is there any other information for General Casner before I proceed?"

When nobody contributed additional thoughts, Jenna welcomed her to occupy the designated seat beside the master light mage. She became familiar with the routine over the last couple weeks and promptly sat in place to get comfortable. While the council murmured about a new topic of discussion, Grace accepted Jenna's hand so the woman could offer her energy, which amplified the ability.

*Are you ready?* she sent in order to warn her partner as she closed her eyes.

*{Whenever you are, my lady.}*

With the master mage's permission, she extended her mind in the direction she knew to be north along a route that brought her to the aforementioned general's main camp. The process took nearly an hour the first time she attempted to contact the man; however, she cut the length in half thanks to her earlier experiences. Many minds, presumably the soldiers and mages stationed along the border, met hers, though she avoided connecting with any except her target's.

General Casner typically stayed in his tent with his assistant and other leaders in the area at that point in the day, as the council established early on when Grace agreed to participate. She brushed against his mind as a signal of her arrival yet hesitated when she sensed a troublesome amount of anxiety. Before she could question it, the man addressed her by name.

*{Ambassador Zelnar, are you there?}*

*Good morning, general. How fares your company?*

A pause followed where she worried about the concern he projected; his response didn't make her feel any better.

*{Apologies, but you'll be relaying quite a bit to the council.}*

*

By the time Grace broke the connection with General Casner, her forehead and temples throbbed enough to where she needed to drop her head into her hands. She already imagined the impression doing so made on Aaron, her uncle, and the others in the chamber, but the update proved to be worse than she expected.

*They were optimistic about the near future too*, she reflected against a wave of regret at being the person to spoil their moods.

"My lady, are you all right?" Jenna asked from her side, leading her to open her eyes and gaze at the curious faces around her.

"I will be fine," she managed to preface before clearing her throat. "The Nim-Valans stole the demon's body his troops had been guarding."

Despite the outbursts and shocked reactions, Grace continued by explaining how the northerners attacked in order to retrieve the creature they believed to be their advisor while doing as much damage as they could before fleeting. She listed the casualties, how the general found out, and the current situation at that camp and others he sent a messenger to spread the word to. Finally, she concluded by stating the options he asked her to deliver with the hope of gaining feedback from the council.

"General Casner has been fortifying his location and sending a warning to spots along the border where the soldiers can strengthen their defenses. He wants to avoid any sort of march into Nim-Vala since he believes they only aimed to recover one of their own, but he suggests you attempt a letter to their king with the advisor's true identity."

"Recover one of their own," General Tont grumbled while shaking a fist. "That's rich!"

"To the northerners, that's what the creature is," General Perry countered, though with a sense of disgust. "Master Byron and Commander Evern said as much when they faced the demon."

All eyes glanced between the mage and Yeluthian until the former picked up the conversation.

"The being mentioned those who serve it are aware of its identity, but I question how much the Nim-Valans know about demons. We have every reason to distrust their kind after what one did to our country, not to mention decades ago when the alliance with Yeluthia was founded."

"Even if we hope to help by informing them, I doubt they would listen to an enemy nation," Aaron commented, prompting nods from around the table.

"I concur, especially since their so-called advisor formed a bond with their king and is willing to support their interests in exchange for servitude."

When the space quieted, Grace struggled to dismiss the urge to drop her aching head back into her hands. She wouldn't recover enough to manage another connection with the northern camp for at least a couple days, which she shared with the man before she departed; however, she traded off speaking with General Casner and Assistant General Calin in Dala. That meant she would be prioritizing one over the other, though the southern base would not be aware of her choice and the current issue.

"Unless anybody else has another idea, I motion to attempt sending a message to King Syrus in Nim-Vala's inner circle," Aaron began and met each member's eyes. "The demon's recovery is not cause to invade and start a war, but I believe we may need to strengthen the border. Intimidation served us well in the past, especially with mages. My hope is their leaders will understand and manage the situation; my fear is the creature will tear Nim-Vala apart from the inside out. In either case, we protect Asteom."

Most of the table shared their agreement with nods or grunts, reflecting Grace's own mentality.

*Focus on ourselves and our allies first. Nim-Vala might need assistance, but we cannot waste resources and energy by attempting to force them to listen.*

"I'd like to bring up another concern right away," Byron interjected after. "If the northerners remove the ancestral weapon from the demon's body, its energy will be released and find hosts."

"That's how those demonic creatures are formed, right?" General Terrell asked, reflecting the majority's lack of understanding.

"Correct. Depending on the results, our troops may be facing more than just ordinary humans and animals."

"What do you suggest?" Aaron pressed when no one added additional comments.

Byron crossed his arms, glanced at Lydia beside him, then back at the others with a slight smile. "I had a feeling I would be returning to the border if this became the case, so I volunteer to monitor that area until we're certain it's safe. Allow me to officially retire from the council and appoint Lydia as my successor."

Many mumbles followed his proposal, yet Grace didn't sense any sort of malice or desperation in them. *The council must have known their time with Byron was limited. They did request he rejoin, at least that is what I heard from Coura when she returned.*

"I will honor your request," Asteom's king replied, drawing everybody's attention again. "From this moment forward, Master Lydia shall act as representative for the dark mages and be our contact with the academy in East Hoover."

Grace chanced a look at the woman on her other side and found the emerald eyes shining with a sense of pride. Still, the new master mage merely bent forward in a bow from her seat and thanked Aaron, who addressed Byron.

"You aren't under any obligation to travel to the northern border, but your service is appreciated. We will continue communicating with General Casner and keep an eye out for demonic creatures."

The meeting seemed to reach its end then until King Arval spoke. "Master Byron, if you feel it necessary for one of my commanders to join you should the issue escalate, inform the council at the next opportunity."

His comment spurred a smile from Grace as Byron agreed to do so.

***

Because of the unpredictable end time for the king's council meetings, Coura struggled to stay occupied until she could get an opportunity to speak with her supervisor. Detrix remained at King Arval's side during such affairs yet usually went off on his own business during the afternoons and evenings, like her father. This meant she needed to be nearby in order to catch him before he disappeared or guess when he would be available.

*I should know better since Byron never shuts up about these sessions,* she grumbled in her mind and released a displeased huff that drew the attention of the guards. They ignored her the first three instances she passed by to check on the chamber, but she wondered if they grew suspicious of her intentions yet. *It's been a couple hours. I wonder what's taking so long.*

She continued down the corridor with the intent to meditate in the queen's garden after training that morning; however, her gut told her to keep the area in sight. Part of that anxiousness stemmed from the update she would be giving regarding her dismissal from General Terrell, and she hoped Evern wouldn't be curious enough to stick to his fellow commander's side while she explained.

*I don't know how he'll react. That's what scares me most.*

Shuffling from the soldiers had her spinning around, yet it took another minute before anybody emerged. Lydia and Byron exited together alongside the new master light mage named Jenna and turned to stroll in the opposite direction. When King Arval appeared between his three guards, she slipped behind while making enough noise to alert them all of her presence. No one paid her any attention as she followed them up to the fourth floor. Then, her father broke away while Detrix and Isan retreated into their leader's room.

"What is it?" Evern inquired without hinting at trouble or accusing her of initiating it.

Coura replied with a sincere smile. "I need to talk to Detrix when he's free. How was the meeting?"

Although she asked as more of a polite inquiry and to avoid giving him an opportunity to press her about her reasoning, her father averted his eyes. The unexpected movement hinted at an issue brought up during the council's meeting.

Her curiosity piqued, though the door to King Arval's space opened a second later. To her surprise, both Detrix and Isan exited. They noticed her and Evern and approached without hiding their interest.

"How are you, Coura?" the former began and smiled while the latter crossed his arms. "Did you need the exercise, or is there a purpose for your visit to the fourth floor?"

Before she could answer, Isan interjected while addressing her. "His Highness is resting, so there will be no interruptions until we are summoned again. Commander Evern will be keeping watch."

"I assumed as much," her father muttered with a nod.

"I actually need to talk to you," she answered and faced Detrix. "It's about my position and a new assignment."

By not continuing, she hoped the other two would leave them alone. Instead, the commanders looked at her and waited for more.

*Is it rude to ask them to go away? Not everybody in the palace needs to know I'm being punished.* Coura ignored the mixture of irritation and chagrin the thought prompted.

"General Terrell will be sending you a message with an update. I'm under your command only now, so I wanted to request a leave. I can share the details when I-"

"Wait, hold on," Detrix interrupted with a slightly bemused expression, causing her heart to sink. "Has your position changed?"

She nodded and remained silent, which led him to tilt his head, Evern to frown, and Isan to release a sigh.

"If this is a personal matter, I will step aside for my break," the oldest of the commanders stated before continuing down the hallway.

In response, Detrix glanced at Evern and pointed a thumb over his shoulder. "Would you not prefer to resume your shift?"

For a moment, Coura wondered if her father would actually leave, and another bit of her spirit rose. Then, he answered.

"I am rather intrigued by this, especially given what was discussed during the previous meeting."

The pair returned to staring at her after, and she just barely resisted the urge to roll her eyes, mainly due to Evern's comment.

*What did he mean by that? What did the council bring up that would relate to me?*

After pausing for a deep breath, she decided to reveal the general's decision. Her father's eyebrows rose, reflecting his alarm, and she could only imagine what he thought of her demotion. On the other hand, Detrix's face relaxed into a neutral expression, as if he assumed as much took place. His next words confirmed it when she finished.

"It is a shame, but I understand their need to maintain a sense of justice."

Evern shot him a minor glare. "They did so without comprehending the potential danger and Coura's intentions."

"I disagree with you, my friend."

Detrix didn't elaborate, so she cut in before the two could continue bickering.

"In any case, there's a bigger issue I need to resolve." She hesitated when she anticipated her father's reaction but went on despite the imminent outcome, sharing Soirée's disappearance, how she gave the ancestral weapon to Aaron, and her plan to track the demon down. "Since you're my supervisor, I figured I should request your permission so you don't expect me to stay around Verona."

While she spoke, neither commander appeared disturbed by her retelling, which seemed odd considering her involvement with the dark creatures and their power. They shared an unreadable look after, and Detrix responded first.

"It seems circumstances are not in our favor."

"What do you mean?" Coura pressed, leading Evern to join the discussion.

"In addition to your news, the Nim-Valans recovered the demon Master Byron and I assisted in defeating."

Every bit of blood in her veins went cold. "What? How?"

"They attacked General Casner's troops who were guarding the creature and managed to steal the body. We assume they did so to continue following who they believe to be their advisor."

*Lupin is… And Soirée broke free…* Although she struggled to control her emotions on the inside, Coura knew they faced more trouble ahead.

"Master Byron will be returning to the border," her father added. "Should the ancestral weapon be removed from the demon's torso, he can alert the general."

*This is becoming a mess.* She crossed her arms and glanced at the ceiling. *Lupin's aim is focused on Asteom as a whole, or Aaron in particular. He said he's after me too, but not as a primary target. I'm sure if he's given the opportunity he wouldn't hesitate. On the other hand, Soirée and Lupin are enemies. I doubt she'd linger around the border, so I might lead her there if I go north.*

"It may benefit you to remain here and monitor the situation with the rest of us," Evern told her after, drawing her eyes again. "Your experience can benefit the troops, both those belonging to Yeluthia and Asteom, and you would not need to travel alone."

"On the other hand, you would not be caught in the middle of a potential battle," Detrix interjected. "This is your business, and we will be made aware of that demon's location as soon as you discover it, correct?"

Coura nodded, causing her father to frown.

"What if the creature hinders your return?" he countered. "I sense many unknown parts of this plan."

*I figured he wouldn't want me to leave.*

Detrix huffed a laugh at Evern's comment, though he addressed her. "Despite the danger, I imagine you considered the risks. If you did not, you would not be standing in front of me now. Because of that, I approve your request. Make sure you are prepared and keep in touch, if you can."

"I'll do my best," she replied immediately. "I expect to depart in the morning. Thank you, sir."

Coura hesitated in case her father continued the discussion. His expression reflected his annoyance with his fellow commander, who avoided looking away from her; however, neither uttered a word. She expressed her gratitude once more, wished Evern well, and turned on her heel to head for the staircase.

*That seemed too easy,* she admitted to herself. The pair's low voices filled the corridor at her back at a volume that prevented her from discerning the words. *I bet Father wouldn't have let me go or would have tried talking me out of going if he were my superior. I'm surprised Detrix let me leave without at least questioning my next steps or where I'll be. Perhaps I earned the opportunity to be off without an interrogation.*

Although the day wore on until that point, she forced herself to pack for the journey ahead and prepare a route across the southern half of the country. She put together something of a list before a knock at the door had her stepping away and calling for the guest to enter. As expected, Byron appeared, took his usual seat, then raised an eyebrow at her once she dropped onto her bed.

"What's all this?" he began with a hint of amusement. "Are you going on a vacation?"

Coura rolled her eyes yet smiled at his remark. "You can call it that."

"I stopped by earlier, but you weren't here."

At his prompt, she shared her previous whereabouts, as well as the results of her meeting with Detrix. He didn't appear bothered by her decision, yet she knew he would give his input when she finished.

"Let me start by saying I understand your connection to the first demon makes you believe you should go after it," Byron responded and held her in place with a stern look. "Still, you have no obligation to act now, and I'm sure the king's council will arrange for a group to accompany you. I'm also not sure why you won't wait until we secure one of the two ancestral weapons we're aware of. However, you're free to go with Commander Detrix's blessing. I won't claim I would grant you permission if I were in his shoes, but it is what it is now."

Coura crossed her arms as a physical means of standing her ground before recalling what else the Yeluthian mentioned. "You'll be returning to the border then?"

"That's right. In fact, I was going to invite you along."

"Really? Why would you..." She paused mid-question to reflect on the situation, which revealed the answer. "You're worried the Nim-Valans will remove the ancestral weapon from Lupin's body."

"If they haven't already, it's bound to happen soon," he replied, confirming her guess. "I'm sure I can sense the demonic energy, but you were able to utilize it and track the source."

"It's not that simple."

"It never is."

The two sat in silence for a minute while simply savoring the quiet moment to think. Coura took the opportunity to lie on her back and stretch her arms above her head, relieving any stress building in her muscles.

*If Soirée wasn't involved, I wouldn't hesitate to go along.*

With a huff, she pushed herself up again. "You take care of the border, and I'll protect Asteom from within. Once I handle the demon here, I'll head north."

Her former mentor sent her a displeased glance, shook his head, and shrugged. "I suppose I can't stop you. Remember, Grace will continue acting as a messenger between General Casner's camp, the palace, and the Dalan base. Just be careful."

"When have I ever not been careful?" Coura teased to lighten his mood.

In response, Byron rubbed his temples, though not without a slight smirk. "How many gray hairs do I have on my head?"

# Unfortunate Circumstances

nlike his previous ventures around Asteom and Nim-Vala's border, Will felt comfortable trusting his senses to guide him thanks to the crude map he created when he and Clara previously assisted Finn. The movement that resulted in conflict emptied some areas while others held less people. Still, the locations didn't change too much, allowing him to proceed without issue. He also made sure to pack food for several days, which kept him with enough energy to not drag his feet.

*If the situation wasn't as dire as it is, this would make for a fine hike*, he couldn't help but think as he studied the vegetation during a break to eat. *Maybe one day traveling between countries will be possible. We have so much to learn from each other.*

The notion soured his mood a bit when he considered what life would be like without demons meddling in their affairs. Since he couldn't do more than sulk when that came to mind, he stood and set out again.

Before the morning stretched into afternoon, he spotted a familiar structure in the distance and released a sigh of relief. The log cabin he recovered in after Finn began helping him and the light mages rested farther ahead, signaling how short the remainder of his trek would be. By that point in the day, he figured he could use the shelter for a respite from the chilly weather while planning his upcoming conversations.

His footsteps crunched in what leaves and twigs littered the uneven path as he drew closer. This didn't bother him until he paused to locate a route around a couple bushes blocking the way ahead and the noise continued. Once he realized what that meant, he hurried ahead to dive behind the foliage for cover.

*I'm not alone!*

The sound of rustling seemed to surround him, increasing his concern and leading his heart to hammer against his chest;

however, what voices he heard a minute later came from the cabin. He reviewed his map again to confirm no enemy camps had been established near that area before slowly adjusting his position to peer through the brush.

Two men identical to most of those he recently faced stood at either side of the lone door to the wooden structure while three entered. A stream of smoke rose from the opening that ventilated the inside since a bonfire pit had been built at its center. Although he strained his ears when he noticed the pair's lips moving, the words remained too quiet to discern.

*If the enemy retreated this far north, they've likely come into contact with Muld.*

That left him struggling to respond for several minutes, both due to his personal feelings on the threat to the people there and the weight of his self-appointed assignment. Only when a single man emerged and began walking around the back of the building, seemingly to patrol the perimeter, did he decide to move.

*I can't stay here, but I need to know if the town is safe*, he decided while placing a shaky hand on the hilt of the short sword buckled around his waist. *If I'm lucky, I'll run into Finn there or learn if he went to the inner circle. I also wonder if the enemy who recovered the demon's body would keep it there. Would they even know the truth about the advisor?*

He didn't believe anybody would share such a detrimental fact regarding their leader, especially with people who weren't putting their lives on the line for Nim-Vala. In a way, that secrecy pushed him forward as he retreated from the bushes to proceed northwest at as much of a hurry as he could manage.

*

The sun already set by the time Will reached Muld, shrouding the town in darkness except for spots where lamps had been lit along the road. His cautious approach cost precious time, yet he told himself the sacrifice far outweighed the potential disaster that would befall him if he got caught. He snuck around homes and buildings while listening for any sign of another person; however, no one else lingered outside. Plenty of spaces held multiple people, which he picked up on through what voices came across in the evening. The barn where he spent his first night sounded extra loud with plenty of grumbling.

*I wonder if the troops are taking refuge there*, he thought after pausing to contemplate his next steps. Several names came to mind of people he could confront about the situation, but part of him worried where the leaders of the enemy soldiers stayed. *Unless I choose correctly or scope out their home beforehand, I'm putting myself at risk.*

Because of the hour and lack of immediate danger, his former host came to mind next. Her likeliest reaction to seeing him again sent a shiver down his spine since he didn't believe she would be as welcoming given the circumstances. Despite what scenes he conjured of her berating him, he also knew she wouldn't turn him away, prompting him to head to the house at the farthest end of town.

A sense of relief greeted him after he observed the structure for a couple minutes and found no wandering guards. He hurried to the front door before lightly knocking thrice.

*Please be home*, he silently begged while avoiding the urge to cower against the wood. Standing in the open made him feel exposed. *Please, Geneva...*

As he raised a fist to knock again, the knob turned, and his heart skipped a beat.

"Good evening," he heard the older woman begin as the door opened. With just two words, her displeased tone came across clearly. "How can I-"

At the sight of Will, who offered a tentative wave, her mouth hung open. She wore her nightgown and held a lamp in one hand. The rest of the house remained hidden by darkness.

"Hello, Geneva. It's been a while since-"

"Get inside," she interrupted and stepped away so he could slip through the doorway.

As soon as he did so, she shut the door without a sound and whirled around. Will didn't get a moment to breathe before she balled her empty hand into a fist and struck him firmly on the top of his head.

"What are you doing?" she demanded as she did so. "You shouldn't be here!"

He attempted to apologize while rubbing the spot, which lightly throbbed, but she brought her fist down again when he moved his hand. Both flew up to cover his head after, though he ducked away.

"I'm sorry," he managed to say when she didn't continue. "I needed someone to talk to about what's going on, and everywhere else held Nim-Valan troops."

The older woman's scowl had him expecting another blow, yet she merely released an annoyed huff before pointing at the kitchen. "Have you eaten?"

He shook his head.

"You should remember where everything is," she went on while her feet brought her toward the opposite side of the space. "It's late. We can discuss matters in the morning."

With that, she left him standing bemused but relieved by his luck.

*

Will didn't intend to sleep in as late as he did the following day, which he attributed to his appreciation for a comfortable bed. When he did stir, he found his unwilling host preparing an assortment of breakfast items and tea in the kitchen.

"This is a lot for just the two of us," he commented as he dropped into one of the chairs at the table.

"I should hope so," came her response while she worked. "We will not be eating alone."

A sense of alarm pierced through his guard until she faced him, put both hands on her hips, and elaborated after noticing his concerned expression.

"Settle down. It's just a couple people from town who want to air their grievances in a safe place."

What grumbling followed about why they decided to bother her instead of somebody else let Will know she wasn't pleased with that intrusion. His lips instinctively curved upward at her harsh personality though.

*I see she hasn't changed.*

He selected a few, lighter options to nibble on, then a knock at the door alerted them of their guests. Geneva didn't even hesitate to warn him to hide or prepare for danger, so he remained where he sat and continued eating even as two, familiar men entered. At the site of the unexpected addition to their conversation, they hesitated to accept seats around the table until the older woman scolded them for being impolite.

"I'm sorry for the cold greeting," the taller of the pair began while their host served them tea. "It's been so long since I last saw you. How are Mary-Ann and Bryn?"

Will smiled at the names of his friends who previously worked under the man's wife, the local seamstress. "They're doing well."

"And what of Zelma?" the other asked. He maintained the largest farm in the area, and the light mage assisted with the labor until their group's departure.

"She is well too." Before Will could share how his friend often wondered about the farmer and his family, Geneva took a seat and added her input.

"Everyone is well, now let's move on. Why are you two here?"

"Thank you for having us," the first man named Karlson began despite her rudeness. It seemed they all were accustomed to her personality. "I noticed the outsiders haven't been here and wondered if they gave a reason. Everybody else has been dragged into their business except you."

The older woman folded her hands on the table, relaxed her posture and expression, then glanced at Will. "About three-dozen men dressed in all black arrived a few days ago. They claimed to be soldiers from the inner circle who were driven away from the border by enemy forces."

"I assumed as much," he commented when she didn't go on. "Their camps are scattered all across the area between here and Asteom."

After she nodded, her eyes went to the farmer named Calab, who picked up the explanation.

"Because of their positions, they demanded we house and feed them. We've never seen soldiers from the inner circle before, but they are not what I expected."

"Same here," Karlson added before crossing his arms. "As the days pass, they demand more from us. We oblige since we aren't able to chase them off and can tolerate the complaining. What's odd is they left Geneva alone."

Will looked at their host. "Is there a reason?"

After sipping at her tea for a few seconds, she dipped her chin in confirmation. "They visited me the first day, just like the others' experienced. When they asked for my occupation, I told them. They left after poking their noses around my home and claiming they don't need a medicine woman. That was that."

"Does that mean they have their own?" Karlson wondered aloud. "Those I've seen never bore any sort of injury or seemed like they carried equipment for treatments."

The men bounced ideas of what that meant around while Geneva listened, allowing Will to consider the odd decision. *I don't recall any sort of healer aiding them during the previous fighting. If they had a person to treat wounds, I believe I would've encountered them already. General Casner also never mentioned any sort of medical support. Could they have received help after the last confrontation?*

The thoughts swirled around his mind as he attempted to consider all angles until a stray comment from Calab drew his attention.

"If I had to put my coin on it, I'd wager their medicine man is one of the three staying with me or a neighbor."

"Why is that?" Karlson pressed without masking his doubt.

"I noticed a few of them messing around with a knife, playing a sort of game where they stab the ground when another's hand is flat in the dirt. I didn't quite understand, but a poor fool managed to get the blade clean through his hand. The sight had me rolling my eyes and going about the rest of my day; however, the next time I saw that man, he had no injury."

"Are you sure you saw the knife clearly?"

"I've observed worse throughout my life, but a wound doesn't vanish. At the very least, he should have had bandages wrapped around his hand."

Both sets of eyes went to Geneva, as if she held the answer. Instead, she frowned and shook her head.

"In my years of medicine, I have yet to stumble upon an immediate cure for a stab wound."

"Nim-Vala doesn't possess light mages who can heal," Will muttered when the three fell silent to contemplate the puzzling situation. "That would have been my first guess, but I doubt these men would accept light energy when their advisor is a..."

"What do you mean?" Calab asked when he didn't go on.

*I shouldn't tell the people about Lupin's real identity. Even if they care about an advisor from the inner circle, bringing up a demon could cause them to panic. This is a sensitive topic for a town unfamiliar with magic. I also wonder if the enemy can heal because of the creature's energy, like those who fought against General Tio and the Dalans outside Verona.*

"It's complicated," he began and adjusted his expression to reflect the severity of what he prepared to share. "Something tells me magic is involved. Not the kind anybody is familiar with either. That's why I suggest you tell the townsfolk to remain peaceful and cater to those men until they leave. They're dangerous and know how to use the weapons they carry."

The stunned reaction from all three left him feeling uncomfortable for tiptoeing around the subject, and they pressed for more information after; however, Will refused to budge. In order to stress his point, he chose to mention how he fought those on the border alongside Finn. When he repeated his previous recommendation, Calab and Karlson seemed to understand that no one in Muld could defend against such threats.

There wasn't much to say about the situation after that, so the two took their leave once they let Geneva know they would keep an eye on her property, just in case. Will pushed his empty plate away and rose to stretch hoping the movement would ease the tension knotting his insides.

"Doting on an old woman," he heard his host grumble as soon as she shut the door. Then, she turned around and fixed him with a stare projecting her suspicion. "And you. Why did you not tell them the whole truth?"

"W-What do you mean?" Will kicked himself for stuttering and revealing how the question surprised him before reluctantly going on. "The advisor from the inner circle, the one Finn has been chasing, is a demon."

Geneva's eyes widened. "What? How?"

"It's a long story, but the creature slipped into the king's circle and is manipulating the men along the border. The soldiers I fought alongside managed to defeat and trap it for a while, but Nim-Vala's troops retrieved their leader."

He decided to explain the current state of the conflict when she asked about the risk to Muld next. Fortunately, she appeared to relax after he mentioned how only the town's guests would pose a threat since he didn't believe the demon would bother with that area.

"Is that why you're here then?" the older woman continued while dropping into her chair. The lines of worry etched across her face showcased her age more than ever. "You came to warn us?"

"I was actually wondering if Finn stopped by. He planned to return to the capital with news that the advisor has been defeated."

"Departing before a job is complete isn't like him."

"At that time, we thought it was."

Geneva lowered her gaze and shook her head slightly. In that moment, Will pitied her for the trouble he caused by updating her on the conflict at her doorstep.

"Finnley hasn't been back for months," she finally answered and adjusted her eyes to look out the nearest window. "I doubt he would return unless he needed information. If he said he would be heading to the inner circle, my guess is he went in that direction from the start."

"You're right. I just wish I could warn him."

"Me too, but he's never been the type to linger in one spot for too long. Besides, he always turns up when I least expect him."

*He's safer in the capital than around the border anyway*, Will thought as they sipped at the remainder of their tea. *Without Lupin's location, the general and his troops need to keep an eye out for an attack. Either I go after Finn or I aid Asteom from their side.*

"If you don't have business in Nim-Vala, you should return south," Geneva added, as if she read his thoughts. "Those men make it dangerous for you to be here, and I doubt Finnley will see me anytime soon."

"You'll be all right?"

She narrowed her eyes to show her annoyance. "Bah! I'm well off compared to the others in town. Don't let us distract you from your work."

Will dipped his chin with a slight wince. He anticipated the cold parting given the older woman's nature; what he didn't expect were her next words, and in a calmer manner.

"You and your friends can make time to visit Muld when your business is complete."

The comment tugged at his heart, prompting him to meet her eyes and commit to a smile. "Of course."

***

The search for the demon's body yielded no results, leaving Marcus, Calin, and their troops baffled. As the first day passed, a sense of paranoia stirred in Dala, which the assistant generals expected. What they weren't prepared for was the support the citizens offered. People stayed awake beside the soldiers on duty to either keep them company or stand guard with dull or makeshift weapons. Others donated food, mended torn clothing, or offered to repolish what leather padding showed its age.

Such kind actions extended to Marcus, though it took him until the following evening to get used to the treatment. His comrades pestered him about how he felt like he burdened the innocent civilians instead of welcoming them as friends, so he eventually stopped turning away the offers and focused on their main problem instead.

Unfortunately, nothing changed before the assistant generals' next meeting with the king's council. They arrived at the chamber together and fell silent as they took their seats. Waiting for Grace's presence to find them prolonged the sense of dread burrowing in Marcus' chest.

"It's never fun being the bearer of bad news," Calin said to break the tension hanging in the space.

Marcus released a sigh to reflect his mixture of frustration and worry. "Would you like to tell them or should I?"

"You're friends with the Yeluthian ambassador, right? The blow might land softer if you explain."

"Is that really what you think, or are you just scared this will ruin your opportunity at that promotion?"

Calin's frown deepened at the question, which Marcus intended to be a joke. Before he could clarify, a familiar voice chimed in his mind, like an echo of a voice in the distance.

{*Assistant generals, are you both present?*}

*We are*, he thought and expected his comrade did the same.

{*The council is ready, but we have unfortunate news to share before your update.*}

"What now?" Calin grumbled from across the table.

After his comment, Grace proceeded to inform them of a similar issue taking place along the border. Marcus' mind went blank as he listened, though his heartbeat increased until his chest hurt.

*The demon General Casner's company defeated is gone too?* Although he hadn't been actively sending the question, his Yeluthian friend replied.

*{I am afraid so.}*

He hesitated to bring up the second being's disappearance before Calin said his name, as if expecting the reaction.

"Go on and tell her," the Dalan soldier began with more composure than Marcus anticipated. "We'll all need time to process what this means."

He nodded and called to Grace. When she answered, he shared their update with what few details they gathered before waiting for her to repeat the news to the council. His back started aching after, so he stood, stretched, and let his comrade know what was going on.

"What do you think?" Calin pressed after. "Could the incidents be connected?"

Marcus shook his head. "I'm not sure. Nim-Vala is becoming more of a problem than we anticipated, but I doubt they've been hiding in Asteom for long enough to travel this far south."

His fellow assistant general grunted in confirmation before rising and moving to stare out the lone window.

*I wish the northerners would just mind their own business*, he couldn't help but say to himself amid a surge of annoyance. In his heart, he understood their leaders were likely the cause of the trouble, and he recalled the faces of the people in the fort he freed from supposed barbarians alongside General Casner and their company. *Death and destruction over what? Why ally with a demon? They're mending an open wound with poison.*

*{Marcus?}*

He instantly pulled his mind away from the negativity he allowed himself to wallow in. *What is it, Grace?*

A pause followed his question before she spoke in a normal manner, letting him know she addressed him alone.

*{I cannot predict the outcome of the council's discussion, though I believe it will carry on for a while. They are arguing over the next course of action.}*

*Will this stretch into tomorrow, or the near future?*

{*I believe so, but I wanted to let you know we can always set aside another time if you need to talk.*}

The offer startled him a bit since he became lost in the business occupying their time. He thanked her after his spirits rose at the notion; however, his Yeluthian friend didn't reply, leading him to wonder if the council was informing her of their message. A minute later, his assumption proved to be correct as she resumed her professional tone.

{*King Aaron, the generals present, and the master mages have reached several conclusions they wish to enact as soon as possible. First, the southern base should not be left without a clear leader with General Tio's absence. From this moment forward, Assistant General Calin has been promoted to the full status as a general. The council makes this decision unanimously as a single unit because of the lack of a supervisor given the circumstances.*}

During the next break, he glanced at Calin while failing to repress a smile at the man's excited expression. "Congratulations."

"I appreciate your support," the soldier replied and dipped his head in a surprisingly bashful manner. "It's nice to hear they have faith in my abilities."

Marcus expected a joke given their relationship, so the honest remark left him struggling to come up with an appropriate comment. To his relief, Grace drew their attention again.

{*King Aaron would like to reassure you the paperwork will be sent at the council's earliest convenience.*}

Calin groaned at that.

{*In addition to this change, General Tont will be departing for Dala to help with rearranging the troops, including a new assistant general.*}

Although he sensed his comrade's eyes look to him, Marcus refused to meet the other's stare. *I guess I should have expected to be returning to Verona at some point. Father will probably drag me back with him once he finishes his business with Calin.*

{*This concludes the council's meeting. They are departing now, but King Aaron requests to speak with Assistant General Marcus.*}

"Aaron?" he couldn't refrain from muttering. The entire session left him struggling to catch up with his emotions, and his closest friend's invitation sent him off course again.

Fortunately, his comrade figured he needed time alone and departed to fetch them lunch.

*I'm ready when you two are*, he thought while imagining the words floating toward the palace.

{*I will let Aaron know.*}

Grace's casual demeanor returned, which he appreciated considering how they needed to use their formal titles during the conversations. When she spoke again, she didn't hide her growing weariness or juxtaposing interest in the topic.

{*He would like to make this brief since I am almost at my limit. With General Calin's promotion, you may remain in Dala and become his assistant or return to the capital with General Tont. Aaron is leaving the decision up to you and refuses to meddle with your status because he understands your views already.*}

*I would've berated him for that*, Marcus mentioned as he recalled his friend offering to step in and discuss the subject with his father a handful of times in recent years. *He's being respectful of my wishes.*

{*I see. Do you have a preference for where you would like to be stationed then?*}

He didn't answer. The stress of the past few days, the news from the council, and the options presented to him spurred a headache. Because of that, he figured he would need time to sort through his feelings.

*Grace, tell Aaron I'll consider my next steps and let him know when we talk again.*

{*I will pass your message along. Be well until then!*}

The Yeluthian's presence faded while Marcus released a sigh and dropped into his chair. His head rested in his hands, then he closed his eyes and cleared his mind in an attempt to relax until a knock at the door signaled his comrade's return. Calin entered without waiting for a reply carrying a tray laden with items from the kitchen.

"Are you finished speaking with His Highness?" the Dalan soldier asked when Marcus didn't address the man.

He nodded in reply, prompting Calin to take a seat beside him, select a few pieces of diced fruit, and push the tray over. They ate in silence until their stomachs filled enough not to bother them for a while. Only then did Marcus reveal Aaron's intentions.

"So he's giving you just two choices," the newly appointed general began after with an impassive expression that hid his true feelings. "That doesn't sound fair."

"It is," Marcus interjected while recalling the many instances in the past where he would complain about his father's tendency to overlook his actions and successes in favor of his seemingly endless potential. "Assistant generals must meet their supervisor's expectations in order to be promoted. That's how it's been since Asteom's founding."

"Usually the expectations are attainable though."

He clenched his jaw to keep from offering a retort or snapping at his comrade; he wasn't sure which would come out of his mouth if he wasn't careful. *I refused to believe I received special treatment because of Father's position until I became old enough to understand the truth of the world. My rise in status and work with Aaron were not entirely earned, so I doubled my efforts in order to compensate for my privilege. Accepting or arguing for leniency will negate what progress I made.*

Calin released a drawn-out sigh and scratched his head before meeting Marcus' stare. "I won't pretend to care about politics now, but I'll vouch for your combat and leadership skills any day. You're more than a match for me at either despite your age."

"Thank you," he replied and eased up as a weight fell off his shoulders.

"Did you decide what you're going to do? I'd like whatever time I can get to prepare my new assistants."

"I think so."

The Dalan soldier narrowed his eyes, staying Marcus' tongue.

"Before you go on, I want you to hear this from me," the man added into the pause. "The base and city will be fine. We survived this long, and these past years brought the people closer. If you feel you should move on, we will too."

Marcus nodded and even smiled at his comrade's honesty. "I appreciate your support, though you shouldn't let your new power go to your head. It's been about an hour and you're already telling me what to do."

The comment caused Dala's new leader to laugh. "I suppose somebody needs to carry on the late general's memory. You get his humor; I get his authority."

"I'm not sure if either is a blessing or a curse at this point."

***

Although every day in Kercher passed in a similar fashion to the previous, Hendal found he should be appreciative of the mundane lifestyle instead of complaining about its simplicity. His childhood and early adulthood consisted of a boring routine, driving him to depart from the eastern city and venture into the capital where he became the high priest of Asteom. Still, he never felt fulfilled once he learned the truth about his lost potential, which would have led him to become a mage instead of a holy figure. That reasoning pushed him to turn his back on the world as it was for what he saw it could be with the aid of Yeluthian deserters and a demon.

All this he reflected on while meditating in the garden outside the church where he stayed with his nephew and Wesley's apprentice, Lyla. The trio ate meals together yet ventured on their own business throughout the day. While the town's priest performed the regular responsibilities and often sent his niece on errands, Hendal took advantage of the peaceful atmosphere in order to channel what sense of balance the world would grant him.

*This environment is much more favorable than that damp cell,* he thought while staring up at the leaves of the nearest tree.

Their colorful assortment captivated him given his only view had been stone walls for months. *Life goes on despite what we endure as individuals. It will continue doing so even after my time is up.*

The reminder of his impending fate acted like a raincloud to drag him back to reality.

When Coura led him into his hometown, he expressed his reluctance to proceed for two reasons. First, and most prominent, was his desire to remain away from civilization since he would no doubt be brought back to the prison. The time alone without somebody influencing his behavior or mood allowed him to consider his past actions and mindset; part of him wondered if returning to that captivity would benefit him. Still, he savored his freedom with the knowledge he could be discovered at any moment.

The second reason he hated traveling through Kercher had to do with Wesley. He expected to run into his nephew at one point or another in the area because of the priest's duties and relationship with the messenger families Coura sought; however, it wasn't his concern over Wesley's reaction that frightened him. What made Hendal afraid of his nephew related to the younger man's caring nature.

*I knew as soon as he saw me he would listen to my tale and offer forgiveness*, he admitted, prompting his hands to ball into fists while he struggled to refrain from breaking down. *Wesley never once questioned why I did what I did. He merely upholds his kind smile and asks if I need anything. How can he not be ashamed of me? Why does he wish to be associated with a criminal?*

"Uncle Hendal?"

Lyla's high-pitched voice stirred him from the gloomy daze he dropped into, and he looked over to where she approached from the garden's entrance. Like his nephew, the young woman always seemed cheerful, though she acted a bit childish for her age, which he attributed to her underdevelopment at birth.

"Uncle Hendal," she repeated when he didn't offer a greeting. "Priest Wesley says the afternoon prayer will begin shortly. You are welcome to join."

He attempted a smile, stood, and winced at a slight ache in his joints. "I appreciate the offer, but I will be in the chapel until you finish."

She nodded without appearing displeased with his reply, which he figured since he responded the same way ever since he arrived. If anybody learned about him, he believed they would report his location to the guards posted around the city.

While Lyla started preparations for the aforementioned session, Hendal entered the safety of the church and dropped onto one of the benches before returning to his prayerful position. The moment didn't last long as footsteps from the hallway alerted him of Wesley before the priest spoke.

"Has the chill returned to drive you inside, Uncle?" the younger man asked in a lighthearted tone.

Hendal huffed a laugh as he met Wesley's amused gaze. "Your apprentice is getting ready for the afternoon prayer is all. The weather is fairly warm for this time of the year."

"You know you are more than welcome to join us," his nephew added, repeating Lyla's offer. "I won't introduce you, or I can make up a name."

"I appreciate what you're trying to do, but I am better off in here for the time being."

Although Wesley's hopeful expression deflated, the priest left him alone with a promise to begin cooking the evening meal once the group departed.

*I would help if I knew what to do*, he thought after his stomach lightly growled. The reminder of his uselessness even months after deciding to stay in the church added a weight to his shoulders.

The multiple voices lifting their prayers as a single unit soon reached him, so he let his mind clear as he listened, which brought about the most relaxed state he found recently. When they broke apart and chatted with each other after, he rose, went into the kitchen, and set the table before his nephew and the young woman entered. Despite their appreciation for his assistance,

Hendal still considered himself less than valuable to the meal's preparations.

Wesley found enough to discuss with his apprentice between bites to fill their time together, then the three cleaned up and washed the dishes before breaking apart for the evening. Hendal exited to enjoy the cool, fresh air that met him outside, and his nephew soon joined him. Though they hardly spoke, the moment felt reminiscent of their years growing up in the church. Before he could mention this, the priest suggested they return inside given the hour.

After he retired for the night and dropped onto the straw-filled mattress Wesley stuffed into the main bedroom used by the holy man, Hendal released a sigh. He repeated a prayer he vaguely recalled from his childhood before sleep took hold of him. When he stirred again, his nephew's faint snores sounded from nearby in the dark space.

*It must be the middle of the night*, he grumbled in his mind while rubbing his eyes before a yawn escaped him. Unfortunately, his body refused to relax again, even after a few minutes.

In order to avoid cursing aloud and potentially waking his roommate, he decided to venture into the kitchen for water and enjoy the quiet of the chapel, which used to calm his restlessness during his years as Kercher's priest. He tiptoed out the door and down the stairs, procured a mug that he filled with clear, fresh water brought in from the nearest well, and dropped into a seat in front of the altar. His weight caused the aged wood to creak, so he avoided moving around until he finished his drink.

*Given my distain with living here before, it's a wonder this is still my favorite place to be in the entire town*, he reflected before setting the mug aside in order to put his hands together. Then, he leaned back and closed his eyes.

Hendal drifted into a state of near sleep while remaining aware of his location. If he drifted off in his current position, he would no doubt wake with a stiff neck, back, or both. He also believed Wesley would playfully tease him for it somehow. That notion led him to rise and stretch with a slight groan at how comfortable he had been.

The last thing he expected to hear at that hour was a feminine, hauntingly familiar voice.

"Quite the hideout for a convicted criminal."

The sound startled him enough to jump before he spun around. No light brightened the building, preventing him from identifying the source.

Hendal's heart began pounding at the thought of an intruder, especially because of his vulnerability and status. "Who's there?"

For a moment, silence answered his question. Then, the voice returned at a different spot off to his right.

"Your prison cell has weakened your mental fortitude, though I don't remember there being much to begin with."

The laugh that followed those words sent a chill through his entire body, freezing him in place. *I recognize her...*

No matter how hard he tried, Hendal could never forget the presence of the malicious yet mischievous demon he allied with years ago. His hands and knees trembled at the idea of her finding him, mainly because he understood what that meant for his cause.

"Don't worry, former high priest. I am here under friendly tidings."

"Then it really is you," he mumbled with a mixture of disbelief, fear, and curiosity.

A second later, a figure parted from the shadows between the chapel's windows to approach him. He squinted in order to make out the silhouette before a sudden, crimson glow momentarily blinded him. Both hands flew up to cover his eyes while he blinked to adjust to the light, and he gazed forward after to find exactly what he expected.

"S-Soirée," he stuttered as he involuntarily shrank from the demon.

Nothing seemed to have changed concerning the creature standing before him. Her ebony hair and sleek, inky fur blended in with the darkness surrounding her, making her pale face, hands, and feet stand out. Violet eyes assessed him while an amused smile danced on her lips, as if his reaction had been exactly what she hoped for. In the palm of one hand rested a ball of fire, which he recalled her summoning on multiple occasions. The additional light also helped him catch a spot on her chest where the fur seemed to have been torn or burned away, leaving an ugly, white scar the length of his finger.

*This must be a nightmare*, he realized when he remembered hearing of the demon's death from Master Byron and King Aaron at his sentence. They never shared the cause or results from such a struggle, yet he had trusted their claim. *No one would tell me that unless it happened. Why bring it up at all or let me believe she was still alive?*

In response, Hendal buried his face in hands and gently hit his head repeatedly in an attempt to wake from the dream.

"Come now, you look ridiculous," Soirée teased, drawing his eyes again.

"This…is real? You're not…"

"Would you like to continue making a fool of yourself, or shall we move forward with our business?"

His mind went blank at her response. *What is she talking about?*

The creature went on without giving him a moment to reply. "It seems another demon has made a mess we must clean up. I managed to assist a bit, but we will regroup with him before heading south."

"You want me to… But, why?"

Soirée's eyes narrowed, and her lips evened out at his lack of understanding. "You are still of use to me, former high priest. Imagine the country under your thumb again. Besides, you always imagined a world where humans and demons could live together and share power. We have an opportunity to test that resolve."

Hearing her reasoning and how he previously held such outlandish beliefs brought about a sense of chagrin, leading him to dip his head and lower his gaze. *I issued such terrible orders, and for what? The sake of achieving what I saw as peace? She muddled my mind, but I acted of my own volition. I cannot even bring this up to Wesley without feeling such shame.*

During his pause, the demon began explaining some sort of plan involving a new source of power outside Dala; however, Hendal already made up his mind.

"I refuse," he interrupted when she took a breath between sentences.

She closed her mouth and remained motionless for a moment, seemingly to consider his answer. Then, she spoke at a lower volume akin to a growl. "You refuse what?"

After inhaling a deep breath and using his memories of the past to push him forward, he raised his eyes to meet hers. "I refuse to go with you."

The demon's unreadable expression didn't change.

"What I sought were ways to justify my actions against those who I convinced myself had wronged me," he continued despite a rising sense of nausea and the slight wavering of his voice. "I saw my restricted childhood, my unacknowledged potential as a mage, and the limits placed upon me as high priest as chains, so I focused on gathering power in order to ensure nobody could control me again. In my twisted mentality, I aimed to prevent others from being confined to a similar fate. I began believing what I did was right."

"Is that what happened?" Soirée countered without hiding her displeasure with his attitude. "You blame my magic for corrupting your virtuous nature?"

"Not entirely. The problem had been festering within for decades, and the demonic energy led me to follow through with my wishes."

The demon didn't move or respond during the following minute, giving Hendal time to reflect on why he felt the need to enlighten her of his sense of understanding. In the end, his reasoning came down to a single fact.

*My life is no longer my own*, he admitted to himself. *In Kercher, I am but a worthless burden on Wesley who can never reveal myself to the people. The guards across the country are no doubt aware of my escape. My chance to change fled when Coura walked through the chapel door, though I never imagined I would meet Soirée again.*

The thought prompted a slightly frustrated sigh from him. "Why are you here? Why me? You never truly gave me your power."

"Is that what this is about?"

Hendal opened and closed his mouth twice before hesitating to answer. To his dismay, the creature chuckled over his mumbles.

"You're upset because you could have possessed much more demonic energy, perhaps enough to prevent the capital city from slipping through your fingers. I suppose you can blame me for not fully trusting you to utilize what resources were available to you."

"That's not it at all," he snapped before remembering who stood before him.

Soirée scoffed, and he could visualize her rolling her eyes. "The past is the past, *former* high priest. Let us focus on the future. I can elaborate on my plan when we reach the mountains."

"Mountains?"

"Was your hearing damaged along with your pride?" she chided. "Enough talk."

With that, the human-like being turned to exit through the church's entrance. Hendal's body had relaxed enough to where he could follow, yet he intentionally kept his feet in place.

*My life may not be of value anymore, but if I hope to remain here, with Wesley and Lyla, I must not give in to temptations.*

Soirée reached the main door, faced him, then pointed at the ground, like a nobleman beckoning their dog. "It is unwise to try my patience," she warned after.

He inhaled through his nostrils and raised his chin before standing his ground. "I am finished cooperating with beings who desire to sow the seeds of chaos. Leave me be, demon."

His voice wavered as he issued the order, leading him to curse in his mind while maintaining as much of a confident demeaner as he could muster. Despite his reaction, he found he didn't regret what he said. The notion reassured him that even if she ended his life, he would die an honest man.

Soirée's violet eyes studied him until she closed them, shook her head, and huffed a laugh. Then, she opened them to fix him with her characteristic, amused stare. "It seems the person responsible for so many deaths and destruction has found a conscience. Congratulations on finally growing a spine, former high priest."

Before Hendal could come up with a reply, she stepped forward until she reached the nearest row of benches. Her empty hand hovered over the wood for a moment while she offered a devious smile.

"By now, I thought you would have learned not to cross a demon."

From the palm of her empty hand came sparks, which crackled and floated onto the wooden surface. Hendal realized her intentions too late as the flickers swelled into flames that rained down and clung to the bench.

"Wait, stop!" he cried and extended a hand. "You can't-"

"What is the worth of this structure to me?" Soirée interrupted. Her soft, almost-human features sharpened into an animalistic expression reminiscent of a predator cornering its prey. "If you refuse to join me on my new expedition, you are just as useless as the boards this building is constructed of."

*Wesley and Lyla are upstairs*, Hendal realized as the fire crept across the wood. *I can't let her harm them or this place! What should I do? Should I call for help?*

As if sensing his thoughts, the demon closed her open hand, abruptly ending her spell. She shrugged after and resumed a bored gaze. "I can just as easily put out these flames."

He ground his teeth as his frustration rose. "Then do it!"

"Why?"

He prepared to berate her for toying with him, like he used to during their time in the palace, until he recalled her purpose for being there. A sense of panic arose and steadily worsened as the fire spread to cover the entire surface of the bench. In his heart, he knew she would let the church burn if he didn't give her a reason not to, and she only asked for one thing.

"I'll go with you," he muttered against his better judgement and fear.

"What was that?" came the demon's response in a tone projecting mock intrigue.

"Enough games. Put out those flames, and I will leave with you."

Soirée's lips stretched into a grin before she extended her hand again. This time, she summoned an icy blast to snuff out the fire in a matter of seconds.

Meanwhile, Hendal's heart sank as he began to accept his fate. *Why me? Why would she need a useless criminal? Have I not been punished enough?*

More questions swarmed his mind until he heard the door open. When he glanced up, the being stepped through without looking back to make sure he followed. He moved to follow while sending a prayer to the gods for protection and his nephew's forgiveness.

# Locations

Unlike his previous journey to the northern border, Byron didn't need to press his pace. He no longer traveled with a mount yet found himself taking pleasure in the company around him, which included several soldiers and Clearshot. The group got along well enough to volunteer for scouting shifts throughout the day and talked casually during meals. Mainly, the men and women asked about his experience with his friend adding commentary every so often.

*This reminds me of my years in the army*, he mused with a slight smile as they started moving the morning of the fourth day. He felt they would reach their goal that evening, allowing them to ease into a steady hike instead of an urgent march. *Patrol routes around the capital city provided opportunities to learn about my comrades. I wonder where most are now.*

Footsteps to his left signaled someone's approach, and he turned to find Clearshot coming to join him. The man's spirits seemed to have improved despite the obvious weariness that would likely linger for months yet.

"Daydreaming?" his friend inquired while raising an eyebrow and offering a genuinely amused smile.

Byron shook his head. "Just savoring the peace and quiet. The general's camp is always too loud for me."

"Too much activity, you mean."

"That's never going to change, even if nothing is happening."

They focused on continuing forward with the others for a minute. Then, he heard Clearshot's voice at a lower volume akin to a mutter.

"I give it half a year."

"What?"

The archer glanced at him with a mischievous look. "Before you get bored in East Hoover."

Clearshot punctuated the comment by laughing as Byron opened his mouth to respond, closed it, and shook his head again.

"Have you forgotten I used to live there?"

"That was a peaceful time though. Now, I would bet you're used to the hustle and bustle."

"We'll just see." He went on to share several memories from his time in East Hoover before he accepted Symon's request to act as the academy's spokesperson when King Hernan started demanding mages. Although he appreciated those years, he couldn't help but look forward to not traveling as often and having his partner beside him.

"It sounds like you're ready to return," his friend added afterward. "When do you plan on finalizing your retirement from your position in Verona?"

Byron hesitated to answer, which caused Clearshot to click his tongue in a disappointed manner.

"I've been concerned about that you know," he continued while rubbing his eyes. "The kingdom will always face conflicts of varying degrees. At some point, we need to be able to step back and let the next generation of soldiers, mages, and ordinary leaders handle these issues."

The words sparked a conversation Byron had forgotten until that moment, prompting him to smile and raise his eyes to the clouds above. "General Tio once told me something similar."

"He was sharper than most of us gave him credit for."

"You're right. I needed to hear that others are just as skilled or prepared to manage the problems we face, or they will learn and develop new ways to combat what arises."

Clearshot elbowed him in the side but sent a reassuring grin. "I just want to make sure you're being stricter with your schedule. You deserve to leave whenever you want. Cintra's waiting for you too."

Byron dipped his chin in confirmation to acknowledge the support, so they left the conversation at that.

The rest of the trek went as expected. They prepared for the cooler temperature ahead of time, preventing them from struggling after the sun set; however, their lead scout returned with directions to the nearest camp. His update spurred sighs of relief and eager remarks, even from Clearshot and Byron.

As the group met with an ally from that site, they learned about their location compared to the border, which didn't prove to be any closer than a full day away. Then, the woman shared grimmer news.

"We captured a dozen Nim-Valan soldiers sneaking around over the course of the last week," she explained with a less-than-amused frown. "General Casner's orders are to keep them as hostages for the time being, but that puts a strain on our supplies. You'll be added to the rotation to monitor them and the perimeter."

Byron considered several questions regarding the enemy troops but kept them to himself. *The general must be doing this because so many got past Commander Evern and I when we faced the demon. I'd be surprised if they send additional men considering they're being captured at such an efficient rate.*

As his companions broke apart for the evening, their leader, the scout, and a man from the camp came to speak with him at the same time.

"We would like a word with you, Master Byron," the first began before looking to the two others.

"About what?"

Instead of answering, the soldier remained silent, allowing the stranger to speak while extending a hand.

"I'm Uriah, the person in charge at this location," he revealed as Byron accepted the gesture. "I expect you won't be staying with us for long and prefer to hear your plan in case the surrounding sites ask."

"He's quite popular," Clearshot interjected before Byron could respond, reminding him of the archer's presence at his side.

He shot his friend a halfhearted glare without denying the truth. *It's beneficial for these people to know where I am since I'm powerful but also likely to become a target if the demon returns.*

No matter the reason, he accepted the invitation. The four crossed the camp, approached an empty area hosting a bonfire, and sat before somebody brought bowls of porridge. Byron choked down enough of the familiar, bland mush to appease his stomach during the conversation. Then, he desired nothing more than to rest.

He would return the main camp, likely with Clearshot in tow, and be stationed wherever the general proposed due to the Nim-Valans' ambush and capture of their advisor's body. Part of him understood the curious trio's hope to predict the near future; however, in his heart, he wasn't certain they would be able to do so.

*There's the issue of the ancestral weapon being removed and releasing demonic power*, he reflected after everyone relaxed for the evening. *If Coura joined me, she would have been a valuable resource. I hate myself for thinking that, but it's a logical component of this fight. Now, unsuspecting troops like those in this camp might be facing what beasts that energy creates.*

Instead of letting his mind wander on the subject, Byron decided sleep would be more beneficial. The dream world soon overcame his mind, but to his dismay, it was filled with shadowy monsters.

***

Although the lack of conflict around Dala and the southern towns meant the humans living in those areas would soon return to peaceful lifestyles, Grace understood her usefulness to the king's council became limited.

"You're availability is essential during a crisis like what we've been facing," Aaron had told her after their previous conversation with Marcus and General Calin. "Thankfully, we'll be able to steadily decrease the frequency of our interactions with the southern base and focus primarily on General Casner and the northern border."

His words came to pass in the days that followed. Instead of contacting one area, waiting a day, then reaching out to the second location, she had been told they planned to utilize her goddess gift every third day. The additional time allowed her to recover what energy she expended better, yet the length of each discussion shortened as well.

*Why do I feel so upset by these changes?* she wondered as she lied on her bed the evening after she had been summoned. At that meeting, the council mentioned adjusting their contact with General Casner and General Calin to every fourth day, lowering her spirits further. *I should be pleased with the lack of harm befalling Asteom's citizens. Who would wish otherwise?*

As she considered the circumstances and how her responsibilities changed over the years, somebody knocked on her door. She sat up and rose to open it before hearing Dianne's voice on the other side.

"My lady, may I come in?"

"It is only you," Grace muttered with a relieved smile, as if her guard could hear her quiet voice. Then, she raised it in order to tell the woman to enter.

The soldier slipped inside while she dropped to sit on her bed again; however, instead of entering farther, Dianne lingered by the door. "Ambassador, how can you see anything without a lamp?"

Until that moment, Grace didn't realize the sun nearly finished setting, shrouding her space in near darkness. She excused herself to light the candle on her desk, which she would use for the lamp, but her guard snatched it first, grumbled about her absentmindedness, and exited. After a few minutes, the woman sat opposite her in the newly illuminated room.

"Honestly, sometimes I worry about you, my lady," Dianne chided, though in a lighthearted manner.

"You do not need to refer to me so formally; at least, not when it is just us. My other friends make it a point to abandon titles in favor of casual conversation."

"I'm sure they're not also your guards."

"They would still protect me as such."

The soldier huffed a laugh yet didn't pursue the subject. They sat in silence for a moment before Grace asked about the sudden visit.

"I'm sorry. It's late, and this could probably wait until morning, but it's been on my mind."

She raised an eyebrow. "What is wrong?"

"I want to ask you that," came the woman's response. "You've seemed bothered lately. I'm not sure if you have people readily available to talk with about your troubles, so I thought I would make it clear I'll listen. Unless this has to do with the council's business…"

"No," she clarified before finding herself giggling. "It is not that important."

"All the more reason to have someone you can vent to."

*This seems familiar*, Grace thought as she pondered the invitation. *When I first met Coura, she acted similarly. Although I do not have any siblings, their consideration is what I imagine an older sister would provide.*

The notion both amused and comforted her, allowing her to respond with her issue. By the time she finished, they began trading yawns.

"I can understand why you're conflicted," Dianne picked up afterward. "Plenty of people feel the same way when a certain task is no longer needed. I remember hearing about soldiers who wished for another battle after what took place in the southern field. For them, returning to normal wasted what skills they honed, and they couldn't see how much better our lives are without drama."

"What did you advise them to do?"

"I didn't say anything, but if I did, I would tell them to move on and find another way to keep themselves occupied. Train harder, learn a new technique, or try wielding a different weapon. Work with the mages to get used to spells being flung around. They could even take up baking for all I care!"

Grace imagined soldiers in the crimson uniforms splattering flour all over themselves while learning the process and laughed. Still, Dianne's message came across clearly. "I should look for a new means of keeping busy then."

The woman nodded. "Whether it's to assist the council, guide your people, or simply for your own enjoyment, the purpose should satisfy you."

After those words, another yawn escaped the soldier, and she stood to bow and depart so they could both sleep. Despite that, Grace remained awake to brainstorm options until they soon blended into her dreams.

*

A full night's rest and breakfast began recovering what power she used the previous morning. With Dianne by her side, the two wandered through the queen's garden, returned inside, and got her to her room so she could change before a meeting with the noblewomen in town. It had been a while since she received an invitation from somebody in Verona given the impact of the massacre on the families of the wealthy. When she did, she declined to attend because she wasn't certain how she would respond.

What prompted her to accept had to do with her intervention in the private dining hall. Nim-Valans snuck in, harmed Coura, and motivated her to cast the strongest binding spell she had ever used. That sense of courage sparked by her desire to stop others from being hurt left her realizing just how much she could do with her limited power and authority.

*Even if I do not use magic, I can still make a positive difference*, she told herself as she entered with her afternoon guard by her side. *The people impacted by the tragedy might benefit from my optimism.*

Nothing about the gathering felt different except for a few missing faces. Most notably, Lady Katrina's. Grace repressed the grief that arose at that thought in order to push forward.

Fortunately, the other, familiar women fed off her positivity and chattered enough to fill the afternoon. She even found time to speak with Marcy, who officially moved in with a nobleman and expressed interest in those in the palace. Given their shared experiences and relationships, the two caught up as friends, and she promised to visit again.

The following day held no plans, which proved to be a blessing when she decided she could practice magic in the newer training ground. Ever since Emilea's passing, she refrained from doing so because of her mixed emotions the memories arose; however, visiting the noblewomen who already seemed to continue with their lives and business despite the tragedy motivated her to do the same.

*It has been weeks since I spent time on my spells, yet I managed to bind that Nim-Valan man and help the guards capture the rest*, she recalled once she stood out in the open with Dianne. *Staying sharp and working with my magic will keep me prepared in case I find myself in a similar situation.*

Her guard didn't protest the training or question what would take place. Instead, she appeared intrigued by the process, making Grace wonder how often the woman encountered magic.

Dozens of other mages took to practicing while she followed several exercises the former light mage walked her through before, and she soon took pleasure in the freedom her energy provided. By the time she finished for the day, sweat covered her brow, though she made sure not to use too much of her power given her summons the next morning.

"Are you done for today?" Dianne called from where she sat in the grass to observe. "It's almost lunch, so we can head to the mess hall when you're ready."

Grace nodded and prepared to accept the invitation until she heard a familiar voice farther from the palace's stone walls, leading her to scan the open area. As she thought, Commander Detrix stood nearby offering instructions to a group of about a dozen people, both human and Yeluthian. What words she picked up interested her since she didn't recognize the spell he described.

"Could you wait a moment?" she asked the soldier when her curiosity won out. "I would like to watch their lesson."

Dianne pushed herself to her feet, agreed to the request, then trailed behind while Grace approached the circle.

"Remember, this is not a series of spells you shape instinctively," the commander advised as Grace slipped behind someone who would hide her from his sight. "You can think of it as a binding of sorts, which requires intense focus. Start there, and we will adjust as necessary."

Many affirmative comments followed from the rest of the mages before they broke apart to work independently. Meanwhile, she stayed at the edge of their circle and studied those around her.

*If Commander Detrix described a binding spell, they would need to practice on one another to both understand how to manipulate the energy on a living creature and what the complete process feels like from both sides. These light mages are positioned as though they are casting a shielding spell.*

Each individual extended their arms in front of themselves yet away from the nearest person. For some, the air in front of themselves shimmered a gold hue, but the fragments never solidified or melded together. This continued until Commander Detrix paused the lesson to demonstrate. Only when he managed to form three sides of a triangle did she recognize what they aimed to achieve.

*That is a prism sealing spell! I have not seen one since the former high priest was captured, though I recall the king's council discussed training light mages to learn how to summon both that and the goddess fire in case the demons return. I wonder how long this has been taking place.*

Despite her piquing interest in the session, Grace's stomach finally growled and tightened, as if protesting her decision to delay her next meal. She refrained from frowning but returned to her guard so they could eat together. By the time they returned to the field at her request, the commander and his students were gone.

*

Every day after her initial visit to the southern training ground, Grace spent half the time at the back of the group learning the prism sealing spell and practicing what she could with her remaining energy. Many mages picked up on the formation and

72

managed a basic section or two, including her, yet she spent time after lunch continuing in the safety of her quarters. This left her exhausted enough to sleep through the night, and she even visited the healers for a recovery potion when she needed to attend the king's council meeting the next morning.

By the following week, she caught up to those who could form all sides. It was then she understood the hefty price of the spell and why they struggled to maintain the fragments for long.

"Shaping the prism sealing is half the battle," Commander Detrix shared at the end of that session. "Once you craft the three sections, it becomes an endurance test. Light and dark energies naturally repel each other, which is the purpose of this mixture between binding and shielding. Consider this as casting two spells at the same time and what that requires from your body. Just like physical stamina, you must practice to strengthen your center."

A few individuals mumbled their confirmation, but they all wore themselves out. This seemed to amuse the commander, who chuckled and pointed at the palace.

"Use tomorrow to rest. In a couple days, we will begin your instruction on casting the goddess fire spell. I will warn you, that requires even more focus and can backfire if the output is too great. I intend to start small and build the flames, so be prepared to be patient."

Again, those who weren't exhausted replied before their instructor dismissed everybody. Grace turned to where Dianne sat on the nearest bench closer to the stone walls until she heard her name.

"Lady Zelnar, a moment of your time please."

When she faced forward again, Commander Detrix approached. The request startled her given he hadn't acted like he noticed her participation. "Of course, sir."

His serious expression lightened at her response. "If I knew you wished to learn these spells, I would have arranged for a private lesson. My apologies."

"It is no problem!" she hurried to reply and offered a reassuring smile. "I was not aware of the sessions until recently when I began training again, and working in a group allows me to observe their progress. I believe I understand better when I am not figuring out solutions on my own."

"I see. If you have any questions going forward, please do not hesitate to ask."

"I will, and thank you."

"Do you intend to return now that the prism sealing lesson is complete?"

She tentatively nodded and noticed his lips curve downward before he continued.

"Are you sure?" he asked and continued before she could answer. "I strongly advise against this. Such a powerful spell will always put the wielder's life in danger; that is just its nature as a wild force. Even I spent years building a tolerance to the burns in order to increase the amount of energy I put into it. Yeluthian and Asteom mages can do so since they participate in combat and risk their lives. You are our ambassador."

As he spoke, her spirit deflated, yet she refused to lower her gaze or avert her eyes in any way. *If I give up now, I will never forgive myself for backing down.*

"I sincerely appreciate your concern," she began once she put together a plea in her mind. "I am not a soldier, so I have no reason to prepare for a fight, and I remain in Verona. With that being said, my life was in danger not too long ago. If I had not learned how to wield what energy I possess, a few humans would be dead. I might not have survived either. That is what drove me to continue training and join your sessions. I wish to possess the skill to assist when I am needed. Even if that time may never come again, and I hope it does not, I would rather be prepared than be useless."

Some part of her words resonated with the commander, for his hardened expression softened, and he bowed his head a bit. "My lady, I respect your decision and admire your tenacity. I could never place myself in your position, but I understand what you desire given the situations you have been forced into."

"Thank you," she felt compelled to add.

"With that being said, the pair of spells requires practice to master. You are more than welcome to join going forward, but please speak with me if you need anything."

After promising to do so, Grace returned to Dianne, who inquired about the conversation, and she explained on their walk to the mess hall.

***

After spending the night in Fester, Coura ventured west and steadily moved south with the intent to explore the entirety of the area before the Western Woods. No magical presences interrupted the peaceful atmosphere, which she figured was in part thanks to Terran's defeat and the Dalan troops' intense defenses.

*How much do the Yeluthians assist with those efforts?* she wondered as she shifted her direction to the east where the base lied. *Commander Detrix and his soldiers are in charge of monitoring from the sky, so they might've had more of an impact than I realized. Does he plan on assigning me to a patrol route when I return?*

She wrestled with her feelings on being dismissed from Asteom's army as the days stretched into weeks until almost a month had gone by. While she had been granted freedom in a sense, she would be bound to Yeluthia's rules yet remain a citizen of both kingdoms. Those who knew her from her work likely questioned her position given how often she departed from one location and reappeared in another anyway.

Her mind lingered on the mundane subject and other, less urgent ideas, allowing her to suppress the fears recalling her fight with Soirée rose. Worst of all, she had no clue what the demon planned to do now that the traitors in Verona had been apprehended and Hendal abandoned the capital.

Fortunately, Coura soon recognized Dala in the distance as she trekked during the afternoon, which startled her a bit considering she hadn't stopped since she departed from her campsite that morning. The sight prompted her to increase her pace, especially when her mouth began watering at the thought of a hot meal.

*I have enough coins to spend at least a couple nights at an inn*, she told herself while remembering the trio of pouches on her person. The first included her savings, the second a standard amount from Commander Detrix for the assignment, and a third gifted to her by her father. *Maybe I'll treat myself a bit tonight and find Marcus tomorrow. He might use most of it to get drunk if I offer to buy.*

The memory of their first time in Fester replayed in her head as she entered the city and melded with the bustle of its people. A sense of relief steadily overcame any anxiety she felt from returning after the previous fight upon finding the area back to normal. The damages had been mended or were in the process of being repaired, what crimson blood splattered on the walls no longer marred the plain surfaces' color, and the citizens' natural behavior didn't hint at trouble.

*I should mention this to Marcus and Calin. They did an admirable job with the recovery efforts.*

Because she arrived earlier than anticipated, Coura decided to purchase a snack and wait to eat a full meal until she could speak to the assistant generals. Her desire to be alone for dinner dwindled as she watched families and friends around her laughing or chatting with one another, reminding her of her recent solitude. She managed to finish her food while crossing the open field and stood before the bridge leading into the southern entrance of the base. Her feet hesitated to go farther due to a sense of curiosity regarding Terran, so she acknowledged it by turning toward the field and scanning for what guards patrolled the body.

*I don't see anyone out there*, she thought and shaded her eyes from the overhead sun. *Did they decide to relocate him?*

A voice from across the moat interrupted her assessment and called for her to state her business, so she figured she could ask her friend about that later. After confirming her identity and requesting to speak with the assistant generals, the man supervising the area cracked a smile before ushering her forward where they entered the structure together.

"I recognize you from your training here and the battle in Verona," he shared once they were inside. "I've been a soldier for almost two decades now, but I've never seen any sort of fighter like you, mage, angel, or whatever. It's good to have you back."

The stranger's comment left Coura fumbling for an appropriate response. In the end, she thanked him and switched topics by mentioning her observations in the city. He apparently picked up on a lot from his routes, for he spent the rest of their walk explaining the recovery efforts before the pair stepped out into the centermost space used as a garden and training ground. She admired the spring flora while dozens of men and women occupied the open area beyond and practiced weapons work.

"I'd say we got off easy," the guard muttered as they approached the edge of the sparring section and scanned for a familiar face. "Except for the demon's disappearance, nobody can complain anymore."

"I doubt the effects of that will reach this far south, at least not for a while."

"What are you talking about?" He pointed in the direction of the city beyond the stone walls after. "It was lying in the field outside Dala."

Coura's feet abruptly stopped. "You're not referring to the one on the northern border?"

The soldier noticed she didn't follow and glanced back with a perplexed expression. "What does that have to do with us?"

While her mind went blank, her heart started racing despite all the blood draining from her face. *Terran too?*

"The generals and assistant general are over there," the man went on, oblivious to her shock. "I better return to my post."

Even though she intended to thank him, the words wouldn't form, so he returned to the entrance without waiting for her to pull herself together. She inhaled a shaky breath to calm down but only succeeded in shortening the next several.

*I can worry about that later. Maybe Marcus and Calin already have a lead or a plan in action.*

That optimism didn't sound as sure in her head as she would have liked; however, she pushed herself into continuing to where she saw the two conversing with a third man. Upon closer inspection, she recognized him as Marcus' father, General Tont. She wondered why he was in Dala as she waved to catch their attention, adding to the already lengthy list of questions on her mind.

"Back so soon," Calin began by way of greeting before she stopped in front of the trio.

She nodded, but before she could elaborate and request a private meeting, the general addressed her.

"What business brings you here? I was under the impression the Yeluthian troops are all traveling on various routes unaligned with Dala."

The way he phrased his words led Coura to believe he already knew about Terrell's dismissal, so she figured she didn't need to bring it up to the others at that moment. "Commander Detrix granted me permission to work on a special assignment involving the recent, demonic encounters."

"Did he now?" the man grumbled in a tone reflecting his doubt.

To her relief, he didn't press for details, allowing Calin to speak.

"General Tont and I have some paperwork to go over before it gets late," he admitted while glancing at Marcus. "You two can catch up, and we'll reconvene tomorrow morning."

Her friend offered a curt nod to acknowledge the message yet only properly greeted her when they stood alone. Then, he faced her with his normal, casual smile. "I didn't think I'd see you again for a while."

"Me neither," Coura replied and returned the gesture. "If it's not too early, we can catch up over dinner."

Marcus accepted the offer, leading them to exit the base, hike into the city, and select a tavern on the far side of Dala. That spot didn't look busy, which she appreciated given the nature of their discussion, though she imagined it would fill with customers by the time night fell. She waited until after the pair received their meals to drill him about Terran's disappearance, even if braving the subject ebbed her hunger.

"There's not much to tell," he began after a frustrated sigh as he poked at the vegetables on his plate with his fork. "Calin and I received word of an ambush on the guards surrounding the creature's body and rushed to the scene. Nobody was seriously hurt, but one soldier sounded like he'd been controlled. Whatever possessed him removed the ancestral weapon, dropped it, and ran off with the demon."

"You haven't noticed anything out of the ordinary since?" Coura asked when he didn't continue.

"Not a whisper. The mages don't sense unnatural energy either."

*What does this mean?*

A pause stretched between the two until Marcus decided to question her next.

"Why are you in Dala again? You mentioned an assignment from Commander Detrix."

Coura averted her eyes while piecing together an explanation, yet she realized she wouldn't be able to lessen the blow of the truth. She proceeded to share her demotion first since she assumed he would hear about it eventually, then she went on to reveal Soirée's disappearance during her recovery of the golden weapon she once wielded, how the item lied in Aaron's possession, and how she requested to search for the demon. Her friend paled a bit despite the dim lighting and didn't speak for a few minutes after. By that point, they finished their food and sipped at their drinks.

"All three demons are free again," Marcus grumbled without raising his eyes from his mug. "How did we go from ridding ourselves of them to having no idea where they're hiding?"

"I didn't believe they were connected before, but now I'm worried."

The assistant general met her stare and raised an eyebrow. "Why's that?"

"Their personalities are so unalike that I can't imagine them working together. They each found ways to manipulate people too, so they'll probably remain separated."

"More conflicts in more places."

Coura nodded as she shoved her empty cup away. "I guess we're back to where we were for the past year, except we know Soirée isn't bound by an ancestral weapon. At least you and Calin were able to repair the damage to the city, and it doesn't seem like the demonic creatures are a problem. Speaking of which, why is the general here?"

When Marcus released an annoyed groan, she understood he wasn't pleased with his father's appearance. He explained Calin's promotion, the need to fill the Dalan soldier's position, and the choice Aaron presented him with all without sounding in favor of any decision. By that point in the evening, the tavern hummed from the noise of its dozens of patrons.

"The scouts and Yeluthians will continue monitoring the towns nearby in case any demons or beasts show up," he concluded after ordering another drink.

"What will you do?"

"I plan on returning to Verona with my father. Calin should be able to handle Dala and the base, and Grace has been connecting us with the capital. He agreed to send for aid at the first sign of trouble."

*Having his father appear after Calin's promotion must leave a bitter taste in his mouth*, she noted. *I would be upset if I were in his shoes, though I'm curious what Aaron and the council will have him do. Would he choose to go to the northern border and support Casner?*

Upon recalling her final memories of that time alongside Byron and Evern, she remembered Will, causing her heart to leap; however, Marcus added another comment before she could surprise him with the news.

"We have a group heading west in three days. Without spare Yeluthians, it would be helpful if you could join them and patrol from the sky until they turn south toward Clearwater. You're free to do as you please after since they'll regroup with the troops posted at that location."

"I appreciate the opportunity to assist," she replied while struggling to hide a grin. "Is there anything else?"

He noticed her odd behavior and narrowed his eyes to show his suspicion. "No. What's gotten into you?"

Coura leaned forward, prompting him to do the same. "I forgot to tell you who I ran into when I was on the border with Casner's company…"

At the mention of Will's name, Marcus' eyes widened in disbelief. She savored his dumbfounded expression, as well as the stunned silence that lingered when she finished sharing their supposedly dead friend's adventures in Nim-Vala.

"He's really alive?" the soldier mumbled at last before lowering his gaze and rubbing his eyes.

"He volunteered to remain there, but I'm sure he'll come back to the capital once the conflict is over," she added. His reaction didn't appear as elated as she expected, but she knew she spent a few minutes in a daze once she stood face to face with Will. "If you don't stay in Verona, you can catch up with him in a new location."

When Marcus straightened and began digging through his coat pocket, Coura reached into the pouch buckled to her waist, removed several coins, and tossed them on the table. The assistant general glanced at her with a minor sense of alarm, as if he didn't expect her to pay for his meal and drinks too.

"Consider this my treat for the information and assignment," she clarified before rising to stand and stretch.

"I should be buying for you based on what you shared," he protested but ultimately left the money on the table.

They exited and moved toward the base by following the lamps' light until Coura considered staying at an inn instead of the base.

*Do I even belong there since I'm not part of Asteom's army?*

The unexpected question came from a dark corner of her mind and slowed her steps. Marcus noticed the changed pace from where he walked ahead and halted with a concerned expression.

"Is something wrong?"

Coura shook her head yet averted her eyes. Although she longed to dismiss the uncomfortable sensation that arose, her training with the Mintelians had her facing her problems instead of bottling them up. "I'm not a soldier anymore."

The assistant general tilted his head. "What does that matter?"

"You don't get it," she snapped before she could control her mixed emotions. "Do ordinary citizens pass through the base?"

"You're not an ordinary citizen, and Yeluthian soldiers are welcome too."

"I…I shouldn't…" She fumbled for the words to express what she felt but struggled. Eventually, the jumbled message faded when she abandoned the attempt.

Meanwhile, Marcus merely waited for a response without comprehending her strife.

*How would he know?* she told herself to combat her annoyance with his lack of understanding. *He's lived his entire life around the army. I grew up differently, which is why my position meant so much.*

"What's bothering you, Coura?" he pressed in a gentle tone. "Nobody at the base needs to know about the adjustment, and I doubt any of them will care."

She paused to take a deep breath, then she braved the explanation that came from her heart. "For years, all I learned was how to become a better fighter and mage. I belonged somewhere, even if I followed my own path. Not being restricted to the rules and assignments doesn't bother me, but I feel like I lost part of myself. I don't fit in at the base."

Marcus stared at her with obvious surprise and didn't respond despite opening and closing his mouth twice.

The sudden confession left her mentally fatigued. That combined with her physical weariness spurred a yawn, so she glanced around to find the nearest inn. "It's late, and I brought enough money to spend on a room in the city anyway. I'll head to the base in the morning to find you so you can point me in the direction of the group you want me to accompany."

"I should be apologizing," she heard him say at a lower volume, piquing her interest enough for her to face him again.

"For what?"

"I'm your friend and comrade," he began with more confidence. "That means I should be supporting you no matter what. I could tell what you just said was hard to admit, but I couldn't come up with an appropriate reply."

"That's not your problem," she interjected only to be chided.

"I just reminded you I'm your friend and comrade. Not only that, but you're a Yeluthian soldier. All allies of Asteom deserve our respect and to be treated as equals. With that being said, I can never comprehend how you feel, especially because you trained at the MAA, but I'm here for you. I'll listen and do what I can to help however I can."

Something about his chivalrous reaffirmation of their relationship lifted her spirits. *He didn't try telling me how I'll be treated won't change or sugarcoat the truth. My position might be limited, and that will affect my work going forward; however, my Asteom allies won't abandon me. My home is still intact.*

She thanked him for the message before he offered to escort her through the base so she could use one of the spare rooms and save time in the morning. Because of the logical approach, she accepted the invitation.

# A Fated Reunion

The trek with the Dalan soldiers proved to be as boring as Coura anticipated, which didn't wear on her nerves except when she soared above. Nobody seemed to mind when Marcus introduced her the morning following her arrival and mentioned she would be monitoring the area from the air. In fact, she noticed some relieved expressions, leading her to believe they appreciated the extra set of eyes.

Their unspoken gratefulness and polite behavior, or polite by the base's standards, when she joined them during breaks and meals held her impatience in check. Nothing hinted at danger in any direction she explored within her view of the soldiers, yet she needed to remain close enough in case of trouble. This led to her flying in circles like a horse tethered to a post.

After three days, the group reached a bend past the underground tunnel that curved the road south. Coura kept a close eye out for the Yeluthian who would be patrolling that area in case they showed up sooner; however, she landed for the night as the sun set without hiding her disappointment.

"How are the skies?" one man asked from where he sat as soon as her feet touched the ground.

She dismissed her wings, tossed her hair over her shoulders, and came closer before dropping to sit cross-legged beside him and his companions. "No change from the previous days."

The troops expressed their appreciation for the fair weather and left her alone once the regular meals were passed around. By the time everyone relaxed to sleep, the sounds of the nocturnal creatures and insects surrounded them, settling the area into a peaceful atmosphere. This allowed Coura to drift off without issue.

Unfortunately, for the first time in weeks, she woke with a start in the middle of the night. Every muscle in her body grew tense, which she learned over the years meant her senses picked up on a threat. She shifted into a crouch in order to crawl toward the others and rouse them, but before she could do so, the presence revealed itself just enough to identify the danger.

*This is her energy*, she noted with no shortage of panic. *Where is she hiding? Perhaps I should warn the guard or flee and hope she pursues.*

After a few seconds to collect her thoughts, she realized the connection to the demon didn't change, meaning the creature kept its distance while contacting her. Soirée used such a tactic in the past to lure Coura toward her, and that seemed to reveal the being's intentions.

*She doesn't plan on ambushing me here, which saves me from raising the alarm and drawing the soldiers into our conflict. I suppose I should be grateful for that.*

Knowing the demon found her first sent a chill throughout her body, yet she managed to pack her belongings, rise, and tiptoe to the nearest of the three guards patrolling the area. Upon seeing her with her pack, the man seized the hilt of his sword.

"Is there trouble?" he practically demanded, though she couldn't tell if his behavior reflected concern or excitement.

"No, but I'll be departing early. I have some business to take care of nearby. You don't need to wait for me."

Although he appeared to want to question her, the guard relaxed and nodded before wishing her luck.

*I'll need all the luck in the world if she's looking to fight*, Coura couldn't help but think after thanking him. *Now, should I explore on foot or narrow down her location from above?*

Due to the late hour limiting her sight, she decided to utilize her advantage and manifest her wings to make traveling easier. Night flights didn't take place often, but she preferred the open air to the crowded trees and felt comfortable with less threats.

The clear sky allowed her to savor the view of the starry ceiling embellished by a crescent moon, and the wind provided plenty of noise to drown out her negativity. A sense of anxiousness at the inevitable confrontation kept her focused on the power tethering her to the creature, so she utilized that to avoid considering the worst case scenarios.

*She's close...*

Just when Coura began circling back toward an opening she could descend into, the demon's presence flared. The sudden, jarring pull on her center caused her to gasp, and her body grew tense before her eyes darted to the earth below. A second later, a flash of light warned her of an attack.

The area lit up in a familiar enough manner to signal a lightning spell. Because of that instinct forged from experience, she twisted to the side in an attempt to dodge the blast; however, part of the bolt caught her right wing, singeing the skin and burning those feathers away. Pain lanced through her shoulder, yet she forced her body to move in preparation for a follow-up spell. To her relief, none came.

*I bet her aim was to incapacitate me,* Coura noted and growled a curse. *The strength behind her lightning didn't feel like it would have killed me, even if it landed in a different spot. Still, I should get out of the sky. I did come here to meet her after all.*

Without lowering her guard, she cupped her wings in order to descend and searched for a place to climb to the ground. The lack of light prevented her from finding one until she nearly touched the treetops, which raised her nerves enough to put her on edge, yet she eventually slipped under the canopy. Only then did she slow her pace, both for her safety as she maneuvered down the branches and so she could listen for danger.

*I'm completely vulnerable. I can't dismiss my wings until I'm sure I won't fall, my sight is limited until I can summon fire for light, and the noise I make will draw her right to me.*

Coura paused, surveyed her surroundings as best as she could, then took a deep breath before climbing down. This continued until she found herself touching the ground. The weight of her wings lifted once she thoughtlessly cut off the spell while drawing her sword. Few insects chirped given the intruder in their woods; however, the noise picked up as she crept through the brush. During that time, she couldn't help but remember how much she despised wandering in the mass of trees.

The focus she maintained prevented her from keeping track of how much time passed. Unlike their past encounters, she wasn't certain if Soirée would actually aim for revenge or simply wish to control her again. This led her to assume she'd be in for a fight.

Finally, a break in the bushes signaled the edge of a clearing. Coura moved into the space and savored the openness that allowed her to stand straight and extend her arms further. Her feet led her toward the center of that area and stopped.

*If I summon a light, it'll act as a beacon and lead her directly to me, and my sight will be hindered if she attacks and I abruptly end the spell. I suppose calling out would do the trick too.*

She inhaled with the intent to do so, yet the words sat in her throat.

*Quit cowering*, she grumbled to herself. *It's been years since we've seen each other. I've grown stronger. I always have my goddess gift to rely on if the situation becomes worse than I can handle.*

As her resolve solidified once more, Coura returned her attention to the presence still humming between them. She hoped she would receive another warning when the demon struck but doubted such fortune. Both hands clutched the hilt of her weapon, and her muscles automatically prepared for combat, which allowed her to spring into action at the faintest whisper of movement from the surrounding bushes.

Her body and mind remained steady while nothing about the environment changed. Despite her previous concern over drawing Soirée to her, she began to realize the creature likely found her position already and was merely waiting for the perfect opportunity.

*At least I know she still enjoys toying with her prey.*

She told herself then to react to any, unnatural sounds despite the possible causes. Doing so wore on her patience, yet she understood it would likely be her best chance to survive if the being intended to harm her.

That fortitude was rewarded when a whisper of laughter reached her from behind. The low volume could have had anyone else believing their mind played tricks on them; however, Coura taught herself not to ignore such hints. Her body instinctively spun around, and a hand raised to manifest a shielding spell using her light energy. A surge of lightning slammed against the magical wall a heartbeat later, producing a deafening crash of thunder.

With the shield in place, she fed additional energy into it before putting her back to her spell just as the blast ended. A shadow slid around from the right after and darted for her. Coura raised her blade even though she couldn't see the other's weapon until a glint created by the lingering sparks caught her eye. She shifted her sword to meet her enemy's, resulting in a ring of metal that echoed around the quieted woods. What pressure pressed against her did not feel like enough to overwhelm her though, yet she took no chances.

The shadow attempted a pair of swings, which she managed to predict and block, then the figure retreated. Unfortunately, putting distance between the two led Coura to lose sight of the other's sword.

*If this is Soirée, she probably dismissed her weapon. That means she'll resort to magic again or a physical attack.*

The split-second realization prompted her to scan the woods before deciding on another shield in case the demon used magic. Like earlier, she raised a hand, manifested a second wall of light energy, then faced the open space.

*Two shields should be enough*, she rationalized as her eyes struggled to spot the shadow. *I shouldn't put myself in a corner or use too much of my Yeluthian power right away. Should I address her now or-*

A crimson glow from farther ahead sprouted into a wave of fire stretching the length of the gap between her shields. Coura swore under her breath before dismissing both spells in order to retreat and avoid the flames. As soon as they passed by her location, her opponent emerged, though the dim light allowed her to confirm Soirée's silhouette.

As if sensing that, the demon charged to initiate combat once more; however, this time the creature didn't give her a moment to consider using magic. The edge of the dark blade scratched her several times when she lost track of the other's movements, but she limited the damage to those for a while. In a way, the lack of a serious intent to kill came across clearly through their bond, piquing her interest until her weariness became an issue.

Both arms throbbed from the constant exercise, her legs responded slower, and her mind became so focused on keeping up with the shadow that she didn't spare a thought until her opponent disappeared again. By that point, she stood panting.

*I can't continue fighting without a break*, she told herself despite her heart's desire to pursue the being. *If I summon a light, would she pause to discuss her business?*

When nothing spurred another bout, she decided to follow that train of thought and turned the palm of her empty, left hand upward in preparation for a fire spell. The spark she summoned grew into a controlled ball of flame that lit up the open area. To her dismay, the demon was nowhere in sight.

"Soirée, I know it's you," she finally called after finding her voice. "Enough games."

Her words received no response, and she released an annoyed sigh. She planned to mention departing and forcing the creature to locate her again until a rumble of laughter reached her from a spot in the trees to her right. Somehow, she knew a spell would follow and dismissed the fire for another shield. The sudden loss of light prevented her from seeing since her eyes needed to adjust, but she clearly heard a chorus of shatters against her magical barrier, like breaking glass, which she recognized as icicles.

Naturally, she backed away with the hope of listening and waiting to spot the shadow in order to prepare for another attack; however, she didn't notice anything once the blast of ice ceased. Coura spun around to put her back to the wall of energy again and slowed her hasty breathing.

The sound of footsteps rose from the left, so she shifted her position, raised her sword, and scanned that direction for movement. What she didn't expect was a flash of light close enough to blind her for seconds after. What lightning the demon released connected with her sword and arms, sending a burning pain through them and forcing her to release the weapon.

Shock registered first before Coura considered magic, yet she practically felt the demon upon her and had no time to consider her next action. A sense of panic followed.

*I need protection!*

With nothing to do besides react through sheer instinct, her past experience with demonic energy took over her body. The power within her center activated as soon as she triggered it and raced to her currently empty, right hand. A familiar weight rested there once she closed her grasp, and she raised that arm despite the pain to defend herself with the black blade she manifested. Another ring of clashing metal sounded, making her realize just how close she had been to getting sliced through.

Instead of pursuing, her opponent immediately retreated. Coura didn't move even though she had a better view of the shadow. A moment later, the creature's amused laughter filled the clearing once more.

"And here I thought taking you by force would be the easiest option," came the familiar, haunting voice.

Before Coura could reply, the crimson glow of a fire spell returned, and Soirée held a ball of flame identical to the one she summoned mere minutes ago. That minor show of power and nothing more allowed her to let down her guard. Her arms lowered, though she noted the charred flesh on her forearms, then she resumed catching her breath while observing her enemy.

Nothing changed since their last meeting except for a missing patch of fur where Coura stabbed the creature using the golden blade she recently reacquired. A scar rested on that spot, though based on Soirée's confident posture and mannerisms, she wondered if the being saw such a blemish as a trophy of sorts.

The pause invited the demon to approach while going on. "What a combination! Light and dark energy working in tandem. It's unheard of, yet here we are. You continue to impress me, Dear One."

Coura remained silent while studying the creature before her. Fear mixed with a burning hatred for the being, and that with her rising impatience, leaving her itching to find a way to end her opponent's life as soon as possible.

Meanwhile, Soirée pretended not to notice. "It's almost as if we never parted, so let's not waste any more time with a meaningless reunion."

With that, the demon put her back to Coura and began walking away.

"Wait!"

The demon paused and glanced over her shoulder with a smirk, though she didn't reply to the order.

"Where are you going?" Coura pressed after her momentary alarm at the creature's behavior given their previous fight. "What are you doing here?"

"Isn't it obvious? I came to find you."

"Why? What do you want with me?"

"I forgot how exhausting humans are," Soirée muttered loudly enough for Coura to hear while facing her again. "Our venture to the world beneath the surface gave me an idea. A new test, if you will."

Coura narrowed her eyes at the implication. "You mean a new experiment."

"Of sorts, yes."

"What makes you think I'm going to volunteer myself to help you?" she snapped despite her attempt to control her voice. Part of her knew the demon would overpower her with ease based on their confrontation alone, but the other side firmly believed the most beneficial reaction would be to stand her ground.

Soirée's gaze didn't waver, and as Coura hoped, the creature continued speaking instead of using force. "I suppose you don't need to participate, but the other human assisting me might have an easier time if you're present."

"Other human?" she mumbled while struggling to figure out the demon's intentions. "Who would ever want to be associated with you?"

"You did, for one."

Coura ground her teeth at the comment. *She's not wrong, but she also threatened my home. If she mentioned my past, I bet she's similarly backing somebody else into a corner.*

Before she could mention this, the creature again dismissed their conversation by turning away to walk toward the darkness looming beyond the brush. This time, when she shouted for Soirée to stop, the demon ignored her to disappear into the trees. The invisible leash's pull tightened slightly though enough to keep her aware of her target's location, which she assumed was intentional.

*What should I do?* she wondered after cursing the situation. *I planned to find her and report back, yet someone's life is in danger. I also can't guess what she's working on. It could be more dangerous than possessing people and creating pawns.*

The notion that stuck out in her mind and prompted her to follow the demon had to do with Soirée's decision not to kill her or seriously try harming her. She reflected on this as she leapt into the sky to soar from above instead of wander aimlessly through the woods.

*I don't like this. I'd believe she still needs me for her twisted experiments, but I doubt she's not upset I sealed her with the ancestral weapon, even temporarily. The more I learn about where she's hiding and what she's up to, the more detailed my report will be.*

*

Coura didn't need to land until the afternoon of the next day. Although she would have preferred a break to eat, rest her body, and enjoy the lack of pressure and wind in her ears, Soirée never slowed. She imagined the demon would rather hurry to their destination while the sun hovered high in the cloudless sky instead of catering to her.

*I'd like to get to wherever she's taking me too*, she admitted as she ignored the tightness of her stomach brought about by hunger. *How far east does she plan on going? I can see the plains in the distance. Any farther and I'll need to rely on my wings since my goddess gift won't reach Dala.*

The empty fields beyond were a stark contrast to the evergreen forest below. That led her to wonder how her guide would cross the area without cover. As soon as she reached the edge of the woods, Coura got an answer. Soirée's presence remained within the trees, so she decided to descent and land just out of the trees' reach.

"Why did we stop?" she called in the demon's direction while removing her pack. Before departing for any sort of scouting mission, she formed a habit of grabbing extra rations as a snack or emergency food in such a situation where she would be on her own.

The response to her question came just above the natural sounds surrounding them. "We will wait until nightfall to continue."

Coura longed to express her displeasure with the delay but knew she should eat and rest while she had the chance. This prompted her to dismiss her wings, find a comfortable enough spot underneath one of the leaf-covered branches, and consume enough of her provisions to fill her empty, complaining stomach. Then, she relaxed her body after drawing her blade and laying it across her lap.

Sleep took her eventually until she naturally woke when the demonic presence flared. By that point, the sun just set on the horizon, allowing hundreds of stars to decorate the sky.

"Let's go," came Soirée's voice from off to Coura's right while she stood and rubbed her eyes.

The creature's silhouette parted from the shadows before breaking through their cover and into the field ahead. Instead of rushing, Coura took her time sheathing her blade, stretching, and shouldering her bag.

*It's not as if she'll outrun me. Besides, I couldn't rid myself of our bond even I wanted to.*

Her leash tightened then, as if in response to her internal comment, so she manifested her wings and leapt into the air.

While the two moved straight east, her curiosity piqued since the Ghurun Mountain Range grew the closer they came to its frightening stature. If it wasn't for the demon's presence, Coura would have lost her completely in the unorganized layout of boulders and uneven terrain. The sight reminded her of her journey to the Mintelian village where her guide from Kercher followed signals left in natural-looking positions along the way.

*This makes finding anyone difficult*, she noted after realizing Soirée most likely hid among the mountains after escaping from under the earth's surface.

Coura only landed once the demon climbed to a nondescript cliff alongside the mountain that rested a few stories off the ground. When her feet touched the rock, she released the spell on her wings and began walking forward to meet the being, who halted at the entrance to a cave she couldn't see earlier.

What she hadn't been expecting and didn't consider until something moved out of the corner of her eye was for Soirée to not be working alone.

A forceful shove from behind sent her stumbling forward; however, before she could catch her balance or retaliate, the newcomer seized her arm, yanked on it to twist her around, and used the other to strike her in the gut. Although she doubled over onto her hands and knees at the blow, the hauntingly familiar attack sent a shiver down her spine before a deep voice addressed her.

"We meet again."

Coura glanced upward with a wince. *Is that Terran?*

Before she could confirm her assumption, the figure raised a fist and landed another punch against the right side of her face when she turned away. The strength behind his hit had her seeing stars, and the next thing she knew, she lied on her side until a kick rolled her onto her back. Only then did the pain seem to register, along with the realization.

"What are you doing here?" she attempted to demand through the fog clouding her mind. Already, her cheek began swelling, and she felt bruises forming where the attacks landed.

"I should be asking you that," came the demon's retort. "Either way, I don't plan on squandering an opportunity to-"

"Leave her alone," Soirée interrupted in a bored tone.

Despite the lack of urgency, her intervention startled Coura and irritated Terran.

"I didn't agree to sparing humans," he retorted without moving. "Either I kill her now and get one piece of revenge out of the way or I wait to do it later."

"Then do it later."

Coura longed to throw in her input yet stayed her tongue when Terran released a low growl. Fortunately, Soirée's limited sense of mercy reached him, for he rose and retreated to stand near the edge of the cliff with an annoyed expression. Only then did she scramble to her feet and address both demons.

"What's going on? Where is the human you said is working with you?"

She caught Terran raised an eyebrow, yet it was Soirée who responded, and in her characteristically uninterested manner.

"You'll find him in the cave behind me. We'll let you two catch up."

When Coura remained in place, the being rolled her eyes, strolled toward Terran, and shot him a knowing, wicked smile.

"Shall we discuss our business then?"

A hand reached for his shoulder when she got close, but he slapped it away and bared his pointed teeth in a menacing fashion. Their playful yet aggressive behavior reminded Coura of a pack of wolves, though she didn't dwell on the subject as the pair descended down the nearest, narrow trail circling the cliff. She faced the cave and tentatively crept forward until she stood just within the entrance.

"Hello?" she halfheartedly shouted into the lightless space. "Is anybody here?"

No voice answered except a faint echo.

*Could this be a trap?* She didn't put it past Soirée to trick her, yet she also recalled the demon's honesty with her over the years. *Whoever she kidnapped must be farther inside.*

With a flick of the dark energy in her center, she summoned a minor fire spell to light the tunnel before proceeding into the unknown area.

The cave system Coura followed proved to be damp but not unbearably so, though the distant squeaks of bats had her dimming the flame in her hand. As she wandered, her connection to Soirée steadily disappeared, leaving her to process her surroundings without interference. Part of her still distrusted the demon; however, nothing awaited except the next section of rock.

*How far does this go?* she wondered when she reached a fork in the tunnel and paused. *If this turns into an underground maze, I'm in trouble.*

After listening to both sides for any noise, she decided on the leftmost one due to the lack of sound from the cave dwellers. Nothing changed as she proceeded to walk forward until several, dry coughs came from ahead to alert her of the human Soirée mentioned.

"Hello?" she called a bit louder while continuing. "Is somebody there?"

Mumbling reached her in response. She longed to rush ahead when she considered if the person fell ill or had been hurt by either demon, yet she held herself to a slow pace until a figure huddling against the cave's wall came into view. When the glow from her spell washed over them, as well as the back to signal a dead end, she recognized the face of the former high priest.

"Hendal?" she all but breathed. Her nerves reacted to her shock, confusion, and suspicion by warning her to be cautious. "Why are you here?"

The man had raised his pale arms to cover his eyes but lowered them slightly to look upon her. Only when he appeared to identify her did he bumble a reply. "Y-You… I never thought… You're w-working with her again?"

Coura bit her tongue to keep from snapping at him, especially because his behavior seemed dazed and weary. With a sigh, she approached, knelt beside him, and looked for any injuries to be certain he hadn't been physically harmed. No bruises or blood marred his robe or what skin she could see, so she shifted to sit cross-legged in a more comfortable position.

*I suppose I should interrogate him a bit.* Before she could do so, Hendal folded his hands together and bent his head in a prayerful position.

"S-She… The demon came and… I only offered to go with her if she-"

"Calm down," she interjected to end his babbling. Evidently, something disturbed his mentality since she'd never heard him speak so flustered. "What did they do to you? Start at the beginning."

That was when Coura learned what befell the former high priest. Soirée's unexpected visit, her threats to the church and his family, and how she forced him to hike to their current location left her feeling mixed emotions, though mainly anger at the creature's manipulation over innocent lives.

"She left me here and only returned once with a bag of fruit," he finished. The entire time, he averted his eyes, as if ashamed of his behavior.

That response stirred a sense of pity from her. "It's not your fault she returned and brought you here. I met her under similar circumstances."

"You did?" he replied without hiding his doubt. "I recall her mentioning your heritage, but my mind was clouded back then."

Coura paused to remove her pack and offer it to the man, who tentatively opened it before digging into the remaining rations. Although she warned him about the hunting knife she kept inside that would surely slice open his hand or fingers if he was careless, he ignored it, prompting her to continue. "She threatened my hometown if I didn't agree to let her try a possession spell on me."

He glanced at her with an unreadable gaze, prompting her to look away.

"Anyway, make sure you eat enough to get your energy back," she continued indifferently. "I'd like to rest during the night and set out in the morning."

"Where are we going?"

"I plan on confronting Soirée about her intentions involving us."

"And after that?"

"It depends on what she says."

She dismissed her fire to crawl away from him and prop herself against the wall with her sword across her lap. The abrupt end to their discussion didn't bother her since she wasn't certain how the rest of the morning would play out.

*

Because of the cave's thick darkness, Coura couldn't determine the hour when she woke. Only Hendal's snoring interrupted the environment, which she accepted as a positive.

*No Soirée or Terran*, she noted while stretching and rising to sheath her blade. *What could they possibly be doing that requires us to remain here?*

The question swirled in her mind, preventing her from forming a strategy when the beings eventually returned. She mustered enough energy for a light and summoned the ball of fire again before blinking to let her eyes adjust. Once that took place, she left the former high priest where he lied to explore the rest of the tunnel system, ignoring her growling stomach in the process.

She returned to the fork and followed the third path until it abruptly ended with a terrifying hole in the middle of the floor. Although she peered ahead, she couldn't locate the other side, which deterred her from attempting to continue exploring by flying across.

*I should probably wake Hendal and get going*, she told herself when she contemplated their escape from the cave and demons. *This isn't going to be fun. I'm definitely too far to try my goddess gift. I could fly off, but he's stuck to the treacherous trails, though I suppose he managed to climb here on his own. If I bring it up beforehand, will he go along or complain?*

Her suspicion regarding their predicament rose with every step as she returned to the former high priest, who sat up and hugged himself. He studied her and only spoke when she retrieved her pack.

"Where did you go?"

"I explored the rest of the cave," she explained and threw the bag over her shoulder. "There's nothing else aside from this space."

Hendal grumbled to himself but left the subject at that. Coura assumed they would be able to move on with their departure and prepared to order him to rise and stay behind her; however, he cowered when she drew her sword.

"What are you going to do?" he inquired in a frightful manner.

His timid behavior led her to raise an eyebrow at him. "We're going to get out of here."

"We can't! Soirée is out there, and if she decides to attack…"

"I would rather attempt to flee than remain trapped," she proclaimed matter-of-factly. "If we do confront her, you need to hurry to the plains and far away from the mountains."

The hopelessness and fear he projected came across clearly in his wide-eyed expression. Coura turned away to ease her impatience and took a deep breath before addressing him again.

"We'll be fine as long as we're careful not to-"

"What's this?" Soirée's voice interrupted from farther down the tunnel.

The unexpected sound sent a jolt through Coura. She spun around to face the demon who managed to sneak up on them and loomed at the edge of her fire's light.

*I hoped she'd be gone, and where is Terran?*

Soirée clicked her tongue and shook her head before looking between Coura and Hendal. "I suppose I shouldn't be surprised you'd attempt to escape. After all, I often forget humans need to eat in order to survive."

When the creature stepped toward the former high priest, Coura's instincts kicked in, bringing her to slide between the two while raising her sword. "What do you want with us?"

"Us?" the demon replied and tilted her head. "At the moment, you're just in our way."

Before Coura could process the words, Soirée lunged for her. She chanced a swing with the blade in her right hand as she debated dismissing the spell in her left. Doing so would forfeit her sight, but she knew the loss of strength and stability also hindered her combat.

In the end, it didn't matter. The creature accepted the deep wound to her chest, splashing dark blood on the rock floor; however, she managed to reach Coura's left forearm, seize it, and yank forward. The force of the pull strained Coura's shoulder, though she maintained her spell until the demon circled around her and twisted her arm behind her back. Heat from the flames burned her palm when her control slipped, leading her to dismiss the fire.

Darkness enclosed the tunnel then, and she became unable to stop Soirée from taking advantage of the opportunity to overpower her. Sharp kicks to the sides of her knees had her staggering until the demon shoved her to the ground. Although her left arm became free, a sudden blow to her right hand caused her to release her weapon. Without a means of defending herself aside from magic, Coura prepared to manifest flames again until a sudden pressure on her back had her lying face first on the cool floor.

"Now, now," Soirée chided from where she knelt on Coura's spine. "I thought you wanted to talk."

When Coura squirmed in an attempt to free herself, the being gripped the hair close to her skull and pressed her head against the ground, keeping her in place. She tried to come up with a solution but grew distracted by footsteps from nearby. A startled cry from Hendal followed before shuffling signaled a struggle.

"What are you doing?" she growled amid the man's resulting pleas for help.

An answer only came when the noise faded as Hendal had been dragged from that area, though his voice echoed for a few minutes. Coura's heart thundered in her chest the entire time, and a sense of guilt at how she let him be taken away so easily began eating at her conscious.

"Believe it or not, finding a suitable host for demonic energy is quite difficult."

The unexpected comment caught Coura off guard. "What are you saying?"

"The former high priest had the potential to wield magic, but when that goes unnoticed, the energy fades despite the center of power already being established. Humans in those positions tend to be well suited as hosts."

"That's why you sought out Hendal? You want to use him again?"

"Not me."

The resulting silence worsened Coura's spirits as she pieced the situation together. "You offered him to Terran."

"In a way," Soirée replied before giggling. "To put it simply, I taught him how to forge a bond between a demon and human."

"*What?*" she snapped to show her anger. "How could you-"

"That type of relationship allows the collected energy to be shared between the two," the demon interrupted without a hint of remorse. "The former high priest will never expend what power he gathers, allowing Terran to merely increase his."

Coura longed to demand more of an explanation and berate Soirée for toying with the man's life, yet how the being revealed her plan hinted at an underlying motive. After a moment, she stifled her temper in order to brave her curiosity. "What's in this for you? Why wouldn't you possess Hendal? I'm assuming you can't forge more than one bond, or it hinders you in some way, but I would think you'd eliminate a threat to your power. What are you getting out of Terran?"

When Soirée didn't respond right away, she knew the creature was contemplating how much to share. A chuckle rose after before the grip on her head tightened.

"You are clever, Dear One. As tempting as it is to answer, I'll wait and see how this turns out."

In the next instant, Coura felt a blow to the exposed side of her neck, making her lose consciousness.

# The Truth Revealed

slight ringing in Coura's ears greeted her when she stirred. Soirée had disappeared, allowing her to push herself onto her hands and knees before adjusting herself to sit and rub her aching shoulder.

*How long was I unconscious?* she wondered before resigning to figuring out her next steps based on what the demon revealed. *Should I even bother looking for Hendal at this point?*

With a huff, she prepared to summon a light until she heard the former high priest's quiet voice.

"Are you all right?"

"I'm fine," she tentatively replied before braving his condition. "How do you feel?"

"The same I suppose. Somebody brought me to the cliffside, but without a moon, I couldn't tell who he was. I remember him placing a hand on my head then waking here. I didn't know you were there until you moved."

*Interesting*, Coura noted while wrestling with what she learned from Soirée. *Terran kept the matter as impersonal as possible by not even sharing his name or that he's a demon too.*

During the pause, her stomach growled loudly enough to remind her of her eaten rations.

"Did she hurt you?" Hendal asked after without hiding his disgust. "I don't understand what's going on, but I'm sure she's the cause."

"No, but she told me why you're here." Coura proceeded to inform the man of Terran and the spell the creature used on him, including the purpose of the bond. When she finished, she imagined his face paled.

"I-I don't feel different," he muttered in a horrified manner. "Does this mean I can wield magic? Will the demon become aware of what I do? How can I-"

"I know as much as you," she interjected, though in a weary manner.

"Really? Haven't you and Soirée been together for a long time?"

"Over a decade, but as far as I can tell, she never tried breaking our connection. She used me for her own plans before I trapped her in the demonic realm below the surface of the planet. Ever since then, I couldn't sense her presence until she reached out when I came here."

"I see."

"Honestly, I'm not sure what you can do for Terran," she admitted and lied on her back with her arms behind her head. "I could always use magic, so Soirée's demonic energy reshaped my center of power to contain it alongside light energy. You've never wielded any sort of power before, right?"

"She once said I acted as a conduit and that her energy flowed through me. That was how I controlled people." He didn't hide his shame in his final words.

They fell silent and contemplated the matter on their own.

*Now that Hendal and Terran are attached the same way Soirée and I are, I'm not sure what escaping with Hendal will do except make him a target for both the demons and what creatures spawn from them. He can't defend himself, and I won't stay close to protect him. Anywhere he goes makes him dangerous, which is worse since he'll be brought to the capital if he's discovered.*

Although she hated rationalizing leaving the former high priest behind, she couldn't come up with a reason not to go on her own except to stop whatever Terran, and possibly Soirée, had planned. Before she could fully commit to the decision, the former high priest spoke again in a neutral, almost hollow tone.

"Have you considered killing the demons? Of course, it's easier said than done, but will their energy leave us then? Is that the best alternative if we don't know how to break the bond?"

He waited for a reply, but Coura remained quiet. Ever since she recognized the danger Soirée posed when she regained her memories, she wondered about that same idea: Would ending the demon's life free or harm her?

*At the time, I was ready to die if it meant stopping her from causing more trouble and hurting more people in Asteom. I survived our fight though. I continued living while putting the past behind me until Terran appeared. Maybe that is the simplest solution; it would keep them from gathering additional power at the very least.*

The conclusion sounded like the most reasonable if it didn't involve dying; however, unlike her younger self, she wasn't certain she could throw her life away on a chance of success. When Hendal pressed for her thoughts after, she shared as much.

"We don't have an answer," she added when she heard him mutter a curse. "With that in mind, we should be cautious. I plan on escaping this cave and flying to Dala to warn the generals there about Soirée and Terran's location."

"What about me?"

Coura repressed a sigh as she struggled to come up with an excuse for not wanting him along. "Where would you go if I got you away from the mountains?"

"I suppose I shouldn't return to Kercher," he began in a defeated manner. "Several towns in the eastern half of Asteom could house me for a while. That is, as long as they don't possess guards."

Instead of reminding him of how the demonic energy would tempt any creatures attracted to that power, she rose and brushed off her pants, which she imagined were covered in dirt. "If we intend to try leaving, I suggest we go now. Without food, we'll wear away and lessen our chances of surviving."

Coura drew her weapon before manifesting the ball of fire again to light their way. She heard the former high priest scramble to his feet before his wavering voice addressed her.

"You wouldn't happen to have a spare sword? I can't do much when it comes to combat, but I won't be completely helpless."

Despite doubting his last words, she turned around to locate her pack. The bag sat nearer to him where she dismissed it after the man ate her remaining rations, but she pointed at it a second later. "My hunting knife is more manageable than a sword."

She waited for him to retrieve the item and nod before returning her attention to the tunnel ahead. The pair set out at a strictly slow pace in order for her to react to an ambush from the surrounding darkness. Fortunately, none came as they reached the fork in the system and ventured along the right path, which would lead them out.

*They must be lingering at the entrance*, she told herself as they crept closer to a growing, dim light. *I would order Hendal to do something, but I can't predict how Soirée or Terran will act. I should manifest my wings as soon as I can and keep their attention on me.*

With an outline of a strategy in mind, Coura dismissed her spell when she could see clearer, pressed her back against the earthen wall, and motioned for the former high priest to do the same. She had an inkling either demon would have stopped their progress at that point if the creatures were seriously hoping to keep them away. The notion urged her forward until the two stood at the mouth of the cave.

"Are we alone?" Hendal whispered while coming closer, as if he hoped to cower behind her.

Instead of answering, Coura walked forward despite her instincts screaming at her to flee. Nothing about the empty area suggested anybody else was around, yet she knew better than to let her guard down.

That trained hindsight benefited her when a crack of lightning shot from an opening farther up on the mountainside to crash at her feet after she leapt backward. Chunks of rock flew into the air and mixed with what dust arose; however, Coura kept her eyes on the being who climbed down from his hiding spot with ease. If she doubted the figure was Terran, his maniacal laugh reminded her of the limited sanity demons possess.

"What power!" he exclaimed while staring at his hands as he approached. "I'm fortunate you dodged that bolt because it hadn't been my intent to kill you without a proper show."

The being chuckled before his eyes rose to meet Coura's, prompting her to ready herself for a fight. In the back of her mind, she prayed Hendal had the sense to escape. To her dismay, the man's trembling voice sounded a few seconds later.

"A-Are you all r-right?"

"Who are you talking to?" Terran asked in a more playful manner than she ever remembered him using in the past. "It couldn't be me. I assume you feel my presence just as I picked up on your fear. I never-"

"What do you want with us?" she interrupted while repressing the urge to growl a curse. "We'll die without food or water. Is that your intent?"

He shrugged to dismiss her questions and settled into his normal, slightly irritated expression. "Don't think I forgot about our last encounter. Do you know how it feels to be locked inside your own mind? The passing of time means nothing to an immortal being until we're forced to wait for freedom. Now that I have it, I'll make sure to repay you for aiding those humans who stood against my conquest of this country. Then, I plan on visiting them with this gift."

Coura sensed the demonic energy riling around him ever since he spoke, so the sight of ice coating his fingers as he extended them toward her wasn't surprising; what did startle her had to do with the significant amount he flaunted. She raised her free hand to cast a shield in preparation for the snowy blast that followed and made sure to extend it far enough to protect her companion.

*Something is off,* she noted while maintaining her spell against the demon's. *Does he understand how much power he's using? I don't recall him ever wielding magic, and Marcus never mentioned it when he attacked Dala. Does this mean he has more energy because of his bond with Hendal?*

In her heart, she believed this due to her relationship with Soirée. That had her wondering where the second demon disappeared to; however, her time to reflect on the situation ran out.

Terran's ice abruptly ended only to be followed by another blast of lightning, though this time he directed the bolts at the ground. The earth under her feet trembled enough to cause her to lose focus, especially when fist-size fragments of the mountain tumbled down around them. Suddenly, a physical strike against the shield caused it to crack.

*The dirt cloud he stirred is too thick to see through*, she realized with a jolt of alarm before another blow shattered her barrier into pieces.

Despite the impact, Coura readied herself by gripping her sword with both hands and assuming a solid, defensive stance. Terran's black blade emerged from the dusty air first to lunge for her torso, followed by the rest of his body highlighted by a crazed grin. She deflected the attack and retreated instead of retaliating due to her acknowledged limitations.

*I'm slower and weaker for starters. I could manifest my wings and attempt to flee at any time, but I won't leave Hendal if Terran is going to try killing us both. I should stick to my original idea.*

The demon pursued with slashes to the right until she caught on to his repetition and chanced a parry. When he pulled his weapon back for another swing, she adjusted her blade's angle so she could slide it along her opponent's without resistance when he struck. Because of her maneuver, she managed to slice at his hands while slipping under his sword. She immediately backed away after, yet he stared down at his hands, which dripped dark blood from the single scratch.

"I don't understand you," she heard him mutter before he faced her again with an amused grin. "You two are similar but different in many ways."

When Coura didn't respond, he stalked forward and raised a hand again to shoot a fireball in her direction, which she avoided by rolling to the side. The impact of the flames against the rock wall farther behind her sent more fragments to the ground.

"You share a ferocity that fuels you," he continued while sending another blast at her. "You're sensible when it comes to combat, yet she is much smarter. I wonder why you don't fear her like you should."

Coura sidestepped to avoid a third fireball before he moved within striking range. Then, she decided to take the offensive by aiming a swing at his left thigh. The creature used his inhuman speed to pivot away and slash upward, catching her in the arm when she attempted to retreat. Although minor, the scratch bled enough to cover her bicep in seconds, and she recognized how he toyed with her.

*Last time, I had to throw off his mentality by bringing up Soirée. It's a risk given his strength, but it might provide an opening to wound him enough so Hendal and I can escape. Speaking of which, I should tell him to go since it doesn't seem Soirée is here.*

She opened her mouth in preparation to shout the order until the demon in front of her leapt forward and stabbed for her chest. Their blades met again with a ring when she deflected his attack before following with a slice in the opposite direction. Part of her expected him to retaliate and keep the bout going, but he retreated a couple steps instead. In the next instant, she sensed his power stirring, signaling a magical projectile.

With little consideration, she predicted an elemental spell. A slightly gold shield manifested when she wove it together with her Yeluthian energy just as he released a shower of icicles the length of her forearm. Due to how the light spell fed from her center, she didn't expect to have any power left after the onslaught; however, that steady stream allowed her to notice what demonic energy jittered beneath its counterpart. In response, she prepared to reach for it when she could dismiss the wall. What she didn't expect was for that tendril of power to be ready to act despite the current spell she held.

Before she could consider what this meant, Coura spotted Terran's silhouette drawing close to her shield. The icy storm abruptly ended then, and he stood grinning. She also noted how the creature's blood dripped from his hands, as if the magic harmed him in the process.

*Mages without control over their energy output allow their power to lash out*, she recalled upon seeing the dark liquid. *I remember when Byron instructed me to unleash what I could against the beast outside Clearshot and Emilea's home. That was years ago, but I still feel the sting of what lightning recoiled back on me.*

"I hate these walls you humans enjoy casting," Terran began, drawing her attention back to the present. His grin faded while he eyed the light shield with displeasure. "They interrupt a fight. It's not as satisfying when I need to pause."

Coura remained silent while maintaining her spell in case the being reacted with another outburst. This seemed to irritate the demon further.

"Not all humans are this adamant about avoiding confrontation. The most fun I've had involved a man who refused to give up even though he clearly would die. He didn't fear death, and that made him interesting."

"If that's all you're looking for then you should let me recover what strength staying in that cave drained," she replied in an attempt to provoke him into showing mercy. "Either that, or challenge Soirée. Surely she can provide you with enough entertainment so you two can leave Asteom alone."

Her comments caused the creature to throw his head back and laugh. "I could care less about you or the humans, but what's the point if there's no prize? Besides, I already accepted a challenge to conquer this country and am eager to see the results."

*He's referring to Lupin*, she realized upon reflecting on his response. *During that confrontation to the north, Lupin admitted he and Terran were planning on clashing with what people and beasts they could manipulate or control. Is that why he's allying with Soirée? Is this all about ruling Asteom?*

No matter the reason, Coura understood she wouldn't stand a chance against the being alone, especially if he could now wield magic and she didn't possess an ancestral weapon.

"Hendal," she shouted without removing her eyes from Terran. "Get out of here!"

She imagined the former high priest still cowered by the cave's entrance yet refused to linger on the man and waste her opportunity to escape. *If I can't warn anybody about this, the rest of the kingdom will remain in danger. For some reason, Soirée kept Hendal and I alive, so I doubt she would go after him.*

That hope was all she could spare on her companion. If she stayed or focused on helping him, she would risk losing her chance to escape.

Before the demon could act again, she manifested her wings while maintaining her shield and spun around to leap into the sky. The goal became fleeing at a level where the being would not be able to reach with projectiles, which would be easier given the jutting rocks making up the mountain range. This led her to focus on climbing higher in the sky as soon as possible.

The demon's voice reached her, though she couldn't discern the words as she rose. Suddenly, a clap of thunder echoed in the surrounding space just as lightning crashed against the wall to her right. The bolts missed her wing yet caused shards of rock to crumble and hit the feathery limb. Although minor, the impact hindered her flight. She staggered in the air to regain her balance before trying to rise once more.

A second blast of lightning struck the section above her after, producing another, deafening rumble; however, this time she found herself caught in the middle of tumbling fragments of the mountain. Chunks as long as her body startled rolling as the entire side crumbled due to the surge of power that struck to begin a chain reaction.

Coura knew she needed to get out of the way if she valued her safety, but before she could commit to a new direction, one of the boulders connected with her left wing. Unlike the previous disruption, this proved severe enough to break bones, leaving her plummeting to the ground against her will. Meanwhile, Terran continued releasing his spell. Flashes filled her vision while thunder and booms consumed her hearing.

*I need to recover*, she told herself amid the chaos as the earth below grew closer. This forced her to dismiss her shield and focus on landing and protecting herself until the avalanche stopped.

When she quit fighting the urge to stay in the air, her body descended at a safer rate. No fragments of the mountainside that struck proved to be as large as the previous one that injured her wing, which she felt grateful for. Both feet touched solid dirt at the same time to signal her return to the spot near the cave, and she responded to the danger around her by dropping to her hands and knees, dismissing her wings, and casting a shield around herself using what demonic energy waited in her center.

The dome encasing her held despite the continued noise until the relentless boulders broke through at the rear edge near her feet. While the rest of her spell remained sturdy, Coura couldn't keep from releasing a cry as she felt her right ankle get crushed under the weight of what rocks took advantage of the break in her shield.

For what felt like several minutes, she held her breath and waited for the bolts and landslide to subside. The lightning's flashes ended first, followed by what thunder it produced. Soon after, less pieces of the mountain fell until only a cloud of dust surrounded her.

*Where is Terran? I should keep my spell up in case he surprises me. Hopefully Hendal got far enough away not to get caught up in this.*

Her next goal became freeing herself from the clutches of what boulders trapped her foot. As she glanced around, her heart dropped at the sight of a wall at her back, displaying just how much of the mountainside fell.

"Are you still alive under there?" came Terran's voice a second later. The demon's tone suggested he grew bored with the current state of their encounter, which lowered Coura's spirits.

Instead of responding, she waited until the creature's silhouette emerged from the earthen cloud around her. He approached where she huddled beneath her shield, paused, then raised a foot to prop it against the magic's circular shape.

"You just won't die," the demon addressed her with an emotionless expression. "I suppose I shouldn't be surprised."

The sense of superiority he projected kept Coura frozen in place until he manifested his weapon and poised it above the shield. She naturally reacted by attempting to crawl back only to receive a reminder about her trapped leg in the form of a pained jolt. No matter how hard she tried to free herself, the rocks wouldn't budge.

In the midst of her dilemma, Terran brought his blade down to stab through her wall and pierce the ground in front of where she shrank away. Violet shards of the compromised barrier floated around her as her only line of defense crumbled.

*What should I do?* she wondered as her breaths shortened and eyes rose to the demon's face. *I can't get away. Any spells might cause more damage to the mountainside, but he broke through my shield. If I don't do something, he's going to kill me!*

The being's lips curved into a pleased smile at her reaction before he pulled his sword out from the earth. Coura raised a hand to manifest another wall for protection; however, a new voice cut through the tension before she could muster the necessary power.

"What a mess you two created."

Both Coura and Terran glanced toward the edge of the cliff where Soirée stood with her arms crossed and a slight frown. When neither spoke, the second demon continued while approaching them.

"Honestly, I expect this kind of behavior from a human, but why ruin such a suitable location by attacking the mountain?"

Before Coura could consider how to respond, Terran huffed a laugh. "I suppose I got ahead of myself, what with this newfound energy. Now I can take advantage of my surroundings using magic. I caught our escapee after all."

Soirée's eyes slid between him and Coura before narrowing at the former. Then, she uncrossed her arms, and a sense of anger emanated from her expression despite how her smile widened. "I find it hard to believe you would be so careless."

Terran didn't respond to her prodding.

"Who would have thought a human with light-blooded power controls dark energy better than a demon," she added.

That comment spurred a reaction. Terran turned away from Coura and pointed his sword at Soirée. "What's the point of keeping them around anymore?"

"You're so thick," his fellow demon commented and laughed in her sickly sweet manner. "I explained this already. They obtain power we can utilize."

"I could care less about protecting humans," he growled, revealing his annoyance. "Besides, all I need is for mine to stay alive."

A shiver slid along Coura's spine at his final remark, both because of the implication regarding her and Soirée's resulting, chilling glare. *I need to get out of here.*

Before she could act on that thought, Terran began walking toward Soirée, prompting the latter to summon a weapon. She could only watch in horror as the hate-fueled energy between them sparked into flames. They leapt at each other like wolves, slicing with their swords, dancing around the other, and biting, scratching, or using physical blows when an opportunity presented itself. The scene became so chaotic that Coura couldn't see certain strikes; she only knew some attack landed when fresh blood dripped into the dirt.

*I can't linger in this area*, she reminded herself after a minute in order to tear hers eyes away from the captivating yet horrific fight.

Her center still held enough energy for her to manifest her wings, which she appreciated; however, her foot remained stuck between a set of boulders. She first tried pulling it out only for a surge of pain stemming from broken bones and torn muscles to stop her before she could draw attention to herself by accidentally crying out. Next, she focused on pushing the rocks but found them too heavy to dislodge. By that point, she worried she would need to cut off her foot if she hoped to flee in time.

Shuffling footsteps sounded to her left and drew her attention away from the problem despite the ongoing bout spreading to the rest of the area. She was surprised to find Hendal standing beside her with his back pressed against the rubble, his hands clutching her hunting knife, and a grim frown across his pale face.

"What are you still doing here?" she couldn't help but snap when he didn't speak. "You were supposed to get away!"

"I couldn't," he replied immediately, as if spurred on by his terror. "My feet wouldn't work, then the mountain shook and I couldn't walk straight. If I climbed down, I'm afraid I would have fallen."

Coura recognized his behavior from her years of experience and knew it was spurred by fear, though she possessed less patience for the man than she otherwise would have due to the circumstances. She tugged on her right leg again while attempting to find a way to slide her foot out as she addressed him and ignored the clashing demons.

"It's safe to descend as long as those two are distracted. I don't know how much time you'll have, but you need to go."

"What about you?" he countered and finally glanced over. "Do you plan on following?"

When she didn't respond right away, he released an irritated groan.

"You're leaving me behind. I suppose I should expect as much based on the past..."

"That's not it," Coura interrupted. She abandoned her efforts and turned to concentrate on the blood-covered beings. "I need to warn somebody about their location and that they might still be working together. Besides, I'm not sure if I'll be able to get out of here without help."

"What do you mean?" For the first time since he came over, Hendal noticed her predicament, and his eyes widened even more.

"I'm stuck, but I don't think Soirée will let Terran kill me," she picked up. "On the other hand, I don't know what they'll do to you."

When he didn't comment on her assumption, she looked away from the demons and prepared to urge him forward again until she saw his expression. What anxiety he showcased moments ago melted into a calmer gaze as he assessed her before studying the inhuman creatures who paid them no attention. His posture also relaxed a bit, which startled her.

"This may not be an opportune time to discuss the matter, but I've been contemplating what you shared before," he began again. His voice still wavered, yet an internal motivation seemed to push him forward. "The demons might need us alive in order to unwillingly collect energy for them, but why keep us in that cave? Why not set us free and watch through the bond they formed?"

Coura involuntarily shivered at his sudden change of tone before resigning to wait while Soirée and Terran sliced each other apart, especially since each wore crazed grins, displaying their love of the exchange. "They can keep an eye on us from a closer distance in case we're attacked. Is that why you're refusing to run? Because you believe it's safer around them? That's not true."

"Are you sure?"

"You've seen how they treat humans. We're no better than animals to them. If we weren't useful because of that bonding spell, we'd be dead already."

During the resulting pause, she noticed his eyes slowly widen, and he gripped the knife in his hands tighter. Her attention returned to the creatures when they circled each other while panting, signaling the likelihood that they would bore of the fight soon and end their scuffle.

*We don't have time for this*, she repeated in her mind before looking at Hendal, who didn't appear to change. *If he won't go, I have no choice but to leave him behind.*

Her hands returned to her leg as she worked to maneuver it free again; however, the former high priest's next words had her freezing in place.

"All we have in common is that we're bonded to each other. I wonder why Soirée taught the second demon this trick if it means he will grow in power. I wonder why she let you go free for years when you work against her and her kind and why she never tried this spell on more humans after she found success with you. These questions raise more, but it appears we need to try something if we'll get answers."

"What are you talking about?" Coura asked when his body started noticeably trembling. She found herself growing afraid of the answer as he shifted to stare at her with a mixture of hopelessness and sorrow.

"Based on your previous thoughts and their behaviors, it sounds like this connection goes deeper than I originally imagined. I believe they're keeping us alive because it would be dangerous for them if we run into trouble. They're selfish beings; you made that much clear. Is what power this bond collects worth the effort? Since the second demon said he would kill me, my guess is no."

"What are you getting at?" Despite the question, she understood what he implied.

"Soirée wants us alive for more than just that worth," he went on with a new sense of urgency. "If it was not important, she would have rid herself of us by now. If that's the case, what will happen if we die? Will the bond still stand, or will it fade?"

*I once believed ending her would end me as well*, Coura reminded herself as she recalled sharing the confession to Hendal. *When I sealed Soirée in the demonic realm, she adjusted her sword to avoid a killing blow too. That's what haunted me for years. Why show mercy to a human who outsmarted you unless you're worried what doing so entails?*

"Let's say that's the case," she reluctantly pressed after accepting his point. "We can still get away now and face this later when we have support from-"

"Why flee when they'll hunt us down?"

Her mouth hung open at his interruption, prompting him to go on.

"Without answers, the four of us are prisoners of the other. I cannot escape without braving a climb down the mountain, and even then I must find food and water to survive. That is, if I'm not turned in as soon as somebody recognizes me. My life is already forfeit."

"Don't give up so easily," Coura found herself saying as her eyes darted between Soirée, Terran, and Hendal and her head began spinning. "If they need you alive, they won't abandon you without resources. Maybe it's better if you remain here just to avoid getting captured and returned to Verona."

The man didn't hide his sense of surprise with her response and even offered a timid smile, which she ignored by looking away. Meanwhile, Soirée and Terran picked up their fight, though only their weapons met the other's body instead of hands, feet, or teeth.

"I never expected to be pitied by someone who experienced what a monster I became," Hendal added. "Unfortunately, it's too late to make amends for the past; however, at least I can try protecting the future."

Coura became so invested in the nearby combat that she didn't process the words for a few seconds. When she did, her head snapped in his direction, and she caught him with the tip of her knife poised above his heart. Hers sank in response.

"Stop! What are you-"

"My life is no longer my own," he replied, echoing his previous comment. "If it ends, you'll learn the truth about this bond."

"We don't know if that will affect Terran. If it doesn't…"

"Even if it doesn't, you'll have an answer," he finished and lowered his gaze. "Not knowing is often worse than seeing the entire picture. At least I can offer you that much."

His selflessness left Coura struggling to respond, though she refused to allow anybody to sacrifice themselves so easily. "Please, don't give up!"

To her amazement, Hendal's hesitant smile solidified into one projecting confidence as he met her eyes. "I'm not giving up.

Allow me to assist you and potentially hinder or stop the second demon from hurting others in Asteom."

The sincerity in his expression had her averting her gaze and grinding her teeth in frustration until he spoke again.

"If I may request a favor… Can you tell my nephew I'm grateful for what time we spent together?"

His wavering voice reflected a surge of emotion, and she found tears sliding down his cheeks as he stared upward. Before she could answer, he sidestepped away from her, lowered the knife, and began hurrying toward the edge of the area. At first, she didn't know what to think until she realized he wouldn't be within range of her, Soirée, or Terran in that direction.

*He's really going through with this*, she thought while instinctively reaching in his direction.

A call sat in her throat, yet she didn't wish to interrupt the ongoing combat and disrupt the former high priest's plan. Part of her hated how she just accepted his risk instead of convincing him otherwise; however, his commitment led her to wonder if she would even be able to sway him. All she could do was watch as the man reached the edge of the cliff, closed his eyes, and mumbled to himself before plunging the knife into his chest in a single jerk.

Coura felt all the blood drain from her face as his went pale and a single stream of crimson spread from the wound. For seconds, she waited with bated breath until she recognized how the area fell silent. When her eyes shifted toward the demons, she found them both staring at Hendal without hiding a minor sense of alarm.

Movement from the former high priest returned her attention to him. To her horror, he fell backward and over the edge of the cliff. One moment he stood as still as a statue; the next he disappeared. Only then did she gasp for air to satiate her aching lungs.

*He's gone.*

Her mind struggled to grasp what just transpired, yet she found herself focusing on the demons after when Terran dropped to his knees while clutching his chest. Sweat already coated his exposed skin thanks to the previous bout, so she didn't notice a physical change in his appearance. Still, he acted as though he'd taken a hit that strained his entire being.

*The bond he forged with Hendal is reacting to the loss of the human half,* she assessed based on the resulting, stirring energy he projected. *That has to be what's happening.*

"You," the demon shouted while directing his attention at Soirée, who observed the situation with an indifferent expression. "You knew this would happen! I'll kill you for-"

Whatever he planned on screaming next became lost to a mixture of growls and choking sounds as he started clawing at his chest. Coura could only watch as his hands steadily slowed, his eyes went wide and closed in succession, and he finally froze in place. After a frightening minute of silence, Terran collapsed forward onto his face.

*

Throughout the entire ordeal Coura witnessed, her body trembled, though she didn't recognize how weary she'd grown until she could think clearly again. Her trapped ankle throbbed, yet she wouldn't be able to free it without causing additional pain, and her insides felt tight despite her ever-present hunger. In order to ease part of the strain, she adjusted to sit as comfortably as she could manage, fold her arms over her available knee, and rest her forehead against them.

*Hendal's... He actually gave himself up to stop Terran without knowing whether or not it would work. That means Soirée and I are also-*

Approaching footsteps drew her out of her meditation before stopping, prompting her to raise her head. The remaining demon towered over her without a hint of anything other than slight annoyance.

"I suppose you're proud of yourself for ridding the world of Terran," Soirée began and glanced at the spot where the former high priest fell. "How much of the credit belongs to that man? I must admit, he startled me given his previous cowardice. At least he managed to be useful."

The creature's following chuckle wore on Coura's nerves, but she felt too tired to argue. Instead, she dismissed her emotions in order to concentrate on freeing herself.

As soon as she returned to her attempt to maneuver her foot out, she heard Soirée huff in displeasure before the demon seized her arm and forcibly dragged her backward. She prepared to berate the being; however, a blinding pain shot through her body when a single, strong pull tore her ankle out from underneath the rubble. After crying out, she clutched her leg while growling curses.

"Judging by your earlier efforts to escape, I'd think you wouldn't waste time by grumbling," Soirée commented and crossed her arms. Still, amusement danced in her eyes when Coura spun around to glare at her.

Instead of responding, Coura turned her hatred into motivation as she shaped her Yeluthian energy into a healing spell and began working on her injury. The process took longer than she would have liked, but she managed to fix enough to manage. After, she remained on the ground and considered her situation.

*I know the truth now thanks to Hendal, but what does that mean for the future?*

"You must be wondering why I kept you here," Soirée began in a less facetious manner.

Coura chanced a glance and found the demon studying the mountains. "It's not like you'd ever tell me what you're planning without it benefiting you in some way."

"As true as that statement is, I also never doubt your maddening ability to figure out my intentions on your own. So, what do you make of the former high priest's actions?"

She raised an eyebrow and contemplated her response. "We assumed the bonding spell possessed some sort of catch related to our lives. Otherwise, why would you keep us alive? Terran held no restraint, so I'm guessing you never shared that part."

"You're correct."

"Were you using that piece of information to manipulate him into working with you?"

"Yes and no."

When the demon didn't elaborate, Coura sighed and got to her feet. "I don't care about him anymore. He's dead, so that's one less problem Asteom has to deal with."

"Are you sure?" Soirée countered and looked her over. "He would have been helpful to you too."

Coura prepared to ask what she meant but hesitated. *This is the piece Hendal and I were missing. What didn't she reveal to us about why she and Terran were working together?*

They stared at each other until she broke the gaze by assessing the landscape. Finally, she caved in when she figured the demon would continue to dance around the subject.

"I don't know. Terran never seemed like the type to play well with others."

"He's not," Soirée added and sauntered toward the second being's corpse. "However, he isn't the sharpest when it comes to scheming. I always bested him when he challenged me, but the fights were entertaining enough for me to leave him alive."

"You gave him power to rival your own then," Coura concluded. "That explains why you two never finished ripping each other to shreds."

A pause stretched between them for a minute. Then, the demon glanced over her shoulder and narrowed her violet eyes.

"That's not the only reason I showed him how to bond with a human soul."

*What is she hinting at?* Coura wondered before assessing all she heard up until that point. *The spell gave Terran power to rival her own and keep her engaged in their confrontations. She never mentioned the risks, so he was careless when it came to protecting Hendal.*

A sudden realization dawned on her when she considered that statement. "If you purposefully didn't tell him about the potential consequences when it came to the person he was bonded with, then you must have known what would happen."

The demon's lips stretched into a proud grin. "You're finally catching on, Dear One."

"Is that how you planned on killing him?"

"Not exactly."

Coura prepared to demand an explanation until her eyes locked on to the pale patch of missing fur showcasing the creature's scar. When she remembered that encounter and its resulting trauma on her fragile mentality, every part of her body went cold. "You knew about this already."

Soirée clapped her hands together. "Now we're getting somewhere!"

"When we fought years ago, you understood what would happen if you killed me. That's why…you…"

"It was only a suspicion at the time," the demon clarified before resuming a less eager expression. "I never considered such a drawback until you found yourself on death's doorstep when you foolishly challenged the pair of light-blooded scum."

"That long ago?" Coura asked without hiding her surprise.

"You could have easily died if our connection didn't pull my energy to you. Instead of sacrificing more power, I decided to intervene. Although it led to me staying with you for longer than I would have preferred, it proved to be better than the alternative."

*All that time I spent trying to keep her from manipulating others meant nothing. She wouldn't have let me kill her, and she wouldn't have killed me either.*

Soirée continued while she struggled to accept that new fact.

"As for the next part relating to that man and Terran, I needed a means of experimenting without using our bond. After all, a capable researcher never attempts possible solutions on themselves first. I didn't expect the former high priest to protest given his misplaced sense of superiority, but it took a bit more convincing than I anticipated."

Coura refrained from mentioning how the demon threatened his home and family. "You didn't experiment on me because of the risks, yet you let me wander freely until I came looking for you. Why now? Why not wait until you had answers?"

Her question led Soirée to pause and consider an answer. After a minute passed, the creature shook her head. "I suppose all the pieces fell into place. My return to the surface allowed me to observe Terran's behavior around the humans, including his downfall. Meanwhile, I needed to find a suitable host for the spell. When he became captured, I freed him in exchange for his cooperation. The promise of power enticed him enough to obey, for the most part."

"Then you located Hendal?"

"Finding him was actually by chance," the demon admitted before giggling. "My hope had been to scout for another half-breed like you, one to balance both types of energy. The eastern side of this country is closest to where I trailed light-blooded beings in the past. Once I spotted him, I merely took advantage of the situation."

As the laughter continued, Coura recalled leaving the man behind when she went to see the Mintelians. *He mentioned his limited time then too. I think he fully committed to helping when he could or staying out of the way in order to savor what freedom he had been granted.*

Soirée released a final, content sigh. "As interesting as the situation has become, I loathe him for ending my fun so prematurely."

"Is there anything else?" Coura pressed while gazing upward. The sky's blue color began darkening to signal the approaching evening, and she refused to remain in that area any longer.

"Are you tired of me already?" came the playful response, as if the being read her mind.

"I have one question. Is Lupin involved in your plotting too?"

"No."

The direct answer had Coura returning her eyes to Soirée, though she was startled to see the demon frowning. Although she wondered if she would regret broaching the subject, she knew it would be important when she returned north. "He mentioned competing with Terran, which is why they aimed to control people in Asteom and Nim-Vala. Unlike Terran, he has a hold on-"

"Lupin chose his path, and I chose mine," the demon interrupted. "That's all."

*Terran must have been the weakest of the three*, she concluded while musing over the information she obtained. *At least, he had the weakest influence over humans. I bet that's because of his attitude, which lines up with Marcus and Calin's reports. Soirée shouldn't be too much of a problem now that her plan was foiled, so I should return to Dala.*

Without a word, she began walking toward the edge of the cliff where Hendal dropped from. She had no doubt he perished, yet she figured checking wouldn't hurt and allowed her an opportunity to attempt a pyre.

*I owe him that much*, she told herself while manifesting her wings.

"Where do you think you're going?" came Soirée's voice. The mischievous tone solidified into serious interest. "If you stay, I can study our bond closer. At least I won't need to track you down again."

"My next priority is to stop Lupin."

"Are you sure you're comfortable leaving me alone?"

The question had Coura glancing around over her shoulder to where the demon grinned. The violet eyes shone with a familiar greediness she'd grown accustomed to with the creature, yet the reality of their dilemma kept them on even footing.

"I should be asking you that," she countered. "If I'm killed on the front line, you'd suffer too."

"Perhaps I will stay south of the conflict where I have plenty of humans to play with."

*So that's how this is going to be. I need to make sure she's accounted for without sacrificing my position to assist with Nim-Vala.*

After a pause, she pivoted to look at and address Soirée. "What if I agree to help when the fight is over?"

The demon tilted her head to show her interest. "Do you mean you'll return to me when it's convenient for you?"

"You like deals, right? If you promise not to harm anybody except Lupin and those who serve him, I will return to you so we can break this spell."

"Interesting," Soirée muttered while raising her eyes and considering the offer.

The longer the wait, the greater Coura's despair became, though she hid behind a mask of indifference. *I'm beginning to understand what Hendal meant when he said his life was limited. She's too dangerous to leave unattended, but Lupin needs to be stopped. I refuse to sit back and let him continue striking Asteom when my life may already be forfeit, especially since I have the ability to rid the world of Soirée. Until our bond is severed, I'm working with borrowed time.*

Finally, the being answered. "I accept those terms, but if you hope to draw out the inevitable, I won't be so lenient. Your allies will pay for such carelessness."

"Fine."

"Also, don't think I will let you copy the former high priest. I intend to watch you closely."

Coura faced the mountains ahead of her and inhaled the welcoming breeze that caressed her skin. "I never doubted you would leave me alone anymore since your life is in my hands."

When she didn't receive a response, she extended her wings and leapt off the rocky plateau to pursue her next goal.

# Sharing Answers

For the first time since he arrived at General Casner's camp, Byron was able to go off on his own to meditate. The tasks the group's leader assigned him didn't require much effort or thought since they involved monitoring the mages, scouting the southern perimeter, and assisting with whatever business the man came up with, yet his focus remained entirely on the troops. It wasn't until a sunny, warmer day surprised them that he decided to indulge himself by taking a break.

*I need to learn to step away from my work anyway*, he justified in his mind while heading toward a hill he remembered from his patrol that morning. *Besides, my responsibilities aren't jobs somebody else can't do if they have to be done within the next couple hours.*

That lax mentality stayed with him until he reached his destination and dropped to sit in a comfortable enough position where he could let himself drift into a state of internal awareness. Doing so helped mages better understand the power they carried and consider ways to test their abilities going forward. Although he achieved it easily, he found it difficult to teach when he explained it to students, leading him to recommend another instructor for the lesson.

*Most struggle to find a sense of peace when so much is happening around them. Perhaps I should ask someone to share a technique with me to help me guide the trainees in the right direction.*

His thoughts circled around that idea, as well as several others he wished to explore when he returned to teaching, until footsteps crunching the leaves nearby drew him out of his meditation.

"So the uneventful days haven't driven you off," came Clearshot's voice, spurring a smile.

He looked at where his friend approached from the right to sit beside him. "Why would a lack of trouble make me want to leave?"

"Because you're the type to revel in a challenge," the soldier pointed out and began counting on his fingers. "You face problems head on instead of avoiding them or leaving them for others. You're nosy. You can't stay still for more than a few minutes, and-"

"All right," Byron interrupted. "I get it!"

The two shared a laugh at his expense after, then Clearshot began a new topic, one that startled him a bit.

"I think Emilea would have liked this spot. It's quiet, and you can view the entire landscape without climbing more than this hill."

He chanced a glance at his friend expecting the sense of sorrow he'd become accustomed to and prepared to offer words of comfort; however, the reaction appeared milder than normal. The chestnut eyes held pain as they stared off into the distance, yet a sad smile eased the tension.

"I pulled myself away from others and from the world because I kept thinking like that," Clearshot revealed when Byron didn't respond. "Whatever I did reminded me of her or had me wondering how she would react. I realized how dependent I was and hated myself for behaving helplessly. When I worked alongside my children, I felt the same. Why couldn't I be their pillar of strength instead of leaning on them? After all, they suffered too."

The comments had Byron considering if he should intervene, but he stayed quiet. *I doubt he mentioned this to anybody else, not even Mace or Lexie. It's healthy to express feelings into words and cope with others offering support.*

"That's why I chose to leave East Hoover," the soldier continued while raising his eyes to the clear sky. "I hoped to shift some work onto my shoulders, both to keep my mind occupied and to be useful. Besides, Emilea wouldn't want me to sink into despair. I will live for her and appreciate the things she can't anymore. Then, when we're together again, I can tell her all about them."

"An admirable mindset," Byron added when it became obvious Clearshot had nothing left to share. "Not many people can move on after such a personal loss. You managed to reflect on your situation, pick yourself up, and find motivation to continue living."

"It's going to sound admirable when you break it down like that," came the lighthearted reply. "I wouldn't be here if it weren't for a few people who stuck around to make sure I ate, slept, and talked about what happened."

"That's what friends do."

The pair enjoyed the rest of the afternoon before returning to camp and being dragged in separate directions: Clearshot to resume the chores he apparently skipped and Byron to meet with the general for a daily debriefing. To his relief, no news marred the otherwise calm day, allowing him to eat dinner in a timely manner.

*I should grab my coat*, he thought as he prepared for his evening patrol. *It would be odd if we got two warm days in a row.*

With that in mind, he retrieved the thick, multi-layer jacket he received when he first arrived at that location before walking north. A ball of flame sparked in his open left hand once he reached the limit of the camp's light, and he focused on assessing his surroundings as he entered the woods. The sounds of the nightlife met him eagerly with loud chirping, whistling, and gentle rustling in the canopy.

*If I didn't become accustomed to this, my eyes would be darting in every direction. This is definitely not a spot for an inexperienced scout.*

Instead of circling the southern part of the area again, Byron had volunteered to venture in the opposite direction when the sun set in order to ease the burden the previous, less confident soldier had. A handful of other mages who could cast the basic fire spell patrolled at night with a guard for protection, but he vouched for his abilities, even though no one argued with his decision to go alone.

His steady stream of dark energy increased as he willed his spell to grow and produce more light around a particularly dense section of trees. When his eyes didn't catch movement or unnatural shadows, he extended his magical senses to scan for another presence. He immediately felt the nearest mages' because of their spells but nothing more.

With a sigh of relief, he continued on his way, eventually circling around and returning to camp to trade shifts with the next scout. It was during the transition that he noticed a serious-sounding conversation taking place between four people who recently came back as well. Before he could ask the younger men and woman to explain the issue, he recognized the only one wearing glasses.

"Will?" he began, drawing all eyes from the group.

One of the soldiers faced him and answered his unspoken question. "Master Byron, we found him wandering through the northeastern section of the forest."

"I figured somebody would recognize me," came the newcomer's explanation.

The sheepish smile that followed let Byron know the herbalist didn't expect to be cornered. He released a breath through his nostrils before addressing the soldier. "This is a friend of mine who assists the healers in the medical station. I'm sure he has a reason for being out so late."

His gaze shifted to Will, and he raised an eyebrow to emphasize his final remark.

"Yes," the young man replied and nodded when he caught on. "I have business to discuss with Master Byron and General Casner."

By that point, the rest of the group shuffled away, leaving their speaker alone to conclude the conversation they started. The soldier appeared to believe Will though and departed after thanking Byron for the input.

"I appreciate you intervening too," the herbalist added when the two stood alone. "If I didn't call out when they heard me, I think I'd be in a worse condition."

He refrained from commenting how "a worse condition" likely would have been an arrow or blade through the chest if a spell from the mage didn't hit him first. "How long have you been gone? I didn't notice you were still here until now."

"After the Nim-Valans retrieved the demon's body, I decided to search for Finn so I could inform him of the changing situation and warn him about the potential danger to the north if the ancestral weapon is removed."

It took Byron a minute to recall the spy's name and put the pieces together. "Were you able to find him?"

"No, but I wasn't entirely certain he would be around. He planned to return to the inner circle, which is at least a week's worth of travel."

Before he could inquire about the young man's venture in the northern country, a yawn crept up on him. His hand instinctively raised to cover it, yet the distraction had him noticing how exhausted Will looked. Instead of continuing the explanation, he decided to forego the rest of the conversation that night.

"Do you have immediate business to report?" he asked next. When the herbalist shook his head, Byron gestured for them to move toward the mess area. "If that's the case, we'll continue this tomorrow with the general. I assume you haven't eaten a decent meal or slept for a full night, so you can recuperate a bit before we move forward."

Will agreed and fell silent until they parted ways when the young man received food. Then, he found his bedroll and rested until morning.

*

"So, the enemy retreated to lick their wounds."

Byron didn't respond to Casner's comment, mainly because he didn't want to interrupt Will's report. Still, he wondered if that had been all the herbalist intended to share.

That morning, the two met at breakfast and went to the general's tent together, and Assistant General Mattais welcomed them, though not without a suspicious glance at Will. After a brief introduction to preface the update, he stepped back to listen.

Nothing sounded out of the ordinary, yet the amount of time Will spent away from the camp made sense once they learned of the enemy troops' change of location. Because of the unknown positions, he needed to slow his pace and follow the same route he used to cross the border.

"It's been quiet ever since they retrieved the demon's body," Mattais added, as if he sensed concern from Will. "No attacks, no spies around us, and no word about danger from our other sites."

"I'm glad to hear that," the young man picked up. "I wouldn't be bothered, except one of the people in the town I mentioned saw something potentially important. The man claimed a Nim-Valan soldier got his hand stabbed, but the wound disappeared later in the day."

Byron's heart dropped. "Are you saying what I think you're saying?"

"The enemy might be able to heal using the demon's power, just like they could when they fought the Dalan soldiers outside Verona."

Casner muttered a curse, Mattais questioned the past conflict since he hadn't been directly involved, and Byron crossed his arms to consider that new piece of information.

*We're working with a secondhand account, so it might not be reliable. We can't outright dismiss the potential risk either.*

"Did the Nim-Valans you spoke with mention animalistic beasts, like what the south has been dealing with?" the general inquired after calming down.

The question visibly caught Will off guard. "No, nothing about those creatures."

"I take it you didn't notice claw marks, sounds, or damage in the woods during your travels?" Byron asked next.

The young man shook his head. When the discussion ended there, the general dismissed him.

"Interesting," Mattais mumbled before glancing at Byron. "You mentioned those beasts would appear if the ancestral weapon was removed, right?"

"That's correct, though I'm not sure how long such a process takes."

"Can you sense when one is near?"

"That depends on if it's able to mask its presence."

"In any case, we already fortified our defenses for such a problem," Casner interjected. "We can figure out how else we can protect ourselves and encourage the other camps to do the same since they are aware of the creatures, but I'd prefer to keep the matter as private as possible. There's no use scaring our troops when it's just a precaution."

"I agree," his assistant chimed. "It'll be easier when the Yeluthians return to scout from above as well."

Byron kept quiet since he disagreed with the pair but didn't believe their perception needed to change at the moment. *The people should know what they could be up against. Then again, there will be clues if the beasts begin appearing, and we can explain then. Those who are aware of what the Dalan troops faced will understand.*

*

The atmosphere of the main camp remained the same over the next couple days, settling any tension lingering from discussions on the demon, their enemy's potential ability to heal, and monstrous creatures. Byron expected Will to press him for answers since the herbalist and light mages became close to the spy and the townsfolk in the Nim-Valan town; however, the young man hardly stayed in one spot. He figured that was for the best since half the preparations Casner mentioned involved stocking up on supplies.

The next time he met with the general, Mattais found him eating with Clearshot and requested his participation in an emergency meeting. Despite the unexpected gathering, the assistant general didn't project any urgency. He hurried to clear his bowl, return the dish, then meet the men at the centermost tent. As soon as he stepped inside, he understood why they summoned him. Standing beside the camp's leaders was Commander Evern and his subordinate Lavine. Both looked as cool and collected as ever and welcomed Byron when he joined them to sit and start the meeting.

"I thought you'd like to hear their update," Casner confirmed after while addressing him. "They landed about an hour ago but needed time for lunch."

"It's no problem," he assured those present. "Besides, you would have called me sooner if needed."

"Levelheaded as always," the Yeluthian leader commented before jumping into his report. "All is well for the most part. The enemy is being spotted less and less, and we have not sensed malicious energy at work ever since the demon's sealing. I was told our allies along the border are capturing those who escaped into Asteom."

"The capital is also aware of the intruders," Casner shared before mentioning his conversations with the king's council through Grace's goddess gift.

"I cannot see the Nim-Valans striking the capital again without meeting opposition. As for the camps themselves, only one issue has been raising concern. It seems scouts around various locations are disappearing frequently enough to signal a pattern."

"What do you mean?" Byron pressed.

"Several sites reported individuals not returning from their patrol shifts. Lavine and I observed from above after hearing such claims, yet no shadows hinted at the enemy or creatures at that angle."

The general grumbled to himself before raising the volume of his voice a bit. "Not enough to panic over but still an issue to draw our attention."

"Those leading the camps said as much."

*The question now is whether we should use time, energy, and resources to pursue this*, Byron thought while Mattais shared how their site didn't experience missing soldiers. *If we had the enemy troops to worry about, I'd dismiss it as paranoia or alert the other sites so they can take precautions.*

He prepared to share as much until Casner looked at him and offered a suggestion.

"I believe our main focus should be retrieving the demon's body. If its power is as dangerous as you shared, we can't let Nim-Vala remove the sword and release its energy."

"You're right," he found himself adding while turning toward Evern. "I would assume we'd have noticed demonic energy by now if the ancestral weapon was removed, at the very least."

The commander nodded. "You mean to utilize Lavine and I in order to find the being or its likeliest location."

"Your ability to fly keeps you two out of harm's way compared to somebody on the ground, and you can cross a greater distance in a shorter amount of time. I'd also wager you can view an area better from above."

"All correct."

"I suggest your scouting begins as close to the border as you can manage without being seen."

"Perhaps farther," the general interjected, surprising Byron.

"You don't think Asteom would face repercussions for crossing into Nim-Vala?" he countered.

When the man's eyes shifted to Evern, the Yeluthian dipped his chin in confirmation.

"Only if we are seen," the commander clarified. "That can be managed."

"Is it a risk we're willing to take though?" Byron pressed when no one else did. "It's not as if observing their land from above is imperative."

"Are you sure about that?" Evern countered and raised an eyebrow. "Better to prevent an issue than resolve it later, especially since lives are on the line."

"I concur," Mattais chimed before his superior.

When it became obvious he was outnumbered, Byron backed down. "If that's what the majority agrees on, I won't argue further."

With the matter settled, the group didn't have much else to discuss aside from details for the Yeluthians. He exited the tent during the others' conversation since he wasn't needed and couldn't decide if he should find Clearshot and inform his friend of the situation or resume his daily responsibilities for the camp.

***

The spirit of the people in Dala felt significantly different compared to Coura's last visit, which she attributed to the lack of enemies keeping everyone up at night. After locating and burning Hendal's body while attempting some semblance of a prayer, she took her time flying west until she recognized the city. By that point in the day, the noon hour rolled around, leading its citizens to wander through town in search of lunch, company, or business purposes.

Her appetite drove her to the nearest building since she hadn't eaten a decent meal in days, and she practically threw her coins at the woman assisting her. Once she devoured the doughy, jam-filled pastry, she went straight to the base in search of her friend. The soldiers patrolling the area greeted her as she entered but didn't know where to find the assistant general when she inquired. Fortunately, her first guess proved to be correct.

Marcus stood in the midst of a group occupying the training area at the center of the structure. At least fifty men and women worked halfheartedly while he observed alongside a man she didn't recognize until she got closer. Her feet slowed to a stop just outside the activity after.

*What is General Tont doing in Dala?*

Despite her curiosity, Coura figured her report would benefit those in the capital as well and continued her approach. Her friend spotted her seconds later, prompting her to offer a tentative smile before he came over.

"I'm glad to see you're still in one piece," he said by way of greeting as he stopped and placed his hands on his hips. "When we didn't hear back from you, we wondered if you would be returning to Dala."

She prepared to mention she didn't know where she would be at that time, but the deeper, gruff voice of the general joined the conversation when the man positioned himself at Marcus' side.

"Where have you been patrolling?"

Naturally, she straightened and met his curious stare. Due to her inconsistent positions across the country, she rarely came face to face with her friend's father, though she never forgot how he treated his son in the past. This made speaking with the general a bit awkward until she remembered how she only served Commander Detrix.

"I scouted the southeastern part of Asteom after accompanying a group heading to Clearwater."

Tont's face scrunched as he processed her answer. "I didn't believe the Yeluthians' routes extended east."

Coura opened her mouth to comment on her unique assignment and permission until Marcus spoke.

"Calin and I had her escort that company and permitted her to search for the demon who escaped."

"I see," the older man grumbled. He started assessing Coura before continuing. "Your connection to the creatures must put you in a position to locate them easier."

"In a way," she muttered while avoiding the urge to roll her eyes. Instead, she addressed her friend. "I have an update if you want to talk in private. We should include Calin."

The mention of the Dalan general had him raising his eyebrows. "Did you-"

"Yes," she interrupted and shook her head. "I'd rather explain all at one time."

Marcus pointed at an open spot in the garden ring surrounding the soldiers. "I'll go fetch him. Wait over there for us."

With that, the assistant general spun to jog around the pairs and trios at work, leaving Coura and Tont alone. She didn't expect the general to speak to her until the others joined them; however, he made his opinion on her known while walking away, forcing her to follow and converse.

"For the future, an urgent report should be given immediately, not drawn out into a spectacle. General Calin would hear the news eventually, and my assistant and I are more than capable of taking the next steps. We are all busy, so you would do well to respect our time."

"Of course," she replied when he sent her a sidelong glance for not giving a vocal response. When he looked away, she caved into her desire to roll her eyes.

"I know you're friends with my son as well. Such casual relationships lead to a lack of professionalism and lax behavior. I ask that you keep that in mind, especially since he is striving to be promoted to my equal."

Those were the final words spoken until Marcus returned with Calin. Neither appeared anxious by her appearance, but their curious stares let her know her expression likely revealed how the general bothered her. Despite her personal emotions, she greeted the Dalan soldier normally.

"I don't think any of us expected you to return to the base so soon," he commented with a casual smile. "Please don't sour the mood with unpleasant news."

Coura huffed a laugh, shook her head, and returned the gesture. Instead of beating around the bush, she decided to get straight to the point. "Terran is dead."

A couple seconds passed in silence before Calin and Marcus went wide-eyed.

"You're serious?" the latter mumbled while the former chuckled. "When? How?"

"This is the demon you captured before, correct?" Tont interjected to address his son, who nodded in response.

She prepared to pick up the report again; however, recalling what transpired left her hesitating. *If I mention Hendal, I'll need to explain the bonding spell. I might also get in trouble since I knew where he was hiding. They could get suspicious of me because of my connection to Soirée too. I don't think I'm ready to deal with that yet.*

"What's wrong?" Marcus asked when she remained silent.

After resolving to face that discussion with him later, she met his eyes and allowed her smile to fade. "Soirée appeared. I trailed her east until-"

"Who is that?" Tont interrupted with a bit of frustration.

"The first demon who assisted the former high priest," Marcus replied in an impatient manner before Coura could.

"The creature didn't attack you? I'd hardly believe a being like that would leave a Yeluthian scout unscathed."

She bit her tongue to keep from offering a retort, and her friend appeared to be doing the same. Meanwhile, Calin managed a smile and crossed his arms.

"General, please allow Coura to share the entire update before questioning her. It gets confusing having to backtrack, but I can fill you in on the details after, especially since this relates to business from years ago."

"Fine," Tont snapped, though he seemed to settle down.

The three glanced at her again, so she continued without issue. She explained how she followed Soirée using their magical bond, how the demon led her to where Terran hid in the mountain range, and when the beings clashed. That was how she ended the matter.

"One demon took down another," Marcus summarized with a thoughtful expression mirroring the generals'. "Then you fled when you got the chance?"

Coura nodded but didn't add more. *Soirée won't go after anybody in Asteom, so the people here shouldn't need to worry about her. Even though she's a problem, no one else needs to get involved. I'll tell Marcus when we're alone, and he can choose to inform Calin.*

"What an interesting turn of events," Calin picked up and let his eyes rise to judge the hour. "In any case, it sounds as though our problem has been solved."

Tont released a displeased groan and narrowed his eyes at her. "I wish we could confirm the creature's death. It's difficult to believe anything nowadays without some sort of proof. Testimonies aren't always reliable."

She voiced her agreement, though his rational input took her back. *He's right about that. Perhaps I should mention our deal.*

"I don't plan on lightening our defenses," Calin began in a confident tone reminiscent of his late superior. "We held our ground before, and that was without an ancestral weapon. I trust Coura about the demon's death and would think it's too soon for the second to head west and attack us."

"If that's the risk you're willing to take, I suppose that's the end of this business," Tont concluded.

"It's not much of a risk. There's just nothing else we can do besides protect ourselves and this area of Asteom."

By that point in the day, Coura's light meal wore thin, leaving her feeling sluggish and weary. The three men discussed suggestions for adjustments based on Terran's demise but ultimately agreed to let the matter sit for the rest of the day and meet in the morning. Calin wished her well, Tont surprisingly thanked her for her report, and Marcus stayed behind.

"I bet you're starving," her friend commented when they stood alone.

His casual behavior encouraged her to relax, prompting her to wrap her arms around her waist. "I didn't exactly eat enough while I was away."

"You should have said so. That update could have waited."

"Not according to Tont," she couldn't refrain from grumbling.

The bitterness in her remark interested Marcus enough for him to question it. "Did he say anything to you when I went to fetch Calin?"

"Apparently I'm a bad influence on you," she admitted and flashed a wry smile. "Who would have thought?"

The notion visibly startled him, and he projected a mixture of guilt and anger. "That's a lie, but I'm sorry he cornered you."

"I'm fine. It's not like I haven't heard that before."

The pity reflected in his eyes as he studied her led her to look away, then he said her name softly, as if to invite her to discuss her underlying problem. She kept her mind on the current situation in order to dismiss what recent, negative emotions arose.

"I didn't want to mention this in front of the generals, mainly because I'm too tired and hungry to explain my position, but Soirée likely won't return to Dala. She doesn't get along with the demon in Nim-Vala either. I suspect she'll linger in the mountains or go north."

"Are you sure? I trust you, but those creatures mastered the art of deception. It could be a trick."

Coura shook her head. "She wouldn't lie to me."

A pause followed her statement before her friend released a sigh and motioned for them to move toward the nearest door. "Calin and my father won't understand. I'm assuming that's why you told me this now."

"The city and surrounding towns sound like they're getting back to normal. I see a need to maintain defenses, but the troops don't need to wear themselves out if there won't be trouble on that scale."

They passed through the chosen entrance and wandered toward the mess hall in silence only broken when soldiers greeted the assistant general. In a matter of minutes, they collected their meals, dropped into seats away from a majority of the others, and began eating.

"I'll tell Calin what you said about the demon," Marcus shared when their plates were empty and they leaned back in their chairs to savor the contentment of a full stomach. "Without a creature sighting in days, he's less uptight about keeping so many guards through the night. We've also been able to hold off attacking beasts a lot easier than in the past."

She merely nodded. *It's up to them to decide the best course of action for the people here. Hopefully Commander Detrix will be able to adjust the routes of his soldiers too.*

"Are you planning on going after the demon again?" he asked after a moment.

"Not yet. I'm more worried about the one aiding Nim-Vala."

"You'll head north then?"

"Maybe not right away," she admitted. "The commander let me search for her, so I should update him and Aaron on Terran's death and Soirée's appearance. If they'll let me return to the border, I can meet up with Byron and my father."

Her friend chuckled at her response. "You never stop moving. I'm not used to traveling as much thanks to this position, but I suppose I'll get used to it again soon."

"What do you mean?"

"When the council promoted Calin, Aaron gave me the option to remain here or return to the capital for a new assignment. I intended to stay at first, but now…"

"There's no need for a second general?" she threw in when he paused, earning herself an unamused look in the process.

"The entire reason I came to Dala stemmed from my inability to learn while working under my father," he went on. Coura noticed his stare shift to the wall behind her as he seemed to be recalling a past conversation. "I recognized how my understanding of leadership was skewed by my upbringing, which changed when I assisted General Tio and Calin. Now, I'm ready to forge my own path, one that doesn't depend on the title but how I can stand tall in the face of adversity."

His words prompted a smile from Coura, though she kept the reason to herself. *Marcus and Aaron are so similar sometimes. They're selfless and know when to put on a mask of fortitude in front of the people they're protecting.*

Instead of pushing the subject, she inquired about his departure, which would be in a couple days after Calin officially announced the new assistant generals. She didn't recognize the names, yet her friend sounded eager for the duo. After mentioning how they would have a lot to live up to considering their predecessors, she requested a room for the night and imagined sleeping undisturbed until the afternoon.

***

Preparing to depart from the Dalan base felt surreal given the amount of time Marcus spent in the city and surrounding areas, yet knowing he left the troops in trustworthy hands gave him a sense of peace. Calin also hadn't acted as though the past few days would be his last. They ate and drank together the final afternoon until he considered how rough riding horseback would be with a headache or upset stomach and focused on a discussion regarding the last couple years.

To his relief, General Tont didn't bother with them and instead took to managing what he could around the base or observing the training in the warm weather. Calin never hinted at any sort of frustration with his father's arrogant behavior, so he didn't dwell on the man any more than he had to tolerate.

The morning of his departure, Marcus found Coura waiting outside the mess hall with hands on her hips and a calculating expression. When he questioned this, she eased up and even laughed in a lighthearted manner.

"I wasn't sure if you'd be functioning well this morning, but I guess Calin is nicer than Tio when it comes to celebrating."

He echoed her laughter before the two entered, collected their plates, and accepted seats where a familiar group of soldiers ushered them over. Most had been at the tavern as well, though their reddish eyes and yawning led him to believe they stayed longer and enjoyed the atmosphere more than he did. Marcus had invited Coura as well, but she declined without stating a reason.

Once the meal concluded, nobody rose or appeared ready to continue with their day until he stood. All eyes darted to him, and the chatting died down.

"Don't stop on account of me," he chided in a joking manner, leading several people to laugh. "If I don't get out of here soon, I'm afraid Calin will force me to stay."

The comment earned him chuckles and dismissive waves from around the table. Coura was the only person to rise and return her dishes with him before the pair exited, went to his quarters, and grabbed what bags he packed for the journey.

"I didn't think you would have this much," she commented once she shouldered a bag containing several items of clothing. "Did you bring your entire wardrobe here when you transferred, or did your family send this after?"

"Believe it or not, my mother respected my wishes and didn't send packages here. Unfortunately, that was after she gave me a set of shirts before I left the palace. They're still waiting for me on my desk."

Her laughter filled the empty space as they departed for the western doors where he would meet his father and Calin. Coura offered to accompany him there yet declined to join the trip to the palace, stating she would rather not interrupt their time to bond; however, he figured she just didn't want to be around the general.

*I still can't believe Father told her she holds me back*, he reflected as they passed through the surprisingly empty hallways. *My position and work ethic are based on my actions and decisions, not my friends. Besides, she's an admirable soldier in many ways. He just doesn't understand people who don't fit into the molds he casts for them.*

The silence of the corridor leading to the exit grew deafening as he wondered how she felt on the matter and if she took offense given her previous concern regarding her dismissal from General Terrell's company. Before he could inquire about the subject, the sound of voices drifted toward them from farther ahead. Dozens chattered until he spotted figures crowding the path ahead, and his steps instinctively slowed.

Coura continued for a moment before realizing he lagged behind. "Are you coming?"

"What's going on?" he wondered aloud.

"Let's find out."

The lack of urgency in her voice eased part of his suspicion, though he racked his brain for a proper explanation. As soon as one person spotted them, he received a startling answer.

"There he is!"

At the man's announcement, all heads turned in their direction, smiles stretched across the assortment of somewhat familiar faces, and all straightened. A few men and women released cheers or offered words of encouragement relating to his departure while others stood at attention and nodded as he approached. His intent had been to slow his steps, yet Coura proceeded without paying the troops any mind, drawing him forward through the sea of bodies.

*Did they come here just to see me off? Why would they take time to do that?*

Someone at the end of the hallway opened the metal door and held it for them as they passed outside where dozens more met them. Just like those inside, these troops projected a sense of comradery while offering grins and standing at attention. Waiting at the farthest end with the reins of two horses was his father, who proved to be the only person without a broad smile.

"It's about time you showed up," a familiar voice called above the chattering, silencing the group in the process. Calin stepped out from the mixture near General Tont and continued when Marcus and Coura halted in front of the pair. "All preparations have been made regarding your assignment since your superior has the paperwork. You are officially rid of us."

Those who heard the man either laughed, cheered, or feigned an offended scoff at the comment, spurring a smile from Marcus.

"What is all this?" he asked at a lower volume without hiding his amazement. "A sendoff seems unnecessary."

"I mentioned your departure to a few people, and they spread the word. You made more of an impact on the base than you'll ever give yourself credit for, especially after General Tio's death."

Marcus instinctively lowered his eyes and dipped his chin. "Thank you, both for your words and for guiding me during my time here. I can't believe it's been over two years since I arrived. So much has happened since then."

"Time has a funny way of passing without us realizing it."

A pause stretched between them before Tont cleared his throat.

"We should be going," the general pressed in an oddly calm manner. "We have plenty of distance to cover before we set up camp."

Marcus nodded and glanced at Coura. "You'll be departing soon as well?"

"Eventually," she answered with a shrug. "I'm sure we'll meet up in the capital."

"You're right. Safe travels then."

"You too."

With nothing else to say, he stepped closer to his father, accepted the reins for his animal, and prepared to mount until shuffling from those gathered around had him turning. Every individual except Calin and Coura began placing their right fist over their chest in a salute while maintaining positive expressions. Nobody moved as he stared and struggled to compose himself before he opted to look away by climbing into the saddle. When he sat atop his horse and welcomed the sight again, the Dalan general and his friend matched the rest of the crowd.

*All this for me? I'm not worthy of such praise. At least, not yet. I still have a ways to go before I can accept such an honor.*

With that in mind, he mirrored the salute and bent forward at the waist in as much of a bow as he could manage. The troops abandoned their respectful positions to wave when he straightened and heard his father begin riding away, leading him to do the same.

*I promise the people of Asteom I will never give up on bettering myself so I can help this kingdom become safe for everyone. That is the goal of a leader, to always aim higher.*

*

After the months he spent on the road hunting demonic creatures, Marcus grew accustomed to riding and found ways to keep his mind occupied. He reflected on his time in Dala and what memories he made, both positive and negative, before focusing on the future. Part of him wondered whether Aaron would keep him in the palace as a guard or send him north to aid those on the border. He wasn't certain which option he preferred.

*I never imagined I'd get a choice. Usually I'm sent wherever I'm needed.*

The first three days passed as he expected with few conversations during breaks or dinner and plenty of time to rest between keeping watch at night. His father hardly spoke, though he always seemed to be yawning, and the weather remained consistently mild. Overall, Marcus enjoyed the relaxed ride.

On the evening of the fourth day, the pair set up camp as usual, ate, and sat by the fire they built. Their space lied next to a clearing where a trio of other travelers already established a spot and chatted to create noise in the otherwise peaceful evening.

*I would have expected Father to comment on the disruption, but he's been rather quiet lately*, Marcus noted while staring into the flames. *He didn't even mention the fanfare my departure caused. Such a show had to have caused an impression, likely a negative one knowing him.*

His thoughts became disrupted when the strangers laughed loudly enough to fill the entire area.

"Such rowdy behavior," the general muttered without hiding his annoyance. "How irritating."

*How would he react if I asked about his early years as a soldier? Surely he had fun at some point in his life.*

Marcus spent the next few minutes attempting to remember when his father last laughed or genuinely smiled. Aside from a handful of memories with their family, he couldn't come up with one. Instead of feeling discouraged or displeased with that notion, a sense of pity arose, prompting him to begin a conversation.

"How has Mother been these past couple years?"

The man's eyes fixed him with an unreadable stare. "Fine. Your sister fell ill last winter, so the workload fell onto her shoulders. I offered to assist."

"I bet you were turned away," Marcus concluded when the general didn't continue. "I was never allowed to help either. They always said my hands were too dirty, calloused, and not nimble enough for that kind of detailed work."

The hint of a smile graced his father's lips. "I'm afraid you got that from me. Among other attributes."

Marcus didn't expect the discussion to continue, so he fell silent; however, the man picked up in a slightly somber tone after.

"You inherited my physical attributes and dedication to a task but also your mother's sense of compassion."

"Isn't that an attribute a soldier should possess?" he countered. The direction of their conversations usually twisted in this direction, so he wasn't too surprised when the general fixed him with a disappointed look after his question.

"You still don't understand."

*It's been a while since I felt this irritated,* he reflected as a hot anger boiled in his chest. *Calin is right though. I can't keep running away or hiding, even if there's nothing I can do to change Father's mind.*

"What does it mean to be leader?" he asked next. The words seemingly tumbled out of his mouth before he truly committed to braving the subject.

"As I mentioned on several occasions, our family has a history of prestigious soldiers who formed a reputation of excellence in skill, intelligence, and courage. They guided their subordinated through trouble, served the royal family, and established the foundation for how citizens of Asteom view their leaders."

"They made a positive impact on the kingdom then."

"Not only that," the general practically snapped to show his impatience. "The people appreciate those they can depend on."

*Is that all we're fighting for?* Marcus longed to demand. What frustration he experienced steadily melted into bewilderment at the implication his father described. *Those who fight for Asteom only to receive praise don't comprehend the impact of their actions. I don't need their appreciation, but I appreciate their confirmation that I could make a positive impact and help when they need it.*

"I don't think it's compassion that compels me to protect others," he admitted without considering how the man would react. Something about that statement pushed him to share his thoughts, even though he knew they would likely set the general off. "No matter where I'm stationed, those who fight alongside me are my comrades. My position might allow me to command troops or make decisions on behalf of the country, but I am no better because of that. My loyalty is to the entirety of Asteom."

As expected, his father scoffed in response. "That is why you will never achieve more with your position. As long as you consider yourself equal to those with less skill, you'll struggle to earn respect. Soldiers are different than the people we defend. You would do well to remember that and forget whatever nonsense the Dalans filled your head with."

At first, Marcus prepared to scold his father for acting so inconsiderate of the men and women in the southern base; however, the sense of pity remained. That in and of itself told him arguing would achieve nothing since the two would never see eye to eye.

*I always thought Father held himself above others because of his position, but that's wrong. His sense of duty separates him from those who aren't in the army. In his opinion, there are those who protect and those needing protection. I see myself as no better than anybody else, but he views status as a means to gauge a person's abilities and intelligence. Is that why he's upset with me? Because I am adequate as a leader except for my perspective?*

He realized the answer to that question was one they would both be displeased with, yet it relieved what stress built up over the years since their quarrel began.

"I'm sorry," he decided to reply once he considered his father's stance. "I disagreed with you but never took the time to form my own opinion of what it means to be a leader. In Dala, I shaped my experiences alongside General Tio, General Calin, and those I supervised into my beliefs as a soldier. Still, it took me this long to realize there is no, right mold. We're different people living different lives. It stands to reason our views on the world are different too."

The general's gaze shifted between annoyed, anger, and confusion before settling into something Marcus couldn't discern. Then, he cleared his throat before responding. "If you're trying to convince me to promote you, words aren't enough to sway my mind. You still have much to learn about what it means to be a general."

"Then I'll learn," Marcus replied without hesitation and savored the relief his renewed resolve provided. "I might not pick up everything, but I will strive to continue learning what I can and help people with whatever power I have."

His father studied him for a moment before resigning to lie down, leaving him with the first watch for the evening. During that time, he reflected on the discussion with a new sense of confidence he attributed both to his bravery from confronting the man he admired for most of his life and to his ability to recognize each perspective and move on.

# The Sage's Lesson

After the fanfare Marcus' departure caused, Coura spent the rest of the day enjoying what the base had to offer until she returned to her room to rest. Calin had informed her of his intentions beforehand, allowing her to savor the sight of her friend receiving the appreciation she no doubt knew he deserved.

"People around here respect him for not looking down on them or delegating his assignments to his subordinates," the Dalan general had explained when he found her a day earlier to request her help. "He's a loyal soldier who values his position, and I think we all believe he should be promoted; however, General Tont is as strict as they come. General Tio never liked the man because of that, but Marcus views his father in a different light."

She had mentioned how much such a goodbye would mean to him, and Calin agreed before a sly grin stretched across his face.

"I'm a bit selfish though. The assistant general gets praise, but I will also relish the moment when his father realizes what's going on and how much his son is valued by the base. His spite is worth the effort."

Coura chuckled as she recalled that conversation in the garden space where she meditated. *I don't disagree with his intentions, but I hope Tont is able to change his mind about Marcus.*

The next item on her list had to do with Soirée and making sure the demon wouldn't disturb the balance the southern city and towns began to establish. Part of her felt silly for acting so cautious given their relationship, which developed because of such deals, yet the creature's priorities left much to be desired.

*I doubt she followed me here, but who's to say she won't remember what Terran did and try mirroring his attacks and conquer Dala*, she wondered as she gazed at the blossoming fruit trees around her. *Then again, she's not the type to copy what someone else does, especially when it failed in the past. This area remains fortified. That and the Yeluthian patrols will eliminate demonic creatures just like they did over the last year. No, I have a feeling she'll move on.*

Coura inhaled and released a deep breath in order to calm herself after accepting that final statement. In a matter of minutes, she cleared her mind and dove into her meditation. She rarely found the clarity she experienced while with Sage Vidar due to the distractions surrounding her, and this proved to be the case when she couldn't focus enough to look beyond the surface of her dual energies.

When a yawn crept up on her, she abandoned the effort in favor of finding dinner. What soldiers and mages who recognized her ushered her over to sit with them before asking about business in the capital or on the northern border. She eventually finished eating, though more time passed than she preferred, and returned to the center ring for a stroll.

*If I can't study my* chi *alve, I won't get any closer to discovering a solution to my main problem,* she admitted when another attempt failed and she resorted to returning to her quarters for the evening. *Sage Vidar has been the most helpful, but we didn't exactly leave on friendly terms. Would he be able to tell me what I can do to sever this bond with Soirée? Would it be worth the trip to ask?*

In the morning, her questions from the previous night, as well as her understanding of the southern troops' defenses, led her to risk venturing back to the mountains for a conversation with the Mintelian man. She found Calin, mentioned her intent to depart, and accepted his well wishes. The Dalan general didn't inquire about where she would go or what she would be doing. Instead, he mentioned informing those in the capital of Terran's defeat, thanked her for the work she did, and promised she'd be welcomed any time she decided to return.

*

It took three days before Coura worried she would need to abandon her efforts of locating the elusive village. Her rations from

152

the base would last at least another couple days; however, she planned to head north and join those at the border if she couldn't fulfill her current goal, and that would take a full day of flying.

*Perhaps I should return to Kercher and request a guide.* The suggestion deflated her spirits when she considered Hendal and his final words. Picturing the priest and his assistant learning of the man's death would no doubt cause them grief. *I can't tell them... Not yet. Not until I can accept what took place and end Soirée for good. Speaking of which, I hope she doesn't follow me here.*

That new concern grew as the morning stretched into evening and the sun started setting to color the sky in warm colors. During her search, she kept the thought in mind until her eyes caught a house between the jutting rocks. Her puffs of breath increased as her excitement rose, encouraging her to move closer. Several more structures appeared in a familiar layout as she descended. Once both feet touched the ground, she dismissed her wings and paused to let her body adjust to the change in altitude. Her eyes drifted over the area while she did so.

Nothing about the village seemed to have changed, which didn't surprise her. The log and straw shacks serving as houses dotted otherwise open patches of grass with only a single, dirt trail cutting through. Beyond, crude fences kept in goats and sheep who appeared more occupied with munching on their fodder than attempting to escape.

Just like her previous visit, her physical and magical senses dulled. This aided her in focusing in the past yet mentally secluded her from the world around her, like looking through a window but not being able to experience what took place on the other side.

She proceeded to enter the space once she felt ready and went straight to the first home she knew belonged to the sage. Instead of doors, the people used sheets to cover the openings, which reminded her of Yeluthia and the Sie-Kie, so she needed to knock on the wooden post beside it. She raised a fist to do so but hesitated for a few seconds.

*Come on, Coura. You'll never know if he can help if you don't ask.*

The gentle chiding motivated her enough to knock; however, her natural fear of the man who seemed to understand everything about her and used that as a tool to tear her open arose.

No answer came from within the structure, even when she tried again, leading her to wonder if she would find him in the isolated, grassy area where the meditation sessions took place. Her curiosity won out after a minute, so she circled around to move along the trail.

Nobody lingered in the open, which she expected from her previous experience, yet a figure came into view from farther ahead. That startled her a bit and slowed her steps. The person also paused before hurrying forward, and Coura soon recognized the ebony-skinned woman as Harriette.

"You returned," the Mintelian said before she could offer a greeting.

"I came to meet Sage Vidar. Can you tell me where he is?"

Harriette nodded in an enthusiastic yet worried manner. "Yes, of course. He is expecting you."

The comment caught Coura off guard; however, the woman spun around to lead her in the opposite direction before she could ask. Neither made conversation despite the passing time, and soon they entered the tunnel at the end of the village. A minute later, they emerged into what she remembered: an enclosed field under a gray sky. Nothing stood out enough to give it attention, not even the group of individuals sitting cross-legged around the area. Harriette merely gestured to the people before backing up and retreating into the shadowy passage.

*I suppose I shouldn't disrupt their meditation. Let's see where the sage is and go from there.*

Tiptoeing without causing a sound was impossible due to the length and dryness of the grass, so she walked around the Mintelians until she spotted her target, who sat farther away from the others. At the sight of his peaceful expression, her heart began sinking as her doubts surfaced. Still, she managed to slip beside him.

"Sage Vidar," she practically whispered when he didn't react to her presence. "I would like to speak with you."

"Sit and join us," came the immediate reply in a neutral tone.

Coura obliged and assumed the same position, one she perfected after the weeks spent among their people. The peacefulness of the quiet space allowed her to easily relax and slip into a trance where she could assess her center clearly. Like normal, both sets of energy followed their own paths while intertwining, creating a swirl of light and dark unlike anything she'd ever felt. The experience had always fascinated her given her power's unique characteristics, yet her current situation had her wondering about the demonic influence.

*Not many people know I can wield both types of energy,* she reflected after retreating to think and simply appreciate her surroundings. *It's not an issue, but it does make me useful in multiple ways. Then again, I might end up putting more burdens on my shoulders. I'm not exactly adept at switching between the two yet either. I should also keep Soirée in mind if I intend to throw myself in danger. She'd likely appear to make sure I don't get myself killed.*

Anxiety steadily gripped her chest and tightened its hold at that point. Until then, she hadn't seriously considered the future beyond arriving at the northern border. Part of her longed to dismiss the subject, but ultimately her mind drifted in that direction.

*Should I tell somebody about what happened to Terran and Hendal? What would they be able to do except worry? Byron, Will, and the others tried stopping me from sacrificing myself when I only assumed I'd meet that fate; now, I witnessed what will happen. I'm a distraction if they focus on protecting me, a risk to keep around if Soirée decides to follow me, and I would imagine Father and the other Yeluthians will view me as a disgrace. That is, if they don't already.*

Such ideas floated around her mind as the time passed until shuffling from around the field caught her attention. She opened her eyes to find those in the area rising and exiting through the tunnel. Only Sage Vidar appeared unbothered by the movement, leading her to believe he would remain with her. In response, she abandoned her position, stretched her stiff legs, then lied on her back with her arms behind her head. The cloudy sky hid what stars shined above, to her slight dismay.

"You returned," came the Mintelian's voice a minute later. "Surprising since you left in such a hurry."

"I'm sorry. I was needed elsewhere."

"Are you needed here?"

Despite the lack of emotion in his voice, Coura knew he remained bitter about their last meeting and winced. "I doubt you or your people require anything from me, and I'm grateful for what you taught me before, but-"

"Then why return?"

She sat up and found his amber eyes studying her carefully, which lowered her spirits. "I need your guidance again."

Instead of elaborating, she waiting for his response. The sage always seemed to know what she planned to ask before she could utter a word, and he'd interrupt her if she didn't get to the point. She hated having to walk on eggshells during their conversations, especially since it put her in a submissive position where she had to adapt to his line of questioning.

Fortunately, he didn't berate her for being indirect and proceeded to inquire about what brought her back. Coura shared how the demons had been captured and freed, her search for Soirée, and finally Terran's death. Unlike her explanation in the Dalan base, she didn't hide what took place with Hendal and how the former high priest's decision rid the world of the creature.

"He discovered how to end a demon's life, so the one bonded with me is looking to break the spell connecting us," she concluded. "I'm returning to assist those fighting Nim-Vala, but I thought you might be able to help figure out a solution."

Night crept over the area while they talked, which she appreciated since it hid the Mintelian's gaze. They sat in silence after until she heard him release a sigh.

"My suspicion was correct," he began in the displeased tone she became familiar with.

"What do you mean?"

"Before we go any further, you should know you never completed the soul cleansing process."

Coura's eyes widened. "I didn't?"

"Far from it. Your bond with the creature runs deeper than mere possession. At this point, it's inevitable that you will die if you cannot understand the spell tying you together. I sense your fear and hopelessness as well."

"Did you know about that all along?" she asked without hiding her disbelief.

Instead of answering, he rose and began walking toward the exit, prompting her to jump to her feet and follow. They went through the passageway and approached his home before he spoke again.

"I am but a guide. My assistance aids you in discovering how to accept what damage the demon did and understand the best method to move forward; nothing more. From the details you shared when you first arrived, I sensed repercussions from this bond, though I intended to address that when you could control your magic and willingly set foot into your center of power."

She couldn't think of anything to say after. A mixture of hatred for his secrecy, guilt for abandoning the counseling she desperately sought out, and dread for what the future would bring overwhelmed her to the point where she struggled the think clearly without blowing up on the man whose advice she needed.

"We will discuss this in depth tomorrow afternoon," he continued, though in a gentler manner, as if he picked up on her inner turmoil. "I suggest you visit the river in the morning. When you are ready, meet me in the meditation space."

With that, he disappeared behind the curtain. Coura wondered if she should return to the hut she used in the past and managed a few steps in that direction before Harriette emerged from the same opening. The woman instructed her to follow behind, then they went to a different, similar structure.

"You will stay in here," the Mintelian instructed while holding the cloth entrance aside. "I assume you remember the layout of the village and your chores?"

When Coura nodded, Harriette wished her a pleasant evening and departed. The events of the day caught up to her then, and she trudged inside to rest.

*

Nothing about the Mintelian village changed since Coura last stayed, including how the people behaved, so much so that she slid right into her previous, regular routine when she woke. The sun took time to rise high enough to illuminate the area thanks to the surrounding mountains, allowing them to leave the torches lit along each path. Breakfast consisted of bland porridge and pear-like fruit slices, and no one gave her more attention than a passing glance.

*It's as if I never left*, she thought as she returned her dishes and exited. The comment spurred a shiver down her spine, though she didn't understand why the concept made her uncomfortable.

Instead of following the rest of the individuals heading toward the nearby tunnel for a morning meditation session, she strolled farther away until she reached the stream used as the village's water source. She spent plenty of evenings soaking muscles and washing blood off her body after her spars earned her wounds and bruises. At the moment, she dropped to sit on the bank and stare at the moving water.

*I wonder why he told me to come here this morning. Why not let me meditate around other people?*

She became preoccupied with the question since she assumed the sage's intent had been for her to reflect on her own that the sound of footsteps startled her into rising and searching for the source.

"Good morning," came a man's voice at the same time before she spotted Rydar approaching from where he walked alongside the water. "You finally returned."

Coura tilted her head. "You knew I would be back too?"

"Not exactly. Sage Vidar just informed me this would be happening, likely sooner rather than later."

When she couldn't come up with a response, she opted to focusing on their surroundings. He did the same, which intrigued her since she expected him to leave her alone, as was their people's tendency. The silence soon got to her, and she faced him again.

"Are you usually around here in the morning? Sage Vidar said I should go to the river but didn't mention what I should be doing. I used to join the meditation sessions after breakfast, but I'm not sure why he wouldn't want me there."

His expression didn't look as confused as she imagined given how little they conversed in the past. He even seemed to be seriously considering her question before replying.

"Are you certain that's why he sent you?"

"He didn't just get me out of the way?"

"I cannot guess his reasoning, but he has a point for every order he gives."

As she considered this, she recalled what she shared with the older man the previous evening. *I'll die if I don't figure out how to break this spell tying me to Soirée. That's one way to get rid of her and help Asteom though. Still, I can't give up my life without at least trying to find a solution. I just don't know how I can free myself.*

"Why did you return?" Rydar asked to continue their conversation. "Perhaps this might be the best spot for you."

"What do you mean?"

He averted his eyes by fixing them on the flowing water. The resulting pause stretched for long enough to have her wondering if he intended to be involved in her problem; however, his expression shifted into one projecting a hint of sorrow.

"My father and I lived together in a town no grander than this village. We were inseparable, especially when he began teaching me how to wield a sword like a soldier. That's what I longed to become so I could stay at his side. When he fell ill and died, my world fell apart.

In my childish mindset, I told myself I would climb to the highest peak of the mountains we used to gaze at in the distance and drop off. Such a grand effort would surely earn me a proper death, and we would be together in the afterlife."

"What happened?" Coura pressed when he stopped for a minute.

"I climbed as high as I could before my hand slipped, dropping me into a stream similar to this one."

"You survived a fall like that?"

"I wouldn't have if it weren't for Harriette." His lips curved into a slight smile after those words. "My body instinctively fought against the current until I pulled myself onto a bank and collapsed. Next thing I knew, I woke with her beside me. My legs were hurt, but she healed them enough for me to limp to a safe location. After she fetched Sage Vidar, he welcomed me as one of his own people. I've been here ever since."

As Coura listened, she sensed his strife. *I bet this is the first time he recounted that experience. The Mintelians here keep to their own business, so it's appropriate he repressed those memories.*

"That time feels so distant," he continued in the same manner. "I used to hide that part of myself, both because of the pain and my shame, but Sage Vidar got me questioning my behavior. If I intended to end my life because I had nothing left to lose, why would I crawl to the stream to quench my thirst? Why would I flounder toward the safety of a sandy bank? My mindset shifted when Harriette healed me and he accepted my story. Before then, I fought to stay alive without realizing it."

She struggled to respond due to the weight of his words, prompting him to turn, study her, and go on.

"I'm not sure why Sage Vidar sent you here or what you are struggling with, but we all have a natural drive to survive. I believe it is part of what makes us human. Whenever I doubt that or negative thoughts suffocate me, I watch the water and note how it continues moving forward."

With that, he began walking upstream. Coura's mind fell silent while he spoke, but his departure pulled her out of that quiet contemplation. She didn't know whether to thank him or show sympathy given his past, but while she struggled to decide, the man continued on.

*

Unlike the morning's encounter, her afternoon with Sage Vidar proved uneventful. The man proposed several questions regarding her bond to Soirée, which she had already been contemplating, then she meditated until dinner.

The next week followed a pattern she became familiar with during her previous stay: She would join the rest of the villagers in their session to monitor her soul space then practice magic with Harriette and Rydar present. The latter part of the day surprised her since she hadn't been expecting to return to spellcasting, yet she soon realized how much she needed the exercise.

"We left off with switching between wielding your light and dark energies," the sage recalled during the first afternoon. "Did you utilize that skill after you departed?"

Coura nodded while remembering her time on the border with Byron. "I did a little. Not enough to have difficulty with my mentality."

"In that case, we need to increase your output."

"Why? What does this have to do with my situation?"

The Mintelian narrowed his eyes to show his impatience, yet he must have sensed her genuine curiosity with that method, as opposed to her previous, belligerent attitude. "It is imperative you understand the effects of magic, both on yourself and what ties you to the creature. Your power is split between light and dark, or what you naturally possess and what you allow into yourself, and the two established balance. I would like to see how that adjusts when one half is utilized more than the other."

That idea led him to guide her through several spells ranging in output. For periods of time, she would maintain shields, controlled elemental spells, or the black blade using one type of energy before switching to the next. As expected, her attitude when casting with the demonic power shifted, leaving her reluctant to abandon what confidence and stability she found, yet her Yeluthian energy comforted her to the point where she would hesitate to change mindsets. The sensations only grew worse when she increased the strength of her spells.

On the seventh day of the exercise, Coura finally dropped to her hands and knees from exhaustion. Her center steadily drained as the afternoons passed but required additional time to recover depending on how much was expended. By that point, she needed a break.

"We're finished for today," Sage Vidar stated as a dismissal.

She looked over at the man and attempted to stop panting. "I just need a minute to catch my breath."

"That is not necessary. I have seen what I needed to and will share my conclusions tomorrow."

When she didn't protest again, he departed with Hariette and Rydar trailing behind.

*I wonder what he'll say. This isn't a test I haven't done before, though the extent is greater. How is this going to help me figure out what to do about Soirée?*

Coura longed to doubt the sage since she couldn't comprehend his intentions with the exercise; however, he never revealed details to her before. All she could do was prepare for their discussion.

The anticipation drove her to clean up, eat, and sleep after her chores, and she rose with less weariness stemming from her center. Nobody paid her any mind as she hurried through breakfast and wandered into the enclosed space. There, the sage sat alone in his usual, undisturbed manner.

"Sit," he instructed when she came over. When she did, he opened his eyes and fixed her with his usual, unreadable stare. "I would like you to describe your connection to the demon once more. Specifically, focus on what you say is a bond you share with the creature."

"When I first discovered her and my ability to wield demonic energy, she acted like my shadow," Coura began while lowering her eyes to focus on the memories. "She would linger in my head and communicate with me through my thoughts. It sounded like she became trapped, but I believe she could enter and go as she pleased. Once I was stabbed with an ancestral weapon, she disappeared. It felt like she had been torn away from my body. I could still sense her presence, and she would use our connection to draw me toward her, like a leash."

"This began after you decided to hunt the beasts misshapen by the unnatural energy, correct?"

"That's right. I also relied on what I gathered to avoid eating and sleeping. Looking back on it, I wore myself down enough for the energy to influence my mentality."

"You were also certain you would die in the fight," he stated before continuing without her confirmation. "Consider that connection again. How do you feel when you acknowledge it?"

She paused to put together a coherent response. "I can only pick up her presence when she's near enough, and I can't hear her thoughts or sense her physical state. Sometimes, I catch her emotions, like when she is eager to draw me toward her or amused by my persistence. It's hard to explain."

"Are you able to communicate through that bond?"

"Not as often as we used to, but she disappeared for the last couple years."

"Finally, are you able to pull energy from the creature?"

Again, she needed to recall her encounters with Soirée and what the two shared before answering. "No, I can't."

His expression shifted as he frowned at that response. "You never mentioned attempting this."

"I shared her power until the incident that separated us," Coura admitted while rubbing the back of her neck. "When I could use dark energy again, I never bothered to test whether or not I could through her."

"And what about the other being you said could draw power from you?"

"I don't know how, but Terran was able to do that too. He extended a hand and manipulated what energy I held into himself."

When the sage produced a low, thoughtful hum and ended his questioning, her interest piqued.

"My knowledge of demons is limited," he prefaced while closing his eyes and assuming a relaxed position again. "The creatures are born from the planet, thus they use what energy comes from the earth. I doubt they naturally produce their own because of this. They also possess living beings in order to consume and corrupt what power their hosts carry. You made as much clear during your explanations."

"What does that have to do with me?" she countered when he paused.

"Did your moments of self-reflection not reveal how this type of energy flows into and out of your body?"

Her eyes widened as she processed his words. "Are you saying…"

"You are not the same as a demon, but how you manipulate dark power is similar to their method. The ancestral weapon damaged your soul space, and the bond weakened; however, you adapted to house that energy. Because of this, I believe your bond with the creature tied to you runs both ways."

"What does that mean?"

"You consider the connection as something similar to a leash, but a leash requires a master at one end to act as the leader. This sounds closer to a chain binding you together. Energy only belongs to a being if it is tied to their lifeforce, so it should disappear once they are no longer alive."

Coura dismissed her shock to confirm her suspicion stemming from that realization. "If what you claim is true, then I should be able to command the demonic energy like she does and pull it away from her."

"It's possible."

*Does Soirée know about this? If she figured it out already, that might explain why she kept her distance. I never thought I could do something like that, but I suppose it gives me an advantage, especially since I can also wield my Yeluthian power.*

Once she felt comfortable continuing the analysis, she returned her attention to the sage. "What about a way to break the bond?"

"What I just shared is all I know about that spell," he concluded, to her dismay. "What the creature formed is beyond our understanding of magic, though it seems the demon is not certain of what took place either. Tying souls together dives farther into one's body than their center of power and may require extensive observation from both sides."

Coura leaned forward to rest her chin in her hands. "You think I should go back to her then."

"If you intend to free yourself without dying, that may be the simplest course of action."

*If working with Soirée is simple I would hate to hear what he imagines as difficult*, she grumbled in her mind before releasing a sigh. *Still, I told her I would go with her when Lupin is gone. Whether or not she keeps an eye on me to make sure I follow through with that remains to be seen.*

"Don't be disheartened," Sage Vidar chided in a gentler tone than she expected. "Your control over yourself when wielding magic has significantly improved since our first exercise, and from what you told me before, you have loved ones willing to fight at your side. You are not as helpless to fate as you believe."

His sympathetic comments lifted her spirits a bit, and she thanked him afterward.

*

The next morning, Coura began heading to the meditation session like normal only to run into Harriette, who beckoned her closer. Without a word, the Mintelian led her in the direction of the dirt circle where she worked on spellcasting.

"Am I practicing magic this morning?" she inquired before covering a yawn.

"Sage Vidar wishes to speak with you," came the answer.

She sensed more beneath the words given the woman's timid voice but opted to hear the reason from the older man instead of pushing. They soon spotted the sage and Rydar chatting at their destination, and the pair fell silent when Harriette and Coura approached.

"Good morning," Sage Vidar began as he studied her. "I called for you because I'd like to hear what else you intend to work on while you are here."

Coura tilted her head a bit. "What do you mean?"

"As I mentioned yesterday, the bond cannot be shattered by the strength of one half because the two ends must be observed. You also seem to comprehend how to shift between the types of energy and merely require experience in order to adapt. What you learned must be put into practice."

"Is that what you plan on having me do next?"

"Only if that is what you desire."

At first, his answer confused her until a realization dawned on her. "Is my soul cleansing process complete now?"

The older man nodded. "Now that you understand your center of power and how the energies behave, you need only to become accustomed to them as spells. I doubt you will focus on that specifically unless you are here due to the conflict you hope to help stop, so you are welcome to remain for as long as you wish."

As he spoke, Coura gazed beyond to where the river was located and considered both options. *I left this place before because Lavine mentioned trouble with Byron. Nobody is requesting I depart. The Mintelians will tolerate me if I stay, and I can practice control over my power. Unfortunately, Soirée can track me down if she comes close enough to the village. Who knows how much damage Lupin will cause by that point. Besides, I shouldn't delay the inevitable to postpone my struggles.*

"I think I need to go," she admitted and curved her lips upward into a sad smile. "I have people waiting for me."

Harriette attempted to hide her disappointment yet lowered her eyes to the ground, and Rydar returned the smile, which looked more like a wince thanks to his effort not to frown. Meanwhile, Sage Vidar nodded, seemingly in understanding, before meeting her eyes.

"Good luck then," he finished, though his stern expression didn't support the words. "Don't be reckless if you intend to survive whatever encounters await you."

"Yes, of course."

"You are welcome to return if you find yourself lost once the bond is severed."

Although his final comment startled her given his standoffish demeaner, Coura appreciated the offer and thanked the older man again. None of the three added additional words, so she took their silence as a dismissal and backtracked toward her hut. After collecting her few items of clothing and food from the mess area, she summoned her wings, leapt into the sky, then moved west.

# Purpose

In the weeks following her conversation with Commander Detrix, Grace needed to remind herself why she attended the sessions in order to avoid growing frustrated and quitting altogether.

The prism sealing spell came together with practice, as he explained, and she found using her power in such a particular way invigorating. Never before had she been able to utilize her energy for a dual purpose, though it did require more attention than an ordinary binding spell. That ate up the duration of her training, as well as what power she could spare.

On the other hand, the goddess fire acted like an energetic creature she needed to keep between her palms. Triggering the flame only took place when the commander fully explained how it would react, what to do when it retaliated, and when to start again.

"You will fail multiple times," he shared on the first day. "Like the prism sealing, the wielder must fully commit to the spell; unlike that process, balance is not naturally obtained. Finding a safe output takes trial and error, which is why we start small. If the connection is not powerful enough, the fire will not manifest; if you give too much energy, the flames will go out of control. Finding stability is the key."

She had not quite understood what he meant until they began; then, she found she didn't understand for completely different reasons. The spell would not take shape for her on the first day, even when she practiced in her room after the session. On the second morning, sparks would form and fizzle out, which he claimed to be normal and countered by encouraging a tiny addition to what power she fed it. After that, a flame formed and either disappeared when the unexpected sight startled her or flared until she dismissed the spell. The later result often singed the surface of her palm.

Just when she or another mage grew displeased with the result, Commander Detrix would suddenly appear to reassure them their progress was on track. Still, no one came close to accomplishing the goal.

Despite the slow development, Grace needed to break often since her conversations with General Casner, his assistant, and Byron on the northern border also depleted her energy, both magically and mentally. If it weren't for her guards offering to fetch meals, she would likely remain in bed sleeping without food due to exhaustion.

Dianne even pointed this out one morning and blocked the door so she couldn't leave.

"My lady, you'll run yourself into the ground at this rate," the woman chided when Grace covered a yawn with her left hand and rubbed her eye with the other. "I doubt your training will go well if you can't stay awake long enough to focus."

She wanted to argue but knew that was true. As a result, she dropped onto her bed to remove her boots. "I suppose I should listen to you."

"Stay there while I fetch your breakfast."

The door closed before she could respond, so she lied on her bed to evaluate her resting power within her center. In the next instant, her guard shook her shoulder to rouse her.

"It seems you're going to sleep through the entire afternoon."

Dianne set a tray of sliced fruit, pastries, and warmed bread on the bed, and Grace noticed a second assortment on her desk when she sat up. Together, they ate and considered the day ahead.

"The dinner for the private dining space's unveiling is tonight," the woman reminded her when she neglected to mention it.

Grace popped an apple slice into her mouth. "Is it summer already?"

Dianne released a weary sigh, either because of her lack of manners or her forgetfulness regarding the special event. "Does wielding magic affect your mind as much as it does your body?"

When Grace laughed to hide her embarrassment, her guard joined in before they finished their meals.

*The dinner will be nothing new, just the setting has been renovated*, she recalled when the soldier removed their trays. *I did not even receive a formal invitation. Aaron told me I could go if I wanted, though I wonder if he wishes for company.*

That thought motivated her to accept and ignore what discomfort stirred due to her previous experience in that space.

*I must not look back on the worst moments except to learn from them. Like my visit to the city, others may need my strength so they can pick themselves up.*

*

As she expected, the private dining space's atmosphere hadn't changed compared to past events. Several, new individuals introduced themselves to her before food was brought out while those she recognized made it a point to be seen with Yeluthia's ambassador in a favorable manner. Part of her took pleasure in her status, but she mostly grew tired of their behavior and remembered when she first arrived and became overwhelmed by the politics.

The greetings ended once the servants came around baring trays of finger foods and glasses containing various drinks. Grace accepted one before hurrying to her seat beside her uncle. As she approached, she noticed Marcus standing in line with his father and Commanders Isan and Detrix. Although she masked her surprise, he managed to catch her eye and offer a smile before she took her seat.

*I forgot he would be returning to the palace. This is welcome, but I did not expect him to be here, and not so soon.*

The meal remained as delicious as she remembered while the chatter seemed to consist of comments and compliments on the new artwork, which she partially supervised after the Nim-Valans' ambush. King Arval mentioned several references to their culture as images of angels adorned sections of the sky-blue ceiling, allowing her to share her input and notes to the artists. By the time dinner finished, she found that to be the most relaxing time she spent in the space.

*Perhaps this is a sign of what the future will bring*, she thought and savored the peace.

As if in reply, a string quartet started a lively tune to draw everybody's attention. It took less than a minute for several couples to occupy the center area.

"Would you care for a dance?" came a familiar voice from behind.

Grace instinctively smiled as she rose to turn and face Marcus, who stood behind her chair and extended a hand. Instead of accepting right away, she wrapped her arms around his waist in a casual greeting. Only when he returned the embrace did she step back and curtsy.

"I did not know you would be here," she shared after he led her out where the others swayed and twirled. "When did you arrive in Verona?"

"Yesterday. Aaron practically begged me to come to dinner even though I'm still recovering from the ride."

"A soldier's work never ends," she pointed out as more of a joke and even grinning when he narrowed his eyes at her.

"Don't go spreading that around!"

The two laughed and caught up before returning to the head table where the others remained. After a while, her uncle and his commanders departed, and Aaron had the same idea. Grace followed him out with Marcus, General Tont, and a handful of guards behind, including hers.

"I'll be returning to my quarters to catch up with Marcus," he shared at a lower volume once he gestured for her to walk beside him. "You're welcome to join us."

"I would love that," she admitted.

By the time they reached the king's room, only her guard and four of Aaron's remained to stand outside while she entered after her friends. The assistant general immediately went to the oversized bed and flopped onto the mattress.

"What a day!" he exclaimed as he stretched his muscles.

Grace giggled at his lax behavior and accepted one of the two, cushioned chairs. Meanwhile, Aaron dropped into the seat at his desk, removed his crown, then ran a hand through his hair.

"You can say that again," he muttered.

At his prompting, the three shared their opinions on the newly decorated dining hall before Marcus told her about his trip from Dala. For the most part, nothing sounded noteworthy; however, she sensed some reservation but couldn't pinpoint a reason.

"Will you be staying in the palace from now on?" she asked after.

He shook his head and scratched his bushy chin. "I'd like to return to the northern border to assist General Casner's efforts. I worked with him in the past, so that cooperation could lessen the burden on his and his assistants' shoulders. Besides, I'm sure they can use all the help they can get."

"That depends on a few factors we don't need to discuss now," Aaron interjected.

When he rubbed his eyes in a weary manner, a sense of pity stirred within Grace, and she decided to change subjects. "At least you were able to be here for tonight's event."

"You're right," Marcus picked up. "I needed a simple task like guard duty to give my mind a break. It's been a rough couple years for the southern base."

"You should stay until you feel strong enough to continue outside the capital," she added while projecting sympathy. "It would benefit nobody if you overworked yourself."

The assistant general sent her a reassuring smile. "Thank you, but I'll be all right. I don't plan on leaving for a few days."

"You're that worn out?" Aaron asked and raised an eyebrow. "Usually you jump straight into an assignment. Are you getting soft?"

His final question had been meant as a jab, causing Grace to grin at Marcus' expense. Still, the soldier rolled his eyes before elaborating.

"If you're going to be nosy, I was wondering if Coura would come here first. After the demon's defeat, she mentioned stopping by to report to Commander Detrix before returning to the northern border. I figured we could travel together."

*She will be joining the fight there then*, Grace noted while her friends moved on to another topic regarding the troops' arrangement under General Casner. Something about hearing her friends continue to defend Asteom seemed to light a fire under her. *I am learning the necessary spells to stop a demon, and my light magic is adequately trained already. Others like Commander Detrix are also in the palace to defend Uncle and Aaron. Why should I sit around when I could be helping too?*

"Grace?"

Her head snapped up. "Yes?"

Both of her friends stared at her with a hint of worry, but Marcus addressed her first.

"Are you tired? It's getting late."

"No! I just..." Her hesitation to continue intrigued them more.

"What's wrong?" Aaron pressed in a gentle tone. "You seemed bothered after we started talking about the conflict with Nim-Vala. I know you've been indirectly involved, so I can understand your concern."

She looked between them and struggled to bite her tongue on the subject. Finally, when she realized they would likely offer advice if she explained her conflicting mentality, she caved in. "It may be selfish, but I wish to leave and assist those fighting too."

Aaron appeared completely taken back, but Marcus merely tilted his head, as if curious about her intentions.

"It's not as heroic as it sounds," the latter responded. "Remember when we joined the Dalan troops to fight for the palace? We camped outdoors with the threat of an attack every night, had to eat rations for energy, and dealt with dead and injured comrades. Being on the solider is worse because the activity is spread out. The woods hide the enemy as well."

"Of course it will be a new experience, but did I not assist those at the camp then? At least I am trained to cast shields and heal now. I am also practicing the prism sealing and goddess fire spells. If the demon attacks, then-"

"Grace, slow down," Aaron interrupted and assumed a serious expression. "You're our friend, but you're also Yeluthia's ambassador. You have no obligation to defend Asteom in your position. Should anything happen to you, where would that leave your people?"

She lowered her gaze to the floor. *People like my parents would blame this country's leaders for being reckless, even though it is my decision. With that being said...*

"An ambassador must represent their people," she began while finding the courage to argue. "If I wanted to, I could visit other places in Asteom and provide information about Yeluthia. Is that not correct?"

"I suppose so."

"My people are brave and will protect humans. The alliance is proof of that."

"It's a bit more complicated," her friend mumbled. He glanced at Marcus, as if inviting the assistant general to share input, yet they paused to let her go on.

"Even so, this is my decision. I cannot stand by while others suffer when I can contribute to a solution. No one needs to know who I am anyway, right?"

"Keeping your identity hidden is smart," Marcus agreed and crossed his arms. "I would also suggest bringing a trusted guard to watch your back."

Aaron shot him a displeased glare. "You're encouraging this?"

"No, but I can advise her."

When Grace expressed her gratitude, Aaron addressed her with less intensity.

"I can't imagine why you would want to be involved with that conflict, but I see you're passionate about helping others and upholding your kingdom's reputation. It will also complicate your position. I do agree you shouldn't be limited to the palace or capital. Asteom has never had an ambassador before, and they're supposed to act as a presence across the country."

"What else are you thinking?" Marcus pressed when he paused to consider that.

"I'm wondering how much jurisdiction I hold over you," her friend finally answered and met her hopeful gaze again. "You should speak with King Arval about this. Even if he agrees with me on not letting you go north, I'm sure he'll have ideas about outlining your role."

Bringing up the subject with her uncle crossed her mind before, yet she had no idea how he would react. *He might be lenient, like he was with regard to my parents' behavior, or he could put his foot down and forbid me from getting myself in a position to be hurt. I suppose it is worth asking though.*

She thanked her friends for their honesty before departing for the evening. Marcus lingered in the space, and she presumed the two still had much to catch up on from their time apart. With her lone guard beside her, she returned to her quarters to rest and brave the conversation she intended to pursue the following day.

*

"I must admit, this is not a discussion I thought we would ever have."

Grace avoided the urge to duck her head or bite her lip and reveal her nerves as her uncle turned over what she shared in his head. She visited him in his room when she knew he would break for the afternoon, though she felt guilty for stealing one of his precious free hours. For the first time in years, she saw a startled expression take over his facial features when she began before it settled into his usual, stoic gaze. When she finished, she couldn't read his reaction until he spoke.

"I also never imagined my quiet, timid niece would request to leave the comforts of Yeluthia for the unknown world below," he added after another minute passed. "Yet here we are."

She allowed herself to smile as his gentle tone let her know he wouldn't stomp out her pursuit of answers; at least not right

175

away. "I learned much since I moved to Asteom, including how to advise on the kingdom's behalf and introduce our culture to the humans."

"You also grew up," he pointed out. "As you know, your parents practically threw you at my doorstep like a sacrificial offering. You entered a new world and made this palace your home. I had no doubt the royal family would take care of you, but it was because of their reputation more than your drive. You were just a child after all."

"I cannot dispute that," she admitted and recalled the missing letters explaining why he sent her. "If it were not for my friends, I would not have survived alone."

"You sound like Quinten. My son is gaining invaluable experience leading the kingdom in my absence yet attributes little to himself."

"He will make a fine ruler one day."

Her uncle smiled at the compliment. "Returning to your request to travel outside the capital, I was inclined to deny it until I reflected on the adult you grew into. I also would not be as understanding if you had not stood up to your parents."

"Really?"

He nodded. "You proved where your loyalties lie: They are to yourself, your position, and those you care about. It is admirable, especially given what you endured since arriving in Asteom."

"I do not hate Father or Mother," she clarified after his compliment spurred a blush. "I love and respect them dearly, but staying and not agreeing to an arranged marriage was what I desired most. They will definitely disagree with adjusting my position so I can travel, and if I get hurt again, I know they will blame Aaron and his council before hearing the truth. It is more reason for them to claim they were right about there being danger if I stay."

"You will be in greater danger if you leave these walls."

"That is true as well," she agreed. The spark in her chest that motivated her before flickered to life once she recalled her training. "What is also true is that you cannot grow without taking a risk. I can wield my energy adequately. Commander Detrix's lessons helped me manifest the spells to assist with stopping demons and their creatures. Even though I have experience facing conflict, I know never to go off alone. I will walk alongside guards instead of marching ahead or cowering behind them."

Her uncle studied her for a moment. "What about acting as an ambassador? This sounds like a personal journey, which is not the primary focus of your position."

"Yeluthia established itself in the capital city and positively impacted the humans here. Allow me to extend that influence beyond the palace. Our people should be welcome everywhere, yet understanding requires informing and introductions. Does that not sound like the role of an ambassador?"

The pause that followed her question stretched while she forced herself to keep her chin high despite her heart hammering in her chest. Never before had she argued with King Arval, but she believed she managed to state her point and stand her ground.

*This feels similar to my conversations with Father and Mother. Unlike them, Uncle is reasonable but must carefully consider all angles of a proposal.*

"You truly have grown, Grace," came his response in a softer manner accentuated by the slight, upward curve of his lips. "I worry about your safety, but as family instead of a king to his ambassador. Your position should not be restricted to the palace at this point."

"Does that mean you grant me permission to act on my own?"

When he nodded, she couldn't contain her elation. "Thank you!"

"I expect updates in writing and through your goddess gift," he added and resumed some of his strict composure. "You will state where you intend to go, the routes, and who you interact with. I would also add timeframes for travel and durations of your stay."

Grace agreed to each point he raised, as well as those he mentioned afterward. Meanwhile, her mind wandered to her next steps, including requesting her guard, packing the appropriate clothing, and asking for riding lessons. The rest of her day consisted of noting those thoughts and more, which steadily shifted her excitement into anxiousness. She remembered her purpose for requesting the change whenever she grew overwhelmed, and that eased her nerves.

By the time she prepared to depart a week later, she felt fully prepared. A warm breeze met her as she passed through the front gate in her new, riding uniform, though she slowed to allow Dianne to catch up. Convincing the woman to accompany her had been one of the easier parts, mainly because of the soldier's loyalty as her guard.

They crossed the bridge together, turned right, and approached where Marcus stood holding their horses' reins. His mount already bore the burden of his items, and he assisted with their packs before boosting Grace into her saddle.

"Are you ready?" he asked as he surveyed her, the animal, and her bags. Like Dianne, he hadn't protested King Arval's decision to let her travel but instead promised to protect her while they were together.

She looked at her guard, who seemed eager to be on the road, and met his eyes. "Let us be off."

With that, he climbed onto his animal and led them into the city.

***

It was both a relief and an ill omen when Byron spotted the Yeluthians' white wings against the puffs of clouds dotting the sky. He had not been actively looking for the angels, yet his routine left him with time to wander to his favorite hill, lie on his back, and relax. As soon as he recognized the beings above though, his instincts kicked in.

*They wouldn't hurry back unless they need to report to the general*, he noted while hopping to his feet and jogging toward the site. *It's only been four days since they departed, which means they'd have to rush here if it takes at least two to reach the edge of*

178

*Asteom. Since they were only patrolling the area, I figured they wouldn't return for at least a week.*

Evidently, the commander's appearance drew plenty of attention. Concerned mumbling met him as the troops conversed with one another, and many came closer to the centermost tent, presumably where Evern and Lavine went. He paused outside the opening to attempt a knock on the wooden post holding up the front before announcing his presence.

"It's Byron."

Any more words or a question would only waste time, so he waited for someone to call for him to enter. When they did, he refrained from bursting through the cloth, instead stepping in as casually as he normally would.

The general ushered him over to where he sat gathering what paperwork and maps lied around his person. Evern and Lavine still stood, yet their slight slouching and heavy breathing gave away how exhausted they felt. Although he longed to ask if they flew directly from Nim-Vala without pause, Byron stayed his tongue and joined the tent's final occupant, Mattais, beside the man's superior.

"My apologies for the intrusion," the Yeluthian leader began, though in a half-hearted manner that showed the comment was meant as a formality only. "We bring an urgent update from farther north. It seems our enemy is concentrating their soldiers at a single location."

"How many did you count?" Casner all but grumbled as his face scrunched into a scowl.

"At least eight hundred."

"That's manageable for our forces," the assistant general added, as if to reassure the group.

However, Evern's next sentence shattered any optimism they held. "We sensed a significant level of demonic energy among their ranks."

While the general and Mattais muttered curses, Byron ground his teeth and considered the potential reasons for such a wave of dark power.

*The ancestral weapon was removed, there's no doubt about that. Did they sense demonic creatures then? We never picked up on the being's presence before, so I don't believe that all stemmed from it alone.*

"What are your thoughts, Commander?" Casner pressed after the pause. "Not only were none of us present except you two, but Master Byron is the lone mage who would be able to summarize the implications. We need to defer to your judgement."

"Thank you for your support. I believe we must consider all aspects of our observations. First, the Nim-Valan troops are gathering together instead of remaining spread out along the border. Next, their location is due north from here, meaning they are likely to strike us if that is their intent. Finally, the demon's energy has been released."

"What does that mean for our forces?" Mattais interjected. "Will the creature be leading them again?"

"I am certain of that. I also would not be surprised if its power spawns beasts similar to what formed in southern Asteom."

"There's another problem we need to take into account," Byron added, drawing their gazes. "The Nim-Valans probably possess the ancestral sword."

"You are correct," the commander replied with a nod. "I doubt the enemy would leave behind such an item, even if they do not fully understand its ability."

"A weapon is a weapon after all."

They turned their attention to Casner and awaited the man's next order.

"Either we remain where we are or mirror their strategy," he began without removing his eyes from a spot on the ground. "This might be the opportunity we need to squash their forces instead of letting them roam east or west."

"We'd need to alert our camps as soon as possible," Mattais added before Byron could.

"Even then, you would be taking a risk," the commander pointed out. "Placing all your troops here would leave the rest of the border unguarded."

Casner voiced his agreement and met the Yeluthian's eyes. "If we continue utilizing our eyes from the sky, we hold an advantage. You and your subordinate can patrol the line in both directions in case the enemy intends to cross. I'd also make sure several soldiers remain to maintain those locations."

Byron considered that strategy before shaking his head. "I suggest you keep more than several people in the camps but agree to strengthen our site as much as possible. Remember our previous assumption? If the demon is defeated or recaptured, the Nim-Valans should retreat again."

"This can be our final stand."

"Exactly. Eliminate the main threat while chasing the human enemies back. We should also send for the ancestral weapon in the capital."

The discussion continued while they put together a plan involving summoning their allies across the border, sending Lavine to the capital for the golden sword Coura retrieved, and relying on Evern's monitoring for updates until their forces could march north. By the time they reached that conclusion, their stomachs growled fiercely enough to rival the demonic creatures Byron confronted in the past.

*I just hope they're tamer than what the first being's power produced*, he thought before wishing the others a pleasant evening despite the circumstances.

***

Will started to believe he'd become adept at adapting to change; however, that optimistic view shifted when he received word about the Nim-Valans' movements to the north. He imagined he would be able to fight for Asteom without conflicted emotions, but part of him worried about the people in Muld, the inner circle, and the still-missing spy.

*If Finn is around the advisor's location, his life is in danger*, he couldn't help but note as he assisted with unpacking the medicinal supplies in the healers' section of their new camp. *I hope Geneva and the other townsfolk aren't forced to become involved.*

*Perhaps the soldiers will leave them alone in order to focus on us, or-*

"Are we all set?" came a woman's voice, one he recognized as the head healer.

He glanced around to where she stood at the front and surveyed those working. After scolding himself for losing focus on the task at hand, he hurried to organize the remaining potions, rise, then depart.

The rest of the camp appeared somewhat established, as displayed by bedrolls and blankets around recently lit fires. No one smiled or seemed enthusiastic about the trek, but Will assumed they were more attentive than annoyed.

*This may bring us closer to a permanent resolution.* He clung to that notion as he searched for Clara and the other light mages near their established sleeping spot.

To his surprise, he found them chatting with Byron and Clearshot present. All sat on the ground with bowls in hand and waved or greeted him verbally when he approached.

"The station is well stocked and ready to function when necessary," he shared while accepting food from Clara, who apparently saved a portion for him.

The master mage and soldier exchanged an unreadable look before the former replied.

"We were just warning your friends about what we expect to happen."

"What do you mean?" Will tentatively asked and abandoned the gruel he prepared to slurp down.

"General Casner is waiting for the Yeluthians to return from alerting the other camps along the border, and we don't anticipate those additions for at least a week. Whether or not the enemy noticed our new position already, we want to prepare for conflict before then."

"That makes sense."

"Our mages should especially be ready with shielding spells. If the Nim-Valans can heal like you warned us about, the best strategy would be to exhaust their magic and search for the source."

*This is similar to what took place in the capital*, he recalled without continuing the conversation. *The Dalan soldiers drew the enemy troops away while a group broke into the palace to deal with Hendal and the demon there. I wonder if Byron and the general intend to maneuver like that.*

He decided not to push the subject due to the evening hour approaching, as well as the exhaustion on their faces.

*

For three days, Will, his friends, and their comrades remained on edge. The new environment hovered just along what he believed to be the line separating Asteom from Nim-Vala, which had him reviewing his crude map of the enemy camps until he offered the parchment to Byron as insight for the general. That earned him enough appreciation from the master mage to wonder if the troops' leaders had any idea about the risk of an attack.

Nothing else changed about the regular routine aside from that tension. He assisted with identifying what plants would be useful to the healers and offered to patrol with several others in order to fill the time between meals. Only when a scout on the northern end returned with a warning did he consider much else.

"The enemy troops are moving in this direction!" somebody announced at a distance he could hear, drawing him closer. "Prepare to march and assume defenses!"

As usual, his mind went blank until he shook himself out of that daze. *It's time to find out what the enemy has been up to. This may change the tide of the conflict so far, especially if the demon is with them.*

Will hadn't been requested on the front lines, not that he expected to be put in that position, so he remained to the rear of the soldiers. General Casner had them trek north and away from the camp before forming a ring to concentrate their combatants to the north and sides while the dark mages supported at a distance and the light mages kept an eye on the south. Should the Nim-

Valans prove too much, they received strict orders to retreat while the magic users crafted shields to cover their backs.

*I suppose turning tail is better than attempting to stand and continue should circumstances become worse than we can handle*, he told himself as he shifted in place. He carried only his sword since additional weapons and shields hadn't been brought along. Thankfully, the thought of being in danger didn't cross his mind due to the nearby mages, including both Byron and Clara.

The newer environment didn't appear much different than he traversed before and blessed them with even ground. Although the trees looked thick, none bunched together too seriously to hide their view of each direction. Lastly, the weather cooperated, which he knew was a rarity during the rainy season.

A deep shout from the front had him and everyone else glancing ahead before the sound of footsteps, grunts, and clashing metal alerted them of trouble. For a few minutes, he didn't see their enemy, leading him to grip his sword's hilt tighter in order to repress his nerves. Then, the burly, dark-haired men of the north emerged from either side in an instant.

Will joined the charge of Asteom soldiers who engaged with the Nim-Valans and soon fell into a mindset where he could swing, duck, and block while focusing on the immediate task at hand instead of thinking about the larger picture. This allowed him to land a couple strikes on two men who raised their dull blades at him, sending them to the ground.

The tide of the fight didn't change until he glanced away from the second. Before he could decide on who to approach next, a sharp pain shot through his right leg stemming from his calf. Shock more than the injury had him stumbling forward and falling onto his hands and knees.

*I thought I killed that one*, he absentmindedly commented as he swung his head around.

Finding his previous opponent glaring at him while blood coated the man's chest revealed the truth. If that sight alone didn't, how the figure staggered to his feet while Will climbed to his despite the pain left little room for doubt.

*Calab was right. These Nim-Valans possess the ability to heal!*

Instead of panicking, he faced the enemy, backtracked as carefully as he could without letting his right leg give out, and attempted to lure the man closer to his allies. The idea worked, for a comrade stepped in to lunge at the recovering figure when he became focused on Will.

"We need to retreat," the soldier told him after and turned to face the next trio of Nim-Valans.

Will longed to aid his comrade but understood how limited his movements were with the wound, and how much blood he continued to lose. Fortunately, those around them seemed to get the idea. Asteom's forces steadily backed up toward their side, and various, glimmering shields crafted by the mages soon rose from all directions.

The entire scene came together around him until he lost his footing and fell onto his backside. No enemy troops lingered nearby at that point, yet he worried he would be trampled in the retreat. Before he could seriously worry about that fate, a taller man seized his arm and hauled him to his feet.

"Let's get you to the healers," the stranger announced as he slipped Will's arm around his shoulders. "It looks like we're done here for the moment."

"R-Right."

All sense of direction left him as they traversed what seemed to be the entirety of the space alongside their allies. Before he knew it, the soldier set him down, and Byrn appeared to tend to his calf. He prepared to thank her and ask about the status of the troops, but she finished without fanfare, sent him a brief smile, then moved on to her next patient.

*Are the light mages that busy?* he wondered as he paused to observe his surroundings.

None of the injuries he saw looked devastating enough to not be healed, and the men and women around him chatted in a casual manner, though still with enough caution to keep the enemy in mind. The exhaustion from the fight, as well as what it took to fix his calf, left him weary enough to remain sitting for a few minutes longer.

"Those of you who are ready can return to camp," a voice addressed the troops. Will couldn't see the source, but he thought it sounded like the general's assistant. "The mages are going to keep these shields up until we're all set and sure the enemy is gone."

While others replied in confirmation and began shuffling together, he couldn't wrap his head around how short the fight lasted or the outcome. *Did they retreat too? I swore the man I stabbed was dead, yet he rose after striking me. Is this all there is to an ordinary attack?*

He shook his head and decided to wait until somebody else could explain what took place. Part of him longed to remain with the healers after he dismissed his questions. The mages continued working without appearing tired, so he decided it would be best not to bother them.

*I guess I should go back with the rest of the soldiers*, he admitted and pushed himself to his feet. The bloody area on his right leg only ached, and he made a mental note to thank Bryn when he saw her next.

As he trudged with the others, he found himself becoming fixated on the shimmering walls the dark mages upheld along the perimeter of their original ring. He couldn't locate Byron yet assumed the master mage led the efforts given the man's extraordinary power. His eyes continued gazing over the shields since that helped settle his mind; however, in the next instant, he thought he saw a Nim-Valan on the opposite side. The shadowy figure had him halting, though those around him merely avoided the obstacle in their path.

*Are they still near us? Why are we not pursuing them?*

Will understood his tactical sense would never compare to a general's, yet the longer he stared, the more sure he became. Silhouettes seemingly danced between the trees and foliage without nearing. It became so distracting that he found himself wandering toward the mages' spell and stopping to observe. When he did focus entirely on the other side of the shield, his body shivered as he heard a low growl.

His head snapped to the magic wielder off to his left, yet the young man merely frowned and continued outstretching his arms to maintain the wall of energy.

The noise quieted after a minute as Will instinctively returned his gaze to the scene beyond the shield. Only a single shadow moved at a slower pace, as if it were stalking the people nearby. His suspicion was confirmed when he caught a pair of violet eyes staring back at him.

# Return to the Border

The atmosphere of the northern woods didn't seem to change in the years since Marcus passed through them, yet he refused to lower his guard. His primary focus remained on Grace despite the other soldier who stuck to the Yeluthian's side; however, in the back of his mind, he couldn't help but remember his previous experience.

*The Nim-Valans betrayed our trust and ambushed our troops, both in Asteom and after we supposedly aided their people. How much of that was due to the demon manipulating their outer circle?*

He spent quite a while considering that question as he racked his brain for information he heard from Aaron, Coura, and others involved with the border's conflict. The report he received from his father on behalf of the council summarized the situation well, but he knew the dark beasts were not simple beings. In fact, he anticipated a similar scenario to what he and Calin managed on the opposite side of the country.

All thoughts remained in his head though since he refused to involve Grace any more than what she volunteered to do. Unlike his closest friend, he wasn't as startled by the ambassador's desire to assist outside the capital.

*She always acted interested in the city and humans in general*, he reflected while adjusting his horse's reins so the animal would follow a less rocky terrain. *Besides, not all of her time spent in the palace was positive. She obviously thought through her reasoning if King Arval approves this, so I'm in no position to argue.*

It helped his case that he spoke with her on several occasions before their departure, and she stood her ground every instance. Keeping an eye on her kept his mind off of what awaited them at the general's camp. The ride remained consistently uneventful, which he always recognized as a blessing, and they soon spotted a scout patrolling the edge of what appeared to be their destination. Marcus called a greeting to alert the man of their arrival before dismounting, leading Grace and her guard Dianne to do the same.

"Afternoon," the soldier began and saluted. His eyes studied their Yeluthian companion for a moment before returning to Marcus. "State your names and business."

The introductions didn't seem to surprise the man except for Grace, though she merely mentioned her first name and unofficial status as a light mage.

"You're welcome to enter and make yourselves comfortable," he said after and pivoted so they could proceed forward. "You won't find much, but somebody should be around to update you on the troops' whereabouts."

Marcus thanked the soldier and continued while repressing his curiosity. To his slight amusement, Grace held no such restraint.

"What did he mean by that?" she asked him once they moved out of earshot.

"I'm not sure," he replied with a shrug. "It's possible General Casner marched farther north to secure the border, but we'll know why once we settle down and eat."

For as casual as his response sounded, he couldn't dismiss a sense of unease stirring within his chest. *If the general is willing to leave his main site alone, there must be trouble that can't wait or that he can't risk bringing into Asteom.*

A younger woman greeted them as soon as they neared the closest bonfire to rest and offered to take their horses, which Marcus permitted. One by one, she led their mounts away, presumably to tie them up at an established post, before returning to fetch them food.

"Two soldiers and a light mage then," she pointed out after he introduced them and inquired about the status of the camp. "Unexpected but not unwelcome. You're late to the party though.

General Casner took most of the troops north because the Nim-Valans are gathering. It sounded like the enemy was preparing to strike a single spot, which would be right here."

"You do not sound bothered by that," Grace pointed out.

Marcus nodded and swallowed his mouthful of the oat-based porridge. "I would assume the general intends to keep the fight as far from Asteom citizens as possible."

The woman shrugged. "I'm not sure, but it sounds like both sides expect this to be the final stand. Why else would they call their forces together from along the border?"

*Interesting. General Casner would rather leave less defenses across a wider area. I assume this is in response to the enemy's behavior as opposed to a preemptive attack or mere suspicion.*

With the update complete, the young soldier wished them well and walked away, allowing the trio to converse.

"I don't like this," Dianne muttered and set her empty bowl aside. "We're teetering on the edge of the pan and diving straight into the fire if we go to them."

"Is that not why we are here?" the Yeluthian countered. "We heard about the danger and hope to stop the demon instigating it."

"Yes, but charging into battle isn't exactly what we planned."

"Plans do change," Marcus couldn't help but add while meeting the soldier's eyes. "I wasn't expecting a grand-scale fight, yet that might end the conflict sooner and put more people out of harm's way. In any case, they can use our help here and farther north. I suggest we organize our next steps and proceed in the morning."

The brief discussion afterward had them all agreeing to join the rest of their comrades, not that he expected any different. What did pique his interest was when Dianne began speaking as soon as he offered to collect and return their dishes. The woman's stern look as she ordered Grace to stay at her side, speak up about concerns, and not act recklessly pushed him into hurrying away lest he become caught up in the lecture.

*

Noise from their comrades reached the trio first and pushed them onward through the darkening environment. Although Grace and Dianne hesitated to make their presence known before spotting their destination, Marcus grew accustomed to the sounds of an ally camp and reassured them to hold a steady pace. By the time the three encountered a scout monitoring the perimeter, the entire area became shrouded in shadows with only the site's fires lighting the area. The solider requested they verify their identities, just like at the previous location, and they were permitted to enter.

"Where can I find General Casner?" Marcus asked after thanking the scout.

In response, the man pointed ahead. "His tent is located at the center. If you continue in this direction, you should reach it, though he's likely in a debriefing."

He considered pressing for details regarding the conflict but decided he would hear the entire story soon and led his companions forward.

"That seemed too easy," Dianne muttered, drawing his attention.

"Why? We gave all the information they need to confirm our purpose for being here."

Her eyes darted around the space in a manner reflecting skepticism. "I never imagined they would let us in given what trouble the enemy caused in the past."

Before Marcus could remind the woman of his position, Grace chimed in. Her tone suggested she wasn't pleased with her guard's distrust.

"If we needed to convince them further, I would have demonstrated my goddess gift. Just be thankful we are not considered suspicious enough to cause a fuss."

"I suppose you're right," the soldier replied after a moment.

The trio left the conversation at that, allowing Marcus time to observe their surroundings and the troops' condition. Weary expressions showcased how recent the fighting took place, though he felt grateful few men and women wore bandages to cover injuries. Nobody looked their way except to wave, and he made sure to return the gesture. Several tents came into view after.

"Which one belongs to General Casner?" his Yeluthian friend inquired, prompting him to pause and listen for the man's voice.

Unfortunately, the continued noise drowned out what discussions took place within the secluded, private spaces. This had him approaching individuals around them to ask. He received a clear answer from the third person, so they stood outside while he knocked on the post. Part of him worried about interrupting a potentially important session, and he readied an apology in response; however, the call to enter came right away without any sort of irritation.

"Good evening," he prefaced as he stepped inside first. "Assistant General Marcus, arriving from Verona with two companions."

The self-introduction earned him startled looks from those occupying the space, including the general, Byron, Assistant General Mattais, Commander Evern, and several others, and he bowed alongside Grace and Dianne.

"Isn't this a surprise," General Casner said after and stroked his beard. "We weren't expecting reinforcements from the capital, especially not you."

"Especially not Lady Zelnar," the Yeluthian added in a neutral tone.

Marcus prepared to share his explanation, which he rehearsed at least a dozen times throughout the day, until the general addressed the rest of the people in the tent.

"Our business for the evening is concluded. If you need to discuss any details of this afternoon's conflict and our plan for tomorrow, find me in the morning."

Various responses, grunts, and nods followed. The three newcomers slid to the side and away from the entrance so everyone else could exit until only Byron and General Casner remained.

"It's good to see you," the former began when they were alone. "Once I heard the conflict in Dala subsided, I wondered if you would wander north."

The comment spurred a grin from Marcus. "I suppose I'm a glutton for action. Without much taking place aside from the recovery efforts, I returned to the palace before requesting to join here."

"It seems you picked up a couple stragglers." Byron's gaze shifted to Grace and Dianne, who lingered behind Marcus.

"We volunteered as well," the Yeluthian picked up with her normal, polite smile. "This is my guard, Dianne."

The soldier bowed again without a word. A displeased groan from the general put a damper on their reunion during that pause.

"I'm not entirely comfortable with an ambassador residing in our camp, and so close to Nim-Vala at that."

"I agree," Byron added and crossed his arms. "Not only are our lives constantly at risk, but you'll be a target if the enemy finds out you're here."

Marcus considered defending his friend until he remembered how adamant she had been about accompanying him. *She must have known she would need to justify her decision when she committed to coming along. As much as I wish to protect her, I can't be the one to argue for her choice. She needs to do that herself.*

Fortunately, she remained as prepared as she had been when she spoke with him before their departure from the palace. He noted how her smile never faded, and her confidence could be heard in every word she used in response.

"I appreciate your concern; however, I am here as a mage on behalf of my people. Not only is my goddess gift constantly available, but my light magic can assist with healing the wounded.

I do not intend to put myself in a position where my life is in peril either. My limit still allows me to help where I am needed."

Byron nodded at the composed reply while Casner released another groan.

"I guess it's too late now," the latter mumbled. "In any case, I'll provide a summary of our current conditions since we'll need your support and the assistant general's leadership."

For the next few minutes, the man shared an overview of what their forces dealt with, which included the Nim-Valan troops gathering, their ability to heal, and how demonic creatures hid in the woods to pick off those who wandered too far from the group. He could paint a clear picture of what trouble such a strategy caused, and Byron jumped in after to mention their decision to summon their allies along the border.

"Commander Evern and his subordinate just returned from their routes," the master mage concluded. "New soldiers and mages are arriving practically every couple hours."

"That must be why the scout we met let us through so easily," Dianne mumbled loudly enough for them to hear.

Byron nodded. "They're not being lazy though. It's just that they're constantly speaking with people from various locations."

"Is there anything else we should be aware of?" Marcus asked when the mage didn't go on and his stomach lightly growled.

Casner and Byron shared a look before the general shook his head; however, Byron's next words contradicted the movement.

"You should also know the demon we previously captured hasn't revealed itself to us. Since its creatures are active, we assume its subjects removed the ancestral weapon used to seal the being."

Such a jarring shift in tone sent a shiver down Marcus' spine, yet he merely thanked the duo for the information. One side of his mind focused strategizing and began inquiring about the plan for the following day until his superior scolded him for doing so given the hour. The general ordered the three to eat and rest in order to assume their roles seamlessly, which they couldn't help but agree with. They left the discussion there and followed Byron out of the tent after Casner dismissed them with a wave.

"I'm sure you would prefer to be around familiar faces," the master mage commented as he led the trio through the camp. A second later, he glanced behind at Dianne to offer a polite smile. "At least, I know Marcus and Grace will see familiar faces. You are more than welcome to join us."

His sincerity and warm gesture spurred a blush from the woman, who expressed her appreciation before mentioning her duty to guard the Yeluthian ambassador.

As they passed the fires and what troops occupied them, Marcus allowed himself to relax as the setting reminded him of working alongside the Dalans. *I've grown comfortable with being surrounded by allies despite the circumstances. That and I feel no pressure to act a certain way because of my reputation as an experienced soldier.*

He prepared to consider the notion further until their guide promptly halted and pointed ahead to where a couple people sat around a bonfire. One he recognized as Clearshot while the other he believed to be Will, which caused his muscles to grow tense. Neither paid attention to them, yet the sight of the friend he believed to be dead for years gave him mixed emotions.

*It's my fault he wound up in such a mess. If I had stopped him from joining the company, or even kept searching after the ambush, he wouldn't have gone missing.* Such thoughts plagued him ever since he spotted the charred remains of the previous camp, and he wasn't certain how to deal with them.

"You can stay in that spot," Byron clarified and lowered his arm. "I have scouting duty for part of the evening, so you don't need to wait up for me."

All three thanked the man before he departed, allowing them to move closer until their comrades noticed them. As soon as Clearshot's attention shifted to the newcomers, a wide grin stretched across his face, and he rose to stand and approach them.

"Well, isn't this a nice surprise!"

First, he bowed to Grace, who expressed how she appreciated working with him, then he offered a hand to Dianne. The woman accepted and introduced herself before Clearshot extended the same gesture to Marcus.

"You're looking well," the archer commented when he accepted the firm handshake. "It seems the Dalans aren't slacking off without General Tio."

"They have Calin to worry about now, and I could say the same about you."

He planned to elaborate on Clearshot's livelier appearance, but the man pivoted to face Will, who timidly crept forward with his head dipped and a sheepish smile. Nobody spoke for a few seconds, as if they all were considering what to say. Finally, Marcus heard his friend's familiar voice.

"It's been a while, hasn't it? I owe you both an explana-"

The sentence abruptly ended when Grace charged forward to throw herself at him and wrap her arms around his waist. Marcus caught her shoulders shaking as she carelessly wept and heard muttering about how the herbalist worried her. The sight of Will's baffled expression before it shifted into relief eased the concern Marcus held as well.

"I'm here now, Grace," their friend attempted to reassure her. "I'm sorry it took this long."

The Yeluthian broke off the embrace, stepped back, and pointed a finger into his chest. "You should be! I suppose that is all in the past now though. Please, do not scare me like that anymore."

While the herbalist promised not to do so, Marcus approached his friends. Grace seemed satisfied enough to step away, allowing him to offer a hand and meet the other's eyes. Will stared at it without comprehension as he wrestled with his guilt; however, his friend's response took him back.

"I'm sorry," Will began as he averted his gaze. "I can't imagine what you went through after the ambush. For months, I never thought I would return to Asteom, and when I did, I didn't reach out. I became so preoccupied with-"

"I'm sorry too," Marcus interrupted without lowering his arm.

The words prompted Will to look up in alarm, so he shook the still-extended hand a bit. As soon as his friend accepted, he pulled the other into an embrace and held on while the message he kept in his heart up until that point spilled over.

"I'm sorry I couldn't protect you. I regret letting you go along, and it's my fault for leaving you alone. You should have been able to trust your comrade, not suffer because of my lack of attention."

He didn't expect his friend to ever understand or forgive him, yet Will's arms tightened in response. The less bulky frame even trembled, and he heard how the other's voice wavered.

"I'm safe. I could protect myself because of what I learned from you and the rest of the soldiers, so don't be upset. Don't blame yourself over what neither of us could control."

"Only if you do the same," Marcus added and broke off the hug.

The weight on his shoulders from years of doubt, guilt, and shame lifted as soon as his friend met his eyes and smiled. Tears slid down both Will's cheeks, prompting the herbalist to remove his glasses and wipe his face with his forearm.

With the reunions complete, Clearshot ushered them over to the bonfire and offered to fetch dinner with Dianne so the three could catch up, thus improving the evening further.

***

For days after she departed from the Mintelians, Coura wondered if she made the right choice to leave. Her apprehension about Soirée's whereabouts ultimately drove her off lest the demon suddenly appear and threaten the innocence of the village. She also considered Lupin's reaction to Terran's death and if he would harbor resentment toward her for it or offer his gratitude.

*Neither reaction would surprise me at this point. Demons are such strange creatures.*

The flight allowed her to clear her mind and simply enjoy the environment, which she savored after remembering what awaited her when she landed. Summer meant the greenery deepened, flowers and plants blossomed, and the wildlife came alive to greet the warm weather. During her breaks, she often noticed rabbits or deer before they fled; however, no people were around those locations.

On the fourth day of traveling, she reached the main camp where Casner and most of his troop stayed, though she descended outside the perimeter and proceeded forward until a scout caught her. Fortunately, the man recognized her from her entrance with Evern, Byron, and Lavine, allowing her to arrive in an uneventful fashion.

What she found startled her enough to instantly raise her guard.

"Where is everyone?" she asked and glanced around the nearly empty space. Most items, such as bags and bedrolls, disappeared, only a handful of fires remained lit, and those who lingered didn't seem bothered.

The scout scratched his chin as he surveyed the area, presumably in order to avoid her concerned gaze. "You must not have heard what the enemy's been up to."

It was then Coura learned what awaited her, including the Nim-Valans' gathering farther north, how Casner regrouped with his soldiers along the border, and the general's decision to meet the men head on. After the explanation, her escort pointed her toward a spot where she could eat and returned to his post.

*I don't know what to think*, she admitted once she procured the expected gruel and started slurping it down. *Why would Lupin form a single unit instead of continuing to spread out? I have no doubt the change is his doing considering how little the northerners have acted without his influence, and the previous strategy had been working. That must mean something is different now that he's free from the ancestral weapon.*

No answers revealed themselves in the following minutes, so she decided to abandon the effort in favor of rest. In the morning, she requested whatever information she could on the general's whereabouts, details regarding her father's location, and anything dealing with their enemy. All that earned her were repeated answers lacking more than she already knew.

*It sounds like nobody fully understood the situation before they went to confront the Nim-Valans. As much as I dislike Casner, I have to admit he's usually more cautious than this. Unless... Does he believe meeting the enemy would benefit our side? Maybe he can predict what the Nim-Valans will do if they remained here.*

She rubbed her left temple and abandoned the effort when attempting to comprehend the strategy became too complicated. No matter the reasoning for their move, she understood she should regroup with her allies in order to assist them first.

*

It didn't take long for Coura to locate her allies' forces due to the amount of bodies crowding one of the only open areas in sight from where she soared above. Unfortunately, what she witnessed didn't reveal much aside from how the enemy utilized the landscape. Figures dressed in the darkly dyed leather seemed to emerge from the trees to strike before staggering away when they were wounded.

*They just keep coming*, she noted while struggling against her instinct to jump into the fray. *I suppose the scout at the main camp did say the enemy gathered all their forces together. It's risky, but if their numbers overwhelm Asteom's, they'll eliminate the biggest threat.*

For longer than she was willing to admit, she balanced in the air until her drive to act had her descending through a break in the canopy. Diving to the ground in the middle of the conflict would no doubt result in distracting the men and women working to protect themselves but likely earn her cuts or bruises from those who didn't recognize her right away. As usual, her hesitation when dropping through the branches, dismissing her wings, and climbing down cost precious time, yet she released a sigh of relief when both feet touched grass.

The nearby clashing of weapons accompanied by a symphony of grunts, pained cries, and curses let her know the conflict didn't change; however, a sound she didn't expect in that moment was the low growl of a predator. The rumbling came from behind, leading her to spin around and draw her sword.

*Who's there?* she mindlessly wondered before four glints of violet caught her eye, instantly souring her mood. *I should have known.*

One of the pair leapt at her without warning, revealing a misshapen mass of fur she assumed had once been a wolf. Unlike those she faced in the past, the beast didn't appear to look much different than its original form aside from the miscolored eyes and green-tinted saliva dripping from its jaw.

Coura sidestepped when it neared and lunged to stab straight through the middle of its torso. When she removed her blade from the lifeless body a few seconds later, she stepped backward in preparation for a follow-up attack only to feel something wrap around her ankles. A sharp yank after swept her feet out from under her, sending her to onto her side in the dirt.

*A coordinated attack?*

Without time to rise, she sat up and poised her sword at the bushes in front of her, which produced a fierce hissing noise. Instead of the single set of violet eyes she had been expecting, five appeared, and the tentacle-like limb binding her legs slowly dragged her forward. A grunt escaped her when she sliced at it and cut through tender flesh, yet the lack of strength behind her blow resulted in a wound too shallow to weaken its grip.

As Coura prepared to try again, the hissing abruptly ended, and the hold loosened from her ankles. She pulled her legs away only to find the limbs limp.

*What just happened?*

"Your feather-headed mindset isn't aggressive enough, Dear One," came a voice from beyond the brush. "You should know not to underestimate such creatures by now."

She wasn't as alarmed as she thought she would be when Soirée stepped out of the bushes to stand over her. In one hand were two, oversized heads of what appeared to be snakes.

"What are you doing here?" she grumbled instead of replying to the previous comments while pushing herself to her feet.

The demon tossed the remains aside. "I figured you would arrive sooner or later, though I didn't imagine you would take your time. How many humans died while you relaxed in the mountains?"

"Shut up. I doubt you even care about that."

When she looked away from Soirée to regain her sense of direction, she noticed a couple bodies lying in the grass nearby. Her instincts drove her forward at a jog while readying her light energy and throwing herself to her knees before them; however, it was too late.

"That's at least two," the demon chimed from behind.

*I'd bet this situation is different than what anyone expected*, she noted after growling a curse. *The Nim-Valans are a controllable problem while beasts like that wolf and those snakes are unpredictable and probably intimidating to those who have never seen them before.*

She rose to her feet in silence and considered whether or not to locate her father or Byron for orders. As she did so, Soirée continued chattering about the danger to her comrades. Finally, she decided to follow her gut and join the fight, which would likely lead her to one of the two anyway.

"Where are you going?" the demon snapped when she began moving toward the conflict.

Coura didn't answer.

"Do you honestly believe ignoring me will-"

"If you don't have any useful input, then you're only a distraction," she interrupted in a harsh tone to show her exhaustion with the being. "I'm helping my allies right now."

Part of her expected some sort of physical retaliation from Soirée as a result of their bickering, leading her to ready a shielding spell. The other side of her mind wondered whether or not the demon would keep their bargain or choose to drag her away. To her relief, neither took place.

"As long as you remember Lupin is still around, then I could care less about interrupting your heroism," came the being's response.

Coura slowed to a stop and turned around to face Soirée, who hadn't moved from where she emerged earlier. "I'll face him with the troops if he does show up."

The two stared at each other for a moment longer, and she noticed the demon's lips curve into a slightly amused smile before the violet eyes looked away.

"Be careful if you reveal your presence to him," Soirée added in a surprisingly cautious manner. "Remember, he's not just after you."

When she didn't elaborate, Coura left the discussion at that, both due to the ongoing commotion and a sense of unease stirred by the ominous warning.

# Battle Preparations

Engaging with the Nim-Valans felt reminiscent of Marcus' recent time spent in the south, as well as his experience fighting alongside the Dalans outside Verona. The enemy approached less enthusiastically since he regrouped with General Casner's forces. They would be cut down and rise to continue throwing themselves at him and his comrades, which became less intense than he remembered.

*I must be getting used to this type of opponent*, he thought absentmindedly while piercing through the leather covering one man's throat. *We should be thankful for this part being monotonous though. That means we can start figuring out what to do about the creatures.*

When he first arrived with Grace and Dianne two days ago, he hadn't been expecting to find their enemy actively able to heal using the demon's power; however, that didn't surprise him given his knowledge of the beings. The troops needed to adjust their focus to defending and retreating in order to put together a means of holding the northerners in place and locating their leader.

Unfortunately, the dark power acted as Byron and the Yeluthian commander predicted by bonding to various animals dwelling within the forest surrounding them. Anybody who parted from the mass of soldiers disappeared in an instant only to be remembered back at camp and pronounced dead. Already two dozen met that fate.

Marcus longed to remain at his comrades' sides near the front instead of lingering at the center of the conflict; however, his personal desire to keep an eye on Grace outweighed that sense of duty. At the reminder, he glanced over his shoulder to where the Yeluthian stood alongside the light mages who maintained a shield covering the eastern perimeter. She never seemed to notice, and her companion Dianne fulfilled the role as guard admirably.

Whatever attention he could spare instinctively went toward Will. Instead of remaining with the healers at the rear, his friend fought as equally far out as him, which meant they likely faced a similar number of enemies.

*He's doing fine so far, but he's not entirely trained. I should advise him to stay by the mages when we regroup tonight.*

Marcus' blade found three opponents during the next couple minutes, allowing him to catch his breath and survey Grace's position again. Before he could proceed into a space where a trio engaged with men rushing forward, he heard someone calling for him and turned to find General Casner approaching at a walk

"Assistant general, we're about to signal for a retreat."

"Already?" he couldn't help but mutter while gazing up to judge the time. The previous days had similar results yet seemed to stretch until evening. "How's the front line?"

"The same," came the older man's gruff reply. "I'd like to discuss options since it doesn't look like this fight will shift in our favor anytime soon."

*I mentioned last night that the conflict in the southern field outside Verona became a battle of attrition,* he reflected as he nodded and began ordering his troops to retreat. *If the Nim-Valans don't grow exhausted and continue healing, we'll never make progress. I'd bet that's the demon's goal, to draw this out for as long as possible.*

Once the soldiers shuffled south together, the mages adjusted their shields to protect the entirety of the mass. Marcus appreciated the tactical maneuvering on their part, which Byron organized, yet he couldn't dismiss the bodies of what allies perished. The healers would remain to take care of those who were still alive; however, the dead lied where they fell.

"It would be too risky to return for them, and lingering there wastes time and energy," his superior argued when he and several others mentioned it back at camp. "Every time we returned to that spot, they're gone anyway."

That fact both haunted and hurt those present, though they understood circumstances were not in their favor.

While he attempted to dismiss what unease that discussion arose, he heard somebody saying his name again before a hand grabbed his arm. The sudden touch startled him given how he cut down enemies who did so earlier, yet he refrained from reacting and was glad he did when he saw Coura standing beside him.

"I've been calling to you," she began in an annoyed tone that matched her expression. "I thought you could catch me up."

"When did you get here?" he asked without hiding his surprise. He imagined she would make a scene with magic or run into him before then until he remembered he kept to the southern section of the area with less activity.

His friend gestured toward the others with her chin to usher them on before answering. "I went to the main camp first since I wasn't aware of the ongoing conflict and left this morning to come here."

"You've been fighting for a while then."

She nodded. "Has it been this bleak every day?"

At her prompting Marcus proceeded to inform her of the current issues and his comparisons to the first conflict with healing Nim-Valans. The camp came into view when he finished, so they remained silent to contemplate what he shared as they entered.

"I need to debrief with the general," he told her after.

Part of him expected her to request to join, but she merely asked where she could get food and rest. He informed her of the layout and also warned about the amount of people likely searching for the same, then the two broke apart.

The remainder of his assignment passed smoothly since everybody felt exhausted and lacked solutions to their problems. General Casner encouraged them to turn in early so they could pick up the discussion in the morning, and Marcus exited behind Byron.

"You didn't want to stay longer?" he inquired while they strolled toward their shared bonfire. "Usually you add more after we finish business."

That earned him a chuckle from the master mage. "Is that why you left? You knew I wouldn't continue the conversation?"

"Pretty much."

"I have another person I'm interested in talking to tonight," Byron revealed and let his smile fade. "Coura's back, isn't she."

Marcus nodded.

"I thought I saw her near the frontline."

"Do you believe her input can help us understand the enemy's abilities?"

"It couldn't hurt to ask."

They approached their section of the camp after those words and found their target around the fire with Will, his friend named Clara, Grace, Dianne, and Clearshot.

"Quite the gathering you assembled," Byron said to nobody in particular to announce their presence.

"The ever-important leaders finally make their appearance," Clearshot replied and held up his bowl as a sort of salute. "Care to fill us in on our next steps?"

"I would if we had any."

The master mage's honesty dampened the mood, and he and Marcus took seats in the circle.

"We're just going to repeat the same charge tomorrow?" Will ventured with a raised eyebrow. "That doesn't sound beneficial."

"It's not," Byron admitted and shrugged. "However, sitting around repeating what we already know isn't terribly helpful either."

"Should we contact the palace?" Grace added a bit timidly, making Marcus wonder if she would be able to given the energy she expended.

"Not yet. We're going to meet again in the morning, which gives us an evening to recover and clear our minds before figuring out a plan." His eyes shifted to Coura, who didn't appear as bothered as the rest of them. "I'd like to have a chat with you about the demons you encountered recently."

"I figured as much," she replied before releasing a sigh. "What do you want to know?"

Byron cleared his throat and crossed his arms before elaborating. "When we last faced Nim-Valans who could heal on their own, that power stemmed from Hendal, who in turn pulled power from the first demon. I believe we'll need to repeat our approach this time around."

"What does that have to do with Terran?"

"We can't risk relying on the ancestral weapon alone. Without a means of ending the being's life once and for all, we'll merely find ourselves delaying the solution. I want to hear how the demon from Dala died in order to assess how we can make that happen if we send a select group to confront it."

Marcus knew the idea stemmed from several discussions in the general's tent that the master mage put together; however, he had been too preoccupied to consider Coura's position. The notion piqued his interest, along with the rest of the group, prompting them to study her closely for an answer. Meanwhile, his friend licked her lips and stared into the fire.

"There's not much to tell," she admitted after a moment. "I followed Soirée east and into the mountains where she was hiding. When I confronted her, Terran showed up, they fought, and she managed to defeat him."

"Through sheer strength in combat?" Byron pressed.

She shook her head yet paused before continuing. The entire time, she kept her eyes fixed on the flames. "Soirée managed to disrupt the energy he possessed. I'm not sure how, but that had him struggling to fight. After she wore him down, his power seemed to fade."

"That doesn't sound promising," Clearshot picked up when the questioning stopped. "The first demon probably did something new if you're not familiar with it."

Coura nodded but didn't comment.

*We can't rely on what we don't understand.*

He imagined the others shared his thought; Byron confirmed that a minute later.

"I hoped we could learn and formulate a plan based on what you shared, but I suppose I was being optimistic," the master mage summarized. "I will still report this to General Casner so we're all aware."

"There's something else you should add," Coura interjected and glanced at him for the first time since the conversation began. "Soirée is hiding in the woods surrounding us, though I doubt she'll be a problem since her goals don't align with harming Asteom."

Marcus' muscles tensed, and his eyes wandered to the shadows outside their light. Everybody else did the same while mumbling their concerns.

"What makes you so sure the demon won't attack us when our backs are turned?" Clearshot demanded. "Your trust in its words isn't worth the price of our lives."

Coura rubbed her eyes. "I know, and I didn't tell you so you could let your guard down. She's goal-focused, so as long as our troops aren't in the way, she shouldn't be a problem is all."

"Can you still sense the being's location?" Byron asked next.

"Yes."

"In that case, you'll need to warn us when it appears."

She nodded as she raised her eyes to scan the sky. "I should tell Evern before tomorrow."

"I was just about to recommend that."

Even without a vocal confirmation, Marcus sensed her trepidation. *The Yeluthians might attempt to track that demon down or argue against such a lax mentality. Plus, Coura's in the middle of the issue because of her dark power and relationship to the commander.*

He longed to support his friend yet felt he would only be a burden if he jumped into her business. She practically confirmed this when Grace and Will mentioned going with her when she rose to stand and stretch.

"I appreciate the offer, but he should hear about this from me. Besides, I can take his scolding and argue with him until he accepts."

"Good luck," he heard Byron mutter, leading him to do the same.

***

For the first time in months, Evern found himself frustrated with the direction of the conflict he assisted in managing, which he hid behind a mask of indifference as he and the general waited for their other participants to arrive. The previous night's discussions worsened his mood, each in different ways.

First, and most prominent, related to the conditions of the combat. The dense canopy above the humans prevented him and Lavine from summoning their wings to assist from the air while the crowded space left him unable to fight as fluidly as he liked. This hindered his ability to incapacitate their foes efficiently. His subordinate echoed his thoughts at dinner while pushing for more from the generals and mages, yet he could only order the young Yeluthian to be patient.

His second issue unsurprisingly had to do with his daughter, who showed up without warning the previous morning. He only caught glimpses of her during the activity, then he needed to meet with the other leaders in their camp and abandoned his questioning for the time being. The group accomplished nothing, souring his mood, so he rejoined Lavine and prepared to rest.

As soon as he felt himself relaxing, Coura showed up with new, unpleasant information. The subject of demons already made him upset, yet he thought he handled her determination and his temper well by promising to consider her points.

*I suppose postponing a serious lecture was the best I could do*, he reflected as the assistant generals entered the tent together. *No one would have benefited if we began a verbal bout. Depending on the direction of this meeting, we may need to trust her connection with the being, as much as I hate admitting that.*

The rest of the participants soon joined, allowing General Casner to begin the meeting. Evern listened as the man requested suggestions and opened the floor for discussion. For the most part, the main focus dealt with locating or drawing out the demon controlling the Nim-Valans; however, they also needed to be careful about respecting the northern country's boundaries. Such parameters also bothered him since Yeluthia never dealt with limits in the sky.

When he found an opportunity to speak, Evern volunteered himself and Lavine again. Their eyes from above would keep the others updated, and Lady Zelnar was becoming an invaluable asset given her goddess gift. They noted his idea without confirming, so he remained silent instead of pressing for an immediate reaction.

Assistant General Marcus took the floor next. "I wouldn't put it past this demon to draw out the battle. That's how the one in Dala behaved. It utilized what demonic creatures it controlled to wear the troops down. We only managed to defeat it by taking advantage of its hubris, and that didn't even kill it."

"I recall as much from the first demon's influence over the former high priest," the general added.

That comment led Byron to segue to a new topic. "Speaking of which, Coura returned with an update."

Evern listened as the master mage shared what he already heard, including how his daughter trailed the wicked being she bonded with, watched it kill the creature plaguing the southern half of Asteom, and its whereabouts in the forest they currently occupied. Internally, he seethed at her reckless behavior and desire to keep the demon involved; however, he did appreciate that she didn't seem to hide any details from him, as proven by the summary.

"So only she witnessed what took place," General Casner muttered loudly enough for them all to hear. "Interesting. She was present during both the conflict in Dala and here as well."

"I'm sure she intends to stay involved until this matter is put to rest," Assistant General Marcus added after.

"I suppose so. Perhaps we should have her target the Nim-Valans' inhuman advisor. The first creature might follow and assist by-"

"I disagree," Evern heard himself interrupt even before he could wrap his head around the idea. "If what she claims is true, it will not bend to the whims of your kind by ridding us of the main threat."

"My thoughts exactly," Byron said after, alleviating some of the building tension in his chest. "Besides, the demon will likely retreat into Nim-Vala, and where does that leave us? That's not to mention the political consequences if anyone is caught across the border."

A pause followed his remark before Assistant General Mattais picked up the discussion. "What other options do we have?"

"Not many, and only a handful worth trying," his superior began. "We can organize a specialized group to search for clues or spy from the woods, but we would be putting their lives at risk as long as the beasts continue roaming freely. The current routine would allow Commander Evern and his subordinate to locate the demons from above, which could help us identify a means of stopping them."

"Unfortunately, we cannot guess how long that will take," Evern countered. "As much as I prefer the open air and trusting in my senses, this might be too time consuming to bet your troops' lives on."

"You're right. My final suggestion is to focus on the enemy soldiers first. If we can immobilize them somehow, we can turn our attention to their leader."

The atmosphere changed during the resulting seconds of silence, as if those present wordlessly agreed that would be their best route. The master mage cleared his throat first before crossing his arms, drawing everyone's attention.

"I wonder if one of the Yeluthian spells would benefit us if we could somehow remove the dark energy healing the northerners."

The others' stares shifted to Evern, prompting him to reply. "It might be worth exploring, though the cost of using such powerful magic is great. The mages will surely need at least a full day to recover."

"Even so, confining the enemy sounds like our best bet," the general summarized. He prepared to elaborate until Assistant General Marcus released a thoughtful hum and caught Byron's eye.

"Years ago during the conflict in Verona with the first demon, the former high priest placed possessed guards outside the previous master light mage's home. I was present when she used a binding spell to hold a pair of soldiers, and I tied them up to physically restrain them. After a half-hearted attempt to break free, their bodies jerked around before stopping. They regained their humanity after waking."

"I remember Emilea once telling me about that," Byron grumbled with a nod. "When the men became bound and useless to their master, the host likely removed the demonic energy in order to avoid wasting it. We couldn't come up with another explanation for why the spell would have that result."

"In any case, capturing the Nim-Valans and restraining them might benefit us in that regard."

"Even if the creature's power lingers, they would be useless except to spy on us from where they will be kept."

"What do you suggest?" the general interjected and scratched his chin. "I'm in support of those means, but we need to strategize if we intend to hit them at once."

During the second half of that conversation, Evern mainly listened and threw out comments in favor of or against certain ideas. His experience didn't necessarily apply to human troops, and everyone would be stuck on the ground, so he chose to defer to his comrades. In the end, he felt comfortable with the resulting plan.

***

For the first time in months, Coura found herself with nothing to do as she occupied Casner's camp. Her flight and participation in the conflict the previous day allowed her to sleep well despite the cooler weather compared to what she became used to in the southern part of the country, and she ate enough to satiate her lingering hunger. Her friends and father were all moving around the camp on various assignments ranging from meetings with the general to scouting duty to assisting in the medical station. When she inquired about helping, they turned her down due to the amount of people already in a familiar routine and claimed she could use the additional time to continue building her strength.

*I feel useless just sitting here though*, she grumbled in her mind while staring into the fire she recently fed. Nobody else occupied a seat around the flames or would do so for hours. *Maybe I can patrol from the sky. It would be rough to start given the lack of a clear opening in the canopy, but I'll manage.*

Despite the idea, she remained comfortably in place and opted to reflect on what she learned since she arrived.

*The Nim-Valans can heal again, are hiding Lupin somewhere across the border, and they march south to engage in combat with Asteom's forces. Demonic creatures also watch from the shadows to keep a barrier around the fighting. I still don't believe Soirée will become involved unless Lupin appears. Even then, she might not reveal herself to anybody but me.*

Coura released a weary sigh and rubbed the side of her nose before remembering how the demon's looming presence meant she would need to continue hiding the truth regarding Terran's death.

*They don't need to hear about Hendal right now*, she had rationalized the previous morning during her flight when she considered how much Marcus knew and who would likely ask. *Explaining his connection to Terran, and what that means for Soirée and me, won't benefit our current issues with Lupin. Besides, I would need to deal with their pity. They would want to avoid killing Soirée or be cautious about her involvement even more than they already are. Other people's lives are at stake if Lupin decides to target beyond our group.*

None of her friends seemed to notice her reserved responses, and her father's hatred for the demons led him to never consider that she would lie. For the time being, she didn't need to face those conversations.

"Is something wrong?" came a familiar voice from her right as footsteps approached.

Coura turned to find Byron strolling over and waited for him to drop down across the fire before dodging the question by asking about his meeting.

"We actually have a plan, which is a relief given the past couple encounters."

"I'm sure that will raise everybody's spirits."

Her former mentor nodded, leaned back on his hands, and closed his eyes, seemingly to savor the warmth and peacefulness of their spot. "Why are you here alone? I figured you would find a task to keep yourself occupied."

"I tried," she replied and shared how her morning went until that point. ""The soldiers and mages have a well-run system in place, so I decided to stay out of the way."

"That's not like you at all."

She huffed a laugh. "I'm more considerate than you give me credit for."

Byron opened his eyes to shoot her a look that projected his doubt, though she knew he still took pleasure in teasing her at every opportunity, as showcased by the slight, upward curve of his lips.

# Unexpected Magic

y mid-afternoon, the entire camp looked ready to initiate combat with the Nim-Valans. Coura learned about their strategy from Byron before he departed to prepare, and soon her friends returned to their spot intermittently to do the same. Meanwhile, she readied herself with the proper armor and enough clothing underneath to keep her warm without causing her to overheat or struggle to move. Her next goal became finding Marcus since the two would be in the same group.

*He's leading the eastern half with Mattais and Evern, and Casner and Byron will be doing the same on the other end,* she repeated in her mind in order to pass the time. *Will said he'll be guarding the healers, and Grace agreed to stay back with him. The troops will split to circle around the Nim-Valans. Once they're surrounded, we use whatever means necessary to restrain them. After that, we'll see if Lupin retaliates.*

The last part had been the most concerning to her since she fully expected the demon to intervene at some point; however, the entire plan relied on their mages' ability to keep the beasts occupied. That was where she would be, both because of her magic and experience.

She remained at Marcus' side once she found him issuing orders to procure any items that could be used for binding the enemy troops. Once they finished, everybody lined up efficiently enough to let her know they became used to doing so over the past few days. Evern appeared beside her then and instructed her to join him near the front of the troops.

"The assistant generals will be supervising the middle and rear sections while I monitor the front for signs of demonic activity," he shared as they crossed through those standing at attention. "It would be beneficial to have you near me in case we need to pursue or become distractions."

"We're not supposed to go after Lupin?" she countered when he didn't continue.

"Not at the moment."

When he didn't elaborate, she figured he didn't agree with that decision; however, she wasn't surprised since the main goal would be to focus on the enemy soldiers. *Take care of one problem before moving on to assess the rest. That makes sense unless an opportunity presents itself.*

A shout from the general minutes later signaled the march, which went smoothly since they only needed to travel a short distance to their goal. As expected, the area where they fought the day before looked empty, and Casner ordered them to halt about halfway across. Coura readied herself for a wait, but the shadowy figures, both from the north and each side of their formation, appeared sooner than she anticipated.

Evern moved first to initiate a shielding spell where the demonic creatures shuffled in the bushes along the perimeter, prompting her and the others in their group to do the same. None of the beasts came close enough to reveal their unnatural eyes or bodies, which intrigued her until the Nim-Valans reached them to initiate combat. After, she fell into a rhythm of swings, lunges, and swerving to dodge what attacks aimed for her.

*They didn't seem to train much in the time I've been away,* she noted when the three who targeted her fell within a minute. *I suppose the motivation isn't there when they don't need to worry about dying. Was I like that before?*

She dismissed the thought when a scowling man around her height threw himself at her and poised a short sword at her chest. Her blade met his when she brought it up to knock his away, then she sidestepped his body entirely before stabbing him in the side. Already, another opponent she previously felled stood at her back and inched closer for a surprise strike, but Evern took care of the man before she could fully turn around. His resulting look seemed to warn her about leaving herself unguarded, a sentiment she ignored given her awareness of the Nim-Valan.

For what seemed like hours, the fighting continued in the same manner, though the duration wound up benefiting their plan. The two groups steadily drifted away from each other in order to create an opening in the center where they forced a majority of the enemy soldiers. Coura remained at the southernmost point with her father but caught glimpses of the Nim-Valans being physically restrained on the ground.

*At least that part is working*, she told herself during a pause where she could observe the rest of her comrades.

Throughout the conflict, she noticed no demonic creatures attacked her shield and saw the same proved true for those maintaining their spells. What shadows she caught moving beyond the foliage merely paced back and forth, though they remained too far away to see clearly. Meanwhile, sounds from the opposite end of the area began cutting through the surrounding noise. She heard growls and scratching against the magical walls on that side, leading her to wonder if the beasts only attacked from the west. Why that would be the case, she had no idea.

Fortunately, she faced fewer enemies as they were driven into the center of Asteom's forces, which began closing around them. The Nim-Valans who noticed their strategy attempted to flee only to be cut down and dragged into the middle. Part of her longed to ensure no one would escape; however, she noted how Evern remained close to his shield and figured she should do the same.

*It would be easy for the demonic creatures to strike when our backs are turned, especially since the mages are likely adjusting the flow of energy as the battle wears on.*

Coura had been keeping her back to her spell as she watched the ongoing movement nearby and shifted to study the beasts beyond in case she would need to recraft the magical wall at some point. Her eyes gazed over the perimeter, yet she couldn't identify the shadowy enemies.

Just when she prepared to mention this to her father, a flash of light from the woods in that direction illuminated the entire forest for a split second. The sudden brightness blinded her and those around her momentarily, even after a crash of thunder and the unmistakable sound of shattering glass followed. When she could see again, she felt the blood drain from her face at the sight of the mages' destroyed shields, several bodies on the ground, and dozens of allies' ruby faces and limbs.

*That must be Lupin*, she realized after racing in that direction behind Evern. *The Nim-Valans have no one else who wields magic, and the strength behind that spell was strong enough to-*

A second clap of thunder interrupted her frantic thought, and the next bolt brought down her portion of the shield. What mages could still assist attempted to reconstruct the barrier; however, the shadowy figures she observed earlier made their appearance once the opportunity presented itself. Instead of demonic creatures, additional Nim-Valans charged out from the trees to strike the nearest, vulnerable men and women.

Coura hurried forward to meet the enemy soldiers while shouting at those around her to retreat toward their allies at the opposite end of the area. The surprising amount of people targeting her for standing against them resulted in several strikes that bruised or deeply scratched beneath the armor, but she knew she wasn't alone in defending her comrades. She caught Marcus fighting to her right and heard him issuing orders for the mages to reform the shield, which some started. On her other side, Evern managed to create a barrier with those around him and began driving the enemy into the center, like they did previously.

The chaos soon appeared to be becoming manageable, yet she knew not to underestimate Lupin. Her concern came to fruition when a surge of the demon's power arose from the center of the area instead of where he previously targeted from the east. No flashes of color or light indicated he used an offensive spell, which confused Coura until she spun around to find a shield as tall as a house cutting through Asteom's forces. Interestingly, the magical wall kept what Nim-Valans her allies captured on one side, along with the demonic creatures; this also meant her group would face what northerners emerged, and likely Lupin, alone.

"Marcus!" she called and glanced at her friend, who shoved his latest victim off his sword.

"I know," he replied in an annoyed manner as he scanned the layout of the opposite direction. "The enemy is using our strategy against us."

"What should we do?"

His resulting silence made her worry. Those around the pair looked to their leader for answers as well, ultimately prompting him to come up with a new plan.

"Fall back!"

"Back where?" someone cried.

"We'll need to carve a path to the south if we're retreating," came Mattais' voice before the man emerged from the growing crowd. "That surprise attack left us vulnerable enough to get surrounded."

"We can't put ourselves against the demon's shield," Marcus countered.

Coura prepared to agree when a second wave of the defeated Nim-Valans rose to continue the fight. During that bout, she overheard multiple arguments regarding the injured who would ultimately be left behind due to the pace of the battle, how they should find a way to rejoin their comrades, and that the mages could target the wall keeping them separated.

*The longer we struggle in one spot, the weaker we get*, she admitted to herself and located the assistant generals, who didn't seem to be on the same page either. *At some point, we'll need to make a sacrifice. We're just postponing a decision and increasing the risk of losing more than we already have.*

A sudden jolt of pain shot from her left side, causing her to stagger and allow her current opponent to seize her weapon-bearing arm. As she attempted to free herself, a growl escaped her before she placed her empty palm in front of his face and released a blast of fire. The man's resulting yell told her the spell landed as intended, so she yanked her other arm free, pierced through his chest with her blade, and turned to where the second opponent towered over her. Without a distraction, she easily slipped around his hulking figure while avoiding what wide swings he attempted and cut down his legs. A stab through his throat followed.

The effort left her panting, though nobody else challenged her in that moment. Because of that, she placed a hand on the still-stinging wound in her side to begin a healing spell.

"Are you hurt?" a woman nearby asked while limping closer.

Coura recognized her as one of the mages who maintained the previous shield. A stream of crimson poured from a gash in her head, and her pupils looked unnaturally large. "I'm fine, but you need a-"

Another crash against the thin barrier protecting them and their allies interrupted her comment and had her looking away. When Coura faced the woman again, the mage had dropped to her hands and knees.

"We need to get back," she halfheartedly told her injured comrade and lowered herself in order to begin a healing spell. Unfortunately, what she sensed felt too overwhelming for her to handle at her level of training. A wave of helplessness washed over her at that.

"Let me…use my magic…"

She studied the figure, who stared at her without seeming to comprehend their situation, and an unmistakable determination radiated from the hardened expression. Something about that motivated Coura to rise and search for her father since she knew he would possess the skill and energy to care for the woman.

To her dismay, the commander engaged in holding the easternmost line. She mustered what dark energy she could into a wall that appeared right in front of him before calling out. "Evern! I need you!"

His head shot in her direction upon hearing her voice, and he jogged over after. His own power seemed to have diminished since they started, yet she had no doubt in his abilities.

"What is wrong?" he practically demanded while looking her over.

Although his gaze lingered on the bloody armor covering her previously injured side, Coura pointed at the woman on the ground. "She needs medical attention."

His sapphire eyes widened a bit before glancing at the wounded figure. When they returned to her again, they projected sympathy that matched the tone of his next words.

"We cannot save everyone."

"She's a light mage and can heal those who can't walk," Coura pressed and sidestepped to raise her arms and craft another shield to protect them. "I'll cover you."

In her heart, she worried he would dismiss the plea for the sake of their assignment, which was why she averted her eyes by keeping them glued to her spells. She also knew the request irritated him and wished to avoid drawing any more attention to it. Thankfully, he knelt beside the woman, initiated the healing, and rose a minute later.

"She is well enough to retreat," he explained while studying the area.

Coura finally looked over and thanked him after.

"It was nothing," he replied before moving on. "It appears all sides are occupied. If the assistant generals have not suggested this already, we should condense our numbers, form a sturdy barrier, and head south."

"I think that's what we're trying to do, but you and I can start on the shields."

Her father nodded in response. Without another word, the two crafted their spells side by side. A third section soon appeared, leading Coura to glance over to where the once-injured mage summoned her light energy.

Their decision to use magic again spurred a reaction from those around them, who either hurried to gather their wounded comrades and retreat toward Lupin's wall or cast shields to strengthen the current layer. Various voices ordered the troops to regroup again, resulting in a somewhat coherent and unified message.

Meanwhile, the Nim-Valans on the opposite side pounded their weapons against the solidified mix of energy. Those who remained a threat were immediately cut down, allowing Coura, Evern, and the other mages to backtrack before establishing another line of shields. After the third round of spells, they found themselves close to the demonic wall alongside the others. Even though they all got a break to catch their breaths, Lupin's lightning lit up the forest again to shatter parts of the barrier. Fortunately, the reorganized mages could continuously maintain at least one layer of magic to protect the group for the time being.

*How long until we tire though?* Coura wondered after the second blast and reformation. *I refuse to use my Yeluthian power now in case I need it for healing later. Besides, Lupin can summon at least three spells at once. Marcus better lead the retreat soon, or else...*

In the mix of explosions, yelling, thumping, and other noise, she heard somebody shouting her name. Her attention left her shield so she could locate the source, which proved to be her friend with the second assistant general limping behind.

"Good, you're together," Marcus began with a brief glance at Evern, who kept some attention on his spell since it remained tethered to him. "We intended to head south and around the demon's barrier, but its creatures are blocking the way."

Coura refrained from muttering a curse, especially since neither soldier sounded too distressed by the update.

"Our allies on the opposite side seem to be continuing their part of the mission," Mattais picked up and pointed at the glimmering, violet wall of energy. "I doubt we can hold out until they're able to help us."

"If you have a suggestion, I encourage you to share it now," her father interjected after a bolt struck his shield, prompting him to cast another in its place.

Before Coura could assist in fortifying the barrier, Marcus addressed her.

"Can you use that portal spell to transport us back to the camp?"

She ground her teeth and looked around at the dozens of people on their side before shaking her head. "I wouldn't be able to go that far with what power I have left. Besides, we'll need mages to stay until everybody else is through. Unless we time the moment perfectly-"

An eruption of thunder punctuated her point and had just about everyone covering their ears before the mages scrambled together another round of shielding. The assistant generals discussed their next option, which involved having Evern or Coura fly to the opposite side to muster the other group's support; however, doing so would lose them a mage. As they shifted to a plan involving marching through the demonic creatures or going around the northern end, the expected blast from Lupin began sounding like a death toll.

*My goddess gift would work for a short period of time and probably result in the least amount of casualties*, she reflected after evaluating her remaining tendrils of energy. *I don't know how useful I'd be after, and I need to be able to get through the portal, but we can't waste any more time.*

Coura prepared to share her decision with the assistant generals and her father until the sight of a frail section of their defenses had her thoughtlessly casting a shield for cover. In that moment, as she looked between the new spell and what she previously manifested, and idea came to mind.

*Light magic requires the energy to remain connected to its host*, she recalled as she stared down at her hands, mirroring the instance when she struggled to understand this concept. *I couldn't figure out how to use my Yeluthian power because I was familiar with wielding dark energy, which separates from a mage's center when a spell is cast. Since that's the case, I might be able to maintain my goddess gift while summoning shields so everyone else can get through. The worst that could happen is my shields don't form, and we're back to the original outcome.*

The notion solidified her resolve to try whatever she could to save as many people as possible.

"Marcus," she called to get her friend's attention again. "I'm going to create a portal to the opposite side so you can join Casner's group. I don't know how long I can hold it open, but it's going to require all my focus. You need to get everybody through."

"What about you and the mages?" he countered. "I thought you said-"

"Don't worry about me. Just get as many people across as you can."

His expression reflected his doubt in leaving her behind; however, she didn't expect her father to comment on the plan.

"I will remain as well," Evern added. "My wings are strong enough to carry two."

Her friend started to question the additional detail until Mattais interrupted and pointed at the still-active Nim-Valans striking the barrier.

"We don't have a better idea, so let's go."

The urgency he projected pushed Coura into initiating the plan. Without losing any more precious seconds, she faced the demon's shield, extended an arm in front of herself, and reached inward for the Yeluthian power warming her center. As usual, it leapt at her invitation to extend beyond its confines, filling her body with a strength stemming from its sense of security.

Those huddled around the four began shuffling out of the way when her spell took shape, and a moment later, the oval portal manifested amid a golden glow. In its center reflected the opposite side of the area, though from a new perspective.

"This will take you to where we marched from earlier," she explained as the pull on her center began draining her reserves. "Hurry up!"

To her surprise, Mattais was the first to go closer to the mirror-like image before ordering the troops to follow him. He then passed through, prompting a mix of confused and worried muttering. The resulting hesitation eased when Marcus stepped forward next and ushered soldiers and mages along by mentioning the enemies who would soon break through the barrier. The reminder had Coura tentatively glancing over her shoulder. Evern remained where he had been in order to continue fortifying his shields, along with about a dozen other mages. Her eyes returned to the group utilizing her current spell before she heard another round of crashing and thunder.

*Don't get distracted*, she told herself and closed her eyes in order to focus better. *They can handle that for now.*

The words repeated in her head as the noise refused to die down, increasing her anxiety as she knew escaping the enemy would become impossible if their protection disappeared.

Despite what outer forces bothered her, the Yeluthian energy kept humming its support throughout her body. She held onto that warmth in order to maintain her goddess gift; however, a second presence, one she already became familiar with, emerged as the light power slowly faded.

*My dark energy is acting up now that I'm giving attention to my center. I can't let it overwhelm what control I have.*

For a while, Coura struggled against the urge to dismiss her spell in order to prevent the demonic power from disrupting her ability, yet nothing happened except the consistent humming. A memory of her time under Sage Vidar came to mind as she studied the different tendrils.

*They won't react to each other*, she recalled and felt some of the tension in her muscles settle. *Since they can't interact, they coexist through avoidance. They'll never cross the opposite's path, which is how I can wield both energies. I wonder if that's why the dark power is so active.*

An idea started sprouting as she observed them before opening her eyes. Marcus no longer guided the men and women through her portal, and one by one her allies filed into it without hiding their emotions. She ignored them all to instead look at the remaining shields the mages maintained. Only her father seemed to be able to muster the power necessary to repair what damage Lupin caused, leading several Nim-Valans to slip through. Although the enemy soldiers were struck down immediately, the lack of a proper defense wouldn't keep them back for much longer.

*Sage Vidar had me switch between light and dark spells until I could do so fluidly. Since my Yeluthian power is tethered to me, am I able to manipulate the demonic energy if it doesn't come in contact with the other tendril? What's the worst that could happen if I try?*

Part of her worried her goddess gift would quit at the interruption while another believed the barrier she envisioned simply couldn't form with another spell in effect. No matter the outcome, she dropped her weapon in order to raise her other hand and released the dark power itching her palm just as another fraction fell to Lupin's lightning.

What Coura didn't expect to find once her wall solidified in front of the weakened mages was a sense of balance comparable to what she normally witnessed within her soul space. Neither presence reacted to the other but instead intertwined to exit along the path she set, resulting in the dual casting. Several sets of eyes shot her way, including Evern's, yet she kept her concentration on only the light and dark energies she manipulated.

Mere seconds later, the results of her decision began affecting her. First, and most concerning, had to do with the power she expended at such a high rate. Her goddess gift continued pulling from her center, which she expected, while the dark energy remained at the level it was earlier. Next, the movement around her on both sides of the walls blurred together, forcing her to close her eyes in order to avoid losing focus.

She relied on her hearing for a while in order to know when to rebuild a shield. Every so often, she would open her eyes and find less people in the area huddled around the portal, and she would adjust the distance of her next dark spell. What sections she didn't cover were apparently being maintained by others, so she relaxed again, shut her eyes, and became engrossed with her breathing.

Coura had no idea how much time passed during the process. All thoughts silenced, and she didn't pay much attention to what went on. The cost for both types of spells made her center ache enough to have her becoming aware of her weariness that would likely leave her completely drained and useless; however, that didn't seem to matter. Only when a weight fell on her right shoulder did she snap out of her trance.

Both arms dropped to her sides while her eyes opened and closed to refocus, though her vision remained blurry. Still, she noted nobody in the area directly in front of her, and each spell faded.

"Everyone went through," she heard her father say. "It is our turn to leave."

The urgency in his voice came across clearly, yet Coura's legs refused to work. When the sound of multiple pairs of heavy footsteps grew louder, she attempted to turn around only to find her vision going dark. The next thing she knew, she rested in Evern's arms without remembering him scooping her up.

"Just relax," he instructed.

What followed became a mess of noise as unfamiliar, deep voices growled in indiscernible sentences, thunder echoed nearby, and wind filled her ears. Coura opened her eyes once after that to welcome the sight of clouds overhead in the open air, then the dizziness returned to have her squeezing her eyes shut.

*I...can't even...stay awake...*

She stirred again only when the cool wind stopped slapping her in the face and the arms holding her set her on the ground. One eye cracked open after the other, revealing the camp the troops departed from that afternoon. Naturally, she attempted to sit up but couldn't due to her weakened state.

"Take it easy, Coura," her father chided from where he knelt beside her. "You fulfilled your task admirably. Allow the rest of us to finish this mission."

With that, the commander rose, extended the wings he didn't dismiss after their flight, and leapt into the sky. She released a huff at the sight while abandoning her effort to adjust herself.

*I should see if someone can bring me food before I pass out*, she noted as the pain in her center returned twofold.

Unfortunately, looking around gave her enough of a headache to abandon the effort, so she drifted off after closing her eyes.

***

Byron had a feeling maintaining his shield on the western side of the area wouldn't be as easy as he was led to believe, even after the enemy fell into their trap. Like the previous days of conflict, the demonic creatures stalking through the forest beyond loomed just out of arm's reach to hold the mages' attention, keeping them focused on their spells instead of the activity at their backs.

When he did venture a glance behind, he could only tell about half of the Nim-Valans were being restrained on the ground while their comrades fought on. The urge to transfer his section of the barrier to the dark mages at either side grew with his desire to ensure the enemy wouldn't be as much of a problem.

*Keeping our shields in place doesn't drain energy as drastically as participating in the action, which is one positive, but I doubt the beasts nearby will abandon us if we capture the demon's pawns. I suppose I need to trust my allies for the time being.*

The thought repeated in his mind minutes later when the noises and movement didn't subside. In fact, he worried it became louder on their side.

His suspicion proved correct when several, startled cries cut through the sounds of battle off to his left, drawing everybody's attention. What he hadn't been expecting, at least not so soon, was for the creatures to find a way around the shields protecting their troops. He caught a trio of dog-like shadows leaping onto unsuspecting men and women, dipping their heads to snap at their victims, then rising and repeating the process.

*They don't appear to be aiming to kill*, he noted when the bloody victims rolled over or scrambled to their hands and knees. *In fact, I'd venture to guess they're only here to act as a distraction. I wonder if that's due to their stature.*

Even at a distance, Byron could tell the beasts were nowhere near as misshapen as the ones he faced in the past. All looked like wolves; however, their behavior let him know the creatures still possessed some intelligence. Instead of targeting a single opponent, each attacked duos or trios, slashing and biting at ankles, arms, or faces.

*They're not intent on dealing lethal blows. I wonder if that means their master commanded them to act as a distraction instead of a serious threat. Unless their claws and teeth possess venom, I doubt the aim is different.*

The thud of a strike against his spell pulled his eyes away from the conflict to where a hissing serpent the length of his body swung its tail with enough force to break bones. After the second attempt, the creature slithered into the bushes, piquing his interest.

*That's as much of a distraction as I've ever seen. Does that mean-*

A sudden release of demonic energy interrupted the question and had him spinning around to locate the source. Although he didn't spot the being, its handiwork in the form of a wall cut through the mass of people and beasts. The explosions booming from the opposite side of the field following the spectacle lowered his spirits after.

"Master Byron!" the mage on his left shouted a second later. "What should we do?"

*Another disruption? How far does its shield cut across the area? I can't tell from here.*

He glanced at the young woman yet raised his voice so those around him could hear the instruction. "Maintain your spell! It's up to us to make sure our comrades are safe from what enemies lie in wait beyond."

The mages who heard him replied with vocal confirmations before focusing on their barrier. Byron attempted to do the same, yet his eyes constantly wandered back to the fighting. From what he could tell, the demon targeted the eastern section of their troops from the other side of its shield; however, the restrained Nim-Valans remained on the western end. This kept them out of the conflict. No matter how hard he tried, he couldn't wrap his head around the being's strategy until a shout from within the mass of bodies reached his ears.

"Don't let them escape!"

*That's it,* he realized and glanced back at his spell. *The distractions are to hinder us from stopping their retreat!*

"The enemy is attempting to flee," he alerted those around him. "I must find the general. Cover my shield if it falls."

Amid the nearest mages' replies and well wishes, Byron spun around and began jogging into the chaos while drawing the sword at his waist. He didn't expect to be engaging in combat with either man or beast, but he did sent blasts of flames to scorch what demonic creatures wandered in his path. Their pained yelps were followed by growls as they turned tail and hurried in the opposite direction.

It seemed the activity picked up again as the previously restrained Nim-Valans attempted to escape, yet he felt their forces were holding their own. Before he could consider doing more, a chorus of battle cries sounded to the south, drawing his attention. Dozens of Asteom troops charged in various directions, both encouraging and frightening those in the area.

*What's going on?* he wondered even as his feet brought him in that direction. Soon, he caught a faint glow and understood when he spotted Marcus among the group. *That must be Coura's goddess gift. She used her magic to transport those on the eastern side of the demon's spell, uniting our forces.*

Underneath his relief, Byron worried how his allies fared against the being if it forced them to abandon their efforts. He told himself not to consider that yet and joined the charge against the remaining beasts and Nim-Valans fleeing north. What weak, elemental spells he used encouraged the enemy's retreat instead of aiming to kill or capture them. The entire process ended minutes later when those around him erupted into cheers and relieved sighs. He allowed himself a moment of reprieve before someone called his name, prompting him to turn and find Marcus approaching at a weary jog.

"Don't push yourself," he warned when he noticed how heavy the young man was breathing.

"I appreciate your concern. Did you assess the results yet?"

Byron shook his head. "Would you like to accompany me?"

The assistant general agreed, so they headed for the captured Nim-Valans first. Along the way, the duo issued orders for the uninjured to tend to their wounded comrades or carry the immobile south toward the healers. They spotted Mattais and Casner already instructing the transfer of what prisoners remained bound, leading them to inquire about the numbers instead of counting themselves.

"If I had to guess, I'd say we captured about a third of the enemy troops," the assistant general commented while his superior continued monitoring the soldiers. "The beasts' intervention lost us half of that at least."

"This should still make an impact on the enemy's forces," Byron added.

"True. We'll see how their leader reacts, especially since they don't seem responsive."

During the brief conversation, Byron noted how the Nim-Valans either stared ahead blankly or averted their eyes; the former concerned him more. *The demon must have some influence over these men. They aren't changing at all, whereas the rest who are purposefully looking away have control over their actions.*

He intended to consider that point further until Marcus' next question drew his full attention.

"Did those northerners die?"

The assistant general pointed to their left where a group of about a dozen, enemy soldiers lied unmoving. Mattais scratched his cheek while contemplating a response.

"I suppose so. We're dealing with the live ones at the moment, but we'll double check for a pulse when we finish."

Byron tried to shake the uncomfortable sensation the sight prompted, yet he couldn't avoid thinking about what that likely meant. *If they died, they didn't have the demon's power healing them anymore. Judging by what blood and torn armor I see, they probably possessed the ability until their capture. Did the being remove its influence when its pawns became useless to it?*

Instead of sharing the assumption right away, he decided to wait until the evening's debriefing in order to help with the prisoner transfer.

***

The pleasant nap Coura took ended sooner than she would have liked, which meant she had to endure the results of expending her reserves. Every part of her hurt, though mostly from exhaustion rather than wounds or bruises. Somebody placed a blanket over her while she slept, but the lower temperature still had her longing for the days under the sun in Verona.

Before she could reminisce about the weather, a startled cry interrupted the quiet atmosphere, sending a shiver along her spine. Grumbles followed, then several screams. One after the other abruptly ended while the sound of hurried footsteps passed by from various directions.

Coura already struggled to sit up and managed to do so just as the smell of smoke tainted the air. Only then did she truly process that the camp was under attack.

*The Nim-Valans are here? How long was I asleep? What about the others fighting to the north? Did these men escape capture?*

Questions swirled in her mind to cloud it, prompting a curse. She shifted to her hands and knees despite the confusion and struggled to rise. By that point, the enemy soldiers wandering through the area noticed her. One pointed and shouted at his comrades, who proceeded to march in her direction faster than she could scramble to her feet and flee. The fiery tents in the background made the scene look like a nightmare.

*Run! Move, Coura!*

Despite the pleas, she remained too weak to do much except raise her hands as a minor defense. She expected death then, or at least to be struck by the swords and clubs they carried; however, a man grabbed her wrists while the other removed a bag hanging on his belt. Each spoke to the other in a rushed manner, as if they were afraid of being caught.

Coura's curiosity about this vanished when the sack wound up being placed over her head. Her sight disappeared, the sounds around her became muffled, and multiple, pained groans escaped her lips when the Nim-Valans forcibly moved her limbs to tie them at the wrists and ankles. Then, her world spun as somebody picked her up and presumably threw her over their shoulder. She hoped to cry out for help when her captors began walking but could hardly make a sound thanks to the pressure on her midsection worsening her center's ache.

*What do I do?* she whimpered in her mind. *Where are they taking me?*

Nothing hinted at answers, though they halted twice to converse at a hushed volume and move her to be someone else's burden. She tried causing them discomfort but knew she would pass out again if she overworked herself. This led her to turn her attention to relaxing and building her reserves during the breaks.

The poor strategy she developed proved to be useless the next instance the men stopped. Whoever carried her pushed her off his shoulder, causing her to land on her side and knocking the breath from her lungs. Although she noted a wooden surface beneath her, the sudden jerk had her seeing stars, and she lost the will to force herself to stay awake any longer.

# A Demon's Meddling

**B**yron's thoughts during the trek to the main camp revolved around the enemy's strategy to utilize the demon's creatures and sacrifice them in order to escape. He no doubt understood the being could care less about what beasts died during the conflict; however, Marcus' assumption had proven correct.

*As soon as we began restraining the Nim-Valans, the demon intervened*, he noted while glancing behind to where the captured men were being led along. *Even its creatures didn't seem to be targeting us. Instead, it focused on freeing those it could before taking back its power. What does this mean for us?*

He wondered how many others reached that conclusion as most of the troops remained silent during the twilight hour. By the time they reached their goal, night shrouded the land in darkness, prompting him and several others with the strength to summon flames for light until they spotted the familiar bonfires ahead. What he and his allies hadn't been expecting until that moment was for the camp to be vulnerable to an attack.

The tents that once held supplies and rations had been flattened or burned, producing thin streams of smoke. Meanwhile, what packs and sleeping rolls the troops left around their area found themselves as fodder for the nearest fire, though most didn't seem to be damaged too severely. Worst of all, less than half the people who remained behind emerged at the sound of their comrades' return.

Casner slowed the march to a stop when they neared the site, yet a handful of people approached to converse with the general, easing some of the concern. Part of Byron longed to push his way to the front and listen to the explanation, yet he knew he would be informed as soon as someone called him for a meeting. Still, the scene spoke for itself.

*I wonder if this was the Nim-Valans' intent from the beginning*, he thought once they moved forward again. *The survivors' accounts should provide an answer, yet I doubt that's the case. First, they wouldn't have enough soldiers to spare to do more than petty inconveniences, like burning tents and supplies. The fact that they left right after striking also means they only invaded with a goal or two in mind. Otherwise, why not take refuge here and wait for us to return?*

The longer he considered those points, the surer he felt in that conclusion, which he would present to the general at the earliest opportunity. Fortunately, their leader dismissed the troops after another minute. Marcus and Mattais ordered everybody to locate their belongings before compiling a list of what would be needed and finished by mentioning the camp was safe to stay in.

Byron heard displeased muttering from the people around them before a familiar voice called his name. He turned to find Will jogging over with Grace, her guard named Dianne, and another, blonde girl trailing behind.

"What happened?" the herbalist asked before he could offer a proper greeting.

"I'm not sure. I have yet to speak with General Casner, but it appears the enemy tore through our camp."

The young man's exasperated expression let Byron know he already put that together. Of course, he didn't comment on the redundant answer.

"I suppose you aren't aware of the medical station's status," the girl added as she slid to Will's side.

Byron shook his head and only then recalled her name and position. "No, but I assume they'll need their supplies restocked based on the rest of the area."

She nodded before turning away to hurry in that direction. Will looked after her for a second, then thanked him and followed, leaving Grace and Dianne to stand alone.

"If you have no other business to attend to, would you mind returning to our bonfire and taking stock of our items?" he requested. This would both give them a job and allow him to relax after his discussion with Casner.

He released a relieved sigh and expressed his gratitude when they accepted, then the three broke apart. Those around him seemed to be finding similar tasks, which helped piece the site back together, and he spotted Clearshot lingering near where the general's tent once stood. Several individuals did so as well, but the man's attention remained fixed on his current conversation with a pair of women.

"It's about time," his friend chided with a frown. "Would you like an update?"

Byron raised an eyebrow. "How much did you overhear?"

"Enough to help you, but there's not a lot to tell. The healers who remained behind with their assigned guards said only a dozen of the Nim-Valans snuck in. As soon as our soldiers saw them, the healers focused on protecting the injured, so that side of the camp is relatively unharmed. Oddly enough, the enemy seemed more preoccupied with causing damage than pursuing them."

The notion caught Byron by surprise. "Really? Why attack at all then?"

"That's just it. This doesn't sound like an attack."

"What's that supposed to mean?" he grumbled yet let the subject drop when Clearshot merely shrugged.

When he found an opportunity to speak with the general, the man summarized that information before requesting Byron's presence at their meeting after dinner. The lack of urgency let him know the incident didn't hinder their rations, supplies, or numbers enough to be concerning, so he agreed and departed with his friend.

"I hope the food is ready by the time we get there," Clearshot commented and wrapped his arms around his stomach. "Then again, I'm sure we'll be waiting in line anyway."

"It could be worse," Byron added with a chuckle at the mundane complaint. "We have enough rations to last at least…"

The words on his mind faded when he noticed a figure at the edge of the area pacing away from the rest of the troops.

Although he relaxed a bit once he recognized Commander Evern, his curiosity led him to change directions.

"Where are you going?" his friend practically demanded without following.

"I'll find you later."

Clearshot let him wander farther before presumably continuing toward the mess area. The amount of people and firelight lessened as he walked toward the perimeter and broke away to approach the Yeluthian. In order to avoid startling the commander, he called out when he came nearer.

Evern paused to glance behind and offer a wave. "Good evening, Master Byron. Is there a problem?"

"I was about to ask you that." He left the response as his answer, which succeeded in keeping the conversation going.

"I suppose you recall what took place with the eastern half of our troops," the Yeluthian began and crossed his arms. "When the demon used its magic, our forces struggled to maintain what ground we had, resulting in Coura needing to utilize her goddess gift."

Byron scratched his chin and noted how the commander refused to look away from the looming woods. "I didn't know the details, but that sounds about right."

"The spell took all her energy, so I flew her back to the camp to rest and be out of harm's way. I have not been able to locate her since our arrival."

"What do you mean?" The sapphire eyes finally shifted to meet his.

"I made sure to place her near the medical station, yet they do not recall seeing her after the Nim-Valans' arrived. Additionally, I patrolled the camp in case she stirred but found nothing."

"I doubt she'd be able to move around in her condition," Byron muttered once he remembered how much energy such a spell drained. At the thought, his hunger ebbed as a pit formed in his stomach. "Maybe she managed to crawl and hide somewhere during the attack."

Evern didn't reply, though he didn't look pleased with that answer either. Before Byron could offer to join the search, he heard a feminine voice interrupt. Instead of easing the troubled mood, it doubled the tension in the air.

"The obvious answer is usually correct."

The Yeluthian already drew his sword before the sentence finished and lunged at the trees directly in front of them. Byron heard a gushing sound, as if the blade connected with flesh, and readied his magic in preparation for either a shield or lightning.

"So sensitive," the voice practically purred a second later before a chilling laugh followed.

From the shadowy brush in front of them emerged a hand, which held the edge of the commander's weapon despite dark blood dripping to the ground. Evern pulled his sword back in a single motion and poised it to strike again as the source of the voice fully revealed itself.

If Coura hadn't prepared him for the original demon's return, Byron would have started panicking from standing so close to the being. Its black fur and hair blended in with the environment so well he could hardly make out its silhouette. Meanwhile, a wide grin showcased pointed canines across its pale face as it casually inspected the wound on its hand.

"Of course you light-blooded scum act before thinking," it grumbled and directed a glare at the Yeluthian, who did the same. "If I visited under different circumstances, you would already be dead."

"What do you want?" Evern demanded before Byron could.

That seemed to amuse the creature. "I thought you were interested in your daughter's whereabouts?"

"What did you do to her?"

"Nothing," the being answered and released a displeased huff before continuing. "Well, I did offer her a warning, but I suppose my words fell on deaf ears."

The commander prepared to argue more until Byron extended an arm in front of him to halt further bickering. When the sapphire eyes shot to him and narrowed, he shook his head.

*We know how tricky demons are, so it's likely toying with us, especially since their kind and angels don't get along. If we want the truth, we need to be direct and not let our emotions get the better of us.* Although he wished he could share that message aloud, he decided to avoid wasting time and tempt the creature into bouncing around the subject.

"What was your warning?" he asked while lowering his arm.

The demon clapped its hands together. "The human is more patient than the pigeon."

Evern growled a curse but didn't physically retaliate or protest, to Byron's relief. When neither became distracted, the demon's grin faded into a slight smile.

"Fine," it continued a second later. "I let her know Lupin would come after her if she revealed her presence. Weakening herself to that point made it easy for him to order his pawns to snatch her away."

"The demon in Nim-Vala… It kidnapped her?"

"I'm afraid so."

Byron went cold at the thought, allowing the commander to pick up the conversation in a less-abrasive manner.

"Where is she now?"

"Likely on her way to the main city. Surely you could fly straight there for a rescue."

Evern didn't respond, which Byron expected given the current situation they faced.

*Anybody who enters the northern country not only puts their life at risk but also tempts further conflict between the kingdoms. A Yeluthian being spotted would no doubt be traced back to Asteom.* As much as he hated to admit it, he understood they would not be able to help without stirring trouble.

Movement brought his attention back to the being as it turned around to retreat into the trees.

"Wait," Byron began, causing the demon to pause, pivot, and face him. "Why tell us anything about Coura? What are you after by remaining close to her?"

He fully expected a snide or dismissive comment given their kind; however, it assumed an unreadable expression as its violet eyes bore into him.

"Let's just say I would rather avoid a repeat of what took place with the former high priest," came the unexpected response.

"Hendal? What does he have to do with this?"

At first, he worried the man had somehow gained power once more and caused trouble without being caught, leading him to consider several issues. Above all, he wondered if it intended to assist the man in ruling Asteom again. The being stared at him in a strange manner, like it became suspicious of his prodding. Then, its response startled him into silence.

"She didn't tell you," the demon said as more of a statement than a question, as if it figured something out.

"Enough riddles," Evern interjected and took a step closer. "What is going on, and why mention the former high priest at all?"

The creature looked between the two before lingering on Byron, and the sadistic smile returned. "How did Terran, the demon creating beasts in the south, meet his end?"

He wasn't certain what the other being's involvement meant, but he recalled the explanation. "You were responsible for its death."

"As much as I would love to take credit, I must share that with the former high priest. You see, the man and demon forged a bond like what I currently share with Coura. He didn't quite want to wait until I found a way to break that spell, so he threw himself off a cliff, thus killing Terran."

Byron's head spun at the sudden amount of information he tried wrapping his brain around.

Meanwhile, the commander slowly lowered his sword. "If what you claim is true, then this bond…"

"That's right," the demon interrupted in a giddy manner, showing how much pleasure it took in confusing them. "The man revealed the ugly truth about bonding souls."

*That means Coura's life is tied to this creature*, Byron realized. Whatever emotions he held in check until that point steadily seeped through until he caught his hands shaking and balled them into fists. *I still don't fully believe a demon, and we have other problems to address.*

"Are you going to rescue her?" he asked when he could control himself.

The being scoffed. "Of course not. She got herself caught, so she can suffer the results. Besides, Lupin won't kill her."

"What makes you so sure?"

"In short, he's using her to draw me to him, presumably to kill me, take my power, or tempt me into fighting him. I have no interest in such trivial goals."

Byron ground his teeth yet kept his head instead of losing his temper.

Unfortunately, Evern reached his limit and addressed the creature once more while raising his sword. "Is there anything else you are hiding, snake?"

"Perhaps I should repeat that if I die, your daughter dies too," the being replied in a low voice akin to a growl.

Instead of answering, the Yeluthian leapt forward to swing at the bushes, though the demon slipped away and disappeared into the shadows before his blade touched the first branch.

*It really did just come here to tell us about Coura*, Byron noted and rubbed his eyes. He had no idea what to think after that. The amount of crucial information presented in such a short amount of time left him struggling to figure out their next steps, both related to the kidnapping and his former student's fate. Beneath that, he found himself hurt by her lies. *Why wouldn't she tell us the truth about the demon and Hendal's deaths?*

Only when the commander sheathed his weapon did Byron repress such feelings. Still, neither spoke for a few minutes until a cool breeze reminded them of the hour.

"We should return for the general's meeting," Evern announced before beginning to head back into their camp.

"Are you sure you're willing to step away from this?" Byron halfheartedly asked as the Yeluthian passed him.

That caused Evern to halt. Even though he didn't turn around, his next question came across clearly. "What should we do?"

"I don't know," Byron hesitantly answered without hiding his weariness.

"How can we save my daughter from either creature?"

He noticed Evern's shoulders sag, yet nothing about the commander's tone suggested he was bothered. "I don't know, but we'll find a way."

"Since that is the case, I believe we should keep this conversation between us for the evening. The general and his subordinates do not need to learn of such a personal matter until we are prepared for tomorrow and the potential conflict that awaits."

Byron found himself agreeing with that point and said as much before the two reentered together, crossed through the troops, and arrived at Casner's tent; however, his mind instinctively returned to the problem as the meeting wore on.

*

For all the trouble the previous evening brought, Byron slept relatively well and without interruption. The general had arranged for the prisoners' care and supervision while arguing they should avoid returning north for a couple days at least. That led to some disagreements as Byron, Mattais, and a couple others who would be monitoring the Nim-Valans didn't want to take the chance of attracting conflict in Asteom. Despite those points, they ended up reaching an agreement when they assessed the number of enemy soldiers and their remaining rations. The group also planned to summon Grace and have her inform the king's council for their input.

*We get extra time to recover*, he noted as he rose, stretched, and began preparing for the day. *We're not necessarily hurting, but our mages expended plenty of energy to maintain those shields against the demon. The additional guards Casner assigned should warn us of trouble as well.*

Since the group wouldn't reconvene until after lunch, Byron assumed his usual duties before returning to his meditation spot to relax. That break provided him with a clear mind, yet his thoughts didn't remain on the conflict for long. The conversation with the demon replayed in his head, as if he attempted to learn a new clue to help rescue Coura, until footsteps nearby allowed him to hope for something new to focus on. To his dismay, it was Evern who approached.

"Good morning, Master Byron. This is quite the hiding spot."

"You could call it that, or a space for meditation."

"Of course." The Yeluthian lowered himself to sit beside Byron. "I would like to discuss what we heard from the demon last night and how to broach the subject with General Casner."

*I figured as much,* he grumbled in his mind before the commander went on.

"My preference would be to fly into their capital and search for Coura, but my duty and the alliance make that impossible without severe risks."

"Not to mention, you would be entering unfamiliar territory without backup."

"Correct. That led me to consider speaking with those who stayed in Nim-Vala's southernmost town near the border."

The notion caught Byron off guard. *I never thought to ask Will or the mages about the inner circle. Would they have helpful insight even though they didn't go there?*

"If the spy we met was here, I would have already inquired about this," Evern continued. "They are the next best option."

"Perhaps we can rely on them a bit more than gathering information."

"What do you mean?"

Byron crossed his arms and let his gaze wander while formulating a request for the young man and women. "First, we need to know how much they learned about the capital city and if they have connections. I imagine the spy has visited that spot, but our allies likely have not."

"Then let us seek them out."

Evern rose to stand and head back to the camp, leaving Byron to follow, which he wasn't too surprised by given their shared concern. The pair returned, made their way to the medical station, and inquired about Will or his friends' whereabouts. In a matter of minutes, they were able to pull the young man away from his work on crafting various potions.

"What's wrong?" were the first words out of his mouth, which matched his worried expression.

Although Byron attempted to ease his stress with a smile, Will didn't appear convinced.

"We would like to discuss your time in Nim-Vala, as well as if you could guess where the spy is," the Yeluthian shared without any sort of reassuring gesture or tone.

"Finn? Why would you-"

"It's a long story," Byron interrupted. When he glanced around and figured they wouldn't be overheard, he decided to share what took place the previous evening. If this bothered Evern, the Yeluthian didn't show it. Meanwhile, the herbalist's face went as white as a sheet.

"Coura is… She was taken to…"

"Yes, I'm afraid so. Commander Evern might be able to fly into their capital to search for clues, but we'd like to learn about the inner circle before sending him."

During the resulting pause, Will looked between the two before staring at the ground. Byron assumed the young man debated their situation but lacked enough information to be useful, leaving him to scan his memories for any pieces that would help; however, he recognized the calculating manner with which the herbalist assessed the problem and kicked himself for underestimating his friend and comrade.

"If Finn wasn't in Muld, he likely returned to his master in the inner circle," Will began mumbling loudly enough for Byron and Evern to hear. "He would definitely know where Coura is if she's there."

"How can we get in contact with him?" the Yeluthian asked a bit optimistically.

"I don't think we can. At least, not through magic or letters."

Byron sensed a scheme forming. "What are you thinking, Will?"

The herbalist finally glanced up and offered a timid smile. "I'll go."

"We do not expect you to put yourself in danger," the commander replied before Byron could.

To their surprise, that comment made the young man chuckle. "Maybe I should have mentioned it earlier, but I've been to the inner circle a couple times already."

"You're joking," Byron chided. "Why didn't you say so?"

After apologizing, Will offered a brief summary of his time acting as a medicine man, allowing him to venture into the capital city, treat the sick, and observe the wealthier Nim-Valans' lives. The entire story amazed Byron, though he understood how the herbalist and spy grew to become friends.

"Next to Finn, you sound like our best option," he added and raised an eyebrow. "The commander is right though. You're under no obligation to accept, and no one besides us and the general will know where you are or what happened to Coura. This is a risky assignment."

"That's true, but how can I not accept when my friend is in trouble? She would do the same for any of us."

Such a statement removed any doubt about their shared resolve, so Byron allowed himself to place his trust in the young man. Will promised to depart as soon as he could, leaving the matter at that.

Next, Evern suggested they inform the general before his assistants and Grace arrived for their meeting with the king's council. It proved difficult to forget what went on in the background regarding the demons, his former student, and now the herbalist and spy, yet Byron kept his chin raised while vowing to uphold his part in their plans.

# Part Two

# Nim-Vala's Prisoner

All Coura knew from the moment she woke to when sleep took her again was the darkness the sack on her head caused, grumbling she didn't understand, and the uneven movement of the wagon she rode in. At least, she assumed that was where the strangers kept her considering she could also hear hoofbeats.

The men would pay attention to her every once in a while by sliding a thin piece of metal under the cloth to pour water into her mouth. She protested the liquid at first since she tasted a bitter undertone she figured had to be a sedative given her constantly foggy mind; however, they would then hold her head in place and force her to drink. She never received food, which worsened her tightened stomach and aching center, yet she wouldn't die as long as she had water.

*I can't live on that alone*, she noted after the first day, or what she guessed was the first day.

Unfortunately, her condition and mentality only grew worse as time went on. What rope bound her hands and ankles wore the skin away when its rough texture rubbed against them, and she soon found herself thirsty every second she remained awake.

Nothing about her world changed until she noticed the bumps steady into a smoother ride. Part of her wondered whether or not she'd begun losing her mind, yet more voices surrounded her. When she attempted to listen, she learned all were in that unfamiliar language.

*I must be farther into Nim-Vala.* That thought, the first coherent one she'd had in a while, gave her a bit of hope that she would be able to learn about her current whereabouts soon.

The next change came when the wagon stopped completely and the environment quieted. Somebody grabbed her arms to haul her into a sitting position before picking her up by throwing her over their shoulder. When she instinctively released a grunt at the pressure on her empty stomach, a man made a shushing sound off to her left. Coura remained silent after yet focused as best as she could on listening for clues. Immediately, she heard a door open and pattering feet on solid flooring, including those of the person holding her. The temperature also felt warmer, and she swore the area grew lighter beyond the bag over her head.

*I must be inside a building. How long have we been traveling?*

The culmination of her physical and mental weariness had her heart pounding faster as the footsteps continued in the silent corridor she unwillingly passed through. Before she could fully panic, another door opened, raising the temperature further, and a loud, boisterous male voice filled the space around them. The newcomer even startled the man carrying her, as showcased by how he jumped at the sound.

Of course, Coura had no idea what the words the stranger practically shouted meant, but they succeeded in drawing her captor closer. A conversation seemed to pass between the two for long enough to make her dizzy from how her head hung upside down. Just when she accepted that she would likely pass out in seconds, the man moved to set her on her side. The soft surface where she landed took her back until someone pulled the bag off her head in an abrupt motion. Her initial reaction to the new environment was to squeeze her eyes shut and shake what hair had clung to the cloth away from her face, which succeeded in causing the room to spin. This led the louder man to laugh as well. As he spoke, she tried observing her surroundings.

The brightness from the room's jarring, white wallpaper and gold-colored furniture nearly blinded her, especially since she grew accustomed to a lack of light. Several lamps kept every corner lit and revealed the faces of her captors. As expected, they appeared just like every other Nim-Valan man she'd encountered with dirty, paler skin and black hair and beards. They looked at her in a dismissive manner, like she was merely a burden they wished to get rid of, so she mustered as much of a glare as she could.

Again, the newer voice laughed and spoke in an entertained manner. This drew her attention and curiosity; the latter piqued when her eyes fell on the source. She never considered the nobility of the northern country, among many things, but the man draped over a pillow-covered couch reminded her of those in Verona. Jewelry adorned his fingers, wrists, and neck while gold rings dangled from where they had been pierced into his ears and nose. The only plain aspect seemed to be his colorless hair since the various shades of purple and gold in his outfit practically screamed for attention.

Her head throbbed by that point, forcing her to close her eyes and relax as best as she could given her restraints. Meanwhile, the supposedly wealthy man talked in a casual manner. When she looked at him again, she found him speaking to her instead of the other Nim-Valans.

*I don't understand*, she longed to say. *Why am I here? Who is he?*

It seemed he realized her dilemma then, for his oddly gleeful tone and expression shifted into annoyance before he addressed the awaiting soldiers. From what she could tell, he berated them while growing more irritated. Two of the other men replied to something the individual said, then the supposed nobleman dismissed them with a wave of his hand.

Coura could only look on throughout the unknown conversation and ignore the remaining man's resulting, interested stare after. She took note of four guards keeping watch at the lone entrance before her taxed senses needed a break.

*

A sharp poke in the back startled her awake what felt like moments later. She didn't remember falling asleep, yet she didn't recall the people around her shifting positions. The Nim-Valans who kidnapped her had disappeared, and a set of four guards stood in front of the doorway. When she peered over her shoulder at the source of the jarring sting, one man in their people's armor hovered over her with a spear in hand.

After a minute passed while she hoped her cloudy mind would clear, she realized somebody had been speaking and located the source. It didn't surprise her to find the bejeweled, jolly leader talking, though he continued addressing her despite her lack of understanding.

All she could do was stare at him as he rambled until her weariness brought her closer to sleep again; however, a single word he uttered mid-sentence caught her full attention.

"…Soirée…"

"Wait," she croaked after catching the demon's name. Her voice sounded hoarse, and she struggled to raise her head and respond, yet she managed to do so. "Soirée. Where is she?"

Coura prepared to demand the information until both her lack of energy and another poke in her shoulder blade caused her to abandon the effort.

No answer came from the wide-eyed, decorated man for a few seconds, as if her quiet outburst shocked him. Then, he chuckled before grumbling in a frustrating manner. That irritation rose until he shouted at his guards. She didn't catch any familiar words after the demon's name, so she abandoned her attempt to reach out.

The next thing she knew, a jab along her spine roused her.

*I…can't keep…staying awake…if…*

Whatever thoughts she had wouldn't manifest. Each part of her body ached from a mixture of hunger, being bound, the guards' prodding, and her empty center. She couldn't even assess her magical power without drifting off. Instead, her eyes scanned the space.

Her host had vanished, leaving only the soldiers at the entrance and one beside her. As soon as she stirred, the man closest to her called to his comrades, and another came over, knelt beside her, and removed what appeared to be a waterskin from around his waist. It didn't take much effort to get her to drink in her current condition, though she longed for more after emptying his portion.

The pair talked in a hushed manner as she refrained from begging when her thirst persisted.

*They must know I can't survive without enough water and food.*

Even the thought of something as simple as a piece of bread caused her stomach to growl. In order to prevent further outbursts, she allowed herself to nap amid the ongoing conversation.

*

Although she began expecting the spear's tip in her back to rouse her before she fell asleep, Coura still jumped every time. Her eyes were heavier than normal, but they landed on the wealthy man occupying his couch and a new individual standing beside him. Unlike the guards, this additional Nim-Valan didn't possess much muscle and wore no armor. His dark hair had been cropped off, and he was the first person she'd seen from the north to bare a clean-shaven face.

The newcomer's timid personality came across clearly after her observations when the first man's voice filled the room in a tone suggesting he was issuing orders. The leaner Nim-Valan nodded during the lengthy lecture of sorts, kept his hands folded in front of him, and only spoke once the deep voice stopped. By that point, Coura had relaxed her body and found a spot on the wall to fix her gaze on. She didn't expect anybody's attention, which led her to be completely bewildered by a greeting she could understand.

"H-Hello. You are f-from Asteom."

Her eyes widened a bit before darting to the source, making her a bit dizzy in the process. The new man studied her in an intense manner, like he hoped to appear intimidating, as he repeated the message.

"I am," she practically whispered at the lack of strength behind the words. "Who are you?"

Instead of answering right away, the Nim-Valan repeated her response to himself, mumbled in their language, then fell silent for a minute. His next sentence confirmed his identity. "I match you speak with me."

Despite the confidence behind the statement, Coura could only stare without comprehension. *What does that mean? My speak... Could that be our languages?*

That much thinking used up whatever mental fortitude she possessed, yet she believed he had been trying to introduce himself as a translator.

When she didn't reply, the Nim-Valan shifted his attention to the seated man, who proceeded to talk for a few minutes without hiding a sense of displeasure. What she learned next would have shocked her if she hadn't grown so weary.

"He is King Syrus," the translator began with more difficulty. "Soirée makes him eager to see you since he first learned. Lupin is not here. Where is Lupin?"

*That's right. Lupin is acting as an advisor and mentioned he's a demon. Is the king wanting him back for his power? Why are they interested in me at all?*

The Nim-Valans continued watching her, so she figured she needed to comment; however, nothing came to mind except her current situation.

"I don't know," she admitted with as much sincerity as she could muster. "Please, I need food and water."

To her surprise, what she said appeared to frighten the translator. He shook his head and mumbled about not understanding. When she remained silent after, he spoke to the king in a flustered manner, causing the royal figure to shout, jump to his feet, and point at her. Coura had no idea what the ensuing yelling from the man meant, so she again let her eyes wander. By that point, her body's weariness let her know she would likely pass out again soon despite the noise. The translator threw out words to rouse her when he was left to his work.

"Lupin should be here. Too much time is gone. Where is he?"

Her mind already lost track of the message, and soon the words spun into a jumble of sounds she eventually ignored in favor of rest. This resulted in several, light stabs in her back that she stopped responding to, even after she acknowledged the sensation of blood trickling down her back.

***

As Will slipped through the gates of Yukin's estate, he needed to pause and catch his breath, both because of how physically taxing the journey had been and to calm his frantic heartbeat. Fortunately, he blended in with the citizens enough to avoid detection, so he continued keeping his head down under the hood of his cloak until he could duck behind a bush.

The seven-day trek he promised Byron had been an estimate given his drive to depart as soon as possible and only rest when he needed to stop. Clara tried talking some sense into him when he found her to discuss the situation, but he remained adamant about being the one to search for Coura.

"Aside from Finn, I'm the only person who went to the inner circle," he argued when she questioned the self-appointed assignment. "Not just once either. They recognize me as a medicine man, so I can-"

"You're just after Finn, right?" she interrupted.

When he nodded, she merely advised him to focus on that instead of acting as the hero, dug through her belongings for a bottle of the hair dye she hadn't used up, and wrapped her arms around him in a tight embrace. She didn't keep him any longer since he needed to collect provisions for the hike, and he departed before noon.

*All things considered, I should be fortunate the weather remained dry and decently warm*, he reminded himself while scanning the entrance to the main house. *Crossing the border again was the most difficult part until now. Hopefully Finn is here or Yukin knows where he is.*

His footsteps hardly made noise as he approached the front door and knocked. Almost immediately, an older man he believed to be a butler opened it, fixed him with an unreadable expression, and asked him to state his name. Will decided at some point that he would resume his façade as a medicine man who lost his hearing in case somebody recognized him from his previous visits.

257

"L-Lord Y-Yukin," he stammered while assuming an innocent expression in order to appear as helpless as possible. Then, he raised a hand to tap on his right ear and shake his head, signaling his supposed lack of hearing.

The butler's expression didn't change. "Be off, young man. The lord and his family have other business to attend to."

With that, the man promptly shut the door.

Will stood in shock at the sudden rebuff until voices from the entrance reminded him of the guards keeping watch. His mind raced as he scrambled back to the gate and into the street beyond.

*What should I do now?* he wondered while lowering his head. He waited to try answering this question until he found a spot along the road to stand out of the way. *If I speak, I abandon my ruse. Would they even believe me if I claim to be a friend? Most of the staff didn't see or interact with me when I stayed there.*

His next idea revolved around sneaking inside during the evening; however, he possessed no skills aside from minor sword work, and he abandoned his weapon in favor of a lighter, less noticeable knife. That lack of stealth would likely get him killed if he were caught.

*I suppose I can wait in case Finn or Yukin pass in or out of the estate. As long as I avoid the guards, patience might be the safest option.*

With a basic plan in mind, he continued lingering on the edge of the road until his legs ached, prompting him to walk around yet make sure the gate remained in sight. The men who patrolled kept an eye on him the entire time.

Hours passed while he shifted from one spot to another until the sun dipped behind the inner circle's stone barrier, shading the city and lowering the temperature. Will intended to dismiss the discomfort nighttime would bring until his stomach growled.

*I'm sure the evening guards will chase me off if I sit or sleep around the estates. I'll need to find a place to rest. Maybe I can slip onto Yukin's property. That would be risky, but at least I can stay close.*

As the thought came to mind, a figure passed out from the gate and into the mix of citizens so seamlessly Will thought he imagined it. That in and of itself drew him toward the individual, and he hurried to catch up.

*Finn is the only person I know who can remain inconspicuous in a group of people. Who else from Yukin's estate would be skilled enough?*

He let his instincts push him into a brisk walk, which he prayed wouldn't catch anybody's attention. Still, it seemed he never got closer to his target. When he considered jogging or calling his friend's name, the figure took a sharp turn onto a path at the start of a garden of sorts. His heart dropped, prompting him to abandon his stealth, run ahead, and slip onto the same trail. There, he slowed when he found himself alone.

*No, I lost him!*

Instead of rushing forward, Will resumed a speedy walk as he assessed his surroundings. Orange and scarlet flowers practically littered the yard beyond, and well-trimmed hedges standing as high as his shoulders lined the dirt path. He spotted what guards patrolled nearby, though none paid him any mind, allowing him to continue searching for the individual he pursued.

The lack of the figure already supported his guess as to his target's identity though. He prepared to quietly call out and prayed his friend hadn't vanished already until something from behind wrapped around his neck and tightened. His hands flew up to pull at it before he realized what was happening, then a blow to the back of both legs one after the other sent him to his knees. Without the ability to brace himself, he landed hard.

"Make a sound, and I'll snap your neck," came a low grumble as the stranger remained at his back.

Despite the warning, he choked out the first words that came to mind. "Finn, it's Will!"

Nothing happened for a moment, leading him to believe he would lose consciousness or be killed for a wrong assumption. Luckily, the pressure on his throat eased, allowing him to breathe clearly again.

"You better have an explanation," the voice said after, though at a loud enough volume for him to recognize it as the spy's.

Will rubbed his neck and trembled at how close he had been to finding himself in serious trouble, yet a glance at the familiar, plain face reassured him at the same time. Despite that relief, Finn's piercing glare displayed the Nim-Valan's anger with his appearance.

"I came looking for you," he began before hesitating to continue. "Are you sure it's safe to talk here?"

"That depends on what you're about to share."

"It has to do with the fight on the-"

"Let's go," the spy interrupted as he stood, turned, and followed the path farther out, leaving Will to catch up.

Neither spoke again until Finn stopped them beside a brick building surrounded by a dense patch of pine trees. At the Nim-Valan's prompting, Will revealed all that took place in the previous weeks, including Lupin's disappearance, the enemy's invasion of Muld and ability to heal, and how Coura had been kidnapped. He even shared her connection to the original demon in order to emphasize the impact of her disappearance.

"You assume your friend was brought to the capital because the creature bonded to her said so?" Finn summarized once he finished recounting the experience. Despite the spy's ability to hide his emotions, a hint of skepticism slipped through. "Trusting a demon is dangerous. Why believe such a claim? It could be using Asteom to target the inner circle. Besides, even if your friend is here, is her life worth risking yours or tempting further conflict?"

Will raised his chin. "I won't give up on her, just like I wouldn't give up on somebody else I care about."

The honest, passionate plea didn't seem to faze the man. "You should know by now I'm not going to stir trouble or take risks if the reward is as minor as saving one life. Soldiers die every day. What is special about this girl other than she is your friend?"

Although he understood Finn's rationalization clearly, Will refused to back down. He considered the situation from an objective standpoint instead of focusing on his personal feelings, which reminded him of another point he recalled Byron briefly mentioning.

"Why do you think Lupin would bring Coura here?" he countered and raised an eyebrow. "She's bonded to another demon who can easily break into the inner circle and cause chaos before it even finds her. We both saw what their kind is capable of!"

"It would have already done so if it intended to search for your friend, right?" the spy argued.

"Are you willing to wait until it does?"

That question hung in the air when the Nim-Valan didn't offer a rebuttal.

Will released a sigh in an attempt to ease the tension his muscles developed throughout their conversation. "I don't trust demons either or understand magic, but the master mage and Yeluthian commander we fought alongside heard it mention Lupin's intent to draw it into Nim-Vala. I'm here to rescue my friend *and* stop that from happening."

After a moment, Finn looked off to his left. "It would be a problem if dark magic worms its way into Nim-Vala more than it already has. That's the only reason I'll agree to assist you."

"Thank you! I know it's-"

"Yukin needs to be aware of this as well," the spy interrupted without acknowledging Will's gratitude. "If he or Elena noticed something off in the king's estate, that could be our first clue."

"Can I ask you one more question?"

The chestnut eyes darted back to him and narrowed. "What now?"

"Why are you staying here when the conflict on the border continues? I know you're loyal to your master and want to protect Yukin, but is there a problem keeping you in the inner circle?"

Finn's annoyed stare relaxed before he answered. "Hopefully not, but Elena is worried about King Syrus. According to her, he has been shutting himself in his private chamber, the one you visited, and is acting strange. I've been accompanying Yukin or his father to dinners there and exploring the estate but haven't discovered any concerning details. She is adamant that I figure out what is wrong with him though."

*I wonder if Lupin is affecting the king like what the first demon did to the high priest in Verona*, Will thought after contemplating that information. *It's definitely a possibility.*

"It's late," the Nim-Valan commented after he filed that concern away. "We should return to Yukin so you can explain what you shared. He might come up with an idea or at least be able to schedule time to see Elena. She'll need to be aware of your arrival and intentions as well."

As the two emerged from their hiding spot and casually strolled closer to the lord's estate, Will focused on putting together a coherent description based on what he and Finn discussed.

*

The next couple days in the inner circle passed by in a blur. Will caught the young lord up on what took place and why he was present, ending with his goal to enter and search the area with Finn. Unlike the spy, Yukin's emotions seeped into his expression, which reflected a mixture of frustration, doubt, and disbelief, and his words after the summary were directed at his partner.

"I'm surprised you agreed to this. It's reckless, even for you."

"I take offense to that," Finn grumbled and crossed his arms. "Rarely am I reckless without fair cause."

"At least only your lives are on the line. That is, if the advisor doesn't lure a demon to us."

Will kept his comments to himself since the success or failure of his assignment relied on the help of what Nim-Valans he allied with over the years. As if in response to that fact, Yukin met his eyes and offered a sympathetic smile.

"Even though I'm putting my position and country first, I'm sorry about your friend. I don't want to be involved, and I know Elena will say the same, but I owe you for saving my life.

The least I can do is get you and Finn into the royal estate for an audience with her."

"I wouldn't ask for more," Will answered with a polite bow.

After that, all they needed to do was wait. The young lord's letter received a response within a few hours, and the king's wife agreed to welcome him and his trusted guards. She added a unique note about how interesting their dilemma sounded, which Finn took as a positive sign.

The following morning, the trio set out for the king's estate. Like his previous visit, Will dressed identical to Finn and trailed behind Yukin after a brief carriage ride. Despite the corridors appearing as he remembered, a strange, eerie sensation haunted the hallways. When they reached their destination and entered a room containing a table and four chairs, he released a deep breath.

*This place doesn't feel normal. I don't know how to explain it, but I wouldn't want to be caught wandering alone.*

Their trio accepted the seats and remained silent as they sat alone. A pattering sound soon came from the lone entrance before Elena's familiar figure stepped inside and promptly slid the curtain over the opening.

"It's a pleasure to see you again, Your Highness," Yukin began while rising and bowing, prompting his guards to do the same.

"I would imagine so," came the unamused response, though at a quieter volume. "None of you seem to visit unless you need something from me."

Will noticed her eyes slide to Finn and wondered how often the spy actually reported to her. Then, the woman's gaze went to him.

"Speaking of which, I am curious why your medicine man is with you."

"He can inform you of his reasoning while I search the estate," Finn replied.

Although Will had been expecting to explain the situation, he didn't think his friend would leave and worried he would need the additional input since Yukin probably intended to stay out of the conversation; however, Elena proved to be more patient with him than he anticipated. She listened attentively as he shared the issue of Coura's disappearance and how this posed a threat to the inner circle, then the room fell silent.

"Talking about demons sounds like an ill-fated omen," the queen began in a reserved manner quite unlike her usual, confident self. "I am sure Finnley and Yukin mentioned this, but Nim-Vala has never dealt with demons or angels. I'd prefer to keep it that way, which is why I agreed to meet with you."

"Thank you," he felt obliged to add even though she ignored the words.

"Since you three owe me a favor for this meeting, I have a job that might benefit us all. My husband has been acting out of sorts lately. I haven't received a summons from him in weeks, and my guards mentioned he's holed up in his lounge. An unfamiliar man has been present for the last week or so."

"This isn't a private matter, is it?" Yukin inquired in a tone suggesting he had other thoughts about the unusual direction of their discussion. "Forgive my suspicion, but Finn and Will shouldn't waste time on questionable relationships."

Elena narrowed her eyes. "Perhaps I should continue before you make additional, outlandish conclusions. Those he posts at the lounge's entrance chase away anyone who comes near, preventing my guards from picking up information. When my husband does emerge, he goes straight to his quarters to rest. All meals are in either location, so he hasn't attended a dinner for months."

Will considered this before venturing a comment. "My friend was only kidnapped a week and a half ago. If this is the advisor's doing, it's been taking place long before now."

"That is exactly why I would like you to investigate."

Before he could ask how to get around the constantly patrolling soldiers, Finn reappeared at the entrance and announced his return. They waited for the spy to join them around the table again before asking about the stroll.

"Nothing out of the ordinary from where I could explore," he answered before his gaze shifted to Elena. "The only locations I couldn't access were the king's chamber and lounge, but you knew that would be the case."

"I did," she replied and proceeded to repeat what she mentioned to Will and Yukin.

*If the king is being manipulated by Lupin, the demon doesn't need to be present for it to control him. Is that the advisor's goal? Why lure the first creature to the inner circle then?*

"What are you thinking, Will?" Finn pressed when he found himself fixated on the center of the table.

He looked up to find their eyes on him, which increased his nerves about overcomplicating the situation. "I'm wondering whether Lupin is actually here or not. If he aims to draw the demon to my friend, does he expect the creature to attack the city?"

"Does that not fit their kind's reputation for mischief?" Yukin countered.

"You're right, but that would damage a place it considers useful."

Elena scoffed. "What does that mean?"

"It's hard to explain," he admitted while reflecting on his knowledge of the beings, as well as Coura's experiences. "They cause trouble but are prideful, so they wouldn't abandon a scheme they spent years designing. I just can't see Lupin risking his position with King Syrus."

A pause followed his sentiment.

"Perhaps that's his goal," the spy all but muttered and rubbed his chin in a thoughtful manner.

"What is it, Finnley?" the woman pressed with a hint of impatience. "Do you believe the advisor is in the capital already?"

"Not at all. In fact, I would venture to claim he isn't going to be around unless the inner circle is attacked."

"Enough dancing around the subject."

Finn raised his eyes to glance at each of them. "If what you said about the bond your friend and the original demon share is true, then Lupin would rid himself of the latter if she dies. On the other hand, keeping her here would lure the creature and likely lead it to cause damage to the city. It would stand to reason that your friend's captor is putting their life in danger."

Will's heart dropped as a chill swept through his body. "You're implying the advisor wants the demon to kill the person holding Coura captive, which we assume to be King Syrus or the man with him."

"Exactly."

Elena growled a curse and balled both hands into fists on the table. "That monster!"

"Calm down," Yukin warned while extending a hand to cover one of hers. "We have yet to confirm whether or not Will's friend is even here. She may also die before we get to her, preventing an attack."

Will noted how the young lord purposefully avoided his eyes after that. *He's right about the results, but I'm not giving up.*

Finn addressed the queen next. "We need to get into those closed-off spaces. Is there any way to do so without causing a scene?"

While she considered this, the spy turned his attention to Yukin. "You should also leave as soon as possible. If your household is tied to what will happen…"

"I understand," his partner practically interrupted. "Just make sure not to be followed if you return to my father's estate."

Elena stood after Finn agreed. "If you plan to depart soon, these two will need a change of clothes. I will have a servant fetch some."

They left the discussion there so she could make the request. In a matter of minutes, Will found himself stripping off the uniform tying him to Yukin in favor of a plain, tan shirt and pants. Finn did the same, then the woman stuffed their discarded items into a sack the servant also brought before handing it off to the young lord.

"Did you come up with an answer to my question yet?" the spy asked his master when their group seemed ready to act.

The woman crossed her arms and looked away. "I did, but it's one I'm not satisfied with. As long as my husband's guards continue patrolling the entrances to both rooms, I don't believe you can enter unnoticed."

"I assumed as much."

"With that being said, I will check his bedroom while you two slip into the lounge. He didn't establish a routine, so we can't predict where he will be at the moment. Perhaps he only goes to his chamber to rest."

"Fine. You should go before Will and I investigate."

"And Yukin before me," she added with a sideways glance at the least-involved member.

With that, their plan went into motion. Will watched as the young lord wished them well and departed. Several minutes later, the queen took her leave after offering a similar message, which felt a bit out of character. Only when Finn approached the entrance and motioned for him to follow did they emerge and begin moving at a steady walk.

"We lack weapons, but the guards only carry swords," his friend shared at a quiet volume. "They also looked less attentive than normal, which means we should be able to enter without issue. If your friend is there, let me carry her out. I doubt you have the strength to run and support someone on your shoulders."

Although true, Will almost mentioned how the spy didn't need to acknowledge his physical weakness. He instead agreed to the strategy before asking how they would be able to exit.

"That's where it gets tricky. Speed is our main ally, as well as intent. The guards will stumble after us if we make deliberate decisions."

"I think I get it."

"Just stay by my side and listen to my instructions, especially if your friend isn't there."

By that point, his heart beat frantically in his chest, and he worried he wouldn't be able to keep up thanks to how his arms and legs trembled slightly. Part of him argued they should abandon the attempt until they could be sure of the king's location, yet time was not on their side. He then began doubting his ability to remain safe without a weapon.

"We'll be fine," came Finn's voice again in an unexpectedly gentle tone. "I will do my best to make sure all three of us get out unscathed. I'm trusting you to uphold the same resolve."

Will didn't know what to say after, so he remained silent. The winding corridors continued to confuse him; however, the spy knew exactly where to go. Soon, they saw four men in uniform standing in front of a closed curtain. Without warning, Finn rushed ahead, leaving him to follow. Their sprinting caught the guards' attention, yet none reacted until his Nim-Valan ally slammed into the closest one. The sudden force caused his target to stumble into another soldier and provided an opening for Finn and Will to slip inside.

*That felt too easy*, he thought before briefly observing their new surroundings.

He had only been in the lounge once when he eavesdropped on King Syrus and Lupin, but the layout appeared as plain as he remembered with several couches and chairs taking up most of the space while cushions and pillows occupied the rest. The brightness of the golden wallpaper threw him off at first, but that helped his eyes go straight to the darkest part in the room: the black hair of a figure lying on the farthest sofa.

Finn already knelt beside the person before Will confirmed it was Coura, though he had no time to assess her condition as the guards entered the area behind them. His feet brought him beside the spy, and together they managed to throw her over the Nim-Valan's shoulder.

"She's unconscious but breathing," the spy hurried to clarify when Will began inquiring about her. "We need to get out of here."

As they stood, two of the soldiers stalked forward and drew their swords. Neither moved faster than a walk, which intrigued him, but Finn took off around the nearest couch and toward the doorway before he could consider that further. Meanwhile, the remaining guards already held their swords as they blocked the exit.

"Split apart," he heard his companion order when they slowed to a stop.

Will obliged by sidestepping to his left, drawing the man closest to him in that direction. The same, lethargic energy came from the Nim-Valan's movements and emphasized the blank expression. That pause allowed him to recall what seemed so familiar.

*The soldiers outside Clearshot and Emilea's home acted just as unattentively. They were being controlled by the former high priest through the demon's power, which must mean the king is able to manipulate that energy too.*

Such an implication worried him; however, he also remembered how easily the enemy troops were cut down without the drive to fight. With his heart in his throat, Will charged forward, anticipated how the guard would react, and focused on adapting to maneuver around the blade. His guess proved correct when the man halfheartedly raised the sword and brought it down in a single motion, allowing him to dodge by leaping to the side. Nothing followed, so he ran past the figure and through the opening.

At first, he didn't spot his companion and wondered if the Nim-Valan was able to get away. His eyes darted back into the room where the guards began shuffling toward him, but someone called his name from his right. Farther down the hallway stood Finn, who spun around to continue their escape as soon as Will looked. That motivated him into a sprint.

Fortunately, he managed to keep up and not get lost in the maze of corridors. Yelling from various directions echoed in the areas around them, yet the noise didn't seem to disturb the spy's focus. Will told himself not to be bothered by it either since his friend could ignore the shouting.

*Are we almost there?* he longed to ask after a minute of running. *How long until somebody discovers us?*

As if in answer to his question, a trio of soldiers with weapons drawn came into view from an intersecting path, leading Finn to practically slide to a stop, pivot, and head through the nearest hallway. Will did so less gracefully, though he caught the men pointing at him before the stone walls cut off his view. By that point, he panted heavily and avoided the urge to hold his side at the start of a cramp. His guide slowed significantly as well, either from weariness or to make sure he kept up, but halted suddenly enough to warn him of another interruption. What he didn't expect was to hear a deeper voice yelling for guards.

"What's going on?" he inquired between breaths.

Finn glanced over his shoulder without answering, allowing Will to observe the scene ahead. A shiver went along his spine at the sight of King Syrus stomping toward them with a furious expression. The Nim-Valan leader appeared to be wearing his nightgown and no shoes or slippers. In one hand, he held a knife covered with enough crimson to be noticeable at a distance.

Immediately, Will remembered facing the former high priest and witnessing a similar, crazed glare. *He must have sensed us because of his guards!*

In the midst of his thought and the man's yells for them to be apprehended, a woman's voice cut through the noise.

"Run!"

Both Will and Finn looked behind for the source of the cry and found Elena hurrying toward them.

"Go," she ordered without slowing. "You must get away from him!"

As the queen passed them, Will caught blood along her forearm and prepared to tell her to wait with the intent to assist or protect her. Still, he knew time remained an enemy too.

"We need to get out of here," he mustered the strength to tell the spy.

When he looked to his friend, he found Finn hesitant to leave the woman, who reached her husband and grabbed for the knife only to be shoved aside. The blade then found its way into her stomach, and she slid to the floor while holding the wound.

Will seized Finn's arm and squeezed. "Let's go!"

That snapped his guide out of the daze. The Nim-Valan pulled his arm free when he turned to head in the opposite direction, leaving Will to follow once more.

Nothing interrupted the remainder of their escape. What guards they heard or saw proved to be too far away to pose a problem, and the pair soon slipped into an empty room. Before Will could inquire about the space, the spy climbed out the lone window carefully enough not to lose their prize. He did the same, accepted he had no idea where they were, and crept through the brush until they emerged into a garden of sorts.

*Where are we? We've been wandering for a while.*

The sound of a door opening startled him into freezing until Finn pointed ahead without a word. They continued at a walk after, and Will soon spotted Yukin standing in front of a building.

"It's about time," he heard the young lord whisper when they came close.

Nobody spoke after that, allowing all four to enter silently. The unknown layout of Will's surroundings confused him until he recognized parts of the estate he previously occupied. Yukin had let them in through a back door, and they slipped into a new bedroom identical to where he stayed.

"She was inside," the young lord began as Finn laid Coura on the mattress. "Tell me what happened."

Will went to inspect his kidnapped friend while the spy explained their escape. He only paused when he noticed the Nim-Valan stop speaking mid-sentence.

"What about Elena?" Yukin pressed with a sense of horror. "She's not…"

"I don't know," Finn answered. "A stab in the gut isn't an injury you can walk away from without immediate treatment."

The implication of that statement had all three paling.

*Elena put herself in harm's way to protect us*, Will reflected when the two began discussing the king's erratic behavior. *I didn't see the wound up close, but she will definitely need help.*

Despite that, he turned his attention to his current patient in order to evaluate her physical condition. It became clear that her captor hadn't been feeding her or giving her enough water, leading her to faint. He wondered how often that took place during the days since her disappearance. When he could gently turn her over, he found bloody holes in her shirt.

"Is she hurt?" Yukin inquired while moving to stand beside Will.

"These don't look too deep, but the sores are growing worse."

"They likely forced her to stay awake," Finn added, drawing their attention. "If she's a mage, I would wager they planned to keep her weak enough not to cause trouble."

"How awful," the young lord mumbled as Will returned to his work.

With what medicine and tools the household had on hand, he cleaned, applied a salve, and bandaged Coura's back to mend the damage. Then, he focused on mixing nutritional potions that would help increase her strength. The entire process took less than an hour, during which the Nim-Valans' conversation regarding their next steps escalated into an argument.

"Someone needs to check on Elena," he caught Finn practically growl due to the deepness of his voice and serious tone.

Meanwhile, Yukin raised his voice a bit to project disbelief. "You two just got out of there by the skin of your teeth! The royal estate is probably in an uproar. How do you expect to locate and treat her without being recognized?"

"I'm a spy, remember?"

"It's too dangerous."

"You would let her die?"

"Do you even know how to mend a stab wound?"

Although Finn attempted an affirmative answer, the question got Will thinking about what he could do while Coura recovered.

*For the most part, she needs to drink these potions and rest, so she's safe here. I might not be a healer, but I can take care of Elena better than anybody else.*

He let himself believe that as he stood, wiped his hands on the rag he kept tied to his waist, and face the duo. "How likely is it that someone in the royal estate can tend to the queen?"

Yukin and Finn shared a look before the former replied. "They have medicine men and women available, but the question is whether or not one will reach her in time. We discussed this earlier while you were working, but King Syrus might not make them aware if it damages his reputation."

"If those who live there or serve the royal family become aware of his unhinged mindset, that would cause a commotion," Finn picked up. "Worst case scenario, they drag her away and clean up the mess, preventing others from knowing what took place."

"Then it would be better for one of us to go since we can sneak around without causing a fuss," Will concluded and pondered the situation.

"Us?"

He nodded.

"You should stay with your friend," Yukin said after a moment in a sincere manner befitting a gentleman. "She needs you."

Will scratched the top of his head, glanced at Coura, then returned his attention to the pair. "Actually, she should be fine. I'm not sure when she'll wake up, but her condition is weak due to malnutrition. As long as she gets fresh water, eats, and takes the medicine I prepared, she'll recover in a matter of days."

While the young lord expressed his amazement with that timeline, the spy narrowed his eyes and addressed Will.

"You're under no obligation to remain here when she is well enough to travel."

"I know."

Neither Nim-Valan responded, which caused him to smile and elaborate.

"It wouldn't be right to leave without ensuring Elena is safe as well. She put herself in harm's way to make sure we escaped. The least I can do is treat her wounds."

The young lord appeared baffled by the selfless offer, and Finn scoffed while shifting his gaze to the door.

"You and your people are so naïve," the spy commented, though not with malice. "You stick your nose into others' business when you don't need to."

"I consider you two friends and Elena an ally is all."

A pause followed before Finn returned his attention to Will. "It's beginning to get dark. We should move and return the same way we left."

Before Will could express his gratitude for being allowed to accompany the man, Yukin interrupted and pointed at Coura.

"If you both are gone, who is going to explain everything to her when she stirs?"

Will hadn't considered the question until that moment, mainly because he slipped into each language with ease, and glanced at Finn. When Yukin did the same, the spy shot a glare between the two.

"How is our medicine man going to enter and move through the estate without being seen?" he countered. "Nobody will trust him if he goes alone."

"He won't be alone," the young lord interjected as he placed a hand on his chest. "Her servants and guards recognize me as well, so he won't need to sneak around."

"It's too risky for you to leave."

"Why? It sounds like I shouldn't be bothered as long as I stay away from the king. I also don't plan on going where I've never been before."

The thought of facing hostile soldiers again reminded Will of how he compared them to the two outside Clearshot and Emilea's home. He decided to share that observation in order to inform his allies of the potential advantage, which left them speechless.

"The men we interacted with before going into the lounge area seemed normal," he added after. "I would wager King Syrus only used the demonic power to control those he needs."

"Which means Elena's guards can help," Yukin finished. "That settles it. I'll prepare the carriage and meet you when you change into a uniform."

With that, the young lord exited, leaving Will and Finn looking after him. The spy appeared to want to argue, which was to be expected, yet kept his mouth shut.

*I wonder if Yukin feels helpless when Finn goes off on missions across Nim-Vala and Asteom*, Will thought with a bit of pity. *When my friends would do the same, I'd worry too.*

He forced himself to dismiss the past in order to pack what medicinal items and ingredients he would need. His Nim-Valan friend assisted before fetching the aforementioned clothing. By the time he changed and instructed Finn on Coura's care, dusk lessened the amount of light out the window.

"Are you prepared?" his friend asked while looking him up and down.

"Almost."

Will hurried to locate paper and a writing utensil from the bedside table's drawer, scribble a message, and fold it into thirds. All the while, he felt the spy's eyes on him.

"Give this letter to her when she's attentive enough to read," he instructed and set the parchment on the nearest chair.

The Nim-Valan raised an eyebrow. "Fine, but what is it?"

"Hopefully this makes things easier for you. To be honest, I don't think she'll cooperate when she learns where she is until she's familiar with someone. Coura's always been headstrong and impatient, but hearing from me might calm her down."

He followed the remarks with an uncomfortable laugh when Finn's unreadable expression didn't change. Then, the spy's next words left him fumbling for a response.

"If you trust me with her life, I trust you with Elena's. Please watch out for Yukin as well."

After promising to do so, Will departed for the front gate where the awaiting carriage lingered in the road.

# Manipulated Minds

As usual, Marcus stirred before the sun rose and dressed in order to be ready for the general's meeting despite the lack of activity over the last week or so. His attempts to stay focused steadily dwindled whenever he considered the currently absent demon, which led him to recall his missing friends.

The day after their last encounter with the Nim-Valans seemed to turn the conflict upside down because of how personal the matter became. Byron explained Coura's kidnapping to him, Grace, Dianne, and Clearshot when all were present during the evening meal, which prompted questions and mixed emotions. When he shared Will's decision to return to the inner circle, Marcus nearly lost his temper.

Even though time passed, reflecting on the herbalist's thoughtless actions still had him simmering. *Does he not understand the danger he is in as an Asteom citizen sneaking across the border? If he gets caught or hurt, we won't know. Nobody will be able to save him, and we just got him back!*

His hands instinctively clenched into fists, yet he shoved such feelings aside as he entered the general's tent where his superior, Mattais, Byron, Commander Evern, and the Yeluthian's subordinate waited.

"Sorry for the delay," he apologized once everyone's eyes found him.

Fortunately, nobody commented on his tardiness, allowing him to take a seat with the others.

"Let's start with the most promising update," Casner began with a gesture to the younger angel. "Lavine returned from the palace late last night, so I figured this meeting could wait."

"Thank you," the aforementioned messenger began while shifting to grab a bundle of cloth from where it laid behind him. Then, he set the wrapped item in the center of their circle. "The king's council agreed to relinquish the ancestral weapon they held in order to aid our efforts here. In exchange, they encourage those stationed along the border to finish this fight as soon as possible."

"Easier said than done," Byron muttered before Marcus could.

Lavine nodded before continuing. "I informed them of the last encounter, as well as the enemy troops' capture. They implore us to utilize Lady Zelnar's goddess gift for updates."

The commander thanked his subordinate for the report, then they watched as the Yeluthian peeled away what fabric covered the aforementioned blade. Watching pieces of gold steadily shine until the entire sword was revealed lit a fire under Marcus.

*Not all hope is lost as long as we have a means to stop the demon.*

"With your permission, I request to keep the ancestral weapon on my person," Commander Evern said after and to no one in particular. "Its ability to amplify Yeluthian energy could prove useful if we face the Nim-Valans and their leader sooner."

"I'm inclined to agree with you," the general replied, though his tone reflected a sense of displeasure. "You'll need to remain within the camp."

"Yes, sir."

"It's a shame we can't locate the other sword," Byron added afterward and crossed his arms. "I doubt the Nim-Valans would use it considering its effect on their leader, but I wouldn't put it past the being to have them hide it from us."

Marcus mumbled his agreement. *At least we can protect ourselves if the first demon wandering around decides to intervene. I know what Coura said, but I just can't bring myself to lower my guard.*

The group reviewed additional items related to the camp's resources, their captured enemies, and maintaining a defensive position until Casner dismissed them. With nothing else to do, Marcus decided he could patrol the perimeter and check in with the scouts until lunch; however, what he learned during the rest of the morning hindered his appetite.

Several individuals noticed a shadow moving around the southern area, though nobody could clearly identify the source. Instead of revealing the identity of the creature his friend warned him about, he assured his comrades they were doing the right thing by mentioning the disruption and not acting. That part of the conflict bothered him as well, yet he hadn't planned on bringing it up to anyone until Byron and Clearshot joined him for lunch and inquired about the routes.

"I hate knowing that monster is lurking within hearing distance," he concluded after sharing the update. "It would be a waste of energy to strike unless we can be sure of success, but…"

"We faced that demon once before and lost," his fellow soldier stated in a calmer manner than he anticipated, as if the man accepted the results of that encounter. "If it doesn't plan on fighting us now, we should count our blessings instead of picking a fight."

"I suppose so."

Marcus found his gaze land on Byron, who continued eating without acknowledging their conversation. Clearshot also noticed and addressed him when the trio fell silent.

"What's wrong? No advice for our young comrade?"

The master mage tilted his head back to stare at the sky with an oddly melancholy expression before replying. "Just leave it be for now."

"You spoke to the demon with Commander Evern, right?" Clearshot pressed with narrowed eyes. "Is he going to ignore it now that he has the ancestral weapon?"

It didn't surprise Marcus to learn the soldier already heard about how the Yeluthian possessed the golden blade given his relationship with Byron. Still, he found himself wondering about the angel's intentions after the master mage's next response.

"I hope so."

"Why?" he countered without sounding too impatient.

Byron's emerald eyes studied Marcus before he released a sigh. "This stays between us. The general and Will are also aware, but I'd prefer to keep the matter private."

Although he wondered what could possibly be the reason for such secretive behavior, Marcus listened as the master mage repeated what the creature shared about its bond to his friend, which it discovered thanks to the former high priest. His body went cold at the realization, and the words he prepared for a rebuttal throughout the explanation left his mind by the end.

*Hendal and the being tormenting Dala were connected too? That's what happened, and Coura is... What kind of spell ties souls together?* He longed to ask but figured he wouldn't receive an answer. *I remember how it also targeted her because of her lineage. Was that intentional?*

A growled curse from Clearshot drew him out of his confused state.

"We can't touch the demon without putting Coura's life in danger," the archer repeated with a scowl directed at his empty bowl. "What a horrible thing to do, especially to an innocent child."

"I agree, but it didn't seem like it wanted to start trouble now," Byron added.

"What makes you so sure?"

"It mentioned what happened to Coura and where we could likely find her because it didn't intend to help, leaving us to do something about her kidnapping. The demon also taunted Commander Evern but didn't seem inclined to fight."

"The guards notice it wandering around the perimeter," Marcus reminded them as his gaze shifted to the trees beyond their fire. "No disappearances or deaths have been reported, so it stands to reason the creature is observing for now."

The master mage nodded. "Exactly like Coura said it would."

They fell silent for a few minutes to contemplate and eventually accept their situation; however, the being's presence became less prominent in Marcus' mind once he recalled his friend's explanations. In order to ease that building tension in his chest, he admitted his feelings aloud.

"Why would she lie about what happened?"

Neither comrade offered a response, pushing him to dive into the question.

"In Dala, she told Calin and I the demons fought, and the one we struggled against had been defeated. She never mentioned the former high priest or any magical connection. Why not tell the truth so we have a direction to work toward?"

"I'm not sure," Byron grumbled. His tone revealed his frustration with that dilemma. "I intend to confront her about the matter when she returns. That is, if her father isn't planning on it already."

"Are we the only people aware of the previous demon's real cause of death?" Clearshot interjected before Marcus could volunteer to join the Yeluthian commander and master mage.

"We informed the general in case the creature around here decides to act. Will also heard the truth before he departed."

The archer rubbed his eyes before releasing a yawn. "Only six then."

"That's exactly where it stays unless anybody else needs to know."

Marcus caught the underlying message and nodded to show he understood. *If word spreads about Coura's disappearance and her bond with the being, she might be thrown out for putting the troops in danger by luring a demon closer to us. Then again, if both die when one's life ends, she could become a target by those paranoid enough to want the creature gone.*

It proved difficult to dismiss the subject outright, yet he attempted to do so since they wouldn't get any closer to a solution until their friend returned.

***

As Grace exited the general's tent alongside Dianne, she held her head high despite the sense of weariness plaguing her after communicating with the king's council in Verona. Such a distance put a strain on her ability, especially given the recent conflict she

281

assist with, yet the days of rest prior allowed her a moment of reprieve.

"Lavine recounted our encounter with the enemy troop and the results," General Casner explained after summoning her that morning. "This will be an update on our status and the lack of activity. Hopefully, we can discuss the conflict with them every four days, even if we only offer brief reports."

She replied that she understood and stretched her goddess gift until she felt the familiar minds awaiting her in the council's meeting chamber. As usual, Aaron expressed his relief that she was unharmed and faring well before reassuring her nothing changed in Verona from Lavine's departure. Because of that lack of news, she prepared to dismiss the connection; however, her friend mentioned King Arval's return to Yeluthia at the end, which she shared with those present in the general's tent. Mainly, the message had been for the commander, who didn't appear surprised.

She reflected on the message when she sat around a fire with food in hand and her guard beside her. *Uncle expects to return to Yeluthia with Commander Isan and the troops not assigned to Commander Detrix's company. With Quinten supervising the kingdom in his father's absence, I am sure Uncle hoped to solve the issues involving demons. The conflict is contained to the northern border, and the main threat is in Nim-Vala, meaning we are doing all we can at the moment.*

Her thoughts continued processing their circumstances until Dianne said her name, drawing her eyes away from her empty bowl. "What is it?"

"Don't overthink the situation," the woman advised with a chuckle. "It is what it is, and those in the capital are doing just fine."

Grace tilted her head. "Yes, I know. I am assessing King Arval's reason for returning to Yeluthia is all."

"That's right," Dianne muttered, as if she forgot that part of the meeting. "Are you worried what will happen when they're gone?"

"Not at all. In fact, I am grateful they stayed in Verona for as long as they did."

"Really?"

The sense of pride she had in her kingdom spurred a smile while she replied. "Of course! Now that the alliance has been reforged, my uncle and his commanders strive to establish peace by ridding the world of demons. This requires working alongside humans instead of above or separate from them. Each kingdom has learned from the other, which strengthens our forces. If the king and Commander Isan feel the time is right to leave, then they must believe Asteom is in a position to handle the problems it faces."

"What about the other commanders?" her guard pointed out. "You mentioned they'll be here, but why keep them around if we humans can manage?"

"Commander Detrix formed his company consisting of humans and Yeluthians to act as a symbol of unity between the two kingdoms. His assignment keeps him tied to Asteom, so I assume he will not return until he can delegate the role. As for Commander Evern…"

Grace paused when she considered his main reason for remaining behind. *It could not be for Coura's sake alone, could it?*

"I'd bet he plans on staying until the demons here are dealt with," Dianne added during the pause. "Why leave when you're this involved? That wouldn't earn you any favors."

"Yes, exactly."

The duo finished their meals and decided a trip to the medical station for a potion to help Grace recover what energy she expended couldn't hurt. She had been avoiding the area due to Will's disappearance to search for Coura, a problem she wished to help resolve; however, she already accepted her current role and refused to waste her energy by worrying.

*Byron made it sounds as though Will has a means of tracking her*, she reflected after the pair departed with a handful of vials from the healers. *I did not press for details, but maybe I should have. Then again, I am sure it is at least a week's worth of travel to enter and explore the northern kingdom. I should put my faith in him.*

The thought proved to be more difficult than she expected, lowering her spirits. She masked her concern around Dianne though due to the woman's knack for confronting her at the first sign of distress, a quality she both appreciated and despised at certain times.

As they prepared to cross through the mass of people huddling around bonfires and tents, Grace noticed a trio of men donning their armor pass by to seemingly exit the camp. Her eyes instinctively followed them, which slowed her steps to a halt.

"What's the matter?" came Dianne's voice in a tone suggesting she hoped to return to their spot for a break.

"Where are those soldiers going?"

Her eyes went to the woman when she didn't receive an immediate response and found her guard studying the woods in that direction.

"I'd guess that's where the enemy troops are being held. They're probably on duty to patrol the group."

Something about the idea of being close to the Nim-Valans bothered her, though she couldn't identify the reason. *I should not hate them for their actions because of the demon's influence, yet it is difficult to overlook the past. Are they aware of what took place in Verona's palace? What if some of them were involved in the massacre.*

The notion left a sour taste in her mouth. She spun on her heel to head straight for the familiar section of the site, dropped beside the fire, and pulled a blanket over her shoulders. Dianne didn't comment on her behavior or attempt conversation, allowing them to relax until the noon meal. By that point, Grace's stomach rumbled loudly enough to have her guard laughing and offering to grab their bowls, which she appreciated. What lack of activity around her brought her mind back to the earlier, hostile feelings she attempted to dismiss.

*Although I do not agree with their decision to follow a malicious being, they are still people. How much of an influence does the creature hold over them anyway?*

At that, she considered what she knew about demonic energy. This led her to recall the instances where she came into contact with a possessed human's mind, whether intentionally or not, and had her sitting straighter.

Dianne returned before she could commit to pondering the subject, and they ate while making casual conversation until Marcus appeared to join them. After the assistant general informed them of his uneventful morning, Grace did the same yet hesitated once she recalled watching the trio of soldiers exit the camp.

"Are you not feeling well because you used too much power contacting Aaron?" her friend asked to catch her attention again.

She hadn't realized she ended with her decision to visit the medical station and shook her head. "No, I only requested potions to assist with replenishing my energy. I will be fine after I drink them and rest tonight."

"If it's too much, you need to speak up."

"I let her know already," Dianne interjected as Grace opened her mouth to reassure him.

That prompted him to nod in a pleased manner and with an amused smile, which she rolled her eyes at.

"If you must know, I was considering the Nim-Valan prisoners being kept separate from us," she ventured to ease their worry regarding her health and segue to a new topic. "Do you remember when we captured the guards forced to monitor Lady Emilea?"

Her friend's brown eyes widened a bit. "I do. Some of these men had a similar response to being bound during our last encounter while the rest seem unresponsive. Are you suggesting…"

"Yes, I am," she answered wholeheartedly without considering the process or risks. "If I can use my goddess gift to free them from the demon's influence, perhaps they may cooperate."

"What makes you so sure they won't turn on us? They might have willingly offered themselves to their leader."

"That may be true, but we will never know. Besides, they cannot heal without the dark energy."

Marcus bit his lip yet didn't turn her idea away. Meanwhile, Dianne didn't object or agree, leading Grace to believe her suggestion could actually help.

*I hope I can make a positive difference, if only to ease the burden on those engaged with the enemy.*

"Let me bring this up with the general," her friend finally confirmed and rose to his feet. "Your safety is our main priority, so I wouldn't put you close enough to be harmed."

"I understand."

"If we can remove their healing ability, we hold more of an advantage. The only downside I can think of is that the demon will regain that power."

"It already seems strong enough to impact our numbers," Dianne added. "What would more change?"

The assistant general looked to Grace, who could only admit her uncertainty. He departed after promising to return that evening with an answer.

*

"Are you sure about this?"

Grace glanced at where Dianne stood behind a tree off to her right. The woman's eyes became glued to the restrained Nim-Valans beyond the brush where they hid, and a hand rested on the hilt of her sword.

"We should be safe here," she said to calm her guard while propping herself against a different trunk. From where she sat, she wouldn't need to worry about being seen or growing stiff too soon.

The previous afternoon, General Casner approved Marcus' request to have her study the northerners' minds in order to remove their ability to heal. While everyone else seemed to worry about her safety despite those on patrol and the enemy's inability to physically retaliate, her main concern had to do with the demonic presence she would no doubt come into contact with.

*It cannot harm me and will likely retreat or plant itself firmly in their heads*, she concluded after considering her experiences with possessed humans before. *As long as I maintain my sense of self, I cannot falter.*

"Are you ready?" she asked her companion with as much of an optimistic smile as she could manage.

Dianne looked at her and nodded. "I should be asking you that."

Grace giggled at the comment, closed her eyes, then focused on relaxing her body. Once comfortable, the light energy in her center sprang to life, as though she destroyed a dam blocking a stream. It flowed from her when she extended her mind in the direction of the Nim-Valans. The enemy troops were easy to locate by their mass of consciousness, which seemed like colorful lights with their own, individual presences.

As she steadily observed each mind by gentle brushing against one, it became obvious who remained under the demon's influence. Those without that shadow hanging over them grumbled in a language she didn't understand, yet she picked up muted sensations, including boredom, uncertainty, and hunger. For the most part, they seemed as ordinary as anybody in Asteom's army.

Those under the demon's influence were a stark contrast to their comrades. She couldn't discern their thoughts or emotions amid a cloud of dark energy, which acted like a fog to shroud their consciousness. When she attempted to dive deeper, the being's hold weakened slightly, though she knew it would take effort to go farther, let alone rid the human of the parasite.

For what felt like hours, she bounced from individual to individual performing the same evaluation before accepting the results. The Nim-Valans would not be able to understand her, and she could not figure out their thoughts; attempting to speak with them became a risk because of this. Those effected by the demon could not be freed unless she expended more energy than she was willing to at that point.

*What would freeing one mind do? I do not know their language, so I would not be able to speak with them, and they are already bound. Even though they may not be able to heal, is using my power worth that?* She couldn't justify doing so and returned to her body shortly after.

A groan escaped her once the ache in her temples took effect. While Dianne said her name, she dropped her head into her hands in order to ease part of the tension. Fortunately, her guard knew this happened whenever she exerted her goddess gift thanks to the various meetings with the king's council, both in the capital and at their camp. Neither spoke in order to keep the environment as quiet as possible until she felt well enough to explain her findings. When she did, the woman sat beside her and offered a waterskin, which she nearly emptied.

"I can see why you're hesitant to free their minds," came Dianne's response when she finished talking. "Unless we are planning to rid them of that healing ability as a precaution in case they escape, it doesn't sound like it's worth the effort."

"Exactly. I do wish I knew part of their language so I could tempt them into revealing useful information."

"Like what you did at the underground market?"

Grace nodded. "I would never try conversing directly, but hinting at a particular topic might cause them to think about it and subconsciously share important information.

"Perhaps the general might find that useful," Dianne ventured while rising and offering her hand. "You'll need to share the results anyway, right?"

After agreeing, she accepted the woman's assistance to stand, then the pair returned. They soon found Marcus, who awaited their update, went straight to his superior's tent, and knocked on the wooden post. A deep voice from inside ordered them to wait, and a few minutes passed before a burly man Grace had seen before and the head healer departed.

"Who's next?" came General Casner's grumble as they entered. Papers littered the ground in various piles except for those in his hand.

Marcus saluted at the invitation. "Good afternoon, sir. Lady Zelnar wishes to update you on the status of her investigation into the Nim-Valan prisoners."

He waved his empty hand as a signal for Grace to continue, which she did in simple enough terms for a non-mage to understand, like with her guard. Once she finished, the general rubbed his chin but didn't otherwise look interested.

"You're saying we'd benefit from a translator," he concluded before releasing a low hum in thought. "That might not be as farfetched as you'd imagine."

"What do you mean?" she asked when he didn't elaborate.

"The assistant general can fill you in on the light mages who survived the ambush on our troops a couple years ago. From what I gathered, they lived in a town just beyond the border, so they might be able to discern the northerners' language."

Grace's eyebrows rose at the memory of being reunited with Will, and she glanced at Marcus, who shot her a knowing smile.

"Thank you, sir," he picked up after returning his eyes to the man. "We're familiar with the survivors and will reach out for assistance."

"Should I push for any information in particular?" she added as a final thought.

General Casner paused to consider her question for a moment. "The demon's location and plans are our main priority, but you could try seeing if they recall the ancestral weapon. We still don't have an answer as to how they knew to remove the sword and where it is now."

"That would be beneficial," Marcus muttered, prompting a nod from his superior.

"For now, we'll move forward with your assessment on those items. We can do so again and adjust our goals depending on their responses."

The three took their leave once the discussion came to a close. Although Grace longed to pursue their assignment, the soldiers both ordered her to eat and rest for a bit due to her weary appearance, which she dismissed.

"Let me speak with the light mages," her friend offered. "There's no need for all three of us to go."

"I suppose you are correct," she mumbled without hiding her disappointment.

Her tone caused him to chuckle and lay a hand on her shoulder. "You're more determined than most soldiers, you know that? We won't be trying your goddess gift again until you recover, so get plenty of sleep in order to be at your best."

Dianne took her by the arm to drag her away after, as if the soldiers coordinated their actions. A meal followed by a nap led to a lazy evening where she chatted with anybody who joined her in front of the fire, including Byron and Assistant General Mattais. Her guard went to fetch dinner when Clearshot took a seat beside her to talk about his day and returned with Marcus in tow.

"How are you feeling?" he inquired as they all dove into their food.

"My energy is steadily recovering," she answered without reminding her friend of how often she went through the process of using her goddess gift.

"I'm glad to hear it."

"Do you have an update on the light mages?" she pressed when he didn't continue speaking.

"Yes, but I didn't want to rush you if you're not-"

"I know not to overexert myself," she interrupted and let her impatience show.

Instead of being offended, the assistant general laughed at her stubbornness, along with Clearshot and Dianne.

"Let's not keep the young lady waiting!" the archer exclaimed before grinning at her. "You're so polite and professional I often forget you're just a child."

Grace's cheeks heated at the comment, but she refrained from pointing out her adult age. Luckily, Marcus' reply saved her from more jabs.

"One light mage from that group of survivors pointed me toward another until I met them all. Half didn't feel too comfortable with the language when they lived in Nim-Vala, and none are confident they would be able to translate at the level we believe you need."

"That's not reassuring," Dianne commented and crossed her arms.

"All five mentioned a couple others who can assist," he continued, though with a wince. "The first is a spy who rescued them and actually fought alongside Byron and Commander Detrix to capture the demon. Unfortunately, he returned to Nim-Vala shortly after."

"And the second?"

Marcus' eyes met Grace's. "Our friend named Will also survived with the mages."

She lowered her gaze. "He is still in the north as well."

"Those I spoke with claim he learned the language better than any of them. I'm afraid we'll need to wait until one of those two comes back."

Nobody argued with him, though Grace desired to brainstorm other options; however, she released a sigh and admitted they reached the end of what they could do on their own.

*What we are attempting to do is a delicate matter. The enemy troops might close off their minds to me if they realize we are using magic, or the demon could react at the first hint of my presence, especially since I prodded them before. Why must relying on others often require such a frustrating amount of patience?*

# A Brief Recovery

With every instance Coura woke, she felt less pain and a clearer mind. The usual, looming figure forced her to drink water and a new concoction, then she would rest. No jabs in the back caused her to stir in the middle of those naps, and she soon realized there were bandages covering her back.

*Where am I? This isn't the same place with the Nim-Valan king.*

When she was awake enough to assess her surroundings, she took pleasure in the sight of a window allowing plenty of sunlight to enter the space, which appeared to be an elegant bedroom. Nobody else occupied the area at the moment, so she sat up with some effort and focused on her center. Although both types of energy recovered a bit, she became disheartened by what she currently possessed.

*I should be able to cast minor spells, but my goddess gift still drained my Yeluthian power. I doubt I can use it again until I eat and rest more. Speaking of which, how long have I been away from the border? Am I still in the king's palace?*

Part of her doubted that since she had been moved near a window she could easily escape through; however, she mainly hoped to find answers regarding the enemy's intentions and Lupin's involvement. Before she could dive into that mystery, the lone door's knob clicked and twisted. The sound had her preparing to leap up until she recalled how much better she felt.

*Whoever is taking care of me must want me conscious enough to speak with, at the very least,* she told herself as her hands gripped the bedsheets. *I still have my magic if it's not a friendly conversation.*

The man who stepped inside closed the door without a sound and went straight to a chair at the farthest side of the room. He only looked at her when he sat and crossed his arms.

*He's not like the Nim-Valans I've encountered so far*, she noted after observing his plain appearance, including chestnut hair and eyes instead of the common, dark features.

"How are you feeling?" he asked after a moment.

Coura opened her mouth to reply before realizing he spoke clearly in Asteom's language. Her eyes instinctively narrowed while her lips pressed together. *Is this a trick?*

"You can call me Finn," he went on when she remained silent. "This is a safe location, so you should continue to recover your strength. Those potions were mixed to ensure you receive what nutrients you were deprived of, but I can also fetch solid foods if you prefer."

His polite tone made her more suspicious. "Who are you, and where am I?"

"We can discuss that later. For now, you should rest."

"I'm tired of resting, especially surrounded by the enemy," she shared as a fire lit in her chest. In response, she threw the sheets off herself, stood with wobbly legs, and went to the window. "If you won't answer my questions, I have no reason to stay here."

"I can name several, but most relevant to you is that Will should be returning soon."

Coura paused with a hand on the sill and turned to face the stranger, who remained in his seat with the same, unbothered expression. "Why is he in Nim-Vala? What are you doing to him?"

Instead of replying, he glanced at the bed then back to her. She caught the signal, trudged over to the mattress, and sat on its edge while repressing an annoyed sigh.

"It seems the drug's effects wore off," he began after. "I needed to make sure so I don't have to repeat myself or deal with a confused patient. As you noticed already, you were kidnapped and brought to Nim-Vala's inner circle, seemingly under King Syrus' orders. Will ventured from the border alone to find me and ask for my help. Together, we managed to locate you and escape to an ally's estate. Unfortunately, an individual was wounded, so Will and that ally went to tend to the individual."

The sudden amount of information left her with dozens of questions, yet she stared down at her hands to put her thoughts together before commenting. "I assume you were left to care for me because you can communicate with me."

"That's correct."

"I also sense you don't want me involved with whatever Will is doing."

This time, the man didn't answer.

*Would Lupin or the king use him to lull me into a false sense of security?* she wondered and looked out the window again. *Is Will even around here? This could be a trap.*

"If you don't believe me, there's a letter from your friend confirming what I just shared," he added.

Coura caught movement from the stranger and found him pointing at the other side of the bed where a piece of paper occupied a second chair. Despite her suspicion, she climbed over the blankets, plucked up the parchment, and skimmed the words before rereading the message, which included what her caretaker said.

"What Will didn't mention was our conclusion regarding the king's reason for bringing you into the inner circle," the man shared when she set the letter aside.

"I assume Lupin is involved?"

He nodded before going on to propose how the demon intended to draw Soirée into the capital in search of her, causing damage in the process, and then the Nim-Valan advisor would steal power at the cost of the king's life.

*Not a bad idea, but I doubt Soirée would be that careless. It would be surprising if she came to rescue me before I neared death, which means I would be suffering longer.*

"Do you have other questions?" he asked when she didn't share her thoughts. "If not, we can see about getting you into the bathing chamber."

She hadn't realized how grimy her skin felt until that moment, especially beneath the clothing she wore ever since her capture, and nearly winced at the idea of how horrible her hair likely looked. Still, picturing her friend among the danger in the royal estate drove her to assist him first. "Where is Will?"

"You don't need to worry about him now."

In response, Coura rose and shot a glare at the Nim-Valan. "Do you really expect me to ignore how he's-"

"You are not fully recovered," he interrupted. "Your life would be at risk, and then his attention would be on keeping you safe instead of the job he set out for."

She considered this for a moment. "He's tending to an injured person, right? I possess enough power for a healing spell. Let me use my magic on them and get Will out sooner."

It seemed her words caught the man off guard, yet he stood and covered his alarm immediately after.

"It would be foolish to push yourself. Besides, security in the royal estate is high given our escape."

"How did you get in before?" she pressed.

"Our ally has connections. As I mentioned, he is aiding Will."

"Is it difficult to sneak inside? How did you two escape with me?"

"I doubt it would be as simple given the commotion your rescue caused."

Although his expression and tone remained neutral, she could tell he'd grown annoyed with her persistence; however, she refused to let her friend remain in a situation where his life was at risk. Coura walked to the window again and threw it open only to be met by a cooler breeze than she expected, causing her to shiver.

"What are you doing?" the Nim-Valan practically snapped, though he made no attempt to go to her.

"I appreciate your help," she began as her eyes scanned the outside world. "I'm going to find Will and get us out of here before the king or Lupin has a chance to act."

In the midst of her assessment, she faintly heard footsteps, and the man seized her left forearm. He then pulled her back without releasing his grip, closed the window in a single motion, and faced her. The slight scowl he wore reflected his frustration, yet his next words didn't hint at the emotion.

"Nobody in the inner circle must know you're here. Not only are you unable to understand anyone, but you're a mage. If the king and his guards don't recapture you, you'll be arrested as an enemy if you're lucky and killed on the spot if you're not."

"I can take care of myself," she attempted to reassure him and tugged her arm free, though he loosened his hold. "I'm worried about Will. You're right about me not belonging here too. You and your allies shouldn't be associated with us if that puts you in danger."

Some part of her plea resonated with the Nim-Valan, for he averted his eyes by glancing out the window and stepping away from her. A minute passed in silence before he released a sigh.

"He gave a similar reason," she heard him mutter and was surprised to find a slight smile gracing his lips. It vanished when he pivoted to walk toward the door.

"Where are you-"

"You should drink the potions Will left for you and plenty of water," he advised without looking back. "I'll see to a bath, new clothes, and food to make sure you are adequately prepared to depart this evening."

The support raised her spirits, and she thanked him before he disappeared through the doorway. Once alone, Coura tested the strength in her muscles with a few, simple exercises and stretches that revealed how stiff she'd grown. She then repressed a groan as she uncorked her friend's medicine, drank it all without pause, and winced at the bitter, herbal aftertaste, which she rid herself of by finishing what water her caretaker left. By that point, she looked forward to scrubbing her body clean and ridding herself of the disgusting clothes that practically stuck to her skin. A gentle knock let her know when the Nim-Valan returned. He cracked the door open and gestured for her to follow without speaking.

*I should probably keep quiet*, she noted while taking in her surroundings. *I'm sure he'll avoid bringing me around people, but I don't want to push my luck.*

What hallways they crossed eventually led to a single corridor with a humid chamber at the end. A wide tub holding clear, steamy water sat in the middle, and stacks of towels, bars of soap, and bottles had been neatly organized on a nearby shelf. She also noted multiple puddles on the stone floor, revealing how someone had recently occupied the area.

"I will keep watch," the man assured her.

When he retreated to guard the space, Coura peeled off her clothes and practically jumped into the bath where she dunked her head several times and savored the warmth. Once she felt content, her eyes went to the various bottles containing liquids likely used as perfumes. Her curiosity piqued at the thought of testing them, yet she remembered she needed to remain inconspicuous around the northerners. With that in mind, she selected a bar of soap, washed and rinsed her skin, and exited to dry off when the water became lukewarm.

*Didn't he mention I would get new clothing?*

She searched the chamber for the extra items and found a pile sitting beside the door. Although a bit large, they felt comfortable enough to move in and matched her caretaker's, which she discovered when she exited to find him waiting. Together, they returned to the room where she had been staying. Bread, apple, and carrot slices, some kind of jerky, and a jam mixture awaited her on a tray.

"What time is it?" she inquired as she went straight to the food. Her stomach growled at the sight before her mouth watered once she popped a piece of fruit into her mouth.

"Early evening. It will be dark in about an hour."

Coura hadn't noticed the dim lighting until then, prompting her to glance out the window where the sky had darkened. The man didn't show interest in her food, so she figured he already ate and polished off what he brought while attempting conversation.

"How did you and Will meet? Was it during his time across the border?"

"Yes."

Part of her wasn't surprised when she didn't receive more of an answer. "What did you say you're name is?"

"You can call me Finn."

"I'm Coura. Are we returning here once the wounded individual is healed?"

"Ideally. It depends on various factors."

She decided to leave the planning at that since he seemed to only share what he wanted her to know. By that point, she finished eating and transitioned to sitting cross-legged on the bed. Finn retrieved the empty tray and left her alone again. When he returned a few minutes later, he tossed her a ball of fabric she soon recognized as a hat thick enough to hang over her head.

"Keep that on at all times," he ordered while strolling to the window.

"Why?"

"Your eyes are a dead giveaway that you're from Asteom. Avoid looking directly at the people we pass, and stay behind me."

"Do I get a weapon?" she halfheartedly asked.

"You shouldn't need one. Focus your energy on following me before we reach our goal."

"Do you even know where they are?"

"I have an idea of their location."

Coura longed to grumble a retort about how they would be searching all night but refrained from doing so since he proved trustworthy so far. *It'd be foolish to make him an enemy at this point, especially while I'm hiding in Nim-Vala. Besides, if Will managed to befriend one of them, I suppose it's not impossible to work together.*

***

Footsteps from the corridor beyond the room where Will worked had him growing tense and pausing until the sound faded. Only then did he release a breath before continuing to rebandage the stab wound Elena suffered from. Meanwhile, Yukin poked his head out to search for potential danger before returning to the queen's opposite side.

"All clear," the young lord whispered as he dabbed at his sweaty forehead with the back of one hand.

Will nodded but didn't remove his attention from his patient.

The pair had been inside the royal estate for three days by that point, and most of their time was spent huddling over the injured woman. Yukin's sudden arrival hadn't caused a stir like they thought; however, the guards on patrol in Elena's wing shared a look when he requested to meet with her. They led the pair to her empty room before one mentioned finding her in a hallway near the king's quarters.

*If they didn't retrieve her and patch the wound enough not to bleed, she wouldn't have survived this long*, Will reflected after he leaned back and wiped his hands on a spare towel. *I just hope I wasn't too late.*

Unfortunately, that had been the limit to what the men could do, which he expected. They took turns sneaking food into the room where they hid her since the king seemed intent on locating the intruders and his previous prisoner instead of tending to his wife. The medical men and women they reach out to in the royal estate were either preoccupied, away from the building, or refused to acknowledge the guards due to their status. Their lone bit of fortune had been recognizing Will from his earlier visits tending to Elena's daughter.

*I'm sure somebody would help eventually, but we don't have time to waste.*

"How is she?" Yukin inquired while inspecting the pale face.

"The wound is healing, and she isn't bleeding now that she's stitched up. Our problem is that she needs to recover what she lost in order for her body to repair itself. This is a slow process, especially since she isn't able to eat or drink for strength."

"We can only wait then?"

He nodded while anticipating the obvious reaction.

"The entire area is searching for you, Finn, and your friend. We can't remain here for long without someone wandering by."

"I understand, but without another person who can monitor and care for her, she may not make it."

In the midst of their conversation, the sound of footsteps returned, though the increased noise signaled multiple people. Both hopped to their feet.

"Hide!" the young lord ordered, forcing Will to crawl under the bed where they planned for him to stay thanks to what blankets draped over the sides.

As soon as he slid into place, he saw the curtain move followed by two sets of boots. He held his breath when Yukin gasped.

"What are you doing here?" came the Nim-Valan's harsh whisper. "Who is that?"

"One of Elena's guards told us where to find you," a familiar voice said after.

Will knew it was Finn's and stuck his head out. The unexpected movement from the floor startled the spy and whoever stood at his side, which made him chuckle despite the circumstances. Once he emerged and got to his feet, it was his turn to be surprised. Even with clothes matching Yukin's father's household and an oversized hat hiding her hair, he recognized Coura when he peered closer and caught her sapphire eyes and casual smirk.

"What are you doing here?" he practically demanded in his native tongue and at the same volume Yukin used earlier.

His friend immediately removed the cap at his response before shaking her dark hair out. All the while, she fixed him with a grin. "I'm glad to see you too."

"You should be in bed! Why-"

"How's Elena?" Finn interrupted in the other language, likely to include Yukin.

Will paused to recall his most recent assessment. After repeating it, both Nim-Valans went to the bed where the young lord mumbled his concerns. Meanwhile, Coura crossed her arms and waited until he faced her again to speak.

"You sure sound like them," she commented as her eyes wandered toward the queen. "Is that the person you're treating?"

"That's one of King Syrus' wives named Elena," he decided to share. "He stabbed her when she stopped him from pursuing us during our escape with you."

"How bad is it?"

"She's stable but needs rest in order to recover what blood she lost before the wound was treated."

Coura stepped around him to approach the sleeping woman on the other side of the Nim-Valans, and Will joined her. He figured they would begin discussing their next steps or if she should remain in Nim-Vala while her strength recovered until she knelt and laid her hands on the bandages.

"What is she doing?" the young lord snapped while backing up behind Finn.

The spy shot a glare at Coura. "What are you doing?" he repeated so she could understand.

"I told you I would heal her," came the indifferent response.

"It's dangerous to use magic here. What if the demon picks up on it?"

"If Lupin isn't here, we should be fine. Now be quiet so I can focus."

Finn's eyes snapped to Will, who could only shrug helplessly.

"You brought her," he couldn't help himself from muttering in the Nim-Valan tongue, earning him a fiercer look.

Switching between languages gave him a headache, so he took a seat and relaxed when the space quieted. Neither Yukin nor Finn moved while Coura worked.

*I don't believe for a second she's well enough to be using magic*, he thought after a moment when he caught his friend's breathing become slight panting. *Why is she pushing herself?*

The faint glow emanating from her hands soon faded, then she opened her eyes and rubbed them with both hands.

"Is she healed?" Finn asked in the neutral tone Will became accustomed to when the spy wanted to hide his emotions.

Coura nodded and glanced back at Will to address him. "You did a great job. All I had to do was speed up the process. It was easy with what little light energy I had and my lack of skill."

While he thanked her for the compliment, Finn pushed for more of an update.

"Does that mean the wound is mended?"

"See for yourself," she retorted and pointed at the bandages.

The Nim-Valan hesitated for a moment before removing the wrappings, revealing unmarred skin beneath. What stitches Will added would need to be removed, yet he had no doubt the internal damage had been tended to as well. Despite the positive outcome, Finn and Yukin still eyed Coura suspiciously.

"At this rate, Elena may stir tomorrow," he said to the pair to lighten the mood. "I should stay nearby, just in case."

"I'll see about rooms and dinner then," the young lord commented and sidestepped to the opening.

As soon as he slipped through, Will heard Coura chuckling to herself. "What's wrong?"

"It's been a while since people felt the need to tiptoe around me."

He didn't press for more when she left it at that. Instead, he went to take out the stitches before Yukin returned. Finn silently monitored the corridor from the entrance, and Coura lied on the floor to seemingly rest during the break. By the time he finished, footsteps sounded to signal their companion; however, the spy exited to converse with those on the other side.

"What are they talking about?" Coura whispered from where she sat up and faced away from the opening.

Will struggled to hear the conversation beyond the curtain. "I'm not sure. I would guess Yukin needed to request a servant's assistance but wants Finn's input."

She produced a hum in response and rested her chin in her hands.

About a minute later, the Nim-Valans entered together. Finn scooped up the cap Coura abandoned, tossed it to her, then ordered them to get ready to depart. Will prepared to ask how far he would be from his patient until a knowing look from the spy had him nodding.

*I shouldn't underestimate his consideration for my work*, he noted while helping Coura to her feet. *That, and he cares for Elena. He knows I should be near enough to step in if her condition worsens.*

The four exited after, keeping quiet until they reached their destination just beyond a right turn. Even though the directions didn't reveal where in the estate they were, the room appeared like those he had been in, except with four beds instead of one or two. When they each selected their cot, Finn went to the doorway.

"I'll fetch us dinner," he announced in Asteom's language, likely because he informed the young lord earlier. "Don't make too much noise. Apparently, the soldiers have been ordered to arrest any unknown individuals or those wandering where they shouldn't be."

"But you'll be fine?" Coura countered and raised an eyebrow.

Finn merely nodded.

*Maybe I should let her know he works on both sides of the border*, Will thought as the Nim-Valan stepped out. *She might already suspect as much.*

During that brief moment, his friend kicked off her boots, lied on her chosen mattress, and visibly relaxed. The idea of her sneaking into the palace in order to use what limited power she possessed left him curious about her intentions, especially given her violent interactions with the northerners up to that point.

In the end, he abandoned those feelings in favor of giving his mind a break.

# Escaping the Estate

What food Finn brought and a full night's sleep sufficiently eased the hole in Coura's center from expending her Yeluthian energy. When she first inspected the stab wound, she knew it would be possible to mend completely thanks to the work Will put in with cleaning and stitching the injury; however, she didn't have much to spend from the beginning.

She hoped her friend wouldn't notice how weak she actually felt since she decided to invite herself along and heal the Nim-Valan woman, which seemed to be the case when he left her to herself during the following morning. Only Finn stayed with her otherwise until the four regrouped for lunch. That was when she heard how the woman began stirring and asking about her husband, the king responsible for her wound. Will shared that much, then he conversed with the northerners, which both excluded her from the discussion and let her figure out her opinion on the matter.

*I only came here to ease the burden on his shoulders and pay the queen back for helping them escape with me. I'd be amazed if the woman didn't mind us sticking around. We're the enemy after all. How long until the soldiers find us?*

She refused to be captured again since that meant she would be put into the same position as a hostage for Soirée, which led her to conclude she would need to return to the boarder. Flying would no doubt get her noticed unless she departed at night, yet she'd leave Will alone to travel on foot. That didn't sit well with her given his journey to locate and rescue her.

Movement from the lord's son introduced as Yukin drew her attention when he rose and addressed Finn in a tone suggesting they began arguing. The second Nim-Valan stood in a calmer manner before the pair exited. In the following silence, Will released a sigh and rubbed his eyes.

"What's wrong?" she inquired when he didn't elaborate.

In response, he fixed her with a gaze reflecting his uncertainty. "It sounds like the king's servants are creeping closer to this wing of the estate. I didn't know this, but where we are is positioned beside the rooms belonging to Elena, the injured woman you healed. Her guards have been warning Finn, and he believes we should depart as soon as possible."

"What's stopping us?"

"Yukin is concerned about leaving the queen after what she endured. It's obvious King Syrus is not in his right mind. She once mentioned how distant he's become too."

"Why not bring her with us?"

"Where would she go?" he countered with a glance at the opening. "Finn refuses to get her more involved and lose his freedom by being bound to protect her while Yukin believes the opposite. It's complicated."

Coura shook her head and refrained from rolling her eyes. "It's always complicated, isn't it?"

That earned her a sympathetic smile from Will, who returned to rubbing his face.

*I wonder if there is a safe location I can transport us to,* she thought after evaluating her center. *It couldn't be far, but we wouldn't need to risk sneaking around. The issue is I've only been to the lord's house and don't remember much to offer options. Would that help our dilemma?*

Even though she anticipated his reaction, she shared the suggestion.

"You're not serious!" he practically snapped with wide eyes. "How much power do you have after such a short recovery? I don't just mean the last day or so either. You can't push yourself to the point of exhaustion whenever you-"

"What's the alternative?" she interrupted and crossed her arms to defend her stance.

"We sneak out together or separate."

"How likely is it someone will recognize us outside this place? Why take that risk at all?"

Will seemed to be biting his tongue, which she figured had to do with his ability to consider an option fully before ruling it out. Because of his hesitation, she decided he might cave in if she expressed faith in her magic.

"If you're only against the idea because you're worried about me, don't let that stand in our way of reaching a safe location sooner. I wouldn't offer my ability if I didn't believe I could handle it, and I'll have time to recover afterward, right?"

"I guess so."

"You would just need to make sure they trust the portal I summon since I won't be able to maintain the spell for longer than a few seconds."

"That sounds more difficult than convincing you not to use magic," he mumbled.

The comment had her smiling, though he promised to speak with Finn about utilizing her goddess gift. That gave her time to solidify her intentions, which proved invaluable when the Nim-Valan returned, listened to Will, then addressed her.

"I'm not familiar with magic," he prefaced with a slight frown. "A majority of Nim-Valans aren't either, so I doubt Elena and Yukin will agree or cooperate. The time limit doesn't help."

Coura had considered their people's views and attempted to explain the process as simply as she could. "It's powerful but not harmful to anybody who passes through. With a portal, we can be transported back to the room where you kept me to recover. No one should be able to trace the destination either."

"You're saying there's no risk."

"Except for slight disorientation, we'll be out of here in seconds."

While he contemplated the option, Will chimed in.

"Convincing Yukin and Elena should be the hardest part, but they witnessed Coura's magic firsthand. They can trust her."

"That's not the part I'm conflicted about," the Nim-Valan mentioned while staring at the wall across from him. "Our next steps will have to take the new location into account, including the lord, his family and servants, and the guards around the inner circle. If Elena goes missing and is discovered there, Yukin's family will be ruined."

*Of course it's a political issue. Nobody would understand what she went through. They only care about how such drama benefits them.* She kept her mouth shut since she didn't have the skill or patience to maneuver through the minds of the nobility.

Eventually, Finn took his leave with Will in tow to presumably reexplain the proposed plan, so she chose to try and sleep until dinner. She managed to drift off for what felt like a few minutes before rising with a yawn at the sound of voices in the room. The Nim-Valans and Will returned and started eating what food a servant presumably snuck over, so she joined them to appease her growling stomach.

"We're going to move forward with your spell tomorrow," Finn said to break the silence as his eyes shifted to her when she dropped to sit beside Will.

She tore off a piece of bread, popped it in her mouth, and chewed for a moment. "It was that easy to convince them?"

"The guards are wandering through these halls now. We don't have time to waste."

Coura glanced at the covered opening and ignored the uncomfortable sensation that arose from the idea of soldiers searching so close to where she had been sleeping. "Whether or not everybody goes, I'm not staying another night."

Those were the last words on the subject for the day.

*

Coura's optimism the morning of their departure steadily waned when the four entered the queen's room to find her up and active enough to talk. Her babbling continued and reflected a slew of emotions that ranged from frustration to heartache, though it varied based on who spoke in between. Of course, Coura didn't understand what was happening, leaving her to keep watch at the doorway until Will came over to clarify the problem.

"She's not as cooperative today," he shared in reference to the woman. "Not only is she nervous about being near a mage and making contact with your spell, but she also wants to help her husband and be with her daughter, who's in the care of a nursemaid."

"Then leave her here," Coura replied with a shrug. "As long as she stays away from the king, she won't be in harm's way. At least, that's what I can tell."

"They don't believe she will."

"Why wouldn't she? If we find and kill Lupin, he should lose what power the demon has been lending him."

"Are you sure he won't…" Will seemed bothered by the notion but didn't finish his sentence or reveal the reason.

He even opened and closed his mouth twice before Finn said his name, ending their discussion. The Nim-Valan seemed to give instructions, then her friend nodded and addressed her again.

"They're ready to start when you are."

"Finally," she muttered as she stepped away from the opening. "You should go through first so they can follow. I need to be last and can probably keep it up for ten seconds."

She made sure to speak loudly enough for Finn to hear since he could also understand her, though he didn't respond. Her attention shifted to the side of the room with the most space after. Like every other instance when she used her goddess gift, she raised both hands and dove into her center of power. What Yeluthian energy she recovered immediately released to begin forming the oval ring that lit up the room, prompting fearful comments from the northerners.

As soon as the image of the room she remembered waking up in less than a week ago formed, she shouted for them to go. Will hurried forward at her signal, gestured for the rest to follow, and passed through. Next, the lord's son and queen stepped closer and hesitated until Finn practically growled something in their language. One managed to stumble in after the other, allowing the final figure to disappear as well. Only then did Coura throw herself into her spell just as her power faded.

***

Will had never truly seen his friend's goddess gift at work, let alone experienced what it felt like to be instantly transported

308

from one location to another, yet as his feet touched new ground and his stomach turned, he prayed he would never need to do so again. What steps followed his landing brought him to the nearest wall where he collapsed with his back pressed against the solid surface. He needed that to help the world around him stop spinning.

Several footsteps and thuds sounded from the rest of the room, but he only opened his eyes when he relaxed enough to test his sight. Everybody else appeared in a similar position except Coura, who managed to fall onto the mattress and remained unmoving.

"D-Did it w-work?" Yukin asked with much effort, as if he were attempting to not vomit.

All three sets of brown eyes found Will after the question, leading him to respond as he wiped his damp forehead.

"It looks like it."

"What do we do now?" Elena whimpered quite unlike her normal, commanding self. When nobody answered right away, she crawled to where Finn sat and hugged his arm. "What do we do about my husband?"

Surprisingly, the spy looked at Will instead of replying.

*She's safe here, they made that much clear*, he recalled as he reflected on their previous discussion, the one that convinced the queen to join them. *Yukin promised to protect her without revealing her identity to the rest of the household, and Finn said the same. I'm not sure if there's much reason for me to stay if our next goal is to free the king by defeating his inhuman advisor.*

He knew bringing up the demon would cause Elena distress, which was what happened when the spy tried explaining King Syrus' erratic behavior before they left, so he approached the subject cautiously. "Leave the rest to those of us who can fight the source of the trouble. With Coura free from the royal estate, no harm should befall the inner circle."

"You're referring to the creature possessing my husband," the woman commented after a moment.

He noticed how pale her dark skin grew and what unshed tears caused her eyes to glisten; however, shying away from the truth would only sugarcoat the effort needed to stop the being. "That's right. The only option we have is to kill Lupin."

"Will Syrus return to his normal self?"

Will instinctively glanced at Coura only to find her still lying on the bed and unattentive. *Byron and the commander mentioned what the demon shared about its bond with her. If one dies then...*

"I don't know," he muttered and lowered his gaze to the floor.

Fortunately, Finn picked up the discussion while rising and offering his master a hand to pull her to her feet. "The advisor's hold on Nim-Vala must be severed by any means. What follows is inevitable at this point."

"Yes, you're right," Elena replied and accepted the extended hand. It seemed his words shook her out of her frightened mentality, for she addressed Yukin next. "If I am to be staying at Lord Crowmald's estate, I will need to know where I sleep, bathe, and eat, as well as any parameters regarding the servants' routes and assignments."

*Back to her old self so fluidly*, he noted with some amusement despite the circumstances. *Still, I'm sure she's masking her troubles in order to appear assertive.*

The young lord climbed to his feet and offered to lead her to her new quarters, which she accepted while keeping a hold on Finn. When the three departed together, Will took a deep breath, closed his eyes, and leaned his head against the wall at his back.

"Are they gone?" came Coura's voice during the silence.

He hadn't been expecting her to be awake, so the sound startled him enough to jump. "They went to get Elena settled."

His friend shifted to sit up, though he noted her slouched shoulders and weary expression.

"Can you ask them to bring me something to eat when they get back?" she requested before covering a yawn. "I shouldn't rest on an empty stomach after using that much energy."

"I thought you already were asleep."

"I'm forcing myself not to doze off, but I can't concentrate when you all keep talking."

Her slight annoyance prompted a smile from Will as he recalled her usually headstrong attitude. *I wonder how much input she would have if she could understand the Nim-Valans' conversations.*

The notion made him chuckle, which drew her attention, and he agreed to speak with Finn about a meal once he returned. That satisfied her for the time being. While he pushed himself to his feet to go to the chair at her bedside, she uncorked one of the remaining potions on the table and drank the entire bottle at once. Her resulting grimace spurred a laugh, leading her to berate him for making the concoction so unapologetically bitter.

*

The day following the group's arrival seemed to stretch for an extra hour or two because of the lack of activity. Will left Coura alone since she spent most of the time sleeping, he had no reason to speak with Elena, who remained in her room, and Yukin had disappeared. He assumed the young lord needed to make an appearance to the rest of the household, figure out how to hide and accommodate the kingdom's missing queen, or both. Finally, Finn only delivered meals.

Due to his friend's use of the lone bed, he made do with some blankets and a pillow on the floor, which left him with multiple aches when he stirred; however, he accepted that he had been spoiled during his time in Yukin's estate. He also knew they would be resting on the ground and without a roof over their heads when they returned to the border, leading him to take pleasure in the shelter.

He ate breakfast, chatted with Coura about their expected departure, then crafted potions with what supplies he left in the space when she drifted to sleep. Only a knock at the door disrupted that peaceful atmosphere. Instead of calling for the person to enter, Will rose and went to it since his friend didn't stir. Finn stood bearing a tray of the usual meat-and-cheese sandwiches on the other side and practically shoved him out of the way to enter without a greeting.

"What's wrong?" he decided to ask after the rude gesture.

The Nim-Valan set the tray on the bedside table, faced him, then pointed at the door. Although the lack of words confused him more, Will followed the spy out and down the hallway. His first thought was that they encountered a problem with Elena, yet he soon realized they were exiting into the estate's back garden. There, Finn gestured to a pair of metal chairs and only sat when he did.

"How is your friend?" the man asked first as he fixed his eyes on Will.

"She's recovering. According to her, as long as she sleeps well and continues eating consistently, she should be well enough to move around tomorrow."

"Good. You two need to leave as soon as possible."

The sudden comment caught him off guard. "Is something wrong? Yukin isn't in trouble, is he?"

"Don't panic," Finn practically scolded him with a look reflecting his lack of patience for such fretting. "No one is in trouble at the moment. Yukin wishes to stay away from you, your friend, and Elena in case any of you are discovered. I'm sure you understand."

"I do. Speaking of which, how is Elena?"

"We've done all we can do for her except stop the advisor."

Will sensed pent-up frustration and decided to press the subject. "I'm sure the leaders fighting the creature are putting together a plan to stop it. When we return to the border, we'll be updated on-"

"I'm not departing with you."

Again, he paused at the unexpected interruption. "Why not? I thought you-"

"I am needed here."

Although he wanted to encourage the Nim-Valan to join him, Will bit his tongue. *He serves Elena, and she's relying on him for protection and guidance while she is in hiding. I can tell he would rather fight Lupin, but he wouldn't turn his back on the person he's loyal to.*

That final thought had him considering the other side of the spy's duties. When the silence stretched, he decided to indulge his curiosity. "What about your master in Asteom?"

"What about them?" came the indifferent reply.

"Aren't you supposed to report in every so often?"

"Yes and no."

*I should have known.*

By that point in their relationship, Will became so used to the Nim-Valan's preference for making such vague remarks that he could only huff a laugh. The sound earned him a suspicious glance from Finn, though the man didn't respond or reveal additional details.

"Coura and I can probably leave tomorrow afternoon depending on how she's feeling," he continued to reassure the spy. "Her condition is significantly better, and I don't plan on traveling at a rushed pace. Knowing her, she might request we hurry anyway."

During the update, his gaze wandered around the garden to various plants decorating the space. He allowed himself that moment of peace before facing Finn again and found the chestnut eyes studying him. Before he could ask what was wrong, the Nim-Valan looked away while speaking.

"My master is the leader of the Reddock household located in Verona."

Such an unprompted piece of information startled Will into silence, allowing the man to continue.

"Those of us who are born to a Reddock go through training as children in order to serve the royal family. Our only purpose is gathering intel from around the kingdom and beyond then reporting back. I never learn whether or not what I share reaches the king's ears or what the rest of the family learns. My assignments dealt with Parnic until I showed enough potential to be allowed to enter Nim-Vala."

"That must have been when Elena caught you."

"I survived for months by making allies before that point. By forming a circle, I protected myself until I had the resources to enter the royal estate."

*Geneva mentioned how Finn rescued her and that he did the same for plenty of people in Muld,* Will recalled. *I had no idea he mainly did so for his own benefit.*

"The work I perform in Nim-Vala and along the border keeps me occupied enough not to need to return to Parnic," the man continued in his emotionless tone. "Besides, the household relies on the intuition of its spies. They receive my reports when I return with valuable information. This conflict has given me enough to be involved in, which the head of the family should understand."

"What an interesting structure," Will mumbled as he considered the insight. "It reminds me of the families in Kercher who acted as messengers between Yeluthia and Verona and raised the next generations to do the same. Many abandoned their traditions when communications ceased years ago."

"I'm not familiar with them, but I can assure you the Reddock household is strict."

He sensed enough tension in those words to make him wonder how much conditioning went into training the spies. It also reminded him of the man's relationship with Yukin, leading him to believe Finn didn't particularly enjoy being tied to the family. "Does anybody else know?"

Finn shook his head without replying.

"Why tell me?" he asked next and glanced at the Nim-Valan. The question arose as soon as he considered how little he actually knew about the man before the pair entered the garden.

For a while, the Nim-Valan seemed to be contemplating how to answer. The building pressure as Will worried he would become entangled in the spy's personal matters deflated when Finn met his eyes and replied.

"I suppose I enjoy talking with you because you're ordinary."

He opened and closed his mouth twice. "What?"

The befuddled expression shifted into disbelief when Finn's face relaxed into one projecting amusement, complete with a slight smile.

"Throughout my entire life, the people I interacted with had a motive for keeping me close. Elena uses me whenever she gets the chance, and even Yukin has his reasons for allowing me to come and go as I please. Compared to those around me who act strategically in order to protect their image and pursue their interests, you're like a breath of fresh air. I would never condone the individuals involved with my upbringing or my masters, but it's nice to know some people are simply interested in an honest relationship."

The blush that developed at Finn's honesty burned Will's cheeks to the point where he dipped his chin and muttered a thank you. When he looked up a few seconds later, his friend resumed the usual, indifferent expression while staring at a spot across the garden.

"You know you're welcome to join Coura and me," he added in order to change topics. "Your assistance before helped us seal Lupin with the ancestral weapon. We could use your skills, and you have every right to want the demon dead."

"I must prioritize Elena's safety," the spy immediately replied. "Until she can return to the palace, I will protect her."

Will longed to point out how the woman wouldn't be in harm's way while under the lord's roof given her lack of attention, yet he didn't believe Finn would budge on the subject. *Perhaps that's part of why he shared a few details about his past with me, so I would understand how he is bound to his master and can't leave.*

It sounded like the most probable reason for the man's stubbornness. After releasing a sigh and accepting the rejection, he raised his eyes to the sky and ventured a final comment. "When the demon is defeated and King Syrus' mind is free, I hope we can meet again to talk without worrying about the world."

Whether or not his words resonated with the Nim-Valan didn't matter to him, just that he made it clear he considered the two friends. Finn never addressed the comment before they moved inside shortly after.

Coura continued dozing when he returned, so he inquired about Elena's condition and decided a final assessment couldn't hurt. The spy led him to her quarters where they found Yukin visiting, but the woman declined any sort of physical evaluation, claiming the wound healed and that was that. Nobody pressed for her to accept, so he abandoned the attempt.

*I suppose all that's left to do is plan for our departure tomorrow*, he thought during the walk back to his and Coura's room. The idea of leaving hadn't weighed on his heart until that moment when he realized that would be his last time in the inner circle, specifically his last time around Finn and Yukin. *I know I don't belong here, but it's still bittersweet. Maybe one day Asteom and Nim-Vala can establish an alliance that welcomes people between the kingdoms. How far off is such a dream?*

His friend sat up and rubbed her eyes when he entered alone, went to the window, and leaned against its sill to enjoy what limited sunlight poured in. "Good morning."

"It's not morning," came her grumble, which spurred a smile.

"Good afternoon then."

She shot him an unimpressed look before covering a wide yawn. "Is everything the same?"

"Yes. No news from the royal estate."

"When do you plan on departing?" she asked next after throwing aside the blankets to rise and stretch her arms upward. "It would be better if we leave as soon as possible."

Will refrained from chuckling at how Finn gave the same insight earlier. Instead, he agreed and mentioned slipping out in the morning. That seemed to satisfy his friend, who peered around the room for a minute before joining him in front of the window.

"How likely is it I can get my clothes back? I shouldn't wander around in the uniform of a Nim-Valan lord's servant."

"That's a fair point. I'll ask Finn when he stops by." Considering how he would soon never see the spy again dampened his mood, though he hadn't meant to make the sentiment so obvious.

Coura studied him for a moment. "Are you not ready to go?"

"It's not… I don't know."

"You're going to miss them," she stated in a sympathetic manner and with a fitting smile for reassurance. "There's nothing wrong with that."

For some reason, admitting the truth made him blush. "They're our enemy, aren't they? I killed others during the fighting along the border, and I'll probably do that again when we go back. Why did I even help them? Why do I want to…"

He became so fixated on his mixed emotions that a pinch in the arm from his friend startled him into jumping and recoiling from her. When she laughed at his reaction, he scowled while rubbing the afflicted skin.

"What was that for?"

"They're your friends, aren't they?"

He tentatively nodded.

"Why not fight for them the way you fought for me, or the rest of Asteom?"

When he continued staring at her instead of responding, she stepped back, put her hands on her hips, and frowned.

"I can see you made a positive impression on Finn, the lord's son, and the queen. You were also staying in a town near the border, right? Do you want to protect those people?"

"Of course."

"Then strive to bring peace between our kingdoms. Lupin's involvement needs to be stopped, but imagine the potential when he's gone. I doubt these people will fully accept mages or magic. They might refuse an alliance because of the conflict and paranoia. Still, you showed it's possible to forge a bond through understanding. Don't ever forget that when you remember them."

This time, he nodded with confidence. "I'll try."

Another yawn from Coura drew the discussion to a close. She went to sit on the bed while Will picked up what items he left lying around and outlined their journey back to the border. Just when she brought up supplies, a knock sounded at the door before Finn slipped inside with the usual food for dinner.

"Are you prepared to depart in the morning?" the spy asked once the two dove into their meals.

"I think so," Will answered and took a bite of the warm sandwich in his hand. The Nim-Valan's next words nearly caused him to choke on the food.

"Our bags are in the kitchen to grab on the way out. I asked the cook to prepare enough for at least a week, so we won't starve."

"You're planning on joining us?" Coura asked before Will could compose himself.

The spy averted his eyes by glancing out the window. "Is that a problem?"

She shrugged but didn't press the subject.

Will felt it would be inappropriate at that moment to express his surprise and relief since neither of his friends seemed to feel the same, though he made a mental note to tell the Nim-Valan when the two could be alone.

# Venturing Alone

yron had no expectations for Will's return and told himself not to put too much faith in the herbalist for that reason. Although he believed in the young man's determination, he also understood the risks, which led him to keep his hopes realistic. That allowed him to not dwell on the subject or waste his time worrying about the future. On the other hand, when he and Clearshot spotted Will, Coura, and Finn surrounded by several people, including Casner and both assistant generals, he wasn't sure what to do.

His feet slowed to a stop as he contemplated whether or not to insert himself in the ongoing discussion. Meanwhile, his friend held no such restrain. Clearshot strolled right into the group, waved, and began chatting about their return.

*Does he ever stop to think about whether or not he's wanted in a meeting?* Byron wondered and rolled his eyes before moving to stand beside the soldier.

"We've been on the road for five days," he caught Will explaining. "Traveling is much easier when there's no rain to turn the earth into mud."

"I can imagine," Clearshot added. He kept quiet after, allowing the general to pick up the conversation.

"If you're in shape for a debriefing, I'd like to discuss your observations in a private setting."

All three nodded, so Casner addressed Byron next.

"Would you mind bringing Commander Evern with you when you join us?"

"I'll go fetch him now."

With that, their circle broke apart. Clearshot followed him toward the Yeluthians' spot in the camp before excusing himself, leaving Byron to locate and inform the commander of the impromptu meeting. Evern didn't show any surprise at the request nor his daughter's return, which seemed odd given what the two learned recently.

*I should make time to have that conversation with her*, he noted as they headed for the general's tent. *Her insight will no doubt help us understand the entire scenario, but we should keep it a private matter. I anticipate she wants it that way.*

The pair entered to find the four and Mattais sitting in a casual manner, prompting them to do the same.

"Now that we have everyone here, can you summarize your time in the Nim-Valan capital city?" Casner began without looking at anybody in particular.

Byron expected Will to do the talking; however, Finn cleared his throat to signal his intent to shoulder that burden. The spy shared how King Syrus' mentality wore away, leading one of the man's wives to investigate the ruler's odd behavior. That had been when Will arrived, and the two soon discovered how Coura had been kept within the royal estate in order to lure the original demon into the capital. He finished by explaining their assumption regarding Lupin's involvement, mainly the being's hope to murder the king.

"Did you pick up on any clues related to this plan?" the general asked Coura after.

She shrugged. "An amateur translator mentioned Soirée's name, and Syrus sounded upset his advisor wasn't present. Otherwise, I have no idea what they were saying."

"That's in line with what we know about demons," Byron added. "I wonder how much involvement the creature had if its influence is already affecting Nim-Vala's leader."

They contemplated that notion for a minute before Evern changed subjects.

"In any case, that plan failed. The demon acting as an advisor is not in the inner circle, correct? Our next priority should be finding it before it can retaliate against us."

Casner, Mattais, and Finn expressed their agreement, then the former provided an opportunity for the spy, Will, or Coura to share additional information or suspicions. When nobody did, the general dismissed them all for the evening. Byron didn't plan on staying since he knew he would see the herbalist and his former student later, and he noticed Finn linger to converse with the general and Mattais alone.

Immediately, the Yeluthian commander led Coura away, leaving him to guide Will back to the fire once they grabbed lunch. There, they found Clearshot and Marcus, who both rose to welcome their companion with pats on the back and questions regarding the northern country. While the young man repeated the update, Byron savored his meal before excusing himself for his afternoon meditation and scouting sessions.

*

*Where is everybody?* Byron thought as he returned to the familiar sight of his bedroll beside his designated bonfire. He expected others to be gathered around given the lack of light as the sun set beyond the woods; however, he found he was the only person present at the moment.

After his uneventful patrol, he ate an early dinner with a few mages he came to know over the years before deciding a walk would help the food settle and wear him out. He fully prepared for additional conversation before sleep, yet the area was empty. With a yawn, he positioned himself close to the flames, wrapped his blanket around his shoulders, and became lost in the dancing crimson whisps. His mind cleared as he did so until multiple pairs of footsteps sounded from behind, drawing his attention.

"You're all alone?" came Clearshot's voice before he spotted the soldier approaching with Marcus. "Did something happen?"

Byron huffed a laugh. "I'm just learning to enjoy my free time."

His friend dropped to sit on his right and slapped him on the back. "That's the spirit!"

"There's not much taking place right now," Marcus pointed out and occupied the space on Clearshot's other side.

"I suppose that's better than too much activity."

Before any of them could broach a new subject, a woman's laugh reached them from across the fire, and Will came into view alongside a young light mage Byron recognized as one of the herbalist's closest friends. The duo requested to join them, which amused him given their casual relationships with one another. Marcus evidently knew the light mage's name, identifying her as Clara, and she mentioned what work went on in the medical station. During the update, Coura slipped into their circle around the flames without more than a brief greeting, and Grace arrived shortly after with Dianne.

*Mere minutes ago, I sat by myself,* Byron reflected with a smile while he listened to the Yeluthian's idea to utilize the Nim-Valan prisoners, which he was already aware of thanks to the general. *They say there's never a moment when peace can't be disturbed in a war, but I won't complain about this type of interruption.*

"The captured enemy troops are already restrained," Clearshot pointed out to bring his attention back to the discussion. "Is this a precaution?"

"In a way," Grace replied without hiding her optimism. "The less of a connection they have to their master, the better, yet I see more potential if their minds are not clouded. For example, they may point us toward the missing ancestral weapon or their leader's location."

"I'll be assisting with Finn to translate their thoughts," Will added.

Byron hadn't had an opinion on the method of utilizing the Yeluthian's ability, mainly because he trusted her not to abuse her power, so he kept quiet. Meanwhile, Coura spoke for the first time since she sat down.

"Where is Finn anyway?"

Will raised his eyes in thought with a contemplative hum, but it was Marcus who answered.

"He's staying near General Casner's tent. The two discussed options for him since he plans on being around from now on."

"I see."

"That reminds me," Clearshot interjected with a glance at the assistant general. "Are we going to sit around and wait for the Nim-Valans to strike us here, or do we have another strategy?"

"I'm not sure. To be honest, it's difficult to predict our next steps when so much is up in the air. The enemy can heal, but we outnumber them now. Then there are the creatures surrounding us beyond the trees. Those are more harmful, and the demon…"

His eyes found Coura after the pause, and Byron caught her look away with a frown.

"Perhaps the captured soldiers will reveal something useful," Dianne began to ease the building tension. "Who knows. At least we're able to build our strength and prepare our defenses."

Grace shook her head with a slight smile. "That is optimistic."

"Why shouldn't we try thinking positively? Our leaders are carrying the weight of our lives. The least we can do is trust in them and hope for the best."

"I suppose so."

"The trouble is what we can't control," they heard Will mutter. "King Syrus, the demons, and then…"

Byron leaned back to stare at the sky when the young man fell silent. "The Nim-Valans are responsible for their own kingdom. We're only involved because of their advisor's manipulation. Perhaps their ruler and the men we're fighting will return to their normal selves once the creature's influence fades."

"What if that's not the case?" Coura asked in a neutral tone, cutting through the calm evening.

Byron turned to stare at his former student and found her studying him. "Even if there are consequences for allying with a demon, Asteom cannot meddle in their affairs. Why do you ask?"

"I'm just curious," she replied and crossed her arms. "Given the previous attempts to help when an alliance was on the line, I wondered how far we would be expected to extend our reach."

"That's a completely different matter, one to discuss when the current conflict concludes and the border is safe again."

"Should we be worried about backlash from the demon's death?" Marcus asked Coura before she had a chance to respond.

"How should I know?" came the expected retort.

"What about the first demon and former high priest?"

*Is he going to confront her about that now?* Byron thought with interest as he watched her narrow her eyes. *Not all of us are aware of what the being shared. I'm not even certain she knows we interacted with it.*

"From my understanding, Hendal used Soirée's power, and it seems like that's true for Syrus and Lupin," she answered in a less aggressive tone than he expected. "Other than their sanity, they might not be effected."

"The only danger is if a human bonds with a demon then," Clearshot pointed out.

"At least our enemy's leader is around here and not farther into Nim-Vala."

Grace's voice reflected her concern as she added to the conversation. "What about the other being? Will it continue to stay uninvolved?"

Coura released a weary sigh when all eyes returned to her. "I already told you what I know."

*Not everything*, Byron longed to comment. It took all his self-control not to grumble the words; however, part of him wasn't surprised when someone else pushed the point.

"What if you were harmed?" the assistant general pressed. "Would it not come to your aid?"

"She didn't when I was kidnapped. Besides, our focus should be on Lupin."

"Are you sure that's wise?" Will interjected. "Ignoring a threat on our doorstep might hurt us later."

"Trust me. She won't become involved."

"What makes you so sure?"

Coura didn't reply.

"Sorry, but I'm not about to leave my friend's life in the hands of a demon."

"What's that supposed to mean?" she countered.

Will lowered his gaze to stare at his hands, prompting her to slowly look from person to person. Everybody seemed to mirror the herbalist or avert their eyes in some way. When she glanced at Byron, he managed not to hide from her, though he instinctively dipped his chin a bit.

"I should have known," she mumbled after while glancing off to her left.

He decided to clear the air when the others remained quiet. "The original demon told us the Nim-Valans captured you and were likely traveling to the inner circle."

"Did she say why?"

He nodded. "Commander Evern was present as well."

That caused her to pinch the bridge of her nose. "Not him too."

During the resulting pause, Byron noticed Grace, Dianne, and Clara looking between them without comprehension. *Those three were not informed of what the creature mentioned. I shared the details with Will, Marcus, and Clearshot, in addition to Casner. I'm sure Coura won't be pleased with us learning that.*

Because of the thought, he fully expected her to snap at him for prying and dismiss the subject altogether; however, she sat straighter before addressing those seated around the fire in an unbothered manner.

"Our main goal is to stop Lupin and the Nim-Valans under his control. We can talk about Soirée when that's finished."

Byron, Clearshot, and Marcus all began responding at once, but the assistant general's words sounded passionate enough to catch her attention.

"Is that why you hid the truth about the former high priest? You're going to disregard that demon's death to protect yourself?"

Coura glanced at Byron. "How much did Soirée tell you?"

"The being mentioned how his death brought about the other's because of the bond they shared, which is the same as yours."

Grace gasped and mumbled something he couldn't discern, so he ignored her. On the other hand, Coura's eyes shifted to assess the Yeluthian and the rest of their group. Her expression never changed as she did so, nor when she shared the truth after.

"I followed Soirée into the Ghurun mountains, and she already had Terran and Hendal waiting. Before I knew what she was up to, she showed Terran how to bond his soul to Hendal's, allowing him to grow in power. When we tried escaping, Hendal took his own life so I could learn how deep the spell goes. Terran collapsed and died too, which Soirée assumed would happen, meaning such a bond effects both lives."

"The demon doesn't know how to destroy the spell then," Byron commented against the twisting of his gut upon hearing the full explanation.

"I told her she can remain close enough to study it if she doesn't become involved in the conflict. It sounds like she isn't inclined to come into contact with Lupin, so that's one positive."

"Is that why the creature didn't pursue you into the inner circle?" Will asked next.

She nodded. "If I had to guess, she assumed he would be using her in some way."

"Finn and I figured as much."

"I don't understand," Clearshot snapped, practically interrupting the younger man. "All we can do wait for the demon to find a solution? What about the danger to you? What if you're hurt and it intervenes, or it dies and you…"

"This is exactly why I hid the truth," Coura replied without a hint of frustration. "You're all distracted because you're worried about me when you don't need to be. Lupin and the Nim-Valans present a greater risk. Besides, I hold some power over Soirée because of our bond."

"Don't you dare suggest-"

"I'm just stating a fact," she clarified while rising. "You're the ones who are snooping for information."

Nobody could deny that, so they remained silent while she procured her blankets and pillow, dusted them off, then addressed the group again.

"Since Evern's aware, I'll make sure he hears the entire story too."

With that, Coura wandered through the camp, leaving Byron to consider her behavior further.

*The only times I sensed irritation were when we prodded for answers. I want to question her about her mentality and make sure she's stable, yet I would bet she'd scold me for doing so.*

The rest of the group mumbled various thoughts on the subject before lying down to rest for the evening. He did the same, though his mind soon started reflecting on his former student's past with the demon, including how she broke down to him after sealing the being below the planet's surface.

*I could never forget how I held her while she wept*, he recalled and gripped his blanket tighter. *She mentioned being ready to die if it meant ending the creature's life and felt torn because it supposedly spared her. Neither of us could have predicted how accurate that decision was. Is that why she's so calm? Does dying not bother her anymore because she learned the truth?*

In his heart, Byron knew the answer to that question, yet he still refused to accept losing her to the demon's spell. His mind etched possible solutions to sever the bond in response, keeping him awake into the early morning.

***

When Coura stirred the morning following her confession to her friends, she readjusted herself to savor what warmth the blankets provided. Evern already rose and began feeding the dwindling fire, and Lavine sat across from her while eating his breakfast. Neither made much noise, which she appreciated; however, she wasn't certain if they were quiet to avoid waking her

327

or because of their naturally swift movements. For the time being, she longed to enjoy the peaceful atmosphere.

Her father and Yeluthian friend reacted similarly to the others who heard the truth the previous evening, which she expected. Both questioned her about her decision to remain in the fight, allow Soirée to linger nearby, and what threat the demon posed until she convinced them nothing would happen as long as Lupin and the Nim-Valans remained the main concern.

*Their grudge with the source of opposing energy keeps their anger focused on Soirée instead of making them worry about me. I prefer that to being fawned over because of my connection to her. Either way, I'm going to have more eyes on me.*

That had been her main point of contention: If she became a distraction, they would be putting their lives in danger while risking their goal to stop Lupin.

*It can't be helped now*, she admitted while sitting up and rubbing her eyes.

"Good morning," Evern said as soon as did so. "Hopefully we did not create too much noise. It is rather early."

"It's fine. I'm usually up by now."

Within the next hour, the sun fully rose, she had a full stomach, and she felt prepared for the day ahead. The three talked about the Yeluthians' patrol route, leading her to inquire about joining them, but an unexpected guest approached their fire before she received an answer.

"Good morning," came Mattais' voice while footsteps approached off to her right.

Immediately, her father was on his feet. "Assistant General, to what do we owe the pleasure?"

The sudden reaction caused the man to laugh. "Nothing urgent, Commander. Actually, the general sent me to fetch your daughter."

Coura raised an eyebrow at him when he turned to face her. "Me?"

"That's right. General Casner wishes to speak with you when you have a free moment."

Unlike Evern, she stood with less enthusiasm and brushed off what dirt collected on her pants. Only when she felt decently prepared did she tell the man to lead the way, which he did without another word. Part of her expected her father to insert himself into the discussion by offering to join; however, he remained silent as she followed Mattais straight into his superior's tent.

"Sir, I have Coura Galdwin," the assistant general announced upon entering.

"Both of you may take a seat," came the gruff voice she'd become familiar with. Over the years, it didn't grate on her nerves as much unless he addressed her specifically.

She lowered herself beside Mattais while the general finished rummaging through a sack and joined them with a rolled-up piece of parchment in one hand.

"Let's get this business started," Casner began.

*It's just us three?* she wondered when he paused to scratch his head.

"As you're aware, a demon not affiliated with Nim-Vala is lingering around our camp. Master Byron mentioned this and that he and Commander Evern communicated with it regarding your kidnapping. This creature was at the center of our conflict in Verona's southern field, correct?"

She nodded when he waited for a response. "That's right."

"Such a threat is a risk to our mission, as well as our lives," he continued and narrowed his eyes at her. "I recall you defending your relationship with that being."

"I wouldn't say I was defending her."

When he shook his head in an impatient manner, Coura sensed how he tried not to snap at her.

"Not the demon itself, but more like your ability to sense where it is and what it's doing."

*How much does he actually know about my bond with Soirée? It sounds like he's repeating what Byron or Evern attempted to explain. Is he interested in utilizing the connection somehow?*

"What are you getting at?" she decided to ask and looked between the general and his assistant.

"I won't pretend I understand your magic," he prefaced after, confirming her suspicion. "In my opinion, all business with demons and their power is evil and should not be sought out. That's why I called you here to organize a private assignment away from Asteom."

Coura felt her eyebrows raise at the sudden proposal. "A private assignment? What do you mean?"

The man leaned back and let his eyes wander around the tent while he answered. "From what I gathered, your business with the demons is a separate matter from our conflict with Nim-Vala. The only exception is their advisor's influence over the soldiers' minds. We already have the Yeluthian ambassador working on a solution, but based on our previous conflict regarding the former high priest, eliminating the source would surely free their minds."

"You want me to target Lupin?"

"Would it be easier because of your connection to the first demon?"

Although she wanted to outright dismiss the assumption, she took a minute to consider what she could do in her position. *If I try finding him, would Soirée follow? Even if I manage to locate him, would he kill me or wait for her? He's probably aware of our bond's depth based on his decision not to return to the inner circle, but I never got the impression they want to fight each other. Unlike Terran, Lupin's strategizing has been more manipulative. I'm mostly curious how Soirée will react since she doesn't seem interested in confronting him.*

"If it helps, we have a map of the Nim-Valans' previous camping sites," Mattais added and pointed to the paper in his superior's hand. "It's from a few weeks ago, but I doubt it changed that much."

The general unrolled the parchment, revealing a crude map with the aforementioned markings.

"This is a copy, so you can take it with you," he shared as her eyes scanned the image.

"What if I can't find Lupin?"

When she returned her attention to the man, he wore a calm yet stern expression.

"Even luring one demon away will keep the being uninvolved with Asteom."

*That's his actual goal*, she realized in that instance. *Casner shouldn't justify doing whatever he wants simply because he can claim demons are to blame. Nim-Vala doesn't feel the same or understand, and they would have even more reason to hate Asteom if we killed because of magic. They don't comprehend the danger they're in, so our forces must keep the demons separate from Asteom, and even Yeluthia.*

The considerable weight that fell on her shoulders after that assessment left her wondering if she should act alone or confer with her friends. Ultimately, their concerned reactions pushed her in one direction.

"I'm fine leaving the camp and attempting to draw the demons together," she admitted and procured the map. "I can't promise this will work or that I won't die, but I'm willing to try."

Casner nodded. "I figured as much. You're free to depart whenever you'd like, but this is a private assignment."

With the plan laid out, she accepted their well wishes and exited the tent.

*

Throughout the remainder of the morning, Coura considered when she would leave and what to bring. She selected several items normally used for camping, food, and extra clothing and dropped them off at the Yeluthians' empty spot to avoid raising suspicion from her friends. Fortunately, she finished her preparations by the time anybody pulled her aside for a conversation. She fully expected most, if not all, of her companions to corner her at some point given her confession the previous evening, and it began with Will when she visited the medical station for bandages and a healing salve. The herbalist greeted her like normal until they were alone.

"I'm sorry for not noticing something was wrong," he began and lowered his gaze. "I should have reached out when you recovered in Nim-Vala. It's no wonder the advisor and King Syrus planned to manipulate you."

"That's all in the past now."

"What if they target you here? As long as Lupin is free to continue leading the enemy troops, we don't know what he's capable of."

Any further attempts to reassure him fell on deaf ears. She sensed his compassion for the northerners, which didn't surprise her given his selfless personality, yet the conversation returned to her struggles against their kind. This only ended when an older woman called him over to assist with some task. Her friend apologized again, promised to help however he could, and left her at the entrance.

Whoever she ran into throughout the remainder of the day acted similarly, though she forced herself to be patient. Clearshot and Marcus inquired about Soirée's intentions during lunch and vowed to not give up on freeing her before they departed for their afternoon assignments. Grace and Dianne arrived before she could leave that area, which led to the soldier asking dozens of questions regarding the existence of demons and what her bond to one meant. Meanwhile, her Yeluthian friend projected more pity than anyone.

*She's probably recalling how Soirée led me away from my parents and lineage*, Coura thought as Grace went on to promise they would free her from the being. *I shouldn't be surprised everybody's focus is on the past instead of the future. Maybe leaving is for the best so they aren't distracted by that.*

By the time she broke away from them, she wanted nothing more than to be alone and wandered through the woods for a spot where she wouldn't be bothered. It took several attempts to avoid what scouts patrolled the area, but she eventually settled on a hill overlooking part of the trees. The open space tempted her into flying; however, she decided against it and lied on her back instead to let her eyes scan the clouds above.

*Their behavior isn't going to change*, she admitted to herself after a moment to reflect on the day up to that point. *I don't think they'll ever understand how much I desire to rid the world of her, even if it means sacrificing my life. If I mention that, I'll never hear the end of their concerns. I'm not planning on giving up, but Soirée isn't the main issue. I don't want their pity; I want everyone to work together to stop Lupin and bring peace to the border.*

She then wondered if departing from the camp would actually hinder her friends' resolve since they would likely attempt to search for her. Just when she considered telling one person or leaving a note behind, a familiar chuckle sounded from off to her right, drawing her attention.

"You found my hiding spot," came Byron's voice before she caught him slipping out from the brush.

"Your spot?"

He casually approached as she sat up. "It's perfect for meditating away from the main camp. I try visiting every afternoon before dinner to unwind."

"I can see why. If the weather were warmer, I'd fall asleep right now. In fact, I should bring a blanket next time."

"Don't get too comfortable," he warned and dropped beside her to observe their surroundings. "I'll kick you out if you disrupt my session."

Coura huffed a laugh but didn't argue. Instead, the pair sat in silence for a few minutes to simply savor the peaceful atmosphere. She nearly let down her guard enough to not suspect him of approaching the subject she faced all day; however, a sidelong glance let her know he intended to discuss it.

"How are you doing?" he began without a hint of emotion, as if he hoped to assess her honest reaction.

The question caught her off guard, and she looked away with a chuckle.

"What's wrong?"

"You're the only person who asked me that," she shared and let her eyes wander upward again. "I'm managing."

"I take it you've been pestered enough for today."

She shrugged yet didn't give the obvious answer. Still, her former mentor read every movement.

"We will find a way to break the demon's spell," he told her with a hint of sympathy.

"I know."

"Then what's bothering you?"

"I'm tired of everyone pitying me." The statement hung in the air for a second before she felt compelled to look at him and continue. "I dealt with Soirée for the majority of my life, so I trust her not to interfere with what we're doing here. Why can't we focus on Lupin and the Nim-Valans? They're the main threat."

Byron's lips curved into an amused smile. "We all care about you, Coura. If any of your friends were in this predicament, wouldn't you want to save them?"

"That's not the point," she muttered against a blush. "I wish they would trust me to take care of myself."

"Well, you did just get kidnapped."

Her eyes narrowed at his jab, but she let him continue with a more serious response.

"Plenty of factors are at play beyond your involvement. There's the demon, the unknown aspects of this bonding spell, and outside threats that could kill either one of you. I'm sure everybody trusts you, but how can we sit by and pretend the rest of the world will let you be?"

Coura stared down at her hands. *I suppose he makes sense.*

"What I'm worried about beyond that is your mentality," he shared after as he crossed his arms. "I believe you're determined, but I don't want you to think there's only one path forward."

When he didn't elaborate, she knew he hoped she would figure out the other options on her own.

*If I'm being honest with myself, Soirée and this spell aren't preoccupying my mind yet. I hope I don't need to address her for a while because I'm not sure what I'll end up doing. Byron's right though. I shouldn't assume I need to die in order for this to stop.*

They remained on the hill until sunset after she thanked him for the reassurance. Being the ever-studious master mage, he avoided conversation and appeared to be meditating while she went back to relaxing with some attention to the energy in her center. In the end, she decided against informing anybody of her assignment from Casner since she figured the man would share his reasoning with others at a later time.

The two returned to join their friends for dinner and brief conversation, then Coura left for the Yeluthians' area to grab what items she left there. No one questioned her decision to go, yet she sensed they didn't expect her to spend another night away from them. On the other hand, her father and Lavine merely asked about the bag when she appeared and believed her when she said she forgot it on accident. Nothing hinted at a departure, so they soon drifted off. She hardly slept before naturally stirring during the early morning hours. With nothing holding her back, she collected her pack, donned the additional clothing, and exited the camp without a sound.

# Spying on the Enemy

Grace fully expected to be uncomfortable during her time among the Asteom soldiers due to living outdoors and sleeping on the ground; however, as the days passed, she soon grew accustomed to the adjustment. Her stiff muscles no longer bothered her enough to make note of, and the bland taste of the regular porridge didn't seem as off putting when she considered how it ebbed her hunger. Best of all, she never felt useless among the humans, who always acted respectful and appreciative of her work.

She considered this one morning as she sat around the bonfire her group of friends claimed. General Casner had her contact the king's council and offer an update on their situation earlier, then she was dismissed for the day.

*I hardly spent any energy on that*, she noted with a hint of vanity. *Perhaps practicing extends the duration of my goddess gift. This is definitely the most I have used it, and I still possess plenty to spare.*

Before she could commit to monitoring her progress going forward, footsteps from behind alerted her of Dianne's return from the mess area. The soldier dropped to sit cross-legged beside her with a huff and handed over one of the two, steaming bowls in each hand.

"What rotten timing," the woman began to initiate a conversation. "I swear everybody in camp planned on getting their food at the same time."

Grace offered a sympathetic smile. "We are not in a hurry, and the weather is quite warm."

"It's easy to be patient when you're not elbowing people out of your way."

She chuckled at her guard's comment before the two dug into their meals.

As they ate, Dianne brought up several observations she found worthwhile to mention, including how the supplies had been reorganized, the addition of an extra group monitoring the perimeter, and her intent to inquire about joining the latter during the evenings. Her enthusiasm with that final point piqued Grace's interest.

"You sound eager to be on patrol," she told the woman after setting her empty bowl aside. "Has guarding me become less exciting?"

"No, my lady. That responsibility is the highest honor I could hope for. I just wish to serve however I can, even in my free time."

After a pause, Grace ventured a guess as to the reasoning behind the soldier's attitude. "You enjoy being here with your comrades. Is that why you long to work alongside them as often as you can?"

"I suppose so," Dianne admitted without hiding her surprise with the guess. "Of course, my main job is unique and more important than the regular tasks around the camp."

"Please do not exhaust yourself. This fight is not over, and I could not bear to see you hurt. I worry enough about my other friends."

The woman studied her for a moment, spurring a blush she attempted to hide by glancing in the opposite direction. Then, she heard her guard's voice in a lighthearted tone.

"I appreciate your concern and promise to be careful. You know, there's another reason for my extra effort."

Grace returned her gaze to the soldier and raised an eyebrow. "Really?"

"I can see how each person makes a visible change. In Verona, the job focuses on maintaining peace. Here, we rely on each other in order to survive. Even fetching water or walking around the perimeter to scout contributes to our overall success. I guess it's a matter of perspective."

"That makes sense."

"You're helping in a way only you can too, so supporting you puts us closer to our goal."

After that statement, Dianne plucked up their bowls and departed to return them to the mess area, leaving Grace alone with her thoughts again. The relaxed atmosphere eased her into a meditative state she worried would tire her enough to nap until a familiar voice from across the flames had her straightening.

Will caught her eye first since he had been the person speaking, and she waved when he approached with Marcus and their new companion named Finn. She had noticed the man hanging around her friend and the general on separate occasions ever since their return from the Nim-Valan capital city but never spoke with him. He usually appeared uninterested in whatever they discussed, which led her to avoid attempting conversation.

"You're here all by yourself?" the assistant general asked as they took seats off to her left.

"Dianne went to return our dishes from lunch."

He nodded once then crossed his arms. "Should we wait for her before discussing business regarding the Nim-Valan prisoners?"

The reminder sent a jolt through Grace's body, as if somebody had poked her in the back with a sharp object, and she instinctively leaned forward to show her interest in the subject. "Is it urgent? She should be back soon and may offer insight, but we do not need to if time is of the essence."

Her physical reaction and verbal response must have made her intrigue obvious, for Will and Marcus laughed a second later.

"He just caught us up on the situation," the former explained, as if reassuring her. "Finn can translate better than me, but we'll both be present when you use your ability."

"You just want to snoop," the assistant general added while rolling his eyes.

Will rubbed the back of his neck without denying the accusation. "That's all we needed to share."

"When do you plan on visiting them?" she ventured after.

The three shared a look before Marcus addressed her again. "We were going to ask you since you'll be using magic and have been assisting General Casner."

During the resulting pause when Grace contemplated a time, Dianne slipped beside her and released a weary sigh.

"Already back to work?" the woman teased with a playful smirk.

She frowned in response. "You were the one who mentioned accepting additional responsibilities around camp."

"I suppose so. Now, catch me up on what you discussed."

"There's not much to tell," Will prefaced before repeating his and Marcus' previous points. "Whenever Grace feels prepared, we can be ready to translate."

Dianne faced her then. "And what did you say?"

Instead of saying that she hadn't given an answer, she closed her eyes and bowed her head to assess her remaining energy. What pride in her power she felt earlier steadily dwindled when she recalled how much effort monitoring the prisoners took, and how she would need to maintain a sharp mind in order to repeat what they share.

Although she longed to act tough so they would begin sooner, she opened her eyes and shook her head. "If I did not speak with Aaron and his council this morning, I would be willing to assist right away. My energy is not depleted, but it would be wise to make the attempt with as much as I can build."

"That's understandable," Marcus replied without a hint of disappointment. "I didn't expect to do anything today on such short notice. When do you think you'll be ready?"

"Perhaps tomorrow afternoon."

"Isn't that fairly soon?" Will asked, though he appeared to be the only person surprised by her estimation.

She smiled to ease his concern. "The Nim-Valan soldiers will not be far enough away to drain my power as rapidly, which allows me to focus on their words and what emotions they project. Repeating them is what I fear can take the most time."

The assistant general nodded and addressed the entire group next. "Shall we plan on meeting here tomorrow after lunch then?"

Everybody voiced their agreement, and after discussing a few details related to the prisoners' location, they concluded their business for the day.

*

Unlike her previous experience surveying the captured northerners, Grace became inexplicably nervous as she sat against a tree trunk near the men's location. Her four companions remained standing on all sides of their secluded section of foliage, which kept them hidden from any prying eyes. Of course, the guards on patrol were aware of their intentions thanks to Marcus' update, yet she had no idea how much of their plan he shared.

*It is my responsibility to focus*, she told herself as soon as she got comfortable. *I must avoid overusing my ability by needlessly making mistakes or not remembering the information I pick up.*

A few deep breaths helped calm her body and mind enough to disconnect from the world, allowing her to activate her goddess gift. The bright, warm energy swirled around her, and she took pleasure in its comforting embrace before extending her mind toward her targets. Just like her previous session, Grace let her presence float over the Nim-Valans in order to observe their mentalities before slipping closer. Those she witnessed while using the spell appeared like flickering flames of a candle as they wavered, inflated, and dwindled based on the person's emotions and attitude. Only when she felt comfortable attempting to spark a thought did she begin selecting enemy soldiers and linger close enough to project various words or images. Nothing out of the ordinary came about as a result, leading her to retract her mind for a break.

As soon as she returned to her body, she blinked to adjust her vision and took a deep breath. Will sat beside her while Marcus, Finn, and Dianne assumed positions to keep watch. All four turned to her when she raised her arms upward to stretch her back and draw their attention.

"How did it go?" her guard asked before the others could.

"About the same as last time. I did not understand what I heard, but I could sense their boredom and impatience with the situation."

When she repeated what words she could remember, Finn confirmed they merely had to do with their curiosity about the weather, their imprisoners, or the length of time spent in captivity.

"Should I try pushing for responses using a list of words or visuals?" she ventured next. "It would be like whispering in their ears and listening for their reactions."

Her companions paused to contemplate her suggestion, then Marcus released a long, thoughtful hum, drawing their attention.

"I trust your ability to observe without sparking trouble," he prefaced. "With that being said, how likely is it they'll pick up on your pronunciation of Nim-Valan words?"

"I wonder the same," Finn added after.

Grace shook her head helplessly. "You have a point. Perhaps I will need to stick with images."

The others agreed, prompting them to discuss options for her to use that would be plain enough not to suspect her of influencing their minds and causing a scene. Ultimately, their main pair of visuals came down to a cloaked, pale figure meant to represent Lupin since she hadn't seen him before and the ancestral weapon.

*No human who has seen a golden blade would forget it, especially so soon.* She held onto that notion as the five wrapped up their brainstorming and let her return to her work.

As soon as her presence returned to the enemy soldiers, she honed in on a single man before projecting the sword first. She anticipated only those who knew about the item would react, which proved to be the case when he didn't respond and dismissed her image, so she moved on by switching to the demon.

Her hope had been to embellish the shadowy being with a hint of malice in order to spur more of a reaction; however, the thought of the creature was enough for the Nim-Valan. She sensed a frightened chill sweep over him, then silence. After a few seconds, all the fear and guilt he experienced caused her to retreat in order to avoid the surge of emotion.

*He is utterly terrified of his leader*, she realized once she could process his response. *His failure seems to be the reason for this. How much control did he have over his thoughts and actions while under the demon's influence?*

Grace filed the question away as she moved on to her next target and continued the process. Only a couple men recognized the ancestral weapon but associated it with Lupin, leading her to assume the golden blade lied with the main threat. On the other hand, every person reacted to the being's image in various ways. Some behaved like the first while many revered the figure, leading them to hope for a swift rescue in the near future. Their desire to be associated with it disgusted her enough to pull away lest they pick up on the emotion. Still, she continued her assignment until each Nim-Valan had been tested. The effort left her exhausted by the time she could return to her body and reflect on what she learned.

*Those who expect to be saved hinted at a hideout in a rocky section to the northeast. At least, I believe that is a hideout. I do not recall General Casner mentioning any sort of specific location where they have been staying.*

The strain caught up with her when she dismissed her ability, and she dropped her head into her hands, causing a couple of her friends to gasp. After a shuffling of feet where they presumably came closer, someone gently laid a hand on her back.

"I imagine you used most of your power?" came Will's voice. "Here, drink this."

She lifted her head enough to see him holding a vial filled with an emerald-colored liquid. Tentatively, she accepted the medicine and swallowed it before returning to her previous position.

"Clara worked with me to perfect this recipe," he went on to explain. "Believe it or not, most of the energy-boosting properties also contribute to the taste, like basil and rosemary, while the rest are too subtle to-"

"Perhaps we should let Lady Zelnar rest for a minute or two," Dianne interrupted.

Grace silently thanked the woman for her consideration. The hand on her back lifted as Will apologized for his eagerness and offered a sheepish chuckle before the sounds of shuffling signaled their movement. For a while, she waited for her body and mind to relax by savoring the quiet atmosphere disrupted only by hushed voices or chirping birds and insects. The natural noise lulled her into a near-sleep trance until she remembered where they were and that it was likely close to dinnertime. As if to punctuate that point, her stomach lightly rumbled.

*I knew what to expect when I volunteered my magic*, she reminded herself. *This discomfort is only temporary. I should not keep them waiting.*

With what energy she could muster, Grace raised her head, covered a yawn, then spent enough time blinking to clear her blurred vision. The ache in her center outweighed her hunger and the tightness building in her shoulders, yet Will's potion dulled part of the sensation.

"I am well enough to continue," she announced, though her tone didn't sound as confident as she hoped.

Despite that, her companions came over and sat in a circle so everybody could hear. The report she gave consisted of all her observations, as well as her opinions on the Nim-Valans' hideout. Marcus asked a few questions regarding the location but ultimately abandoned the subject when she couldn't give additional details.

"It would make sense for the enemy to bring the ancestral weapon back to their camp if it's a threat to their leader," he shared after. "It also stands to reason the demon would be hiding there at the moment."

"It's dangerous to assume that's where the advisor is," Finn added with a neutral expression.

The assistant general nodded yet stood his ground. "I can't imagine the being would be anywhere else except along the border. You, Will, and Coura confirmed it wasn't farther into Nim-Vala."

"The men also thought about their camp at the mention of the creature," Grace repeated and raised her chin a bit. "It felt as though they expected to be rescued, even if they feared punishment for being captured."

Finn didn't appear to believe her, but he kept silent, allowing Dianne to continue the conversation by addressing Marcus.

"Sir, I would venture to guess this is our best lead as to their leader's position and perhaps the weapon you're searching for. Why not send spies east along the border to scout for the enemy's camp?"

Grace and the rest of the group watched him close his eyes and pause to consider that option. Finally, he opened them, raised his gaze to the overcast sky, and replied.

"If it were my decision alone, I wouldn't take the risk. Our soldiers on patrol have yet to suggest the northerners are plotting an attack, so we would have time to try this again and hone in on a specific location before rushing into a fight. With that being said, unpredictability is a factor in battle. We may not have as much time as we hope."

"Spoken like a true assistant general," Will commented with a grin.

The comment had Marcus returning his eyes to their circle. "I should confer with General Casner and Assistant General Mattais."

"Would you like me to join you?" Grace felt the need to ask despite her weariness.

Her friend got to his feet and offered her a hand, which she accepted, prompting the others to rise as well. Only then did he answer her question.

"I should be able to remember what you reported, but thank you for the offer. I'd imagine you want to rest and eat to start building your strength."

She nodded and hoped the gesture didn't appear too desperate. *I am exhausted enough to sleep as soon as we return to our bonfire, but it will be much more satisfying on a full stomach. Of that I am sure.*

***

During her first day of hiking north, Coura didn't know what to expect and kept her guard up at all times. Part of her worried about an ambush, either from the enemy troops or a demon, yet none came. Not even the beasts that stalked her allies from beyond the camp's perimeter paid her much attention. She thought it was odd until she considered they likely obeyed only their master's command.

*As long as I'm not in the way or actively attempting to disrupt them, perhaps they don't see me as a threat,* she reflected that evening once she settled into a well-protected nook in a rocky section of the terrain. *I could care less about them now. Finding Soirée is my main goal, and I'm sure she'll appear soon if I search for Lupin. Would he still be on the border or return to Nim-Vala's capital city?*

The next morning, she set off after studying the map Casner offered her. For the most part, the sites to avoid appeared spread out enough so their scouts wouldn't overlap with each other, which left a slim trail she could maneuver through. The uneven, hilly path soon evened out, allowing trees to occupy most of the space and make her more alert. Nothing brought about danger through the afternoon, so she found a suitable spot to rest that evening.

Two more days of similar traveling conditions piqued her curiosity when she considered the lack of northerners.

*I should have at least seen a scout,* she reflected while scanning her map during the late morning. *They did mention Lupin condensed his forces to strike as a single unit, but I didn't believe he would completely abandon all other parts of the border. Then again, he would be cautious if he actually cared about Nim-Vala. He only desires entertainment by testing his power and manipulation.*

With a sigh, she rolled up the parchment, returned it to her bag, and rose to stretch her legs. The peacefulness of the environment helped ease whatever concern followed her out of the camp, though she refused to relax enough to be surprised by an enemy or demonic creature. In fact, as she continued hiking, she acknowledged how free she felt away from the confines of her comrades.

*I'm not pleased to be surrounded by the woods, but this is a journey set at my own pace. Nobody is here to tell me what to do or order me to behave a certain way. It's not that I hate fighting alongside others either. I don't know how to describe it.*

Her mind lingered on that subject until slight rustling in the bushes ahead had her halting to throw herself behind the nearest tree trunk.

*An enemy wouldn't naturally move so quietly unless they saw me already,* she noted with a hand on the hilt of her sword. *It might be one of the beasts, but would it reveal itself to their prey? What about a coordinated attack?*

While her thoughts naturally raced over various possibilities, she kept her breathing slow and muscles ready to spring into action; however, the dark energy in her center recognized the presence that emerged through the shared bond a second later. Her body relaxed as she stepped away from her wooden shield to find Soirée standing as unbothered as ever in front of the bushes.

"What are you doing here?" Coura began without hiding her displeasure.

The demon tilted her head yet didn't appear to be her normal, playful self. "I should be asking you that, Dear One. Are you aware you crossed into the northern kingdom?"

"What does that matter to you?"

The violet eyes narrowed. "Your stubbornness mirrors stupidity, not bravery. That must mean you decided to go off on your own for some reason."

Coura couldn't tell if the being understood her purpose for departing from the camp or not, but she saw no reason to hide her intentions. "I'm returning to stop Lupin. If I can draw him away from the-"

"A fool's errand," Soirée interrupted while studying her fingernails. "Do you honestly believe he won't figure out what you're up to? Besides, you are no match for his magic."

"Then why not help me?"

The question seemingly startled the demon into silence, allowing her to go on.

"Did you forget about our deal already? If we defeat Lupin, the Nim-Valans' minds will be free, they'll retreat, and the border will be secure again. We can work on severing the bonding spell after."

"Of course I remember," Soirée replied with a scoff. "I merely wonder if you realize what you're getting yourself into. Honestly, your lack of awareness will get you killed if you're not careful."

Instead of pressing for an explanation, Coura didn't respond, prompting the creature to elaborate with feigned exhaustion.

"Lupin rarely thinks for himself, which makes him predictable. At least Terran remained true to his instincts and primal behavior."

Coura raised an eyebrow. "What do you mean?"

"I would rather not dive into our entire history together, but Lupin proved to be more trouble than he's worth. When I learned all I could about magic, I abandoned him to stay in the southern kingdom. His grand ideas about ruling over humans didn't interest me, but I worried about his lust for power."

"He's stronger than you then?" she ventured. Part of her expected the demon to snap at the assumption, yet Soirée only shifted to gaze at a spot in the woods behind her.

"Do you recall how the others of my kind behave?"

Coura struggled to come up with an answer when she remembered her encounters with Lupin and Terran and hesitantly nodded.

"They tear each other apart in order to consume flesh containing demonic energy," the being added. "The strong feast on the weak until they become sentient enough to pull the lifeforce from another."

*She's not referring to Lupin or Terran*, Coura realized with horror. *The creatures I saw in my nightmares, those who roam in the demonic realm, are still her kind.*

"Some, like myself, grow out of such a mentality," Soirée continued and fixed her with a serious look. "Others indulge until they lose their sanity, becoming no better than the beasts you've faced."

"You're saying Lupin is in the latter group."

"I'm afraid so. His desire to strengthen himself magically has made him a dangerous spellcaster, but his mind will erode if he gains power at greater levels."

*I wonder if that's what happened to Terran. As soon as he formed a bond with Hendal and could wield magic, he dismissed Soirée's warnings and threw around lightning.*

"How do we stop him?" she ventured after processing the information. "You don't want to confront him or let me go because he could steal your energy. How can we weaken him enough to defeat?"

"An excellent question, one I am not certain I wish to answer right now."

"Why not?"

"In the years we've been apart, he surely learned more about spellcasting and dark energy. I would hate to waste such a valuable resource without picking his brain."

Coura bit her tongue to prevent herself from muttering a curse. *Of course there's something in it for her. If she won't kill him, I suppose I'll need to settle for the next best option.*

"How do we weaken him enough to restrain?" she asked after.

The violet eyes studied her for a few seconds as a sly grin stretched across the demon's face. Instead of responding, Soirée turned to point into the trees she emerged from. "Farther north is the nearest, enemy camp, which may be where he is hiding. If we draw him out, he should abandon his pawns to pursue us."

"Then what?"

The being shrugged in her coy manner. "Who knows? At least you'll learn where he is."

"That won't be useful if he kills me right away," Coura grumbled but considered her position. "I guess I can report back with his location at the very least."

Before she could fully commit to sneaking closer to the Nim-Valans, the demon returned through the brush and disappeared into the shadows beyond. Only a tug from their shared connection let her know the creature cared about her following.

*

"I don't see Lupin."

"Perhaps I should send him a greeting."

Coura shot the demon an unimpressed look. "Are you sure he's here?"

Soirée didn't respond except to toss her raven hair over one shoulder and emerge from where the two lingered beyond the edge of the woods. By the time they noticed the enemy's camp in a somewhat flat field, night approached to darken the entire area. Coura struggled to locate the Nim-Valans' leader but felt no energy stemming from the site, which lowered her expectations.

"Where are you going?" she snapped at her companion when Soirée continued forward.

The being glanced over her shoulder and pointed at the group of nearly two hundred across the open area. "He is likely masking his presence to avoid drawing attention to this spot. Observing from a closer distance would be more helpful."

"And what if someone sees us?"

"Simple. We silence them."

With that, Coura watched as her companion stalked through the tall grass like the beasts around Casner's troops. Her instincts told her not to become too relaxed, yet nothing screamed at her to flee.

*I suppose I must commit to finding Lupin, no matter the means*, she told herself before creeping out of her hiding spot. *My assignment is to keep the fight between the demons. If the Nim-Valans become involved now, I'm not sure I can escape without summoning my wings, which ties me to Asteom and Yeluthia. I'll need to be considerate of my next move.*

By the time she reached Soirée's side, she needed to lie flat on her stomach in order to avoid being seen by the men at the edge of the site. Dim fires had been lit and would soon grow into ones with enough light to reveal their location, so she prepared to press the demon for their next steps until the being's quiet voice reached her.

"They don't appear to suspect us. Slipping closer shouldn't be a problem as long as you keep up."

Coura's heart leapt into her throat, though she managed not to physically react beyond whispering an irritated response. "We're close enough. If he's here, we'll see him without him noticing us."

"For now. It's becoming dark enough for them to feed their fires into lighting this entire clearing. We go closer, we take cover behind the nearest tent; we remain here, we risk getting caught by the human scouts."

*I can't argue with what I already realized.* Again, she struggled to wrap her head around their maneuvering yet never doubted the demon. She considered this while Soirée practically slithered just out of reach of a supply tent. *It's because I trust her. If she didn't like our chances of sneaking in, she would have said so. This must mean Lupin is actually here, right?*

Coura swallowed her rising anxiety, took a couple, deep breaths to calm her mind and body, then crawled through the grass at a pace where she wouldn't disturb the blades too much. Pebbles often pressed into her palms and knees, but what earth she passed over proved to be firm and even. All the while, her eyes remained on what silhouettes she could catch.

"It's about time," Soirée chided when she finally reached the demon's side. By that point, the Nim-Valans talked and ate in the warm glow of their bonfires. "Any longer and I'd be worried about daylight exposing us."

Instead of offering a retort, Coura adjusted herself into a crouch matching her companion so she could draw her sword at the first sign of trouble. The duo peered ahead at the figures and assessed what they could for several minutes until Soirée spoke again.

"It appears their layout is similar to your allies' camp. Since that's the case, and especially because no women are among their ranks, passing through unnoticed is out of the question."

"What if you reveal your presence enough for Lupin to notice?"

The demon produced a drawn-out hum, as if she contemplated that option, and ultimately shook her head. "I'm tired of the methodical method. It's too boring."

Before Coura could process the words, Soirée noiselessly rose out of the grass with a wide grin.

"What are you doing?" she whispered without restraining her alarm and frustration. "If we're caught, we'll be-"

"There is no 'if', Dear One," the being interrupted at a normal volume. "When we are discovered, we'll show them the true extent of our power."

In the next instant, a bright ball of dancing flames manifested in the being's hand, causing Coura to glance away despite the shock that reverberated throughout her body. The loud crash of an explosion followed, and when she looked up immediately after, the tent covering their bodies crumpled underneath the weight of the creature's fiery blast. Soirée's haunting laughter filled the air above the crackling fire then as she stood unbothered by the activity her spell spurred.

The noise, as well as the immense wave of heat and light, prompted action from the Nim-Valans, who shouted at one another while pointing at the burning tent. In a matter of seconds, the men procured their weapons and charged in that direction.

At the sight, Coura abandoned her position, scrambled to her feet, and turned to flee; however, a grip on her right forearm as she spun around held her in place.

"What are you doing?" she practically screamed at the demon restraining her.

Although she attempted to pull herself free, Soirée didn't budge. No explanation came either, which frightened her into nearly panicking until she attempted to draw her weapon with her left hand. At that, the being yanked her around before shoving her backward and releasing the grip, sending her stumbling straight to the edge of the tent's fiery remains.

*What is she doing?* Coura repeated in her mind with disbelief as she glared at the demon.

Whatever the answer was, it remained a secret when the black blade appeared in Soirée's hand and the violet eyes shifted to the enemy troops. Coura hurried to arm herself at the reminder of their position and the thundering of footsteps at her back. Then, she pivoted to locate the nearest Nim-Valan, who already raised his broadsword in preparation for a powerful strike.

Her instincts honed from years of experience kicked in at the sight, sharpening her mentality enough for her to set aside her shock and react appropriately. Instead of meeting the metal head on, she sidestepped just enough to dodge the attack, which allowed her to follow up with a stab through the man's gut. She raised a hand after and prepared to cast a shield when several opponents charged forward at once; however, a blast of dagger-like icicles pierced their bodies in various spots from Soirée's next spell.

*I don't know what she's thinking, but we can't survive an onslaught from a couple hundred Nim-Valans*, Coura noted as she removed her blade from her first victim. *They can heal too, which limits our time and expendable energy. Should I retreat or wait in case Lupin appears?*

The question remained on her mind while the next batch of enemy troops reached her. Like every other encounter she'd fought through recently, she allowed herself to settle into a steady rhythm of strikes and dodging while avoiding the most dangerous attacks.

She still earned plenty of scratches, most deep enough to need stitching, yet it wasn't until the Nim-Valans nearly surrounded her as she backtracked farther into the field that she needed a new plan.

*They'll wear me down by the time I reach the woods,* she thought amid her panting after slicing across a man's thighs in a single, sweeping motion. *I hate bringing attention to Yeluthia and Asteom, but I don't know if I can escape without using my wings at this point.*

Before she could commit to the idea, a shadow in her blind spot had her preparing to twist around until something struck her right shoulder, sending her onto one knee. The blow also knocked the breath from her, and the sensation of blood trickling down her back revealed the weapon possessed spikes that pierced through armor.

The source of the strike, as well as a trio of their allies, leapt closer in order to take advantage of the situation. Without a means to retaliate with her sword, Coura dove into her dark energy for the first time and crafted lightning she scattered in all directions. The Nim-Valans cried out once the bolts connected, dropped to the ground, then remained motionless. All who watched backtracked with frightful mumbling, allowing her to climb to her feet.

*I'll be dead soon given the shape I'm in and the number of enemies. My magic can only keep them at bay for so long.*

During the pause, she considered fleeing until Soirée's voice cut through the otherwise quiet environment.

"Tired already? Perhaps you should fix the root of the problem instead of floundering around."

The taunt didn't draw her attention, but her eyes found the demon when she heard footsteps and felt another wave of fire off to her right. The being sauntered closer in as casual a manner as ever, huffed a laugh, then raised a foot to kick one of the fallen Nim-Valans so he rolled from his stomach onto his back.

"Lupin's stench fills this area," Soirée shared while wrinkling her nose. "I'm surprised you didn't notice."

"You're referring to their healing ability," Coura replied when the being seemed to be waiting for a response.

"That's right. Since these humans are bound to him, his power will flow through them as long as he wills it."

"We can't stop that from happening unless we kill Lupin."

A series of shouting from their surrounding foes let them know their time for chatting was up, prompting her to raise her weapon against a painful sting in her injured shoulder.

Instead of joining her, Soirée knelt beside the Nim-Valan she kicked and placed a hand on the man's head. "Defeating Lupin is the most efficient way to end his possession, but we have another option."

Before Coura could question the comment, a surge of demonic energy rose suddenly enough to have her sidestepping and facing the being in alarm. The power didn't prove to be immense, yet it felt as noticeable as the lightning that shot through the clearing minutes ago. Even the approaching soldiers hesitated to proceed and muttered to one another. As abruptly as it started, the sensation ended.

"What did you do?" she asked when the creature rose.

Soirée didn't offer an explanation. Instead, she poised her sword above her target and stabbed downward, piercing the man's chest. He already began stirring and placed his hands on the blade in an effort to pull it out; however, his attempts grew weaker, his face paled significantly, then both arms dropped to his sides. He remained motionless even after the demon removed her weapon.

The entire time, Coura watched with a sense of unease. *Marcus, Will, and Clearshot all mentioned how Hendal removed his influence over a pair of his guards once they became restrained, which is what they're hoping will happen with the captured Nim-Valans. In this case, Soirée must have torn the energy from them until Lupin noticed and cut off that connection. The enemy troops won't be able to heal if she keeps doing that, but how power hungry does she plan on getting?*

Soirée met her eyes then, as if the being heard her question. "Do you understand?"

"You're going to steal his energy until he retreats from their bodies," she replied and looked at the remaining men.

"We'll be here all night if I do so alone."

A shiver slid along Coura's spine, and she refused to acknowledge the implication of the creature's words.

To her dismay, Soirée pressed the subject. "Since your center can house demonic energy, you should be able to draw it to you just as easily. Doing so will allow you to finish off your opponents."

"And how soon will I lose my mind?" she practically interrupted without hiding her disgust. "If Lupin doesn't show up, I plan on flying out of here. I refuse to get involved with you anymore."

The last sound she expected to hear in that moment was the being's laughter, yet it cut through the tension and even appeared to unnerve their looming opponents.

"You're so dramatic. You once possessed nearly the same amount of power as me without sacrificing your sanity, remember? That is what makes you so unique and interesting to study. Such a balance is unheard of. Why should that have changed?"

Coura bit her tongue to stop herself from arguing further. *Sage Vidar said something similar, but the risk has to do with my mentality. The more I focus on demonic energy, the more difficult it becomes to dismiss it.*

Their precious minutes of peace ended then as the enemy charged. Soirée remained close by and continued drawing Lupin's power from the fallen Nim-Valans between halfhearted spells while Coura struggled against a dizziness brought about by her injury and the pain it spurred. Steadily, her right arm's aching caused it to raise and lower less efficiently, resulting in less impactful motions.

*Perhaps I should go now. If I grow too weak, I won't have the strength to-*

A jarring sting from a slice across the back of her left knee had her staggering while shoving another's sword aside. She shifted her weight to avoid putting the majority on the new injury; however, she became vulnerable when the men took advantage of the opportunity to finish circling around her. The grip on her sword tightened in response, and a stream of curses echoed in her mind.

Without a means to physically keep up, she turned to magic. A shield formed as soon as she gave her light energy permission to act, blocking those at her back. The Nim-Valans struck the magical wall in response, so she instinctively made a mental note to continue feeding the spell while facing the four who charged at once. The first she interacted with held a club he swung with reckless abandon, which benefited her for the moment due to his comrades' reluctance to get too close. Unfortunately, her body's weariness, along with the wound in her leg, prevented her from acting as fluidly as she liked.

*I need a break to heal*, she admitted when her opponent's wild swings forced her to retreat until her back pressed against her shield. The thuds against her spell seemingly matched the thundering of her heart in her chest. *Magic is my best option at this point. I managed to use my goddess gift while shielding before, so I should be able to utilize both types of energy.*

Coura let herself believe this to be the case lest she cave into her doubts. Without a second to waste, she reached for the dark power eagerly dancing in her center while raising her free hand. A blast of fire similar to Soirée's earlier performance enveloped the closest Nim-Valan and scorched those behind him. She ignored their resulting screams and immediately placed the palm on the back of her knee to begin a healing spell. This required her to disconnect from her shield, yet the relief she experienced more than made up for that sacrifice.

By the time she stood straight again, the enemy was ready to continue their pursuit. Those beyond the magical wall hammered away, causing it to crack, and the men in front of her ignored their burned comrades to march forward. Without a means of keeping her opponents at bay, she repeated her series of spells. A new shield formed at her back just as the former shattered into fragments, then she continued using flames to hold off the Nim-Valans in front.

*I'll never be able to escape if I can't get away. My energy might not last until Soirée intervenes to take the demonic power either. What should I do?*

The question repeated in her mind several times over the next few minutes as she wielded elemental projectiles to hold off her attackers. When she scanned the surrounding space for Soirée, she couldn't find the being, raising her concern. Nothing changed from her perspective until the troops began yelling in a manner she recognized.

*They're rallying together*, she understood with a sinking feeling. *My magic keeps them away because of how vigilant they are. If they rush at once without worrying about getting hurt, how long until they reach me?*

Coura figured the answer was what she expected and summoned her wings despite the amount of activity. Unfortunately, the men charged as soon as she did so, preventing her from leaping into the air and forcing her to raise a shield using her dark energy in order to maintain the one at her back. The amount of strikes that followed cracked the wall in a matter of seconds, yet she could only think to manifest another. All around her, indiscernible voices, the clanging of metal, and thuds sounded. Her head spun as she glanced back and forth before settling on the sky above.

*I need to go!*

Just as she crouched to jump and climb into the sky, as she envisioned departing the scene and settling somewhere quiet for the night, a sharp pain shot through her side. The startling sensation had her glancing down to where one of the charred Nim-Valans at her feet healed enough to prop himself up with his left arm and stab his sword just below her ribs with the right. She stepped backward to pull her body away from the weapon with a wince and pressed her empty hand against the wound. While she initiated the spell to mend the bloody flesh, the soldiers on the ground began rising, albeit slowly.

Coura anticipated how long it would take for them to attack, as well as how much time she would have before the shield behind them would break, while the healing ended. Her body's exhaustion grew due to the strain, yet her focus didn't falter until a second, almost identical surge of pain arose from her left shoulder blade amid the sound of shattering glass. The source removed itself right away, so she spun around and dismissed her wings to ease the blinding discomfort their weight exaggerated. It was then she remembered how she cut off her connection to that shield in order to heal the stab wound, allowing the men to weaken the wall until they could pierce it. A crimson-coated spear tip protruded from a hole in her spell, and a grinning Nim-Valan didn't even attempt to hide his pleasure with the result.

Instinctively, Coura raised another shield, though her dark energy responded to her boiling frustration, producing a violet-tinted wall instead of the slightly golden one she'd grown accustomed to. Both the sight and her situation led her to growl a curse as she faced the opposite side where the burned Nim-Valans crept closer.

*What should I do? I need to heal my shoulder before I can manifest my wings again or else I'm not sure I'll have the strength to get into the sky. Perhaps I can clear the way again with flames or lightning. They might not care and continue toward me anyway.*

From deep within her chest, beneath the aching of her muscles and shortening breaths, she felt a tug on the invisible chain tying her to Soirée. That nudge from the demon held obvious intent, though she struggled to dismiss the temptation to utilize her dark power.

*If I'm able to pull Lupin's energy away from these men, they won't be as eager to charge toward me, especially since I can use it against them,* part of her rationalized. *On the other hand, I don't know how that will affect me.*

All the doubt and fear she held in check began seeping through her tired mental state; however, she managed to raise her sword against the nearest Nim-Valan when he lunged for her with a gurgled cry. Because of his already weakened body, Coura easily knocked the short blade out of his hand before delivering a stab through the gut. His comrade took advantage of her limited movements to rush at her left side just as she tore her weapon free. Instead of attacking, he resorted to seizing her elbow and attempting to slip around her, presumably to pin that arm behind her back.

What he apparently forgot was her ability to wield magic, which she did as soon as she figured out what he planned. Her wrist twisted so the palm faced him before she released a bolt of lightning straight into his chest. The thud of his body dropping to the ground let her know he wouldn't be a problem for the moment, so she kept her eyes on the next duo approaching.

As a pair of Nim-Valans charged to initiate combat, the previous spell's lingering hum in her veins added to the already-present aggravation driving her forward. The pain and weariness in her limbs began increasing with every movement, her throat burned from breathing so hard, and her hearing only picked up on the obvious pounding against her shields and the enemy's footsteps. In her mind, she could only focus on the people in front of her.

The next man fell once she hurried to slit his throat, resulting in a slice across her right forearm, and the second followed suit after she utilized a series of icicles to puncture his torso. After that, the shield beyond them shattered, forcing her to hurry and cast another.

*Judging by the amount I put in, my magic is starting to run out*, she admitted with dismay as her eyes went to the cracked wall at her back. *Either I escape soon or they wear me down enough to overwhelm me. If I hurry, I can manifest my wings again and get into the sky.*

By that point in the evening, the area became enveloped in twilight. Darkness nearly covered everything in shadow, leaving only vague silhouettes of trees and people. Coura paused to evaluate her remaining Yeluthian power yet couldn't distinguish it from its active counterpart. This concerned her for a second before she noticed the Nim-Valans on the ground starting to twitch their limbs. Before she could come up with a new strategy, the shield behind her shattered. Dozens of cheers from the men beyond lowered her spirits.

*Can I run faster than they can move? If they catch me, I'm dead. If I stay here, I'm dead. I can't trust my light energy if I can't sense it.*

Amid the frantic thoughts, Coura instinctively avoided considering Soirée's location and Lupin's power. The former would likely intervene only when she came close to death, though what the creature would do after dragging her away remained a mystery. Meanwhile, the Nim-Valans' leader's presence hovered over the entire clearing like smoke to irritate her senses. The urge to cave in and claim what dark energy the northerners held grew with every passing second thanks to how hopeless her situation became. Still, she knew there would be no turning back if she committed to wielding demonic power.

Unfortunately, without another plan she was left at the mercy of her own, limited capabilities. Another, violet shield followed in each direction, sending a chill through her veins, and she prepared to flee from the camp and remove herself from the mass of enemies; however, as soon as she took one step, a jolt of pain shot through her right leg. The unexpected sensation had her falling onto her hands and knees.

*What just happened?* she absentmindedly wondered before glancing at the spot.

Her entire body went cold at the sight of a knife hilt embedded in her calf. On the other side, the tip of its blade protruded from her skin. Coura considered removing it yet knew she would struggle with a healing spell due to how her dark energy acted up to that point. Then, she contemplated how far she could get before she bled out, leading her to want to keep the weapon in place. The discomfort also deterred her from touching it.

*What should I do?*

Unlike the previous determination fueling her thoughts, a wave of hopelessness accompanying her exhaustion left her with less motivation. She couldn't decide on her next course of action and only felt frightened when the Nim-Valans she felled started crawling toward her.

The nearest who likely threw the knife grabbed for her as she shifted to sit instead of remain on her hands and knees, allowing her to poise her sword for a strike. As soon as he got hold of her ankle, she plunged her blade into his shoulder then kicked him with her uninjured leg. The follow-up motion helped her remove her weapon, and she prepared to do the same to her next opponent until one of the shields shattered.

Coura raked her brain for options as she looked between those barreling closer, the few healing on the ground, and her bleeding calf, yet her mind went blank. Although her body began relaxing in response to the inevitable defeat, the energy in her center flared to life, just as it had when she trained with the Mintelians.

*It overwhelmed my mentality*, she recalled and savored what determination arose. *Sage Vidar warned me about letting my center become unbalanced. At this point, I can't survive by relying on my Yeluthian power or what demonic energy I can control at a single time.*

Against her better judgement, and while ignoring the active connection to Soirée, she reached over to place a hand on the Nim-Valan she just wounded. Her senses picked up on Lupin's presence immediately, so she honed in on it, secured the tendril of dark power as if it were her own, and pulled.

# Risky Endeavors

Coura didn't entirely know what to expect when she stole Lupin's power from the enemy soldiers. In the past, when Soirée and Terran took demonic energy from her center, the ache felt as though she were being torn in half without pain. The memory of such discomfort stayed with her for years, and she recalled it as she claimed the tendril within the Nim-Valan.

He possessed a minor amount compared to what she normally held; however, his connection to their leader was evident. The looming presence hardly attempted to interfere with her extraction, allowing her to finish in a matter of seconds. As a result, the man groaned, stared at her with a horrified expression, then trembled wildly enough for her to notice.

*I need to make his death a spectacle for his comrades*, she noted while the new power increased the humming in her veins. *My goal now should be to convince them to flee before I kill them.*

With that in mind, she decided to climb to her feet using no shortage of effort, poise the tip of her blade above the wounded man as he crawled in the opposite direction, and stab downward through the center of his back. Her eyes went to those charging forward before she raised a hand to summon a shield and block their approach. When nobody seemed to acknowledge the unmoving soldier at her feet, she removed her weapon and limped toward the nearest Nim-Valan.

Unlike the previous man, this one could rise and challenge her. Still, the constant lack of real motivation behind the effort allowed her to easily seize his arm and repeat her previous tactic. The results proved to be the same, but she got a twisted idea to make the others aware of her ability.

Removing Lupin's energy from the enemy soldier had an effect on his mentality, just like with her previous opponent. She took advantage of his dazed reaction by raising and dropping her blade in a vertical slice that cleanly cut off the arm she held just below the elbow.

His horrified expression and accompanying scream drew all eyes as he stepped backward, released his weapon, and cradled the injured limb. A stream of words followed in his language, which she assumed were curses against her.

Meanwhile, Coura waited while attempting to ignore the pain and discomfort in her calf. She soon noticed how pale he grew before he turned to seemingly retreat. Three steps later, he collapsed.

In order to keep the momentum of her actions going, she stepped closer to the remaining Nim-Valans she could reach. The knife wound prevented her from walking without a limp, yet the enemy troops didn't allow her to complete her approach. All four stumbled toward her at once with weapons raised.

How her mind shifted afterward set the pace for the rest of the conflict. Every thought quieted in favor of savoring the euphoria from the dark energy, which eagerly activated at her command to form whatever elemental or shielding spell she desired. At the same time, her body moved instinctively to cut down each target while taking minimum damage. Her goals became simple: disable, steal, then kill.

Those on the opposite sides of her shields also took notice of the result. The noise from their strikes quieted significantly as they watched their comrades permanently fall, and their grumbles sounded more concerned than hostile. Despite their behavior, Coura knew not to let up in her current predicament. She shifted her attention to the soldiers at her back who caused the most damage to the magical wall, as shown by multiple, deep cracks on its surface. Her mind flew through several ideas for how to manage them before settling on the most productive, yet riskiest method.

Her feet led her closer to the shield, which prompted the Nim-Valans to find their courage and continue attacking it until it caved in and broke into fragments. During that pause where they hesitated to come into contact with the glittering pieces, she raised her empty hand and released a system of scattered bolts that shot across the open area. The bodies her spell connected with were thrown backward or froze from the shock before dropping to the ground.

The lightning didn't stop once she succeeded in causing disarray among their ranks. She sent wave after wave as she approached to kneel beside the fallen men and pull the demonic energy into herself. Every ache and pain soon dulled and became replaced by pure exhilaration matching the confidence that silenced her doubts. All the while, her mind felt at peace.

What bolts she sent eventually morphed into crimson flames, then burning blasts of ice when she grew bored; however, she started waiting so a handful of opponents could rise and challenge her. Once she defeated them, the process continued. Only when the Nim-Valans' numbers dwindled and they turned tail to retreat into woods beyond their camp did Coura recall the opposite side of the area containing the other half of their ranks. To her dismay, that part of the clearing appeared nearly identical to hers with bodies littering the earth. A single figure stood among them holding a ball of flame in one hand.

*Soirée.*

The demon's name was the first coherent thought she'd had in what felt like hours and seemed to bring her back to her present situation. She turned with the intent to approach the being but stumbled when her right leg wouldn't lift enough to manage a step.

*That's right*, she recalled with a glance at the knife in her calf. *How am I supposed to hike back to the camp with this?*

Instead of reacting or pushing through the injury, she decided to wait so she could calm down. What demonic power she stole from the dozens of men didn't seem to decrease as the evening wore on, resulting in the same, euphoric state that drove her to fight. Although dangerous, she found she appreciated the internal support, which she knew saved her life. Unfortunately, the energy continued jittering in her veins no matter how hard she tried to dismiss it.

"Why not remove that thorn so you don't trip over yourself?" came Soirée's voice during her attempt.

Coura looked up from where she had been staring at a spot on the ground to find the demon halting toe to toe with her. Instead of replying, she decided to inquire about Lupin's location.

"He must not be here," Soirée's responded before she scoffed. "How careless. Leaving behind fresh lambs for the slaughter."

Silence hung between them for a few seconds. Then, Coura straightened and narrowed her eyes at the being.

"You knew he wouldn't be here."

"What makes you so sure?" Soirée countered with a smirk. "The evidence suggested this was his base of operations. You could sense his presence overwhelming the living creatures, right?"

*Of course she'll dance around the accusation*, Coura thought once she realized bickering would get her nowhere. This led her to scan the nearby camp for any signs of activity. *I hoped to confront Lupin and have those two eliminate each other, but I guess I was being optimistic. I need to report back to Casner. At least we managed to make a dent in their forces.*

With nothing left to do, she turned her attention to the blade in her leg. The dark power continued numbing her calf, yet she noticed how it seemed to be waiting to act, piquing her interest. After a moment to prepare herself, she firmly grabbed the hilt.

*I'll bleed out if I'm not prepared to heal this.*

The notion led her to evaluate what light energy she possessed, but to her dismay, her Yeluthian power retreated deep into her center. She bit her lip in response while her heartbeat picked up.

"What's wrong?" Soirée asked with feigned concern.

Although she figured she didn't need to answer, Coura did so anyway. "I overused my magic. What power I have for healing won't respond due to the overwhelming amount of dark energy in my body. I'll need to find supplies in their camp to stop the bleeding until I can mend the wound."

She rose to her feet during the explanation yet hesitated to infiltrate the Nim-Valans' site when the demon produced a low hum.

"You do recall your time with my power, correct?" came Soirée's next question in a hauntingly calm manner.

A shiver slid along Coura's spine once she understood the hint; however, the being moved before she could vocalize her displeasure with allowing the demonic energy to heal her as it did years ago. In a swift motion, Soirée dropped to her hands and knees, reached for the knife, and yanked it from the flesh as Coura began demanding the creature leave it alone. The startling movement and resulting sting had her stumbling a couple steps backward before falling onto her side where she clutched her leg and cursed the demon.

"You'll be thanking me here shortly," Soirée promised and tossed the weapon aside before standing over her.

*I can't give in*, she told herself despite how the dark energy started mending the damage. Already, she appreciated the power's ability to know how to work without her direction. *If I can't control myself, I'll lose what balance I achieved. My center will go back to the way it was, and then I'll become the monster I've been fighting.*

Despite the pleas, she took pleasure in what sense of confidence the strength provided. Her calf soon healed, prompting her to rise and dust herself off amid Soirée's prodding.

"See how easy that was? You also have a means of preventing the enemy from recovering. I would say the evening's struggle was worth the effort."

"I need to get back," Coura mumbled and glanced at the sky. "Lupin is still out there. As long as he manipulates the northerners, he continues to pose a threat to Asteom."

The creature rolled her eyes but didn't argue.

With nothing else to discuss, Coura attempted to reach inward and manifest her wings only to find the energy slipping through her invisible fingers. Her second try yielded similar results, leading her to instinctively stare down at her hands and repress what gloom stirred.

*My Yeluthian power isn't responding at all. I could always summon my wings though, which means I pushed myself too far.*

Her hopelessness boiled into rage spurred on by the dark energy when she reflected on what brought her to that point. Both hands balled into fists before she addressed Soirée, whose violet eyes studied her under the moonlight.

"You knew this would happen, didn't you?" she practically screamed without restraint. "You showed me how to steal Lupin's power from the Nim-Valans because it would repress my own!"

Her questions spurred a laugh from the demon. "You give me far too much credit, Dear One. Your potential amazes me, which is why I remain close. That, and the bond keeping us together."

"You wouldn't have stopped me if you believed I would lose my ability to wield my light energy."

"Of course not."

The truth wasn't shocking, yet the anger it spurred led Coura to consider several retorts that would continue the argument. In the end, she clamped her jaw shut, spun around, and closed her eyes while taking deep breaths.

*This is what Sage Vidar warned me about. I can wield both types, but they'll respond negatively to each other of one becomes greater. What's done is done. I need to focus on-*

Her reflection abruptly ended when she felt a slight weight fall on her shoulders where Soirée's hands rested. From them, the alluring power flowed into her body.

"Why not pursue Lupin and his followers?" the demon practically purred close to her right ear. "Together, we're strong enough to defeat his forces and grab his attention. Imagine the energy he possesses. That would surely benefit your friends and their kingdom."

Against her better judgement, Coura savored the sensation of stability between the two as she processed the words even though the offer disgusted her and she fully intended to refuse.

Only when she could mentally tear herself away from the demon's grasp did she spin around, raise an arm, and slap the creature's hands. Soirée didn't appear offended by the rebuff and grinned while stepping back.

"It was only a thoughtful offer."

"Quit wasting my time," she snapped before summoning a light and traversing the area to head into the southern woods, ending their conversation. Once she located the pack she abandoned in the bushes when they arrived, she mustered her energy and set out for the trek ahead.

***

As Marcus crouched behind a boulder just barely wide enough to hide his entire body, he forced himself not to reconsider his decision to volunteer for his current assignment. He already expressed his wariness about what Grace reported regarding the ancestral weapon and their enemy's leader; however, his superior had a different take on the information.

"If they're recovering from losing at least a quarter of their forces, now would be an ideal time to strike," General Casner explained during the meeting following his Yeluthian friend's involvement. "I'm in favor of aiming to disable as many northerners as possible and destroying their rations. Their leader is another problem entirely, but one we can hold off with magic."

The man had looked to Byron for confirmation, prompting the master mage to agree.

"An unexpected attack would also look appropriate at this time," Commander Evern added after. "If our main goals are to confirm the being's location and recover the ancestral weapon likely hiding among their camp, the latter would be the most difficult without additional insight."

The following day, both Yeluthian soldiers spent hours flying above in order to confirm the site's position along the border and memorize its layout. From that information, Marcus had volunteered to lead a search group into the site during the chaos. They eventually concluded three, limited squads could cover more ground and moved forward with the plan.

*Of course I would offer my services without considering the necessary skills*, he thought while pointing ahead as a signal for the four individuals under his command to move. *I'm not exactly built for sneaking around. We'll be lucky if we're not seen before we step foot near one of their tents.*

Despite his pessimistic mindset, he still had faith in the other groups. The general had suggested Finn due to the spy's experience slipping around dangerous environments, and Commander Evern volunteered his subordinate, Lavine. Although Marcus didn't know much about the Yeluthian, he knew he wouldn't need to worry about that squad's safety thanks to the soldier's combat abilities and knowledge of the area.

*I need to focus on my own troops now.*

None of the soldiers who crept behind him possessed any particular skills that made them unique; however, all had been regular scouts during the night, so they felt comfortable wandering in limited light. At that point in the day, twilight covered the land, hinting at the darkness to come.

Marcus avoided wincing as each, slow footstep crunched what dry grass lay underneath his boots even though the sounds of battle in the distance likely held everyone's attention. He continued forward until he could slip behind the cover of the nearest tent. His hand instinctively went to the hilt of his sword, which he refused to unsheathe until a threat presented itself. One comrade, a young woman who rarely spoke, would keep watch and warn of danger anyway.

As soon as he faced those hiding in the brush and nodded, the four scattered in order to distance themselves from each other. His strategy took advantage of the enemy's lack of troops to cover more ground in a shorter amount of time, which he knew would be risky if not every Nim-Valan engaged with his allies.

*Each squad member has a partner except me, but I'll be staying between them so they can survey the perimeter of our search. We need to be as efficient as possible since the general will call a retreat at any time.*

He slipped inside the tent after confirming the lack of people around that spot and dug through what bags he could get his hands on. Fortunately, the space held dry rations, so he could simply dismiss it and move on to the next. While he did so, he struggled to avoid considering the risks he and his comrades faced, mainly how a separate group with dark mages would be charging through to summon flames and burn as much of the Nim-Valan camp as they could. This wouldn't take place until the retreat; however, there would be no warning.

*I understand the desire to remain unnoticed by the enemy, but how can we make sure the squad members are clear of the fire?* he wondered before shaking his head and moving into the next tent. *I suppose it's our responsibility to remain aware. As long as we continue to keep an eye out for danger, we should notice when the area brightens.*

That was all the time he spent on such thoughts. For minutes, he scoured through what bags and items he could get his hands on, which included blankets, waterskins, coats, boots, and other, non-threatening supplies. He hurried to finish then snuck outside once more. Shadows of his comrades passed in and out of view, but he paid them no mind. Instead, he approached one of many bonfires that cooled into glowing, flickering embers before dropping to his hands and knees.

Just like Asteom's forces, the Nim-Valans left their belongings lying around since they couldn't afford to waste energy on more than crude piles. He didn't expect to find such a precious weapon among their clothing and miscellaneous possessions, which proved to be the case when he stood emptyhanded once his inspection was complete.

A silhouette off to his right caught his attention, and he readied for an attack when he heard the figure approaching at a run. Fortunately, the person spoke before he could react.

"Assistant General," came a man's voice he recognized as one of his squad members. "The northern section of their camp is clear."

Marcus glanced in that direction. "I appreciate the update. Stay at your post and keep watch for our mages. You can give them extra protection while retreating together."

"Yes, sir!"

With that, the soldier backtracked at a jog, leaving him alone once again.

*If those two completed their search already, I should receive an update from the others. I doubt Lavine or Finn's groups will linger once they're done, so our squad can remain to greet our allies.*

He decided to continue searching while moving east in order to meet up with his remaining group members. Nothing of interest caught his eye among the enemy's belongings, but soon the sounds of combat could be heard from farther ahead, leading him to wonder if any Nim-Valans remained behind to protect the site. Although he longed to rush over, confront the trouble, and aid the others, he repressed the urge.

*We're all focused on our own parts of the mission*, he reminded himself while turning his attention south. *Everybody knows their role for this to be successful. I would just cause confusion, especially if I'm not needed.*

His concern shifted to the amount of noise coming from the camp, which raised into grunts and shouting as loud as the clashing, metal weapons. Despite his attempt to ignore the voices, he wondered about the demon's return should their location be compromised. Such a threat pushed him on until he spotted a shadow approaching and prepared for an attack.

"Assistant General, it's only me," the figure replied in response to his shifted stance.

Marcus recognized the feminine voice as one of his squad members, the woman who rarely spoke, and relaxed. "Are you finished with your search?"

"No, sir. We noticed one group fleeing the site and the fight taking place across the area and thought to find you for further instruction."

"Did you recognize anybody who fled?"

She shook her head.

"I expected as much," he grumbled before gazing east. "It doesn't seem the noise will die down soon, but I'm expecting our mages to appear without warning. Have you and your partner depart as well."

"We didn't complete our search yet," she protested, more out of alarm than displeasure.

"If you two are in a safe enough position to do so, then leave once you're done."

"What will you do?"

Marcus raised an arm to point north. "I'll be with the rest of our squad along the perimeter. We can protect the mages when they arrive and retreat together."

The woman's resulting pause had him believing she would request to join; however, she didn't pursue the subject. With well wishes, she spun around to jog back to her original position.

"I should go too," he muttered to himself after. No small shortage of reluctance followed as a sense of guilt added weight to his shoulders, mainly due to his group's lack of success. Still, he reminded himself of his part as one of several pieces in motion and went to find his lingering pair of comrades.

When he reached the final tent at the edge of the enemy camp, Marcus prepared to call for the soldiers until a bright light directly ahead had him shading his eyes with one hand and reaching for his sword with the other. A second later, he processed the source as a ball of fire being held by a wide-eyed man. Several others cast a similar spell alongside the mage, easing the tension.

"Were you trying to alert the enemy of our arrival?" another snapped at the first, causing the mage to bumble an apology.

Marcus returned his arms to his sides while making sure to move deliberately enough for them to notice him without perceiving him as a threat. As he stepped closer, he then let them know his identity.

"Assistant General," the man who scolded his comrade began and straightened, as if startled by a superior officer's appearance. "Master Byron ordered us to strike the camp despite the ongoing fighting."

He raised an eyebrow. "Ongoing?"

"It sounds like the enemy is holding our forces at a standstill. We mages didn't act until we received the order to depart for this location. Honestly, I wasn't expecting you to still be here."

*Byron sent this group ahead even though they could help with the conflict. Does that mean their reaction is different than what he expected. I wonder if the general is aware of his decision as well.*

"In any case, we should continue with the mission," he told those around him. "Two of my squad members are lingering around this side of the site, and I heard the sounds of weapons clashing on the east end. Whether or not our allies are still around, we must hurry. I'll join you during the escape."

Some among the newcomers looked surprised by his offer, yet most expressed their thanks for the support. With nothing else to waste energy on, he ushered the mages forward to fulfill their purpose. What fire they held caught on to the tents, blankets, clothing, and various items in their path as they marched through the camp. Marcus merely watched in order to follow at the rear. There, he reunited with his squad members who seamlessly slipped beside the mages.

"It's going according to plan," one mentioned after a brief greeting. "At this rate, we'll be out of here in no time."

"Don't let your guard down," Marcus warned, drawing their eyes. "The enemy could return at any moment. Besides, at least a few were guarding the eastern end. I wouldn't put it past them to engage with us should they still be standing."

That silenced the pair, though they nodded to acknowledge his words.

Throughout the march, his eyes darted around while a hand rested on the hilt of his sword. The eerie hush surrounding them was broken only by crackling objects consumed by flame, and an orange glow lit up the area. What shadows arose as a result increased his concern of an ambush; however, none came. The mages paused at the southern end of the camp to await further orders from their leader despite a forming cloud of smoke, which caused them to rub their eyes and cough.

"Our assignment is complete," he heard the man from earlier announce. "We can start heading back to the-"

Before Marcus could process the pause in the mage's words, numerous cries of alarm sounded from the front. He instinctively drew his sword, glanced at his fellow soldiers, who did the same a second later, and found his voice.

"Return to our camp, and stay together!"

Those who heard him either took off in the direction of their site or hesitated for long enough to glance at him before following their companions. This resulted in a mass of people frantically heading west, like a herd of startled deer.

Marcus didn't linger to supervise them. Instead, he charged forward to face what danger awaited at what had been the front of the group. First, he noticed a violet wall signaling the use of a shielding spell from a trio of mages. The three shouted similar commands for their allies to flee, yet plenty appeared intent on staying to join in defending their comrades. Next, he spotted several figures on the ground, including the man who had been leading them. Arrows protruded from their torsos and limbs, though no body held more than one or two. Some of those standing also had bloody spots from wounds he couldn't identify.

On the opposite side of their shield were Nim-Valan men who practically blended in with the shadows. Their swords, spears, and crude maces pounded against the magical wall to produce wide cracks. He only counted a dozen, but they already made their mark.

*I bet they knew they couldn't stop us from burning their camp, so they waited to attack until we prepared to depart.*

With that thought in mind, Marcus tightened the grip on his weapon and faced the pair of soldiers at his side. "We defend the mages so they can escape with the injured. The enemy can likely heal, so aim to draw out the combat."

"Yes, sir!" they replied in unison without a trace of fear.

He didn't bother instructing them any further. Instead, he closed the distance between himself and the remaining men and women before shouting orders for them to retreat. A handful began protesting until he interrupted their replies.

"Our mission is complete. We have no reason to stay except to die at either the northerners' hands or the flames consuming their camp. The wounded need you now."

As if to punctuate his point, the wall of energy shattered to better reveal the men beyond. The trio of mages began backing up once the Nim-Valans rushed forward, so Marcus hurried to intercept the closest opponent. In a matter of seconds, his blade found itself lodged in the chest of that target. He pulled his sword out then swung at the legs of the next man, who tumbled to the ground like a sack of grain.

*We're lucky this group behaves as unattentively as the others we've encountered,* he noted and raised his weapon again to knock away another aiming for his head.

At either side, his fellow soldiers engaged with their own opponents and found success just as easily. Marcus took advantage of the support by glancing over his shoulder at the mages who hadn't retreated yet, either due to stubbornness or panic.

"I won't ask again!" he shouted. The slight frustration he felt at the sight of their disobedience motivated him to add more. "If you fight, you'll get in the way of our retreat. I don't plan on staying much longer, but if you do, that's your life you're willing to risk."

His next target came into view as he finished speaking, pushing him into combat once more. Whatever happened at his back was up to his allies. Despite his inability to control that, he hated dismissing comrades when they were in danger; however, how he stood his ground as their superior eased some of the burden on his shoulders.

*It's just like with Lavine and Finn's groups,* he realized while disarming a Nim-Valan and slicing through the man's thigh. *Our success relies on everybody doing their job. I can help organize the plan, guide others toward our goal, and defend them until my last breath, but keeping the mission on track takes priority when our lives are on the line.*

He made a mental note to consider that point in the future when he had the luxury to relax and returned his attention to the task at hand. The pair of soldiers remained at an equal distance, so he adjusted to steadily back up when an opportunity presented itself. His comrades did the same, and he spared a moment to look at where the mages had been, though to prevent himself from tripping over them rather than to ensure they departed. Fortunately, nobody occupied that space. Even those on the ground had been carried away.

"Everyone else is gone," he told his companions while allowing himself a smile. "Should we follow suit?"

"What about the enemy?" one asked between breaths after felling his opponent.

Marcus took a moment to assess the northerners still on their feet, as well as the majority lying in the dirt. His throat and eyes burned from the amount of smoke, yet the environment didn't seem to bother the Nim-Valans. After disarming another man, he responded to the question.

"We won't be able to defeat them, and this area is getting too dangerous. Fall back, but keep them in sight. We'll need to make sure they're far enough away from the mages anyway."

With that, the trio spun around to sprint for the westernmost patch of trees. The brush had Marcus pausing in order to adjust his eyes to the darkness and his skin to the cooler temperature, but he didn't stop moving until the crimson light became barely visible between the foliage. His fellow soldiers noticed when he halted and did the same, then they watched the camp for any sign of the enemy pursuing them.

None did so, though he didn't let down his guard. Quiet instructions had them continuing their retreat at a slow enough pace to look and listen for trouble. All the while, Marcus wondered whether or not the other squads escaped safely and if either group managed to do so with the coveted prize.

***

The aching of Byron's muscles steadily grew as he forced himself to remain still behind the cover of a wide pine tree where several mages awaited orders. Farther east, the faint sounds and sights of battle let him know the conflict continued despite the late hour. Still, he kept his head against a rising sense of concern.

*What is happening over there?*

"Master Byron, should we intervene?" the woman to his left asked in a whisper without masking her impatience.

He shook his head. "Not yet."

"If not now, then when?" a young man practically demanded from his other side. "The spellcasters with them can only provide so much light. We should–"

"We should wait for the general's signal," he interrupted without removing his eyes from their comrades, though he did raise the volume of his voice so the entire group could hear his next words. "If we act too soon and the demon is watching, it'll make sure we regret our decision to enter without a backup plan. Remember, we are the support, not the distraction."

A few people mumbled their agreement, but most stayed quiet. Their behavior didn't bother him though, especially since his reasoning resonated with his desire to assist as well.

Their attack had multiple purposes, which would only be achieved by splitting into various groups with their own assignments. Such a strategy was risky, as Casner admitted during their plotting session; however, no one could deny they needed to take a chance if they hoped to make some sort of progress.

*The creature shouldn't expect such an intricate fight right now. We captured some of the Nim-Valans and drove them away while holding our own against its magic. If anything, this can be considered our attempt to squash their forces. In reality, we need the ancestral weapon in order to defeat their leader, and we need to learn where it is hiding.*

Byron motioned for his group to sneak closer as he crept forward toward the next, needle-covered mass of branches. His position sounded rather simple in the grand scheme of things since he would only act when the general let him know their enemy's leader became involved.

*I was also supposed to wait to send the squad into the Nim-Valan camp, but I refuse to waste that opportunity*, he reflected once he paused behind his new spot. *I trust Marcus, Lavine, and Finn to work efficiently enough not to linger in such a dangerous place. Either the weapon is there or it's not, so there's room for doubt, but burning their supplies will absolutely hinder their ability to remain near the border.*

His mind returned to the present where the ongoing conflict continued. Unlike those targeting the site, the general wanted to make his part a matter of stamina. Casner and a majority of their soldiers, along with a group of mages, would act as a distraction to draw the northerners into combat. Then, they would remain to keep the fight going until the demon appeared.

*When the creature arrives, one of their spellcasters will signal to us by sending fire or lightning upward. That is, if we don't spot the being's handiwork first. I understand the general's desire to keep magic as uninvolved as possible if their leader won't show up, but it possesses enough power to cause trouble before we can reunite.*

Byron rubbed his nose while dismissing the rising concern again. His eyes followed what movements he could see in order to distract from how much time the situation drained from the evening. From what he could tell, the Nim-Valans acted no differently than their previous encounter, resulting in each side trying to wear down the other.

"Sir, please," the mage from earlier began with a greater sense of urgency. "They could use our help."

"Not yet," he replied with the intent to repeat his previous explanation.

Before he could do so, a flash bright enough to fill the area in front of them erupted, blinding everybody and causing the mages to cover or avert their eyes. Byron did the latter, rapidly blinked to clear his vision, then returned his attention to the conflict where continuous blasts followed. A maelstrom of lightning, fire, and ice cut through the darkness and revealed the silhouettes of both allies and enemies. Bodies were flung into the air or thrown aside from the force of the spells. Additionally, an overwhelming presence swept through the area, like thick poison infesting a pool of water.

Byron called for his group to emerge and join their allies despite how the being's energy affected his senses. His legs felt heavier as he charged toward the soldiers, yet every hair on his body stood up as his skin crawled.

*I thought I'd gotten used to this sensation from working around Coura for years, but the amount of energy this demon is releasing is insane. Is it doing so to intimidate our forces, or is it simply that much more powerful?*

Instead of considering an answer and options based on his conclusion, he raised his arms to summon a shield in front of the nearest bunch of Asteom men and women along the perimeter. Most sat or lied on the ground, as if they lost their balance, which he attributed to the creature's immense presence.

"Let's get a wall going to separate our forces!" he shouted with a glance behind at those who followed him into the fray.

The mages didn't react to his orders as well as he'd hoped, yet they soon slid into the right mindset in the next minute when they caught up. They fell into line with him and mirrored his spell, creating a shimmering barrier that stretched from one end of the space to the other. Byron dropped out before issuing instructions for the healers to continue assisting the injured, a select few dark mages to provide additional light between shielding, and the rest to steadily move farther into the mass of people. Meanwhile, he kept part of his attention on the onslaught across the area.

*The direction of its spells keeps changing, which means it's jumping from one spot to another along the eastern end. It isn't sparing its own troops either. I'm assuming they can all heal then.*

Minutes passed without change, both reassuring and bothering him until he decided to act on his own. Those he considered his direct underlings during his time along the border remained by his side, so he prepared something of a plan before issuing his next orders.

"Keep watch on this section," he yelled while glancing between the nearby faces, drawing their eyes. "Your only goal is to maintain the line until the general decides to retreat. If that takes too long, start falling back."

He sensed their displeasure with his instructions; however, nobody protested. This left him able to bring down his spell, charge across the line, and reestablish it from the opposite side. From then on, he recognized himself as an enemy to the dozens of northerners awaiting fresh meat.

*My goal is to locate the demon*, he reminded himself as his eyes scanned the battlefield. *This is my assignment. At least, unless I run into Casner first.*

Unfortunately, his plan didn't involve strategizing beyond conceptualizing his next steps. Those who approached with ill intent found themselves struck by whatever elemental projectiles he conjured while a continuous formation of shields at his back prevented anyone from sneaking up on him. His footsteps led him farther into the chaotic mess of metal weapons and various vocalizations from grunts and shouting to cries of pain or groans from the afflicted soldiers.

Byron had grown accustomed to such scenes despite how off putting some of the sights were. What allies he spotted in need he assisted by sending a bolt to have them facing less opponents or a wall to protect them from an unexpected blow. His mind shifted into a state reminiscent of his time at the academy where he always kept part of his attention on his more vulnerable students yet still allowed them to try at their own pace.

*Such guidance builds confidence and morale without directly keeping them reliant on me. If I hadn't learned that early on in my career, I'd be holding everyone's hand until my last breath, both because of my sympathetic nature and their perceived need for support.*

The thought left his mind when a man obviously hoping to reach him barreled forward with a club raised in each hand. Dark fur covered most of the Nim-Valans' bodies, yet the figure nearing him appeared to have his own coat, like a bear on its hind legs.

Before Byron could react to the new enemy, the earth underneath his feet shook violently enough to have him losing his balance and dropping to one knee. Most everybody did the same or landed on their sides, backs, or rears.

*What was that?* he wondered as he pushed himself up.

As soon as he did so, another tremor rocked the ground. He didn't stagger this time though, allowing him to search for the source. A flash off to his right had him looking that way before instinctively raising his arms to cast a shield. The sight not only revealed the cause for the quakes but also let him know where his target hid at the moment.

The bolts ceased seconds later, filling the area with near silence after what loud claps of thunder deafened both friend and foe. He dismissed the aftereffects in order to dismiss his spell and begin jogging in that direction before any potential opponents rose to challenge him.

What he didn't expect was for someone to take his arm while saying his name.

"Master Byron, enough!"

The words didn't register right away, leading the person to shake him by the bicep until he acknowledged them. When he glanced over, he met Mattais' tired eyes.

"The general is calling for a retreat," the man's assistant continued while releasing his hold.

Byron couldn't comprehend the purpose for such a decision and voiced as much after. "Why now? Our mages are ready to join the battle, the demon is giving its location away, and-"

"It's been hours since we initiated combat. Our troops are worn, and General Casner doesn't like what's going on with the flow of battle."

That comment caught him off guard. Instead of arguing further, he requested to be taken to their leader, which seemed to be what the soldier was waiting for. Together, they crossed through the growing mass of bodies that stood to continue the fight until they reached the edge of the forest surrounding them. This made Byron even more curious due to how they separated themselves from the majority of the action.

"Sir," Mattais called and turned his head from side to side. "Over here!"

Both glanced at a figure lying on the ground at their backs. Immediately, the assistant general threw himself to his knees in order to prop his superior up. From there, Casner removed his helmet, revealing a bloody mess underneath.

"We don't have time to waste," he began by addressing Byron. "You can't pinpoint their leader's location, correct? I'd be amazed if you could given that's what we've been trying to do for hours. Well, that seems to be its plan for the time being."

Byron helped the general to his feet when the man struggled to do so with Mattais' assistance alone. "What do you mean? What troubles you?"

"Our Yeluthian ally has been sprinting after the demon to no avail. We've been failing to do so too thanks to what enemies stand in our way. Besides, the beasts haven't shown up either. I'm concerned the being is waiting for something."

During the resulting pause, Byron attempted to wrap his head around the situation until Mattais spoke.

"It's obvious their leader is toying with us to wear down our numbers. Look at how the northerns are acting. They're not marching to overtake or surround us."

"That's a fair point," Casner added and spat. "We drew them away from their camp, so why not chase us away?"

Byron nodded as the reasoning became clearer. "The enemy is at a standstill. Whether or not they're waiting for something to happen, they likely won't change their tactic anytime soon."

"Exactly. I'm worried about the safety of our forces if we stay. We didn't intend for this to be a battle of attrition."

"I understand."

The general pushed himself away from them and straightened with a wince. His weary panting didn't bode well for his current condition, yet Byron knew better than to fawn over the hardened soldier. Together, they split apart to begin issuing orders for a retreat.

Those who heard the call finished off their opponents before turning tail and hurrying in the direction of the mages, which Byron used as a way to tell what direction he faced.

*It's the middle of the night, likely closer to dawn than dusk. We still need to march back to our camp and pray the Nim-Valans don't follow.*

During their retreat, the demon's spells continued. He managed to protect those he could and even picked up on Commander Evern's presence amid the unnatural smog the being produced. He imagined Coura fought alongside her father since he hadn't seen her for days and silently wished the duo well. The added support convinced him to remain one of the last people on the battlefield in order to keep shields up alongside his ally. Others joined them the farther east they wandered until he nearly tripped into a bush along the perimeter. Only then did he yell for them to fall back completely.

His comrades did so until he stood alone observing the troops on the other side of his spell. The blasts of flame, lightning, and ice abruptly stopped during that part of their retreat, which intrigued Byron; however, what baffled him most was the men's behavior. None crossed an invisible line separating the two sides. In fact, they looked to be standing at attention.

*What a strange turn of events*, he thought as he pivoted to spin and head into the trees behind his fellow mages.

# Back to Basics

lthough she worried the hike back to her allies would be arduous, the lingering effects of the demonic energy kept Coura going without issue. The morning after her confrontation with the Nim-Valans left her feeling sore above all else, especially in her previously injured leg. Fortunately, her hunger and thirst ebbed enough to spur her on until the middle of the afternoon. Only then did she recognize how the dark power continued humming in her veins. She dismissed it altogether and forced herself to eat, drink, and sleep as best she could.

*The last time I ignored my body's needs in favor of Soirée's power, I wound up in worse shape when it faded*, she reminded herself as Emilea's resulting lecture echoed in her mind. *I don't know when Lupin's energy will leave me, but I can't rely on my light magic until I'm sure I can cast it without issue.*

She spent a few minutes during every break doing just that: reaching inward past the active tendrils in search of what lied deeper within her center. The warmer presence remained, but it refused to react to her beckoning. After the attempts, she moved on.

Her only solace throughout the next three days was the lack of interference from Soirée. The demon seemingly disappeared once Coura departed from the area where they slaughtered nearly all two hundred northerners, which both relieved and bothered her.

*She asked me to join her in stopping Lupin directly. I became so frustrated with my unbalanced center that I didn't consider it, even though Casner and Mattais sent me away to do just that.*

In the end, the lack of their target and destruction of an enemy camp seemed to justify her decision to return for the time being.

The uneventful hike concluded when she spotted a pair of soldiers scouting the woods at dusk on the fourth day. Instead of approaching right away, she looming just out of sight until it became dark enough to justify a fire spell to light her way. She waited a while longer just in case before emerging from her chosen hiding spot, casting the ball of flame in her hand, and wandering toward the nearest duo on patrol.

"Who goes there?" one called, though they must have figured she didn't pose a threat due to her ability to wield magic.

Coura came close enough for them to fully see her before introducing herself. "I'm returning from a private assignment General Casner gave me. If you'd like, you can escort me to him for verification."

The two glanced at each other, then the first without the lamp pointed a thumb over his shoulder at the camp's location.

"I'll go with you," he announced and spun on his heel. "The general's still recovering from yesterday's battle. I suppose you didn't hear about that, right?"

She shook her head and kept to the man's side as he held a casual pace. He shared how the troops targeted Lupin's hideout in order to quell the remaining Nim-Valans and the damage resulting from the conflict. All the while, Coura couldn't comprehend why their leader would make such a rash decision.

Few people aside from the guards appeared to be up, which she appreciated given the hour and her own desire to rest around a warm fire, so they reached the general's tent without issue. The soldier knocked against the wooden post before a grumble from inside prompted them to enter. Immediately, her escort straightened and saluted the figure hunched over various papers and maps.

"Sir, one of our mages on a private assignment has returned. She wished to meet with you right away."

Coura glanced at the general, who looked up for a second before addressing the guard.

"Could you find Assistant General Mattais and tell him to see me. After that, you're dismissed."

With nothing else to add, the man agreed to the order and exited the tent. All the while, Coura observed the many bandages covering Casner's head and hands and imagined more beneath his clothing.

*Why would he choose to go up against Lupin?* she wondered again.

The general seemingly ignored her while they waited for Mattais to show up, so she remained standing until the expected knock came followed by the assistant general's appearance. He wore no armor and kept a blanket wrapped around his shoulders, making her believe he had been lying down for the evening.

"General, you summoned me," he began before recognizing Coura.

"Sit, both of you," came their superior's response as the man collected and set aside his papers. When they did so, he finally gave her his full attention. "I wasn't expecting you to return so soon. Is it because you didn't run into the demon leading the enemy troops?"

"I didn't encounter Lupin, but I did engage in combat with some of his men."

She proceeded to inform the two of her experience without hiding Soirée's involvement since they were aware of the being's presence. When she finished, she crossed her arms and waited for their reaction.

*I'm sure I'll get an earful for not sticking to my assignment. I can't even guess where Lupin is hiding with the rest of the Nim-Valans, so I'm not giving much of a report.*

To her surprise, a wide grin stretched across Mattais' face while a deep chuckle sounded from Casner. The latter commented on their unusual responses after.

"I should've known you wouldn't hear about our recent endeavor before now," he began and allowed his smile to fade. "Thanks to the Yeluthian ambassador, we were able to narrow down the location of the ancestral weapon and figure out the numbers surrounding it. In order to retrieve it, as well as confirm the demon's presence in that area, we organized an attack that lasted throughout the evening."

"Just for the ancestral weapon?" she muttered in disbelief. "That's risky."

"Even so, we sent a message," Mattais interjected with a serious, side-long glance. "Asteom isn't backing down. Commander Evern's subordinate and his squad reclaimed the golden sword on the eastern side of their camp, and we confirmed their leader's position while limiting our casualties."

"I suppose you get some of the credit," Casner grumbled while snatching a map from the pile of documents he had set aside. As he continued, his finger traced an invisible circle around part of the layout. "The Nim-Valans must have sent for reinforcements halfway through the night. None showed up, preventing them from committing to a full-scale attack."

During the resulting pause, Coura considered Soirée's motives and what she initially thought of the conflict. *I guess the credit goes to her, as much as I hate to admit it. I wouldn't have gotten close enough for a fight if she wasn't certain about pursuing Lupin's energy. Everything worked out for us.*

"In any case, we don't plan on acting again without cause," the general picked up. "We're still holding some of his troops hostage, you took care of another group, and their leader should be scrambling together what's left of their forces. We'll strengthen our own soldiers for what I expect to be the final confrontation."

"You want me to stay here then?"

He nodded. "I'll summon you again if we need to utilize your abilities and connection to the creatures. Just make sure the one looming beyond our camp doesn't intervene."

Despite the urge to comment on how she can't control Soirée, Coura agreed and departed with Mattais after Casner's dismissal. The assistant general had little to say and parted ways with her soon after while wrapping the cloth tighter around his shoulders. By that point, she began feeling effected by the lowering temperature and hugged herself against its chill.

*I left my stuff by Evern and Lavine's fire, but I would rather avoid being near them now*, she admitted after noticing a dull ache in her arms, like bruises covering her skin. *They'll notice the demonic energy before anybody else and demand answers. Byron and the others will pester me too, but I don't think the presence will bother them as much, except for Grace. At least I can avoid their scolding until I'm well rested.*

With that in mind, she considered her current condition next and believed she would benefit from a sleeping potion given how the active power kept her awake without her consent. She avoided making much noise, reached the medical station, and tiptoed around the dozens of sleeping men and women lying on the ground with bandages covering various parts of their bodies. Once she spotted a healer working on his stitching by lamplight, she approached and quietly cleared her throat to get their attention.

"Can I trouble you for medicine?" she began at a lower volume out of respect for the tent's occupants.

The young man raised his eyes without hiding his own weariness and inquired about her needs. After a brief conversation where she explained how she couldn't sleep, he retrieved a pair of vials from one of three bags at his feet and handed them over. The instructions matched what she remembered about the mixture, and she thanked him before departing when he finished.

Without another task for the evening, Coura returned to where she recalled her friends' bonfire being, found them asleep, then retrieved a couple blankets and a pillow from the nearby supply cart. She slipped between Will and Clearshot, who both snored peacefully, while noting Grace and Byron's position across the dimming flames.

*I doubt the distance will matter, but I'll attempt to be respectful. Hopefully they aren't completely alarmed by the demonic energy when they stir. I can't really help what happens.*

The wax seal on the first vial in her hand broke easily, and she tilted it back to swallow its contents before setting the glass aside. She decided to wait in case the effects weren't as promising as she needed, which proved to be the case when she only sensed slight mental fatigue minutes later. After consuming the second potion, she lied down, wrapped herself in the blankets to get comfortable, and cleared her mind until sleep swept her away.

***

For one of a few times in his life, Marcus was the first to rise with the sun and start his morning routine early. The previous days' adventures surprisingly didn't wear him out too much, resulting in a fulfilling night's rest. He attributed this to the success of their mission, which earned them the ancestral sword in addition to finding the enemy's leader and gaining insight into the Nim-Valans' remaining numbers.

*That seemed too easy*, he reflected as he splashed water from a basin onto his face and shivered at its shocking yet refreshing chill. *When Lavine removed the weapon from its sheath and told us exactly where his scout found it, the enemy's appearance made sense. Still, I would think they'd assign more than a few guards around that area.*

The Yeluthian's squad had infiltrated the private space without knowing what to expect; however, the fact that Nim-Valan soldiers patrolled the farthest end of the camp seemed to hint at a prize worth protecting. Nobody questioned the golden sword's location after the explanation, but Marcus couldn't believe their luck.

Their efforts shifted to recovering after the battle. He learned what the rest of the troops faced and became just as confused as the general about the demon's intentions. In the end, they agreed not to linger on the being's reasoning, yet caution would be their ally going forward. His thoughts then focused on helping his comrades recover, fortifying their defenses, and whatever other tasks Casner or Mattais gave him. Both men agreed not to meet with anyone during the morning in order for them all to rest and eat in peace. Marcus fully intended to take advantage of the break.

After cleaning his face, beard, and hair, he went straight to the mess area for breakfast. He savored the heat from his warmed porridge during the walk back to his bonfire before dropping to sit beside Will, who appeared to have just woken up.

"Good morning," he began while offering a smile.

His friend yawned then grumbled a reply. The lack of energy had Marcus chuckling to himself, though he dove into his meal instead of commenting on it.

A minute later, Will rose and moved away from the area, presumably to wash and grab food. Without the herbalist's presence, Marcus noticed how quiet the area grew, and an odd, uncomfortable sensation hung over him, like a raincloud blocking the sun. He didn't think much of it until he surveyed those remaining around the dwindling fire and noticed an extra body to his right.

*Is that Coura?*

Byron and Clearshot were gone, which he expected given how early they normally rose, and only Grace remained bundled in blankets across the fire, as showcased by her whisps of white hair. This meant Dianne was already awake and left only one person who would still be sleeping.

*I imagine she stayed with the commander and his assistant during the conflict since she never returned here. Did something happen between them to cause her to come back? We were all pretty flustered by her news regarding her connection to the first demon, so I don't blame her for wanting to avoid being bothered.* The reminder of how she nonchalantly brushed aside their concern stung, but he told himself he would get an opportunity to speak with her about it again in the near future.

Footsteps crunching in the dry grass alerted him of Will's return and pulled his eyes away from his other friend. The herbalist yawned before dropping to the ground beside him.

"I take it you were up for most of the night?" he inquired as he considered the amount of wounded soldiers and mages near the medical station.

"The healers needed the help," came Will's mumbled response before he slurped at his food.

Marcus didn't continue the conversation until they finished and set their bowls aside. He then asked about the status of that area, which fortunately didn't sound too overcrowded, and if his friend would be returning to assist during the afternoon.

By that point in the morning, Dianne rejoined them just before Grace stirred. The Yeluthian offered a brief greeting yet appeared as though she didn't sleep well, as showcased by a frown and pale complexion. The two departed from the fire right after. Marcus didn't get a chance to comment on this since a bothered groan from Will drew his attention immediately following the women's departure.

"What's wrong?" he pressed when the herbalist crawled closer to Coura.

Instead of answering, Will plucked up a pair of objects from the ground, faced Marcus, and held them out.

"They look like vials for medicine," he noted with a shrug.

His friend scoffed at his response. "Yes, they are. I'm upset by what these likely contained and the fact that they're both empty."

Marcus raised an eyebrow to show his lack of understanding, prompting an exhausted sigh from Will.

"See the colored residue on the inside? I recognize this as a potion used to help with falling asleep. You're not supposed to take more than one within a certain period of time, but knowing Coura, she probably didn't listen. That's how you wake up with a headache."

"If it's that painful, she should learn from her mistake."

Will didn't appear convinced with his logic but abandoned the subject for the time being. The two chatted about the previous nights' events and what their days entailed before Grace and Dianne returned. Their Yeluthian friend still didn't seem entirely relaxed despite her guard's upbeat attitude. When Marcus inquired about this, she merely claimed to still be tired and kept quiet after.

Nobody else joined them over the next hour or so, and their conversations eventually turned to their responsibilities for the day. Will mentioned finding Finn before resuming his position at the medical station since he hadn't seen the man after the battle's conclusion. Meanwhile, the general requested Grace's appearance so they could update Aaron and his council on their recent success. Dianne would accompany her as usual.

"What about you?" the soldier asked him when they stood to go their separate ways. "Are we continuing to build our strength?"

Marcus nodded. "I'll be monitoring the recovery efforts until I'm needed elsewhere."

"That shouldn't be too exhausting," Will added while stretching his arms upward. "I'm sure you prefer this to all the action."

"Of course, but you never know how long it'll last."

The three agreed with him and parted ways without wasting another second of their valuable free time.

***

An earthy, bitter taste greeted Coura when she stirred, emphasizing the dryness of her mouth. Of course, she wasn't surprised given the potions from the previous evening; however, a dull ache gently pounded against the back of her head as an added result of her impatience to fall asleep. She remained bundled in her blankets for a while longer and hoped the grogginess would fade, but her growling stomach soon had her sitting up to begin her day.

*I can still sense how much demonic energy I possess from Lupin's troops*, she noted first as she rubbed both eyes with her knuckles until she saw colorful spots. *It's not suppressing my hunger or weariness at the moment, probably due to the medicine's dulling effects. I should find breakfast while food is still appealing.*

She prepared to throw the covers aside and rise until she caught the sound of footsteps close by. Then, a familiar voice spoke from above, prompting her to glance upward.

"I wasn't sure if you'd be moving much today considering how late you joined us," Clearshot began with his characteristic, amused grin. "It's almost noon anyway. Slow morning too."

Coura didn't respond. Her eyes became fixed on one of two bowls he held that presumably contained his lunch, though she noted nobody else around them. After a few seconds, he chuckled, looked between her and the food, then extended the wooden dish toward her; however, when she eagerly reached for it while preparing to thank him, the soldier pulled the bowl away.

"Not so fast," he warned without losing a hint of humor. "Care to share where you've been hiding during all the excitement?"

"I wasn't hiding. Casner sent me on a private assignment."

Her casual reply had him raising an eyebrow before offering her the food once more. This time, he allowed her to accept it and dropped to sit so they could talk over the meal. She appreciated the conversation that followed, which included her recounting her meeting with the general, how she slipped into the Nim-Valan camp after Soirée, and the results. Clearshot didn't appear bothered by any part of the mission, though he didn't ask questions or make comments to show curiosity or concern.

Once she finished, he summarized what she had heard from Casner and Mattais the night before. Lavine's group found the ancestral weapon Lupin placed under guard in his camp while the demon put up a fight to seemingly keep Asteom's forces in an isolated spot. Whether or not the being intended for this to be a distraction, she couldn't decide, yet what she and Soirée accomplished no doubt contributed to her allies' successful retreat.

The archer rose to toss a couple branches onto their fire before releasing a groan and stretching his back. "It sounds like we're nearing the end of this conflict."

*I hope so*, she longed to comment, but the words stayed in her throat when she considered what that meant. *I'd like to make sure Soirée is dealt with after Lupin and Nim-Vala. If I can't kill her, I might have to return east. That's a problem to face later.*

The thought steadied her mind for the moment, allowing her to lie on her back with her hands behind her head and relax. Although she heard Clearshot huff a laugh, he left her alone in order to return their bowls.

Without a plan for the afternoon, Coura contemplated savoring the lack of activity by napping or meditating, which would further help her center return to its original, balanced state. Part of her considered that a waste of time because of how much demonic energy she carried and knew utilizing what advantages it provided would benefit their forces.

The idea rolled around in her head until she noticed a pair of figures approaching from the southern path. As soon as she glanced over to identify them, she understood how continuing to harbor such malicious power would only hinder those closest to her.

Byron and Evern walked side by side before stopping on the opposite end of the flames, prompting her to sit up and wrap both arms around her legs. Neither spoke right away, though her father crossed his arms with a frown projecting disgust.

*I already assumed they wouldn't be pleased with me, but now I have to face them together. Did they plan this, or am I just that unlucky?*

"Clearshot was just here," she decided to share while pointing in the direction of the mess area. "Nobody else has been around."

"That's because some of us have responsibilities," her former mentor replied in a lighthearted manner.

Coura rolled her eyes. "Does scheming really require that much effort?"

"You know it does. I won't berate you for resting though. The general shared what took place with the second division of Nim-Valan troops."

That seemed to be an invitation for her to elaborate on her assignment. Just like with Clearshot, she didn't refrain from explaining the original intent to find Lupin and confront him alongside Soirée so the two would fight each other. As she shifted to discussing what actually ended up happening, Byron circled around the fire to sit closer. Evern remained in place without moving a muscle.

"I figured Lupin wasn't around, so there would be no point in lingering farther north," she concluded while letting her eyes wander. Behind her father, she noticed Clearshot heading in their direction.

Byron followed her gaze before speaking at a quieter volume. "You'd better be careful if you continue wielding demonic energy. Remember what happened last time?"

Coura stared down at her hands in response. She had no doubt the bruise-like markings she first received years ago were hiding beneath her clothing simply based on how much dark power she acquired. A slight stinging also arose when she paid them any mind, like a burn that continually irritated her skin.

*This is just another change I must accept*, she told herself when she considered the impact of stealing the enemy's unnatural ability. *If they can't heal, they're as human as Asteom's soldiers. Instilling a fear of death might be the best way to force them back. Would they continue listening to Lupin if he can't protect them?*

By that point, Clearshot reached the trio and announced his arrival with a chipper greeting. The mood lightened after when their conversations focused on the camp, its resources, and their next steps. Coura found herself unwinding since no one addressed her, allowing her to simply listen and make comments on the mundane topics.

Evern eventually slipped away before Marcus, Grace, and Dianne returned with their evening meals. She noted how her Yeluthian friend stayed away and avoided eye contact with her but otherwise acted normal. On the other hand, the soldiers didn't seem to notice what changed. The assistant general brought up her assignment, so she summarized what took place for a third time. When she finished, Byron immediately changed the subject by inquiring about Casner's report to the king's council.

*I guess it's appropriate to move on*, she thought and got to her feet.

Her growling stomach led her to fetch dinner, though only after Byron asked where she was going and if she could bring him food as well. She decided to oblige, but her first goal had her heading toward the medical station for another sleeping potion. The healer looked her up and down upon hearing the request before retrieving a satchel and fishing out a vial. Coura accepted it while contemplating whether or not to ask for two until somebody called the light mage away.

*I'll come back if I need more tonight.*

With that in mind, she moved to the mess area next for a pair of warm bowls filled with the usual porridge and wandered around the tents and bonfires until she recognized her friends' spot. Her steps instinctively slowed when she didn't see Byron right away, then they stopped when she noticed him chatting with her father at the edge of the firelight. Her curiosity about their conversation away from the others tempted her to eavesdrop until her stomach rumbled loudly enough to shake her out of her suspicion.

*They're probably talking about Casner's report for Aaron and the other generals. Either that or some strategy involving the Nim-Valans. Evern looks calmer than before, so I shouldn't worry.*

Despite the attempt at self-reassurance, something about watching the two converse piqued her interest, as well as her nerves given their tendency to scheme. This hung over her after she rejoined her friends, ate her meal, and impatiently waited for her former mentor to return for his food.

***

"I am worried about my daughter."

*There it is,* Byron thought and licked his lips while avoiding the urge to interrupt Commander Evern in favor of dinner. *I figured he had a reason for pulling me aside, though is this personal or related to her private assignment?*

When Coura's father returned to join the group while she went to fetch food, he didn't suspect the Yeluthian would be planning on having a discussion with him; however, the soldier requested they speak alone and led him around the site before bringing up the matter.

"Is it because of the obvious?" he countered.

The commander eyed him without a hint of concern, like someone genuinely seeking advice. "Probably. I did not bring up the demon's energy to her considering how she has been acting. I suspect she is already aware of the influence such a malicious presence has on others."

"I agree," Byron muttered while rubbing his chin. "That's not what bothers you though, is it?"

"Not directly. It is her willingness to become involved with that power. She understands the risks yet allows herself to stroll headlong into danger. The long-term effects could harm her body and soul beyond repair."

"You're right, but that's how she's always been."

Evern narrowed his eyes without a word, prompting Byron to elaborate.

"I'm not saying I'm fine with her careless mentality. I just doubt that will change, especially given what we know about her connection to the first creature."

He expected to be defending that statement, yet the Yeluthian merely released a low hum in response before leading them in the direction of their starting point. Those around the fire either greeted them with smiles or ignored the pair in favor of continuing whatever they had been discussing. Byron prepared to join them until his companion grabbed his arm to halt his steps.

"Please, may I borrow another moment of your time?" came the polite request.

Although his stomach growled its own protest, he didn't see Coura with the group and knew he would be waiting for dinner anyway. The commander dropped to sit at the edge of the fire's light after, prompting him to do the same.

"Thank you for your insight regarding my daughter," the Yeluthian soldier began in a relaxed manner, which startled Byron a bit. "I would like to request another favor."

"What is it?"

Evern's sapphire eyes scanned the area before he replied. "I do not believe the enemy will attack for a few days at least. Our previous strategy, as well as what Coura accomplished, disorganized their ranks. We also possess the ancestral swords, meaning we have a way to hinder the creature directly."

"I agree with your assessment," Byron added during the following pause. He caught the commander's gaze lingering on a point near the fire and traced it to where his former student now sat between Clearshot and Marcus.

"With the time that is available to us, it might be beneficial for me to continue her training. May we utilize the space you visit for your meditations?"

The innocence of the question and the Yeluthian's resulting, friendly look nearly had Byron laughing before he composed himself. "Of course. It's not as if it belongs to me."

To his relief, Evern chuckled in an amused manner. "Yes, I understand. I only wished to warn you in case you stumbled upon us when you hoped for privacy."

Byron expressed his gratitude while considering the soldier's idea. *Coura's progress has significantly improved in recent years. If it hadn't, she wouldn't be one of their troops. Still, I wonder what her reaction to the commander's training will be. He didn't provide a reason for the decision, but I would wager it has to do with helping her rely less on demonic power and more on her own skills. Whether or not she'll listen is another issue entirely.*

Instead of lingering on the future, he decided to resolve his current problem first. He thanked her father for being considerate of his thoughts while rising and offered the Yeluthian a hand. Evern accepted, dusted himself off, then wished Byron a pleasant evening before departing, finally allowing for an opportunity to eat.

***

The second morning since returning to camp left Coura with a minor headache thanks to the sleeping potion she needed late into the previous evening. As she expected, her companions were all awake and either eating or away on their own business, prompting her to rise, complete her morning routine, and fetch breakfast. No one bothered her while she did so; however, she noted how warm the weather grew as the sun rose, which seemed to put everybody in a better mood.

*Is it summer already?* she wondered once she finished her meal and lied back to soak up what rays escaped the canopy above. *No, it hasn't been that long. I'll enjoy the heat wave anyway.*

What felt like minutes later, she noticed footsteps close by and cracked open an eye to find Evern standing beside her. He wore an amused smile and chuckled at her lax behavior.

"Napping already?" he asked after while crossing his arms. "Your mother would say you take after me for sleeping at the first opportunity."

She sat up with a grin, stretched her arms upward, then offered a retort. "You make that sound like a problem."

"Only when responsibilities are being shirked."

"Is there something I should be doing?" she asked when his comment resonated with her.

In response, Evern pivoted and gestured for her to follow him. "Bring your sword."

The mention of a weapon piqued her interest. She practically jumped to her feet, hurried to retrieve the blade she had been using during her time along the border, and went to his side. Despite her curiosity, she avoided interrogating him since she knew he would likely avoid bringing up an assignment until they could speak without being overheard.

*This must not be urgent. Father isn't in a rush, and he actually doesn't look like he's focused on following an order. Is he planning on scouting from above? I mentioned how I can't wield my light energy because of Lupin's power. Did he forget already? No, I'm guessing it doesn't involve flying.*

Her mind continued evaluating the possibilities when he didn't speak, which increased her curiosity further when they exited the camp to follow a trail into the surrounding forest. She soon recognized the direction and wasn't surprised when they emerged into an open area along a hill, a spot she knew Byron frequented for meditation session. The master mage didn't occupy the space when they entered, so Evern continued until they reached the center.

"I would like to take this time to resume your combat training," he explained after halting and facing her. "It has been a while since we did so."

As he drew his weapon from the sheath buckled to his waist, Coura felt her excitement deflate. "I don't understand. We've been fighting here for weeks already."

"Yes, but a life-or-death struggle hardly qualifies as training."

She longed to dismiss his lesson yet didn't argue again. *Perhaps this is a way for him to unwind. Byron used to do that when we first arrived in Verona, though I only figured that out because he never restrained himself. Wooden weapons only cause bruising or broken bones. I should be careful if Evern is serious.*

With that rationale in mind, she readied herself and mirrored his position. The match began as soon as he shot forward to initiate swordplay. Her mind remained calm in order for her to assess each movement and block or retaliate; however, the lack of strength behind his attacks let her know he didn't intend to imitate one of the life-or-death struggles he previously mentioned. She soon found she enjoyed the exercise.

Neither marked the other for several minutes as metal met metal until her father scratched her in the arm when she attempted to utilize the nearby incline. The sacrifice allowed her to separate from him, causing a break in the session she used to catch her breath.

"Are you warmed up?" he asked while raising an eyebrow and lowering his blade.

Coura couldn't tell if the question had been meant in jest, so she nodded and pointed her weapon at him. "I'm awake now, if that's what you're wondering."

"Good. We can start with your training."

Those words seemed to trigger a new attitude from the commander. She noted how his expression hardened, and his body straightened, reflecting the tightness of his muscles. He fixed her with a stare projecting hatred, as though she were an enemy, which startled her a bit. Unlike his usual demeaner, this abandoned any lightheartedness.

*This must be what he wants to do*, she realized while warily readying herself. *I suppose I should take this seriously now too.*

Although she attempted to muster the same emotions that would help her focus, she couldn't seem to copy his intensity. This came back to bite her when he lunged to initiate the bout. Every swing held twice as much weight as before, and his movements proved to be as sharp and precise as she remembered. That let her know he was treating the lesson as a true fight. Coura couldn't do much more than prevent his sword from reaching her due to his swiftness, which led her to remain on the defensive until he backed away. While she began breathing heavier, he looked as cool and composed as ever. She opened her mouth to inquire about his change in behavior, but he charged before she could make a sound.

What followed became a battle of stamina. Instead of taking the offensive, she remained trapped by his constant strikes, unable to act for herself. This ended when he swiped for her face, grazing her left cheek in the process, and brought his opposite side close enough to shove her backward without touching her weapon. The unexpected, physical blow had her stumbling before he raised a foot to kick her in the stomach. Despite the minor pain, his attack knocked the breath from her, leaving her to drop to her knees while wrapping an arm around her midsection. A second later, she felt the edge of his weapon against her throat.

"Get up."

Her temper didn't flare until his unbothered words reached her. She pushed his blade away and stood without considering if he planned to continue immediately. "What was that?"

His sword returned to her throat after, but she didn't react. All the while, his demeaner remained estranged.

"Ready yourself," he warned instead of answering.

"You're treating this differently than a sparring session, and I won't be bullied around if that's all you intend to do."

She swore she noticed a hint of concern cross his face before the antagonistic expression returned. The weapon then lowered as he reset his position and poised to attack again.

"You are mistaken if you believe this is anything more than training," he said after.

The response didn't sound deceitful, though it still confused her, so she decided to swallow her retorts and prepare for the next bout.

Just like before, his vicious, uncharacteristically barbaric method left her with little time to react. She managed to counter his strikes during opportunities, yet he always landed a worse attack, leaving her with cuts and bruises that healed thanks to the power she carried. Unfortunately, the commander steadily restrained himself less when she would recover, which resulted in deeper wounds. This only succeeded in causing her frustration to grow.

Twice more she wound up on the ground, and twice more she rose after he ordered her to do so. The entire situation confused her, though her temper prevented her from confronting him until she let down her guard and was knocked onto her backside. As expected, the cold metal pressed against her neck a second later.

"Get up." By then, even he panted and wiped away beads of sweat.

Coura shook her head. "I'm done."

"Get up."

"Why not tell me the truth? Why hide why you brought me here? It's obviously not to train since you said a life-or-death struggle hardly qualifies as training."

His sapphire eyes pierced her like daggers, yet she stood her ground. When he understood she wouldn't proceed with his game, his weapon lowered.

"How do you expect to defeat a demon when you cannot win against me?"

The question hadn't been what she expected.

"Furthermore, the skills you honed during your lessons with myself, Commander Detrix, and your comrades fall to the wayside when dark energy is involved. You fight as though you do not fear being harmed because of the healing ability, and magic is always an option readily at your fingertips. Such a mentality weakens your need to trust in combat prowess."

During the resulting pause, Coura fumbled for a reply. She naturally longed to argue with him about the benefits of utilizing what power she possessed, yet he spoke true regarding her lack of attention toward her weapons training.

*He's right. I was useless against Terran, my magic doesn't compare to what Lupin can do, and Soirée could kill me with her sword alone. I suppose I didn't think about how the demonic energy impacts my mentality beyond the emotional toll.*

At that notion, another realization came to mind, and she raised her eyes to meet his unreadable stare. "You weren't fighting like yourself on purpose."

"No," he answered while shaking his head and frowning. "It disgusts me to consider a demon's strategy, but we must do what we can to prepare ourselves, even if it means resorting to such vicious methods."

Whatever frustration she held melted away at his response, leaving her feeling foolish for doubting his faith in helping her. A bit of fear rose in its place after when she considered how easily either remaining demon could defeat her if she didn't put her entire being into a confrontation.

Movement from her father pulled her away from such worries for the moment. He approached to stand in front of her and offer a hand with none of the animosity from before.

"We will break for lunch and return to continue with clearer heads."

Coura accepted the gesture, allowed him to pull her to her feet, then they sheathed their weapons before departing for the main camp together. The mess area appeared as busy as she expected, yet they managed to grab their food in a matter of minutes and head to Evern and Lavine's bonfire. The other Yeluthian wasn't present, which had her wondering where he could be, but they ate and returned to the clearing without wasting the precious hours of sun.

As soon as the pair emerged from the brush, she spotted two figures standing atop the hill. Her feet instinctively slowed to halt, yet her father continued as though he expected them to not be alone. Upon closer inspection, she recognized Byron and Grace, who waved once they noticed the newcomers.

"Good afternoon," her former mentor began with his hands on his hips. "I hope you don't mind company."

"Are you here to meditate?" she halfheartedly asked before eyeing Grace. "Did Byron drag you along?"

Her friend giggled at the accusation. "I can assure you I agreed to assist."

"Assist?"

When Grace nodded, Coura sensed the Yeluthian's energy at work.

*{Byron and Commander Evern would like to keep your training as private as possible, so they requested I monitor our communication.}*

She didn't understand the need for such caution until she considered who they needed to avoid interacting with yet. *You're referring to Soirée.*

*{Yes, the first demon we encountered. You mentioned it wanders around the camp to watch you and study your connection, correct? Are you able to tell if it is nearby?}*

Coura crossed her arms and turned her focus inward next. After following the direction of her tether to Soirée, she glanced to her left. *She's farther in that direction. Not close enough to be able to observe or listen to us right now.*

*{I see. I will share your update with Byron and the commander.}*

A moment of silence passed between the four while Grace conversed with the others before the master mage addressed Evern.

"We'll be here if you need anything."

"I appreciate your participation," her father replied with a nod at both Byron and Grace to acknowledge each of them.

With that, he led Coura to the bottom of the incline, drew his weapon, and resumed their training. The session went smoother thanks to her willingness to view him as an enemy, yet she still struggled to find the rhythm she once established when she worked in Verona. By the time they ended for the day, she grew determined to win at least a single bout, if only to muster her faith in her abilities; however, a new thought came to mind during dinner, one she hadn't considered until she could reflect on the day.

*If they're preparing me to face Lupin and Soirée, they must understand I'm going to confront each demon*, she noted against a tightness in her stomach. *Lupin and the Nim-Valans are enemies of Asteom, but Soirée is my responsibility because of our bond. Evern, Byron, and probably everybody else hated the idea of me confronting her before. Now, they've accepted what needs to happen.*

The thought of no one stopping her or encouraging her to hide relieved her immensely while simultaneously increasing the pressure to succeed.

***

The amount of time that passed between the last conflict didn't register with Will until he found himself staring at the restocked potions in front of him. His free time over the last week consisted of creating a list of what items the medical station needed, gathering ingredients, and concocting mixtures for the healers. Those who were injured recovered and went on their way during the process, and the light mages who treated them took time to rest and replenish their energy. Only he seemed to be constantly working over the last couple days.

"Is this it?" he muttered to himself and grabbed for his list.

After reviewing each vial in the assorted bags, he set the parchment down, tilted his head back to stare at the top of the tent, and rubbed his neck. *I guess I became so set on restocking medicine that I lost track of myself.*

As if in response to the thought, his stomach growled, signaling his regular break for lunch. He chuckled before rising and exiting the station with a parting wave to the attendants lounging near the entrance.

The rest of the camp seemed to be in the same, relaxed mood, so he decided it wouldn't hurt to take it easy as well. He grabbed his portion of food and set out for the fire his friends frequented during their time along the northern border.

*I wonder if Clara or Finn would be there. Clara and her friends normally keep me company during their shifts, but I haven't seen Finn around for more than a minute or two. It's almost as though he stops by to check on me before running off to work on some task.*

Will then considered Marcus, Coura, Grace, and the others who appeared and disappeared just as often. Due to his self-appointed duties, he didn't give himself time to converse when they were together, though the lack of activity limited what they would discuss. The only person sitting around the group's fire when he arrived was the assistant general. The soldier held a half-empty bowl in one hand while leaning back on the other in a casual manner. As soon as he saw Will, he raised his wooden dish in greeting.

"Are you alone?" he asked before dropping to sit cross-legged across from his friend.

Marcus nodded. "I was, but only for a few minutes. Byron, Grace, Dianne, and Clearshot just left to meet Commander Evern and Coura."

"Are they patrolling together?"

The question seemed to bemuse the soldier for a moment, then he huffed a laugh. "I forgot you haven't been around lately. At least, not when I'm here. The commander has been sparring with Coura every morning and afternoon. Byron and Grace go along, I guess to practice their magic, and Dianne and Clearshot accompany them sometimes."

"What about you?"

"I join them when I can. General Casner requests I attend most meetings he holds, which usually involve the other leaders, but they take place in the morning. After lunch, I either patrol the camp, check on supplies, or find another task to keep me occupied."

"Are you free this afternoon?" Will ventured when Marcus paused to finish his meal. "I ran out of chores at the medical station, so I don't really have anything to do."

The assistant general considered this before nodding. With that, the two cleaned their bowls amid idle conversation, went to return the dishes, then exited the site through a trail he didn't remember existing. Still, the worn path proved how often it had been used. Eventually, the pair emerged into a clearing holding their friends, which he anticipated given the sounds of clanging metal and quiet voices. His eyes immediately went to Coura and her father, who fought with more intensity than he expected, resulting in scratches that would no doubt require stitching and blows that instantly caused swelling.

Unlike him, the sight didn't seem to bother Marcus. The soldier continued around the session toward a hill where the other four observers sat together. Byron was the first to acknowledge them when they came close enough to converse.

"Come to unwind with the rest of us?" the master mage inquired and pointed a thumb at those beside him.

"You could say that," Marcus replied before turning his attention to the weapon-bearing combatants. "It feels wrong to be lying around when those two are working up a sweat."

Will prepared to agree until Clearshot interjected.

"Don't say that. You make us sound lazy for enjoying a beautiful, spring day."

"You are being lazy," Byron added without skipping a beat. "Grace and I are monitoring the area and our energies, and Dianne is technically on guard duty. You're just here so you don't get roped into a patrol route."

When the archer could only pout and deny the accusation, Will, Marcus, and their Yeluthian friend shared a laugh.

"That is not necessarily a problem," the latter picked up in a sympathetic tone. "We should all be able to enjoy the moments of peace before battle."

Although the others nodded, Will's attention returned to the sparring match when he heard a grunt followed by a thud. His heart dropped a bit as Coura lied on her side, presumably after being knocked down by her opponent; however, she managed to deflect the commander's next attack, land a strike at his exposed leg, and leap to her feet in a matter of seconds.

*Just watching them makes me tired*, he admitted to himself when the pair continued without a break. *My combat skills aren't the best, but could I benefit from training too? Should I have spent time on that instead of restocking the medical station?*

His thoughts lingered on those questions before a frightening notion came to mind, one he had been subconsciously repressing until he found himself concerned for Coura's safety against the commander despite the Yeluthian's awareness. *The demon she's bonded with is hiding around the woods, and she mentioned killing it once the conflict with Nim-Vala is settled. She must be working with her father in order to prepare for that confrontation. What happens then? If she defeats the creature, won't she die too? Is it even possible to single-handedly beat one of their kind?*

Will's hands clenched into fists as he wrestled with his emotions until a light weight fell onto his right shoulder. He glanced over to find Marcus' hand resting there, and the assistant general offered a smile, as though he sensed the direction of Will's thoughts.

"When was the last time you trained?" his friend asked while removing the hand. "I could use the exercise if you're up for it."

As Will opened his mouth to respond that he hardly touched his sword even after he returned to Asteom, Byron commented on the suggestion.

"You two can spar near where you entered the clearing. Grace and I should return to our meditating."

"My body's been growing stiff without much activity," Clearshot added while rolling his shoulder. "I'll be on the opposite side working on my aim then."

Their Yeluthian friend addressed her guard after, but Marcus led Will away before they could learn what the woman would be doing. Clearshot trailed behind as they crossed the area, then he selected a spot to practice his archery without disrupting anybody else. The assistant general halted them at the farthest edge after.

"This should be fine," he said and faced Will. "We can use sticks instead of swords."

They split apart to acquire their desired, improvised weapons from the environment surrounding them and reunited in a matter of minutes. Once they felt prepared, Marcus initiated the session at a pace familiar to Will. He could keep up with the soldier's movements, yet any he attempted to parry were blocked.

*He's obviously going easy on me so I can get used to the motions again. I should have known I'd lose some skill over the months I spent in Nim-Vala.*

Although disheartening, the realization helped him focus on relearning what he could in their brief time together; if not for his own survival, then to help his comrades and friends when the time came to face their enemies.

# The Last Stand

The days Coura spent with her father succeeded in both reminding her of her previous training under the Yeluthian commanders while keeping her mind occupied on current circumstance. She didn't allow herself to stop thinking about combat, the ongoing battle with the northerners, or Soirée and Lupin except during meals with her friends. Their support never involved bringing up what they would be dealing with in the near future, yet knowing they worked to hone their skills while remaining by her side lifted her spirits.

When their group returned in the evening for dinner, they were thrown back into the reality of their situation.

Amid the lighthearted conversations around the fire came Mattais' voice before the assistant general came into view. The man panted and wiped his forehead with the back of one hand, as though he had been hurrying around the camp before stopping at their location, though he still managed to offer a brief greeting.

"Assistant general, Master Byron, and Commander Evern, General Casner requested I bring you to his tent for an emergency meeting."

All three stood upon hearing their names, though Byron alone inquired about the purpose.

Mattais shook his head in a helpless manner. "I'll explain on the way."

With that, the four departed from that spot, leaving Coura and her other companions confused and concerned about the reason. They finished their meals over a discussion about the enemy's potential movement until Will offered to return their dishes on his way to the medical station.

"I'd like to check on our supplies," he elaborated when Grace mentioned his lessened involvement around the healers.

"The general's unexpected meeting might mean an upcoming fight, so we should be completely prepared."

Nobody argued with his logic; however, Clearshot rose to steal a stack of the wooden dishes when the herbalist struggled to carry them in both arms. They strolled away after, leaving, Coura, Grace, and Dianne to continue chatting. A few minutes later, only the soldier returned.

"Where is Will?" the Yeluthian inquired once Clearshot rejoined them.

"Please don't tell me he actually plans on working this late," Coura commented and crossed her arms. "He makes it sound as though the station will run out of potions within seconds if he's not there to supervise."

The archer chuckled at her assessment. "You're not wrong, but I'm afraid he may actually be needed overnight. His friend, the light mage who's been around here several times, caught us on our way across camp and mentioned a rumor of enemy troops marching east."

"That must be why the general called an emergency meeting," Dianne added, prompting a nod from Clearshot.

"The medical station is preparing for an attack at any moment, so the healers will be gathered until that happens or we learn more about the Nim-Valans' intentions."

*This will likely be the final confrontation with Lupin*, Coura realized as she continued listening to the three throw around ideas and predictions. *I can't imagine he would drag this out with what men he has left. Besides, I believe he only wishes to cause chaos for Asteom. If he expects to crawl back to Nim-Vala's capital and continue worming his way into their politics, he won't risk falling to the ancestral weapon or being captured.*

The four lied down for the day as she reflected on the demon. More questions arose the deeper she dove, which kept her awake even after the others fell asleep. Fortunately, her exercise throughout the morning and afternoon caught up with her, tiring her body enough to draw her away from her thoughts.

*

The increased amount of activity woke Coura earlier than she would have preferred, though she knew she should be grateful for the noise rousing her since she could get ready for what the day would inevitably bring. After fetching herself breakfast, she dropped beside Marcus, who didn't appear to have gotten enough rest.

"How was the meeting?" she pressed before beginning to slurp down her food.

The assistant general released a sigh as her question drew the others' attention. "General Casner ordered the soldiers to get into position despite the distance between our location and the enemy troops. According to the scouts, they aren't trying to hide their presence, and the demon hasn't used magic."

"Speaking of which, what about the mages?" Byron asked next. "You mentioned our soldiers, but I assume the rest of us will be given a separate assignment."

"That's correct. We discussed various lines and strategies, but the general seems unsure. He might request your input before reaching a decision since you've been assisting with that."

Although Byron didn't respond, Coura had a feeling he already expected to be involved in the plotting.

Their group finished their meals in silence before beginning to split apart with Marcus supervising the preparations, Clearshot accompanying him, and Will returning to the medical station to join the healers. Meanwhile, Dianne remained at Grace's side like normal while Coura chose to stay near Byron.

*I assume I'll be placed with the mages, so I'll wait until we're given a position in this fight*, she rationalized after inching closer to the fire in order to savor its warmth. *The real question is how close I should be to Lupin. My center can handle stealing his power and exposing the Nim-Valans, but I hardly fought him during our last confrontation due to my previous injuries. I might just get in the way.*

"Master Byron, you are still here."

At her father's voice, Coura glanced over to find the commander approaching her former mentor. He dressed in the non-metal armor matching every other soldier and wore a fitting, unreadable expression. She also caught a glint of gold from the ancestral weapon buckled to his waist, which she hadn't seen during her time along the border despite both swords being in their possession.

"I am," came the response as Byron stood. "Were you sent to fetch me?"

Evern's lips curved into a slight smile. "By the general's order."

"Let's get on with it then. Who knows how much time we can spare on building our defenses."

He walked onto the path that would take them toward the center of the site yet hesitated to continue when her father didn't move. Instead, the commander's eyes shifted to meet hers, and his smile vanished.

"General Casner requests your participation as well."

The sudden summons had her raising an eyebrow until she put together why he would need her input. Whether it was her connection to Soirée and demonic energy or her ability to remove the enemy's healing ability, she understood her worth to their leader. With a huff, she pushed herself to her feet and followed Evern while dismissing the shred of disappointment at having to leave the warmth of the flames.

No one spoke as they crossed through the busying camp, allowing them to put together their thoughts before the meeting. As soon as they reached the tent, her father entered without announcing his presence. Byron did the same, so Coura slipped in last. Casner's space didn't look messy the last time they spoke; however, papers, supplies, and various pieces of armor took up enough of the ground to prevent them from sitting. He stood beside a woman she believed to be in charge of the medical station and offered a grunt in greeting as they shuffled in and formed a circle.

"Thank you for fetching them, commander," the man began and addressed Byron next. "I'm sure you've heard what's going on from Assistant General Marcus or one of the other soldiers managing the troops. Our priority now is to organize the mages and figure out some sort of plan to deal with the demon."

"Do you have any ideas for where to start?"

"I already spoke with Master Massie about the healers and light mages."

He paused as an invitation for the woman to pick up the explanation, which she did in a dignified yet soft manner.

"Since we won't be moving far to engage the enemy, I don't see a need to keep any of my mages around the station. They are trained to act as healers and defenders interchangeably, so I suggested they do so on their own terms in groups positioned in the east and south."

"You would rather not have them outside the fighting?" Byron asked after. "The northerners' relentlessness puts us in a position where endurance is key to victory, so we can't risk danger befalling our healers."

"Normally I would agree, but I'm told we may not need to worry about endurance."

The woman's gaze shifted to Coura, prompting the three others to look at her too.

"You're referring to the demonic energy," she replied in order to clarify for the group.

Instead of waiting for the light mage to answer, Casner responded. "This battle will have both sides focused on wearing down their opponents. Because of this, I doubt the camp will be at risk. If it is, it'll be at our backs, meaning the enemy would need to go through our forces anyway. That's why we agreed not to keep mages away."

"The main issue remains the demon then," Evern added.

"Exactly. Our soldiers kept up with theirs before until the creature used magic. This time, I'd like to wipe out their men while a few individuals locate and deal with the enemy's leader."

Silence filled the tent for a minute while they considered that plan. During the break, Coura wrestled with her desire to go after Lupin and what task she would likely be given thanks to her ability to possess the being's power. It didn't surprise her when Casner brought up the connection after.

"If we can weaken the Nim-Valans like Coura did in their easternmost site, I imagine they will be defeated easily or retreat north."

"I can remove their healing, but I can't promise how long that will last or how many of their soldiers will be affected," she interjected when Byron and Evern began to speak at once. "It's just me too, and I promise Lupin won't pass up an opportunity to intervene if interfering with his spell hinders their success."

"You're saying we shouldn't rely on using that strategy?"

"I don't mind trying to limit their healing as much as possible, but it's unpredictable."

He crossed his arms while narrowing his eyes a bit at her; however, he didn't argue. This allowed her father to continue the discussion.

"General, it sounds as though we should establish two parts of this fight. The first will deal with the Nim-Valan troops, and the second involves the demon. We have two ancestral weapons, so I believe it would be in our best interest to target the creature directly."

"I agree," Byron shared after. "Besides, we haven't brought up the potential for the demon's creatures to be active this time. Let the mages handle shields, the soldiers keep the enemy occupied, and the selected individuals work on locating their leader."

Coura noted how Casner contemplated the suggestions before responding. In the meantime, the light mage named Massie expressed her approval. That seemed to help the general move forward.

"We formed the outline of a strategy and now need to finalize some details, mainly who will be sent after the demon, though I already have an idea of who is going to volunteer..."

***

From the moment the sun rested on the horizon to when it reached the opposite end to set, Byron never paused for a break.

415

Even meals consisted of snacking on dry rations while donning his armor after passing along the general's orders and appointing supervising mages who would be leading each group. He spent most of the morning with Casner, Evern, Massie, and Coura simply plotting where the troops would be positioned in a space just beyond their location so the enemy would march into their current route. Despite the simplicity of the overall strategy, his main concern would be entrusting the mages' safety to others while he would find and engage with the demon.

The sunset's vibrant colors along the clear sky above caught his attention as he gazed upward through the canopy and considered that. *Nobody seemed surprised I agreed to separate myself in order to go after the Nim-Valans' leader, but four people hardly constitute as an intimidating force.*

When it came to selecting individuals for the special assignment, he threw his name in first, followed by the Yeluthian commander. Evern also suggested his subordinate accompany them and that he continue carrying one ancestral weapon while Casner holds the second, which nobody argued with. The pair of angels would keep to the sky until the demon showed itself. Finally, Coura's participation was necessary, according to her, which didn't sit right with him or her father.

"I doubt he'll just let me steal his power," she explained after they argued against her involvement. "If you want the enemy soldiers to stop healing, I have to intervene. Lupin will likely show up at some point then. Use me to draw him out of hiding."

*Of course she would suggest being the bait*, he reflected as he heard footsteps approaching from behind. *I don't doubt she assumes she has nothing to lose since her life is tied to the other creature. Speaking of which, I wonder if it would show up to protect her. Would it confront the northerners' leader like it did with the demon targeting Dala? Is that what Coura is hoping for?*

He longed to ask but dismissed the question when he turned around to face her and realized how out of place the subject felt in that moment. His former student took the opportunity to speak after.

"Evern and Lavine took off to catch up with Casner," she shared while adjusting her right arm's brace. "We're the last ones to depart."

"All according to plan," he muttered in response. "I'm ready whenever you are."

Instead of replying, she continued fiddling with the leather armor on her forearm before it eventually settled into place. During the process, Byron noticed bruise-like markings above her wrist when the skin was exposed, reminding him of their previous journey around Asteom. The two had discussed that alone after the general's dismissal, and she made it clear she understood the danger.

"I don't intend to overwhelm my center with demonic energy," she startled him by mentioning in a calm manner after he lectured her on the risks. "My Yeluthian power still isn't responding, so I won't hold my breath that I'll be able to use it. With that in mind, my body will heal on its own. If I monitor what I take in and wield, I can make sure I stay within my limits."

*That's all she shared, but I'm not entirely sure I trust her to understand what she can and can't do when under its influence. Demonic energy is different than any presence I've encountered. I know the commander feels the same way, if not more suspicious.*

His worry ebbed when she met his eyes, nodded, and placed a hand on the hilt of the sword at her waist. "We should hurry."

The pair began jogging through the woods without concern for what noise they produced due to their late arrival to the conflict. Either the troops would already be stationed and in position, or they would be engaged with the enemy. Byron made sure to keep his eyes peeled for any sign of the demonic creatures in case the beasts targeted them as well.

For what felt like nearly an hour, they traversed the uneven terrain while avoiding the rocks, branches, and foliage hindering their speed. Their progress didn't seem to matter as much once they heard the sounds of battle farther ahead.

"Prepare to slow down and enter on my signal," he ordered and shifted from a jog into a brisk walk.

"Got it."

A second after those words, Byron heard rustling and uneven footsteps from behind. He instinctively halted and spun around only to find himself alone.

"Coura?" he called as his eyes scanned his surroundings. "Coura, where are you?"

When he received no response, his heartbeat picked up. His first thoughts revolved around the creatures, prompting him to draw his sword in preparation for an ambush. Then, he clearly heard his partner's voice, though at a distance.

"Let go of me!"

His feet moved in that direction before he could consider who would target her. A smooth, feminine voice had him stopping in his tracks once he recognized it as the first demon's.

*It's here already*, he thought against a chill sweeping over his body.

Fortunately, the surprise delayed his reaction for mere seconds. He gripped his sword tighter and proceeded ahead until he spotted Coura and the being. It held her by the collar of her shirt with one hand and pressed her against a tree trunk, keeping her pinned in place. Despite that, she attempted to pry herself away from the being's grasp and wriggled in an effort to escape.

"What do you want?" she demanded in a tone possessing more annoyance than fear.

Meanwhile, the demon's expression projected anger as it addressed his partner; however, its following question sounded unbothered. "Do you expect me to let you get yourself killed?"

"Don't you want to find Lupin?" Coura countered.

"Finding him is one thing, but allowing you to throw yourself into his clutches is another. Didn't I warn you about being careless?"

"I'm not rushing in alone."

"I assume your role involves utilizing his power, which will create a confrontation you won't survive. Remind me how you fared against Terran?"

"He's dead now, isn't he?"

Byron considered approaching to assist, yet the lack of tension between the two as they spat questions and retorts at each other stayed his hand.

"This is our opportunity to corner him while his troops break apart," his partner stated and stopped fighting against the being's hold. "If we don't stop him now, when will we get another chance? The entire conflict can end tonight. Wouldn't that benefit you?"

The creature's malicious gaze relaxed into a glare, but it didn't refute Coura's argument, allowing her to add more.

"Why not help us? Together, Lupin doesn't stand a chance if we-"

"Remember what I shared about my kind and gaining power?" the demon interrupted while releasing its grip in order to step backward. "He is beyond what you would consider sane thanks to his possession of the northern men. Who do you think he will go after in the mix of blades and magic?"

"The biggest threat to its success," Byron answered. His response drew their attention, and he sheathed his weapon while moving closer. "You're implying the enemy's leader will go after one of you two because of the demonic energy you carry. Multiple targets would distract it."

The being huffed a laugh. "On the contrary, Lupin won't focus on anything other than one of his own kind. His narrowmindedness is partially why I broke off our partnership decades ago."

"He'll be aiming for revenge then."

"And you humans will just get in our way," the demon finished with a proud, devious smile that sent a shiver along Byron's spine.

On the other hand, Coura didn't seem affected by its behavior. "I doubt you'll admit to being weaker than him, but you could still end this sooner by fighting alongside us. Everybody would stay away from-"

"Sorry, Dear One. I am more interested in watching than participating despite what thoughtless danger you throw yourself into. Just know I won't hesitate to interfere if you find yourself at death's door again, and I could care less who winds up in front of my blade."

The warning hung in the air as the being retreated into the brush before disappearing in the shadows beyond. Byron continued studying the spot where he last saw it out of instinct until Coura waved a hand in front of his face to pull his focus away.

"Don't worry about her," she advised without appearing bothered by the unexpected conversation. "If Soirée says she won't intervene, we don't need to worry about her. The others are waiting."

He cast a final glance at the trees, nodded, then adjusted his attention toward the west where the sounds of battle rang out. After urging her to stay close to him, the two set out in that direction.

***

The ringing of metal in Marcus' ears became familiar over the years, settling him into a mindset where he could act and process the situation at the same time. That had been one of the first lessons he learned when he became his father's assistant.

*"Keep your head about you,"* the familiar voice repeated in his mind as he swung his blade across the nearest enemy soldier's thigh. *"If you can't move, you're useless. If you can't think, you're in no position to lead."*

He noted how he hadn't considered his father's words for years before diving back into the mass of bloodied bodies alongside his comrades.

For the most part, the current conflict mirrored their previous encounter. The troops engaged with one another as soon as they came in contact at the designated location, Asteom's forces continued to hold their ground, and the Nim-Valans merely rose every instance they were cut down. With the mages' support, Marcus felt comfortable maintaining that position.

"Any news from the perimeter?" he heard General Casner shout from off to his left.

Before he could answer, Mattais' voice sounded from his right.

"The beasts are out there and attempting to break the walls. Those mages will be occupied."

*As expected. The demon isn't restraining its creatures this time.*

He returned his attention to the men stumbling toward him with crimson staining their hands and faces. In a matter of minutes, he stood alone once again. The pause allowed him to scan the area in order to assess their progress.

Like earlier, he recognized few differences between the fight from over a week ago. The first had been the extra threat occupying the magic wielders' attention, which forced them to maintain shields instead of contribute to the battle. He would have been more concerned if he didn't catch what Coura, Byron, and the Yeluthians were up to already.

Even at a distance, he spotted flashes and glimmers from the spells his friend and the master mage used to take down several foes at once. What bodies fell to the ground sometimes didn't rise again, but he recalled Coura's recollection of her fight against a secondary set of Nim-Valan troops farther north. Although he disagreed with her decision to manipulate the demon's power, he couldn't deny how it benefited their cause.

Meanwhile, the angels preyed upon unsuspecting Nim-Valans by pouncing like aviary predators, either landing suddenly enough to incapacitate their chosen opponent or swooping lower and slicing at multiple enemies. He imagined their role required the most patience out of everyone's due to how they would be repeating the process until the enemy's leader appeared. When that would happen, he couldn't guess.

Marcus allowed himself to ease into a regular routine of attacks since his assessments didn't yield new, useful information. Out of the corner of his eye, he made sure to watch his comrades in case any struggled against their opponents; however, the northerners' sluggish behavior allowed them all to stay on top of the Nim-Valans' movements.

For what felt like hours, he didn't question the lack of strategy from the enemy. His limbs burned from exhaustion, though not enough to deter him from their goal, and the sun soon set to shroud the area in darkness. Fortunately, the mages were able to start torches or hold balls of fire in their hands to light the entire circle of combat. The teamwork they used to do so while making sure the barrier around them remained impressed him, and he made a mental note to comment on it to Byron later.

*For now, I need to uphold my role alongside the other soldiers*, he reminded himself while selecting his next target.

Before he could act on that thought, the northerners changed their tactic.

A set of startled cries sounded from farther behind, alerting Marcus and those around him of trouble. He craned his head around to find dozens of men barreling through the ranks of Asteom soldiers and turned to raise his blade against the nearest who swung a dull broadsword. Metal met metal when he blocked the northerner's attack, but the strength behind the blow had him backtracking a couple steps. In response, his opponent's mouth curved into a mad grin.

*He's different than the others*, Marcus realized while adjusting his stance for the enemy's follow-up swing. During the process, he caught a scratch along the man's forehead and understood. *Of course! It's because he isn't being manipulated by the demon. He still has control over his mind, but how?*

While he tried to come up with an accurate explanation, he ducked under and sidestepped the Nim-Valan's following attacks, which were wide enough to predict despite the lack of demonic influence. An opportunity for a stab presented itself during the next, vertical swing as the broadsword rose and dropped near Marcus' left shoulder. He instinctively slid in the opposite direction, pointed the tip of his sword at his opponent's gut, and thrust the weapon forward.

His metal pierced through the weaker, leather padding easily; however, the man had released one hand and shot for his throat at the same time. He hurried to let go of the hilt, step back, and seize the Nim-Valan's wrist to stop the strike in response. What physical combat skills he picked up over the years kicked in as soon as he caught a glint from the man's hand. His foot lifted to make contact with the side of his opponent's knee, causing enough of a distraction to lighten some of the strength behind the northerner's arm. Marcus used that to his advantage by shoving it aside and pulling back a fist before landing a punch against his enemy's exposed jaw.

As he retreated, the figure dropped to the ground and remained unmoving. Someone called to him after, yet he refused to leave until he knew the man wouldn't get up again.

*They shouldn't be able to heal unless the demon is possessing them*, he remembered after. The notion eased what tension hung on his shoulders, and he retrieved his weapon without issue.

"Assistant General!" came the shout again as soon as he dismissed the Nim-Valan.

Marcus glanced around until he spotted a soldier hurrying toward him without regard for the fighting surrounding them. That lack of caution irritated him given the risk to his comrade's life.

"What is it?" he snapped and prepared a lecture on being aware of the enemy at all times. The words became lost in his throat when he heard the reason for such impatience.

"General Casner has been wounded!"

Marcus' mouth hung open as he processed the update. "What happened?"

"Assistant General Mattais sent me to fetch you," the man continued between breaths. "The healers are working on him, but it doesn't sound promising."

"Take me to him," he demanded despite the overwhelming urge to push for more of an explanation.

His comrade took off through the continuing chaos around them and managed to avoid what stray weapons would have otherwise interrupted the trek. Marcus wasn't as lucky. Twice, somebody stepped in front of him as a challenge, forcing him to outmaneuver the individuals just enough to incapacitate them. All the while, he ground his teeth in order to avoid screaming in frustration.

Finally, after what seemed like too long, they broke away from the main fighting and into the safety of the area containing their healers. Those who weren't tending to patients stood with arms extended and manifested shields to separate themselves from the combat. He soon spotted his fellow assistant general standing beside two, kneeling women working on their superior.

"Sir, I found Assistant General Marcus," his guide announced while slowing in front of Mattais.

Marcus went right up to the man without waiting for any sort of greeting. "How is he?"

Mattais' eyes reflected distress as they met his before lowering to the body on the ground. "Not well. The new troops targeted us before we recognized them as real threats."

"What do you mean? Where did they come from?"

"According to the mages, a second wave of Nim-Valans arrived from the east. We believe they were our prisoners due to how normal they behave, though we're not sure how they escaped the guards and their bindings."

"Could it have been the demon?"

"I don't know," his comrade replied in an exhausted manner, as if he had been raking his brain for answers already. "They targeted us and broke apart. Before I realized what happened, General Casner could barely stand due to a wound on his arm."

The unexpected reason baffled Marcus. "A wound? How could-"

"It's a potent poison," a voice from one of the women interrupted, drawing their attention. "They knew what they were doing when they scratched him. We can only hope they just used it on one person. Otherwise, we're in trouble."

*The Nim-Valan with the broadsword held another weapon,* he recalled after her words. *Was that an attempt to do the same to me?*

"Is there an antidote?" he asked next while trying and failing to hide his desperation.

"We sent somebody to fetch it from the camp. He mentioned preparing a few vials a while ago but didn't think to bring them. Our magic is keeping the general stable for now, but he's in no condition to move."

Marcus released a breath in order to ease the ache in his chest. *General Casner should live. That's a relief, but…*

He returned his attention to Mattais, who didn't appear as reassured. "This shouldn't be cause for a retreat, right?"

A pause stretched between the two for a minute. Amid the regular, ongoing noise came the sound of thunder.

"The general would scold us for overreacting to the loss of one man," came his fellow assistant's response. "Besides, you have enough experience to lead our troops."

The comment caught Marcus off guard, and his startled reaction prompted a weary smile from Mattais.

"Don't you agree the bravest, most skilled, and responsible person should be in charge?" the man continued.

"Yes, but I'm just a-"

"I can't do it."

Again, Marcus found himself at a loss for words.

"I'm not ready to step into my superior's shoes," Mattais went on at a quieter volume yet without a hint of shame. He even held up his hands, which trembled. "I may be older than you, but I still have plenty to learn and confidence to build. I'm only in this position because General Casner's previous assistants were promoted, but you've been training for this your entire life."

Although he couldn't deny that fact, Marcus shook his head. *Father refuses to believe I'm ready for such a role, and I trust his judgement. Perhaps this is the opportunity I've been waiting for. Still, so many lives are in my hands.*

"It's now or never," his comrade added with a glance at the general. "We don't have anybody else."

He followed Mattais' gaze while contemplating their issue. Part of him couldn't fathom assuming their superior's role as leader, yet he couldn't come up with a valid reason not to do so given General Casner's condition. That, along with how the troops continued risking their lives as they stood around, helped steel his resolve.

"The plan doesn't need to change," he began while utilizing his newfound strength. "If the new group of Nim-Valans are the prisoners from our camp, most won't possess the demon's power, meaning they won't be able to heal. Those who rise can be managed until their leader appears. Otherwise, Coura's been taking its energy."

"What about the beasts around the perimeter? The mages might not be able to hold them off for the entire evening."

Marcus let his eyes wander over the nearby conflict as his mind worked to process the question. "This fight serves two purposes: to eliminate the enemy troops and put an end to the demon. If the creature doesn't show up by the time we need to retreat, we can assume it abandoned its pawns."

"What makes you so sure?" Mattais countered.

"Why lend its power at all if it doesn't plan on utilizing the men it manipulates? From what I learned about demonic magic over the years, if a possessed human dies, the energy either doesn't return to its host or the host gathers a lesser amount. It doesn't make sense to waste resources."

"I see. We hold our ground then?"

"For the time being. If the demon does show up and cause problems, we'll need to reevaluate our strategy in order to support those targeting it."

He became so engrossed by his thoughts that he jumped when his comrade placed a hand on his shoulder, drawing his eyes.

"An admirable assessment," the man commented with visible relief. "Just tell me what to do, sir."

Marcus couldn't refrain from huffing a laugh in response. "How about you stay close to the mages in case anything here changes. I'll return near the frontline to issue orders based on what takes place."

He managed a single step before Mattais grabbed his arm to keep him from leaving. When he sent the man a look to reflect his confusion, his fellow assistant general frowned.

"We shouldn't risk losing you too. Who knows if the enemy still carries poison-coated weapons. You're safer here."

The caution sounded reasonable, yet Marcus found himself struggling with the concept, and he wondered why. *Perhaps I'm used to being involved in the action. Then again, why would I train if becoming a general means standing on the sidelines? Is my own safety that far above the rest of the soldiers?*

He attempted to remember how his father responded to such a situation; however, he suddenly realized he had never seen General Tont in battle. The man's combat and deductive skills were equal to the others in his position, which kept him on the king's council, but he never experienced a fight like what currently took place.

*I suppose he would agree to issue orders from a distance*, Marcus told himself despite how the notion deflated his spirits. *There shouldn't be a right or wrong answer, and plans change, but I refuse to value my life as greater than anyone else's. Maybe that's what I needed to learn.*

He knew his father likely shared a different opinion and wondered if General Casner thought the same. In the midst of his reflection, Mattais released his arm and shot a reassuring smile.

"Let me return to the frontlines," the man suggested and gripped the hilt of his sheathed sword. "I'll be the soldier mad enough to charge into the fray."

He followed his statement up with an awkward laugh, but Marcus ignored it as the comment spurred a memory from years ago. In it, he charged behind General Tio and Calin during the conflict in Verona's southern field. The Dalans arrived to help stop the former high priest's manipulation of the Nim-Valan soldiers, and he couldn't deny he had thought the base's leader was crazy.

*Not only then. General Tio lost his hand against the rogue angels and challenged the previous demon alone. He never shied away from participating if it meant he could defend his people. Calin is the same, though not as vocal. I always admired their courage and how it inspired their troops. That is how I imagine a leader.*

Without realizing it, Marcus' feet moved on their own toward the battle beyond the mages' shield.

"Wait," came his comrade's voice. "I thought we agreed you would remain here."

He paused, pivoted, and found himself grinning as his heartbeat picked up with a sense of confidence reminiscent of his time in the southern city. "Sorry, but I can't do that. I'd be a disgrace to my mentors if I didn't give my sword to our cause. Don't worry; I'd also be a disgrace to them if I die here."

Instead of staying for a response, he returned to approaching the shield and drew his blade before charging into the mass of allies and foes.

# Adapting to Danger

Like every battle Coura previously participated in, her mind settled into a calmer state once she fell into a familiar rhythm and understood her opponents. What nerves arose during the trek to the scene dissipated once she and Byron selected a spot away from their comrades where their magic wouldn't interfere with the ongoing fighting. All it took was a single bolt of lightning to draw the enemy's attention.

*So far so good*, she told herself while evaluating the energy humming in her center. *I'll take a break after these two.*

The men who approached at what she generously considered a walk held emotionless expressions as they halfheartedly swung their weapons. At their movement, she cut them down without a second thought before stabbing her sword into the ground, placing each hand on their arms, and reaching inward to extract the demonic energy within. Lupin's power never seemed to resist her, leading the process to take less than a minute.

As she rose to stand straight, she couldn't help but wince at the stinging along her limbs where the dark energy escaped without her control, which let her know when to pause her efforts. She retrieved her weapon while glancing at the Nim-Valans she just felled in order to confirm they were truly dead.

"How are you holding up?" she heard Byron call from nearby where he lingered next to a trio of torched enemy soldiers who twitched as their newest injuries healed.

Coura refrained from rolling her eyes but didn't answer.

*That's about the twelfth time he's checked on me since we started*, she reflected and let her eyes wander across the area before thoughtlessly lowering her gaze to her wrist. Despite the darkness surrounding them, she could clearly see the bruise-like pattern where it peeking out from underneath her padding. *I wonder how long it will take before Lupin appears. I can't do much compared to Soirée, but I don't believe he'd wait until a majority of his troops are defeated. Is he planning on exhausting them before coming out of hiding?*

The sound of footsteps from the direction of her partner had her glancing over to where he closed the space between them. He halted a noticeable distance away though, reminding her of the demonic power's influence on other people.

"It's been a while since we arrived," he began in a cautious manner, as if he didn't trust the current situation. "General Casner intends to remain here all night, but I'm not sure when we should rejoin the troops."

"What do you mean?"

"Without the demon present, we're being underutilized. I wonder if merging into the heart of the conflict would either draw it out or cause the northerners to retreat."

"We don't want them to retreat though," she added before a group of shadowy figures off to her left caught her eye.

The six or seven enemy soldiers lumbered in their direction before she raised a hand to send lightning their way. What demonic energy she released overwhelmed her control, as it had in the past when she carried too much, producing a wider blast than she intended; however, the result was still what she intended. The lone downside to using such a powerful spell remained what lashed back at her. In that case, the shock numbed her arm, and what minor bolts connected with her hand and forearm charred her skin.

"Maybe you should stick to manifesting our shields," Byron commented in an unimpressed tone when she returned her attention to him.

She frowned in response. "I'll be fine. What were you saying about merging with the others?"

"Essentially, we're not facing the majority of the enemy troops. You're also limited with how many you can bring down permanently, so their leader could be waiting until we tire before acting."

"I think you're right," she muttered without hiding her displeasure. "Did you notice the demonic creatures?"

"They're only targeting the southern and western sides around our forces."

A pause followed where they assessed their surroundings and what recently recovered Nim-Valans attempted a charge from multiple directions. Coura gripped her sword tighter against a surge of frustration stemming from the unnatural energy in her veins. Once she recognized it, she reminded herself why she needed to avoid manipulating her dark power for a few minutes. Instead, she rushed forward to engage with her chosen targets, shifting the magical influence into motivation for her physical strength. Her blade swept through each man seamlessly, which she appreciated given how little attention she needed to give them, before she stood alone again.

The temptation to steal what energy they held had her considering abandoning her previous resolve until she recalled her partner's partially sarcastic words about shielding. After sheathing her sword, both hands rose so she could craft as tall and wide a magical wall as she could along the northern border. What power she expended didn't compare to what remained, yet she walked closer to inspect its durability.

*This should hold if the beasts or Lupin show up. Perhaps I can work on fortifying the perimeter to ease some of the burden on the mages. If Byron and the others cut the Nim-Valans down, I'll be able to take whatever energy I need.*

The idea became more appealing once she considered how productive such a system could be if Casner intended to remain in the area for as long as possible. With that in mind, she spun around and began heading toward where her partner continued cutting down and incinerating the enemy.

In the next instant, a violet shield appeared an arm's length away from her face. Her feet stopped before her mind considered the source of the spell, but once she felt the dark power emanating from it, her heart dropped.

*It's Lupin! He's here to-*

"Who would have guessed you'd be the thorn in my side this time."

Coura pivoted toward the familiar voice on her right while both pointing her blade at the newcomer and raising a hand in preparation to summon flames. Unfortunately, her reaction proved to be too slow. Before she could process her opponent's appearance, the figure lunged and seized both her wrists. His movement caused her sword to pierce through his left shoulder, but what fire she cast in the short amount of time scattered into a puff of smoke due to her alarm.

The being grinned as the gray cloud blew in his face, making his nearly white skin even more frightening. For the first time since they encountered one another, he abandoned the cloak, allowing her to assess his true appearance.

Unlike Soirée and Terran, Lupin possessed no hair on his head, and any inky fur was covered by the clothing he wore, which matched the Nim-Valans' armor. She didn't believe she would have recognized him upon first glance if he decided to wear a helmet to mask his pale complexion; the thought sent a shiver down her spine against the fear his sudden arrival spurred.

"I fully expected Soirée despite the weak imitation of her power," he continued as she fought to tear her wrists away. "You both enjoy meddling with my business even though it doesn't concern you. Why not savor what precious time you have left instead of spoiling my fun?"

"Asteom is my home," she growled in response when he seemed to be waiting for a reply. In the midst of their spat, she heard Byron's voice from beyond the nearest shield yet dismissed it in order to focus on their main enemy. "Besides, I know you don't care about Nim-Vala or its people."

"Of course not," he practically interrupted while letting his grin widen. "My lone investment is their ability to entertain me. Where else will I find humans foolish enough to trust a demon? Now that Terran is gone and Soirée turned her back on me, I expect to exploit their kingdom for as long as possible."

*Soirée mentioned how power corrupts a demon's mind,* Coura recalled after his explanation. *Without one of his kind to challenge his reign, he must intend to remain tethered to Nim-*

*Vala's ruler and corrupt its kingdom from the inside. What's the point of involving Asteom then?*

Before she could ask, the being leaned closer and continued.

"If you wished to join me, all you needed to do was beg."

His words didn't register until she felt Lupin's energy shoot into her body from where his hands held her arms. The sensation immediately reminded her of when she tracked down the demonic creatures spawned by Soirée's loose power and took the energy into herself, except he controlled the transfer. Every second brought about immense pain thanks to her overflowing center, as if she were being stabbed in various spots at the same time.

She froze after dropping her chin to her chest and squeezing her eyes shut. Any urge to move left her since it resulted in a worse sting than she already experienced. Meanwhile, Lupin cackled at her reaction.

"Poor humans with such frail bodies," he teased amid the laughter. "Such weak creatures to fall for the-"

Whatever he planned on taunting her with next abruptly ended, though she couldn't lift her head to see the cause. He released his grip on her wrists a second later, and as she dropped to her hands and knees when her legs buckled from the strain, a gust blew by. Her mind struggled to keep up with the world around her due to the lingering demonic energy producing a ringing in her ears that prevented her from discerning the voices she picked up on.

The frustration with her condition, as well as the ongoing pain, had her internally cursing her lack of attentiveness until she pried an eye open in an effort to remain conscious of her surroundings. In the next instant, her negative emotions shifted into surprise when she spotted a detached, pale hand on the ground in front of her beside a pair of white feathers.

***

It took far longer than Byron anticipated for him to shatter the demon's shield using what magic he could muster after the being's presence filled the air. He hadn't seen how it snuck close nor how it managed to grab his former student, but he didn't panic until the power suddenly amplified into a terrifying amount. Coura's reaction to the surge, as well as her lack of attention to his resulting calls, let him know the energy affected her beyond her control.

A stream of curses flowed through his mind as he shot bolts from one hand and icicles from the other until cracks covered the barrier; however, it still wouldn't budge. Part of him couldn't help but marvel at the structure's durability despite his frantic attempts to take it down. Only when the demon's cackling reached him did he finally throw caution to the wind and send a more powerful blast of lightning than he would have risked otherwise. Its deafening crackling filled his ears while flashes occupied his vision, yet he swore he heard the unmistakable sound of shattering glass amid the noise.

The spell also backfired on him due to the limited control. What bolts broke away from the main blast cracked like whips against his arms, chest, and face, no doubt resulting in burns ranging in severity. He dismissed the discomfort as he prepared to rush forward through the smoke, yet his feet slid to a halt before he managed more than a handful of steps.

Beyond the dark, steadily thinning cloud in front of him, he spotted the unmistakable sight of angel wings. The first set extended in front of Coura, who fell to her hands and knees during the chaos, while the second lingered farther behind her. Of course, he recognized them as Evern and Lavine, though the hatred their expressions projected seemed quite uncharacteristic.

"It's about time you showed up!" their enemy cried with a sickening amount of enthusiasm. "I was beginning to wonder if you'd finally abandon your so-called human allies."

"Be silent, monster," the commander replied with as much disgust as his glare reflected. "Your interference has gone on long enough."

When he lifted the golden weapon in his hand to point the tip of its blade at the demon, Byron caught a dark liquid staining its surface. *Did he manage to land a scratch?*

His eyes went to the creature after. It didn't appear affected except for how it cradled its right arm against its body, but it raised both in a shrug after, revealing its missing hand. The sight both raised his spirits and put him on edge due to the potentially rage-filled reaction.

"I could say the same for you and your kind," it continued without a hint of anything other than amusement. "Your obsession with humans is sickening. Always involved in their kingdom's affairs, though I suppose you yourself have more of a personal investment. Is she the only reason you're fighting? You realize she's fated to die, right? If it's any consolation, I never planned on being the one to kill her."

When Evern didn't respond to the taunts, Byron decided he should join his allies before the situation escalated even further. He made sure his footsteps were loud enough to draw the three's attention, but his eyes never left their opponent.

"Commander, I'll protect Coura," he began at a lower volume that had the demon tilting its head to show its curiosity. "Allow me to support from the sidelines while you and Lavine use close combat."

"I appreciate your input," came the Yeluthian's reply. "We will try to make this quick."

With that, Evern charged forward. Lavine followed a second later, and Byron manifested as tough a shield as he could form in front of himself and his former student, cutting them off from the resulting fight.

It became evident the Yeluthians had formed a strategy beforehand as soon as they neared the demon and split apart. The younger of the two leapt into the sky, though not high enough to stay out of the way, while his superior remained grounded to initiate combat. As expected, their enemy manifested a barrier to block his nearest opponent's first strike, then it raised its eyes to Lavine.

As soon as it launched a wave of ice upward, Evern abandoned his attempt to break through the shield in order to sprint to the side and slip around the wall's edge. This had the demon glancing away from the airborne Yeluthian, who then dove for a swing at the creature's exposed back.

*They're utilizing the distance between themselves to divert the being's attention*, Byron noted with some amazement at the fluidity of their plan. When he considered how the angels normally fought, the tactic made sense. *Their soldiers never stay in one spot anyway, both due to how they manipulate their stamina and their ability to occupy the ground and sky simultaneously.*

Unfortunately, the continuous back and forth attacks were easily managed by the demon, who would summon a barrier when Evern could approach and dive into a new, wider space when Lavine swooped. All the while, it wore a haunting grin to show its enjoyment with the fight.

*I've seen this before. Combat is like a game to their kind. They savor the thrill of battle, but when that wears off, they change tactics. We need to predict its next steps, otherwise we're reacting to its decisions.*

Byron considered this as the Yeluthians' continued their attempts to reach the being. His greatest concern, and what he kept returning to, had to do with how overwhelming demonic energy could be. Its intimidating influence wasn't as potent thanks to his exposure to what Coura possessed over the years, yet it made his skin crawl enough to be distracting if he let his guard down.

With that in mind, he believed their enemy wouldn't expect his participation so soon in the fight. His feet brought him around the edge of his shield, then closer to the hectic movements of the inhuman figures. Meanwhile, his eyes followed the transparent walls, which appeared and fragmented at the demon's whim.

*I can't get close enough to fight with a weapon even if I wanted to*, he noted as he evaluated his options. *That leaves magic. The demon's power is greater than my own, and I need to avoid putting Evern or Lavine in harm's way. Perhaps I don't need to rely on attacking then.*

The notion of becoming a distraction didn't often occur to him because of his usual involvement as a leader and mage; however, he understood his current position wouldn't allow him to do much else. Despite that, he knew he would hinder his comrades' progress if they remained unaware of his intentions.

*I'm sure they will figure out why I'm here if I act at an opportune time. It won't take long for the demon to either, but if I adapt to its reaction, I may be able to contribute more than flashy spells.*

With something of a strategy in mind, Byron hurried to stand behind the nearest shield controlled by their enemy, focused on his options should the creature remove its barrier or attack him, and watched where the commander engaged with the being. Evern's blade never touched the demon, who slipped away from his strikes while summoning a new wall. As Byron studied the pattern before Lavine dove for an aerial attack, he couldn't refrain from noticing how the creature's previous spells remained, filling the area with a maze-like collection of violet that shimmered in the surrounding light of the others' torches and fires.

*That's where I'll begin,* he decided as he mustered his courage and charged forward past the first pair he encountered.

The lack of direction and separation between shields forced him to slow his progress, though he found he appreciated the protection he could use against their opponent. Finally, he slid to a stop behind where the demon and Yeluthians continued the bout, then he raised his hands.

"Over here!" he yelled above the noise while releasing what lightning he summoned.

His call had both comrades glancing at him before their enemy halfheartedly looked over its shoulder. By that point, a blinding flash from his spell filled the area, though he limited its output severely due to only needing the brightness.

*That's as obvious a distraction as I can make. Evern and Lavine should realize the point of my intervention, and a couple more times should be enough to lower the being's guard. Then, I can switch tactics.*

The lack of power behind his bolts didn't damage the shield in front of him enough for it to break; however, he wouldn't risk being caught in that spot should their opponent retaliate. He sidestepped to the space possessing another, sturdy wall as the fight continued in the same fashion as earlier and prepared an explosion of fire at his fingertips. To his slight dismay, nobody tore their eyes away when he shouted again.

*I'm already being ignored*, he thought before releasing the flames, which increased the amount of light without overwhelming their sight. *I suppose it's time to move on to the next phase.*

Instead of abandoning his position, Byron mustered a greater amount of energy into a single ball of fire he could manipulate easier than lightning or ice shards and waited for his opportunity.

Lavine climbed back into the air after returning to the ground for a frontal assault, which the demon blocked by producing another shield. This left the commander free to attack, though the creature manifested its blade and knocked the golden weapon away, driving Evern away. At that moment, Byron yelled for a third time. He waited for the being to turn its back on him since the three combatants didn't respond, which it did a few seconds later. The opening motivated him to release his spell with as much force as he could reasonably control, shattering the violet wall and shooting forward like an arrow.

His flames, which remained contained to the size of a melon, still decently lit up the space enough not to prompt suspicion from his unsuspecting target. This resulted in a direct hit to the demon's upper back with enough force to send the being stumbling forward, and a hole burned through its armor and clothing, revealing pale skin matching its head.

To his relief, Evern managed to stay out of the way until that took place, whether or not the Yeluthian became aware of his intentions. The commander leapt into action in order to take advantage of the opportunity after by lunging for their enemy. His golden weapon flew for the exposed section on the demon's body, and Byron found his spirits rising.

That unwarranted optimism deflated in an instant when the creature seemingly erupted into a storm of flames and bolts. The sudden rise of spells emanating from the being contained enough power to interrupt the Yeluthian's attack, leading to a scratch instead of a stab when it dodged by tumbling forward. After scrambling to its feet, the being dismissed the fire and lightning, whirled around to face Evern, and snarled. In response, Lavine dropped to stand beside his superior, and both poised their weapons at the enemy. A heavy silence hung between them, leading Byron to ready a shield since his previous means of protection had been destroyed.

What caution he felt morphed into apprehension that had the hair on his arms standing when the being's snarl morphed into a sick grin. Then, the creature threw its head back and laughed in a crazed manner quite unlike its composed behavior from their earlier encounters.

"What fun," it began as the chuckles quieted, though Byron couldn't tell if the words were meant to be sarcastic. "It's not often I find myself being surprised anymore. The humans I surrounded myself with are not the brightest and are fueled by desperation and greed. Not to mention, my hatred for the flyers influences my passion for this battle."

Neither Byron nor Evern commented on the unprompted sentiment, which seemed to amuse the being further.

"Do you know what I enjoy most about our interactions? For you, this is a life or death fight to protect your home, dignity, or whatever mundane beliefs you hold. On the other hand, I find this to be a challenge of sorts. A game through which I can test my abilities and power. What I learn guides me to continue on. That is the value of keeping yourself untethered to dead weight."

*It's not wrong, but it also doesn't fully comprehend the desire to care for another.*

"Master Byron, I apologize for squandering such a perfect opportunity," he heard the commander comment at a volume only the three could hear.

The words tore him away from his thought, especially since neither Yeluthian moved. "I figured the demon wouldn't pay much attention to me. At least we're all on the same page."

"We cannot guarantee such luck going forward."

Their enemy's laughter reached them again as sparks flew from its empty hand. Meanwhile, Byron noticed a coating of ice formed over the wound on its other arm, stopping the bleeding, though he had no doubt the creature would still be able to utilize magic.

"Should I let you strategize for a moment?" it taunted before releasing a disappointed sigh. "How uninteresting. We demons fight through instinct, not pausing to figure out our next steps like some game."

"This is a game to that monster," Lavine growled with repressed rage.

Evern said the younger angel's name in a stern manner. "We must not let our emotions influence our actions lest we become distracted."

"That's what the creature wants," Byron added, prompting a nod from the commander. "We're fortunate to have this time and outnumber our opponent three to one. I'll continue using the shields around us for cover and focus on distracting it."

"We will repeat our previous formation, though I intend to utilize the air," Evern picked up with a glance at his subordinate.

As soon as Lavine nodded, the Yeluthians charged forward without warning, leaving Byron to hurry and duck behind the nearest barrier. A second later, the wall began crumbling as the sounds of clashing metal reached his ears.

*It must be changing its approach*, he noted after grumbling a curse and manifesting his own shield. *If it's able to dismiss the spells surrounding us, I'll be forced to create my own protection or remain exposed. Hopefully Evern and Lavine can keep it occupied while I work.*

Those hopes were dashed in the next minute when their enemy launched a blast of knife-like icicles toward the commander, who had been positioned parallel to Byron's spell. The Yeluthian leapt into the air in response; however, the surge of ice shot straight ahead and connected with his barrier. Several projectiles became embedded in the solidified energy, compromising its integrity and forcing him to abandon the manifestation spell.

His next idea involved returning to one of the being's remaining walls and becoming a distraction again. Without so much as a thought, he allowed his shield to shatter while sprinting for the nearest source of protection. His eyes remained locked on his comrades and enemy the entire time.

*I might be better off as a target*, he admitted to himself and halted behind his destination. *At least part of the demon's attention must be on me when it dismisses its barriers. Evern and Lavine are its true opponents, so I need to support them as much as possible.*

While he worked to plan his next steps, his heartbeat refused to slow, resulting in heavy panting that burned his throat. The uncomfortable sensation lingered despite his efforts to ignore it, yet he reminded himself of what the rest of the Asteom troops and their Yeluthian allies were facing, as well as the importance of their mission.

The indirect motivation pushed him into action once more. Both hands raised to summon a series of blinding lights, which the figures didn't seem to pay attention to until he released the bolts to either side of him. The sparks flickered and went out before touching the ground; however, their movement had been unexpected, resulting in their enemy backtracking in the opposite direction and his comrades' hesitation to pursue.

Although he wished he could assure the angels of his control and that he wouldn't use spells unless he knew he wouldn't harm them, Byron accepted the situation as it was. The demon's focus shifted to him when it pivoted to face its shield, revealing its intent to dismiss that spell. He already built another surge of lightning in those seconds and released it as soon as the first crack in the violet wall in front of him appeared.

What followed became a mass of noise as thunder and shattering glass filled his ears, light from the attack, and heat where the bolts bounced back to singe the hairs on his skin through the clothing and armor. He kept his attention across the clearing despite the discomfort while readying himself to leap away from the being's retaliation.

*Find another shield next*, he told himself before cutting off the spell.

As soon as it ended, Byron readied his legs to work while his eyes darted around for protection. To his dismay, fragments of the demon's shields floated to the ground amid the looming darkness. The realization that the creature dismissed every wall it summoned in a matter of seconds left him feeling cold.

His struggles didn't appear to effect the three though. Evern and Lavine both occupied the ground on either side of their opponent, who used its ebony blade to defend from the former while its frozen stub conjured flames and ice to keep the latter away. All the while, it wore a wild grin to project its excitement, which let Byron know they needed to end the fight sooner rather than later.

Nothing changed while he studied the combat until Evern unexpectedly leapt into the air again. The creature swept its sword across the sky in response, and he swore he caught the blade slice flesh. Still, the commander climbed higher before sharply descending to initiate another series of dives and swipes. Lavine managed to back away from the attacks yet remained on the same level with his weapon pointed at their enemy. The Yeluthian only crept close enough for an attempted stab when his superior ascended.

*This doesn't feel right*, Byron noted after a few minutes passed without change. *Lavine isn't attacking anymore; he's defending Evern while the commander rises higher. We can't rely on a single individual against a demon.*

His feet brought him closer to the chaotic scene before he committed to participating more than he had been doing with the intent to offer a warning. Unfortunately, his timing was off. The words never left his mouth when the airborne soldier flew lower to glide above the ground for another strike. Just as the golden blade cut for their enemy, the being dropped to its knees, pulled its black sword over its head, and threw its upper body forward in a powerful, vertical swing. Byron watched as the commander attempted to dodge the retaliation by sliding to the right, but the strength it put into the blow became evident when its weapon connected with the angel's left wing. Evern had been moving too fast to control his extra limbs beyond an instinctive reaction, resulting in about two thirds of the feathery addition separating from the rest of his body. Without the support, the Yeluthian rolled in the air before colliding with the ground where he tumbled to a stop amid what crimson liquid poured from his wing.

By that point, Byron's couldn't stand still. His heart hurt for his comrade because of the injury, yet he knew who would be the next victim if he didn't act fast.

As expected, Lavine retaliated by hurrying ahead as the demon rose to its feet. The opportunity it left seemed like an obvious trap since it kept its back to the younger Yeluthian, which proved to be the case when it spun around and stabbed for Lavine as soon as he came within reach. Only then did Byron intervene. The shield he manifested in that instant appeared between the two suddenly enough to have both weapons slamming into it with matching clangs. Fortunately, he poured plenty of energy into the wall so their strikes wouldn't damage it.

*I should keep my spell up for now. Lavine needs to calm down, and Evern...*

He struggled not to glance over to where his comrade remained on all fours with blood coating multiple places. Part of him wondered how damage to a manifested limb impacted the rest of the body, but the question vanished as soon as their enemy turned its attention to him. The amused smile disappeared, leaving a cold, emotionless expression.

For what felt like minutes, they stared at each other until the tension in the air became too heavy to ignore. The younger angel didn't move either, halting the fight.

*I'm no match for a demon, in magic or physicality. Either I wait for Evern to recover and rejoin us, or it's up to Lavine and I to figure out a way to win. Neither option is ideal.*

Their time ran out then as the being charged toward Byron while dismissing the shield and Yeluthians entirely. In response, he summoned a barrier for protection and prepared another for the inevitable; however, the creature slid to a stop just before reaching him, flashed an amused, beastly smile, and turned around. He hadn't noticed Lavine closely chasing the demon and cried for the angel to stop as soon as he understood the danger.

Despite the warning, his Yeluthian comrade remained too close to their enemy, who anticipated the distance between each of them. The black blade appeared again without Byron realizing it vanished earlier, and his heart sank. In response, he shoved aside his concerns regarding his own safety, dismissed the shield in front of himself, then sent a blast of fire toward their enemy. The lack of true strength behind the spell merely served to interrupt the demon's attack. Lavine could only halt and raise his weapon in defense while his wings tightened against his body.

On the other hand, their opponent seemingly predicted his reaction. The creature stepped backward to just miss what flames caressed its body before both arms moved at once. Its icy stub pointed at the Yeluthian and summoned a barrier extending wider than any up to that point in the evening as the other released its sword to launch a snowy wave of wind in Byron's direction. Instead of blowing him away or piercing him with icicles, the chill stung his exposed face, then his hands when he raised his arms for protection. His mind went to another shield immediately after, but the unforgiving wind had him squeezing his eyes shut against the frozen bits that would no doubt blind him if he dared a glance.

*I need to try something*, his mind urged at the thought of what the demon planned.

He raised his left hand against the continued blast and prepared a magical wall directly in front of himself until the power he mustered abruptly disappeared amid a shot of pain. It proved enough to have him release a startled cry just as the being's spell ended.

*My arm... I didn't see what happened, but my energy won't respond.*

His frantic thoughts quieted into silence when he glanced at the spot only to find the limb missing from the bicep down. Blood leaked from the open wound, and both the sight and loss made his head spin.

"I considered killing you on the spot," their enemy gloated from where it stood a safe distance away. "However, the light-blooded need motivation to fight me without restraint."

The words rang hollow in Byron's mind as he struggled to tear his eyes away from the missing limb. After a moment, he found himself dizzy enough to fall onto his knees before he realized what that meant.

*I'm losing too much blood. If I don't find a healer, I'll die shortly.* No emotions accompanied the facts, like he watched this happen to another person. Only when he heard his name did he bother looking up at what took place around him.

The demon no longer loomed above as Lavine initiated combat with enough force to drive their opponent away. Byron noticed the younger Yeluthian struggling between the being's ability to utilize magic and a weapon in tandem. Meanwhile, it was Evern whose voice he heard as the commander knelt beside him to inspect the wound.

"Master Byron, stay with me," the angel urged in a tight voice.

Although he longed to tell his comrade not to fuss over him, Byron remained aware enough to know he was dying. His mouth worked, yet no sound came from his lips, and he could only imagine how foolish he looked.

"I healed your arm enough for it to not continue bleeding. You must lie down and rest until this is over."

Part of him became drawn to the missing limb again, and he nearly fell into a trance when the crimson pool at his feet hypnotized him; however, a grunt from Lavine and laughter from the demon threw him back into the present. Without thinking, he met the Yeluthian's eyes, narrowed his, then shared what their enemy revealed.

"It's using me to enrage you two into fighting recklessly. Don't give it an opportunity to overwhelm you."

His hoarse voice didn't carry as much weight as he hoped, yet Evern still nodded. Despite that, Byron sensed uncertainty from his comrade and reached over to seize the commander's chest plate with his lone hand. A new sense of urgency filled his veins, prompting the action and leading him to press his warning.

"I'm serious," he growled. "Time is running out. It's not physically stronger than you or Lavine. If you can maneuver around its spells, you can win."

The sudden emotion visibly startled the Yeluthian until Byron's weariness returned, forcing him to release his grip and lower his head in order to catch his breath. He heard no response after that. Shuffling signaled Evern's rise and departure from his side, then he closed his eyes and simply listened.

For a while, nothing out of the ordinary caused him to become invested in the fight. Metal blades met their equals, snickering and taunting from the demon continued, and the sound of flapping wings let him know the angels didn't plan on remaining grounded. He envisioned the beings soaring above the battlefield, leading him to wonder if they enjoyed the position as aviary predators.

*I must be losing my mind now.*

He huffed a laugh at the notion before his shaky, right hand rose so his remaining fingers could brush against the newly healed skin on his other arm. Based on his halfhearted inspection, he knew the commander prevented the injury from bleeding but could do nothing more. The thought of their kind being limited when it came to light magic left him feeling bitter despite his appreciation and admiration of the Yeluthians.

*They're experts at manipulating energy to the point where they can fly, and they're fluid combatants. You'd believe they would find a way to reattach limbs with their goddess' blessing.*

That negativity sparked further displeasure as he found himself opening his eyes to watch the ongoing fight. His frustration elevated when Evern received a scratch along the cheek before their enemy danced away.

*Some all-powerful being. They were hailed as heroes for defeating the demons decades ago. Was that just embellished to improve their reputation? Did they grow weaker without people to protect?*

Byron knew such rude comments were childish, yet he couldn't stop in his current state where the unfiltered thoughts didn't seem to matter. Every part of him ached, especially his left arm and shoulder, as his body involuntarily relaxed due to the lack of activity. This both discouraged and irritated him.

The ongoing fight didn't help his attitude. Neither Yeluthian could make progress between physical attacks and spells, as if they couldn't predict which their enemy would use next. Meanwhile, the being never hid its wicked glee. A curse escaped his lips in a grumble when Lavine's imprecise swings resulting in a parry that allowed the creature to pierce the angel's midsection.

*We put our faith in them*, Byron couldn't help but recall with a sense of gloom as Evern stepped in to allow his subordinate a moment of reprieve. *The ancestral weapon is our only means of stopping a demon, but we'll never get close enough to utilize it. We should have planned better. The commander can't land the final blow without help because of our enemy's ability to slip away unscathed.*

At first, he found himself spiteful at his comrades for underestimating the being's cunning and physicality, which allowed it to avoid taking damage; however, as he observed what took place nearby, a realization steadily dawned on him. When he could piece it together, he found himself sitting straighter with new interest.

*The demon never stops moving*, he discovered while keeping his eyes glued to the being. Just like his Yeluthian allies, their opponent rarely remained in a single spot for long, backpedaling and sidestepping enough not to stay still. *I remember observing Evern and Coura's training and learning about the angels' style of combat. It relies on movement; to win is to avoid keeping grounded to a single location. Each method has benefits, but the commander and Lavine are essentially engaged with one of their own who can also use elemental magic at an expert level.*

His head pounded from the strain of thinking too much in his condition, yet a sense of excitement arose at the notion of figuring out a means to victory.

As he continued watching his Yeluthian comrades attempt to best the Nim-Valans' leader, he soon needed to admit his limitations in order to plot accordingly. The hand on his wounded arm dropped to his side, and he struggled against the urge to shut his eyes.

*I'm physically incapable of much. I'll likely wear myself into an earlier grave if I try moving around or fighting. My energy isn't completely depleted though, but it's nowhere near as powerful as our enemy. What could I do to restrain the being anyway?*

His next idea involved somehow communicating with Evern or Lavine in order to ask them about a binding spell. Unfortunately, such a discussion would waste valuable time on an ability he wasn't certain they could perform.

*Binding spells require extreme focus to adjust to the victim's reaction. I doubt either Yeluthian could manage that, let alone doing so while the other holds the being's attention. Magic is our best option since we can't physically restrain it, but who could wield it unnoticed and with enough strength to…*

Byron suddenly remembered their fourth comrade and scanned the area. Off to his left, Coura remained on her hands and knees just as he'd left her.

*She only possesses demonic energy at the moment*, he recalled while probing with his senses. The surrounding, unnatural presence filled the field thanks to the creature and its hold over the Nim-Valans, allowing what she held to blend in. *The creature also poured more into her before Evern and Lavine stepped in. Her body might not be responding, but she's our best chance at a surprise spell.*

The next obstacle he found himself facing was how to get to his former student. His blood loss continued affecting his head, leading him to wobble and drop to his knees when he attempted to stand. Colorful spots also blotted his vision in response, and he muttered a curse while clenching his jaw.

*Take it slow. I shouldn't rush, especially when I'm not a target.*

He prayed that remained true as he pushed himself to his feet. There, he paused to catch his breath and adjust to the unexpected shift in weight caused by his missing limb. When he could look at the action, nobody seemed to be paying attention to him.

*A walk would draw less interest than if I try running or jogging*, he rationalized before one foot followed the other toward his goal.

Despite the lack of speed, he stumbled several times and fought off a wave of dizziness accompanying his weakened mentality and hurting body. He imagined the demon sending a bolt of lightning in his direction when the noise seemed to grow louder, yet nothing interrupted his arduous trek.

Before he realized it, he stood in front of Coura. Even a brief glance proved enough for him to understand what the overwhelming amount of demonic energy did to her. Sweat coated her face and dripped onto the ground at regular intervals while every part of her became paralyzed by the immense pressure he no doubt knew she experienced.

*When this happened outside Clearshot and Emilea's home, she experienced enough pain to prevent her from moving or talking. I needed to render her unconscious to even allow someone to pick her up and bring her inside.*

Despite the memory, he knelt beside her and stifled his pity for the sake of their mission.

"Can you hear me?" he asked first to gauge her awareness.

To his slight relief, he caught her chin dip a bit.

"If you can, you're going to have to help us. Evern and Lavine are holding the enemy leader's attention, and I can't fight or use much magic. That creature gave you its power, right? I need you to restrict its movements so the commander can deal a finishing blow."

Her strained panting became the only sound between them for a few seconds.

"I remember before when you were like this," he added in a gentler manner for reassurance. "I can only imagine how much it hurts, but you need to rid yourself of the energy your body can't handle. Otherwise, it will act like a poison and kill you."

Byron held his breath after those words and hoped for some sort of confirmation. His eyes returned to the combat when he didn't receive a response, though his mind raced for other ideas until he forced himself to stop due to a headache. Finally, he closed his eyes with a sigh.

*I suppose I got ahead of myself.*

After a minute, he opened his eyes and returned his attention to the ongoing struggle. The trio of combatants steadily rotated around the open area, which had him wondering if he should manifest protection should a stray spell wind up his and Coura's way. He raised his hand with no shortage of reluctance at how he longed to simply sit and rest his strained muscles until a pained growl escaped the figure beside him. When he looked at her after, he found her struggling to lift her right arm, which hovered just above the grass. The surge of elation at her effort hurt his chest, yet he leaned over to offer his assistance.

"Let me help," he ordered while placing his available hand under her upper arm. "Go slow. I'm sure this isn't going to be easy on you."

Again, only her labored breathing acted as a reply.

Byron refrained from speaking anymore and pushed upward as best he could given his weariness. Despite that, her strength proved to be enough with his support. Her hand eventually rose to where she could aim across the field, and he sensed the demonic energy stirring.

"We need to wait for the right opportunity," he reminded her before she could release a spell. "Wait for my signal."

When that would be he had no idea. The commander seemed adamant about challenging the being on the ground, but it returned to utilizing barriers and separating the two. Meanwhile, Lavine lingered farther back, as if waiting for a moment to rejoin the fight.

*Come on you two. Lead our enemy in this direction.*

He hoped his silent plea would somehow reach the pair, especially when he noticed Coura's arm trembling.

"Just a bit longer," he attempted to reassure her, though the words also resonated with him.

Evern and Lavine soon traded off attacking and continued the rotation amid a laugh from their opponent. Byron imagined the demon taunting its prey when he caught the creature's voice, spurring a reaction from his allies. He reminded himself of how patience would be their greatest asset if used correctly and held his breath.

Finally, he saw the setup for their chance to act. The demon retreated like normal yet in the direction where they waited. He wasn't certain whether or not it spotted them or recalled first encountering Coura there, but he allowed himself to believe it wouldn't bother with the humans. This seemed to be the case as it never turned around when the Yeluthians pursued.

"Get ready," he warned his companion at a lower volume. As soon as the being pivoted to shift directions, he seized the opening. "Now!"

The power Coura had been building released at his command, though not exactly as he imagined. Instead of a blast of lightning or fire, a series of walls to block in the creature, or some other means of restraint he expected, she conjured wind carrying icy fragments too tiny to damage a target. Like a contained snowstorm, the spell crossed the distance between them and their enemy in seconds before connecting with its lower half.

Immediately, the demon spun around to glare at its unexpected attackers; however, what ice already caked its legs and feet weighed it down. To Byron's relief, Evern and Lavine pounced once this took place, forcing their enemy to summon walls for protection against them instead of Coura, who kept her power steady throughout. This allowed her spell to remain at a constant pace.

Byron kept his attention on their target without letting his cautious mindset relax since he expected retaliation at any moment. This came when enough shields prevented the Yeluthians from reaching their opponent. The being twisted at the waist due to what ice formed along its legs, manifested a series of fireballs, and launched them at him and Coura with a snarl. At that, he removed his hand from Coura's arm in order to craft a wall to protect the pair. This didn't interrupt her spell, so the wind struck their side of the barrier; however, it blocked the demon's magic. Once the flames ceased, he dismissed his shield in order to allow her icy blast to continue.

With Evern and Lavine's pressure, their opponent couldn't spare a moment to retaliate again. Byron allowed his former student to release what power she held since it succeeded in restraining the being enough for it to stay in one spot and readied his energy for another barrier should the need arise.

He became so focused on the series of events taking place that the commander's sudden change in tactics threw him off. The angel sidestepped into Coura's spell, startling Byron into yelling at her to stop, before crouching and lunging for an upward stab. Because of the shards in the wind, he practically disappeared in the snowstorm-like mixture. Their opponent didn't see the strike coming, either due to his cover or Lavine's attacks from its other side. In the next instant, the golden blade passed through the being's stomach.

At first, Byron remained startled into silence. Coura ended her spell at his previous shout, allowing him to observe the results. Ice covered Evern's back as he knelt in front of the creature. The ancestral weapon in his hands didn't move, and neither did the being they ensnared.

For a heartbeat, nothing happened. Then, the demon began falling forward. He heard the commander call for Lavine, who looked as dazed as Byron felt, and the two traded the golden sword's possession while carefully lowering the creature's body to the ground.

*We did it*, Byron thought through a sense of disbelief. *We actually...caught it...*

His acceptance of the results released any sort of control he held on his mind up to that point. The weariness he had been fighting off overwhelmed him instantly, and he unwillingly dropped onto his uninjured side. Still, an exhausted smile graced his lips.

He glanced at Coura and hoped to share the news with her when he realized she hadn't moved. Although her breathing didn't sound as frantic, he noticed ice coating her entire hand and most of her right arm. The sight wasn't surprising considering how she needed to release the spell with as much force as she possibly could.

*Hopefully that...expended...enough...*

When the thought wouldn't fully form, Byron knew he needed rest. His eyes closed after acknowledging that, and soon the world around him faded away.

# Predictions

espite his mental and physical fatigue, Will's high spirits kept him going as he shifted from person to person while examining every injury he could. He switched from acting as a warrior along the healers' side of the area to a medic when it became obvious the Nim-Valans were retreating and the demonic creatures scattered. Various cheers from farther ahead let him know their plan succeeded, so he sheathed his weapon and began tending to the wounded.

What took place next remained beyond his field of vision. Everyone seemed to be moving in all directions, and the light mages became overwhelmed with patients being carried over. Instead of interfering in their work, he decided to hurry around the battlefield with others and mend what they could without the use of magic. For the most part, they remained undisturbed except when soldiers approached to request their attention or offer to help.

*It's not my responsibility to direct anybody in one spot or another*, he sheepishly thought after instructing a man twice his age on how to bandage and apply pressure to a bleeding injury on their comrade's thigh. *I only know what I know and do what I can to help. I'm not a leader like the general or his assistants, or even Byron and Clearshot. Even Clara steps up to fill the role.*

He noticed his friend utilizing her power earlier and left her alone before venturing out into the field. Dozens of enemy soldiers' bodies lied unmoving alongside their own, which piqued his interest until he started treating those in his path.

Evening passed without him realizing it until the sunrise lightened the area and those holding torches or fire spells dismissed them as soon as they could. Will paused to stretch the tight muscles in his back with a wince, remove his smudged glasses, and wipe them on the cleanest part of his shirt. Although it removed the worst spots, he found himself longing for a spare rag and new clothes.

*Now isn't the time to fuss over that. I need to-*

The thought was interrupted by the rumbling of his stomach, which he hadn't acknowledged until that moment. Part of him didn't want to consider eating given the sights he'd seen over the course of the last few hours, yet he was experienced enough to know he shouldn't ignore his body's needs. After promising himself he would search for breakfast as soon as he could, he picked up where he left off by kneeling beside a groaning soldier.

For a while, he became consumed by the recovery process. The sun rose fully as the activity around him slowed before a hand dropped onto his shoulder once he paused for a break. Of course, he expected another request and reluctantly turned around only to find Clara assessing him.

"What are you doing this far out?" he asked without hiding his surprise at her unexpected appearance.

His reaction prompted an amused smile, which seemed to ease her demeaner. "You do know the fight is over, right?"

Will stared at her before letting his eyes wander around the space for the first time that morning. Only the dead occupied the ground, and their allies already worked on creating piles for pyres. Meanwhile, the Nim-Valans' bodies were being lined up at the northernmost end, presumably in a respectful gesture. He also noted how no one lingered around the area.

"Those who weren't ordered to assist already began returning to camp," Clara mentioned before releasing a sigh. "I volunteered to stay with the remaining healers since I'm not completely drained, but I wanted to make sure you were safe."

Her following smile heated his cheeks, and he thanked her for her consideration. After clearing his throat to mask his emotions, he briefly shared what he had been doing to treat those unable to move to the light mages.

His friend nodded when he finished and glanced back toward the medical area. "Your work didn't go unnoticed. Master

Massie thought of you when we had people being carried over with bandages and stitches. She said they would have died before then if they continued bleeding."

"That's a relief," he muttered in response while purposefully avoiding taking credit. "I intend to circle around the battlefield again for anybody else in need. After that, I think I should retreat for something to eat."

"Sounds like a reasonable idea. Before I forget, Finn wanted me to tell you he'll be back this evening or tomorrow afternoon."

He raised an eyebrow when she didn't elaborate. "Where did he go?"

"I assume he fought alongside our troops, but once we knew the demon had been defeated and its creatures fled, he mentioned speaking with the general before trailing the Nim-Valans."

"I'd bet he's making sure they return across the border."

Clara expressed her agreement. "He caught my attention when I could spare a second and asked me to let you know."

"I wonder why he thought to tell me that," Will mumbled. When he couldn't come up with a reason and figured it didn't matter, he shook his head and thanked her again.

"Come find me when you're ready to head back," she instructed as she stepped away before walking toward the eastern end of the area.

The update and realization that they were almost done in that location filled him with a sense of determination to finish his role. Fortunately, he found no others in need of assistance during his resulting trek around the field. Those who remained continued dealing with the bodies, so he resigned to removing himself from the open space; however, as he began heading in a new direction, someone caught his arm with such force they nearly pulled him off his feet in his weary state.

"I'm glad I found you," came a familiar voice as he turned around.

As expected, it was Marcus who grabbed him by the elbow. The assistant general upheld a confident expression, though Will sensed tension and concern behind the chestnut eyes.

"If you're not busy, can I ask a favor?" his friend continued.

"I suppose so."

Instead of elaborating, Marcus gestured for him to follow while pivoting in the opposite direction. The motion and lack of details intrigued him, especially when they moved toward the unoccupied section of the field.

"When Commander Evern's subordinate shared the demon's fate and the enemy soldiers began retreating, I went to find Grace," the assistant general shared before they halted. Then, he faced Will and frowned. "I'm sure you heard about General Casner. Mattais agreed to work with a team to transfer him back to our camp and begin the recovery process while the Yeluthians and I handled the Nim-Valans' leader."

"Is it really…"

"It is. Grace used some sort of powerful fire spell to burn the corpse into ashes, just as we planned."

A sense of relief spread throughout Will upon hearing the news, though he wondered what he would be doing if the creature was truly gone. Fortunately, Marcus noticed his curiosity and pointed across the area, prompting him to peer ahead to where a dark figure seemed to be on their hands and knees. He had overlooked the person on first glance and kicked himself for not realizing they likely needed medical treatment.

"Can you check on Coura and help her back to the camp?" the assistant general asked.

Something about the question didn't sound right to Will, and he pressed for more information when he noticed Marcus' gaze linger on their friend. "Of course, but what's wrong? Why isn't she healing herself like before? Why didn't anyone go to her before now?"

After releasing a sigh, the soldier rubbed the back of his neck. "To be honest, I don't fully understand it either. Commander

Evern mentioned how demonic energy is off putting, so it would strain the mages, especially the healers. He suggested we leave her alone for a while in case she could recover on her own."

"Is she hurt?"

"I don't know. I doubt he would leave her if she was physically wounded."

Will looked between the two before brushing aside the uncomfortable feeling that arose from the limited explanation. "Don't worry. I'll see for myself."

"I appreciate your help."

"Just make sure not to overwork yourself," he added to lighten the mood as he stepped forward.

Marcus promised to do so before they split apart.

With each step Will took into the open space, he felt his nerves rising at being farther from the safety of his comrades. The thought of being ambushed by the enemy soldiers, or even the beasts under the demon's control, made the hair on his arms stand; however, his feet continued toward Coura.

*This is odd. I wasn't worried about going to her until I left Marcus' side. I've been alone for hours, yet something about lacking protection around me is concerning.* He wondered about this before recalling the Yeluthian commander's message to his friend. Then, the reasoning resonated with him and eased part of the building tension. *It must be the dark energy he mentioned. I'm not completely affected because I'm not a mage, but its presence is still strong enough for me to notice.*

Underneath his disgust for the being, he found himself pitying his friend, who didn't react as he approached and knelt beside her. Immediately, he heard her wheezing, as though she'd exhausted herself, leading him to investigate before attempting to touch or move her.

"Coura, it's Will," he began in a calm manner. "Are you hurt?"

He contemplated whether or not she heard him when she didn't reply right away, leading him to consider if she had been struck by some sort of magic that hindered her senses. When he placed a hand on her back after, he gasped at how her entire body trembled and felt hot through her damp clothing.

"I think I've seen this before," he muttered more to himself than to her as he removed his hand and dug through his satchel for what remaining potions he carried. "It's an imbalance of energy. You must have exerted yourself."

A sigh of relief followed when he found a pair of vials, removed them, and broke the wax seals before adjusting his position to sit in front of her. To his dismay, he figured he would need to get her to move if she were to drink the medicine.

"Can you lie down or at least lift your head so I can give you a pain-numbing potion?" he ventured and fully expected silence.

Although he didn't receive a vocal answer, he noticed her shaking arms steadily lift a bit as she shifted her weight to her knees. He soon understood what she attempted to do and hurried to guide her into a sitting position while ignoring her sharp gasps and groans. As soon as she looked stable, he lifted the first bottle to her lips before tilting it back. Part of him worried she wouldn't have the strength or control to drink the medicine, yet he watched as she did so. Her resulting wince made him chuckle.

"One more," he promised and repeated the process. "We don't have any spices or fruit to sweeten the flavor."

"You could have warned me."

Hearing Coura's voice after the second dose, albeit at a volume akin to a whisper, lightened Will's mood after his initial shock. He apologized while adjusting to sit with his legs straight in order to give his knees a break. The weariness he dismissed throughout the morning loomed over his body, and his stomach continued rumbling.

"Just let me know when the numbing starts so we can head back. It's about time for lunch."

"Is that why you're here?" she asked after a pause.

He caught her head rise a bit so she could look at him. Beyond her tired expression, she projected a slight sense of guilt, likely for needing assistance. In order to quell the self-blame, he offered a sincere smile and opted for honesty.

"I've been working with the healers on tending to the injured. It seems you're the only person who's not on their feet. Marcus and I figured you might need help."

She huffed a laugh and stared at the ground again. "You could say that."

The mixture of emotions he picked up on during those few minutes left him unable to determine what to say next. Fortunately, she slowly extended a trembling hand toward him after, revealing her desire to stand with his assistance. He scrambled to his feet before taking it, hauling her up, then hurrying to place himself under her arm so she could lean on him for support.

"I hope you know I can't carry you if your legs don't work," he added when the majority of her weight fell into his body. "We don't need to rush."

Coura didn't respond, so he focused on getting them moving in the direction of the camp. With each step, Will heard her either release a hiss or grunt through gritted teeth. It hurt him to know the potion couldn't block out all her pain; however, he avoided lingering on the medicine's limitations by observing the distance between them and their goal.

***

Marcus' stroll through the camp a couple days after his return didn't give him much reassurance in their defenses. Everyone who wasn't on patrol duty slept most of the day to recover what strength they expended, especially since a portion relied on the light mages to mend their wounds. This also left the healers in need of rest. If he hadn't seen their enemies' leader burned away with his own eyes, he wouldn't allow such lax behavior.

*I'm not entirely comfortable with our situation, but this is the best we can do at the moment*, he told himself as he waved at a group of men enjoying breakfast around their bonfire. *I refuse to lower my guard until we're sure the Nim-Valans won't attack again. Who knows when that will be.*

Despite his own weariness, his loyalty to his comrades drove him to uphold his duties while the general recovered. Mattais agreed to remain at their superior's side during this time unless Marcus called upon him since not much needed to be done. The assistant general's willingness to let him act as their leader continued surprising him, but he shoved his personal feelings aside for the sake of the troops.

A message from Casner earlier that morning lifted the weight of responsibility from his shoulders slightly, both because of the return to form and the man's improved health. He readied himself for the meeting as soon as he could before heading toward the centermost tent, which he entered after knocking and receiving permission to do so. Inside, the bitter smell of medicine hit his nose and tickled it as he approached the figure sitting on the ground. The general's slouched shoulders held a blanket that wrapped around his entire body, and Marcus immediately saw how pale the man was even after days of sleep.

"Good morning," he greeted his superior after halting.

Casner waved a hand as a gesture to the space across from him without raising his eyes. "Sit."

Marcus did so and only then noted his fellow assistant general's absence. "Will Mattais be joining us?"

"Eventually. I wanted to speak with you first about a few things."

His superior's eyes lifted to meet his, revealing a heavy shadow underneath them. The comment piqued Marcus' interest, so he remained silent.

"First, I appreciate how you assumed responsibility of the soldiers during my absence. Mattais informed me of what took place and your lack of concern when asked to do so."

"I wouldn't say I wasn't concerned," he replied honestly only to be quieted when the general raised a hand.

"We can discuss that at a later time. For now, you have my gratitude. Next, we received a report from Commander Evern's subordinate Lavine. The Yeluthian has been scouting from above and sees no sign of enemy activity from here to the border. Our spy also returned with similar observations. It seems killing their leader freed their minds and scared them off."

Marcus released a sigh, which eased some of the tightness he had been carrying in his chest. "I'm glad to hear that. Our forces are too weak to fight off an attack right now."

"The rest of our camp's leaders said the same. It seems Lady Zelnar's magic, or rather the magic of her people, succeeded in killing the demon."

Casner's words and the resulting pause didn't sound reassuring despite their implication, prompting Marcus to press the subject.

"Sir, should we be preparing for retaliation?"

"Not right away," came the response as the general shifted his gaze to the left. "From what I understand, our mages don't sense the being's presence outside our site."

Marcus scratched his chin. "Outside our site? Does that mean…"

"The demon is gone, its followers fled, and it seems the beasts turned tail as well. Only Coura possesses that unnatural power bothering the mages, which interferes with their probing. There's also the concern about the remaining demon lurking around this area."

The mention of his friend startled Marcus a bit since he hadn't seen her since he sent Will to help her. *He described how he thought she expended her magic and left her with the healers when they returned. Doesn't that mean she isn't using dark energy anymore?*

"I'm sorry, but I don't fully understand," he added when Casner appeared to be waiting for a response. "I can visit her this afternoon and ask about that. Perhaps she has a way to mask the presence or trace it to a possible threat."

The general nodded yet didn't seem convinced. "I'll be honest with you. I'm looking at returning our forces to their original positions along the border and in Verona should the northerners and beasts remain dispersed. Our resources can't support our numbers for longer than a couple more weeks, so it makes sense if the danger has been dealt with. Should this be the case and that malicious being isn't gone by the time we move out, I'm ordering Coura to stay here."

Marcus prepared to question his superior's comment in defense of his friend before forcing himself to consider the reasoning. *They don't get along, but he wouldn't do this out of spite. If she were to return to the capital, the mages and magic-sensitive civilians would likely react poorly. Not to mention they might not be able to sense if an actual threat appears.*

He found himself agreeing with Casner about the safety of the kingdom; however, he also recalled how isolated Coura felt when she first arrived and stifled what guilt arose.

"I take it you comprehend the situation," his superior added when he didn't respond. "You're more than welcome to inform her of my decision should this issue not resolve itself."

"I plan on doing so when I visit the medical station. It would be unwise to travel so soon anyway. We still have time."

He noticed a faint smile grace the general's lips before they switched topics.

The remainder of their conversation consisted of assessing the results of the recent battle, including the deceased, their remaining supplies, and how many scouts were available. What took place with the enemy troops after was reported by Finn, who then expressed interest in returning to Nim-Vala's inner circle once his work finished. Mattais never showed up, though Casner didn't mention his assistant at all, and Marcus departed when the head healer arrived with the general's lunch and medicine. Although he longed for a warm meal too, he decided it would be in his best interest to visit the medical area and check on his friends.

*Coura deserves a warning about General Casner's intentions, and I should make sure Will didn't work himself into the ground. Grace has been resting in our normal spot with Dianne supervising, and Clearshot didn't act too bothered by his injuries. Then there's Byron.*

In order to avoid lingering on the master mage's condition, he considered the others he knew who would benefit from a visit due to their recovering wounds. This kept his mind occupied until he stepped into the busy space filled with dozens of men and women either sitting and chatting with each other, sleeping, or receiving food. Meanwhile, light mages and volunteers slipped between the rows of bodies to tend to their patients.

No one bothered Marcus as he went straight for the wide, centermost tent temporarily housing the most serious cases and entered behind a young, blonde woman. Inside, the atmosphere felt less cheery. Hardly anybody spoke above a normal volume in the dimly lit space, which he assumed allowed the injured to rest easier, though the majority of occupants appeared to be asleep.

He tiptoed his way around those working while remaining silent so as not to disturb the quiet environment until his eyes caught his first target's familiar face. Fortunately in that moment, Byron sat up during a conversation with an older woman. Both seemed to be chatting in a casual manner, allowing him to approach without worrying about interrupting an evaluation. The master mage noticed him first and offered a halfhearted smile in greeting. This caught the woman's attention, prompting her to look over her shoulder, return her attention to Byron, then rise and walk away after a few additional words.

"I hope I didn't prematurely end an important discussion," Marcus said after watching the light mage begin healing her next patient.

"We were just catching up," came the man's response. His weaker voice revealed just how fatigued he remained after the battle. "I'm sure your update is more important anyway."

"Not really." Marcus followed the response by dropping to sit across from the master mage. There, he shared most of what took place after the conflict, though he purposefully left out details that would raise concern.

"I appreciate the effort to keep me informed," Byron replied after and released a weary sigh.

"Of course. We shouldn't need to act so soon thanks to what took place, so you can consider this a friendly visit."

Despite the lightheartedness of his comment, his spirits sank when the master mage placed a hand on the wounded, left shoulder and looked away. He had been avoiding staring at the missing limb until that point; however, his control slipped at the movement, stirring a sense of pity.

"I'm sorry about your arm," he began as his eyes instinctively lowered. "We knew the risks of a selected group facing a demon, but…"

"There's nothing to apologize for," the man interjected during Marcus' pause.

Byron's gentle, reassuring tone had him returning his gaze to the man's face where the smile returned.

"Injuries are common in battle," the master mage reminded him after. "You know that as well as I do. What's important is my life is still intact. It could have been much worse."

Marcus nodded without pursuing the subject further. He decided he took up enough of Byron's time and said as much while getting to his feet. Then, he left the man to rest and exited through the opposite end of the tent than where he entered.

His second goal had been to locate Will, which he did after a few minutes of meandering around the medical station. It was no surprise to see the herbalist hurrying from one person to another offering potions from a satchel to light mages and patients alike. His friend's constant effort never ceased to amuse and impress him, and he needed to wait for an opportunity to catch his target's elbow mid-stride.

"My apologies, but I'm out of pain-dulling medicine at the moment," Will said in a rush without even looking at Marcus.

This led him to shake the herbalist's arm a bit. "It's Marcus."

His friend looked over, met his eyes, and stammered an apology before he released his hold. Will continued blinking, as if in a daze, letting him know how fatigued the herbalist actually was.

"You need a break," he began once he processed this. "Let's grab lunch."

"I shouldn't leave the-"

"From what I can tell, the soldiers are managing. It's not healthy to overwork yourself, right?"

Marcus chuckled when his friend nodded and the mop-like head of hair flopped out of place. To his relief, Will followed as he led them away from the wounded and into a crowd gathered for lunch. They received their portions then returned to their bonfire where Dianne and Clearshot sat with empty bowls at their feet.

Both greeted the pair before beginning casual conversation. Grace's guard mentioned how the Yeluthian exhausted herself when Will inquired, reminding Marcus he hadn't seen the herbalist in days, then Clearshot asked about Byron. He shared the master mage's condition as best he could, which visibly satisfied the soldier.

"I'm sure he's ready to be back to work," the archer added after. "You have time to linger on your thoughts and regrets when you're not allowed to do much."

Marcus agreed after recalling his first, serious injury during what time he spent accompanying Byron to the Magical Arts Academy. The memory led him to press Will about Coura's condition since he planned to visit her next; however, his friend's timid response had him thinking otherwise.

"Master Massie ordered me to keep her at the farthest point of the medical area, practically along the camp's perimeter. The dark power she holds disrupts the light mages' concentration, so I've just been stopping by to leave medicine, water, and food."

"Is she at least recovering?" Clearshot inquired and crossed his arms to reflect his displeasure with the situation.

"She hasn't been awake when I'm there, but what I leave is gone when I return."

They left the conversation at that. Shortly after, Will expressed his desire to continue his work, and Marcus felt the same. Both departed from the bonfire before splitting apart for their own business.

***

Although the noise nearby brought her out of sleep sooner than she would have preferred, Coura remained bundled in what blankets surrounded her. The pit in her stomach subsided when she allowed the demonic energy to suppress her hunger, which she already acknowledged as detrimental to her recovery when she did so over the last three mornings. In order to make up for the loss, she forced herself to eat and drink whatever Will brought when he visited, nearly making herself sick in the process. What burning her damaged skin experienced ever since Lupin decided to overwhelm her with his power kept her moving as little as possible, both to avoid the pain and give her body time to rest. Even days later, she couldn't sit still from the physical discomfort, as well as the disagreeing presences within her center.

*I can sense both the light and dark energies at odds*, she noted after shutting her eyes and focusing within to where the intertwining tendrils wound around each other, like opposing currents. *My Yeluthian power slips through my fingers, so that hasn't changed. I'm guessing I can't use healing magic or my goddess gift yet. With what Lupin threw at me, it might be a while before I can do so.*

From what she could tell about the camp surrounding her and the fragmented memories of the previous fight, the Nim-Valan leader had been defeated. The troops around her were injured, yet a sense of optimism drifted above them, likely because their forces succeeded without them losing their lives. It pleased her to see how her allies steadily recovered and returned to their duties.

Coura counted six days since Will dragged her to the spot she currently occupied, which felt like enough time for her to want to move around, so she sat up with a yawn while rubbing her eyes. She already noted how far she lied from the rest of the soldiers and considered this as she drank from her filled waterskin.

*This area looked full when I arrived, so I didn't give much thought as to why Will placed me here. Now that I'm able to assess my center, I can tell how much demonic energy I still hold. The light mages must sense Lupin's power and want to keep me as far away as possible. Can't say I blame them for removing a distraction.*

Despite the notion, she couldn't shake how being cast aside bothered her. Her main argument had to do with Lupin giving her dark energy against her will, so she had no say about the malicious presence she projected; however, over the years she'd come to understand that her opinion, the truth, and what others saw her as would never align.

She emptied the waterskin a minute later before tossing it aside just as she heard footsteps and glanced up to find Marcus heading toward her. Like everyone else, he had shadows under his eyes, and his face looked thinner.

"Good morning," he greeted her with a wave. "You're up earlier than I was expecting."

Coura mirrored the gesture before raising her eyes to the unusually clear, sunny sky. "It must be before noon. How late did you expect me to sleep?"

"Well, at least until lunch," he replied after dropping to sit cross-legged beside her. "I asked Will when I should stop by, and that's what he suggested. You never seem to be awake when he brings you food and water."

She confirmed the herbalist's poor timing around her recovery, then she decided to inquire about the battle and its results. As expected, her father managed to strike the ancestral weapon true, sealing Lupin so Grace's goddess fire spell could burn the creature into ashes, and the demonic energy he possessed with him. Meanwhile, Marcus led the efforts against the Nim-Valans when Casner had been stabbed by a poisoned blade.

"The enemy troops scattered for the border once your group defeated their leader," he concluded with a weary yet satisfied smile. "Whether or not their minds were freed, they understood they needed to retreat if they valued their lives without the healing magic protecting them."

"All according to plan."

A pause stretched between them for a while after her words, letting her know something else occupied his mind and led him to converse with her.

"The general is worried about a loose thread," he prefaced and averted his eyes.

His avoidance let her know the problem involved her, which she expected when she considered what else they needed to be concerned about. *I'm assuming this has to do with Soirée then. She's still wandering around, as far as I can tell, but she hasn't reached out since before the battle. Is she satisfied with Lupin's death? I doubt she'll leave me alone now that he's gone.*

A chuckle from her friend drew her attention away from the patch of earth she had been staring at.

"I'm guessing you figured out what he sent me to tell you?" Marcus ventured after.

She nodded. "It's the remaining demon."

"Partly. He's concerned the dark power you hold will lead it wherever you go, as well as bother the other mages."

"That is a problem."

"He plans on ordering you to remain along the border to avoid putting anybody else at risk. I let him know I'd warn you in case there's something you can do about it."

Although she disliked the man, Coura couldn't argue with Casner's point. *Of course he's focused on protecting those who are vulnerable to demonic magic, as well as whatever Soirée might do if she gets close. Now that Lupin has been defeated, I suppose I should figure out my next steps since I said I would go with her.*

She pushed the reminder aside in order to contemplate how she could manage the energy humming in her veins. "As far as I know, I'd need to expend it all."

"What do you mean?"

"Do you remember when we fought the serpent-like demonic creature outside Clearshot's home?" she asked while crossing her arms. "Byron had me release what I could both to pierce its thick skin and use a healthy portion up. If I can find a way to do that again, the presence should fade."

"If you're sure, I'll trust you to take care of yourself," he responded after a moment.

The comment prompted an appreciative smile. "Thank you. I should ask Byron what he thinks though, especially since I need to mask the energy. I'd hate to make everyone even more afraid of me than they already are."

Her friend's concerned expression reflected his pity, which she ignored in favor of rising to her feet. This prompted him to do the same before she requested the master mage's location. The question deepened his frown, and he mentioned the medical tent, sparking her curiosity in the process. The two headed in that direction before he mentioned talking to her later and choosing to walk toward a group of grumbling soldiers nearby.

Coura had never been inside the secluded space and paused after entering to let her eyes adjust to the dimmer light. Unlike the rest of the camp, the atmosphere felt comparable to a church as a peaceful lull hung over the healers and their patients. It also remained much quieter than she became used to, making her self-conscious about every movement.

*I don't remember Byron getting hurt*, she thought as she stepped farther into the layout. *Then again, I couldn't move well enough to check on him. He ordered me to help restrain Lupin, and I recall him guiding my arm through the pain.*

The memory steadily returned as she glanced over each person lying on the ground or sitting up conversing with the light mages. Those who noticed her fell silent, sent glares, or whispered remarks she knew weren't pleasantries, yet she dismissed them. As long as no one confronted her, she forced herself not to care.

She reached the middle of the tent and halted when she recognized the master mage as one of the men lying asleep off to her right. Although finding him resting caused her to hesitate, her next observation sent a chill throughout her body. Bandages completely covered his shoulder and wrapped around a stub above where his elbow should have been. The rest of the limb was gone.

*His arm is…*

During the fight, she didn't recall such an injury nor if he sounded hurt or exhausted. A mixture of sympathy for her former mentor, guilt at herself for not being able to prevent such a loss, and anger directed at the demon swelled in response. Before she could decide what to do next, a woman wearing a light gray dress with golden hair pinned back stomped closer to stand in front of Byron.

"Get out!" the woman growled in a fierce enough tone to startle Coura. "You shouldn't be around the injured."

"How is he?"

"Our patients' progress is none of your concern," the healer practically interrupted while pointing at the opening behind her. "When they're recovered, you'll be able to bother them away from us."

What disgust and fear the woman projected prompted similar stares from those around the tent, and she ordered Coura to leave once more without budging at all. Because of that, Coura spun on her heel with as much dignity as she could muster, raised her chin, and avoided the putrid glares following her out of the tent.

*Just like old times*, she mused with as much dark humor as self-loathing. *I suppose I won't be hearing from Byron for a while then.*

In order to quell her irritation with her situation, she returned to her spot at the edge of the camp where no one would interrupt her planning; however, she noticed a path leading into the woods beyond along the way and shifted directions in order to follow it. The narrow trail didn't look occupied, so she slipped through the brush. The change in scenery eased what tension she experienced due to the dark energy's affects since she walked alone. This gave her an opportunity to reflect on the idea she shared with Marcus.

*Do I really need Byron's advice? I know expending my power will impact the demonic presence, so I should be fine as long as I go far enough away not to be interrupted. I'll need to make sure those back at camp don't pick up on my spellcasting too.*

With that in mind, Coura kept hiking through the forest until sunset. One eye always remained on her surroundings in case an enemy approached despite the lack of threats she could perceive. Even her connection to Soirée didn't react whenever she studied it, letting her know the being wasn't near. Still, the looming canopy and tight space made her feel uncomfortable, as it usually did.

She only stopped when she stumbled upon an area with enough room for her to justify using magic away from her allies. By that point, she pushed her body enough and regretted not bringing a waterskin or food. The power she held suppressed what thirst, hunger, and weariness arose at her command as she considered her options.

*A blast of fire or lightning will no doubt cause a stir and risk flames catching onto the branches and leaves. I could use ice, but how much will that disrupt the environment? Winter is over, or at least it feels that way, so I'd need to condense it enough not to overwhelm the forest. What about a wall of ice instead of shards?*

The idea of a barrier reminded her of her last conversation with Byron, instantly lifting her spirits. Her hands rose after, and she began manifesting a shield while masking the released energy as best she could.

*A barrier surrounding the camp couldn't hurt, especially since we're not anticipating a retaliation from the Nim-Valans. Perhaps I could strengthen the border by doing this to the north as well. Casner should hear about this from me so he's not surprised and it'll be under his authority then. I just hope this fixes my problem instead of causing more trouble.*

# True Friendship

The camp's activity increased over the days since the Nim-Valans' retreat as more troops recovered and prepared to depart. General Casner's orders permitted those previously along the border to return to their positions while those who came from the palace could either go back or request a reassignment. All in all, Marcus got the impression everybody's sense of excitement wore away after the final conflict, leading over half to want nothing more than to resume their regular roles.

This seemed especially evident with the healers, as he witnessed when he visited the medical station to look for Will. People packed their belongings and what items were organized to serve various purposes except for the few who tended to the wounded. Even then, that only accounted for a dozen or so individuals.

After a brief search, he managed to locate the herbalist among a group of young women he recognized as those who survived across the border. He had hoped to find the spy Finn among them for a split second, but his spirits deflated when that didn't prove to be the case. Instead of departing right away, he pursued his original intent for finding his friend and approached.

"Assistant General!" a younger, mousey girl exclaimed upon spotting him, drawing the others' attention.

He offered a casual wave in order to quell any alarm stirred by his appearance. "Good afternoon. May I borrow a moment of your time?"

"Is it really borrowing if you can't pay it back?" another blonde mage countered, though in a lighthearted manner. This spurred the one at her side, who he recognized as Clara from their many encounters, to elbow her in the ribs.

"Don't be rude," she scolded the former before addressing Marcus. "Of course we're free to talk."

He chuckled at their banter. "I appreciate it. Have you seen Finn around?"

All the girls frowned and shook their heads. Will did the same, yet he alone appeared bothered by the question. When Marcus glanced at him, he averted his eyes.

"I see. If he does turn up, please send him to the general's tent."

After they each agreed to do so, he wished them well, turned on his heel, and walked away. His thoughts shifted to others he could ask since that had been his superior's final request for the day; however, a hand on his elbow stopped him from considering this further.

"You're not in a hurry to find Finn, are you?" came Will's voice.

Marcus glanced over his shoulder as his friend let go and moved to stand beside him. "No, it's not urgent. General Casner just wants to see how long he plans on staying near the border and discuss who to report to after we leave."

"That's a relief."

When Will didn't elaborate, he sensed concern from the normally talkative herbalist and decided to pry by asking what was wrong. This earned him a deeper frown as a pause stretched between them.

"I'm worried," his friend finally admitted in a bashful manner.

"I'm sure he's able to take care of himself, especially since the enemy has been dealt with."

Will shook his head. "That's not what I mean."

Marcus didn't understand and waited for an explanation instead of pressing the subject since he felt the reasoning had to be more personal if it didn't relate to the previous battle.

"I'm worried about what's going to happen now," Will continued before releasing a sigh, removing his glasses, and wiping them on his shirt. "The fighting might be over for good, which would be for the best, but I'd imagine Finn plans on returning to Nim-Vala. I have no reason to cross the border again, so we would never see each other."

Hearing such an innocent explanation warmed Marcus' heart considering how few people sympathized with the northerners, and he placed a reassuring hand on the other's shoulder. "Change is scary, but it's for the best. Besides, Finn is a spy for Asteom. He won't disappear. In fact, he'll probably help establish peace between the kingdoms."

Despite his genuine attempt to cheer his friend up, Will's gloom shifted to reflect concern, as if the words bothered him. Marcus removed his hand in response and considered why that would be the case. Before he could reach a conclusion, the herbalist started walking forward while broaching a new subject, forcing him to follow.

The two wandered through the camp and discussed a variety of topics, including the medical station's progress, how many soldiers they expected to stay behind, and the rough timeline. Such idle conversation eased what tension loomed between them earlier, though it threatened to return when Will inquired about his intentions.

*There's another demon lurking around these woods, and it's tied to Coura. I want to refuse to leave when she could use the extra support, but what would General Casner say? Aaron and his council might need my assistance elsewhere. Which is the right path?*

Fortunately, the sight of a familiar face along an intersecting path saved him from diving into that mess. Mattais strolled beside another soldier in as proud a manner as ever before noticing him and waving. When his fellow assistant general pivoted to head their way, Marcus glanced at Will; however, before he could ask if they needed to talk about anything else, his friend already understood the message.

"I should be getting back. The healers aren't as familiar with the medicines I keep, so I'd hate to cause an accidental mix up."

With that, he spun around and began heading toward the opposite end of the camp. Marcus watched him go for a moment, then his comrade's footsteps pulled his attention back to the man.

"If you've gotten enough fresh air for the time being, the general requested I send you his way," Mattais shared without any sort of greeting, though in a casual tone. "I told him I'd keep an eye out during my patrol."

"I'll go to him right now," Marcus promised.

The older soldier nodded and continued on his way without giving the request another thought. This also let Marcus know the subject wouldn't be serious, yet his curiosity piqued. Several ideas popped into his head as he made his way to Casner's location, and he entered after announcing his arrival.

"Come in," the general called while he did so. "That didn't take much waiting at all."

Marcus offered a smile in response but stood at attention without speaking, which he learned was customary around his superiors. The man sat at the center of his tent and ran a cloth over his golden sword, which he laid in his lap before Marcus' arrival. His eyes looked up at his guest briefly before returning to the weapon.

"Join me, won't you. It hurts my neck to have to gaze up during a conversation."

In response, Marcus relaxed and lowered himself to the ground.

"The lack of urgency lately has allowed me to recover," Casner began after. "Not only that, but I'm able to pay more attention to our next steps instead of the immediate future. One of these items has to do with you, assistant general. Do you wish to remain here, somewhere else along the border, or return to the palace?"

The question didn't startle Marcus, yet he hoped to avoid facing that decision due to his conflicting loyalties. He prayed this wasn't obvious as he provided a neutral but honest answer. "I will go wherever I am needed."

A pause followed his words. During that minute, the general finished polishing the sword, set it aside, then met his eyes.

"Just what I expected to hear from you. The truth is, it doesn't matter where you go. I'm curious if you had a preference."

Marcus contemplated how to respond and ultimately shook his head. "I suppose I only want to go where I can be the most helpful."

"I'll offer you a piece of advice," the man continued and dipped his chin a bit. "Too many people will take you up on an offer like that. Consider all options, then narrow them down or put them in order. You won't run yourself into the mud that way."

"Thank you, sir. I will keep that in mind."

"You'd better, especially once you hear why I summoned you."

When Marcus raised an eyebrow at the comment, Casner crossed his arms with a smirk before elaborating.

"Lady Zelnar visited this morning to share an update with the king's council. In it, I had her mention my support for your promotion."

Such a surprise left Marcus at a loss, and he fumbled for a reply. "Your support?"

"That's right. If it came up sooner among the king's council, I planned on pushing for it; however, General Tont never suggested such a thing. I'm sure that's not startling to hear."

Every discussion he'd had with his father seemingly came to mind at once, lowering his spirits after he recalled wanting to mold his own future, even if it meant abandoning his position. "I have faith in my superior's reasoning for the delay."

The rehearsed response didn't appear to please Casner. The general's amusement faded before he crossed his arms and leaned closer. "I'd never insert myself into your relationship with Tont, so what I'm about to share is based on professional observations. The life you've led until this moment prepared you to act as a leader, and after hearing about how you took charge when I was injured, I'm sure you're ready to move forward. I'll vouch for you when you accept your calling."

"I appreciate that, sir."

"On a personal note, the world doesn't function because of one person's beliefs," the man added at a quieter volume, as if to emphasize his next point. "If we only listen to a single opinion, our perspective narrows, and we limit ourselves to their expectations. It's not wrong to challenge this by seeking out additional insight."

Marcus found himself enraptured by Casner's final statement until he acknowledged the silence hanging between them. He hurried to thank his superior for the advice and rose without thinking about whether or not they finished talking. To his relief, the general merely mentioned seeing him the next morning, prompting him to depart and find a suitable spot to reflect on the conversation.

* * *

Although Will told his friend he'd be needed at the medical station, he didn't believe anyone would touch his potions due to their lack of labeling and disorganized arrangement known only to him. He didn't intend for the medicines to get so confusing, but following the previous fight, he simply hurried to keep up with the demands of the healers and their patients.

*I'll head back once I clear my head*, he vowed during a hike through the southern forest. *I'm sure I can forage for extra ingredients while I'm out here.*

His body committed to the task by instinctively searching for and procuring the aforementioned plants while his mind focused on his main concern regarding Finn's location. The spy hadn't been around for days, which didn't normally bother him except the conflict seemed to be coming to a close.

*If he's loyal to Asteom and Nim-Vala, I would bet he's going to return to the inner circle so he can resume his previous routine. Serving both kingdoms must put an immense amount of pressure on him, including traveling for days on end, and it keeps him from Yukin and Elena. I wonder if he'll ever be free to decide where he goes and what he does with his life.*

In the midst of his reflection, a voice, one he least expected in that moment, startled him into dropping what finger-length leaves he methodically collected from a climbing vine.

"I thought I would find you here."

Will's head snapped to where the source stood watching him in a bored manner. "Finn, it's you!"

The spy stepped closer while he scrambled to retrieve the leaves and rise. He didn't know where to begin when his lingering worry caught up to him, but his friend spoke before he could select the appropriate words.

"Do you and the light mages plan on remaining along the border?"

"I'm not sure. Why do you ask?"

The brown eyes looked elsewhere. "I wanted to let you know I haven't found any enemy troops remaining near Asteom. My guess is they retreated and will probably regroup before pursuing their next target."

"That's a relief." Despite the statement, his tone didn't suggest he felt better after hearing the news. Even Finn eyed him dubiously afterward.

"What's wrong?" came the anticipated response.

Will refrained from releasing a sigh yet glanced away and bit his tongue. Only when the silence stretching between them grew too unbearable did he brave his nerves and admit the truth.

"I won't have a reason to enter Nim-Vala, so I doubt we'll see each other again. You shouldn't need to watch the border anyway, right?"

As expected, the spy shook his head without a hint of sympathy. "You're overthinking our situation. My duties keep me bound to my masters in both kingdoms."

"I know, but…"

He couldn't bear the spy's unreadable expression and looked away. *Why is this so difficult?*

After another few seconds, Finn startled him by picking up the conversation in a more relaxed manner.

"I would wager your friends are excited to be returning home after their time in Nim-Vala."

Will nodded before adding, "I am as well. Who knows how much has changed in the past three years."

"Plenty, I'm sure."

"You're always welcome to visit us if you're in the capital."

The comment appeared to startle the spy, which spurred a chuckle from Will.

"I doubt you'll go that far into Asteom," he hurried to add. "I might get dragged away too. That happens often, especially since I prefer working on the road. In fact, I'll probably return to the border once the commotion dies down in order to explore farther west."

Despite his rambling, Finn didn't interrupt or seem disinterested; for some reason, this increased Will's nerves until he ran out of breath sharing his intentions. The two stared at each other afterward before an amused smile stretched across his friend's lips.

"Your life is so simple," the spy mumbled while shaking his head. Then, he fixed Will with a stern look. "I'll continue to do my part to bring peace between the kingdoms so you can explore more of Nim-Vala too."

Will's eyebrows shot up, and his mouth fell open a bit. During his stunned silence, Finn stepped closer to place a hand on his shoulder.

"I promise to fight for that alliance. You shouldn't need to sneak across the border to visit Geneva, Yukin, or even Elena."

As the hand lifted, what unsettling emotions bothering him disappeared, and a sense of security took its place. "You're right. That reminds me, can you thank them for me when you see them again?"

"I suppose so, but I can't say when that will be."

"That's fine," Will replied with a smile while Finn resumed his neutral expression. "And thank you too."

He longed to add more to fully express his gratitude, yet the spy wasn't the type to appreciate long-winded sentiments. Those words seemed to be enough as the two returned to camp together before parting ways for a final time. Still, he felt better than he had in days.

*Even though we don't know if or when we'll meet again, we believe in each other and that dream. We're friends after all.*

***

The sound of footsteps beside her had Grace hurrying to feign sleep. Unfortunately, her guard must have already noticed her previously staring at the sky and savoring the sunshine, for the woman dropped to the ground with a huff before shaking her shoulder.

"My lady, it's almost noon. You shouldn't sleep through a meal."

She repressed the urge to sigh and instead opened her eyes to find Dianne watching her closely with a bowl of steaming gruel in each hand. After sitting up, her guard shoved one into her hands before starting to eat.

"I did not plan on missing lunch," she couldn't stop herself from grumbling.

The woman shot her a displeased look. "Even so, you need to build your strength."

She bit her tongue to keep from mentioning what she had been saying over the previous week and a half since she woke after the battle. Instead, she chose to be grateful for the food.

*Dianne is taking her job far too seriously. In fact, I would argue acting as my caretaker is not part of her responsibilities.*

After she expended her light energy in order to summon the goddess fire and rid the world of the Nim-Valan's demon leader, Grace appreciated how the healers and her guard took care of her. She needed to build her strength more than anything, and they allowed her to do so without becoming overbearing.

This lasted for a few days until she felt decently recovered. The medical station cleared her to resume her duties as General Casner requested her presence when she could use her goddess gift once more, but Dianne didn't seem convinced. The woman refused to let her wander around their camp more than necessary and even requested her meetings be kept to a minimum length.

The consideration for her condition flattered her at first; then, she grew to despise being fretted over. *It is no better than living in the palace. Servants and soldiers never give you time alone or the freedom to act without assessment.*

Despite her negative mindset toward being overprotected, Grace did find solace in her abilities during the recent conflict. Her shielding and healing needed to remain at a level where she wouldn't wear herself out, which kept her attention on her energy level, but everything changed when the demon's life had been taken.

*I sensed its energy dwindle and vanish*, she recalled as she stared at her empty hands after Dianne procured her empty bowl to return the dishes. *Part of the presence remained, though I understood that was what Coura possessed. A shadow lifted from the enemy troops, allowing our forces to control the battle. The lack of urgency once they began fleeing benefited my spellcasting more than I realized.*

Her next assignment involved manifesting the goddess fire she trained herself to control, which she successfully accomplished when the being no longer distracted or frightened her. Watching the resulting flames devour such a wicked creature while obeying her command sparked a hint of pride she had never experienced before. She savored the feeling ever since.

On the other hand, her lack of power afterward prevented her from contributing toward the healers' efforts. She pitied everybody who fought and earned wounds throughout the fight, especially those closest to her. For some reason, what hurt most was learning about their conditions at a later time.

*Master Byron's injury could have taken his life easily. His survival is truly a miracle, along with the general's. I never considered the enemy using venom-coated weapons, but it is a viable option during battle. I do not know how I would handle dealing with a case like that. The healers never appear to panic though. Then Commander Evern...*

Even without the ability to manifest wings, Grace understood the impact of disrupting such a unique, complicated spell. Since it tied to the caster's body, they felt every bit of damage they experienced through an arm or leg; the connection to their center of power took a harder hit.

*I doubt the lingering trauma will allow his energy to hold together anymore*, she reflected amid a surge of sympathy for the Yeluthian soldier. *We are taught about the fragility of magic and how it rebounds on the user if handled incorrectly. I may not comprehend his situation because of the manifestation spell, but I do know he is likely suffering in his own way.*

In an attempt to ease her emotions, she sent a prayer to the goddess before Dianne returned.

"How are you feeling today?" the woman asked in a gentle manner, as if she could read Grace's mind.

"Better, thank you."

"There's an update floating around the camp that might lift your spirits."

She raised an eyebrow in response. "What sort of update?"

"Our assignment should be finished in the next couple days," her guard explained while beaming. "Assistant General Mattais found me to request we join him at the general's tent again. He intends to contact the king's council, share the lack of activity from the northerners, then officially disband our position."

"What if the enemy is not defeated?" she countered halfheartedly. That had been the main point of discussion during her previous communication between locations.

"They received word about what's taking place in Nim-Vala. Apparently, it would be better if our defenses spread out across the border again instead of remaining lumped together."

"I suppose so."

Dianne sensed her hesitation and reached over to place a hand on her arm in a reassuring gesture. "The assistant general didn't mention much, so I'm sure we'll get the full explanation when we meet with them. He also mentioned Master Byron is well enough to join this time."

That bit of information instantly lightened Grace's mood. "Really? That is wonderful news!"

"I thought you'd be happy about his recovery," her guard added with a chuckle. "We can head over there whenever you're prepared."

With the woman's blessing, she hopped to her feet, brushed the dirt off her clothes, and held herself to a brisk walk as they crossed through the camp.

*

What the assistant general told Dianne proved to be true, which he expanded on in detail alongside his superior during their meeting. The spy Grace met once before and saw on several occasions over the last few weeks confirmed the lack of enemy troops beyond the border, as well as additional insight she wouldn't have imagined hearing so soon.

Nim-Vala's king already became aware of his advisor's death, which Byron attributed to an unnatural connection through demonic energy, resulting in the man ordering the inner circle to strengthen its defenses. Most of those present agreed the northerners would resume what tension they built between classes over the years before the demon's intervention, though Asteom would keep troops posted along the border.

"We proved ourselves to be stronger than their men," the general concluded after the conversation wrapped up. "It makes the most sense for the outer circle to retreat and regroup before acting anyway. They'd be foolish to attempt to continue this fight without their previous leader and that healing ability."

The majority of those present agreed aloud while Grace silently wished for that to be the end of their involvement with Nim-Vala, if only for the sake of peace. When the discussion turned to organizing the remaining supplies between the soldiers and mages who would remain on the border, she fulfilled her duty by reaching out to the king's council. The brief update and subsequent comments let her know those in Verona agreed with the assessment.

With nothing else to do, she and Dianne were dismissed. Both grew famished once the excitement wore off, leading them to grab dinner and return to the bonfire where Clearshot, Will, and surprisingly Coura chatted casually. All three offered a greeting before Clearshot pressed the pair for information on the meeting. She let her guard explain what took place while eating and quelling the sense of unease that arose from her friend's unnatural, haunting presence.

Coura hadn't been present for days until recently, and even then she often slipped away before Grace could get settled in a spot across the flames. She hated how she reacted due to their friendship over the years; however, she knew the demon was to blame. That helped calm her down enough not to cave into her desire to leave the area when her friend stayed for longer than a couple minutes.

By the time evening covered the land, Byron, Marcus, and Finn joined the group and provided their own updates and opinions on the situation. The latter ate his meal in silence before conversing with Will, who appeared concerned, then leaving. Grace repositioned herself to sit beside him in the empty spot when his worry lingered.

"Is something the matter?" she asked at a quieter volume to avoid disrupting the rest of the group's conversation.

Will seemed startled by her question but huffed a laugh instead of masking his emotions. "We're fortunate this conflict is wrapping up. It could have ended much worse too, but I feel sad."

Grace didn't know how to respond; however, her lack of a reply allowed him to continue while gazing beyond their circle.

"Finn is leaving tomorrow and won't be back for another week or so. I'd be surprised if he sticks around for longer than half a day."

"I did not realize you two were close."

"He's not the type of person to put relationships over his work, which is why ours surprised me. I've become braver because of my time in Nim-Vala thanks to him. I just can't imagine not having anything to do with them anymore."

Such an honest, personal reason hadn't been what Grace expected to hear, especially due to her own bias regarding the northern kingdom. Still, she refused to dismiss her friend's feelings or doubt his experiences when he needed somebody to talk to.

"I suppose that is the fragility of life," she began in an attempt to ease his troubles. "We get plenty of opportunities to meet people and form our own relationships, but that time is not guaranteed. All we can do is our part in assuring a future for others to do the same."

The brown eyes beneath his spectacles shifted to stare at her with no shortage of amazement, spurring a blush.

"W-What?" she stammered as she glanced away, prompting him to laugh.

"Thank you, Grace. I'll be sure to remember that from now on."

After those words, they fell into the mix of chatting taking place from the rest of their group. Everyone appeared relaxed, yet the positive update from the day kept them full of energy and alert enough to remain awake. Despite that, the shadow looming over Grace steadily crept forward again as she grew tired. She sensed it taking hold of her friends as well before Will finally brought up the problem no one could dismiss.

"Did General Casner mention the demon in the woods?" she overheard him ask Marcus during the duo's conversation.

What other voices filled the air silenced as all eyes looked to the assistant general, showing she hadn't been the only person to catch the question. Meanwhile, Marcus glanced at Coura, who raised an eyebrow, before lowering his gaze and answering.

"We're discussing the matter tomorrow before the first set of troops departs."

"Those soldiers and mages are from the sites farther east," Byron added, drawing everybody's attention and relieving some of the pressure on the assistant general. "We'll be dismissing various companies over the next few days just to be certain the Nim-Valans don't change their minds. Since Verona is last on that list and may take place over multiple days due to the amount of troops returning, I suggest you all determine how long you wish to stay."

Grace didn't intend to add her input since she hadn't considered the situation that far ahead; however, Dianne spoke on their behalf immediately after.

"We'll be heading out as soon as possible," the woman stated matter-of-factly and raised her chin. "My lady shouldn't be kept in a dangerous environment longer than necess-"

"I plan on remaining here until the general does not require my services," Grace interrupted without considering how her response would sound.

This resulted in startled reactions from her friends and guard, who leaned closer with a concerned expression.

"Are you sure? What if the second demon targets you? The northerners might still retaliate too."

"I truly appreciate your concern, but my role in this camp is to act as communicator between our leaders and the king's council. If trouble arises when most of Asteom's forces disperse, how would anyone be made aware?"

"A logical answer," Marcus added when Dianne didn't argue. "You'll have your guard and the rest of us protecting you as well. That is, if everybody else is staying until the end."

The comment spurred a smile from Grace, and one by one each person expressed their desire to remain for various reasons. Will hoped to wait for their spy while Byron would assist General Casner, Marcus, and Mattais. Clearshot refused to go alone then addressed Coura when she didn't add her thoughts.

"You're stuck here, aren't you?"

"That depends," she answered in a neutral tone before crossing her arms.

Grace and those around her waited for more, but she didn't seem inclined to pursue to subject, allowing Marcus to end the evening by promising to keep them updated whenever he could spare the time.

***

Every morning since she returned to her friends, Coura woke with a start due to a tightness in her chest that had her believing she'd stopped breathing at some point. Sweat covered her body and chilled her to the bone thanks to the early, chilly temperature, though fortunately everyone either went about their business or remained asleep. She thanked her luck for that because it prevented her from having to explain the reason or craft a lie, both of which she didn't want to do.

*It's Soirée*, she acknowledged and paused to catch her breath in order to calm her racing heart. *She knows I'm prolonging fulfilling my part of our deal.*

If she doubted this, she needed only to focus on her connection to the creature. Every hour, the dark power tying the two together felt as though it tightened, straining her soul space and causing the sense of panic. This continued against her will, so she ignored it as best as she could while standing, stretching, and proceeding with her day. By the time she cleaned up and returned with a warm bowl of porridge, those around the fire were awake with their own breakfasts or finished eating. Marcus soon departed with Grace and Dianne behind him, then Will mentioned meeting with Clara at the medical station.

"I thought I never stopped working," Byron commented when he and Coura sat alone. "He's putting me to shame."

"At least you have an excuse to not to try so hard," she teased as she watched the herbalist disappear into the mass of tents and soldiers. When she glanced back at her former mentor, he frowned at her.

"A missing arm only limits how I can contribute, not the amount of effort I can expend."

"You're arm? I was referring to your age."

Coura mustered as much of an innocent look as she could, yet her composure crumbled into a smirk when he scowled in response. A few seconds later, he rolled his eyes and chuckled.

"I'm glad this experience hasn't tarnished your sense of humor," he grumbled and let his smile fade. "Have you seen Commander Evern lately?"

The question instantly soured her mood when she considered the reason for her avoidance of him and his subordinate. "No, but I probably won't until I know I don't bother Grace anymore. Then I'll be able to be around him and Lavine without hostility."

"I doubt your father would act that way."

"Are you sure?" she countered while raising her eyes to the clouds above. "You know how energies react. It's not something we can control."

As if in response to her comment, her link to Soirée pulled on her body again, intensifying the ache in her chest. She attempted to hide this by closing her eyes and taking a deep breath; however, Byron already noticed a change in the mood.

"What's wrong?" he inquired with a hint of suspicion.

"It's nothing."

She opened her eyes when he didn't speak again and found his emerald pair studying her. *He's too observant for his own good.*

"I imagine you don't want to tell me," he prefaced a minute later as his expression and posture relaxed. "That's fine, but I'm here if you need to talk about what's going to happen."

Coura nodded and thanked him, which was enough for the moment. She watched as he rose to his feet then plucked up his empty bowl and faced the direction of the mess area.

"I also think you should find the commander. I'm sure he's worried about you since you haven't approached him yet."

When she didn't reply to his suggestion, he accepted that as the end of their conversation and walked away. She savored the solitude by sliding closer to the fire where its warmth soon helped settle her mind and body. This also allowed her to contemplate her situation without becoming distracted by anything outside the dancing flames.

*I can't keep avoiding the problem, but I don't know what to do. My first instinct is to locate Soirée and stop her, though I'll die in the process. If I can't make up my mind soon, I'll be the last person here. She'd come after me then.*

Coura released a sigh before burying her face into her arms, which wrapped around her knees as she hugged her legs to her chest. The unnatural posture caused her back to ache minutes later, so she stood with a wince and decided to listen to her former mentor's advice.

*Evern might come up with an idea I didn't consider*, she rationalized while strolling through the camp toward the Yeluthians' spot. *If not, I suppose I can make sure I see him before whatever happens.*

The notion dwindled what hope remained in her heart as she passed the dozens of individuals on their own business. Some sidestepped out of her path to let her know they felt the demonic presence while others simple went out of their way to send her a glare. Their responses led her to keep her eyes forward, though she became numb to the snubs over the years. In any case, she reached her goal and found her father sitting beside Lavine. Both sets of sapphire eyes already landed on her before she came near, prompting her to wave as she approached.

"Has it been a quiet morning for you too?" she asked them when neither offered a greeting.

"It has," the commander began and glanced at his subordinate, who seemed unusually dismissive. "We need only to build our reserves for our departure. How are you faring?"

"That's sort of why I'm here. Do you have time to talk?"

She kept a neutral tone to avoid hinting at an issue; however, his resulting, sympathetic gaze revealed her attempt had been in vain. Evern pushed himself to his feet without a word, though she noticed how gingerly he moved, and the two left Lavine alone.

"Shall we visit one of the southern trails?" her father suggested when she hesitated to pick a direction to lead them in. "I do not imagine they are occupied often due to the recovery efforts."

"That's fine with me."

"Would you also prefer to initiate this conversation when we are away from the camp?"

The question hinted at his knowledge of her purpose for seeking him out, though she figured she had nothing to hide between her friends and family. This prompted her to share what had been on her mind recently, including Soirée's lurking, how their connection pulled her toward the being, and her lack of a solution to stop the creature without hurting herself in the process. By the time she finished explaining, they wandered along a dirt path worn from the troops' use over the past weeks.

"I wanted to see if you had any ideas," she concluded afterward. Her eyes instinctively scanned the woods around them, but at that moment, she forced herself to look at her father.

Evern didn't appear surprised by her speaking about the issue so openly, which eased a sliver of the tension building in her chest. His thoughtful gaze as he contemplated the situation also let her know he took the problem seriously. After a few minutes, he halted and faced the trees off to their left, drawing her eyes to a spot where wild flowers swayed in the gentle breeze.

"I have never been put in a position like this," he began at a quieter yet calm manner, as if he wished to avoid disrupting the peaceful atmosphere. "If your mother or my fellow commanders were here, they would savor my loss of a reply."

Coura's heart sank in response. "You don't know what to do either."

"I am afraid not. Demons and their powers are foreign to Yeluthia and our people, and this bond you forged is unlike any sort of spell I am aware of."

"I assumed as much."

She huffed a laugh before turning away to mask her disappointment. Before she could accept his reply and contemplate other resources, she felt a gentle touch as her father laid a hand on her shoulder.

"Just because I lack the knowledge to help does not mean I will not assist you, Coura. You should also speak with your friends about this. Such a close support system is rare between soldiers and mages, or Yeluthians and humans. Do not forget your lineage as well. Demons can be defeated, so it stands to reason their magic has a limit."

"You're right," she responded after a minute to process his advice. "Maybe I should stop worrying and go end this already."

"We will never learn if we do not try."

The words echoed in her mind as he turned her from where he held her shoulder and wrapped his arms around her in a reassuring embrace. Her arms immediately rose to hug him back, and she struggled to keep her emotions in check until they returned to camp.

*

That evening, Coura told those around the fire about her decision to confront Soirée the following morning. She strengthened her resolve during a meditation session after speaking with Evern and readied herself for their reactions, which didn't disappoint. While Marcus, Clearshot, and Will argued against what they deemed to be a rash choice, Byron and Grace seemed to be biting their tongues.

*They understand I can't keep putting this off*, she noted amid the resulting noise from the other three. *Those without the ability to sense the demonic energy just don't get why I can't stay around until she acts first.*

"If a demon attacked our camp tonight, how many lives would be lost?" she interjected at a raised volume in order to quiet the other voices.

As expected, the question either startled them into silence or left them considering the outcome.

"The longer I wait, the likelier it is she'll come after me," Coura continued while dismissing that possibility. "Our allies are aware something is out there too."

"Did you speak with the general yet?" Byron asked when none of the resulting grumbles manifested into another argument.

She shook her head. "What's the harm if I disappear?"

"What about those of us going with you?"

That caught her off guard. "You're not…"

"I won't let you do this alone," her former mentor stated with a stern look. "If Evern intends to come along as well, that's a master mage and a Yeluthian commander gone."

"And an assistant general," Marcus added and crossed his arms.

Part of Coura already believed her friends would join, yet hearing them volunteer still left her speechless. Her lack of a response allowed enough time for Clearshot and Will to mention going too.

"We'll need the ancestral weapon if we can even hope to win," Byron picked up before Grace chimed in.

"If we repeat the circumstances surrounding the Nim-Valans' leader, my goddess fire should be enough."

"My lady!" her guard exclaimed after the comment only to be shushed by the Yeluthian.

"Dianne, you cannot honestly expect me to sit by when my spell is our best resource."

"Not if it puts your life in danger. The battlefield contained healers and mages to shield you. You'll be more vulnerable with a small group."

"The reward is greater than the risk," Grace replied and met the woman's firm stare with a stubborn one of her own. "I do not plan on being involved with the fight until the moment arrives when I can summon the goddess fire. With your protection, the creature should not even bother targeting me."

"That, and Evern will be another, tempting distraction," Coura added.

Byron produced a low hum to grab their attention and rubbed his chin while becoming fixated on the flames in front of everybody. "I doubt my magic would be useful given how much combat we can expect to take place, which means I can focus on shielding."

His suggestion fueled the discussion as Will, Marcus, and Clearshot shared their input on what positions they preferred in relation to each other, as well as Byron and Evern. Meanwhile, Coura listened and formed her own strategy. No one pressed her for details on what she would be doing, so she let them talk until the evening grew late. A sense of unease drifted between them after when they each lied down for the night.

For what felt like hours, she tossed and turned without being able to find a comfortable position. New ideas and fears arose thanks to her mind's inability to settle, leading her to sit up, rub her tired eyes, and glance around the fire. Once she confirmed her friends were all asleep, she quietly got to her feet, slipped on her boots, and walked to the southern end of the site.

She hadn't planned on hiking through the darkness until she found herself heading along the trail she and her father used earlier in the day. A slim tendril of dark energy produced enough light in the palm of her hand to keep her from tripping over the few obstacles in her path as she wandered through the woods.

*Is the forest less irritating when it's shrouded in darkness, or am I just numb to my hatred of being under the trees?* she wondered amid the chirping insects. *This may be my last night to enjoy such an experience.*

Her steps paused so she could listen to the noise for a minute; however, an unnatural, light thumping sound had her glancing around to where a figure approached with a torch in one hand.

*That must be the evening patrol.*

Such an interruption didn't bother her except she hadn't come up with an excuse for being out of the site and on her own. An apology sat on her tongue as the man walked nearer; however, she recognized him as Marcus when she could catch a glimpse of his face.

"What are you doing here?"

"I was going to ask you the same thing," he answered before a yawn interrupted his explanation.

Coura noted his half-awake expression and put the pieces together. "You followed me?"

"You didn't notice?" he countered with a weary grin. "I thought you were ignoring me."

"No, but I…" What words she planned to say left her then, so she dipped her chin and averted her eyes.

"What's wrong?" he pressed while projecting sympathy. "Is this about tomorrow? We both need our rest for what's to come, but if you need to talk-"

"You're right. Let's head back."

When she attempted to pass him, her friend raised his free hand to stretch that arm in front of her. The two stood in silence for a moment, as if to emphasize his interrupted offer, before the hand lowered.

"I'm scared too," he admitted without looking away from her. "After our last encounter, I understand how difficult trapping and ending this demon will be. You, Aaron, and others I care about were hurt. I don't want that to happen again."

Coura felt compelled to meet his gaze, though she struggled to hide what emotions arose, causing her hands to tremble. "Me neither."

"We're not as inexperienced as before though, and the ancestral weapons are both available to us. With Grace's magic, our chances to finish off the last of those beings is exponentially greater."

"That's not what I'm afraid of."

Marcus' face fell at her honest response. "I'm sorry. I keep forgetting you're…"

While he fumbled with his reply, she stepped closer and dismissed the spell in her hand.

"This has always been between Soirée and I, but that doesn't mean we're not harming others."

A pause stretched between them, leading her to wonder what he thought of the bond. *I've never been normal since we met. He's seen how powerful I became with demonic energy, and how weak I grew without it. I wouldn't blame him or anybody else if they wished they never met me.*

"Any sort of dangerous situation is going to involve the people you care about," he added then. The resulting, determined expression he wore also startled her a bit. "Whether we're fighting alongside you or cheering from the sidelines, we choose to show our support. I bet you feel the same when our roles are reversed. That's what friends are for, so don't be bothered if you need to lean on us until it's over."

Hearing such a sincere reaffirmation brought tears to her eyes. *In that case, what's the harm in letting my guard down for a few minutes.*

She stepped forward until they were toe to toe, turned her head, and bent forward to press her cheek against his shoulder. The rest of her body relaxed into his a second later, allowing her to quietly cry without strain. As soon as Marcus understood what was happening, his free arm wrapped around her in a partial embrace.

Despite her jumbled thoughts before, her mind fell silent. The wildlife continued its song around them to resume the peaceful setting, and Coura savored the undisturbed sounds. The shaking of her hands soon quelled when the tears ran out, though she wasn't compelled to move away until he removed his hand from where it rested on her back.

"Are you ready to return to camp?" he asked in a new, softer tone compared to when he first appeared. "We're pretty far out, so we should get going if we want to reach the perimeter before sunrise."

She straightened in response and nodded as she noted how exhausted she grew. Only the image of their group's bonfire and her awaiting blankets kept her from falling over after they started walking; however, she made sure to breath in the cool, fresh air surrounding them to remind herself of why she needed the evening stroll.

# A Fated Encounter

Despite what awaited him that day, Byron slept through the night and woke feeling well rested. Only a slight ache in his left shoulder bothered him until he sat up while rubbing the damaged limb. His eyes wandered to the fire, then over the bundled figures circling it before landing on where Coura normally lied. The blankets remained, but she was gone.

*She left*, he realized as a sense of panic jolted him into a more alert state. *I didn't think she would be so reckless. Going off on her own will surely get her killed!*

He threw off his covers and began to rise before a familiar voice off to his right drew his attention.

"Calm down."

Byron glance over to where Clearshot lied in a casual manner and stared at him. An amused smile adorned the soldier's face, and he sat up to stretch both arms toward the sky.

"She went to speak with General Casner before the camp stirred," his friend explained after.

The simple reason, not to mention one they discussed the night prior, immediately eased what tension Byron developed in those brief seconds of alarm. This prompted him to chuckle at his overreaction, which was soon joined by Clearshot's restrained laughter.

"I can't blame you for worrying," his friend added once they settled down and decided not to rise. "Given her record of disappearing and placing the burden square on her shoulders, it's surprising she didn't leave earlier."

Byron scratched his head and released a sigh. "I'd say she's maturing in that regard. You can't forget what she's been through or how many people turned their backs on her."

"That doesn't justify dismissing those of us who stayed with her over the years."

"I can't argue with you there."

They dropped the subject when a groan from one of the boys across the flames let them know the rest of their group would be rising soon. The sound prompted them to do so and begin preparing for the day. By the time Byron was dressed with breakfast in hand, only Will sat in front of their fire with an empty bowl nearby.

"Did you eat already?" he asked the herbalist while dropping to the ground.

"I'm used to the pace of the medical station," the young man shared with a sheepish grin. "It doesn't usually allow for me to taste the food, but what we get isn't exactly full of flavor."

Byron agreed before tipping his dish back in order to slurp up as much of the mixture as he could in a single mouthful. When he finished, he set the wooden bowl aside and leaned back on his arm to settle his stomach. He didn't intend to converse during that moment, but the young man's timid voice addressed him then.

"Can I ask you something?"

"Of course, Will. What is it?"

Given the tone and hesitation, he assumed the question had to do with Coura or what was to come that day; however, that didn't prove to be the case.

"Are you sure you'll be able to manage without your arm? I don't mean to insult your abilities, but such a grievous injury takes time to recover. I can only imagine how much of a change it is to get used to."

Although he'd grown to hate acknowledging the lack of his limb over the past week since his recovery, Byron couldn't blame anybody for doubting his physical capabilities. He straightened from where he sat, and his hand went to the stub above where his elbow used to be. The pain still haunted him, which he expected came across when he returned his gaze to Will with a response.

"Rest assured, a magic user can wield their energy without the use of their arms. I'll likely never try fighting with a sword again unless I have to, but I don't expect to be put in that situation."

Will frowned and seemed like he wanted to argue until his eyes shifted to a spot behind Byron. Footsteps alerted them of others, and Byron looked over to find Marcus, Coura, and Clearshot walking together with their own meals.

"Remember this," he added while turning to address the herbalist once more. "Each of us has our strengths and weaknesses. We must trust one another to fulfill what roles we can't do ourselves."

When the young man nodded, they welcomed their companions back in order to move forward from the topic. Coura mentioned Casner's dismissal of her and well wishes for the group after reluctantly relinquishing the ancestral blade in his possession to Marcus at her friend's request. Grace and Dianne soon joined the circle, then Commander Evern, who briefly flashed the golden hilt of the weapon sheathed at his waist. Within the hour, everybody appeared prepared to set out. He noted a looming feeling of despair setting over their group as their conversations ended and silence filled the space. In the midst of that break, Coura pushed herself to her feet.

"If you're ready, follow me."

She spun on her heel after those words to head north, which intrigued him given the lack of activity from that direction lately. Most of their group acknowledged the waves and greetings they received along the way until they shifted into a line in order to walk evenly through the wooded path.

For a while, they trekked in silence. Byron's thoughts during this time ranged from what to expect, how to counter a magical ambush, and their distance in relation to the border, then how the demon would behave once it recognized those present. He kept any concerns limited to the encounter so he didn't consider the danger they put themselves in, as well as the results if they were successful.

Because he took to the rear with Marcus in front of him, he didn't hear or see a signal to halt from their leader until he nearly stumbled into the assistant general when the soldier stopped. Coura's voice reached him at a quiet, indiscernible volume as she addressed her companions, leading him to adjust his position so he could peer ahead. From that angle, he saw her continue forward into a clearing while the others remained behind the foliage.

"What's going on?" he whispered to the young man closest to him.

"The demon is farther ahead," Marcus shared without shifting his gaze from Coura. "She believes it knows we're all here but wants to draw it out first and gauge its reaction to a fight."

Byron could tell the assistant general disapproved of the method, but it was too late to protest. Seconds later, Coura stood alone with both arms at her sides in a posture that didn't hint at defensive or antagonistic. He also noticed how quiet the forest fell before a clear, wicked laugh echoed around them. The sound sent a shiver along his spine before the figure emerged from the bushes off to the clearing's right.

Despite his previous encounters with the creature, he grew tense and instinctively readied his energy in preparation for a shielding spell. The irritation that arose at being in the demon's presence instantly overwhelmed him and continued to increase when it strolled over to speak with Coura. Such confident strides, along with its broad grin, let him know their enemy would take pleasure in a confrontation.

*We understood this won't be easy from a combat standpoint, but the creature's behavior isn't normal from what we've encountered in an enemy*, he thought as the being leaned closer to Coura so it could speak into her ear. *It should be obvious we're not challenging an ordinary opponent. Any preconceptions might only distract us.*

As it spoke, the demon fixed its violet eyes on their group, shifting from person to person without letting its smile falter. Byron despised the uncomfortable sensation that stirred in his gut in response to how vulnerable he felt; however, it was when the gaze slid to Coura again that his heart hurt for his former student.

*Our lives are at risk, but she's trapped.*

That pity flipped in an instant when the being raised its arms to place both hands on Coura's shoulders. For some reason, the sight lit a flame under Byron, as if witnessing the manipulation firsthand awakened his desire to protect the one person whose life had always been impacted by the creature's existence the most.

*We'll kill that monster*, he vowed and prepared to leap into action. *If it's the last thing I do, I'll make sure it meets its end with us.*

***

Coura was aware of Soirée's presence long before she set out with her friends thanks to the demon's eagerness tightening the tie between them. As she did every morning, she ignored the sensation in order to mask what emotions arose; however, she also wished to avoid letting the being know what she intended to do.

*I have no doubt she'll figure out we're confronting her once we enter the woods. It's a matter of setting the tone for this fight when she shows up.*

That had been why she opted to approach the most fitting clearing alone. At her signal, there would be no turning back.

"What is this?" came the familiar, feminine voice from off to her right. "Offering yourself to me so willingly?"

Coura didn't answer, prompting Soirée's silhouette to emerge from the branches and leaves at the perimeter. As usual, the creature sauntered toward the center of the area without a care in the world before halting just in front of her. Nothing about the demon appeared to have changed from their first encounter except for the lone, white scar across her chest, yet the level of familiarity between them developed over the years.

*I used to be too terrified to speak*, Coura recalled as they studied each other. *Then I'd grow angry in her presence and throw my words at her without considering the risk. With our souls connected, it's not even worth getting worked up over anymore.*

Soirée's grin widened, as if the being read her thoughts. "Did you bring your friends along to watch?"

"They're here to help me kill you."

The blunt response earned her a huff of laughter before the demon leaned close enough to speak quietly into her ear. "What if

I kill them first? I'm surprised you would drag them here to meet such a cruel fate. Let me tell you what will *actually* happen…"

A series of descriptions followed in which Soirée picked one of her friends and came up with ways to hurt them; however, Coura forced herself not to listen. Despite the vicious nature of the acts, two truths kept her from believing in such outcomes.

*They're not as weak as she remembers. I know they wouldn't join me if they weren't confident in their skills. Besides, it's seven against one whose life is tied to mine. The real problem is whether or not we can keep her here. If she runs-*

Before she could finish the thought, Soirée laid both hands on her shoulders without any force that would suggest harming her.

"Are you sure you wouldn't rather enjoy the remainder of your life, Dear One? In case you forgot, I intend to break the spell and free us both. You could return to your mundane life in the palace, grow old with those behind you, and never see me again if that is what you choose."

The idea of such a future had Coura smiling, though it was sardonic instead of reflecting happiness. "You're lying. As soon as you're done with me you'll end my life."

"Is that what you believe?"

"It's what I've known ever since I learned about this bond."

A pause stretched between them before the demon removed her hands and stepped back while a twisted giggle escaped her. The violet eyes bore into Coura, reflecting a furious hatred as the creature bared its fangs in a half-smile, half-snarl.

"Why don't I just take you by force," came the being's next words.

In response, Coura drew the blade at her waist, assumed a defensive stance, and glared with as much intensity as she could muster. "I'd like to see you try."

Neither moved until the whistle of an arrow flew by from over her shoulder. The projectile landed in Soirée's chest, causing the demon to take another step backward. Still, the grin didn't fade.

"I'll be sure to leave you for last so you can watch your friends suffer!" the being growled before lunging forward.

As Soirée outstretched a hand to reach for her, Coura brought up her blade and sliced the tip across the pale palm. What dark blood it drew dripped to the ground as the creature retracted her hand then summoned her black sword. It took two swings, which she blocked, before Marcus appeared at her side to push their opponent back.

Arrows continued flying, though not all landed on some part of the demon's body, striking the shields Byron crafted. After noting the magical barrier's existence, she dismissed it altogether in order to focus on defeating their enemy, as opposed to keeping Soirée in the clearing. This became crucial when Evern joined the mix of clashing weapons with a fierceness he rarely showed except at certain moments during battle.

Coura retreated and paused to catch her breath when her father appeared while the assistant general attempted to sidestep around the two combatants. Despite her desire to locate the others, she didn't dare turn her attention away lest she be caught off guard.

*Clearshot's attacking from a distance, Byron is maintaining the shield and likely ready to step in should an opportunity arise or we need help, and Will and Dianne are protecting Grace. I can't imagine those three would be out in the open. I don't need to worry about anybody except myself then.* The notion had her gripping her sword's hilt tighter.

Just like Marcus, she began circling the ongoing display of bloodlust between Evern and Soirée as angel and demon collided. Part of her wondered if her father would let up at all or maintain his position as their lead fighter, which left her and the assistant general as support. She prepared for this strategy until the demon suddenly changed tactics. Their opponent kept the attacks between weapons until Evern drove her back a few steps after landing a scratch on her forearm, prompting a sneer. Then, her fists and feet became an issue.

The Yeluthian practically dove forward when an opening seemingly presented itself as Soirée lowered her weapon a bit. Instead of lunging, he swung horizontally, cutting through the air as his target ducked under the golden blade. Her empty fist pulled back before she hurried to punch him in the gut; however, he managed to brace for the strike. At least, that was what Coura thought when he immediately retaliated by bringing the ancestral weapon in the opposite direction and at a diagonal angle. The resulting slash had the demon tumbling away. When their opponent remained on one knee after, panting and bearing her fangs at Evern, another arrow buried itself into her arm. The being seemed to have had enough at that point.

Coura expected to be forced into combat at any moment, so it didn't surprise her when Soirée raised a hand to manifest a shield that cut through the limited, open area and split it in two. This separated them from her father and Marcus.

*It won't take them long to get around the spell*, she noted while the demon rose and tossed the raven locks over one shoulder.

Despite their enemy's casual demeaner, she knew better than to let the momentum of the fight die down. This sparked her desire for vengeance, prompting her to charge ahead and initiate another bout. Despite the emotion, she kept her movements controlled due to her friends' and father's involvement.

*If she's looking to wear me out and take me by force, I can't be so hasty. Besides, I'm not up against her alone. Somebody will intervene, so whatever opportunity I can make for them will help.*

Soirée's crazed grin stretched farther while their weapons met, as if the being read her thoughts. Then, the demon freed a hand and seized one of her wrists. Instead of attempting to yank herself free, Coura tried utilizing the closed space by bringing up her right leg with the intent to land a blow using her knee. Unfortunately, she was both too weak and uncoordinated to successfully manage more than a light strike, which caused her opponent to laugh.

A stream of curses flew through her mind as she unsuccessfully struggled to pull her arm free, manage her sword, and attempt another kick. Soirée's continuing cackling also spurred a blush out of embarrassment and frustration, yet it reminded her of just who they were dealing with.

That refocused awareness led her to dive into the stagnant, demonic energy in her center. At her beckoning, it shot eagerly into her right hand, which she released from the hilt of her weapon. Soirée kept a grip on her other wrist, so she left it there and manifested the black blade she rarely needed anymore. Unlike a normal wielding position, her direction summoned the weapon so the blade pointed downward, allowing her to plunge it straight into the demon's exposed foot and into the ground beneath them.

Coura fully expected the being's reaction after such a bold strike; if she didn't, she would be a fool for putting her life on the line so carelessly. This kept her muscles ready to dodge what came next.

A pained, ferocious cry escaped Soirée in response to the wound as the violet eyes darted from the dark weapon to her. The hold on her arm loosened enough for her to pull it free just as the demon's other hand swiped for her face. The sudden, physical retaliation had her craning her head back, though out of instinct rather than by choice, and she stumbled away with less balance than she preferred.

*I didn't even see her weapon disappear*, Coura thought once a stinging sensation resonated where the being scratched her right cheek, likely down to the bone. *A moment later, and she would've gouged my eyes instead of skin.*

It frightened her how close she had been to letting that happen; however, there was no time to linger on the close call. Soirée already held the black blade in one hand after removing it from where it pinned her foot to the ground, and her furious expression didn't change.

Before the demon could stalk closer, a flash of light filled the area, startling Coura enough to jump. The following rumble of thunder eased her worry as she partially covered her eyes with a hand against the sudden brightness.

*That's Byron's magic. He must have been waiting for a moment like this to act, or at least to pause the combat for us.*

A familiar voice called her name once the noise died down, though she avoided glancing around since she knew it belonged to her father. A few seconds later, he reached her side and slid to a stop, drawing her attention.

"Are you hurt?" he asked without removing his eyes from the smoke settling nearby.

Coura shook her head then returned her gaze to where their enemy hid within the gray cloud. "I'm fine."

"Stay close to me from now on. If it targets you again, we cannot let it separate us."

Although she accepted the order, she didn't reply aloud.

Movement off to their left had her preparing for an attack until she recognized Marcus charging forward. He ignored the pair entirely in order to rejoin the fight with a battle cry while swinging his sword. The smoke prevented her from seeing their enemy clearly, yet the unmistakable clanging of metal against metal let her know her friend found the demon.

"What should we do?" she decided to ask her father instead of rushing headlong into the conflict.

Evern paused to consider her question, but before he could answer, a crimson glow erupted from up ahead, signaling Soirée's use of magic. As a wave of heat reached them, the commander stepped in front of her and conjured a shield to protect them. Meanwhile, Coura scanned the area as tongues of flame began seeping in bursts through the dark cloud.

"Where's Marcus?"

"I do not know."

She grit her teeth and struggled not to hurry around his shield in search of the soldier. Fortunately, that tension only lasted a moment as his body became visible amid the fire. He appeared to dodge what spells flew his way without acting on the offensive.

*He's alive*, she told herself in order to retain her focus. *Now we need to locate Soirée.*

Just as the thought concluded, their enemy leapt out of smoke, swinging a black blade in each hand in an erratic manner, both to clear the air and make her movements unpredictable. Marcus reacted the only way he could by attempting to block as many of the swipes as possible. Still, Coura noticed where the cuts landed and bled to shade his clothes beneath the punctured armor.

"We need to help," she told the commander before sidestepping with the intent to slip around his shield.

Evern understood and dismissed his shield after those words. The glowing particles shined as they faded to the ground in a shower of glittering light, though she ignored the energy remnants in order to hurry forward with her father beside her. In the next instant, they slid to a halt when their enemy dropped one sword, raised the empty hand toward them, and sent a bolt of lightning in their direction all without removing her eyes from Marcus.

"Get back!" the Yeluthian soldier shouted as he repeated his earlier spell to shield them from the sudden blast.

Coura covered her ears against the resulting clap of thunder that shook the ground, yet the lack of strength behind the spell felt evident when Evern's shield didn't even tremble. The reason became clear when a wave of ice followed with even less power, causing the shards to shatter as soon as they connected with the slightly golden barrier.

*She's using magic to keep us away so she can target Marcus first. I doubt she'll toy with him for much longer.*

Both hands balled into fists at the realization, leading her to recall the sword she dropped when Soirée seized her wrist. Her eyes followed the one their opponent held, though she noted how her friend kept up with the blade since maneuvering a weapon and magic lost the demon speed. The scene disappeared again when the ice storm picked up.

"We can't just hide here," she growled to show her frustration.

"Do you not believe the creature is tempting us to dismiss our safety?" the commander countered.

His tone didn't suggest he wasn't upset by their situation; however, he didn't budge even when Coura stepped closer to his spell in order to peer through the blast of snowy wind. From there, she contemplated their options, as well as their allies' positions.

*My magic hasn't recovered enough to be deadly, but maybe I can use it as a distraction. That way, Evern can get a chance to attack.*

With that in mind, she prepared to share her suggestion and focused inward on the active, demonic energy. It jittered with enthusiasm, leading her to recall how it did so earlier when she already expended some on the black blade. The recollection had her studying Soirée, or rather the weapon the creature wielded.

*I never dismissed my spell, which means it's under my control. If I manifest it again, would it come to me?*

She watched as Marcus rolled on his side when his opponent tripped him up and stabbed the ground where he had been. Even from a distance, the glistening sweat covering his scarlet face and dampening his hair became visible when he jumped back up to his feet in order to defend himself against the next round of wild swings.

"If you plan on assisting your friend, I recommend doing so now," her father urged, to her surprise. "If our enemy focuses on me with its spells, you would only need to worry about close combat."

Instead of pointing out how he held their other means of success and could keep up with Soirée better than her, Coura's thoughts returned to the weapon the being wielded. Specifically, what she could do to interfere with the pace of the fight given how she had been the one to manifest the sword.

*I can't tell Marcus about dismissing the spell without giving it away to Soirée, so I'll just need to wait for the right moment when he can react,* she told herself and returned to monitoring the conflict nearby. *Evern gave me permission to act too. I'm sure he'll catch on if this works out.*

The assistant general continued blocking what strikes came his way, though some, severe-looking scrapes concerned her, while the lithe creature appeared to be tiring of the exercise. What once was a crazed grin mellowed into an amused smile as the creature began panting, and Coura noticed the violet eyes glance in her direction multiple times when the being drove Marcus back.

They seemed to be shifting toward the commander's shield even as the ice returned to bolts of sparks.

Despite the bleak outlook, she kept her attention on the demon and her friend's motions until she felt confident in predicting the next series of attacks. Soirée used a forceful swing with both hands on the sword's hilt for a moment in order to throw more strength behind the attack, shoving the assistant general away again when he met the metal with his own blade. His arms lowered in response to the effort. Coura held her breath while this took place and readied herself by finding the connection to the manifested weapon. As soon as the demon raised her blade with the obvious intent to bring it down in a vertical slash, she cut off the spell.

What followed would have had her laughing if their lives weren't in danger. Shards of the dark energy scattered just as her father's shield did earlier while Soirée's arms dropped. The unsuspecting nature of the maneuver wasn't lost on the being, who appeared alarmed by the disappearance as it happened. Fortunately, enough muscle had been behind the attack that their enemy followed through with the motion, allowing time for Marcus to react and retaliate.

Before Coura expected him to take advantage of the opening, the soldier lunged forward, brought the ancestral weapon up in a single swing, and released a cry projecting strain and desperation. The upper edge made contact with his opponent's chest enough to create a long gash spewing ink-like blood before she stumbled backward, likely due to the artifact's essence.

Evern decided to take advantage of that break by removing the magical wall since Soirée's lightning stopped when she prepared for her last attack. As the golden barrier noiselessly shattered, the Yeluthian charged toward the creature, prompting Coura to follow when she realized he intended to intervene. Various ideas came to mind since they could fight together, especially since Marcus would need time to recover, yet Soirée didn't remain affected by the wound for long.

The demon's lips curled into a snarl before both hands raised to summon balls of fire that flew in their direction. Just like earlier, Evern created a shield for protection, though this time Coura heard him mutter a curse at the interruption. She also noted the being directing flames across the area off to their right and wondered about the reasoning.

*Is that where the others are hiding? Byron should be protecting the perimeter, but why target them now?*

As the spell continued, she remembered Marcus' vulnerable position closest to their enemy. This led her to creep toward the edge of her father's barrier where the tongues of fire appeared and felt less powerful; however, as soon as she did so, they increased in intensity.

"The creature is keeping us occupied with this nonsense," Evern explained when she backed away with her hands raised to cover her face from the heat. "In case you could not see through its spell, the assistant general is being guarded by Master Byron. I cannot tell what it plans on doing next, but we will not be able to go near enough to kill it if it continues using magic to avoid close combat."

Although she believed the explanation, Coura grew uneasy in response. *Soirée isn't the type to avoid a fight unless it's not worth the effort. Does that mean we're too much trouble to bother with? Will she flee instead of pursuing me then?*

Concerning questions continued rising in her head as she worried the demon would depart and leave her fumbling for a new strategy to sever their bond. In an attempt to ease her fidgeting, she summoned the black blade once again before pacing behind the commander, who looked to be struggling against the offensive magic.

*He's not completely healed from his encounter with Lupin,* she recalled with a twinge of pity. *Byron shared the details of that fight, and Grace tried explaining the impact of severing an angel's wings on their center. All I understand is that he's not prepared for a drawn-out battle of spells. I don't think any of us are.*

With this in mind, she settled on returning to using her weapon and shared as much with the commander.

"How do you expect to get close enough?" he countered, though with curiosity rather than doubt.

"I'm going to connect with Marcus first. That way, if Soirée keeps you here, we'll be able to hold the rest of her attention."

"If you believe that can work, I will not stop you, but you should take my sword."

The suggestion startled her considering he didn't seem to have brought a spare; however, he elaborated before she could comment on it.

"You two should stand a better chance of sealing the demon if you both have a means of doing so."

Coura considered this before shaking her head. "If you can rejoin us, you should. Besides, I doubt I can effectively wield it."

That had bothered her given her past inability to even hold the relic due to the opposing energy she possessed. Despite her personal feelings, she refused to prevent her father from assisting if the elemental spells ceased.

Evern didn't comment on the remark. Instead, he nodded and ended their discussion there.

With what fortitude she could muster, Coura focused her attention on the direction her friend had been in earlier, ignored the concern for her safety against Soirée's flames, and rushed past the golden shield. As expected, the fire kissed her skin to singe hair and skin in various places, yet she remained out of its path for the most part, resulting in less severe burns. This also allowed her to view the area beyond, which appeared mostly as it did before.

Their opponent kept both arms raised to continue sending spells at Evern and Marcus, who now stood behind Byron's violet barrier. The master mage wasn't around from what she could see, yet his presence no doubt impacted the fight. Part of her longed to adjust her path in order to charge at the being until she thought better of it.

*I'd only be throwing myself at her without backup*, Coura noted as her gaze lingered on the demon.

In response, Soirée caught her eye and grinned, as if inviting her to try attacking head on. When she didn't, the creature ended what spells she sent at her friend and father. The unexpected change involuntarily increased her anxiety.

*What's going on?*

To her relief, she reached her goal just as their enemy began sprinting toward the violet shield. Marcus already shouted at her in alarm, but the words faded once they realized the threat heading their way.

"I hope you have a plan," her friend grumbled while readying himself, prompting her to do the same, albeit with a smirk.

"No idea."

She heard him groan with displeasure while stepping closer to the shield. "In that case, stay back. I don't know where he is, but I'm assuming Byron is guarding us."

"Evern will join us when he can too."

By that point, Soirée slowed to a walk, paused in front of the barrier separating them, and raised a hand toward the commander again. From it erupted a series of lightning bolts identical to what she summoned against him earlier.

"You're an annoying lot," the being said at a volume above the resulting thunder. "Why not forgo the support and let us continue our battle of skill? Such interruptions defeat the beauty of combat, and spells are too noisy."

*You're the one using magic*, Coura longed to retort. She bit her tongue to prevent herself from doing so, yet the thought of strictly sticking to sword work didn't sound as off putting as she imagined. *Marcus and Evern have the ancestral weapons, so maybe it's worth the risk.*

The demon manifested her black blade a second later and poised it to stab the shield all while maintaining the bolts. In order to end the spell, as well as move forward with their best chance at success, Coura walked forward until she could go around Byron's barrier. All the while, Marcus called for her to stop.

"Look at this," Soirée practically cheered in an excited manner. "You're ready to stop with such boring games."

"Only if you are," she countered as she gripped the hilt of her weapon with both hands and widened her stance.

In response, the lightning abruptly ended.

# Borrowed Hope

Byron attentively made sure to monitor his mentality during the ongoing, personal conflict due to both his former student's wellbeing and the safety of the rest of their group, yet he struggled to keep a level head when he saw Coura approach their enemy amid a sea of sparks and shields. Although he trusted her not to take on the matter alone, he also knew she would put her own life in danger if it meant helping their chances of success.

*I can't fault her for giving her father and Marcus better opportunities to act since they're supposed to be our main combatants thanks to the ancestral weapons*, he reflected while wiping away the beads of sweat lining his forehead. *I'll need to keep an eye on all angles again.*

Throughout the fight, he utilized the forest surrounding the clearing by circling the edge from within the brush in order to avoid detection once he cast a spell. He only summoned a barrier to protect the assistant general at that point but got the feeling the direction of the conflict shifted.

His legs brought him to the southernmost point, then he paused to assess the situation when the demon and Coura began swinging at one another. Immediately, he spotted Marcus hurrying to join by going around the remaining shield he kept up, prompting him to dismiss the wall. He then readied his power for additional barriers should the need arise despite an ache stirring in his left shoulder.

*It seems we're back to the start but with less stamina. Since I haven't fully recovered my energy, it's expending at a faster rate. I would wager the same is true for Commander Evern, which may be why he's not leaping into the current bout.*

Byron's eyes studied the blades and how they all managed to avoid coming into contact with a living being; however, it also became obvious that the demon didn't take its opponents too seriously. As he began considering whether or not it would harm Coura due to their relationship, the concern he failed to suppress became justified in the next instant when the creature raised a hand in his direction and summoned a shield.

The movement caused him to jump, and he rose to stand when another wall of demonic energy formed at its back. By the time he realized what the being planned, it crafted the final set of barriers on the northern and eastern sides, creating a box keeping it, Coura, and Marcus trapped together.

A curse escaped his lips as he decided hiding didn't matter anymore and emerged to jog over to the nearest shield. The silhouettes of his allies and their opponent weren't clear, yet he could follow the movements well enough to know what took place. His eyes lifted after the brief assessment to measure the height of the structure, which extended far above his head.

*Any sort of magical attack is a gamble when I can't identify what's happening and predict an opening. Should I focus on bringing down one side of the barrier?*

The amount of power to do so would likely leave him exhausted, but he struggled to come up with another idea until the Yeluthian's voice reached him from off to his left. As he glanced over, Commander Evern turned the corner at a run and slid to a stop an arm's length away while panting.

"Master Byron, are you able to destroy these shields?"

"Not without effort," he summarized before pointing upward to where he had been contemplating an attack. "Would you be able to fly through the opening?"

The sapphire eyes looked at the spot, returned to him, then narrowed slightly. "The area within is tight enough that an extra body would make combat even more difficult. Besides, if the demon targets me with the ferocity it showed earlier, I cannot guarantee Coura and the assistant general's safety. It would be better to eliminate part of the shields and create more space."

The commander's final words echoed in his mind as someone was shoved into the violet barrier with a thud. *What would additional space do to benefit our goal? We're trying to keep the creature contained to this clearing, right? Perhaps it gave us the opportunity we need.*

As a new strategy took shape, Byron found himself hating how it disregarded his trapped allies' safety and expected the Yeluthian to feel the same. Still, he faced the soldier while committing to the idea.

"We should use its spells against it."

"What do you mean?" Evern asked without hiding his apprehension.

"Right now, the demon is contained by its own hand. If you and I can fortify that space by placing our own shields beside them, it won't be able to escape so easily."

"Then what? How are Coura and the assistant general supposed to defeat it alone?"

"They won't need to do it alone," Byron clarified as he shook his head. "I'll call for Grace. If she can manifest the goddess fire spell used to kill the previous demon-"

"You would harm our allies in the process?"

"I hate leaving them trapped too, but if the enemy's barrier goes down, I can remove one of mine so they can escape. How else can you see us being able to use the best weapon we have without arousing suspicion?"

Evern pursed his lips together yet didn't offer a rebuttal. Byron took advantage of the time available to them by closing his eyes and calling to the younger Yeluthian, whom he expected to be listening for a signal.

*Grace, can you hear me?*

*{What is going on?}*

Her immediate response spurred a smile despite the situation, and he pictured the ambassador and her guards peeking out at the fight from where he left them farther west. In about a minute, he explained his plan before waiting for her response.

*{I am worried about Coura and Marcus, but I believe you are correct about this being our best chance.}*

*Thank you*, he replied with a nod directed at the commander to signal her cooperation. *I'll place a shield on the side closest to your current position. Once you see me standing there, come over with Will and Dianne.*

Grace agreed to the order before her presence faded, allowing Byron to discuss the final details with Evern.

"I should go to the eastern side then," the Yeluthian said afterward.

"You handle the north and east. I'll take the others. If you get the chance to bring Coura or Marcus out of the space, do it."

With nothing else to add, the two split apart for their opposite positions. Byron caught the remaining trio jogging over to meet him while the struggle continued nearby. It soon became an effort not to get distracted by the figures fighting for their lives beyond his reach.

*Just hold on you two. We'll end this soon.*

***

It took Coura about a minute to figure out what Soirée was up to after the demon manifested walls to surround the trio. Their following fight mirrored the earlier bout with a single exception: Marcus stood farther away and only raised the golden blade to ward off their opponent when the creature came too close.

*I'm sure he's exhausted*, she realized when her friend avoided engaging with the enemy more than once. *If she won't kill either of us, we can buy time for the others to come up with a plan. At least, I hope they get the idea.*

Although she sympathized with Marcus' condition, she didn't feel much better. Her throat burned from constantly panting as the being kept her on her toes with fluid, light jabs meant only to prevent her from resting. What strikes landed scratched her leather padding enough to either bruise or break skin beneath the protection, showing the demon's continued desire for causing them pain.

What benefited Coura, and what she intended to thank her father for, was the brief training he provided before the battle against the Nim-Valans led by Lupin. Such a reminder of her

517

combat progress kept her from dipping into the pool of dark energy resting in her center, which she worried would consume her again if she didn't use it properly. This also meant what wounds she earned didn't heal.

As if in response to that fact, Soirée lunged forward with a wide, horizontal swing from the right, prompting Coura to bring her weapon up with both hands and knock the metal away. Such a direct attack kept her attention for long enough that she missed when her opponent freed a hand, balled it into a fist, and threw it toward her chest. The resulting blow landed against the ribs on her right side. She stumbled back in response with a wince while the being cackled.

"You're more alert than our last encounter," Soirée commented when the laughter died down. "It's still not enough to beat me, but you're more entertaining. I can see why Terran kept you alive for as long as he did."

Coura considered a retort but thought better of it when their enemy pointed the black blade at her.

"As much fun as this is, I would rather depart with you and continue my research. Are you going to cooperate, or should I make you bleed until you lose consciousness?"

Instead of waiting for an answer, the demon charged and brought the weapon down on Coura, forcing her to sidestep closer to the nearest shield until her back nearly pressed against its solid surface. When she lingered in that spot due to indecisiveness after, Soirée took advantage of her hesitation to reach forward and push her into the wall of energy with enough force to rattle her teeth. The switch back to physical attacks had her cursing the creature in her mind.

A glint of gold caught her attention then, stopping her from attempting to retaliate. From off to her right, Marcus stalked forward with the ancestral weapon poised to strike. He didn't appear to be hiding his intent to return to the fight, which led their enemy to face him and frown.

"You must feel terrible for leading your friends to their deaths," Soirée commented without looking away from the assistant general. "All you had to do was leave with me, and their lives would be spared."

Coura realized the words were meant for her even though the demon didn't give her any attention. Before she could consider how to respond, Marcus came near enough to swing his sword, beginning another round of clashing metal. Unfortunately, the soldier's weariness was apparent enough that his opponent could easily toy with him and deliver several, nasty cuts on his arms and upper legs.

*What can I do?* she wondered as she watched her friend struggle to stay on his feet. *She'll kill him if I can't figure out a way to-*

The rising sense of panic gripping her in that moment froze when a shadowy figure beyond the barrier passed along the opposite side. Their hasty speed had to be a sprint, and she followed them with her eyes until they halted in front of the side where she and Marcus previously hid behind Byron's shield.

Before she could grasp what her ally on the opposite side of the magical wall would do, a pained cry from the assistant general returned her gaze to him. Her heart sank as she saw Soirée place the black blade against the side of his head as he dropped to his hands and knees. Crimson coated part of his face and spread across his left leg where the armor he wore had been sliced apart. Soirée clicked her tongue in a show of mock disappointment and slid her violet eyes toward Coura during the resulting pause.

"I often forget how humans tire so easily. I suppose there's nothing left for me to do with this one."

Coura watched as the being brought her sword back slowly in preparation to strike at Marcus' neck. "Wait!"

The plea seemed to echo around them and succeeded in staying the demon's hand.

*I told myself I wouldn't let anybody get killed*, she recalled while releasing the spell on her weapon and dropping both arms to her sides. *If the others can't get through the barrier surrounding us, then it's up to me to end this. I'm the one who should be dead, not them.*

When her blade disappeared, Soirée raised an eyebrow without moving anything else. Coura decided to take a chance by closing the distance between them at a cautious walk. To her relief, their enemy didn't react until she put herself between the being and her friend by standing in front of Marcus. Her hands extended outward a bit, as if she could physically protect him even though the tip of the creature's sword now rested against her chest.

"You win," she added after a moment of silence passed when the demon assessed her actions. "I'll go with you if you-"

"You can't fool me."

The harsh interruption had her fumbling for a reply. "I'm serious."

Soirée huffed a laugh and in a single, swift motion, brought her weapon across the front of Coura's upper leg. The slice wasn't deep, yet it stung enough to have her wincing as blood began dripping from the wound.

"Do you honestly think I care what you want?" the demon asked after in a less amused tone of voice.

Before Coura could consider a response, the blade scratched her other leg in an identical fashion. Still, she held her ground.

"I can take you whenever I please," Soirée continued and stepped forward so they stood toe to toe. "I had plenty of opportunities to end your precious companions' lives, but do you know why I let this play out?"

"Because you enjoy sick games."

That spurred a chuckle. The sound instinctively lowered Coura's guard just enough that when the being pierced her with the demonic weapon in the stomach right after, she gasped. Although the metal barely broke skin, Soirée slowly pushed it farther in while leaning closer.

"This is extremely entertaining," she elaborated before twisting the sword, causing a greater amount of pain. "However, just like with Terran and Lupin, one must earn their place at the top. You and your friends act as though you tolerate my presence instead of fear it, and we can't have that."

To punctuate her point, Soirée removed her blade in a single jerk. A groan escaped Coura then, and she struggled to ignore the growing pool of blood forming at her feet. Her eyes remained locked on the violet pair, which helped her dismiss the distractions.

"If all you need is me, then we can go now," she attempted to reiterate.

"You just don't get it, Dear One."

Again, the demon slashed at each of her legs just below the previous cuts before positioning the tip of the black blade above her center. The sight and implications of a drastic injury to the location of her energies sent a shiver along her spine, as did the being's next words.

"Letting these insects and the pigeon live would only serve to let you feel better about sparing their lives. You'll never learn why you shouldn't stand up to me, and their deaths wouldn't influence others to respect the powerful."

Giggling followed the explanation that sank Coura's spirits.

*I'm not recovered enough to stand a chance in a fight, but maybe I can use my goddess gift for long enough to save Marcus. I wonder if he can move or whether or not I can get to him and drag him through. That's my best chance at survival now, but if Soirée strikes my center, I'll lose what energy I possess.*

Part of her also continued wondering about the shields trapping them together and if a direct attack would succeed in fracturing enough for them to escape or help to arrive.

*I'll get one shot at either option*, she noted after when the demon's amusement died down. *I can't guess how long I can keep a portal up and if we'll have enough time to go through it, so I should stick to a spell that can damage the barrier.*

Soirée grinned and prodded her with the metal. "Are you going to move aside like an obedient girl, or do I need to make you bleed out?"

Coura glared at the creature before scanning the magical wall across from her. *I need somewhere we can get to quickly and…*

What she didn't expect to see was a shadowy figure standing beyond that side of the barrier. She couldn't guess which of her other companions watched from that spot, but they would be in danger if she targeted nearby. This caused her to hesitate, and time ran out when Soirée evidently noticed her shifted gaze.

The violet eyes widened a bit to show awareness of the potential threat. Before she could find her voice and what she would say to prevent their enemy from changing targets, the demon's head snapped to the right in order to glance over one shoulder.

*Is she worried her spell will be destroyed?* Coura thought as her heartbeat picked up when Soirée scowled. *Do I need to keep her attention on me?*

Various options came to mind that would put her at risk yet delay the fight. She still wasn't committed to giving up, which led to an internal conflict regarding standing her ground until the end or aiming for a less violent resolution.

In the midst of her dilemma, and while Soirée became distracted, a solution arose from an unexpected source. One moment, she looked on as the being studied the shadowy figure; the next, she heard a gushing sound before their connection wavered.

*What happened?*

While she attempted to understand the cause for such a rift in the bonding spell, the demon looked down. That was when they saw part of a golden blade in Soirée's midsection stretching from the gap under Coura's right arm.

*This has to be…*

A gentle touch on her lower back reminded her of Marcus.

*He's too weak to fight*, she remembered with no shortage of disbelief as she looked over her shoulder to where her friend now knelt. In his left hand was the ancestral weapon, which he managed to utilize by stabbing through the narrow space, and his right pressed against her in a way that helped stabilize his position.

"I'm sorry it took so long," he mumbled between breaths.

Despite her desire to check on his condition, Coura returned her attention to Soirée. The being froze in place while glaring at the weapon and wound, which leaked dark blood down the polished, metal surface. Marcus' panting a few seconds later led her to catch how his hands trembled.

*The strike must not have landed true if Soirée is still awake!*

Such a realization motivated her to act before their opportunity went to waste. Without a word, she reached around in order to grab the sword's hilt from her friend and avoid it slipping out of position; however, a jolt shocked her hand in response.

*That's right*, told herself after muttering a curse. *I can't wield this because of the demonic energy I carry. Then again, I might be able to manage holding it in place.*

For a second time, she seized the hilt and forced her grip to tighten against what pain shot through her arm. Her jaw locked as she struggled to push the blade in farther, yet it wouldn't budge. Together, she and Soirée remained stuck in place like statues.

Time felt as though it crept by for an hour before a voice cut through the heavy atmosphere.

"Coura, Marcus, get back!"

*Is that Byron?* she wondered after her heart skipped a beat at the unexpected sound. *How can we hear him with the barrier?*

It was then she realized how the shields around them varied in color. What were once sturdy, purple-hued walls of demonic energy now appeared golden on two sides while the third held an untraceable power. The changes told her all she needed to know about their current situation.

*Soirée can't maintain her spells thanks to the ancestral weapon weakening her control. Those must belong to Evern and Byron, but why would they want to keep a barrier around us?*

A light tug on her arm pulled her away from the question.

"Let's go," Marcus urged without attempting to mask his weariness.

Coura shook her head as best she could against the golden sword's affects. "We can't remove the blade, or else she'll be free."

He didn't argue with the statement, though the hand lifted. A moment later, she heard hurried footsteps approach from behind.

"What are you two waiting for?" came Byron's voice in a demanding manner.

A heavy hand rested on her shoulder and attempted to guide her backward; however, she refused to budge.

"Help Marcus," she instructed without turning around. "We have her cornered now. I can't move."

The thought crossed her mind to ask her former mentor to finish stabbing Soirée in order to ensure the sealing magic worked, but one of the pale hands shot toward her before she could do so. In the next instant, the demon held her by the throat and squeezed until she could barely breathe. No words came from the being, yet what hatred and ferocity her expression radiated said enough.

At that, Byron removed his hold. She heard him say her name after in a quiet, concerned manner after, and she longed for the strength to tell him what she had in mind; however, he shared another idea, one she hadn't thought about until then.

"I'll be back for you as soon as I get Marcus away. Don't worry about the weapon. Grace is ready, so we need to go."

*Grace?* The Yeluthian's name sparked a sense of hope once she remembered the unique spell her friend could wield. *The barrier must be to keep Soirée in place so she can't escape. I don't need the ancestral blade to do more than hinder her ability to run or react.*

For a while, she repeated that in her mind while gasping for as much air as she could. Nothing about their enemy changed except for the amount of liquid on the ground, leading her to wonder whether or not the physical damage meant much aside from the weapon's purpose.

*I can't keep this up for much longer*, Coura admitted when her vision went in and out of focus. *Where is Byron? Evern's probably maintaining those shields, and Will and Dianne are guarding Grace. She should just start her spell before it's too late. If I pass out now, the blade will be removed.*

Her hearing seemed affected as well, which she noticed when what voices and sounds around her grew muffled. All she could do was try keeping a level head.

*My body might not be responding, but as long as I can focus and stay sane, we can beat her.*

Suddenly, she sensed a faint presence, like a set of eyes watching over her from above. The recognizable sensation let her know she wasn't alone and motivated her further.

*Grace, can you hear me? If you can, use your spell to burn Soirée!*

Part of her expected to hear the girl's voice; however, she felt too weak to discern the noise. A hint of fear stemmed from the presence, but nothing more.

*Summon the flames you used to kill Lupin. Don't worry about me. I'll pass out soon, then she'll come after you... We don't have...much time...*

The force behind her mental command faded as colorful spots blotted her vision. Her grip on the golden hilt steadily loosened, and if it weren't for her reaction to the artifact, she believed she would have already let go.

Just when she expected to lose consciousness, the hand seizing her throat lifted, alleviating the pressure. This led her to gasp and cough for a full breath, yet the air became tainted by a cloud of smoke. The putrid smell of burning flesh also filled her nostrils.

*She did it*, Coura realized once her sight returned enough for her to catch the scarlet flames consuming the demon's entire body.

What elation she experienced shifted to concern in a matter of seconds as the fire expanded and compressed like a living creature's lungs, reaching her skin and scorching her flesh. Out of surprise, she stepped away while raising her hands to cover her face, which had her abandoning her position and the ancestral weapon. Without a stable wielder, the sword slid out and dropped to the ground with a dull clang.

Her feet refused to cooperate when she became conflicted between retrieving the item and fleeing. The flames continued to grow until they threatened to burn her again, yet growling arose from the figure consumed by the fire. She watched with horror then as the demon's arms and head jerked around, projecting agony and frustration in each, wild motion.

*Soirée's still alive? How long does it take for her to die to this spell?*

Before Coura could consider an answer, someone grabbed the back of her coat and tugged hard enough to yank her backward. The jarring pull seemed to wake her from the dreamlike state she'd been in once she observed the flames, leading her to understand how her position likely affected her Yeluthian friend's focus, as well as how dangerous it was.

She spun around to find Byron already sprinting away from the demon and hurried to catch up. To her dismay, the injuries on her legs, the wound in her stomach, and the inability to clear her head returned with a vengeance. She managed a few, wobbly steps before falling onto her side where her eyes instinctively returned to Soirée. By that point, the figure attempted to follow amid the growling, which morphed into repressed shrieks. The sight paralyzed her until Byron returned. Without wasting time, he took her arm and pulled upward, guiding her to stand.

"Are you able to move?" he asked when she could stay on her feet.

"I think so."

The emerald eyes looked between her and Soirée after her unsure response. His lone hand raised after, and he manifested a shield in front of them yet wide enough to connect with the others on either side.

"This should keep the demon at bay, if only for a bit," he shared without lowering his arm or diverting his attention. "I'll feed it from here so the creature doesn't get away from the commander's walls. Go by Marcus or find Will and get your injuries treated."

Coura longed to argue since the fight wasn't over but couldn't muster the strength. That caught her off guard since her sight returned and she no longer struggled to breathe, though each, short inhale felt off.

*I didn't lose much blood, so why can't I walk straight or talk without effort?*

A scream from Soirée cut through the reflection as the being threw herself against Byron's barrier. The inky fur appeared to have burned away, along with her hair, yet any exposed, pale skin turned black as it charred. As she watched the creature pound both fists against the magical wall amid the sea of flames, Coura remembered their bond.

*Her presence is barely there*, she noted when she traced the connection. What was once a stream of power passing between them merely trickled and flowed in only one direction. *My energy is going to her in an attempt to heal her body. That must be what happened to Terran!*

Before she could fully comprehend the reasoning, her legs gave out, dropping her to her hands and knees. A hand rose to rest against her center as the panting involuntarily slowed and her muscles grew weak. In less than a minute, she completely lost the ability to react.

*This is why if one of us dies, the other follows suit. Our bodies naturally heal because of the demonic energy, but if we run out of power, it begins draining the other source. Hendal's must have been taking from Terran. The spell really is like a chain linking us together.*

The cries rang around her yet steadily faded once her senses stopped responding, leading her to drop onto her side before she realized she even fell. No part of her body would move after that, so she closed her eyes, savored what energy she could before it disappeared, and prayed the fire would put an end to their fight.

***

It took all Will's self-control not to abandon his place at Grace's side, even before his friend began using magic. He would never be able to keep up with Marcus or Coura, and especially not with the Yeluthian commander, yet he needed to remind himself repeatedly not to abandon his position in favor of acting heroic.

*My role is her guardian right now*, he told himself when the fight began and he witnessed the combatants being hurt or tossed aside. *Once she becomes involved, the demon will likely target her, and that's when I can participate further.*

Despite the outline he formed in his mind during the morning, everything changed when their enemy manifested a box to keep Marcus and Coura contained with it. The implications of such a decision didn't hit him until he spotted Byron and the commander conversing, then Grace gasped, as if she were startled.

"What's going on?" he ventured after the sound.

Her concern-filled gaze turned to him while she answered. "Byron requested we go closer so I can cast the goddess fire spell while the being is trapped."

"Is that what's happening?" Dianne interjected in a less bothered tone. She raised a hand to shade her eyes against the sunlight and frowned. "I can hardly tell with those walls up, so I can only trust he knows what he's doing."

"He usually does," came Clearshot's voice off to Will's right.

The archer kept his bow drawn ever since they entered the space and never looked away from the demon; however, Will wasn't certain he would get an opportunity to shoot an arrow at such a distance and with magic involved.

Movement to his left drew his attention back to his Yeluthian friend, who emerged from their hiding spot among the brush in order to hurry toward where Byron now stood alone. All three of her guards followed and readied their weapons before halting in front of the barrier. Beyond it, Will attempted to identify the shadowy figures but had no luck.

"We are ready," Grace announced when they stopped, prompting the master mage to share his plan.

"You'll wait here until I give the signal for your spell. The rest of you will protect her until the demon is dead. Got it?"

Will voiced a confirmation, along with Clearshot and Dianne, before Byron wiped his forehead. Only then did he notice how exhausted the man appeared. He nearly asked if there was anything else he could do to help until the wall of energy closest to them disappeared. What they witnessed on the other side left them speechless: A bloodied Marcus knelt behind Coura as she stood in front of their target; however, the golden blade in his hand stretched between them to pierce the demon.

"They did it?" Clearshot said in disbelief. "Does this mean…"

As the question faded away, the master mage rushed toward the scene. Will could only watch as he reached their allies, briefly conversed, then helped the assistant general up.

*What about Coura?* he wondered when she remained behind to hold the ancestral weapon. A shiver slid along his spine when he noticed the demon's hand around her neck. *How can Grace use her magic if the creature keeps a hostage?*

His thoughts began racing for ways to help his friend before the Yeluthian at his side lifted both arms to extend them toward the opening.

"Wait! Coura's still-"

"She is ordering me to proceed," came the displeased response as Grace's hands glowed a golden color.

"What?"

No other words came to mind, and he received none from his friend. Dianne and Clearshot didn't speak either. Will ground his teeth in frustration yet knew not to interfere with the spell that would rid the world of another monster. Instead, he focused on his assignment and gripped his sword's hilt tighter.

*Don't get distracted. I have to trust everybody, just like they trust me.*

As a burst of flame erupted from the darker figure, all the fear he experienced up to that point melted into awe. He imagined the goddess fire would look like what the mages cast, which it did to a certain degree, yet this radiated a comforting power. Each part seemed to act on its own, waving, twisting, and sparking without a pattern. What heat reached them also felt gentle and warm, like a hand caressing his exposed skin.

*It's beautiful*, he admitted while savoring the sensation.

He became hypnotized by the magic until the barrier reappeared and cut off his view. After blinking to clear his sight, he first caught Byron in front of the wall. Then, he saw Coura lying behind the master mage. His heart sank, yet he avoided moving or making noise that would distract Grace. Shrill cries echoed around them during the process as well, though he didn't realize they stemmed from the demon right away.

"Will, you should go to Marcus," came Clearshot's voice amid the chaos.

His head snapped to where the archer stepped closer in order to place a hand on his shoulder. "I'm supposed to protect Grace. What if-"

"Don't worry," the man interrupted with the most series expression Will had ever seen from him. "Unless Byron's shield goes down, we should be safe. Marcus needs a healer."

He swallowed and found a lump in his throat. "Fine, but shout if you need me."

Clearshot nodded before pointing at where the assistant general lied in the grass farther off to their right.

As he closed the distance between himself and the soldier, Will felt a pang of guilt for not paying attention to where his friend wound up. *I was so entranced by Grace's spell that I didn't even notice what else took place.*

"Marcus!" he called and threw himself to his knees beside the assistant general. "Can you hear me? It's Will."

The half-open, chestnut eyes slid to him while he began assessing the damage. A minute later, he diagnosed several injuries needing immediate attention and slipped off his pack to dig out what bandages, tools, and creams he could use.

"You'll bleed out if we don't stitch these wounds," he mumbled, though more to himself than to his friend. "Let me know if you need a pain-dulling potion. I didn't bring much, but the least I can do is mend some of the deeper scratches."

For a while, he became lost in his work. Marcus never protested aside from a few groans, and he wiped his hands on his pants when he finished. By then, the silence filling the entire area began weighing on his shoulders. His friend seemed to notice as well and attempted to sit up.

"You shouldn't push yourself," Will argued half-heartedly.

"I appreciate your concern, but what happened to everyone else?" came Marcus' reply.

They both glanced around after; however, nothing appeared to have changed except the lack of fire beyond Byron's shield. The notion pushed Will to his feet.

"Stay here until you're well enough to stand," he instructed in as stern a manner as he could muster. "I'll find out what's going on."

Part of him expected Marcus to protest, but the soldier merely nodded, allowing him to return to Grace's side without delay. He appreciated that when he reached the Yeluthian and her guards just as her spell ended. Both arms dropped to her sides before she fell forward. The unexpected motion caught him off guard, yet the others were ready to catch her.

"Easy now," Clearshot began as the two guided her to her knees. "Don't overdue it."

Will didn't believe she heard the words, for she sank to the side immediately afterward and into Dianne's awaiting arms. At first, he released a sigh of relief since he attributed such fatigue to her use of magic; however, once he noticed her pained expression, he dropped to inspect her body for the source.

What he hadn't noticed until he got closer were how her shirt's sleeves completely burned off, exposing scarlet markings across her hands and forearms. White blisters already began swelling in various spots to add to the injuries.

"My control…could not handle….such an amount," he heard her mumble between breaths.

"My lady, it's time for you to rest," Dianne replied before Will could. "Let us care for you so you can recover."

To his relief, the Yeluthian didn't speak again. Her labored breathing continued until he dug out the pain-dulling potion he mentioned to Marcus and held the bottle to her lips. When she drank the entire vial, he began applying a salve to her arms before bandaging them up. His attention remained on his current patient as he did so. Finally, he leaned back on his heels when each arm had been completely wrapped.

"Is she going to be all right?" the woman holding his friend asked just above a whisper.

The pleading in her eyes made his heart ached when he considered the truth. "She needs a light mage to heal her skin right away. If the blisters burst and get infected, that could cause irreversible damage. I'm not sure if her skin will scar or not without one either."

"I understand."

When neither spoke, Will realized how quiet the area remained. He glanced around to find Clearshot gone and pushed himself to his feet again.

"He went to check on the assistant general," Dianne shared a second later. "I can remain here if you wish to join them."

He offered a grateful smile. "Thank you. They should be stable, so I'll see if the commander is available to tend to Grace."

Will expected Marcus to be where he left the soldier yet found the spot empty. He scanned the remaining space after and only then noticed how all sides of the magical barrier had disappeared. Gathered in front of a charred square of earth was the remainder of his group.

*Thank goodness.*

His feet brought him over to the others at a jog, and a greeting sat on his tongue until he got closer. Every thought fled his mind upon seeing their behavior. Byron alone stood facing the opposite end of the field with his back to everyone else. Meanwhile, Clearshot and Marcus sat with defeated expressions, and the Yeluthian soldier knelt nearby. Coura's upper body rested in his arms.

"What happened?" he practically whispered when he halted to assess the scene.

"Exactly what we knew would take place," Clearshot answered at the same volume and without meeting his eyes.

Will didn't understand yet felt pressing for a better explanation wasn't appropriate. Instead, he crept closer to the commander. As soon as he noticed the figure's shoulders rising and falling to signal deep breaths, he paused.

*Should I ask if he can heal Grace?* he wondered as he watched from a distance. *Is he treating Coura now? I don't want to interrupt if that's the case.*

In that moment, as he recalled the previous fight, he remembered the demon. Nobody confirmed its death, yet their lack of urgency led him to believe it was dead. For some reason, that left him cold inside.

*If the creature isn't alive, and it was tied to Coura...*

Will's feet moved without him realizing it until he fell to his hands and knees beside the Yeluthian soldier. His breath caught at the sight of his friend, and tears welled before he could control himself.

One glance revealed enough. Her closed eyes held shadows underneath, emphasized by sunken cheekbones, and her skin took on a grayish tint. Any trace of life disappeared from her expression, giving it an almost peaceful appearance. He raised a shaky hand after and took one of hers in his. Its limpness bothered him almost as much as its chilled temperature.

That proved to be enough to break his composure. Without consideration for those around him or their current situation, he bent forward, held her hand against his chest, and wept. All the while his head spun as he tried to process what their success meant.

***

As Byron studied the charred remains of their final enemy, all the exhaustion he'd been dismissing returned like stones piling onto his body. He expected to collapse at any moment, yet his legs wouldn't budge.

*I wasn't expecting Grace's spell to be so powerful*, he thoughtlessly admitted to himself while reaching over to rub his aching stump. *It took every bit of energy I held to keep the flames contained, as well as the creature within.*

What considerate part of his mind remained active made a note to thank the Yeluthian later. For the time being, he wanted nothing more than to be left alone.

The noise he heard behind him solidified that desire. Various footsteps came near, followed by gasps or comments regarding his former student, then silence and quiet weeping. He already knew what to expect going into the fight; however, experiencing the aftermath hurt his heart enough to have him choking back tears.

So, he fixed his attention on the burning figure until it became undistinguishable from the charred earth. The remains weren't pleasant to assess, yet he grew too afraid to turn around. He had been hoping he would pass out before someone pulled him away to face the results.

*Luck doesn't seem to be on my side. I don't know what to do now.*

A sudden but gentle weight on his shoulder roused him from his uncertainty before Clearshot's voice addressed him.

"How are you holding up?"

The question sounded sympathetic, leading Byron to dip his chin as a display of his pain. No words came to mind, even when the hand lifted and his friend leaned closer.

"You should see her."

"I can't," he muttered without hesitation.

A pause stretched between them for a few seconds.

"You'll regret it if you don't," came the other's response before Byron heard him walk away.

*I hate to say it, but he's right. She deserves a proper goodbye.*

He inhaled and released a shaky breath while mustering the courage to turn around. When he felt prepared, he faced the despondent group seated near Commander Evern, who held Coura. Will had taken one of her hands in his and bowed his head over it, as though he were praying, Marcus sat beside his friend with a downcast expression, and Clearshot remained standing to watch where Grace and Dianne relaxed nearby. Nobody paid him any attention, which encouraged him to approach the Yeluthian and kneel on the side opposite Will.

The pale face of the young woman lying in front of him appeared peaceful, though from weariness instead of a content dream. Nothing hinted at her still being alive, yet Byron's aching heart wouldn't let him accept the fact that she would never again look at him with the bright, blue eyes he'd become accustomed to. She would never smile or laugh, or mock him for his shortcomings, and he would never get the chance to see her blossom into her own person free from the demon's influence.

Before he realized it, tears streamed down his cheeks. He instinctively dipped his chin and closed his eyes in an attempt to mourn without disrupting those around him. The familiar, meditative position soon had him slowing his breathing, and he embraced what tendrils of energy floated in his center.

*I didn't notice this until now, but my senses are dull, like something is hindering my ability to pick up on another presence,* he realized after a moment. Normally, the sensation would bother him, but his current mood left him feeling numb inside. *Could this be the creature's doing? When it died, did it leave an aftereffect of some kind? Perhaps I became so accustomed to its nature that I feel off without it lingering in the air.*

He considered bringing up the subject in case it affected the Yeluthians in a negative way that would disturb their recovery, yet he hesitated to shift to a less sorrowful mentality. Finally, when he looked to where Grace lied against her guard, his concern for her wellbeing outweighed his worry about disrespecting the commander's grief.

"I'm sorry to bring this up," he prefaced while addressing Evern, drawing the angel's red-rimmed eyes. "Are you able to pick up the demon's foreign energy at all? My senses are bothered for some reason, and I'd like to make sure you and the ambassador aren't negatively affected the longer we remain around its corpse."

The question and explanation sparked a bit of life in the Yeluthian, for he straightened and shook his head. "My power was nearly depleted just keeping the shields up, so I cannot tell whether or not the being's presence lingers."

"I'd bet Grace is drained too," Byron mumbled.

When the commander didn't respond to that comment, he considered what he knew about the unique light energy the angels possessed. This eventually led him to analyze Coura's magic, which he didn't fully understand yet heard plenty about over the years.

*The demons' presence overwhelmed her natural, light power against her will, forcing it back. At least, that's how she explained it. She couldn't heal or manifest shields using her Yeluthian energy when they weren't balanced; however, it remained with her when she lost what dark energy she possessed.*

As he continued contemplating those instances, his eyes returned to the motionless figure before he shared his thoughts aloud. "Commander, Coura's power may have been skewed, but she never lost her light energy, correct?"

He glanced at Evern when he didn't receive a reply and found the Yeluthian studying him a bit skeptically. Will also lifted his head, as if the conversation piqued his interest.

"I could never comprehend her ability to wield magic, but that is what I always assumed," the angel shared quietly. "What are you hinting at?"

Byron picked a spot on the ground to fix his gaze on while he organized his thoughts. Despite his best effort, he found himself growing a bit optimistic when he could put the reasoning into words. At that point, he met the commander's eyes again, though this time with a sense of determination.

"If what we know about demons is true, they shouldn't be able to manipulate light energy, let alone the kind Yeluthians use. That means Coura's natural power should still be with her."

"What does that have to do with her now?" Will interjected in a slightly irritated tone. "She's dead. Her bond to the creature we just killed took her life, and you're worried about magic?"

"Not magic," Byron corrected before returning his attention to Evern. "The demon could only take what it can manipulate. Her Yeluthian power might just be slumbering again."

At first, the soldier remained still, as if holding his breath in anticipation for more, then he carefully set his daughter on the ground and laid a hand on her chest. Byron noticed his eyes close and his chin dip in a meditative manner before picking up on a presence stretching from the figure.

*I'm so weak I can hardly sense anything anymore. If I try what the commander is doing, I would only waste what energy I can muster. On the other hand, he might be able to-*

A sharp, startled gasp from Evern pulled his focus back to the situation.

"You are right," the angel began as a pair of fresh tears slid down both cheeks. "It is faint, but her center still holds a bit of our people's power."

"Does that mean she's alive?" Will asked without hiding his amazement.

Instead of answering, the commander took a shaky breath, prompting Byron to add the idea he conceived at the thought of her still housing light energy.

"What if you transfer as much of your remaining power as you can? It might be enough to revive her."

"Even if it does nothing, I would never forgive myself for not trying," came the immediate response in a tone stressing his determination.

After those words, he placed both hands on Coura's chest right above her heart. They began emitting a golden glow just visible against the sunlight, which reflected his weariness. Meanwhile, Byron held his breath, both to avoid bothering the commander and out of suspense, until he grew dizzy. Marcus crawled closer to watch as well, though the assistant general did so quietly enough not to become a distraction and didn't question what Evern was doing.

Minutes passed before any sort of change took place. The commander's light steadily dimmed and disappeared, but he didn't immediately remove his hands. Finally, he opened his eyes to stare at his daughter without a hint of emotion, piquing Byron's interest.

"Did it work?" he couldn't help himself from asking in the resulting silence.

Instead of addressing the question, Evern spoke to Will next. "Would you please check for a heartbeat?"

The young man jumped in alarm, nodded once, then seized Coura's wrist first. After a moment to listen for her pulse, he bent forward to press an ear against her chest. His slightly perplexed expression as he returned to his previous, sitting position again drew Byron's attention.

"Did it work?" Marcus pressed a second before Byron could repeat his question.

Will removed his glasses and wiped them on his shirt as he answered. "I'm not sure. I think I heard a heartbeat, but it's weak."

"What energy I could support within her reminds me of a dying ember," Evern added as the sapphire eyes lowered to Coura with a hint of sadness.

Despite the Yeluthian's shift in mood, Byron found a bit of hope in that comparison. "Blowing a gentle breath on such a sensitive force has the potential to spark a new flame."

The comment drew the others' attention, and he believed they understood what he intended to get across.

"We've done all we can for her. Whether or not she recovers is now up to the strength of her will to live."

***

The aching of Coura's body stirred her before she realized where she was. No part of her would respond, increasing the uncomfortable sensation, so she lied on her back and waited for

538

sleep to take her and end the growing torture. Unfortunately, her mind remained alert enough to ward off the weariness.

*Where am I?*

Slowly, her eyes cracked open until she could blink and clear her vision; however, only an endless sea of white greeted her. It took a minute to remember her previous visits to her soul space, though her current predicament let her know something was amiss.

*What happened?* she soon wondered when her second attempt to rise failed, leaving her to contemplate how she wound up there. *I can't remember anything except what this place is. Even those memories are hazy.*

Attempting to think hurt her head enough for her to abandon the effort, and she closed her eyes again while keeping her breathing steady.

*Am I dead? Is that why I can't move? Maybe it's because of whatever I did outside this space.*

She figured that had to be the likeliest option, prompting her to release a sigh. At the sound, the only noise she heard, she recalled conversing with a voice she previously identified as her inner presence.

"H-Hello?" she tried calling out. To her dismay, the burning of her throat turned the shout into a whisper. "Is anyone there?"

Only silence filled the bland space.

A surge of panic arose at the idea of being trapped until she focused on calming herself with deeper breaths. Although it lessened her stress, the aches didn't ease.

*What's wrong with me? Why is my body behaving this way? I could always move, though I struggled once to rise and run.*

The memory came to mind immediately, along with the reasoning behind her past issue.

*I remember a voice telling me I had been hurt and needed to recover before I could wake up. I healed on the outside, but my soul was damaged. Does that mean something like that happened a second time?*

A jolt shot through her after the question, as if she'd been struck by lightning. No pain accompanied the shock, yet she found herself gasping for air. A ringing arose in her ears at the same time, prompting her to cover them with both hands and curl into a ball in an effort to ease the deafening sensation. Every part of her trembled when various images steadily came to mind until she remembered the demon who bonded to her soul and the memories they shared.

*Soirée must be… Is she really gone?*

Before she realized it, tears streamed down her cheeks. At first, she assumed they stemmed from joy and relief; however, she felt quite the opposite and didn't know why. What emotions stirred as a result continued keeping her incapacitated while the hammering of her heart in her chest nearly suffocated her despite her attempts to calm down.

There was no indication of a change for a long time. By that point, Coura expected to pass out. When she didn't, she began to notice how the aching gradually grew numb until she couldn't feel anything. Tentatively, she uncurled her body before pushing herself onto her hands and knees.

*I can move*, she realized as she looked around. *My limbs are responding now, but why?*

While more questions continued to rise in her mind, she stood and instinctively stretched her back even though she couldn't tell if it was tight, or if that mattered. Her eyes wandered the space in search of any sort of hint as to her current condition, yet she noticed only gray cracks far above. When she understood what they were, her breath caught.

*The demonic energy flowed in and out from those spots. Does this mean I can't manipulate it anymore? Sage Vidar told me my center changed though, so it would never heal. Could this be the result of Soirée's death then?*

At the thought of the creature, the previous surge of mixed emotions and debilitating alarm attempted to take hold of her body. Fortunately, the numbing increased to mask most of the sensation. Coura stared down at herself once she recovered and found a faint, golden tendril of light wrapping around her torso. She considered what it could be as it swirled, lifted into the air, and floated away.

*What was that?* she wondered while the presence vanished into the surrounding environment. *I suppose I haven't seen my Yeluthian power either. My center must be completely unbalanced now.*

The notion left her with much to contemplate, least of all what awaited her when she would wake outside her inner world. Somehow, she knew the aches she experienced came from her physical condition, though the lack of rest as the time passed also meant her mind wasn't clouded.

"If I had to guess, I'd say Soirée's death is taking its toll on me regardless of any injuries I experienced," she mumbled to herself as she wandered into the endless sea of nothingness. "I'm not sure why. My memories returned all at once, and last time that's all I needed in order to stir."

Leaving the space always frightened her a bit due to how its safety comforted her; however, one fact motivated her to move forward despite the fear. It repeated in her head as she moved, and even after she lied down in an attempt to rest.

*I'm free from Soirée. If she's gone, I'm not bound to her. Even if it's not the same, my life is my own.*

# Honest Emotions

It was no surprise to Byron to see Evern occupying a spot in the clearing they frequented so often as of late. After returning to camp, he figured they would run into each other at some point once the group split apart and could recover, so he made no attempt to bother the commander. That had been two days ago, and much changed since then.

First and foremost on his mind remained Coura's condition, which slightly improved with each passing hour. Her father's shared energy seemed to support her weak lifeforce enough to keep her stable despite her reaction to losing her bond with the demon. No one expected her to wake so soon, but just surviving the hike back on Clearshot's shoulders lifted their spirits.

The second distraction came from Casner, who issued orders for the troops to begin dispersing toward their new assignments. He hadn't given much thought as to when he planned on departing and mentioned as much when the general asked.

"You've more than earned your retirement," the man reminded him the previous evening when they last met. "Most of the soldiers and mages returning to Verona will leave tomorrow in order to travel together. You're welcome to join them, wait for the rest of us to go in a couple more days, or head out on your own. I only request you let me know so I can inform the king's council. I'm sure they'd appreciate a notice."

*I suppose I haven't wrapped my head around this yet*, he reflected as he entered the private space and approached the commander. *Our fight is over. The demons are gone, so now we can move on. It's more difficult than I imagined.*

That final thought prompted a smile, which he used to greet Evern once the Yeluthian noticed him.

"Out to enjoy the weather as well?" came the other's response as the sapphire eyes raised to the clear, blue sky beyond the treetops. "This must be the warmest day since we arrived."

"I agree. It would be a shame to waste it by working."

His comment spurred a huff of laughter from the commander. "What work is left for us weary souls?"

Byron didn't reply. Instead, he dropped to sit beside the angel whom he'd come to befriend during their shared time along the border. In that moment though, he wouldn't have been able to tell the being was a Yeluthian aside from appearance.

*I can only sense a bit of light energy stemming from him. He definitely exhausted himself magically. I'd bet he's been resting nonstop ever since we returned. This might be the first time he's been awake for long enough to do something with his break.*

For a minute, he contemplated inquiring about this before deciding to indulge his curiosity. The question earned him a faint but genuine smile.

"As you are aware, it will take weeks for my power to return to normal," Evern shared after. "My wings were already damaged from the battle against the Nim-Valans, which causes issues with the manifestation spell. I doubt I will be able to fly again for at least a month."

He sensed the commander's inner pain at having to admit such a hinderance. "I had no idea."

"It is the risk we take. I am fortunate my loss can be recovered though."

Whether or not the comment had been meant to reference Byron's arm, he chose not to pity himself by mentioning it. This created a peaceful silence until the Yeluthian spoke again in a more serious tone.

"I must travel on foot with the group departing tomorrow at dawn. My king requests my presence as we finish our business in Asteom and transition the training Commander Detrix initiated. Lavine will make the journey from above as well."

"You're fine leaving Coura here?" Byron asked without hiding his surprise. "I understand King Arval's desire to continue your people's work, but she's your daughter. She needs all the help she can get right now."

"Do you believe she would wish for me to stay if it meant delaying my return?"

The sincerity behind Evern's question startled him and helped him accept the conclusion the angel already reached. "No, she wouldn't."

"I desire to remain by her side until she wakes, but that would do nothing except satisfy my personal strife," the Yeluthian explained after. "Without my energy, I cannot help her heal. I would only be occupying another bed and eating what rations remain for those staying along the border. The light mages tending to her vowed they would do their best to help her as well. I must trust in their abilities."

Byron hated removing his personal feelings from the situation, yet the rational side of his mind believed all would be well if the commander departed. He mentioned this, to Evern's visible relief; however, he shared his decision to stay at the camp for a while longer.

"I have no ties keeping me bound to the palace, so I don't need to go immediately. Since that's the case, I promise I'll look after Coura while you're gone. When she's well enough to travel, we'll return together."

His words didn't seem to surprise Evern, yet he sensed how much the offer meant when the Yeluthian thanked him. Because of this, he decided not to mention how he already planned on waiting for her to heal before departing from the border.

***

For a few minutes after her eyes opened, Coura stared upward until she could comprehend that her mind no longer occupied her soul space. What aches her body experienced, as well as the weight on her chest, didn't change, which led her to believe she still slept and merely envisioned parting from the dream-like world. Her gaze steadily drifted over the space after, and she soon recognized she had been placed inside a tent.

*Is this part of the medical station?*

The question, or rather the notion itself, increased her heartbeat. While her breaths shortened against the tightness of her chest, tears arose to slide down her cheeks; she wasn't certain if the realization that she managed to survive or something else triggered them.

*I'm alive... How am I still alive?*

Despite her ability to think, her head seemed heavy, as though she didn't completely wake up. A woman's voice soon filled her ears, but she couldn't discern the words until a set of grayish eyes met hers and tore them away from the tent's ceiling.

"How are you feeling?"

"I don't know," she answered honestly in a grumble due to her voice's lack of use.

Several more questions followed, but the strain on her mind to consider them created a headache that led her to stop speaking. When it became apparent she wouldn't be able to provide adequate responses, the woman offered her a vial and urged her to drink. The bitter solution tasted familiar; however, she fell asleep before identifying the contents.

*

No dreams or visions marred Coura's rest, and she credited this for her alertness when she stirred again. Although the aches lingered, every part of her noticeably recovered except the weight on her chest. She considered this after a different healer came by when she struggled to sit up, assisted her, and brought her a bowl of porridge.

*It's not a physical injury, or else those caring for me would have noticed*, she finally admitted to herself as she set the empty dish aside. *That must mean it's related to my magic, or my connection to Soirée.*

At the thought of the demon, an odd, choking sensation closed off her throat. The hatred she held for the being still remained, yet it began to be overshadowed by a sadness she had never experienced. Before she realized it, the tears returned.

*I don't understand. I'm glad she's dead, so why do I feel so horrible? Could this be because our souls were tied together?*

545

The longer she contemplated the issue, the worse she felt. In the hours that passed as she sat alone, she came to believe the bonding spell was the cause, but accepting the reasoning proved to be more difficult. Only when a woman began lighting lamps to ward off the surrounding darkness did she admit the truth.

*Losing Soirée was like losing part of myself. This pain I'm experiencing is proof of that. No matter how much I desired to rid the world of her, we were forcibly connected beyond our use of dark energy. Why?*

A cheery, familiar voice drew her out of her slump as she spotted Clara approaching with a broad smile.

"You're awake," the girl pointed out and stopped beside her. "That's a relief! We weren't sure if you'd… Never mind. Will asked me to fetch him when you stirred, so I can get him if you're up for a visit."

Coura hesitated to respond; however, her silence evidently meant she was fine with that, for the light mage spun around and practically jogged out of the tent. She contemplated feigning sleep before her friends could shower her with attention, yet knowing they worried about her condition up to that point kept her from delaying their encounter.

In a matter of minutes, Clara returned with Will, as well as Grace and Clearshot, and each took turns giving her hugs and pats on the shoulder. They sat around her after in order to share some of what took place since they last spoke until her mind actually grew weary. Thankfully, a single yawn was all the notice they needed to excuse themselves for the evening, allowing her to rest again.

The morning brought about less stiffness, so she decided to try standing only to lose her balance during the first couple attempts. This caught the nearest healer's attention, and after scolding her for overworking herself, the woman returned her to her previous, sitting position on the blankets. That was when she noticed her father and former mentor looming at the entrance.

*I shouldn't be surprised they'd come visit me*, she noted as she repressed a sigh. Why she felt anxious to see them she didn't know until she acknowledged the conflict within herself. *Who would ever grieve a demon's death? This makes me even more different from the other Yeluthians, which won't please Evern. I might not be able to use magic again either. What will Byron think?*

While these and other thoughts bombarded her mind, only the commander crossed the space to approach while the master mage conversed with one of the light mages. Coura hurried to prepare an appropriate greeting in those precious seconds but struggled to find her voice. As she opened and closed her mouth like a fish out of water, her father knelt and wrapped his arms around her in a single, swift motion, leaving her stunned. No words passed between them for a minute or so while he held her and she hesitantly returned the embrace.

"I was not certain what would happen," he finally muttered into her hair before inhaling a deep breath and pulling away. His sapphire eyes glistened as they met hers, and she noticed the shadows underneath them. "That is neither here nor there. How are you feeling?"

"Fine," she whispered when nothing else came to mind.

"I am pleased to hear that." Again, he pulled her in to hold her against his chest while he continued. "Truly the goddess blesses me. I did not think I would get the chance to speak with you before I go. His Highness and our comrades will be relieved I can end my report on an uplifting note."

Nothing he said made any sense to Coura. Before she could start questioning his words, he leaned back, placed a hand on her head, then took a moment to assess her physical condition.

"You should be well enough to travel soon, according to the healers tending to you. I must depart with those returning to the palace under my king's orders, but Master Byron agreed to wait until you recover to leave. Continue to rest and recover your strength until we reunite. Then, I promise we can spend time together."

With that, Evern rose and turned to walk away. She tried calling for him to wait only to manage a quiet mumble. Her head spun at the amount of information he presented, though she understood he was traveling to Verona shortly. When and why remained unanswered.

*I guess I'll have to wait until we see each other in the capital.* Part of her felt relieved that she wouldn't need to explain what bothered her, so she decided not to dwell on the rushed goodbye.

Meanwhile, Byron came over but stood beside her with a pleased expression instead of lowering himself to the floor. He extended his hand a second later, and she stared at it without comprehension.

"I bet you're starving," he began after. "It should be early enough to avoid waiting in line for breakfast."

Of course, Coura hadn't noticed how hungry she became until he mentioned it, prompting her stomach to rumble in response. She wondered whether or not she should warn him about her earlier attempts to rise; however, he picked up on her trepidation before she could decide.

"Your caretaker just said to take it slow and that you should feel better once you eat."

He shook his still-extended hand a bit to urge her on.

*I'm assuming I'm not the only one who hasn't had breakfast,* she longed to grumble at his impatience as she accepted the assistance.

Once he pulled her to her feet, she needed a moment to balance herself before her legs would cooperate, then they exited at a slow walk. The camp appeared as normal as she remembered, though there were noticeably less people wandering around or occupying bedrolls near what bonfires remained. Byron didn't comment on what transpired while she slept, yet she figured he wanted to wait until they could properly discuss the matter with their food in a more private setting.

This proved to be the case once they accepted their bowls of porridge and returned to the familiar setting where she previously stayed with her friends. Nobody occupied the space at that moment, leading her to realize the sun had just risen.

Once he slurped up about half his meal, her former mentor released a content sigh and glanced around in a casual manner. "Your father, Lavine, Grace, and Dianne all departed at dawn with a group returning to the capital. Most of the troops already left for their previous posts, either along the border or elsewhere in Asteom. The general expects to go tomorrow with his assistant and Marcus."

"What about you?" she managed to ask. The warm food eased her throat enough to motivate her to talk. "Are Will and Clearshot still here too?"

"I promised Evern I would remain until you can travel so you're not left alone. Clearshot wants to accompany Casner in my stead, and it sounds like Will is going to depart with the healers in a day or two when they're ready. I can't imagine how they'll feel after being away from the palace for years."

The two finished their porridge in silence when she didn't continue the conversation. Already, she felt more alert with a full stomach, and the movement reduced what stiffness plagued her until then. To her dismay, the lone problem remained the weight on her chest.

*Will this ever go away?*

She wondered about that while staring into her empty bowl. Although she noticed her companion's head turn toward her and felt his gaze, she couldn't bring herself to look in his direction.

"What's wrong?" Byron asked when she wouldn't budge.

A mixture of anxiety at revealing the truth and shame for her inability to control her response to Soirée's death closed her throat again. Instead of pressing for an answer, her former mentor simply shifted his stare elsewhere. When Coura could muster the courage to glance over, she found his head tilted back and eyes closed as he soaked in what sunlight reached them. Something about his relaxed, content posture reassured her somehow, as did their relationship when she began recounting their history.

*It would be better to get this off my chest than to try burying it. At least, that's what happened in the past.*

"I don't know how to explain it," she began despite her reluctance to do so.

Byron looked her way without a word, causing her to avert her gaze while her cheeks flushed. Once she located a spot on the ground to stare at, what she struggled to understand tumbled out. She described the lost connection as best she could then how that created pressure in her chest likely due to the demon's absence. By the end of the lengthy explanation, she felt worse than before and apologized.

"Who would ever mourn a creature like that?" she muttered as she allowed what tears had formed to slide down her still-burning cheeks. "I hate myself for behaving this way."

She let herself wallow until the embarrassment wore away a bit and wiped her face with the back of one hand. All the while, she never so much as glanced at her former mentor. His lack of a response or any sort of reassurance seemed to support the self-loathing, so she prepared to accept such repercussions.

"I never imagined such a spell would make me consider a demon's motivations."

The unexpected remark, as well as his unbothered tone of voice, had her turning her head toward him out of sheer curiosity. "What do you mean?"

"Was the being's goal to possess, or was there another purpose?" he continued while raising his gaze to the sky again. "From what you both mentioned, it seems like that had been its intent, but I wonder if the years didn't reshape its view."

"I don't understand."

The emerald eyes lowered before meeting hers, and in them reflected patience and sympathy. "Did you care about that demon like you care about your family?"

Coura shook her head.

"What about like me, your other friends, or even Aaron?"

She repeated the gesture, though with a slight sense of bashfulness at how he singled out Asteom's king.

"If that's the case, why grieve the loss of such a creature?" he countered, bringing her mind back to the present. "One would assume that means you miss them, but that's not the case, is it?"

The question had her considering what she felt toward Soirée until the moment she woke in the medical station. "No, not at all. I feared her almost as much as I hated her, but that decreased once I learned our lives were tied together."

Byron nodded, as if he expected that response. "That spell forced you to care about the demon in a way you couldn't control, and I'd wager it had the same effect on the being. However, its view of love was skewed. Their kind doesn't understand complex emotions like respect, selflessness, or admiration. At least, that's been my experience."

"You're saying she tried mimicking a personal relationship?"

"Perhaps not at first. I can't guess what it hoped would happen or what it planned when the possession failed, but what connected you two wasn't real."

The concept, whether true or not, left Coura with plenty to think about. She said as much after a moment, prompting a smile from her companion.

"Whatever the case, you shouldn't feel guilty or embarrassed for how you're reacting to the demon's death," he deduced. "Nobody blames you for what you can't control, especially after what you went through."

She found herself agreeing with his point before thanking him and choosing to believe in that conclusion. *Even if that's not what Soirée planned or how she felt, she's gone now. Time might be the best medicine to sooth the lingering pain. It's my decision to move on with my new life and find the best way to go forward.*

# Epilogue

As he exited the king's meeting chamber for a final time, Byron took a moment to reflect on the years he spent in that space, both discussing the successes and hardships Asteom faced. He knew he would always be sentimental about the experience, yet he couldn't deny how relieved he felt to be free from the burden of his responsibilities as the palace's dark master mage.

*I wouldn't be this calm if I didn't trust Lydia with that role,* he noted as he strolled through the stone corridors. *I never imagined I could pass along such a demanding job without some regret, but she's a perfect fit. The council already trusts her input, especially since she projects confidence when she speaks. I'm impressed with her growth as a leader.*

He made sure to mention as much when the two talked the previous afternoon over lunch. In order to avoid delaying his departure with Clearshot that day, he planned his goodbyes ahead of time with the final group being the king's council. This allowed him to exit the chamber, fetch a meal from the kitchen, and meet his friend in the grand hall before the pair set out for East Hoover.

Because everything went according to schedule, he was able to let his mind wander once he reached the mess area and procured a bowl of stew, a slice of bread, and a glass of chilled cider. First and foremost, he acknowledged Marcus' long-overdue promotion.

*I'm not one to savor somebody's humility, but witnessing Tont suck up his pride and appoint his son as his equal was more satisfying than I ever imagined. Then again, when Casner and Calin mentioned it after their experiences with demons, denying the young man's contributions would have made Tont look foolish. It's a shame he likely only voiced his support to protect his reputation. In any case, Marcus will do well in the position, especially since it isn't much of a transition.*

The former assistant general didn't seem surprised by the news when his superior brought it up, leading Byron to assume this discussion had been in the works since their return from the border a month earlier. In fact, no one treated him any differently after the announcement, justifying the decision.

Byron believed this to be for the best once he heard Aaron's other update, which was shared at the beginning of their meeting that morning. Recalling the king's words instantly put a smile on his face.

*If I didn't know he and Coura bonded closely over the years, I would have fallen over at the mention of an engagement. I do wonder how long they've been planning this, mainly because of her conflict with the demon. Thankfully, that's all in the past now.*

He had congratulated the young man before leaving the chamber and promised to keep the news a secret until it was announced at the upcoming Harvest Festival, which Aaron requested during the meeting. Despite his commitment, he already struggled to contain his excitement and would continue to do so as the event drew nearer. While he silently vowed not to share any details with Clearshot, Cintra, or Symon, the most difficult part would be to avoid giving them any reason to suspect him of withholding information.

The dining area filled up during his reflection, reminding him of the hour and motivating him to hurry to his quarters for the bags he packed earlier. After surveying his room for a final time, he went straight to the grand hall and located Clearshot near the entrance.

"It's about time," his friend chided him with a playful grin. "Any longer and I'd worry you were staying for good."

Byron huffed a laugh while readjusting the pack on his right shoulder. "I'm sure they'd throw me out on the street if I changed my mind again."

The pair prepared to exit as Clearshot expressed his doubts about that until somebody called for them to wait. Both turned at once to find Grace and Will jogging across the space without regard for the others out on their own business.

"What's wrong?" Byron asked when the younger duo slowed to a stop and paused to catch their breaths.

The herbalist straightened and opened his mouth to reply; however, the Yeluthian ambassador answered first.

"We came to say a final goodbye."

"Didn't we go through this yesterday?" Clearshot reminded them, though with an amused smile.

This time, Will was able to share his input before his friend. "That was with dozens of other people around. We agreed a proper goodbye is in order."

"We'll be back in a couple months anyway."

Grace shook her head, causing the loose, white locks to slide over her exposed shoulders and arms, which highlighted the discolored parts of her skin. It took Byron a bit to get used to those burn marks, but he managed not to stare.

*That's the price of such powerful magic*, he concluded when he heard about the results of the goddess fire spell.

Without a light mage present to mend her scorched body after the final demon's defeat, it began healing on its own. By the time they dragged themselves back to camp and could get her tended to, the damage was irreversible. Still, she held her head high during the entire recovery process and afterward when she returned to the palace, a feat Byron admired given how many stares and pity the afflicted skin spurred. That positive attitude and newfound confidence earned her a spot as one of Commander Detrix's appointed teachers though, so he had to trust in her ability to use the Yeluthian magic without fear going forward.

He began to wonder about her eagerness to accept given the traumatic experience; however, the conversation between Will and Clearshot caught his attention.

While Grace would be supporting those in the palace, the young herbalist planned a route around the western half of Asteom in search of new research. Accompanying him would be the light mage named Clara, and the two intended to be away for the next few months. Will shared all this at Clearshot's prompting even though they discussed it before.

"We hope to leave within the next week," the young man finished with a hint of hesitation. "It feels like we just returned to Verona. I'm going to miss sleeping on a mattress."

The others chuckled at his comment.

"After what you've been through, that should be the least of your worries," Byron added, to Will's agreement.

Silence stretched between them once the laughter died down, so he took advantage of the moment by wishing them well and extending his hand toward the herbalist first. Will accepted while Clearshot opened his arms as an invitation for Grace, who fulfilled the embrace. Instead of offering a handshake like Byron, his friend pulled Will in for a hug immediately after, spurring a bashful blush from their companion. Meanwhile, the Yeluthian wrapped her arms around Byron's waist before he returned the gesture. Then, the four split apart in opposite directions.

Once they exited the palace, Clearshot raised a hand to shade his eyes from the relentless sun beating down on the land. They would need to visit the stable for their horses, which Byron appreciated since the moving air kept them cooler than if they traveled on foot, but as their sight adjusted, they noticed a final set of obstacles in their way. Standing nearby were Coura and Marcus.

"Not them too," he heard his friend mutter before releasing a sigh. "It's going to be dark by the time we leave the capital."

Byron offered a sympathetic pat on the shoulder as his former student and the newly appointed general approached. Damp spots on their clothing, sweat covering their brows, and scarlet cheeks revealed they had been training prior to that moment.

"We'll make this quick," Marcus prefaced with a knowing look at Clearshot, who appeared just as impatient as he sounded. "It didn't seem right letting you go without a proper farewell. One more personal than being surrounded by other soldiers and mages. After all, we owe you both for your contributions over the past few years."

"We were just fulfilling our duties," Byron replied modestly. "You understand that."

"Fulfilling your duties and risking your lives are separate concepts."

"It's more like we all threw ourselves into danger," Coura added and shook her head in a helpless manner. "I suppose the kingdom would be different if we didn't do that."

After her response, Clearshot stepped forward until they stood toe to toe, drawing her eyes. "That's an understatement. The peace we assisted in bringing about is worth the effort, even if it doesn't last forever."

Byron noticed a faint blush despite her already rosy cheeks before his friend pulled her in for an embrace, which she returned a moment later. He decided to address Marcus when he heard the two mumbling their goodbyes and extended his hand.

"Congratulations again, general."

The young man's smile stretched as he accepted the gesture with a firm grip. "Thank you for everything. Please don't be a stranger."

"Of course. I don't intend to travel often anymore, but I have every reason to visit when I can."

They broke apart then and faced Clearshot and Coura, who seemed satisfied with their own farewell. Until that moment, Byron hadn't considered what he would say to his former student if they were alone; the thought tightened his chest.

*We shared a brief goodbye yesterday when others were present, but now is different.*

"Why don't I fetch the horses," his friend offered before beginning to walk away with a glance at Marcus.

In response, the general followed behind while adding, "Allow me to escort you."

Byron watched the pair head toward the aforementioned stable and attempted to come up with the words to express a fitting farewell. Coura didn't seem inclined to speak first, so he started with the first topic that came to mind.

"Have you heard from Evern recently? I forgot to ask yesterday."

"Not exactly," she replied while picking at her fingernails. "Mother sent a long, emotional letter when he told her about our time on the border."

"I assume she wasn't pleased to hear her daughter practically died in battle?"

"Let's just say I'm expected to check in on a regular schedule now."

Although he longed to pry further, Byron figured the personal matter belonged between her and her parents and left it at that. This allowed her to change the subject, to his relief.

"They'll be back for the Harvest Festival in a couple months, so it won't be too long. You and Cintra are coming, right?"

He recalled the proposal announcement and nodded, prompting her to cross her arms and look away.

"Nobody needs to get sentimental about being apart when we'll see each other soon. Besides, Aaron knows where to find you if the kingdom is in trouble again."

"Don't suggest that," he said amid his laughter at the idea. "I have faith in the king and his council. The next generation of leaders already has matters under their control. It's time to move forward."

He attempted to project the sincerity he felt with each word in order to eliminate any doubts she held. Whether or not it reached her, he believed in her ability to accept change.

*Perhaps she already has. She doesn't seem as bothered by my departure as I feared, which must mean she's ready to embrace the future. I can't blame her now that she's free to choose her own path.*

The notion spurred a smile; however, his assumption proved to be off when he turned to study the palace for a final time as he waited for Clearshot and Marcus to return. As soon as he moved, Coura stepped closer, wrapped her arms around him, then buried her face in his chest in a swift series of motions. He recovered in a heartbeat and returned the hug.

For a while, they simply held each other. Byron closed his eyes to savor the moment before pressing his lips to the top of her head. "I promise not to become a stranger."

"You'd better not," he heard her reply after a sniffle. "You're always welcome."

He took her message to heart before the sound of hoofbeats reminded them of his departure.

***

Coura and Marcus stood staring after the horses for a while even when the animals disappeared into Verona. As soon as she released Byron and he and Clearshot mounted their mares, she began toying with the ring on a chain around her neck. The engagement gift from Aaron remained under her shirt until she couldn't control herself. In a way, the memory of receiving the item eased what emotions arose.

One of the first conversations she had when she arrived in the capital was with her friend in order to let him know she survived and rid herself of Soirée. He patiently listened to her story, expressed his gratefulness for her return and recovery, then removed the piece of jewelry from the finger it usually occupied.

"I want you to have this," he shared while taking her hand and placing the metal in her palm. "It belonged to my mother. Whenever I found myself struggling with what happened around me, I'd think of her as my pillar of strength. Allow me to support you like that too."

In response, she brought up his proposal and accepted.

*I'm scared, but I'm not alone*, she told herself after recalling their conversation and his resulting elation. *Change tends to do that. I should be used to it by now. Like Byron said, it's time to move forward toward a brighter future.*

Coura released a sigh and slipped the ring back under her shirt before addressing Marcus. "Are you ready for lunch? I expected them to be here sooner."

"Is that why you wanted to spar this early?" he countered with both hands on his hips. "I didn't get a break to eat after the council meeting, so I'm famished."

"Shall I fetch a servant to bring the new general his meal?"

His resulting, unimpressed look had her grinning in a devious fashion. She found she enjoyed teasing him in such a manner about his promotion, though only after she sincerely congratulated him.

"I'm surprised you're still standing," he picked up after gesturing for them to return to the palace. "Lydia mentioned you two trained for an hour at sunrise. I caught her yawning several times throughout Aaron's reports."

"It was the only time she had available."

As the two entered the grand hall and crossed the area, Coura took a moment to assess her center and what tendrils occupied that inner space. She immediately picked up on the light energy since it flowed in a steady rhythm. Meanwhile, its counterpart loomed farther down.

*The lack of Soirée's presence didn't affect my soul space except when she drained our shared power. Without her, Lupin, or Terran around, I don't take in as much demonic energy, but I also don't need to wield magic as often.*

Normally, that would bother her; however, after working with Sage Vidar, she recognized how balanced her center became. Never again would she feel overwhelmed by the dark power or struggle to control herself because, for the first time in her life, what she wielded belonged to her alone.

*I have no excuse not to continue practicing*, she noted with a rising sense of confidence. *Wherever they put me, whatever they ask of me, I'll be prepared. It may not be a battle against demons or a war for the fate of Asteom, but I'll make sure I fight with every breath of this new life I've been given.*

# Glossary

CHARACTERS

Aimes Occaily – an older, former seaman from Clearwater who joins Coura during her venture to defeat the demonic creatures roaming Asteom

Aaron Vanstriann – heir to the kingdom of Asteom and son of King Hernan and Queen Freia

Assistant General Calin – leader of the Dalan base under General Tio

Barnelus Dagger-Diver – son of the Sie-Kie's *shimla* and their people's lead hunter

Bryn Leetle – a light mage who survives the ambush along the border

Byron Rinod – a master mage who wields dark magic and acts as Coura's mentor, an instructor at the Magical Arts Academy, and eventually the academy's representative in the palace

Califer Beackdal – former master light mage in Asteom's palace

Captain Harvey – leader of the Nim-Valan army who visited Asteom's capital

Cintra Amaldi – Byron's childhood friend who lives in Fester and works as a seer

Clara Waterton – a light mage who survives the ambush along the border and befriends Will

Commander Detrix – one of King Arval's trusted soldiers in Yeluthia

Commander Isan – one of King Arval's trusted soldiers in Yeluthia

Cornelius "Clearshot" Bayporter – a distinguished soldier who specializes in archery and Byron's close friend and comrade; he is married to Emilea and has two children: Mace and Lexie

Coura (core-ah) Galdwin – a dark mage and soldier with the ability to wield demonic energy and manifest black wings

Dianne Merker – an Asteom soldier assigned to act as Grace's guard

Drake Telkanar – a rouge Yeluthian working with the traitor in Verona

Elena Taymor – wife of King Syrus, one of Nim-Vala's six queens, and Finn's master

Emilea Bayporter – a master mage who wields light energy and acts as the palace's lead healer; she is married to Cornelius and has two children: Mace and Lexie

Evern Galdwin – commander of Yeluthia's army; he is married to Paulina and has three children: Coura, Odell, and Jackie

Finnley (Finn) – a Nim-Valan spy who assists Will and the light mages across the border

General Casner – commander stationed in Verona who is sent to the Nim-Valan border

General Garvish – new commander stationed in Verona

General Terrell – new commander stationed in Verona

General Tio – leader of the Dalan base

General Tont – commander stationed in Verona and Marcus' father

Geneva – a Nim-Valan woman who houses Will in Muld

Grace Zelnar – Yeluthia's ambassador sent to Asteom's capital; possesses a goddess gift that allows her to speak mind to mind with others

Harriette – a Mintelian woman who serves Sage Vidar and assists with Coura's training

Headmaster Symon – leader of the Magical Arts Academy and Byron's friend

Hector Lauple – a rouge Yeluthian working with the traitor in Verona

Hendal Duers – Asteom's former high priest

Jaspire Uskinor – leader of the rogue Yeluthian group assisting the traitor in the palace; possesses a goddess gift that allows him to heal from a distance

Jurek Younder – Asteom's new high priest

King Arval – leader of Yeluthia

Kline Galbourough – a rogue Yeluthian working with the traitor in Verona

Lady Katrina Neneme – wife of Lord Donovan Neneme and friend of Emilea

Lavine – Yeluthian soldier under Commander Evern who befriends Coura

Lissa Quentile – a light mage who survives the ambush along the border

Lupin Olim – King Syrus' mysterious advisor

Lydia Teller – a dark mage and Byron's second-in-command

Lyla Kroft – Wesley's apprentice and future priest of Kercher

Marcus Tont – an assistant general in Asteom's army and Prince Aaron's closest friend

Mary-Ann Weavu – a light mage who survives the ambush along the border

Marcy Kilguire – a woman from Dala who joins Coura during her venture to defeat the demonic creatures roaming Asteom

Nullan & Elenor Zelnar – Grace's parents and political leaders in Yeluthia

Paulina Galdwin – she is married to Evern and has three children: Coura, Odell, and Jackie

Rydar – a Mintelian man who serves Sage Vidar and assists with Coura's training

Sage Vidar – a Mintelian man who oversees a village and conducts soul cleansings

Soirée (sw-our-ae) – a demon who appears like an adult woman who forms a soul-bonding with Coura

Syrus Taymor – king of Nim-Vala and Elena's husband

Terran – a demon who appears to Coura during a scouting mission in search of Soirée

Thelma Boncarl – a rouge Yeluthian working with the traitor in Verona

Urvin Tsansa – a rouge Yeluthian working with the traitor in Verona

Verdic Ulshritz – former priest in Kercher and Hendal and Wesley's uncle

Wesley Ashre – priest in Kercher and Hendal's nephew

William "Will" Shairp – an herbalist from Clearwater who focuses on medicinal potions

Yukin Crowmald – a Nim-Valan lord and friend of Finn who Will treats and allies with

Zelma Vulan – a light mage who survives the ambush along the border

## LOCATIONS

Clearwater – the southernmost city in Asteom primarily known for fishing

Dala – a city in southern Asteom housing a military base led by General Tio

East Hoover – northern town housing the Magical Arts Academy

Inner Circle – Nim-Vala's capital housing the royal family and nobility

Kercher – an eastern city known for housing messengers between Yeluthia and Asteom

Magical Arts Academy – often referred to as the MAA, this school houses primarily light and dark mage trainees and is located in East Hoover

Medina – a town located in the southwestern section of Asteom and the site of a demonic creature's massacre

Muld – a southern town in Nim-Vala where Finn brings Will, Clara, and the rest of their group

Neston – Coura's hometown located in the forest south of East Hoover

Nim-Vala – country north of Asteom

The Valley Beyond – open area between a series of tunnels connecting Dala, Clearwater, and Fester

Verona – Asteom's capital city

Western Woods – an extensive forest covering most of Asteom's western coast and home of the Sie-Kie people

Yeluthia – also referred to as the City of Angels, this kingdom consists of a people who are closely connected with light energy, allowing some to manifest wings and thus giving them the nickname angels

## MISCELLANEOUS

Ancestral weapons – items gifted to Asteom's royal family consisting of two, golden swords, daggers, and bows; crafted with a sealing spell to protect against demonic energy

*Chi-alve* (key-al-ve) – term for soul space or center of power

Goddess gifts – special abilities used by certain Yeluthians involving telepathic communication, long-range healing, portal manifestation, and other spells

Mintelians – a secluded people who live in the Ghurun mountains and value artistic trades

*Shalma* – Sie-Kie's term for witch, or one who uses magic

*Shimla* – Sie-Kie's term for chief

Sie-Kie (sih-kai-e) – a tribe living in the Western Woods who value tradition over magic

Summa and Izina – god and goddess worshiped in Kercher

# About the Author

Courtney Lillard was born and raised in Appleton, Wisconsin as the middle of five children. Growing up, she loved music and theater, and participating in both allowed her to develop a deeper interest in the arts. She graduated from Quincy University in 2015 with a B.A. degree in Broadcasting and Public Relations Communications and from Western Illinois University in 2018 with a M.A. degree in Communication Studies.

Aside from writing, Lillard is a fan of reading fantasy stories and the classics. Her other hobbies include cooking, playing video games, and doing puzzles, at least until her cats knock the pieces off the table.